THE COMPLETE RED MOON TRILOGY

DIANNA LOVE & MARY BUCKHAM
WRITING AS
MICAH CAIDA

ISBN 978-1940651019

Please Note

This is a work of fiction. Names, characters, places, and incidents either are the product of the author's imagination or are used fictitiously, and any resemblance to actual persons, living or dead, business establishments, events or locales is entirely coincidental.

Cover Design & Interior Format

WHAT READERS ARE SAYING ABOUT

Time Trap, Time Return and *Time Lock:*

"Time Trap is amazingly original and unexpected...I loved every second of reading it!"

~~ Alexandra Fedor, 15, who has read The Book Thief, The Hunger Games, and Anna Karenina.

"Wonderfully written … I've never read anything like it. Excellent!"

~~Adam, age 28

"Time Return will grip you and keep you reading until the very end. The action is undoubtedly exciting, as well as the suspense. You won't want to put it down!"

~~ Brooke McClure, teen

"If I had found books like this [Time Return] when I was a teen, I would have started reading much earlier, instead of waiting until my mid twenties!"

~~ Kay Barnes, adult

"As the thrilling conclusion to the Red Moon series, Time Lock does not disappoint and will leave you in awe…perfection on paper."

~~ Angela Catucci, college student

"Time Lock, and the Red Moon Trilogy, is a fast-paced, exciting fantasy that is so well written that it meets my expectations as an adult reader too! Loved it!"

~~ Sharon Griffiths, adult

"The last book in this trilogy blew my mind. Drop the mic. Walk away."

~~ Amazon reviewer

Micah Caida is a blend of two voices
New York Times Bestseller Dianna Love and
USA Today Bestseller Mary Buckham.

GLOSSARY

ANASKO (uh – NAS – ko)
Be'tallia (Beh – TAHL – ya)
K'ryan (KRY – ahn)
C'raydonians (krah – DOE – nee – ahns)
croggle (KROG – ul)
dugurat (DO – gah – rat)
Etoi – (EE-toy)
furkken (FUR – kin)
G'ortian (GORE – shun)
Hy'bridt (HY – brit)
Komaen Sphere (KOE – main)
K'ryan (KREE-ahn)
Micah Caida (MY – kah – KAY – dah)
MystiK (MISS – tick)
Neelah (NEE – lah)
Phen (FEN)
prantheer (pran – THEE – er)
Rayen (RAY – un)
Rustaad (ROO – stad)
TecKnati (tek – NAH – tee)
Thylan (THIGH-lun)
Uberon (OO-ber-ahn)
V'ru (VROO)
Zilya (ZEEL – ya)

NOTE: This story is appropriate for all teens and often enjoyed by adults.

TABLE OF CONTENTS

TIMETRAP

RED MOON TRILOGY
SCIENCE FICTION TIME TRAVEL BOOK 1

DIANNA LOVE & MARY BUCKHAM
WRITING AS
MICAH CAIDA

CHAPTER 1

PAINFUL STARBURSTS EXPLODED BEHIND HER closed eyes.

Colors flashed wildly. Her body flipped around in a freefall.

She clawed at air unable to grab anything. Suddenly, she tumbled forward and bounced against a rough surface. Heat scorched her arms and legs. She instinctively tucked her head and shoulders.

No help. Sharp stones gouged her back and sand coated her sweaty body.

What was happening?

All at once, she lurched forward and slammed to a stop, flat on her face. Ears ringing, her next breath wheezed out, mouth dry as the hot dust singeing her skin.

Had she fallen? No answer. Her brain hadn't unscrambled yet.

"Get up, girl, if you value your life," someone demanded in a deep male voice that sounded like an elder.

Don't push me right now if you value yours, old man, she silently berated him. She opened her gritty eyes to blinding light and a cockeyed view of an endless desert.

Not a person in sight.

"Get. *Up!*" he ordered again.

If he yelled at her one more time, he wouldn't be happy when she did make it to her feet. Every inch of her hurt. Who was *he* anyway? He could help her. She'd kill for a drop of water. Her head still spun, and her stomach wasn't much happier. Gravel bit the scraped palms of her hands as she pushed up on shaky knees.

Muscles screamed in misery. Her body had been battered like a kickball. She looked around at endless empty land. Still, no one in sight. She wobbled sideways and kept twisting in a full circle.

Not a thing for miles but desert and mountains. She grabbed her aching skull as if that would stop the sickening spinning.

Had she imagined that voice?

Where was she?

Blinking against the harsh sun, she started to tremble. Nothing made sense. She couldn't call up where she'd been minutes ago or how she'd arrived here. Fear slithered through her. *No! Slow down and think.* Rubbing the back of her hand over gritty eyes, she focused harder.

Where was that old man?

Then she looked down at herself. Feet tucked inside short boots made of tanned skins. Familiar, but … not. Buckskin material covered her from shoulders to skinned knees in a sort of tunic. A leather thong was tied around her waist.

She swallowed, waiting for some memory to rise up.

Anything.

Just a hint at what was going on. Sweat streaked down her face and burned her eyes. She clawed at the empty gap in her mind. The longer she waited for answers that didn't come, the more nauseous she got. What was wrong with her? Why couldn't she remember what happened for her to be here?

Now would be a good time to panic.

Her skin chilled even with the heat and sun beating down on her.

She lifted a shaky hand to shove sticky hair off her face and sucked in air faster, stilling with a new realization.

Clutching a handful of hair, she pulled the strands into view. Black. Long, thick and black. She didn't recognize it.

I don't even know what I look like. Her heart thumped wildly. She took another glance at the barren landscape, hoping someone would show up to help her. Her body trembled.

Wouldn't her family miss her?

Wait. What family?

Did she have any? Her vision turned watery, bulging with tears she fought to hold back. Had someone gotten rid of her? Who? Why? Had she done something bad?

Was this empty desert home? She had no idea.

She gripped her shaking hands and sucked in a deep inhale of hot air. It burned her lungs. Didn't matter. She'd do anything to stop her rising panic.

Panic kills.

Someone had told her that once. Who? Still no answers. She had to calm down or she wouldn't survive to learn any answers.

Squinting, she searched for something familiar. Mountains and sand. Nothing but reddish-brown mountains and a blanket of sand. Wait. *Red* mountains. She knew those. Her heart thumped with hope now.

Closing her eyes, she tried to remember anything. Bright colors flashed behind her eyes and a sharp ache stabbed her skull. Grabbing her head didn't help that but … the pain cleared her foggy brain a bit.

Slowly, a word came forward.

Sandia.

She smiled.

That was the name of those mountains. Relief flooded through her so quickly her skin tingled. *I'm just disoriented.* Not a serious problem.

"You waste precious seconds, Rayen."

She froze in place. That had been a real voice and close by. Taking a deep breath, she turned slowly. Someone had better be there.

And who was Rayen?

She kept moving until she found the owner of that gravelly voice.

An old man. She blinked to clear her eyes. No, the shimmering *image* of an old man. An elder, just as she'd thought.

But she hadn't expected a spirit.

He had white stringy hair falling to his bony shoulders, light gray eyes, and gnarled limbs. His body flickered. In fact, the red and tan cliff rocks were visible through his translucent body. Beyond that, an unbroken sky stretched overhead, wide and empty, so intensely blue it hurt her eyes.

Ghost man floated above the desert floor with legs crossed.

Floated. Hmm.

She had been feeling a whole lot better until seeing him, but she'd take help from any quarter right now. "Who are–"

The ground beneath her started vibrating and shifting, killing her question. She stumbled sideways.

"Listen," he ordered, his voice tense and urgent. "Three things you must know." The ghost spoke louder with each word, competing with a heavy, shuddering sound in the distance.

She chugged in a couple deep breaths, as if that would quell her rising fear. With those inhales, she smelled a rotted stench. Cloying decay and smoke. A warning smell she couldn't place, but something she sensed deep in her bones.

Whispering, she warned, "Danger comes." She looked from side to side.

"You listening?" the old ghost shouted.

Like I have a choice? She swallowed, not a spit of saliva in her mouth. To move this along, she gave him her full attention again, but crossed her arms in warning. He needed to hurry up.

The thundering sound in the distance grew louder, reverberating through her body. Adrenaline stirred her blood, urging her to be ready.

"First thing," he enunciated as if she was slow witted. "You die if you eat peanuts, and you are seventeen."

"Peanuts?" she repeated. Who cared about nuts? Also, wouldn't that technically be two things? She sniffed at the air. The burning stink thickened. Her hand went instinctively to her hip, reaching for a knife that wasn't there.

"Second. Your name is Rayen."

I'm Rayen? Now she had a name, which would thrill her if she could believe a crazy hallucination. A new fear paralyzed her.

She didn't recognize her own name ... or what she was doing here ... or where here was.

The ground shook harder. Dust and pebbles scattered everywhere. She rocked back and forth, widening her stance to stay balanced. "What's making that noise?"

That's when she caught the distinct sound of hooves pounding. Hard. Behind her ... and gaining speed.

She jerked around, not believing what she saw.

A beast. Her throat muscles clenched at the sheer size of the thing. Part hairy, part thick gray hide that looked inpenetrable. The creature blotted out the desert landscape behind it, barreling forward, rocking back and forth on three legs, wide head low to the ground. Scary fast, churning geysers of sand and dirt, eating up distance quicker than anything its size should.

Air backed up in her lungs. "What the – "

"Third thing, Rayen," the elder shouted, his voice nearly drowned by the rumble. "*Runnn!*"

CHAPTER 2

GHOST MAN VANISHED AS SHE raced for the mountains at full speed.

Survival instinct took over. She ran, arms pumping, and rocketed away from the beast. Then a quick leap over a stray thorny bush. Don't think. Just keep moving. Her heels slammed hard rock, feet barely hitting the sand.

She spared a fast check over her shoulder.

The beast was gaining, yellow eyes burning for blood.

What *was* that thing? Shouldn't she know?

Didn't matter. Right now, she had no place to hide and no idea how to escape. No trees large enough to hide behind. Nothing.

Just the mountains. They were her safe haven. She knew that, but how? Was there a place to hide in those rocks up ahead? Maybe that beast couldn't follow her up a sharp incline.

Keep moving.

Ragged breaths brushed past her dry lips. Hot air scorched her chest. She gagged on the creature's nauseating smell. She could hear it gaining on her. Shaking the earth even more now.

I'm running too hard. Won't last at this pace. Her lungs were going to burst. *Have to find cover.*

Where?

Stinging sweat poured into her eyes when she looked up to see what lay ahead. Huge boulders had tumbled into a monolithic pile along the nearest ridge, as if stacked by a giant's hand.

Tell me that beast can't climb.

If she could just get far enough ahead and reach the peak on the other side of those boulders, she might escape that thing.

She veered slightly left, pistoning her arms faster and breathing hard as prey being run to ground.

Fifty feet. *Run faster.*

Thirty feet. *Not going to make it.*

Ten feet. *Come on.* Almost there. Almost.

A roar screamed through the air.

She leaped from ground to rock. Slammed a knee. Slapped raw palms against jagged surfaces baked by the sun. Heat scorched her skin.

Ignore the pain.

Climb, climb, climb!

Scrambling fast as a lizard, she reached for crevices, slapping her knees and thighs on every sharp edge.

Another scream rent the air, higher pitched this time but farther away. She risked a quick glance. The thing pawed the ground. Dust erupted, choking the air.

She stretched for the next handhold and pulled herself forward. What *did* that thing want? Was it just in a rampage or did it want her? She slipped and scrambled up, flipping around to catch her breath.

At the base of the rocks, the creature started morphing from a huge, low-to-the-ground beast to a tall, thin canine shape with a short, sleek coat of sand-colored hair.

And talons.

Was that possible? It shouldn't be. *I'm so dead.*

She bit her lip, tasting blood. *Can't quit now.* She sucked in another blast of baked air and clawed her way up the next rock outcropping. Sunlight poked through crevices from the other side. Maybe if she could get to the other side there'd be someplace to hide.

Or people.

Like me? *Where are my people*?

Worry later.

The sun roasted her exposed skin and beat down on her back siphoning away what energy she had. Muscles burned the harder she climbed. Blood pounded in her ears. She didn't want to be eaten by some monster. She jammed the toes of her boots into whatever crack she could find and shoved her body higher, faster. Fingers searching the rough surface, she clutched at a finger hole.

But it was sandstone. She slipped, digging her fingers deeper, and scrambled hand-over-hand.

The sound of loose rocks falling behind forced her exhausted body to keep moving.

Hot breath licked the air below her legs.

Her heart thrashed around.

The beast was almost on her.

A space between rocks gaped to her left. Scrunching her shoulders as thin as possible, she plunged into the narrow V opening, raking her back raw.

A shaft of blue sky yawned on the other side.

Deadly panting echoed closer behind her.

Fighting panic, she made one last shove forward and lunged through the opening too late to see where she went.

Nothing but air.

Her feet flipped over her head. She coughed out a choked screech and tumbled. Blue sky and rusty-brown rocks blurred through her vision. She hit hard, face slapping the dirt.

Pain. She couldn't breathe. It knocked the breath out of her. Her head spun and every bone reverberated. Her next wheezing gasp hurt.

"Son of a bitch!" a strange young male voice called. "Hey, dude, we got a skydiver."

Do I know the name Dude?

She opened her mouth and groaned. The only sound she could make.

"Hey, babe, where's your chute?" the same voice asked, closer now.

Babe?

"Idiot, she fell from the rocks." Another voice that sounded just as young and male joined the first. "She's a mess. Leave her."

"No way she fell. From those rocks?" the first male argued. He whistled low. "Should be dead." Then he whispered, "Hey. Maybe she is. We better go."

We'll all be dead if that beast follows me. She twisted her head enough to look up at the cliff face she'd just dived from.

There. In the crevice of dusty-red boulders loomed a shadow. Long and thin. Waiting.

Even from this distance, she felt the danger. Predator eyeing prey. But what kept it from attacking now? The other people? The distance? Could that thing not shift from land animal to a winged creature and swoop down?

Beware the beast whispered through her mind.

As if she hadn't figured that out? That voice stirred a memory, almost. It had been a feminine voice filled with worry. *Who?* Rayen clawed the sand and rocks in frustration. *Why can't I remember?*

The flicker of knowing slid away faster than dust through an hourglass.

Fear coiled in her chest. *I'm so confused.* The blank spots in her mind terrified her far more than the beast did.

"She's alive," the young nosy guy said. Sounded like he walked off.

Well, she'd gotten her wish and found people.

Rolling onto her back, she sucked slowly to pull in air, but it still hurt. Her entire body hurt. Body slammed twice and feeling as if she'd been squeezed from the inside out.

The second male voice called from a little further away. "Come on, Taylor, move it. We gotta get out of here before—"

A high-pitched screeching noise blasted over the top of the stranger's words, followed by the echo of an older male voice. Not the ghost's voice, a different one. His words boomed through a mechanical amplifier, shouting, "*Stay where you are. Hands in the air. Stop!*"

But instead of stopping anyone, bodies swung into action. She angled her head to figure out who was doing what. She'd thought there were only one or two people nearby, but a dozen plus young ones erupted around her. Running in all directions. Dust devils with legs.

The booming voice barked more commands. "*Stop where you are. Down on the ground. This is the APD.*"

She had no problem complying. Flat on her back, she stared up at an empty, vast sky. Breathing was about all she could do.

Wonder what an APD is?

As if in answer, gravel crunched under approaching steps. A weathered face with skin as dark as that on her arms hovered into view. Indigo blue pants with a knife-sharp crease and dust-covered boots. One boot kicked her hip.

She gritted her teeth to hold back a groan of pain. *A warrior never allows an enemy to see you flinch.*

Had that been another random thought or a memory? One she knew as truth?

"Stay right where you are, kid. No funny stuff and you won't get hurt."

Too late. Everything ached right down to the roots of her hair. And why had he called her a kid? Was that anything like a dude? She dug around in her mind and came up with kid as a baby goat.

Maybe I'm not the only one with scrambled brains.

The boot nudged her again. "Get up. Slow and easy."

She eyed that boot, considering what would happen if she spun his foot to face the wrong way. But he had a black metal object on his hip that could be a weapon, and she still didn't know what was going on.

Breaking his ankle didn't seem too smart.

Rolling to her side, she shuddered to her knees. That settled it. She was in no shape to fight anyone right now. She'd made the right decision not to antagonize this person. Bracing herself, she lurched up to stand and anchored her feet shoulder width apart. Wiping at her arms had been a mistake. Sand and grit clung to her damp skin. All she did was grind it into the raw places.

The man she faced stood barely taller than her. An elder she estimated to be three times her age if that old ghost had been right about her being seventeen.

He had eyes like coarse stone and age seamed this man's face. His voice snapped with anger when he spoke. "What kind of damn outfit you wearing, girl?"

He said *girl* as if she reminded him of a maggot. As for her clothes, what about *his*?

Couldn't place what he wore, but she sensed the meaning behind his words and attitude–authority.

All the elders milling around wore the same covering–blue pants, light blue shirts, everything regulated and unyielding except for the sweat stains at their armpits and lower backs.

She cast another glance around then at her clothes. No one was dressed like her. Not even the others her age. They wore a different type of uniform–unusual words and designs written across their chest coverings-PMS, Mad Cow Disease, Rangers. Loose pants that sagged at their hips, colorful footwear too short to be boots. The more she took in, the less she understood.

She asked her mind again for what was normal or how she'd ended up here and found only cold emptiness filled with dark shadows.

Fear turned into a rabid animal in her chest, fighting to get out.

With no idea who she was or where she belonged, would these people help her?

"You going native?" the man asked me, guffawing. He shouted over his shoulder, "Hey Burt, we got one thinks she's Pocahontas. Looks Navajo, like that other kid you got cuffed."

Pocahontas? Could that be my name, too? No. Judging by the way he'd treated her so far, he didn't know her and didn't care. The crazy old ghost had shown more concern.

A young boy shouted a snarled string of words.

The other elder in this group, a guy called Burt, clasped metal rings on the scrawny one's wrists. He was younger than her and looked more malnourished than dangerous. Her head throbbed with confusion. What had the first elder meant by saying she looked Navajo? What was a Navajo? She fingered her hair again, drawing the strands to her eyes. Straight and black like the skinny kid. Was her face as sharp as his? Were her eyes brown, too?

Acid boiled up her throat.

Not one thing seemed familiar, and she didn't even know what she looked like. Panic darted across the other young faces, but they seemed to know where they were headed and were not happy about it. None of them appeared confused over why they were being captured. No one had that *who am I* look of confusion she was certain sat on her face.

And no one here recognized her.

Blue lights flashed drawing her gaze to a dirty white box with wheels. Was that how the elders had arrived? That form of travel seemed wrong, but she couldn't pinpoint why.

Who were these people? What did they want?

While the two elders talked back and forth, she scanned the cliff face again. Was that beast gone? Or had it merged so deep into the shadow of the rocks as to be invisible.

Turning around, she eyed the male and female elders rounding up the struggling captives. Could the beast thing have morphed into an elder? If so, what were her chances of escaping these people?

"You got a name?" the man at her side barked.

She whispered through cracked, dry lips. "Rayen."

"That a first name or a last?"

She shook her head. Big mistake. Pain shot through her battered skull. The elder waited for her to answer, but the ghost hadn't shared more than a single name. She licked her lips and said, "Don't know."

"Can't hear you."

She got her back up with him constantly yelling at her. "I *don't* know." Talk about the scary truth. An icy ball of terror jackknifed around inside her and he wanted another name. She kept her face passive, trying to figure out what to say when she knew so little. Her eyes watered, but she blinked against tears.

She was not one who cried easily. Strange, but she *knew* this about herself. *Never expose a vulnerability* rolled through her thoughts.

She might not know who she was, but some deep-seated instinct told her to trust herself to know how to survive.

"Where you from, kid?"

Just keep asking me questions I can't answer, chewing up my insides. She shook her head.

"Don't have a last name? Don't have a home? Wrong answers, kid." The elder reached for something in his belt. "Turn around. Hands behind your back."

She'd have no way to escape if he bound her.

As if she had a choice? There were too many of the blue uniforms with the black metal devices on their hips. She knew to respect the danger of those devices. Even if she did try to run, the beast was still out there. She could feel its presence bone deep.

Reluctantly, she turned. She'd wait for a better chance to escape. A narrow strip of rigid material looped against her bruised wrists tightened with a sharp tug.

"That'll keep you." The man sounded pleased. "Where's transport, Davis?" he shouted to someone.

"On the way," came a female answer.

"Captain's going to be glad to know we got this gang corralled before they disappeared into the Sandias," the man next to her bragged. "You were right about these kids holing up this side of the Del Agua Trail."

Del Agua. That name pinged in her brain. She knew of that trail.

Another positive sign, right?

"Folks out at Piedra Lisa Park will be happier," another person said, laughing.

Piedra Lisa Park? Her shoulders fell. She didn't know that name or what they were talking about.

A sudden jerk on her arm sent her stumbling. She couldn't swallow the groan that slid out this time.

"Keep up, kid. No lagging. We got room for one more in this van." The man spoke out of the side of his mouth as he half dragged, half-shoved her toward one of the dusty boxes with wheels and iron mesh windows. This one already jammed full of snarling, angry young prisoners.

Wary glares taut with anger and fear sized her up.

No friendly faces there.

Her arms and legs trembled at the thought of being caged and helpless. And no telling when that beast would attack again. Could it get inside this box with wheels?

Stalling, she asked, "Where are we going?"

"Why we're taking you to the Hilton Albuquerque." The man snickered.

A Hilton Albuquerque? What was that place? Could the beast get to her there?

"Where?" she asked, nerves getting to her.

"Don't be a fool, girl." The man thrust a meaty hand on the top of her head and shoved her inside toward the only remaining single seat. The taint of fear and sweat filled her nose. Heads hung, shoulders hunched. They knew what waited for them and she did not. One more unknown tightened her throat muscles.

She gritted her teeth and asked again, "*Where* are you taking me?"

"Where do ya think we take juvenile delinquents who steal twelve-thousand dollars worth of valuables and destroy a business just for fun?"

Stealing? Destruction? She wrenched at the tight bond around her wrists, panicked.

She wasn't a criminal.

Was she?

CHAPTER 3

WHAT HAD SHE DONE TO end up *here*?

What was this place?

Determined to show a strong front, she held herself erect in the stiff seating. Hands clenched together in her lap hid the terror vibrating inside her.

Artificially cooled air washed across her skin, a welcome break from the heat outside. But the air in this room smelled stale and suffocating. She found it odd to recognize materials like glass, metal, and wood, but being inside a structure with glass windows and wooden doors unfamiliar.

The elders in blue uniforms, called officers, dropped her here alone. What happened to the other young ones going to the place called jail?

Burt had warned her not to screw this up. This being … school.

She knew the definition of a school, or to be schooled on a topic. But the mental path she ran along chasing down those thoughts disappeared before she could find the end.

She rubbed her wrists, glad to be uncuffed.

One of the two doors to the room opened, snapping her to attention.

Three people entered. More elders. Two men and a woman. The woman and one of the men appeared to be around thirty years old. The other male elder appeared to have aged at least twenty more years based on the gray in his hair and deep grooves on his face.

Correction. They weren't *elders*.

She'd heard them called adults.

"I'm Dr. Maxwell," the oldest man said as he folded his flabby body into a seat behind a large table.

In a rigid chair opposite of him, she sat perfectly still and silent.

An elder of his age should offer her some comfort. Not this one. He had stone-cold eyes, which assessed and weighed everything. Dr. Maxwell pointed at the other two. "This is Mr. and Mrs. Brown, the benefactors of The Byzantine Institute of Excellence."

Institute, another word for school, but just as odd sounding as the term *adults*. She kept tucking away every little piece of new information, sick of feeling so out of place and confused, but she lifted her gaze to the Browns.

The two men had much lighter skin color than hers, especially the doctor, with thinning hair and pale skin dotted with age spots. But Mrs. Brown's skin resembled hers.

All three watched her as if waiting for her to address them.

She'd rather wait until she had to speak, but she was tired of being pushed here and there. Tired of being confused. The sooner she got answers, the sooner she hoped to find her way home. "Why am I here?"

Dr. Maxwell sat back, eyeing her with a flat gaze. "The Albuquerque PD said your fingerprints didn't match those found at the Piedra Lisa Park break-in, but neither did your prints pop up right away in their initial run through the database. Since you were captured with the gang suspected of these crimes, you'd normally be held in juvenile detention while they decide what to do with you."

"PD?" she uttered, hating to not understand words.

"Police department," Dr. Maxwell clarified, sounding annoyed, as if he did not believe her confusion.

PD was law authority. She'd heard the other kids whispering about detention and something called juvie. Scared them bad. She held her silence to allow this Dr. Maxwell to continue explaining.

"The police deal with a number of Native American kids every year. Most are no older than you, some are criminals, and some have been turned out of their homes to survive on their own. The Browns–" He nodded at the other two adults as if she'd forgotten their names already. "Sponsor a handful of Native teens every year. The police know to contact them about potential candidates. While we wait to hear back from the detectives about your background check, you've been given the opportunity to remain here ... as long as you behave and don't cause any trouble."

She wanted to ask what a Native American was but decided it might be wise to wait and not sound any more ignorant than she had so far.

At the jail, a worker had called her a savage and shoved a handful of clothes at her. They'd sent her to a small room where she'd washed off most of the dirt. She now wore a thin maroon colored chest cover they'd called a T-shirt. It was soft against her cuts and bruises, plus the blue pants — no, these were known as jeans. She hadn't minded changing.

At least now she felt clean, and people had stopped staring at her.

"Rayen?" The woman speaking to her in a gentle voice had smooth skin, and warm greenish-brown eyes above sharp cheeks. Like what Rayen had seen in a mirro when she changed clothes, but her eyes were a bright greenish blue. She swallowed hard against nausea, recalling how she did not know the face in that mirror.

Mrs. Brown smiled, the first welcoming expression Rayen had seen since opening her eyes in the desert. The woman's sun-colored yellow dress flattered her skin. Compassion in her face reminded Rayen of another woman, one with straight black hair like hers and … she wanted to growl when the image never completely formed.

She realized Mrs. Brown had gotten quiet, waiting for something in response. Rayen went with the simplest reply. "Yes?"

"We're here to help you, Rayen." Mrs. Brown smiled over at Mr. Brown. The tall man had dressed in charcoal gray pants and a matching … jacket. She'd heard that reference at the police building. Beneath the jacket, he wore a white T-shirt. Might not be a T-shirt. It had buttons. Yes. Those were buttons.

While Rayen struggled to grasp any memory, three sets of eyes judged every breath she took. She had to hold her panic back and stay calm when she wanted to rant and scream. She'd been taught discipline by someone. Her elders?

Who were *her* elders? Where were they?

Mr. Brown stood with his back against a wall of books and ...

Colors flashed in Rayen's mind, prodding her to think harder. Those were *real* books printed on *paper*. Her heart thumped faster. Paper was precious because ... she clenched her fingers at hitting a blank spot again. Her next breath shook at failing to piece together yet another shattered memory.

Mr. Brown missed nothing, arms crossed, observing her with the intensity of a wise elder who shielded his thoughts.

When he flicked a look at Mrs. Brown, she moved closer to Rayen, taking the chair on her right. "We've been told you have no identification."

"Yes." Rayen wasn't sure what these people expected for identification other than her face. Eye scan? That triggered another half-memory, which vanished as quickly as it had come. She wanted to pound the chair arm.

"I've been told you are reluctant to share information. Is that correct?" Mrs. Brown continued.

"No." Rayen hesitated, debating over how much information to reveal, but what did she have to lose? "I just do not *remember* information to share."

"Oh." Mrs. Brown paused, seeming perplexed, but her lips turned up in a reassuring way. "I understand so let me tell you about our Institute."

"Why?"

"Perhaps you'd fit in here."

Rayen's heart dropped to her knees. She had no interest in joining her school, but from the minute her hands had been tied this morning, she'd lost all control of her life. She was their prisoner. For now.

To avoid antagonizing her captors, she nodded to appear agreeable.

"Our program is for teens of high school age and is different from other schools in this part of the country in that we have two unique areas of study. We use a selection process based upon the skills of each student. Our diverse program was created to offer students with unusual abilities a chance to excel in areas not often taught in other venues. Or perhaps not taught in as specific a way as how we guide students here."

What was this woman talking about? At a loss, Rayen gave her another nod, prodding the woman to continue talking.

"We pride ourselves on not only accepting students with brilliant minds who are headed for places such as MIT and Harvard, but also those who strive to develop their other senses, like their sixth sense."

Rayen understood most of the words being spoken, but some terms were strange. MIT? Harvard? *Sixth sense* ignited a thought, though. Six senses. Touch, smell, hearing, taste, sight ... and intuition, power, or energy.

Was that correct?

"Do you understand what I'm saying, Rayen?" Mrs. Brown asked, alerting her that she could tell her mind had wandered. Again.

"Yes." That word worked a whole lot better than constantly saying no, as Rayen had been doing up until now. She would play this word game to keep them from binding her wrists again and locking her away. She had to be free to move for a chance to escape.

Dr. Maxwell leaned forward, resting his arms on his desk, but his eyes hadn't warmed at all. Snake eyes. "What Mrs. Brown is trying to tell you is that she and Mr. Brown award a small number of positions to select students from less fortunate homes, depending on how the student tests. We understand that some teens run away from bad situations. We can't guarantee that you'll get a placement here without gaining permission from your family, or if you don't qualify after testing, but if you tell us the truth about who you are and where you're from, we'll assign you an academic advisor and see what we can do."

They wanted her to stay! Here? For how long? Rayen couldn't swallow past the knot of tension in her throat. She didn't belong here.

But she had no idea where she *did* belong.

Mrs. Brown tapped a finger on her arm. "Who's your family?"

A question Rayen couldn't answer with yes or no. She admitted, "I don't know." She was tired of being viewed as a bug with no more sense than to run under the nearest boot heel. She opened her mouth to say, *I woke up in the desert, disoriented and with a beast chasing me*, but her survival instinct kicked in again, warning her that less was more right now.

"Don't know?" Mr. Maxwell's calm face slipped, showing his true feelings. Irritation. Disgust. He glanced at Mr. Brown, his tone dismissing her from this conversation. "*We'll* know who she is by the end of the day once we get the police results on her fingerprints. I think we're done here ... right?"

Mr. Brown's angular face still showed no emotion until he looked at his wife and his blue-gray eyes softened. "What do you think, sweetheart?"

Mrs. Brown swung around with a look of pleading on her face. "We haven't gotten the results of the blood test to review yet, Charles." She turned to Dr. Maxwell. "Would you check on those again?"

Rayen had known what the officers had been doing when they took copies of her fingerprints, even though the ink pad they'd pressed her fingers on had seemed like a messy way to transfer prints. Then they'd jabbed her with a sharp needle.

They'd drawn blood.

Everybody wanted her blood today. What did these people want with it?

Dr. Maxwell flipped open the top of a thin metal case with an apple-shaped emblem on the lid and started tapping at it with his fingers. "The blood results just came through and–" He leaned closer, reading something, then his forehead creased sharply before he turned to Mr. Brown. "Uh, we do need to review this report."

Mr. Brown's eyes lit with interest.

Mrs. Brown slid forward in her chair, anxious, but before she could say anything her husband shot a pointed look at Rayen and said, "You may wait in the next room."

When she didn't move, Dr. Maxwell stood and took a step toward her.

Tired of getting dragged, shoved, and jerked around by strangers, particularly the eld ... the adults, she jumped to her feet, arms loose, hands ready for defense.

Mr. Brown unfolded his arms and reached over as if to restrain the doctor as he spoke to her. "*Please* go to the next room. Wait for us there."

Mrs. Brown stood just as quickly, putting herself between the doctor and Rayen. The woman gently cupped her arm. If either of the men had touched her, she couldn't say what would have happened, but this woman's touch reached past Rayen's need to fight. Her need to protect herself.

Mrs. Brown smiled reassuringly at her and indicated the second door with her free hand. "There's a waiting room right in there. We'll send someone for you in a moment, okay?"

Releasing a harsh breath that had backed up in her chest, Rayen nodded before turning to open the door. As she passed through and pulled the door almost closed, Dr. Maxwell spoke in a low, excited voice, but too quiet for her to understand.

She paused with the barely open door at her back and focused her full attention on his words. Heat bloomed in her chest and radiated out through her body as she concentrated. This felt right even if she did not understand what was happening.

The more she focused, the clearer the voices sounded.

Dr. Maxwell was saying, "... I'm telling you there are markers in her blood like nothing we've had before."

Mrs. Brown asked, "What specific markers?"

"With just one pass through the new software program, her DNA spiked alerts in four of our profile areas with the strongest algorithmic—"

Rayen didn't understand the next part. Just a string of strange letters and numbers. She'd heard of "software" and "DNA" at some point. Software versus hardware. DNA determined bloodline. She could almost hear the words in her mind coming from something inanimate as it instructed her.

Mrs. Brown spoke up. "I say we put her in the computer science program and see what she does."

What happened to *'we can't guarantee you placement without getting your family's permission'?*

And what of Rayen's family? Did they exist? Did they know what had happened to her? Were they looking for her? A dark ache stabbed at her heart. A hole so large it threatened to swallow her.

The door suddenly snapped shut at her back, pushing her a step forward. She opened her eyes, quickly taking in her surroundings.

She stood inside a larger room that had chairs placed around the walls. There were three doors and several small tables that weren't as tall as her knees.

And someone watched her–a young male with a mature gaze.

Embarrassment heated her face at having been so focused on the conversation about her she'd lost track of her surroundings. A dangerous mistake.

This young one might be a teen or kid, but the young ones captured with her had not called each other teens. Might be because the adults had said *teens* in a negative way.

A couple of the boys close to her age had called other males in the area *guys*. That had seemed acceptable to all of them.

Trying to talk like everyone else here could only help her.

This ... *guy* lounged in one of the chairs that appeared more padded and comfortable than the one she'd had in the doctor's room. This new stranger had skin a deeper brown color than hers, closer in shade to that of the drink he held in a bottle with writing hidden beneath his fingers. His short black hair curled in tight circles, matching the color of his pants and shirt, but his shirt had ... *buttons*. Yes, buttons sounded correct.

Brown eyes watched her with an edge of intelligence that demanded others notice him.

Not sure of any order to the seating, she strolled over to the first open chair. One of the small wooden tables separated them. She sank into the soft material, sighing over how good it felt against her abused body.

"New recruit?" the guy asked.

Would there be an end to the questions Rayen could not answer any time soon? She heaved a sigh and flipped through her knowledge to come up with the word recruit. Ah. She had it. The word meant being called to a task. As he waited for an answer, she gave him the only one she could. "Possibly."

"I'm Nicholas. You certainly appear to be new-recruit material since you're adorned with that leg iron."

She glanced down at her leg that still throbbed with pain.

Punishment for not listening to her instincts earlier when she'd first arrived at this school. Those instincts had warned her not to jump at an opportunity that had "too easy" written all over it.

But her gut had badgered her to escape at her first chance.

The officers in blue clothes who'd delivered her to this place had turned their backs for a moment outside, long enough for her to run. The minute she'd stepped through what looked like an open gateway, a bolt of energy screamed through her left leg, the one with the wicked-looking metal ankle bracelet those officers had attached.

She'd fallen to her knees, writhing in pain, then dragged herself away from the invisible field of current and flopped on the ground.

Chuckling, one of the men had walked and pointed to the metal contraption. "Guess I don't have to warn you what'll happen if you try to run with that latched to you. These fine people take in low-life scum and half-breeds like you. Best show your appreciation and don't give 'em no trouble. Or you won't like where we take you next."

Still shaking in pain, that barely registered on her barometer of concern when she had just wanted to close her eyes and pretend this was all a bad dream.

"Hey, just kiddin' with you, sweetheart," Nicholas said in a lighthearted tone, bringing her back to the present with a snap. "Don't feel singled out. Recruits who arrive via government channels rather than being enrolled by family wear a security device until the front office receives all the records. The Institute is responsible for you. No big deal. They can't risk being sued if you wander off the property. Not as though you're in prison or something."

That made sense, except for being sued. What did that mean? Added to the list of information missing from her brain. If this school gathered records, maybe they would figure out where she'd come from and who her people were.

Would they send someone to find her family?

Nicholas leaned forward in his chair. "Where do you hail from?"

This guy didn't sound like any of the kids she'd met earlier. He had a stiff way of talking and sounded more like one of the adults.

She frowned at him. "Hail from?"

"Your point of origin. Home."

She pinched her lips, unwilling to say 'I don't know' one more time so she summed it up all at once. "I know my name's Rayen, but not where I'm from. I have no idea what I'm doing here or if I'll stay. I hit my head in the desert and can't remember anything." She'd heard the kids in the van talking about her.

One had made a comment that she could have lost her memory from the fall.

Sounded like an explanation for the empty spots in her mind.

"Word to the wise, sweetheart." Nicholas glanced at her sideways. "Don't tell anyone you've suffered a head injury."

How could that complicate her life any more than it already was at this point. She had to work through everything minute by minute already. What other reason would she have for not knowing answers?

But this Nicholas was the first person since Ghost Man to offer advice without sneering when he spoke. She asked, "Why not? It was not intentional."

He scratched his ear and took his time as if thinking very hard or hesitant to share. At last, he said, "If Dr. Maxwell thinks you are damaged goods, you'll be withdrawn from here so fast you'll get whiplash. Then you'll end up in the detention center hospital. Those who go there experience *mutatio*."

Hospital? She thought she might have heard that term before but not enough to track.

Rayen asked, "What's *mutatio*?"

Smiling with regal superiority, Nicholas explained, "It's Latin. Means *change*."

Before she could ask what exactly he meant, one of the doors not connected to Dr. Maxwell's room opened and a female young one entered. Rayen caught her thought and made a correction. This young one was a *girl* or *teenager*, based upon what she'd heard at the police station.

This one looked a year or so younger than Rayen. Bouncing happily into the room, the teenager had white plugs in her ears and a tiny pink metal square on her hip. She wore an orange, green and purple dress with wide side pockets. The dress was draped over purple-and-white striped tights that disappeared into scuffed black boots with three-inch-thick heels. She'd twisted her yellow-and-lavender hair into eight or ten ponytails that stuck out in all directions.

Every ponytail had a different color ribbon tied around it and moved with the rhythmic shake of her hips.

Nothing matched on her, including her eyes ... one brown and one green.

Two different color eyes?

The strange teen paused, took one look at her with those unusual eyes, then her lips curled in a quirky half-moon curve full of curiosity. She removed a plug from one ear. Her gaze slid over to Nicholas.

He said, "Where's your broom, Gabby? Wouldn't want you caught with no transportation."

Broom? Rayen couldn't understand the connection with transportation, but she read insult in Gabby's face just fine before the girl covered her reaction with a wicked smile.

"Nick, you're such a flirt. Careful or I might turn you into a horny toad," Gabby replied in a singsong voice, then snapped her fingers. "Oh, wait, someone already did." She laughed, a fluttery sound that danced through the room.

Nick gave her an indulgent smile, one which didn't quite reach his eyes, but he seemed more amused than insulted. "What would we do without eye candy in this place? I salute whoever scours the country to decorate our halls with sweet things to entertain the male student body."

Rayen kept her face neutral, glad not to be the center of attention. Derision in his voice keyed a memory she couldn't pin down beyond the distinct feeling of anger over being ridiculed for her differences at one time. She felt a fleeting camaraderie with this girl who smiled at Nicholas in the face of the demeaning insinuation beneath his words.

Gabby continued swinging her hips back and forth as if to some secret musical beat. "Whatcha doing up here, Nick? Waiting for an optimum snitch opportunity?"

Once again, Rayen suffered being mentally lost. *What was a snitch opportunity*?

Nicholas enjoyed taunting this Gabby in a way that *sounded* harmless, but Rayen had her doubts. On one hand, Gabby acted as if whatever he said was funny when Rayen had the sense he'd struck a nerve hidden beneath Gabby's indulgent smile.

On the other hand, what did Rayen know?

Nothing.

Nicholas chuckled. "What brings *you* here, Gabby? You lose your crystal ball and get stuck having to navigate your way around humans?"

Her laughter tinkled with a sly undertone. "Oh, to be a mere mortal." She pranced past Nicholas and out the last door that opened into a hallway.

"She's schizo," Nicholas muttered. "Stay clear of that one."

How many new words would Rayen have to learn just to get around this place? "What do you mean by schizo?"

"Crazy. Rumor is she hears voices." He spun a finger around his ear.

So? I talk to ghosts, which Rayen kept to herself. No way was she going to admit that to this guy, but she took note of his warning about Gabby.

The door from Dr. Maxwell's office opened again and another girl came into the room, as different from Gabby as the sun from the moon. This one wore her auburn hair straight and chin length, vibrant pink on her lips, and had a round face with such perfect features Rayen peered close to see if she was real. Where Gabby had been a lightning display, this girl came across more regal with her ice-blue eyes and russet-red tunic that stopped at the middle of her thighs. The sleeves on her white jacket were shoved up.

This girl clutched a fist full of papers and held a thick, dull-green book against her chest, then cast a bored look at Rayen. "I'm Hannah. You must be Rayen."

After she gave another nod, Hannah continued in dull voice that sounded imposed upon. "I've been asked to show you around the school and take you to class."

"Class?"

Her eyes rolled with impatience before she said, "You've been assigned to Mr. Suarez's computer science class in room 217."

"Oh." *A learning program*, Rayen mused. But with a *real person* instructing?

"Follow me." Hannah issued that directive as though ordering people around came naturally to her.

Nicholas spoke up and this time his voice had a smooth texture. "How's it going, Hannah banana?"

Rayen studied Nicholas to figure out what had caused him to change from a superior tone to one of lighthearted teasing.

Hannah even sounded different when she addressed him in a soft tone. "Fi-ine. And you, Nick?"

"Never better."

There were undercurrents here, but it was one more thing Rayen couldn't figure out. She stood with thoughts flying through her mind. *Why am I being sent to a class? I just want to find out who I am ... where I came from ... and do I have family?*

The last being the most important.

As she started to move, Nicholas whispered behind her, "Remember, sweetheart. Mutatio. Tell no one."

Lifting a hand to acknowledge his words, Rayen murmured, "Thanks." And she *was* thankful that he'd cautioned her before she made the mistake of adding to her problems by admitting a head injury.

The hospital sounded like a place to avoid no matter what.

Nicholas raised his voice just above a whisper, but she knew he still spoke to her. "Any time. You need anything, you let me know."

The only thing she needed was to fill the gaping hole in her memory and doubted he could do that.

Rayen followed Hannah out into a hallway. Once they were out of Nick's hearing, something Gabby had said nudged Rayen to ask Hannah, "Do you know what *snitch* means?"

She wheeled around with a pinched look as though the question had been how many noses Rayen had on her face. When she realized Rayen was serious, she huffed out a noisy sound, answering as if she recited a definition. "A snitch is someone who takes you into their confidence and acts like a close friend, then shares that information with an adversary or enemy, quite often in trade for something they want. Got it?"

"Yes." Snitch was another name for a traitor. Rayen had one more question. "What do you know about Nicholas?"

Hannah's smile tilted with a smug angle. "He's at the top of his class in computer science. He's very popular with all the girls. And ..." She swept a long look down her nose at Rayen. "And he's off limits to you, but you should be polite to him."

"Why?" Rayen ignored why he had limits and focused on Hannah's last words. "Are people unkind to him?"

"Are you serious? No. He's their *only* child."

"Whose only child?"

"The Browns. They adopted him."

Rayen's stomach dropped. She'd just spoken openly with Nicholas *Brown*, someone who could easily tell his parents that she was damaged goods.

Mrs. Brown had been her only ally so far, but what would happen when she found out Rayen was not suitable for this place?

Closing her eyes, Rayen swallowed hard. She might not have wanted to be here to begin with, but she certainly didn't want to go to that hospital and end up *mutatio.*

CHAPTER 4

RAYEN FOLLOWED HANNAH, WHO HAD stopped briefly in a noisy room filled with teens long enough to eat a bowl of soup.

Matching her guide's pace as she moved down the sterile walkways, Rayen sniffed the air. Everything smelled well-scrubbed but confining. Hannah still carried the papers and the book with the hard green cover. It had to be two inches thick. Rayen's fingers itched to hold the book and touch the papers, but she wouldn't ask.

Hannah barely tolerated her presence.

Every time Rayen said more than yes or no, people looked at her as though she lacked brains. Same as Hannah's perpetual expression.

Rayen's internal defenses continued to bellow for her to escape.

Not going to happen this time until she knew how to leave without getting zapped by an electric charge.

Or knew *where* she was going.

A tone dinged three times overhead from some hidden source.

Waving a hand at rooms we passed, which were full of young ones, Hannah said, "That's the final bell to be in class on time, but it takes a moment for the instructor to get things rolling so we're fine."

She pointed out plaques on the wall touting someone's accomplishments and droned on about what had inspired the creation of the school, but her mind drifted.

Rayen cut her gaze left, then right, taking in each classroom through open doors. Heads turned her way, curious expressions, but not a flicker of recognition on her part or theirs. She'd never been here before or surely someone would have recognized her by now.

What would her fingerprints reveal? And couldn't those be altered? Why not search their records for her face or use a retina scan which couldn't be altered so easily?

She stopped midstride. How did she know fingerprints could be changed ... or about retina scans? No one had mentioned those options. Should she?

Only if she wanted to be treated like a moron again.

Hannah had been in the middle of describing something about the school. Her monotonous voice faded as she kept walking then paused, looked around, and spoke in a snippy tone. "Rayen."

"Sorry." Rayen caught up to her.

Hannah drew a deep breath, expelling the air slowly with a brief shake of her head then continued rambling on. "As I was saying, the Browns are rich. Very rich. They bought this place four years ago for the Institute. *If* you make it through here, you're pretty much guaranteed a spot in a top college. You're fortunate the Browns aren't just loaded, but nice people to be so generous."

Rayen zeroed in on the one word that didn't track for her. "Nice? Then why'd they give me this leg bracelet?"

She glanced at Rayen's ankle where the metal cuff barely showed below the bottom of her jeans, then raised a dismissive gaze. "It's a security measure that Dr. Maxwell requires ... for *some* students. Just until the staff is sure the student is ready to stay here."

Meaning, Dr. Maxwell expected a certain number of students to try to escape. If this place was so good, and the Browns were such nice people, why would anyone want to run away? More questions without answers.

And more reasons for Rayen to get out of here. She who didn't fit in with Hannah's kind.

Stopping in front of the last open door in the hallway, Hannah rapped on the doorframe with her knuckles. She broke out a bright smile for someone inside and said, "I have the new student the office sent you the text about."

Text? Rayen didn't ask.

Hannah backed up, clearing the way for a thin man to step out into the hallway. He wore a white shirt with half sleeves and pants the color of the desert. Strange clothes to Rayen, but from the way everyone had reacted to her simple buckskin sack dress, as described by one person at the police building, *she* was the strange one here. She wished they'd given her back the boots she'd first worn. Those had been more comfortable than the things on her feet now. Sneakers.

Did that mean these shoes made it easy to sneak around? If so, they might be useful.

Altering her voice to a superior tone that reminded Rayen of Nicholas, Hannah addressed the skinny man. "This is Rayen. No last name." She turned, stabbing a serious gaze at Rayen as if in warning. "This is Mr. Suarez, your beginning computer science instructor. The Institute will give you additional classes once they know your academic level and *if* you'll be staying." Her look said that wasn't likely and she didn't care anyway. She handed several sheets of paper to Mr. Suarez then edged a step closer to Rayen and thrust the book she'd been carrying at her.

Surprised, Rayen grasped it in both hands and held the precious material carefully. Her fingers moved with respect and awe over the texture of the cover.

Hannah tapped the hard cover. "You probably won't get time to read much by the end of the day, if you *can* read, but this book will help you familiarize yourself with the school guidelines and programs offered. *If* you stay around, finish it this week. Oh, I almost forgot. You're to be at Dr. Maxwell's office at five o'clock today to meet with them again."

The way she kept emphasizing *if* was starting to wear on Rayen.

Hannah tossed her head and turned away, prancing toward the classroom.

"Why?" Rayen demanded.

Hannah jerked around as though spooked, then recovered to snap, "Why *what*?"

"Why do I meet them at five o'clock?"

"To speak with the ..." She glanced at Mr. Suarez and said, "Need a minute." When he nodded, she closed the distance between them and spoke in a low, tight voice. "Look, I agreed to bring you, but I didn't take you on as an understudy. Did you forget you got picked up by the cops this morning?"

"No." Cops must be another term for police, but how did *she* know all of this?

"Then I'll make this simple. From what I heard, the detectives investigating the Piedra Lisa Park robberies are coming by to speak with Dr. Maxwell. You wouldn't know anything about that now would you, Rayen?"

Ignoring her sarcastic tone, Rayen replied, "No." At least, she hoped not.

"Better not be the case, because if they find anything tying you to the crime spree that's been going on, they'll take you with them." A smug glow lit Hannah's gaze. "Just be sure to be in Dr. Maxwell's office at five sharp or losing permanent placement here will be the least of your worries. You'll be sent ... somewhere else."

She gave Rayen another dismissive glare then walked calmly into the classroom.

Permanent placement? Rayen didn't want to stay here, but neither did she want to be shunted off to someplace worse.

Why had she left her home?

Did she even *have* a home? Her gut said yes.

"Let's go, Rayen," Mr. Suarez said with a cool politeness, lifting his chin toward the classroom. His voice was less hostile than Dr. Maxwell's and not nearly as superior sounding as Nicholas's had been.

Rayen mentally marked Mr. Suarez as not a threat. Besides, like everything else today, she had no choice but to comply.

She hated having no say over her life.

A low murmur clouded the room until she walked in then everyone stopped talking to look. At her. She'd faced a sentient beast out in the desert. This shouldn't be worse, but her stomach kinked at moving deeper into the room. Fifteen pairs of eyes took stock and judged her on the spot.

Not a friendly face among them.

To be specific, there were sixteen pairs counting Hannah, but she hadn't followed their gazes. She'd taken her seat on the right side of the room and had her chin down, focused on setting up a slim rectangular unit on her desk. This one was similar to the unit with the apple-shaped emblem that Dr. Maxwell had used.

Based on the wide eyes and snorts of barely suppressed laughter, especially from the girls in the room, the consensus was that Rayen didn't belong.

She couldn't agree more.

"This is Rayen," Mr. Suarez informed the room, then gave her instructions. "Take one of the two seats in the back on the left, but don't turn on the monitor."

She nodded, ignoring the stares as she passed small metal tables with light colored wood surfaces. Each table held two keyboards and two flat panels … the monitors?

Monitors and keyboards.

Finally, something clicked. She knew what a monitor was, and a keyboard.

Maybe coming in here would rattle her memory.

Most of the kids seemed to be her age. As she approached the last desk on the left with seating for two people, one of the guys she passed studied her with blatant interest. He softly said, "Hel-looo, baby."

Hmm. Rayen might not grasp every meaning, but she did understand that wolfish look, especially when the girl next to him hissed something angry under her breath. He just kept smiling at Rayen.

Some things were universal. But the girl next to him wasted her energy complaining. She could have him. Rayen had no interest in him or any other male here.

All she had to do was stay out of trouble and make it to the meeting in Dr.

Maxwell's office at five o'clock.

Mr. Suarez stepped behind his desk. He muttered something about finishing roll call as he glanced up and down, his eyes searching out each student after saying a name.

Rayen settled into her chair, glad not to be in the front on display any longer.

The teacher scanned the room again. "Where's Tony?"

When no one answered, Mr. Suarez scribbled a note on his paper, placed it on his desk, and said, "Let's get started." He wrote words on a white wall behind him that read:

DEADLINE FOR THE TOP TEN COMPETITION: MAY 15, 2018

Wait, she understood that. The words at least, but not what they meant.

The instructor used his marker to tap the letters. "Deadline for this year's competition. That's two weeks from today, folks."

Rayen toyed with the date in her mind, but 2018 triggered no memories. Surely something significant had happened this year in her life.

The more she studied the date it began to feel familiar. Significant. *Why?*

She was starting to hate that three-letter word.

Every time she tried to concentrate hard on anything, an ache bit into her forehead. She rubbed her temple then dropped her hand, fingers touching the green book.

As Mr. Suarez started talking about the project, she opened the book, reading the first page of introduction. Hannah was right about how long it'd take to get through this thing, but Rayen couldn't get past how special holding a book felt.

Mr. Suarez paused.

The silence drew her attention.

He looked right at Rayen when he spoke. "For those of you who are new, the Top Ten Computer Project's a special event the Browns created where our best ten students in computer science will have a chance to compete for a full scholarship to any of the top ten universities in this country. You'll each be assigned a partner for the first phase."

Excitement flittered through the room, but Rayen sighed. She couldn't have been less interested. She returned to the book, blocking out Mr. Suarez's voice so she could read as much as possible in what time she had.

She started scanning the pages fast, really fast. Then she felt heat, or energy, swirl in her chest. The same type of feeling she'd had earlier when she listened to the Browns and Dr. Maxwell talk behind the partially closed door.

Her heart pounded. She clutched the book tighter. Energy rolled down her arms until her fingers tingled.

Pages fluttered past as if she fanned the pages, but she only held the book.

She caught every word, comprehended every sentence.

In less than a minute, she'd finished the book. And slammed it shut, earning a hard stare from a girl at the next table over. Her gaze ended with a frown and a whispered word. "Freak."

Pushing the book away, Rayen looked at her trembling hands.

Was that normal?

Was *she* normal?

"Miss Landers and Miss Pearson make up the next team," Mr. Suarez said, calling out names to match up partners for the project.

Rayen took a couple of breaths to settle herself then did a quick head count, relieved at the uneven number of students. Was there no one to match her up with?

That suited her just fine. She'd only end up proving how clueless she was about everything in this room and in this school, except for the monitor and keyboard in front of her. She might not know everything about how these units worked, but she was sure she'd seen something like them before.

"Whoa, I know you're not startin' my favorite class widdout me, Mr. S," someone announced as he entered the room. A husky-built guy with chopped-off black hair and an olive tint to his skin.

He looked about Rayen's age but had an attitude of someone years older. His dark brown, calculating eyes searched out each of the other five girls in the classroom, each of which he gifted with a wink and a cocky grin.

Rayen noted that all the girls returned his attention with varying degrees of smiles.

Even Hannah, whose lips quirked when she tossed a brief glance his way.

Mr. Suarez paused to frown. "You're late, Tony. I told you the first day of school I don't tolerate tardiness from anyone."

"My apologies, Mr. S. A young lady needed my personal assistance." His hands moved constantly, as expressive as his I'm-the-one tone. Here, there, touching a silver medallion at his neck, punctuating his words in the air. "Being a gentleman and all yourself, I know you wouldn'ta wanted me leavin' the young lady on her own."

"What kind of assistance?" the instructor asked, wary-eyed.

This Tony guy beamed a sneaky-cat grin Rayen didn't buy any more than she did his grandiose performance.

And what was this guy's strange accent?

Tony opened his hands in a what-else gesture. "New kid from Jersey and Italian, like me. Got lost her first day. I delivered her safe and sound to the front office. But I didn't waste no time humpin' it here. Like I said, sorry I was late, Mr. S, but I'm ready for the Top Ten Project. Seein's how my last name starts with an S, I'm thinkin' I'm paired up with the sweet Miss Georgiana Sanderson, right?"

A look came over Mr. Suarez's face that knocked the foundation out from under Tony's grin. "Miss Sanderson has been paired up. In fact, everyone has a partner. In light of your charitable nature to help new students–"

Rayen sat up straighter *No. No. Don't do it …*

"–you'll be teamed up with our newest student, Rayen." Mr. Suarez pointed in her direction. "Take your seat, Tony."

Tony's eyes finally lit on her. All his smug attitude slid away leaving disbelief. He stepped over to the teacher and lowered his voice, but Rayen's sharp hearing caught every word he said.

"You kiddin', Mr. S, right? You know how bitchin' I am on computers. I need someone who can hang with me, not ..." Tony cut a harsh glance at Rayen, then his expression smoothed, all charm by the time he faced Mr. Suarez again. "Not somebody just off the reservation."

One of Mr. Suarez's eyebrows arched at a sharp angle. "If this was so important you should've been punctual and I'm going to pretend I didn't hear that last comment. Rayen is your Top Ten partner until I say differently. Take your seat."

"But–"

"Now, or you're out of the competition altogether."

That had Tony snapping to attention.

Rayen had grabbed the seat closest to the corner from which she now watched as Tony swaggered down the center of the room, scowling. As he drew closer, she could see part of an image in black ink that crawled up his neck, peeking out from beneath the collar of his shirt. The design was a creature with sharp pinchers.

Some memory niggled at her. Neck markings meant something, but what?

When Tony reached her table, he dropped into the chair and crossed his arms.

The minute Mr. Suarez turned to the white board again, Tony leaned over, a nasty smile on his face when he whispered, "Find a way to disappear or I'll do it for you, sweet cheeks."

CHAPTER 5

"UNFREAKINBELIEVABLE!"

Rayen ignored Tony's latest outburst since they'd left Mr. Suarez's classroom and concentrated on searching the equipment room for a computer to rebuild. She had no idea how to perform that duty, but this gave her time to plan an escape.

She couldn't stop thinking about how she'd read that green book in seconds, yet she now stood here staring in confusion at tables filled with equipment that had monitors.

Wish I could get through this assignment as easily as I fanned through that book.

Much of the terminology in the classroom hadn't clicked for her. When Suarez had explained the principles of what he expected to see built from outdated equipment in storage, Rayen had rolled her eyes. The jumbled words still spun through her mind, some pinging a trickle of memory but others sliding past.

She hadn't minded that Tony dragged his feet to leave the classroom since it meant everyone else had already been to this storage room, chosen the parts they wanted, and left. Now it was only her and Tony.

Not ideal, but easier to escape one than a room filled with other teens.

This Top Ten Project had something to do with taking an old computer and rebuilding it into an AI or Artificial Intelligence unit. She understood those terms, had heard of a computer, and an AI somewhere, but she knew as much about turning a computer into an AI as she did about flying to Mars.

At least, she didn't think she possessed that skill or knew how fly to any other planets in the solar system. Though she did know the planets, and knowledge of space travel tapped at the edge of her mind.

She had no expectations of remaining in this program, but until she met with Dr. Maxwell or found a way to leave, she might as well pick her way through this clutter to see if she recognized anything. The green book had made multiple references to accessing information on the computer, so apparently computers were used to store a lot of documentation and records.

If one of these worked, she'd like to see if she could use it to find out something about herself. Small chance of that happening, but one could hope.

Tony shoved a monitor dusty with age out of his way, grumbling, "I should be with four-point-oh Sanderson, not some mute who doesn't even understand English."

Rayen swallowed her smile. Tony *would* think she was unable to speak since she'd refused to answer any of his obnoxious questions like what tribe had she come from. How much wampum she'd paid to get into this place? Did she have a clue how lucky she was that they let the terminally clueless into the Institute?

Did she even know where Jersey was?

No.

Instead of replying, she'd shrugged in answer, amused when Tony went off on a rant over how he wished he were back in Jersey if this was as good as it got here.

He pitched a thing he'd called a mouse into a box of miscellaneous parts and turned on her again. "You're not screwing up my chance at MIT."

There was that word MIT again.

Crossing her arms, she faced him, more curious than anything to see what this blowhard would do next. He might have two inches on her since she was maybe five-and-a-half-feet tall, but he was the one terminally clueless if he thought his loudmouth intimidated her.

Just then the door over in the corner opened and a girl backed into the room, humming a strange, but interesting tune as she dragged in a cart with cleaning products, a broom, and dust mop.

But there was no mistaking all that bizarre color. Gabby.

Still humming, she turned around and jerked back when she saw us, dropping her can of drink that rolled across the room, sloshing brown liquid everywhere.

Tony jumped sideways. "What the 'ell? Watch whatcha doin'."

Rayen gave him a dark look of warning. The poor girl had been startled. Just an accident.

"My bad," Gabby said, sounding amused until she let out a weary sigh and grabbed a towel from her cart. She dropped to all fours to wipe up the mess.

"What're you doin' here anyhow, sweet cheeks?" Tony asked in his Mr.

Nice Guy voice.

Rayen cocked an eyebrow at him. Were all girls "sweet cheeks" to this guy?

Tony looked around warily as if keeping an eye out for Mr. Suarez.

Gabby drew an exaggerated breath, eyes staring up in serious thought when she answered, "It should be obvious that I'm getting ready for the prom, but I'm still waiting for my white mice and glass slippers to arrive. Until they do, I'm relegated to two hours of cleaning up. An unfair penalty for telling the truth."

Mice and glass slippers? Rayen let that pass.

Tony rolled his eyes, dismissing her with a shake of his head, muttering, "Good practice. World needs more hamburger flippers."

"Your ridiculous opinion has been duly noted." She smiled sweetly at him with eyes twinkling as if she knew her reaction bothered him.

He turned his back on her and mumbled, "First Sacagawea. Now Cindereller."

Sacaga-who?

Shrugging at his back, Gabby bumped her shoulder into the mop hooked on her cart, knocking the stick loose. She had quick reflexes, grabbing the mop handle before it whacked Tony in the head. But when she slapped her other hand down for balance, it landed on Rayen's foot and her finger grazed the skin of Rayen's bare ankle just as she thought, *If I'm Sacagawea and she's Cindereller, that must make Tony the Jersey Jerk.*

"Jersey Jerk. That's too funn–" Gabby sucked in a breath and shoved up on her knees, snatching her hand off Rayen's foot. For a few seconds she sat there, staring ahead, frozen. Silent.

Tony kept muttering to himself. Apparently, he hadn't heard her, but Rayen had caught Gabby's words.

Had she heard Rayen's thoughts?

Weirder things than *that* had happened today already, so Rayen kept her face blank and acted as if she hadn't heard anything. She returned to moving computer parts around on the table.

That must have worked to convince Gabby no one had heard her. Her shoulders slumped, as if in relief as she continued cleaning up the spilled liquid.

The door still stood propped open with her cart half in and half out.

Temptation hit Rayen square in the chest. All at once, she wanted to leave, even if only just far enough to find a place to sit and think. Anything would be better than being stuck as Tony's shadow for the rest of the day, as Mr. Suarez had instructed her to do. She didn't want to build a computer, even if she knew how, or go to another class.

She wanted to go home, wherever that was.

With Tony distracted while removing the cover off one computer, Rayen slipped out the door. Two steps into the hallway, she smelled something rank, and familiar.

The beast. She swung around, looking everywhere until she spied a black bird, a raven maybe, perched on the top edge of an open door at the end of the hallway.

That beast *could* morph into a winged creature. But why hadn't the thing turned into a bird out in the desert?

Instead of questioning her good fortune at escaping it once, she backed up, slowly and stepped into the room again. She tugged Gabby's cart all the way inside and closed the door. Sweat dampened her palms.

Tony turned around, scowling at her, but an undercurrent of worry he hadn't managed to hide tinged his words. Something bothered him. "Suarez finds you here doin' nothin' he's hangin' it on me. You gonna help or not?"

With that beast outside, waiting, she needed to figure out a plan. A way to escape. One that wouldn't get Gabby or Tony hurt. The thing might look like a simple bird right now, but no telling what it could become in the next minute.

Rayen stepped over to the last worktable where she spied a unit similar to Dr. Maxwell's. A laptop. That's what Tony had called the thin computer units that opened like a book. A mix of styles and colors sat open in rows, facing forward like good little soldiers. She started fumbling with the closest one.

Appeased, Tony returned to tinkering with a computer on his side of the room.

Nothing happened to the one she'd chosen. No lights flickered when she hit a couple of buttons. She abandoned it and stared at others on the worktable as if one of the units would choose her. If all the cracked faces and beat up exteriors were any indication of functionality, she had serious doubts any of these were usable. But if she managed to get one turned on, maybe she could send a message for help.

Lifting her head up, Rayen paused. How did she know these things could be used to send messagges? Searching her thoughts ended in a blank again. She felt eyes on her and glanced over at Gabby who still sat on the floor with a curious squint in her gaze but said nothing.

Gabby shot Tony a weighted look then made some decision and stood up next to Rayen, murmuring, "The universe can be a strange and wonderful place ..." She paused, glancing over at Tony for a moment before adding, "If not for those who should have remained a glint in their parents' eyes. Don't you agree?"

Nicholas's warning about Gabby came back to Rayen, but this girl didn't seem dangerous. Just unusual, different from the others, but so was Rayen in their eyes.

And other than Nicholas, Gabby had been the only friendly one around Rayen's age so far.

Nicholas might be *snitching* on her at this very minute.

One problem at a time.

Gabby didn't wait on an answer, moving ahead to say, "We didn't get a chance to meet earlier. I'm Gabby."

Rayen started to offer her hand, a strange reflex that felt like what she should do to greet someone, but she left her arms hanging loose instead, wary of touching anyone.

On the other hand, Gabby didn't reach out either.

Where had Rayen gotten that stupid idea anyhow?

Tony turned halfway, took one look at the taunting smile Gabby sent him and shook his head in disgust before giving them his back.

Ah. Now this made sense. Gabby wanted to poke at Tony by being friendly with the new girl.

"I'm Rayen." She was glad to offer Gabby something in return, even if it was only her name. All she had for now.

Tony paused, shook his head, and muttered something about low placement standards.

Gabby studied Rayen with her odd, mismatched eyes. "I presume you're one of the chosen few offered a spot on the Top Ten Project."

How to answer that? Rayen was none of those things, but she *was* here for the stupid project. Had this project not been offered to others, like Gabby? Falling back on the best answer at hand, Rayen lifted her shoulders and let them drop.

"Ah, the rare humble academic. Found a suitable computer yet?"

Rayen shook her head.

Tony kept his back to them when he said, "Fat chance of Sacagawea pickin' a decent computer." He sent a pompous smile over his shoulder and told Gabby, "Why don't you call up your fairy godmother, sweet cheeks? See if a magic wand can help her."

When he returned to whatever held his attention, Gabby's lips curved up.

She touched her finger to her lips, looking as though a devious idea fueled her thoughts before she whispered to Rayen, "Put your hand out and see which computer calls to you."

At that suggestion, Rayen lifted an eyebrow.

Gabby released one of her bubbling laughs that bordered on scary then lifted her shoulders in a what-can-it-hurt motion.

Sighing in defeat, Rayen turned back to the table. She had no reason to treat Gabby with caution or condescension the way Nicholas had, because she seemed nice and harmless. Rayen stuck out her hand and waved it over the top of each laptop.

"Ah, for the love of Einstein, are you two for real?" Tony complained, crossing the room, a scowl on his face. "What *are* you doin'?"

Gabby rounded on him with an expression of excitement. "Perhaps she'll prove that techno-ites like you are not all full of dull stuffing," she taunted. "Rayen is using her sensory skills to select the perfect computer, which requires the unique ability of energy touch. Please don't try it or you might hurt yourself and I wouldn't be able to help you. My magic wand only works if you possess a heart."

Rayen smiled, playing along with the teasing while she searched for a computer that showed some promise, anything to get Tony off her back. What could it hurt to go along with Gabby? It wasn't like Rayen knew what she was doing anyhow.

Tony smacked a hand on his forehead. "Oh, no, don't tell me you're one of those woo-woo students from the east wing."

Gabby struck a pose with one shoulder cocked up and her chin held high. "Careful or I'll call my flying monkeys."

"For the love of ..." Tony mumbled, pulling out a small handheld device he started thumbing. "Say your name's Gabby, huh?"

Rayen glanced sideways. She'd seen those handheld units used earlier. Communication devices. *A phone.* She got excited. Tony could call someone and–

She moved to reach for him, but her extended hand yanked toward a laptop, jerking her forward with the powerful motion.

Her fingers gripped a scuffed-up machine in the second row that had a scratched black case. *Weird.* She caught Gabby's startled gasp, but Rayen wasn't going to acknowledge it. Instead. she lifted the computer and made room for it on the front of the worktable.

Oblivious to anyone else in the room, Tony waved his phone, chuckling. "Oh, yeah, this explains everything. Gabrielle Lin." He glanced up with a flinty gaze more calculating than friendly this time. “You don’t look Chinese.”

“Oh, dear, really? Because you certainly appear to be the spitting image of an A-hole.”

“Ah ... major screw up.” Tony focused again on his phone screen. “Says here you’re sixteen.” He eyed her up and down as if doubting her age then went back to reading. “Psychological profile ... delusions, antisocial personality syndrome, alien ... they got that right. What planet you from, babe?”

Right then and there Rayen decided that if she ended up staying here she’d figure out how to build a computer from scratch on her own before she asked Tony for anything.

Prancing around happily, Gabby ignored Tony and snagged the wire attached to the laptop that had responded to Rayen’s hand. Not just responded but had pulled her to it. She hadn’t even felt heat inside her chest this time. Did that happen with others ... or just her?

Gabby stuck the metal prongs at the end of the wire into the wall. Must be a power source.

Rayen tried to concentrate on what was happening with the laptop, but her mind still worked on what to do with the threat outside their room. What was that bird-beast doing?

She once again considered using Tony’s phone to call in help, but who would she call? Teachers? Dr. Maxwell? She’d been warned not to cause any trouble. Besides, she knew better than to try convincing the Jersey Jerk that a rabid, shapeshifting, predatory bird was loose in the hallway. Tony wanted a reason to get rid of her and that beast might morph into something else by the time someone showed up here.

Best case, she’d end up looking like a bigger idiot or a troublemaker.

Worst case, the bird could kill whoever showed up plus her, Gabby, and Tony. But the bird-thing had seemed interested only in her. Rayen just needed to keep her head down until five o’clock when she’d hopefully receive some answers.

She realized Gabby was waiting for her to do something. When Rayen didn’t move, Gabby pressed a button near the top of the keyboard.

The computer whirred to life.

Still tapping keys on his phone, Tony talked without looking up from his phone. “Ah, now we gettin’ to the good stuff. Kicked outta the last two schools for disciplinary reasons, but ... wait, this can’t be right. No way Cindereller tested that high.” Tony frowned. More thumb typing.

The laptop in front of Rayen buzzed with energy. She punched a couple of keys, surprised to find that her fingers knew how to form words as quickly as she thought them.

Standing at her right shoulder, Gabby hummed something quietly until an image of circles appeared on the screen. She brightened at that and said, "Ah, you've found the entrance, but do you know the password?"

Was this girl serious. Rayen gave another head shake.

Gabby cocked her head, ponytails flopping to one side and laughing silently. "I like to keep my finger on life's Escape key. Try hitting that, Jedi."

Rayen knew that key but couldn't very well say so after she hadn't thoughts of it on her own. She pressed ESC.

Nothing happened. The three circles of banded colors that mixed with copper, gold and silver, kept spinning and turning, passing over and around each other.

Gabby gave the computer a confused look and leaned closer, mumbling, "Wonder what's wrong?"

Tony appeared on the other side of Rayen. "Nothin' other than two morons do not a computer tech make."

Ignoring the loudmouth, Rayen kept manipulating keys in hopes of clearing the screen, but nothing would let her past those circles.

Gabby angled herself forward, talking across her to address Tony on the other side. "Perhaps there's a better way for a computer savvy one such as yourself to garner the attention of the Browns. Such as letting Mr. Suarez know how gifted you are in hacking confidential records."

Tony dropped his voice low. "You threatenin' me, sweet cheeks?"

"Threat is such an unattractive word. Think of it as inspired relationship building," Gabby said, not the least bit intimidated by Tony.

"Who they gonna believe?" He scoffed. "Me or some psycho babe with zero computer ability?"

"And here I thought you found *all* my records, placing you in the caliber of a true mastermind as opposed to petty thief."

"Yeah, I found them, but records can be doctored. Not that you didn't show an impressive level of skill pluggin' in that power cord. Now you two are pickin' out a computer like itsa Ouija board. Can't wait to see what's next."

Rayen lifted her hands to hold up between those two, or she tried to, but something tugged her fingers back to the computer.

Then she caught a swooshing noise outside in the hallway.

Too intent on arguing, Tony and Gabby missed the flying dark shadow flashing past the glass window.

Rayen had glanced over in time to see black wings flapping. What would that thing morph into next? And would it stay outside this room? Even if it only wanted her, would it harm Gabby or Tony if they got in the way?

Time had run out. Rayen had to get out of here and draw the beast-bird away, then figure out how to not get caught again. Something told her she'd only been lucky to escape it the last time, but she couldn't stay here and be the reason these two got hurt.

Gabby waved a hand, dismissing Tony, and sounding bored with their verbal game. "Some people have the gift of touch, an unfortunate shortcoming in those who don't."

Tony waggled his fingers and eyebrows, smiling. "I got plenty of touch, babe. My fingers can make that laptop sing."

Gabby glanced at Rayen's hands with a knowing look and uttered, "Don't think you've got her touch."

"Ya think? She can't even get the screen to open."

Rayen tried to lift her hands again, but her fingers were heavy as weighted metal and drawn to the keys as if they were magnets. This wasn't helping her immediate goal of escaping the room. More than that, she didn't think this was normal.

Gabby looked up at Rayen, her face calm and sincere. "Just ignore Tony and open your senses to–"

Tony hooted as if he hadn't heard anything so ridiculous in years.

In a surprising change from her earlier teasing, Gabby growled and grabbed Rayen's right wrist as if forgetting her wariness about touching. She snatched Rayen's hand off the keyboard and shoved it palm out toward the monitor, speaking at Tony the whole time as if *he* was the clueless one. "Everything has energy. You just have to–"

Rayen's arm sucked into the screen.

Gabby shrieked and gripped Rayen's wrist tighter, trying to hold her back. Not as hard as Rayen was trying to pull back, but whatever had latched onto her wasn't turning her hand loose.

The raven slammed against the glass window, beating its wings to get into the room. Tony and Gabby were both shouting so loudly, Rayen doubted anyone heard the thing but her.

Tony repeated, "What the f–" He clamped his hand on Rayen's left arm, yanking to pull her back.

He was strong. She hoped he'd win the tug o' war, but her hand kept sinking further into the monitor ... then her arm started shimmering.

In the next instant, she was sucked all the way inside, her body twisting into a kaleidoscope of colors. Heat ripped through her from her arms to her chest then through her legs.

Gabby blurred into a colorful stretched shape on one side of Rayen. Tony's grip tightened on her arm as they all spun into a bright orange-red vortex.

CHAPTER 6

RAYEN SLAMMED UP AND DOWN, over and around, freefalling in a vacuum of cold air. Someone screamed. Had that been Gabby? A foot kicked Rayen's arm, grazing her then gone.

Another shout. Tony?

No time to think.

Slam.

For the third time in less than a day, Rayen crashed into a hard, unyielding surface. This time a knee jammed her spine. An elbow gouged her stomach.

"Get your effin' foot off my ribs," Tony growled from somewhere nearby.

Everything was black. Rayen couldn't see.

She squeezed her eyes tight then cracked them open. Sucking in air, her eyes adjusted slowly. Feeble light and barely visible shapes came into focus.

Another room. This one metal. Round walls. Blinking red-orange light.

Where was she now?

Not any more familiar to her than the desert or school had been. She pulled into a sitting position. No bones broken but bruises on top of bruises. How much could a body take? When her vision adjusted further, she could make out details and see the other two. An eerie red glow washed across everything. She licked her lips, mouth dry as a dust bowl.

Gabby groaned.

"You two okay?" Rayen's words echoed in the cramped space.

Gabby cocked her head one way then the other, sending ribbons and hair flying. "I'll live."

Twisting around to Tony, she found him with his head in his hands. He drew his knees to his chest then lifted his head and grasped the metal disk hanging from a chain around his neck. A talisman?

Rayen nudged him with her elbow. "You alive?"

His head popped up. "Yeah, I'm alive." In a quiet voice, he added, "What the freak just happened?"

"Don't know." Her standard answer for the day and it did nothing to ease her sense of dread. She rolled to her feet, biting back a groan. Complaining wouldn't help anything.

She fisted her hands to stop the trembling. Were these things really happening or was this some bizarre dream? Nightmare was more like it.

Tony and Gabby were real though, so all of this must be, too. At least she wasn't the only one confused this time.

This space reminded Rayen of a large, round version of the thing Hannah had taken her inside of called an elevator, but this space was three times the size. Shouldn't this thing have a door or hatch? Maybe a reverse button to take them back? One she'd jab in a heartbeat.

She stumbled toward an arch of smooth metal with purple light seeping around the edges. Possible entry and exit point? With her hands splayed open, she connected with the cool surface and felt for a button, control, anything, but stopped when the wall began humming under her fingers.

Buzzing metal, a vibration. She wished that would be a good sign, but the noise and vibration climbed up her spine like claws.

Gabby asked, "Smell that?"

Rayen hadn't until now. She caught a whiff of a pungent scent that immediately put her on alert for the sentient beast.

But this was a different smell. Sulfuric.

Even so, some deep, primitive sense of survival warned her that they had to get out of there. Now.

"Rayen?" Gabby's earlier happy voice was gone, replaced by a low guarded tone that transmitted equal concern. "I can't explain it, but I feel this is a bad place to be."

"Agreed. But how do we get out of this thing?" Rayen ran her hands over the arched door again, searching for a release mechanism.

Tony called over, "Wait a minute. Why try to get out of here when we might need to *be* here to go back?"

Taking a deep breath, Rayen glanced over her shoulder, keeping an eye on the other two while she continued touching the metal, hoping to find some release mechanism.

Tony pulled himself quickly to his feet then braced his hands on his knees. "Think I'm gonna puke."

Gabby shuddered. "Eew. Just kill me now if you do."

Tony put his hand on the wall and groaned.

It might have been funny to see the loudmouth brought low if Rayen weren't so concerned about where they were and how they'd ended up here. The last thing she remembered was Gabby sticking her hand on that laptop monitor. Actually, *inside* the monitor.

Gabby unfolded her arms and shifted from the floor to her knees to a standing position, her face pale in the pulsing red haze. But she shook herself, as if preparing for whatever she had to face, and straightened her spine. She stepped up next to Rayen. "Got any idea where we are?"

"No." There had to be a lever or button somewhere to open a door or hatch.

"Either of you ever see anything like this before?" Gabby asked louder but calmly, even though Rayen caught the way she clenched her fingers.

Tony grumbled, "No."

Rayen admitted, "I don't know."

"What kinda answer is that?" Tony's bravado returned in full force. "Either you've seen somethin' like this before or not. It's a yes or no question."

"I *said* I didn't know." Rayen turned back to patting the wall, urgency driving her. Not sure why. The smell? The buzz?

"Look, Sacagawea, now's not the time to be cryptic." Tony stood and stepped toward Rayen, his chin up, his whole attitude set for a fight.

"*Now's* a good time to give it a rest," Gabby interceded in an even tone, but sounding much more serious than she had before. She angled her head, staring as if she tried to reach inside Rayen to get an answer her own way.

If anyone could dig something out of Rayen's mind that'd help, she was all for it. When Rayen said nothing, Gabby just shrugged.

Tony argued, "No, I won't give it a rest. We're here because of her."

"Not really," Gabby corrected. "*I* put her hand on the monitor and I saw *you* grab her arm, so that would seem to implicate all of us equally, don't you think?"

Tony wouldn't relent, studying Rayen as if he couldn't decide what to think. "Whatcha mean when you say you can't remember, Sacagawea?"

Why play with words or avoid the obvious at this point? Besides, Nicholas had probably already told the Browns about her head injury so what could it matter if these two knew?

"I'm saying my mind's a black hole." Rayen's voice burned dark with frustration crowding her throat. She slammed one hand against the metal. For all the good that did. But they couldn't just keep on standing here. Waiting for whatever had caused that smell to return.

Her skin chilled at the idea of being trapped in here. She knew on some primal level that they had to escape. Now.

"Like *amnesia*?" Gabby asked, her tone too bright in the face of Tony's incredulity. "How fabulous. That means you get to start over, clean slate. Make your life whatever you want."

Just when Rayen thought she had an ally she could depend upon. She relented and said, "Yeah. Just like amnesia, but I'd rather have my original life back than a new one."

"Oh, in that case I'll help you hunt for it," Gabby offered as if we were looking for a lost shoe. The red flashing light looked different in Gabby's green eye than it did in her brown eye.

"You can't have amnesia," Tony scoffed, getting his teeth behind his words. "We just got here. No way could you–"

"I'm saying I had amnesia back at the other place," Rayen snapped. "The school. Nothing's changed here." Except for her sense that staying trapped in this space could be dangerous. "Look, we'll talk about that more when we have time. For now, we've got to get moving."

"Why?" Tony asked, oblivious to the red pulsing light that kept increasing in intensity. He held up his hand and huffed out a hard breath as if trying to be reasonable. "Let's use logic. If this thing we're in brought us here, wherever here is, then it should take us back, right?"

He had a point, but the metallic hum chose that moment to grow into a low whine that picked up in volume. What was happening?

Tony covered his ears. "That's frickin' awful."

"Still want to stay in here, Jersey?" Gabby called to him.

Rayen had to yell even louder over the screech. "Help me find a way out. Gabby, you search this side of the room and I'll search the other."

"What're we looking for?" she called back, surprising Rayen when she jumped into action.

"A handle. A button. I don't know–something. There's got to be a lever to open a hatch on this thing."

Tony dropped his hands and shouted, "Oh, come on, you two. Maybe whatever sent us here is *sending* us back. Ever think of that?"

Gabby yelled back, "If you're not going to help us, I'd say it's been nice knowing you, but I'd hate to die with a lie like that on my conscience." She swiped her hands back and forth frantically over the metal faster and faster. "That smell's getting worse, and it feels ... hostile."

The hairs were already standing up on Rayen's arms from the same thought.

"What smell?" Tony demanded, but his voice sounded shaky. "Hostile? You tryin' to pull more woo-woo crap? Tryin' to scare me? Won't work."

Rayen had no idea who he was trying to convince, but she heard the truth beneath his words. Jersey Jerk *was* scared.

Deep down scared.

Gabby coughed, but she'd started pounding the metal wall on her side of the container, working her way back closer to where Rayen pounded the metal.

Rayen whirled around to Tony. "That!" She pointed to the pulsing blood-red light, now beating like a heart on overdrive. "Is going to kill us if we don't get out of here. Now."

"A light's gonna kill us? You on crack? Tell ya what. You two do the woo-woo thing and I'll use the computer in my phone."

Giving up, she turned back to the wall. Missing something. But what? *Think.*

She came up blank. Too many holes in her memory. All she could do was pound her palm then her fist against the wall. A flat, smooth wall that was heating up. Not good. Not good at all.

"I got it," Gabby said, excited, stopping to push flyaway hairs from her face. "Maybe we have to do what we did with the computer."

"Meaning?"

"The two of us," she nodded at Tony, who was busy punching his smart phone and cursing when nothing happened. "We need to touch you. Maybe that will make the door open?"

Tony paused. "Forget about that. I hold hands with girls I date, not two loonies tryin' to get me killed." He jammed the phone back in his pocket.

This wasn't getting them anywhere.

The whine of machinery reached crescendo pitch. Nothing to lose.

"Let's try it," Rayen shouted over the screeching metal.

Gabby moved past Tony where he stood close to the arched panel and stopped. Rayen latched her hand onto Gabby's wrist, feeling static vibration beneath the girl's skin even through her sleeve.

Rayen picked up terror, but determination, too.

Gabby growled a sound of frustration and lurched for Tony's arm. The look on his face said he couldn't decide whether to pull away or not, but he didn't.

Nothing happened.

"Great," Tony snarled. "What now?"

Rayen was fresh out of ideas. And time.

A whirring scream split the room, tearing her brain apart, making all of them double over.

She wanted to jerk her hands up to cover her ears, but she shouted, "*Don't let go!*" Then added, "Think!"

Tony shouted, "*Think?* That's all you got? Think."

If they did get out of this room, Rayen was going to shut him up even if it meant using her foot to plug that yapping hole.

But right now, she had nothing more than what Gabby suggested so she yelled, "Think getting out. Open. Something!"

The room started rocking, gyrating with the three of them.

Gabby tightened her grip. "Open up. Open sesame," she shouted. "Time to go. Beam me up, Scotty."

Tony grumbled something unintelligible.

Lowering her head, Rayen blocked out as much as she could of Gabby's terror and Tony's lack of faith, the stench, the vibrations. She thought simple words as hard as she could. *Out. Gotta get out.*

She leaned her entire body against the wall of metal, tugging Gabby and Tony toward it at the same time. Lights flashed wildly and the noise hit ear-bleeding level.

They were going to die.

All at once, energy burst inside Rayen's chest.

The walls shimmered around them.

Then an opening appeared as all of them tumbled face forward into the purple light.

CHAPTER 7

RAYEN STARED AT A PURPLE sky with green streaks through it.

Where were they now?

She shouldn't just lay here sprawled on her back, but she needed a minute. Strange shin-deep grass surrounded her. Could this really be grass? At least it was softer than desert dirt. Her fingers found a blade and tugged.

It stretched. The rubbery stuff was an odd mix of brown and aqua with bumpy yellow specks. She inhaled a big lungful of warm, moist air, waiting for her racing heart to quiet.

That might not happen any time soon with trying to make sense of that sky.

Green streaks and a big red ball that didn't glow like a sun. It pulsed instead.

A chillingly eerie sight she had no reference for.

"I think we've just gone where no man has gone before," Gabby crooned. "That looks like a moon. It's got shadows ... craters . . . or maybe it's a face?"

"Okay, Sigourney Weaver and Princess Leia," Tony groused, his voice coming from somewhere off to Rayen's left. "Where the freak have you two got us to now?"

Good question. Better question was why hadn't they left Tony trapped in that metal room? A tempting idea. She pushed up and propped herself on her elbows. "Who's Sigourney Weaver and Princess Leia?"

She got a look from both Tony and Gabby at that.

Tony laughed. "You're serious. Ever watch *Alien* or *Star Wars*?"

Rayen shook her head. If she didn't come up with a yes answer soon, she'd get dizzy from shaking her head so much.

Gabby sat up and smiled, unbothered by her answer.

Tony's mouth dropped open, speechless.

Gabby swiveled her shoulders, a dazed look of wonder on her face as she took in her surroundings. "Check out the sick colors in this place."

"Sick, as in unhealthy?" Rayen glanced around in horror.

"Ah, no, that means they're gorgeous and amazing." Gabby smiled, framing a picture with her index fingers and thumbs, clearly someone who lived in the moment. Wildflowers of neon-pink and intense black, some with sharp spikes and even square shapes sprouted here and there.

Tony speared Gabby with a hard look. "You happy 'bout this?"

Gabby muttered something to herself then said, "I'm not entirely sure I'm even conscious and will admit to feeling a bit out of my element right now–"

"A bit?" Tony chuckled sarcastically.

"–but you shouldn't take life so seriously. It's not permanent after all. And to be honest, I was looking for a change of scenery."

Rayen admired the way Gabby had held up so well through this and wasn't bawling her eyes out. As that was one person not giving Rayen a hard time for being here, she could better handle Gabby's strange ways than Tony's abrasive attitude.

He was already reaching for his phone–did he sleep with that thing? At least the phone should keep him content for a moment.

Or so she'd thought.

He squinted at Rayen's leg. "What're you wearin'? A cuff?"

Out of reflex, she looked down. She'd forgotten about her ankle bracelet. Had it stopped working? The thing was still locked on, but she hadn't felt any electric shock, not even a tingle. Maybe it only worked if she passed through the gate opening.

When she didn't answer, Tony muttered, "Suarez stuck me with a freakin' criminal. This day just gets better."

Rayen rolled to her knees. Every muscle groaned in protest. Was being beaten and bruised her normal state?

And landing in strange places, too?

Scanning the open terrain that spread out for a long way, all she found beyond a sea of grass was an encroaching jungle bordering the area on all sides.

A deadly quiet jungle.

No sounds. No breath of a breeze. Nothing.

Tony stood and trudged over to the metal thing, which had spit them out and immediately sealed itself back to a solid cylinder again. He started smacking a palm against the structure over and over, his other hand still clutching the phone he waved around.

"What the freak are *you* doing?" Gabby asked, mimicking Tony's voice as she slid to her knees before standing. "Think your cell provider has coverage here?"

"Look. I'm just tryin' to get back inside. I put more faith in technology than this–" he flipped his hand to indicate the unreal world around them.

"But we just got out–"

"You two wanted out of this thing. Me?" Tony jerked his thumb at himself. "Got dragged along. We came here in this pod thing. Logic dictates it's the only way back. So, you can hang aroun' and sightsee, but I'm findin' my way home."

Just then the metal pod started spinning, causing Tony to stagger backwards. "What the-–"

His last words were swallowed in a bang and puff of red clay dust. When the air cleared, the pod had disappeared.

"*Nooo!*" Tony screamed, his hands thrown wide, his eyes wider. "It can't . . ."

But it could and it had.

Rayen felt as sick to her stomach as Tony looked. Staying inside that thing had worried her, but he'd been right on one point. It *was* the way they got here and the only way back to the institute.

Gabby stared at the open spot for a moment, stunned silent.

Running a hand over her hair, Rayen worked to calm her racing pulse. She'd heard something new beneath Tony's cocky arrogance. Panic. The kind of panic when your whole world has spiraled out of control, and you couldn't stop it.

For the second time today, she knew how that felt, otherwise she might not be keeping herself under control.

Calm on the outside anyhow. If they could look deep inside her they'd see chaos swirling into a tornado, threatening to destroy her with yet one more shock.

Tony gave his phone a longing look then dropped his arm and started circling where the pod had been, his movements getting more and more frantic. He ground out an oath and yelled, "Okay, fine. No 9-1-1 here. No 4-1-1. No electronic connection. What now? And what *is* this place?" He spat the last words in Rayen's direction.

As if I've got all the answers? She bit back her temper, determined to leave her senses tuned to their surroundings. "How should I know? I don't know what happened back in that equipment room or where we are or how we'll get out of here, but I do know our best chance at surviving is if we work together."

Tony's face said he supported no one's plan but his own. Especially someone who didn't know the Princess or Sigourney people. She saw his reaction as simple denial about what was going on and even she understood it to some degree.

She didn't expect a complete change in Tony's personality, but they couldn't survive by fighting each other.

Strength in numbers. Where had that thought come from?

Didn't matter. It made sense. Even if they were only three.

Her instincts told her things and she believed in her heart that she should trust them, especially in this place.

Gabby stood to one side staring at the jungle then swung around looking from Rayen to Tony. "Rayen's right, you know. We have no idea what kind of place we've just been dumped into. Unless you can teleport us with that phone of yours, we have no way back until we figure out how we got here. Can you counter that logic or is bitching and moaning your only plan?"

Whoa. Rayen took a long look at Gabby. Was this the same girl they'd traveled here with? The one who hadn't seemed to take much of anything seriously back at the school? Gabby had laid out Tony's options in simple terms and managed to point out his abrasive attitude without sounding as if she'd attacked him.

After a moment of digesting that, Tony held up a hand. "Enough. I got your point. I'm just sayin' logic dictates that the way back is the way we came. Until that pod returns, I agree. We find out as much as we can about this place and if there's anyone else here. 'Specially if they can help us."

Rayen had been wondering if they were alone. If they found others here, would those people be friendly or a threat? And she had no idea why, but she was sure she'd encountered enemies before — enemies other than the beast-bird. Bad ones.

Tony added, "While I'm stuck here, I want no more touchin' any electronics without clearin' it through me first since neither one of you babes has a clue what you're playin' with. Agreed?"

Hard not to agree with him since computers seemed to be his passion. Rayen didn't care for his "babes" comment but nodded anyhow.

Gabby grinned. "As long as you agree to be open to using our other senses here."

"Sure, sweet cakes. Whatever you say." Tony shook his head and made a snorting sound that indicated how little he thought of *her* suggestion.

Undaunted, Gabby added, "If you want to return the way we came here, keep in mind that the computer screen reacted to *Rayen's* touch and sucked in *her* hand."

Just when Rayen had counted Gabby as a friend she wanted to say, "Let's not keep pointing that out, okay?" but she didn't.

Tony said nothing, but distrust stirred in his gaze.

After playing the whole event back through her mind again, Rayen had no more answers about what had happened than those two did. She'd felt a surge of energy wick up her arm and into her body the minute her palm disappeared into the screen.

Pulling hair away from her face and wiping perspiration off her neck, she rolled her shoulders, ready to talk about something else when Gabby distracted her.

Gabby's yellow-and-lavender ponytails bobbed when she kept turning her head as she looked up, intent on something in the distant sky.

"What is it?" Rayen followed the direction of Gabby's gaze across two hundred feet of open space that ended in a slashing dark line of massive trees. The beginning of the dense jungle vegetation.

"Can you hear that?" Gabby asked, her voice soft, but no humor this time. Something had her entire focus.

Should Rayen shake her head yet again or wait to hear more, but a sound reached her ears right then. A heavy *whap, whap, whap* sound. Rayen glanced around and still saw nothing.

Until Gabby inhaled a quick breath and pointed up.

"What the heck's that?" Tony demanded, his gaze following her finger. "Sounds like—"

Rayen shushed him with a raised hand then moved to stand next to Gabby, both of them facing the direction of the racket. They bumped shoulders and Rayen got a jolt of an image. Not a clear image but a definite sense of danger.

Gabby tensed the way she had back in the equipment room when she'd repeated Rayen's thought about Tony. Probably because Rayen had not exposed Gabby then she didn't react, just continued quietly staring in the direction of the noise.

"Any idea what it looks like?" Rayen realized that Gabby had gifts she kept hidden. Based on her own reception since waking up in the desert, and Tony's taunting just because she was different, she didn't blame Gabby for protecting her secrets.

Sounding serious, Gabby said, "I'm trying to see it in my mind ... but it's not like anything I can explain."

Tony made a disgusted growl. "If you savants are done doin' a mind meld thing, would someone please tell me what the heck is goin' on?"

Gabby's fingers twisted the skirt of her dress. "If you'd *shut up* long enough to hear and look up, you'd know."

The warning in her tone must have worked. Tony froze then glanced in the direction they were staring. "I don't–oh, crap."

That summed up Rayen's feelings as the moving object started taking shape.

Not a single object but objects. A good dozen or so of the largest maroon-and-black bat-like creatures Rayen had ever seen. That surprised her.

She didn't know where she'd seen bats before, but bits and pieces of her thoughts were functioning at times, at least whenever her brain seemed pressed to figure a way out of trouble.

Like now. They had to get away from these big dark flying creatures.

First, she had to determine which direction they were headed.

Those creatures easily had wingspans of four to five feet across, blackening the sky as they swarmed nearer.

"Are those ... bats?" Tony said to no one in particular as the swooping wings grew louder the closer they came. "Aren't bats nocturnal and only eat insects?"

Tony's last words had been more hopeful than reassuring.

Gabby's voice sounded squeezed from her lungs, getting higher by the second. "This could be nighttime in this place with that red moon, and we may *look* like insects to them."

"Let's not hang around to find out," Rayen shouted and turned for the closest trees. "*Run*!"

She didn't have to say it twice as the other two took off with her, but that forest was a long distance across the field.

Tony yelled, "We'll never make the trees in time!"

Rayen checked to the left of them. The bats were still gaining altitude so they might not actually dive down, but her small group was going to intersect their path and end up running beneath the bats before they reached the tree line. She kept moving rather than risk a bad guess that the bats weren't going to fold their wings and plummet toward them.

They'd almost made cover when tiny acidic pellets hit Rayen's face and arms, stinging her skin.

"Ouch!" Gabby swatted the air around her face.

Tony slapped his head. "They're *spittin*' at us."

Rayen thought it was obvious, but still shouted, "Keep your face turned away."

After a hundred feet of running flat out, the grass gave way to thick, vine-strangled vegetation. Plate-sized leaves whacked her face. Gnarled roots, some knee-high, tried to trip her, and thorns raked the skin on her arms. Another hundred feet and they'd reached the tree canopy.

Panting and slowing once all three of them had plowed fifteen feet into the thick growth of trees, Rayen stopped and squatted until she could peer through a break in the twisted limbs back toward the grassy field.

"Gone," she whispered, catching her breath. She scanned the sky, or what she could see of it by moving back and forth until she found a sizeable opening through fat leaves on the towering trees. Deep purple ribbons appeared through gaps, but no green streaks that had been there when she'd first arrived. That throbbing red moon, if Gabby was right about it being a moon, still mocked them though. Inside this forest, they'd entered a world of shiny copper and brown colors, red vines, dripping hollow sounds and shadows that shimmered.

Creepy, but safer than where they'd been. Away from oversized bats.

At least, she hoped they were safer.

That sprint had been no real effort for her, but Tony had his hands on his knees, dragging in deep breaths of the thick, damp air. He whistled. "What's this place? Jurassic Park goes techno? That was close."

Jurassic Park? Rayen gave up trying to figure out things Tony said.

"At least the bats didn't come after us," Gabby pointed out, just as winded as Tony, with hair falling loose from her ponytails.

Tony ignored Gabby, turning to me. "Now what, Touchy Feely?"

"How should I know?" Rayen stood, getting tired of him expecting her to have answers, because he first blamed her for this problem, then complained about the answers he got. "What's *your* great idea, Techno Guy?"

Tony's face screwed up in pure disgust. "Drop me in a city and I'll find my way, but out here? Not my thing. *My* idea would've been not comin' here in the first place. What *did* you do to that computer to make this happen?"

"I didn't do anything," she muttered, but not with any conviction.

"You musta hit a combination of keys."

"You think we're here because of a typo, genius?" Gabby chided. "Oh, yeah, that's scientific."

Tony started pacing a wide oval path between Gabby and Rayen. Couldn't he be still for a minute? He slapped orange-and-blue-striped palm fronds out of his way. "Everything in science has an explanation. We just have to figure out how we ended up here."

Lifting her hands to her colorful ponytails, Gabby started fixing the loose ones. She passed Rayen one of her stretchy loops. "You need this."

"Thanks." It took a few twists to pull her thick length of hair back. At least now it wasn't swinging around, swatting her in the face anymore.

Gabby started in on Tony again. "That's the thing about you science types. So locked into a narrow way of thinking. You just can't wrap your mind around the possibility that all things do not have a tidy scientific answer."

Rayen couldn't accept everything that had happened today too easily herself, but they had bigger problems to worry about. Her mind had been stingy with memories, but now wanted to make it up to her by raising one survival concern after another. "Since we have no idea how long we'll be stuck here, we need a plan to find water and food. And to figure out what's poisonous or not."

Gabby's eyes lit up. "Since Tony clearly doesn't trust our judgment, he can taste everything first."

"Very funny," Tony grumbled, still beating a circular path.

Rayen did a double take at where they'd just come tearing through the weeds and bushes, seeing a potential new problem. The vegetation had already started growing back as she watched, which meant moving around would only get them lost when the path covered over, even if she left markers.

When Tony passed a bush with yellow and orange flowers, he flipped his hand at one, scattering petals everywhere.

Gabby shoved a disgusted look at him. "I don't know what your problem is, and I bet I can't pronounce it."

The squinty glare he shot back at her said he hadn't found that funny, but he did avoid touching the next vine he passed that supported a bright pink flower the size of his face.

Rayen leaned her head back, searching above them for fruit in the trees, but saw nothing obvious. If they didn't recognize something edible soon, what were they going to eat until they found a way back?

When she brought her chin back down, Tony had paused, standing with his arms crossed next to another huge pink blossom.

This one had brilliant green spots.

And petals that moved in and out as if ... *breathing*?

She rubbed her eyes. That couldn't be. Right?

Had to be the wind causing the movement, but she didn't feel a breath of air stirring past her.

She would have dismissed the flower but noticed Gabby studying one just like it next to Tony's left knee.

"We need a plan," Tony said, unfolding his arms and slapping the phone against his thigh in a rhythmic tap.

Hadn't Rayen just said the same thing?

That brought Gabby's attention back up with a sharp chin lift. "How are we supposed to come up with a plan when we have no information to go on?"

Tony swung his arms out. "I don't know. Maybe we start with finding something we can use for weapons."

Strange as it might seem, Rayen was about to say he had a valid point, but Tony swung his hand holding the phone out and back toward his thigh at that moment.

The very instant she realized that flower really *was* drawing a breath.

Rayen yelled, "Look out!" but the pink petals lunged up, sucking tight around Tony's hand and arm before he had a chance to react.

Everything happened in a burst of seconds.

Fast as a coiled snake, a tendril of the vine lashed out from beneath the flower and raced around the wrist that Tony frantically tried to jerk free.

Tony shouted, "*What the–*"

Rayen dove for him but landed in an empty space as the vine snatched him off his feet and slithered away, dragging Tony deeper into the jungle. He made garbled noises.

"Grab him," Rayen shouted at Gabby, who had the best shot at getting to Tony before he passed her and disappeared.

For someone who hadn't looked overly athletic, Gabby lunged for him and managed to barely snag his ankles.

Rayen jumped up and raced after both of them.

"*Raaayen!*" Gabby yelled, flopping behind Tony as his body cut a rough path through vegetation slapping away right and left like a shark ripping through water.

Picking up speed, Rayen caught glimpses of Gabby's hair flying behind her with her face plowing up silvery dirt. Her body acted as deadweight to slow the momentum of the slithering vine, but not by much.

Pushing harder to get ahead of both of them, Rayen leaped over fallen trees and dodged wide bushes, slowly passing Gabby and Tony. Humidity soaked her clothes and sweat ran down her back.

Whipping around a tree, the vine seemed to slow for a second.

Rayen saw her opening and threw herself toward Tony, latching onto his free arm. Got it. Now she and Gabby could both be anchors. Maybe the vine would hit a spot it couldn't pull all three of them through.

Sounded good. Wasn't.

They were getting beat to pieces. Even with her ankle restraint gouging a deep furrow through feather-fine soil and decomposing leaves, nothing slowed them down.

If anything, the vine started moving faster.

"Don't let go!" she yelled.

Her last words hadn't been necessary.

Fuzzy brown tendrils snaked up from the main vine and circled down Tony's body to snag Gabby around her wrist. They were lashed together as if one elongated body.

A second tendril whipped around Tony's arm until it reached Rayen's wrist.

Let go and risk being able to catch up again? Or–?

There wasn't enough time to think it through as the sticky brown length wrapped and triple lashed Rayen's wrist to Tony's arm.

Terror rode through Gabby and Tony's faces.

Rayen couldn't be distracted when she had to find a way to free them.

Like fragile tails tied to a windborne kite, they swept across the jungle floor, bouncing up and down, banging back and forth, being thwacked against plants, small trees and leaves with prickly thorns.

At last, the vine started to slow again.

Rayen raised her head, gritting her teeth against the burning pain of being dragged over the rough ground. She spied a wide-girthed tree ahead, larger than any others nearby. One so big that little grew anywhere in the immediate area except for a huge bush with jagged leaves at the tree's base.

Dark, oozing, orange spots and bumpy shapes dotted the weathered tree bark, some looking uncannily like faces. Small faces.

But the tree wasn't the biggest threat. The bush surrounding its base sported another pink blossom, like the one that had attacked Tony. Only this flower was massive. The petals were wider than her shoulders. They sucked in and fanned out in a breathing motion. The center area had what looked like a pile of black sticks ... that started spreading.

The sticks moved until they lined the opening like teeth, sharp and clicking when the mouth of the plant snapped closed then opened again.

"Tony, watch–" The words choked in Rayen's throat when a vine curled around her neck, tightening.

"*Hellllpppp*!" Tony's frantic plea came out muffled as another vine wrapped his head, covering his mouth and nose.

Rayen had hit her limit of being knocked around and attacked.

Anger shot through her, sending strength to her tight muscles.

Energy started building in her chest, wicking its way up through her arms and down through her legs. Everything slowed. Sounds dulled. She could feel each beat of her heart thrum in her ears.

Then that energy exploded inside her, boiling her blood, hotter and hotter, until her mind and body moved with the speed of a lightning strike.

Purely on instinct, she swung her only free hand in a slashing chop toward the vine branch that was shutting off her air supply. She mentally repeated one thought. *Cut, cut, cut.*

And it happened. She lanced the tendrils strangling her as though her fingers were small knives. Air once again flowed into her lungs.

She had no idea why that had worked, but the vine dragging the three of them stopped moving forward. Instead, it began wrapping layer after layer around Gabby, Tony, and Rayen. Like a spider cocooning its prey.

She wrenched aching muscles, forcing herself to wiggle forward, past Tony and Gabby, struggling until she could yank each of her legs free to stand between them and the host bush. With everything she had in her, she stomped the vine with her foot, focusing on the word *crush* as she did.

Nothing.

Brown tendrils wrapped Tony's forehead, mummy like, leaving only his eyes void of any arrogance, just pleading silently for her to save him.

Gabby gasped and wheezed.

The vine was strangling her to death.

Rayen focused harder. She thought *break* as she shoved her heel down with a vicious blast on the vine.

Again, nothing.

One last effort. Squeezing her eyes until flashes of light burst in her head, she called up all the energy into one last thought as she slammed the vine again.

Kill.

Then she heard it. The shuddering of live wood ripped asunder and an unearthly howl of pain.

The bush screamed.

CHAPTER 8

RAYEN'S HEART SLAMMED HER CHEST with every ear-splitting wail from the massive pink flower at the base of the tree.

Had she killed Gabby and Tony by attacking the vine?

The tension wrapping their bodies snapped.

All at once, thick vines connecting them to the tree splintered as strips of the plant shriveled.

Drawing a breath of relief, Rayen staggered over to reach down and grab them each by one hand. Then she pulled, dragging them from the bindings still wrapped loosely around their bodies. Uprooting one of these trees would be easier. Where had that wild energy gone? She still had adrenaline pulsing through her, but not that hot power. She gritted her teeth and yanked harder.

Their bindings splintered this time, allowing her to drag them clear of the bush.

Tony clawed his hands over his head until every last piece of clinging stem remnant had disappeared, leaving scratches and cuts. His skin was flush, his breathing heavy. He reached into his shirt, yanked out the metal disk and kissed it hard.

"What's that?" Rayen asked.

"Saint C." Tony eyed her. At her blank expression, he added, "You know. St. Christopher. Patron saint of travelers."

No, she didn't have a clue what he was talking about.

Gabby fell over on the ground, hissing, cradling her wrists, which flushed bright red.

Feeling lightheaded herself, Rayen knelt beside her. "Are you okay?"

Gabby released her wrists, sat up, and shoved hair off her face, visibly shaken, but she took a breath and muttered, "I will be after I kill Tony."

"That thing attacked me," Tony mumbled, the fight having gone out of him.

"After you attacked another flower. Maybe it wanted to eat your phone."

"My phone?" Tony lifted his hand, realized he still had his phone and said, "Hallefreakinlujah." Relief spread across his face until he frowned at Gabby. "What the heck are you talkin' 'bout the flower bein' mad? It's a plant."

"*Everything* in any world is alive," Gabby said. "Just because you can't make something fit into memory chips, processors, and motherboards doesn't mean it lacks value or survival instincts of its own. We have to be careful in this place."

"It was a *freakin' flower*, for cryin' out loud. Who woulda thought it'd try to eat me?"

"You've got a point. I'd expect a plant to be more discriminating." She rubbed the raw skin around her wrists.

A leaf fell out of Gabby's hair. She picked it up and shrugged to herself then gave up a half-hearted smile. She did look a year younger physically than Rayen, but that girl had the tough core of someone who'd fought her own battles for a long time. Whatever life Gabby had led had taught her how to adapt, because she'd been taking everything in stride better than Tony had so far.

More than anything, this plant attack proved how much they needed each other. Rayen hoped Tony realized that now. "Let's call this progress on the learning curve and move on. No harm, no ..." She almost had the word, but it vanished.

"No foul?" Gabby smiled, suppling the word.

"Yeah." That sounded right, though Rayen didn't have a clue where the saying had come from. Another crumb from her brain.

Tony muttered something in her direction that sounded like, "I'm gonna have to start callin' you Xena after what you did."

Another name that meant nothing to Rayen.

Once Gabby reached her feet, she dusted off her ripped dress and asked Rayen in the quiet voice of a conspirator, "What *did* you do to that vine?"

Not a question Rayen wanted to answer. Or *could* answer with any confidence.

"Don't know," Rayen admitted, and decided a lie would be better for now until she could figure a few things out for herself. Besides, that battle had drained her to the point it was hard to dredge up thoughts, much less words. Muscle fatigue from the inside out. "It all happened so fast. Everything's a blur."

Though she *had* figured out something just now. Where she'd been out of her element in that school, there was something primitive here that called to her blood. Did her family live in a place similar to this? She didn't think she'd ever seen anything like the vegetation or bats in this place, but she had a strong sense of having survived off the land at some point in her life.

That she'd been expected to fight and protect. Or die.

Gabby stared at Rayen again with that deep look, as if trying to read everything Rayen hadn't said about getting away from the vine, but the sound of Tony thrashing away drew their attention.

"Where are you going?" Gabby called to him then shot a questioning look at Rayen as if she had a clue what that crazy Jersey Jerk was up to now.

"Home," Tony flung over his shoulder, steadily stomping deeper into the jungle, evidently trying to retrace the route the vine had dragged them.

"There's nothing back there," Rayen called out.

Tony stopped as if pulled taut by an invisible wire. He turned partially to say, "Back in this direction is where the pod was. Might come again. Who knows? Gotta be better than dyin' in this hole."

Now he sounded worse than terrified.

He sounded defeated.

She glanced at the quivering bush, the one that had nearly devoured the three of them. Her gaze traveled up the towering trunk where she caught sight of the small faces she'd noticed before. One looked more and more like a sad child in the shadows of the dim forest light.

Gabby's gaze bounced between Tony and Rayen, searching for an answer in a place that held none. "You think we should go with him?"

"No." Rayen meant it. Her gut told her the pod was dangerous. But then, standing around or going deeper into the jungle could be, too. She shook her head and admitted, "But splitting up isn't an option either."

In the few seconds that she'd hesitated, leaves and branches started weaving across the path behind Tony. Once they left this place the chances of finding their way back here, or anywhere else, were dismal.

They were stronger as a unit of three. They could survive this if they kept their heads. She believed that at a level deep enough it drove her to compromise.

She headed for what she could see of the path he'd left. "Let's go, before we lose him."

"We don't have that kind of luck," Gabby grumbled close behind. "But I'm not jumping in again if he gets attacked because of stupidity."

"How long do you think that'll be?" Rayen asked, afraid they'd find out sooner rather than later.

CHAPTER 9

SOMEONE'S GOT TO ADMIT WE'RE lost. Might as well be me.

Rayen paused to lean against a broad tree trunk and dropped her head back, feeling the wood squish around her head. But when she shoved the heel of her hand at it, she'd hit a rock-hard surface. Had the bark anticipated the strike? She wiped sweat out of her eyes and rubbed at her ankle cuff that caused a drag on each step. She might be in better shape than Tony or Gabby, but even she was exhausted and thirsty.

She announced, "This isn't working. I don't think we're getting any closer to where we started out."

She'd hiked over mounds of gnarled roots, hacking bushes with unyielding branches using nothing more than her hands–minus the superpower she'd fought the vine with–and was hungry enough to start gnawing on her own arm.

Gabby slipped into a crouch. The chafed, reddened skin around her wrists hadn't gotten any worse, but no better either. She chugged a harsh breath, her hair now wearing as many twigs as ribbons. "Maybe Rayen's right." She exhaled heavily, looking at Tony. "Not sure we're making any progress going this way."

"What is it about girls? You always side with her. Ever think *I* might be the one who's right?" Tony crowed. Or it would have been a crow if he hadn't been as winded as the rest of them. He stood with his legs braced in a wide V, hands on his hips, his chest heaving.

Gabby cocked her head, tapping a finger to her cheek. "Hasn't got anything to do with gender but let me think about it. You right? No. *You* called her Xena. Change your mind about her being a warrior princess?"

"A crazy one," he mumbled.

If they didn't find water soon, being right or wrong wouldn't matter. Besides, Tony had lost some of his edge after that scrape with death. And to be honest, Rayen couldn't in good faith say that returning to the pod area was a bad idea.

But they needed to hydrate.

Could they find anything in this place that would be safe to drink?

She'd worry about that when they found some liquid. With as much as they were sweating, dehydration was a given. She'd gotten more light-headed with each step and was sure a small furry rodent had slept in her mouth for a week.

"I'm not taking sides," Gabby added. "Nor am I arguing with the logic of going back to the pod area, but I don't think you know where you're going and rushing forward isn't safe."

Tony's gaze turned hard as tempered steel for a few seconds, then remorse washed all that away. Something was driving him even beyond the basic desire they all had to return home. Some fear that hid inside his anxiety and shook beneath his words. "I haven't figured out what the freak happened to get us here or where the freak here is, but I can't be late checkin' back in with Suarez this afternoon. I've got a lot on the line for this Top Ten Project. A *lot*."

"Like what?" Gabby asked, her voice holding no bite.

Tony looked as though he would tell her the truth, but his gaze shifted from worried to arrogant, quickly shielding whatever vulnerability he wanted to keep hidden. He cracked his knuckles, burning off energy even when he was exhausted. "Unlike you two, I *am* going to MIT."

Between dealing with the beast-turned-bird back at the school and getting sucked into this alternate dimension, Rayen had forgotten about her own time pressure. She had to be in Dr. Maxwell's office by five o'clock.

She *had* to find out who she was.

Of everywhere she'd been since opening her eyes today, the school offered her the best place to learn who she was and somewhere safe while she figured that out.

Except for the beast that was still there. But she'd take her chances with it to get Gabby and Tony back to safety. She didn't fit into their world, but she believed they very likely were in *this* world because of her.

And right now, worrying about anything except escaping here and getting back to the school was laughable.

Gabby huffed an exasperated breath at Tony. "You're not the only one with time issues."

"Oh, yeah?" Tony said. "What's pushin' on you, sweet cakes?"

"You, right now." Gabby dismissed him with a wave of one hand, then she started stretching as if she had a routine that relaxed her.

Tony ignored her and pinned Rayen with a "what now?" glare.

She hadn't asked to be in charge and if Tony thought he had all the answers he could start sharing. "Okay, genius, if you want to keep going, we need water. Got ideas on where to find it?"

Tony looked surprised to be put on the spot, but all he offered was a tired shake of his head. "Told you. I'm out of my element here."

Great.

"Gabby?" Rayen asked, not expecting much, but with this girl's gifts she might be able to find water. When she sent back a confused look, Rayen said gently, "You have some abilities. I'm not asking you to share what they are, but I dug my fingers into the ground during the last stop and didn't reach moisture."

Gabby nodded, took a deep breath, and closed her eyes. "I'm not a diviner," she murmured, though Rayen didn't have a clue what that meant. "But I'll give this a try."

Rayen shot a look at Tony to warn him not to ridicule Gabby, but he actually watched her intently as if he hoped she could do something.

Gabby dropped her head back and held her arms out to each side in a motion of opening up to the world. Her lips moved silently then she frowned and lowered her arms. She opened her eyes, frowned, and cocked her head, listening for something. "Hear that?"

"What?" Tony looked around. "You hear water, maybe moving like a stream or river?"

Gabby twisted her head one direction, then another, getting a fix on what Rayen couldn't hear. But Gabby *had* heard those bats before, way sooner than Rayen had, so she turned her head in the direction Gabby faced ... and caught a faint sound.

A high whine that sounded like a cry.

"Is that a child?" Gabby stood straighter, pointing in the direction they'd been heading. "That way."

"A kid?" Tony looked confused. "I thought you were divining for water?"

Gabby turned on him and snapped, "I'm not a magic wand! I hear what I hear and right now it's the sound of a child crying. Some things are more important than you."

Tony jerked back.

Rayen didn't blame him. Their rainbow butterfly had fangs. Had the child crying triggered that reaction in Gabby?

"I hear it, too," Rayen confirmed.

Tony slapped his forehead. "That could be *anything* in this place." He dropped his hand and said in a calm, logical voice, "Computers aren't computers, flowers aren't flowers, so why should a cryin' kid be a cryin' kid?"

He had a point.

Gabby paid no attention to him, her voice turning to steel. "I don't have an answer for you, Mr. Know It All, but that still sounds like a child. It could be hurt. Who's to say someone else isn't here if we are and I'd think you'd be interested in checking it out if that child arrived here in a pod as well."

The gears started turning in Tony's head. "You're absolutely right, sweet cakes. We can't risk that bein' a child left alone in this place. Let's get humpin'."

Surprise at his quick shift in attitude showed in Gabby's face. "Uh, okay."

Rayen almost wished Gabby hadn't handed him such a convincing argument for checking out the noise. Tony perked up the minute he realized the arrival of another person might open the path to go home, which meant he'd go charging forward without thinking about the dangers.

Tony looked right and left, anxious to move out. "Which way, sweet cakes? That kid's our GPS to the pod area."

Gabby turned toward the sound of the child's voice. "This way."

"Wait." Rayen grabbed her arm, feeling sudden determination rigid in her muscles. "It could be a trap."

In the moment that they'd touched, Rayen caught a buzz under Gabby's skin and saw a visual of Gabby as a young child, alone, crying. Who'd left her to fend for herself?

And how had Rayen seen that?

"Or it could be just a child," Gabby said emphatically, shaking off Rayen's hand. "We haven't found water or a way back. If there's a child here, then there may be other people here. Regardless, are you willing to gamble a child's life and leave a vulnerable kid exposed to this place?"

Something inside Rayen shouted, "No," that she'd defended younger ones before, but she had no idea when or where. Nothing felt right in this place. If she were perfectly honest with herself, nothing had felt right since opening her eyes this morning.

"What's it going to be, Rayen?" Gabby asked, fidgeting to get going.

Tony added, "Like you said, we can't split up."

More than that, Tony had just admitted that he trusted her judgment. Something not to be taken lightly. Not if they were going to make it out of this alive.

Were they right to trust her?

She didn't have a reason to stop them from going to the child other than sensing that sounds had been used as bait for traps at some point in her life. On the other hand, she couldn't honestly live with the thought of ignoring a child in need. "We'll go, but if it *is* a child let's not race straight to it without a plan."

"Agreed," Gabby said.

Tony nodded.

Rayen didn't like the thought of possibly walking back toward the clearing where the sound was coming from, not with her gut still screaming the metal pod area wasn't a safe place to be, even if it was their only connection to the school. But she raised a hand, indicating for Gabby to lead the way with Tony following and her taking up the rear.

Not an ideal setup for defense, but she felt better suited for this terrain than those two and could keep an eye on both of them this way.

The hike seemed to go quickly as the cry grew louder, though decreasing in intensity as if the child, or whatever made that sound, was winding down from full pitch bawling to a pathetic whimper.

Rayen noted purple light again through a break in the trees. But this time, the green stripes were back. Could they really be returning to the clearing where the pod had been? The sky looked the same way it had when they'd fallen out of the pod. Call her superstitious, but she had an uncomfortable feeling about that sky.

She jogged past Tony, calling to Gabby. "Wait up."

"What now?" Gabby asked in a snappish tone.

Rayen looked at her more closely. Maybe she'd heard exhaustion. "We agreed to scope this out before walking up to the noise."

A child in distress clearly bothered Gabby on some internal level, but she nodded in reluctant agreement. "As long as ... if it's a child we're going to help it and not just make a dash for the pod, right? If there is a pod."

Rayen nodded. "If it is a child, and alone, we'll take care of it."

"We doin' this today?" Tony stood with his thumbs hooked in the pockets of his jeans, waiting. Sweat beaded down the side of his face, streaking through patches of dirt. He might have been a self-centered jerk at the school, but he'd been working better with them since the flower attack. She could tell he moved like someone capable of defending himself and hoped that was true if they faced a new threat.

Turning back in the original direction, Rayen cautiously eased toward the whimpering sound. When she reached the tree line, she crouched low, waving the other two down, making sure they hugged the multi-colored foliage enough to avoid being blatantly visible to anything in the grass clearing.

And there in a patch of packed-down earth was a small girl. Maybe five or six years old, curled on her side into a fetal position, hiccupping air like someone who'd cried out every last ounce of emotion.

She looked so tiny and alone out there.

But the flower that attacked Tony had been the vulnerable-looking bait of a carnivorous plant and this place was riddled with danger.

The child was dead center in the clearing of the odd-colored grasses mixed with patches of bare ground. She wore a silvery dress, gold jewelry, sparkly shoes and her hair was braided and curled as if she'd been dressed for a party.

Why didn't she look like Rayen's group–ragged from running for their lives?

Had a pod dropped the child here, too, or was she just lost?

Tony whispered in Rayen's ear as he squatted next to her. "There's no pod. Think we're in the same spot where we arrived earlier?"

Rayen shared the disappointment in his voice, since she couldn't deny hoping the appearance of a child meant adults would be nearby and show them the way home. But Tony was being calm, so she answered him by pointing to where they'd clearly beaten down the grass while running from the bats earlier. The trail started from a flat area of grass, roughly conical in shape where the pod had been recently.

Wait. The grass had not grown back out there the way it had in the jungle.

Gabby flanked Rayen on the other side. "What's the plan?"

A battle raged inside Rayen, a tug-of-war between her drive to protect an innocent child and the strong sense that she was right to be wary. "I'll go get the girl. You two sit tight."

"What if the pod comes back while you're there?" Tony asked. "We should all go so we can be together if that happens."

Gabby wasn't agreeing or arguing, but Rayen knew from her response to the child's cry that she'd go along with anything that would allow her to help the little one.

Tired to her bones, Rayen shook her head. "Based on how that metal thing brought us here and left, we'll have plenty of time for you to reach it if it shows up. I need you to watch my back. I can't explain why, but I have a feeling this might be a trap. If something happens to me, I don't want you caught out there, too."

A sudden thrumming started. The vibration came from below ground.

The pod? Or something else?

Rayen fought to keep her balance. *What the–?*

Gabby floundered where she knelt beside Rayen, her arms flapping to keep her balance. Tony cursed and growled.

The earth movement shifted from a tremor through the ground to an eruption of rocks and dirt out in the open space. Something alive emerged from beneath the surface on the other side of the child, near the dark jungle where it bordered the far side of the grassy clearing.

Like a giant crocodile on steroids, the creature's head and long snout burst out of the ground. Huge black eyes stuck off each side of its head. The body kept coming. It used multiple arms to drag itself up. Had to be twelve, maybe fifteen, feet tall when it stood upright on two feet the size of giant palm leaves, but with talons. Thick hide covered in scales and a wide mouth full of pointed teeth.

It let out a wild screech. A metal-tearing-against-metal roar.

Tony sat up on his knees, eyes bulging. "*What the freak is that?*"

Color drained from Gabby's face. She stared open-mouthed at the beast emerging from beneath the ground then squeezed out a whisper. "The child."

A trap. Rayen hated being right.

Just as much as she hated what she had to do next.

CHAPTER 10

RAYEN WANTED NO ARGUMENT AND made that clear with her tone. "I'll go. You two stay here." When Tony stood, she shook her head. "If I don't reach the little girl, you won't either, so don't follow me."

He opened his mouth to argue, but she gave a pointed look at Gabby whose attention remained locked on the kid.

Giving a nod to show he caught her meaning to watch out for Gabby, Tony still clearly struggled to make the right choice. At the blowhard's core, he was male and had probably been raised to protect females but based on what had happened with that deadly vine, they both knew she had the best shot at saving that child. Even Tony had to admit that she was far faster than either of them.

With a reluctant sigh, he said, "Don't hit a pothole, Xena."

The whole exchange took seconds she couldn't afford to waste so she had no time to ask what a pothole was.

Gabby had been paralyzed by the deadly scene unfolding until Rayen gave her shoulder a quick squeeze of encouragement and jumped up to take off running toward the child.

"*Rayen!*" Gabby shouted, a delayed reaction kicking.

There was no turning around at this point. She had to trust Tony to do his part to hold Gabby back and keep her safe. This was now a foot race against the roaring creature that had emerged all the way out of the ground. Dull orange scales with bright blue swirling lines covered its body in dizzying patterns.

It shook off dirt like a wet dog and swung its enormous head toward where Tony and Gabby hovered at the tree line.

Rayen risked a glance over her shoulder, relieved to see that Tony restrained Gabby. They were in the open, but not far from the jungle's edge.

Booming steps rocked the ground.

She whipped her head back into the race.

The strange croco-monster had dropped down on four of its limbs and began heading forward with a side-to-side movement at a thundering speed then slowed. Bulging black eyes streaked with yellow veins flared wildly at Rayen then dismissed her as too insignificant to get in the way of reaching its initial, and easier, prey–the little girl. Two thick arms dangled from the monster's upper body. Hands large enough to rip a human body in half or swat a grown man into next week had three thick-boned fingers with curled claws.

This was not the Beast that had chased her in the desert. This was worse.

Startled by the movement, the child sat up and let out a hair-splitting cry.

With the ground shifting the closer Rayen came to the monster, she had to perform a quick double-step to stay upright.

Forcing her legs to spin faster, she matched pace with the monster and angled her body into a head-on collision course. She waved her arms and shouted wildly for the child to get up and escape.

The child didn't move.

"*Get away. Move. Run!*" Rayen bellowed. Drawing on all of her strength, she sprinted the last few yards.

The little girl twisted to crawl on her knees, staring at the monster. Wide-eyed, her panicked cry was drowned out by the *thud, thud, thud* of the predator bearing down on the tiny person.

With an extra surge, Rayen threw herself toward the child, scooping the little girl against her body and hitting the ground hard, rolling to the right. But Rayen had her safely cocooned. For now.

The ground rumbled and vibrated as the croco-monster catapulted past. It came so close she could smell its sour odor, feel the blast of its hide scrape her upper arms.

Safe?

Not hardly. Maybe Tony had been right to focus on the pod to get out of this place.

Pushing back to her feet and hugging the child close, Rayen made a quick sprint to the closer jungle edge on the opposite side of the clearing from Gabby and Tony. She careened around, facing the back of the monster. It skidded to a stop, snorting, and stomping the ground.

The little girl in her arms quivered. Too terrified to make a noise. Her heart beating fast like hummingbird wings. Rayen stepped deeper into the jungle's edge. She moved behind the biggest, baddest palm-like frond, hoping to soothe the child by being hidden.

Where was the monster?

Had it given up chasing the child? Why?

Rayen heard shouting. Inhaling air into her starved lungs, she shifted the child against her chest and eased back out into the open space until she could see Gabby and Tony. They waved their hands and shouted taunts at the croco-monster.

They were the reason the monster had lost interest in Rayen and the child, but that appeared to be the extent of Tony and Gabby's planning.

How was she going to keep those two from being eaten?

She couldn't leave the little girl alone. Neither could she save anyone if she risked her life by rushing back into the monster's path.

Before she came up with a plan, the creature lunged forward and barreled toward Tony and Gabby. They stopped yelling and turned to run back to the jungle.

Chugging air as if she'd never get enough, Rayen set the girl on the ground.

The child crumpled, clinging to her leg as a lifeline.

"Stay here. You'll be okay," Rayen gasped, trying to untangle herself without harming the child and hoping she understood what Rayen said. She tried again by patting the little girl's feather-light hair to keep her calm. Would she stay put?

A cry of wild noises went up from deep in the jungle on Gabby and Tony's side of the clearing. No time to think.

Frantic, Rayen pulled again at her trapped leg, glancing over at Tony and Gabby.

They stopped shouting and were looking around then suddenly stood transfixed at the edge of the clearing.

Who, or what, was making all that noise?

"*Keep going!*" To punctuate her words, Rayen leaned forward, dragging the child. She waved at Gabby and Tony, shouting, "Don't stop. *Run!*"

Neither one moved, their two bodies as rigid as trees.

What was wrong with them?

In a blink, twenty children varying in ages, sizes, and looks exploded from the jungle on both sides of Gabby and Tony. The newcomers raced toward the monster, rather than away.

There *were* others in this place.

And they were crazy.

None of those appeared younger than ten or older than Rayen. All of them followed a tall male she'd call a boy, who appeared to be seventeen or eighteen. Hard muscle wrapped his body, and he carried a rough-looking spear as a warrior would.

Not a boy. Too dangerous looking to group him with the young ones running around.

He took two long strides on powerful legs and used his forward movement to throw his spear, stabbing the croco-monster between plating in its chest.

The monster bounced back as if it had hit an invisible wall, then fell over on its side, writhing in pain. A couple of the kids levitated, hovering in the air over the beast, shouting taunts and waving sticks and fists.

How'd they do that?

Even from here, Rayen could see the terror in Tony and Gabby's faces.

She pulled her leg free of the child's grip and took a step toward her friends.

Something sharp stuck her in the back and felt like it broke the skin.

Swinging around, she almost tripped on the little girl as she prepared to fight whatever had hit her. Two boys maybe twelve or thirteen at the most. Both pointed lethal looking, if primitive, spears at her chest. Where had these boys come from? The jungle?

Finding more people here would be good news if not for these two trying to skewer her.

The boys wore ragged, mud-splattered tunics to their knees. One youngster had flame-red hair spiraling out from his head. His face, arms, and legs were mottled in leaf-colored hues. Skin colors that shifted and changed from greenish brown to pale yellows. The other boy's tangled brown hair fell to his shoulders. He had glowing purple eyes.

Was everything in this place weird? And deadly? Even little boys?

That red-haired one was the shorter of the two and had a threatening look for someone that young. He ordered, "Get down on your knees. Hands on your head."

Good news? She understood their words. But she ignored his order, demanding, "Who are you?"

They pointed the razor-sharp tips closer to her chest. Red Hair said, "Move, and you die."

And she'd thought the Institute had been a trial?

Her back stung where one of them had already stabbed her once. Nothing worse than a cut ... as long as that stick had no poison on the tip.

She paused. She knew what poison was?

This was not the time to add a check mark to her ongoing list of what she did and didn't know. What she knew for certain right now was that this little warrior meant what he said.

But she didn't care. "That thing." She hitched a shoulder toward the still-roaring croco-monster. "Is going to kill ... my friends."

"Those two are safe ... from the croggle."

"A croggle?" She glanced over her shoulder. Ah, the monster. "If this is just my scrambled brain having a nightmare, I hope I wake up soon," she muttered and gently untangled her foot again from the child at her ankles. When she did, both boys looked down.

Not trained very well to lower their guard so easily.

Rayen twirled around, catching both spears at once and pitching them aside then spun back to check on Gabby and Tony. Same spot.

What was that monster, the croggle, doing?

Nothing, because that band of shrieking children were beating it for all they were worth. They used a net of woven vines, crude three-pronged weapons, clubs and spears like the two boys had held on her. Their mighty leader called out orders and took the lead in beating on the croggle.

Why didn't he just grab another spear and kill the thing?

Did he want to kill it or was he only training his little warriors? The kids I'd seen floating before were no longer in the air. They'd joined the others. Maybe their ability to remain airborne was limited.

She took a step and heard from behind, "Last warning. You move, you die, tecknati."

What was a tecknati?

When she turned around, both kids had their weapons again. How'd they manage that without her seeing them? She'd pitched the long sticks a good distance to her right, far enough she should have heard or seen them going for the spears.

Didn't matter. She had to get to Gabby and Tony. But if she ran toward her friends, one of these two–or both–might gut her with a spear.

Maybe she could move them in that direction. She asked, "Why aren't you helping your friends with that monster?" Neither one answered. "What are all of you doing here?" She glared in case they failed to hear the lack of patience in her voice. "What *is* this place?"

Still no answer.

The little girl huddled in the same spot near her legs, eyes glazed in shock, probably over how she got here since she wasn't dressed like this bunch.

Rayen had a hunch that she'd gotten spit out of a pod, too.

She could appreciate that scared, shaky feeling.

More annoyed this time, Red Hair raised his voice. "Down on your knees. Now!"

"No." She waited to see if either one would make a move. When all they did was exchange a look of confusion with each other, Rayen angled her head around to see how the battle was going.

Their tall leader had a club in one hand and something that could be a sword in the other, not giving the monster–croggle–an inch. Stab. Thwack. Stab. He had golden-brown hair and strange light purplish skin with aqua and dark-blue markings. Broad shoulders and muscled arms that swung a club the size of her leg with no more effort than if he held a thin stick.

But spearing the thick-hided creature with sharp points and clubbing it just enraged the thing rather than scaring it off or killing the monster.

Even stretched out on the ground, the croggle howled all of a sudden and lashed out with its giant tail, knocking two children out cold.

Then it rolled onto its belly, trying to right itself.

Rayen could hear the boys behind her suck in their breaths.

Things were not looking good for the humans–assuming anyone present was human–and here she stood being useless, pinned in place by two half-sized guards.

Not any longer.

She twisted toward the boys once again, surprising them for the second time when she yanked away both spears. "I need these."

Mouths open, they stared at their empty hands.

Nodding at the little girl at her feet, Rayen shouted, "Take care of her."

And she was off. To commit suicide? Not intentionally.

Yes, she could die, but then so could all of them. Besides, she had no choice.

She didn't want to lose Gabby or Tony despite how much Tony annoyed her. She'd been alone in that desert. She didn't want to be alone again.

Slowing to assess the situation, she flicked a glance to where she'd last seen her friends, guessing that kids with spears stood behind Gabby and Tony, too.

The croggle strained and bellowed, trying to get up.

That creature would first kill its attackers then go after Gabby and Tony the minute it got tired of being beaten.

And to be honest, charging toward a threat felt bone-deep right to Rayen, as odd as that sounded. As natural as breathing, she knew she'd done this before ... somewhere.

Rushing forward, she was almost upon the monster before the other kids noticed her. The guy in charge whipped around with shock riding his face then a fierce mask slipped into place. The younger ones seemed confused, as if trying to figure out if she was friend or foe.

No time to explain.

The leader kept his gaze on Rayen, all the while roaring orders at the children, drawing them away from the croggle, and her.

No support there.

Tossing down one spear to free up a hand, she flipped the other spear over in her right hand, a natural position for attack. Energy swirled in her chest, like before, but faster and stronger. Power shot through her arms and legs until she thought it would consume her.

Using her speed to run up the blunt scaly tail of the croggle, she pushed off and landed on its back. When her momentum slowed at the thing's neck, she clenched a curved horn sticking out the back of its head to hold herself steady as it moved underneath her. Her muscles expanded and thickened with every blasting beat of her heart.

The spear began to smolder under her fingers as if burning.

That was new.

She ignored everything with the exception of focusing on killing this threat. She trusted instincts she sensed were as much a part of her as the strange energy building inside. She didn't think she could reach the monster's eyes sticking out the sides or break through the skull to its brain. But she had to try.

When she drew the spear up over her shoulder to strike, a row of scales around the beast's neck flapped out and fell back in place, out and back. Breathing?

Just as had happened in the jungle when she battled the vine, more energy rushed through her, but this time it felt hot as molten lava.

She clutched the spear in a tight grip, holding it poised above the neck flaps.

The monster exhaled. Its scales flipped open.

A shout of "*Tenadori*" burst from her throat. She thrust the spear downward between scales in the neck.

The sharpened stick struck membrane that resisted.

Her muscles bunched. Heat exploded through her body and rocketed through her arms. She powered another shove deeper into the monster until something inside gave with a spurt of stinking gray-blue ooze that spewed out.

The croggle screamed and thrashed hard, tossing her through the air like a leaf caught in a gust of wind.

She slammed on her back, knocking the breath out of her. Pain squeezed her chest. Her lungs begged for oxygen. After a few seconds, she sucked in air, head ringing and the rest of her feeling like a flattened bug. Her body complained from head to toe, but she pushed up on her elbows in time to see the monster spasm again, glow bright then explode into blue flames.

The high-pitched squeal of an animal in agony rolled on and on until the thing shuddered once more and collapsed on the ground with so much force she felt the blast in her chest.

Scales curled back in the intense heat that blew away from the monster and rushed across the flattened grasses, scorching her skin much like the desert had earlier.

That seemed years ago.

Young voices started shouting in anger then a deep male voice boomed orders to back away and said something else she couldn't hear.

Probably the leader.

But the monster was dead. A croggle, whatever that was. Within seconds, the thing turned into a bubbling mass of scorched skin and scales.

She'd never get that acrid smell out of her nose. Her head spun from the effort of pushing herself up to look. She let her aching head flop back to the ground, unable to force her body to move another inch.

Gabby started yelling and chaos erupted.

Rayen should move. Get to Gabby and Tony.

Can't breathe yet. Wheeze, pain, wheeze.

Who were these people, all kids, and that older boy? *A guy,* she corrected herself. Anyone that powerfully built was no boy.

But why did everyone sound so angry? The threat was dead.

Thoughts skittered through her head. She coughed and pulled in air, breathing in short gasps, staring up during brief snatches of lucidity.

Purple sky. Single red moon.

No green streaks now.

She closed her eyes, hearing a groan. Hers. She hoped Gabby and Tony were safe now that the croggle was dead.

Quiet descended.

Then footsteps marched toward her. That same deep voice she'd been hearing ordered, "Stand up."

She opened her eyes. The violet-skinned leader's face suddenly shifted into view. Hair, more gold than brown now, fell to his shoulders. Were her eyes playing games with her? His hair changed to multi-colored browns, grays, and burnt orange, all muted colors. Interesting.

Different, but interesting.

Brown and black straps that looked like leather crisscrossed his chest, if such a thing as leather existed here. Loops on the straps held dagger-type knives and flat metallic discs with jagged hooks. Throwing blades. He wore woven links of the leathery material around his waist like a belt that drooped over a short groin covering created out of a plum-colored tanned hide. A longer blade hung at his hip. Bold aqua and deep-blue designs slashed along legs of roped muscle that stopped at short, dark-gray boots with orange and green fur.

Strange didn't end there.

His eyes were unusual, too. Almost too light to be human and they were first aqua then hazel ... now reddish-brown and glowing with fury. She noted several of the kids with similar skin, but theirs changed as if shifting from camouflage colors to one shade of violet.

Maybe she'd hit her head too hard. Again.

The dark markings, like soft leaf shapes or blobs, on the leader's skin remained fixed in place. She had a feeling that meant something significant about him.

He repeated, "Stand. Up." But with more force.

Hopefully, she could reason with him since she'd helped slay their monster. She forced herself to roll over onto her stomach then pushed to her knees and finally reached her feet. That had taken no small effort.

When she stood, she still had to bend her neck to look up at him.

He studied her from the ground up, much like someone would observe a new species. Had he not seen a female before?

An idea came to Rayen

Back when she first met Gabby, she'd thought shaking hands was a form of friendship. She dug through her brain for any help. She believed it *was* a sign of showing no hostility, so she took the risk of extending her hand.

He ignored her, his eyes burning like hot coals. His nostrils flared in anger.

She'd been sure that shaking was some universal sign of non-enemy, but maybe not.

"Two hands," the leader demanded, voice as grim as his face.

She didn't think she was familiar with this greeting. *Then again, I don't know what I do and don't know.* It wasn't as though she could remember ever being taught protocols any more than she knew where she'd learned how to fight. And she could not remember ever being chased by a morphing beast or fighting a croggle, but she'd survived both. She saw no problem in going along with his request for two hands, even as terse as it had sounded.

She stuck out her other hand, both palms up to show she was no threat.

The leader raised his spear to her throat. "Don't move."

I figured that out on my own.

A skinny kid around fourteen she hadn't noticed before came out of nowhere and lashed red vines around both of her wrists before she could blink.

She glared at the leader. Purple just topped the list of her least favorite colors. "You're being a little unappreciative after I helped you kill that thing."

"You destroyed it."

"Agreed." She enjoyed a moment of pride over having the skill–and strange internal power–to defeat a monster that huge. Something flickered in her memory.

A ceremonial moment after she'd completed a similar kill.

But the look on the leader's face didn't say thank you.

Instead, he snarled, "You destroyed *all* the croggle, leaving not an inch of skin or bones to be used. You *ruined* meat that could have fed our village for two weeks. And now that we have to deal with your arrival our hunting trip is curtailed."

Just. Her. Luck. "I was only trying to help you keep these children safe."

A female, maybe sixteen, stepped up to the leader. Evidently there *were* girls here. She wore a muted burgundy tunic with a braided gold edge that stopped short of her knees and ankle-high skin boots like the rest of them. The boots were made of material that reminded Rayen of animal skin, supple and breathable. The female's hair fell in dark ringlets woven of blond and black, surrounding a stunning face ... until her dull gray eyes slapped Rayen with icy hatred.

Ignoring Rayen's claim about trying to help, the leader spoke to the girl. "Is the child safe, Etoi?"

"Yes, Callan."

"Did you contain the other two?"

"Yes. The second team has them bound and waiting for your signal to return to the village."

Just as Rayen had figured, this group had caught Gabby and Tony.

What little goodwill she had toward anyone at this point was quickly sliding away, but she had to stay calm until she could figure out how to free Gabby and Tony.

And after that, a way for the three of them to escape.

She'd draw on that strange energy inside her when the time came. She just had to be careful around these small children.

This Callan guy wheeled around to address the glum-faced pack of children circling him. They ranged in ages from ten to fifteen with mixed eye, hair, and skin colors as if none were related, but dressed in three basic colors–mostly browns, a smattering of deep-reds, and one golden color.

Their leader might be older than Rayen, maybe even eighteen or nineteen now that she'd studied him more. Hard to tell when someone had the honed edge of a warrior. He told his band of tiny fighters, "We'll find another food source we can defeat, or we'll find something better for food. But now we must return to the village." She heard a couple of rumbling grumbles, quickly suppressed. The leader obviously had the unhappy group under control.

Someone poked her with the tip of a spear to get her moving. "Ouch." Rayen called out to Callan, "Would you tell them to stop stabbing me?"

He again ignored her, striding ahead to lead the way.

Rayen clenched her jaw. Just let her get her hands on another spear and she'd put a couple of holes in him. As she had no choice but to follow, she asked him, "Why are you taking us as prisoners?"

He didn't slow his stride or turn around when he ordered, "Silence, tecknati."

That word again. *What* did it mean?

Hopefully someone at this village they were going to was more open-minded than this guy.

The two boys behind her spoke between themselves. One mumbled, "What do you think *he'll* do with *three* tecknati?"

When the second boy answered, his voice was flush with respect ... or fear. "What would you do if a tecknati killed your brother the way his died? You saw what–"

"Don't talk about that," the second boy ordered. "I couldn't eat for two days after seeing the vid of what happened to his brother."

Rayen's jaw dropped. Who was this "he" they were talking about? Their leader?

Should she be more concerned about being thought of as a tecknati, whatever that was, or finding out what this Callan had in mind for her group?

Both sounded deadly and unavoidable.

CHAPTER 11

THERE HAD TO BE A way to escape without harming a child, but Rayen hadn't come up with it yet and only young ones surrounded her as she walked. Even if she did figure that out, she wasn't sure she could get Gabby and Tony free fast enough before one of these miniature terrors speared them.

And those sticks they used were lethal.

She followed the blond-haired girl called Etoi who plodded along behind the leader. Callan. Nice name that didn't reflect his personality.

Rayen raised her voice. "Where're we going, Callan?"

Not a word or motion of acknowledgment. Again. He just kept marching at a brutalizing pace through the thick and muggy forest. If he followed a path, she was having a hard time detecting it, especially with the way the jungle grew back so quickly. Something niggled in her memory that she should be able to read a trail. But why?

She spoke louder this time. "Who are you people?"

Etoi made a disparaging sound in her throat, "You teks really think we're so easily fooled?"

Rayen was tired of being called names she didn't recognize, but she doubted Etoi would believe her if she argued that she did not know what a tek was. Would this girl answer if Rayen made it sound as though she talked to her this time instead of Callan?

She gave it a try. "Is the village far?"

Silence.

"Is the village your home?" Rayen pecked away at Etoi, going for tiny bits of information in hopes the girl would slip and give up something.

Etoi shook her head until her ringlets danced. She chuckled sarcastically, but finally spoke, emphasizing her words that had a funny accent beneath them. "Don't be a dugurat."

"A dugurat?"

"As if you don't know," Etoi muttered. "You put them here."

Walking third captive in line behind Rayen, Tony spoke up. "Think she just called you a moron in another language, Xena."

She cast him a droll glare over her shoulder.

Gabby, who was right behind her cut in. "Astute observation from someone who has probably been called that in *every* language."

When Rayen faced forward again, Etoi had turned around, walking backwards. "Make fun all you want because you will–"

"*Enough*, Etoi." Callan cut her off.

Her eyes transmitted a promise of retaliation on Rayen for getting her yelled at by the leader, as if Rayen had caused her to be in trouble.

Etoi spun around and stomped away.

"Never thought I'd miss being at school," Gabby murmured as she moved closer behind me.

Rayen gave a quick check over her shoulder at Gabby. She now wore a wary, distant look Rayen started to think might be the first honest face Gabby had shown since they'd met.

The normally cheerful girl trudged along looking like some exotic flower left out in the heat too long. Her ponytails and ribbons drooped, as did her shoulders.

Next to the droopy flower, Rayen probably looked like a wilted weed. But she had a sense this could be her normal state.

Trudging two steps behind Gabby, Tony had a grim set to his mouth and squared shoulders. As if he'd felt Rayen watching him for a moment, he lifted his eyes and gave a half-smile with as much humor as a man going to his death. "The teachers will never believe us *if* we make it back to the Institute."

What could matter so much for him to worry more about a school project than the trouble they faced? She tried to encourage him. "We'll get out of this."

A sharp poke in her ribs took her breath.

She swung back around to face forward and found Etoi walking backwards again with one of the sword-type weapons. Some grayish-brown hardwood with the tight grain of dense wood that had been honed to a lethal edge and deadly tip. Etoi's lips thinned with menace. That's when Rayen noticed Callan had moved several long strides ahead of them, providing Etoi a chance to speak freely again.

Fueling her own expression with plenty of foul mood from a long day chocked with pain, Rayen lifted her vine-wrapped hands in a quick move and shoved the tip of Etoi's sword away from her chest.

The annoying female flipped the blade back in place just as quickly. "I'm not one of the children to easily disarm." Her smile promised pain if Rayen gave her reason to justify slashing her stomach open. In fact, Etoi's expression dared her to fight back so she'd have an excuse. "You have no value here and would be wise to remember such."

Etoi seemed to like hearing herself talk.

Rayen changed her tactic to a more friendly approach. "At least tell me where *here* is."

"Don't act as stupid as you look, tecknati."

Rayen turned that on her. "If you're as intelligent as *you* look, you'd realize I'm telling the truth and have no idea what a tecknati is or where I am." *A pretty consistent state of mind for me today.*

Tight lines across Etoi's face eased in thought. She clearly considered whether Rayen spoke the truth, but in the end, Etoi scoffed. "Don't think to play tricks with me. They won't work. You know very well where you are since there is no way for you to be here without a tek knowing." Etoi's gaze dropped to Rayen's ankle. "What is on your leg? We don't wear any device like that."

Rayen hesitated to answer. She didn't want to say she'd been cuffed as a security measure since that would give this bunch even more reason to think of her as a threat.

Etoi's smug smile deepened. "Obviously another tek device you plan to use against us."

"You're wrong."

Quick as a thought, Callan was once again marching only one step ahead of Etoi, his back an imposing figure that dwarfed her. She didn't realize he'd returned. He swung his head around, dark eyes scanning over his shoulder. His gaze settled first on Rayen, pausing long enough for her to cock an accusatorial eyebrow at him. That turned his face even harder, then his eyes landed impatiently on Etoi.

He spoke in a quiet voice ripe with iron authority. "Take a flank position, Etoi."

She tensed at having been caught disobeying his earlier order to be silent and clenched her lips in a rigid line before nodding. Moving six feet to Rayen's right, Etoi took point over a string of children walking parallel with her line.

Another word caused Rayen to slow briefly, thinking. How had she known the word *point* meant to take the lead? Another puzzle piece slipped through her fractured thoughts.

No one deviated from that arrow-straight direction until they approached a puke-green fog hovering just above the low-growing jungle vegetation. Rayen could probably stretch her hands from one side to the other across that patch of mist.

"Is that green crap what I'm smellin' that stinks so bad?" Tony asked no one in particular. "What *is* that stuff?"

Callan lifted his hand and signaled to his line of children as he angled his direction to avoid the green mist.

Never-let-it-go Tony quipped, "You fight monster croggles, but you're afraid of a little fog?"

When Callan once again didn't respond, Etoi couldn't pass up an opportunity as her group came closer to Rayen's with Callan's shift in direction. Etoi clearly wouldn't be silenced for long, which made Rayen wonder at her status in this group. Her smile lacked kindness when she spoke in Tony's direction. "As if you don't know the fog will peel the skin off your bones ... slowly, and painfully. However, if you wish to pretend otherwise, go ahead and step into it. I'd enjoy hearing you scream."

Tony scoffed at her. "Dream on, babe."

Guess she didn't rank being called sweet cheeks or sweet cakes.

In the next few steps, the fog was just ahead and to the left of Callan as he shifted the line right, giving the stench zone a wide berth.

Rayen wrinkled her nose at the rotting sweet-sour smell. Just how dangerous could a patch of green translucent fog be?

As deadly as a pretty flower?

What gave it the rotting odor?

She tossed a warning over her shoulder to Tony and Gabby. "Let's not test it, okay?"

Tony answered, "Got no plans to touch any of this crap even if it does sound like Amazon girl's only tryin' to yank our chains."

Etoi pointed at a small, pink lizard-looking creature with a perfectly round head and eyes at the ends of two prongs that stuck off the top. "Perhaps the eegak will teach you a lesson." She aimed her wooden sword to prod the funny-looking lizard that had brown and white dots splattered across its pink body. It scurried between the broad leaves of low-growing plants, the pencil-shaped body and tail stretched out the length of Rayen's forearm.

All at once, the lizard paused, head sticking up, tongue flickering. Etoi poked the sword tip again and the lizard took off at a run, bulging eyes locked ahead as it raced and lunged into the fog.

At first contact, the lizard squealed a hideous high-pitched sound as its skin literally peeled off its little body. Small legs kicked at a phantom attacker as it writhed in a grotesque ball of muscle and bone. And then *pifft*, like water hitting a hot surface, it disappeared.

That explained the disgusting smell.

Gabby gagged as if she was going to throw up. "Gross."

Tony just whistled. "Daa-yum."

Out of the corner of her eye, Rayen watched Etoi's calm face during the whole event. "It doesn't bother you to see something innocent die that way?"

Etoi kept marching forward as she spoke. "Most animals know to avoid the fog unless they're being chased, except for the eegak. They are almost as stupid as a dugurat who has no survival instinct." Then she added, "Nothing innocent should die, but–" Her gaze slid to Rayen with lethal intent. "Teks aren't innocent."

Callan must have had enough of her. "Etoi, go ahead to alert Mathias of our arrival."

That must have been something she wanted to do. Lowering her head, Etoi took off, quickly passing Callan and disappearing into the jungle ahead of him at a fast trot.

Would Mathias be the "he" Rayen had heard those boys talking about earlier? The one they were marching toward? The possibility that he might be more dangerous than Callan had Rayen making another attempt at communication. "Is Mathias in charge of this place?"

Callan still ignored her.

At the mention of Mathias, the mottled, colored skin on most of the kids started moving, changing shape and position, even to different colors on some.

But nothing moved on Callan's skin.

She couldn't really fault him for his silence. *A wise warrior reveals little to the enemy.*

Who'd taught her these lessons that fluttered into her mind as if sent on the wind?

Callan lifted his hand and extended one finger up.

The children who had been flanking Rayen's group moved over to their line, some filling in gaps between her, Gabby, and Tony. She glanced back to check on Gabby, who nodded, letting her know she was fine for now even if they were too far apart to hear each other without yelling.

Tony gave Rayen a similar nod and mouthed, *We're with ya, Xena.*

Her heart warmed at that. They might be in trouble up to their armpits, but they were finally in this together. First time she really believed that since they'd landed in this place.

In the next few steps, Callan and the small warriors emerged from the jungle into a wide-open area ... completely shrouded in another green fog.

But this band of green mist was huge, rising three times as tall as Rayen and spreading a half-mile wide.

Had Callan marched them here just to force her, Gabby and Tony into a mist dense enough to kill all three of them? If so, Callan had better be prepared to die, because she wouldn't go meekly to her death, or allow any of her group to step a foot into that stuff without a fight.

"We're not going in there," she warned him.

The stoic warrior finally turned to acknowledge her. "You'll not be harmed if you follow directly behind me and your other two follow you."

Could she trust anyone in this place? No. She didn't know how she'd called up the strange energy that had helped her stop the killer flower and defeat the croggle, but she believed she could call it forth again if someone pushed her to defend herself and her group.

She slowed her pace and asked, "What if we don't follow you?"

Callan took a moment answering, a tight smile playing around his mouth as if he looked forward to a worthy opponent. "Please resist. Not that I need more proof that you are tecknati who have killed nineteen of our smallest children–so far. But it would simplify her life to gain a decision now instead of later. The question is what do you think *I* will do if you refuse to follow?"

In other words, walk forward and risk entering this fog that her group might not be immune to even if Callan and his followers were, or stand firm and end up gutted.

Tough call, since he thought the three of them were tecknati who'd killed children ... and someone's brother. She could understand wanting to punish anyone who harmed those unable to defend themselves, but even without knowing her identity, she was sure she could never hurt an innocent. Especially a little one.

She would *not* willingly die–or let Gabby and Tony pay the price–for someone else's crimes.

CHAPTER 12

FACED WITH CHOOSING BETWEEN ENTERING fog that could flay them alive and facing a pack of weapon-wielding opponents, even if they were kids, Rayen picked what she hoped was the better of the two options.

She told Callan, "I've never harmed a child and I saved that young girl from the croggle. We're not this tecknati thing you keep accusing us of being. A warrior's word is worth his life. If you give yours that you're telling the truth, we'll follow you, but if either Gabby or Tony are harmed, you'd better hope I don't live. Because I will make you pay."

Callan took her measure with a steady, clear-eyed gaze and said, "I give my word that I speak the truth. If you and your friends remain in line along with the others, the three of you will pass through the fog with no harm."

The word *friends* raised something strong within Rayen. A sense of bond she hadn't previously assigned to the brief relationship she'd shared with Gabby and Tony, but at this point they were in this nightmare together and had to depend on each other. And it wasn't as though she knew if she had any friends or not.

Could she accept this unknown guy's word?

It wasn't as if she had a choice at this point? Not really. "Thank you."

He leaned close and added, in a far more menacing tone, "I've also given my word to destroy every tecknati I meet as long as I draw a breath. I swore my life to this vow. Do not test me again."

She knew when she was butting her head against a rock wall and nodded to Mount Callan to show her acknowledgement. Angling around, she snagged Gabby and Tony's attention then called back, "They're going to make a path. Stay exactly behind the person in front of you."

Gabby paled but her eyes sharpened with determination. She swung around, speaking to Tony, then she and Tony faced forward, both giving Rayen tense nods of understanding.

She hoped she wasn't leading them to their deaths when she told Callan,

"We're ready."

The leader gave her another look of promised retribution then turned his back to her and raised his arms. A spear clutched in one hand and the other hand empty. He spoke in a strange language, murmuring until the fog parted, rolling back to the right and left, leaving a three-foot-wide tunnel. Just enough room to move through while still needing to be careful. Then he strode forward.

What had Tony just said a few moments ago? *Daa-yum.*

Rayen followed, tensing when she felt the cool residue of the fog tingle on her skin, but no burning sensation. Fifty steps ahead the tunnel finally ended at a massive cavern-like space enclosed by the towering fog on all sides, but open overhead. Looking up, the sky reminded her of the striking blue one that had spanned from horizon to horizon back at the Institute, except this one undulated from a deep blue-purple shade to a vibrant red-purple. And that blood-red moon glared down on her.

She didn't know anything about the school she'd left, but right now she agreed with Gabby about missing that place.

At least the school had made more sense than wherever they were now. Once Gabby, Tony, and all the warrior children behind them were inside the misty barrier, the path through the fog closed.

With her group safe for the moment, she took in the village. Some of the unusual trees and bushes had been cut down, leaving a few trunks high enough to be stools. But those trunks were strange shades, some mustard yellow and others bluish gray. Vines and branches crisscrossed above, stretching from tree to tree and covering an area three times the size of Mr. Suarez's classroom.

Young children who stood no taller than Rayen's waist moved around inside this area, being watched, or herded, by others who were closer to thirteen or fourteen years old. Some of them sat around a pile of glowing rocks as if hovered over a campfire, but there were no flames. Others pounded what appeared to be plant fibers into cloth. Two little girls stood facing each other, a small orange gourd hovering in the air between them. It was literally suspended in air.

No strings or levers visible.

Another little boy with wild cinnamon hair levitated his body a good foot off the ground. Like the two had done while fighting the croggle.

They all paused to take note of Callan's return and the three strangers. Prisoners, to be more accurate.

Silence swept around the interior walls of the village that appeared to be made of massive feathers strung on a vine running between trees. The feathers hung vertically side-by-side. All the colors imaginable, but there were more dust-brown feathers with vibrant red or orange streaks than any other.

Rayen didn't want to know what kind of bird had a feather as tall and wide as her body.

Callan handed his spear off to one of his half-sized soldiers, then turned to me. "You. Come with me."

"What about my–"

A spear tip nipped her in the back, hard enough to break skin. Again.

She hissed at the new wound but followed the leader through a willowy hallway composed of more feathers. She heard multiple footsteps trailing behind and could only hope Tony and Gabby were being herded to the same place as her.

She needed them close if the chance to escape presented itself, but she resisted the urge to turn around and earn one more hole in her back. She had enough cuts and bruises for one day, and figured she'd hear something if Gabby or Tony were harmed.

And for once, she didn't think Tony would stir up trouble.

But what about this Mathias, who she was pretty sure she was about to meet? Would he be as hardheaded as that brute Callan ahead of her?

Based on her luck today, she wouldn't be surprised.

At the end of the passageway, she followed Callan into a room about twelve feet square. The corners were rounded where the giant feathers, solid mauve and lavender ones this time, overlapped. Just like the rest of the village she'd seen, this space also had no ceiling, open to the sky.

A female teen stood with her back to Callan's approaching group while she listened to Etoi who spoke in a low, agitated voice.

" ... they pretend to know nothing," Etoi hissed. "One has the mark on his neck and a strange smell. Another has some metal device on her leg and still Callan brings this threat back to our village. Why did he not kill them when he could? You must tell Mathias–"

"Zilya." Callan announced his presence with a voice sharp as a knife slicing air.

Still standing with her back to us, the other girl, this Zilya Rayen guessed, said, "That will be all, Etoi."

Color splashed her cheeks, but Etoi donned a calm expression and dipped her blond head at Zilya in a respectful manner before heading out through a different opening. She spared Rayen a terse, just-wait glance on her way out.

Rayen smiled, showing just enough teeth to let Etoi know she need not wait on her account.

A swish of movement drew her eyes back to finally see this Zilya.

She turned around gracefully, looking as though everything about her contained that same liquid quality, and paused. Her attention landed on Callan first, her eyes widening in question. His stern face didn't budge. Her tunic-style gown was an odd yellowish, almost golden, material, not shiny, but elegant in its simplicity. Strange half-moon designs were sewn in a deeper burnished gold down the front. She stood eye-level to me, but her regal posture gave her the illusion of being taller.

Spikey, white-blond hair haloed over her head, so pale it reflected lavender highlights from the sky, luminous against the bright gold feathers of the wall at her back. Zilya had a smattering of little raised, jewel-like dots from tiny to the size of Rayen's smallest fingernail fanning out from her left eye. The dots started as black then shifted to iridescent as they spread across her high cheekbone.

Rayen didn't think she was beautiful so much as compelling, but she knew Tony would be drooling if he were standing here.

What about Callan? Was he as dazzled by her?

Curious at his reaction, Rayen cut her eyes at him.

His eyes flicked in her direction as if he'd sensed being watched. His gaze bumped into hers, hung there a second studying her, then he looked away, frowning as if caught.

Rayen turned back to the girl. Zilya took her in with one long, cool appraisal, but her voice lashed out at Callan. "I understand there are two others."

"Yes."

"Bring them. Mathias will be here in a moment."

Callan didn't move.

Zilya's face softened when she added in a coy tone, "Don't worry. I'll be safe."

That sounded so flirty-sweet it was nauseating. Either she didn't see Rayen as a danger or she felt capable of defending herself. Rayen wondered which it could be.

Callen let out a huff of air. "I'm sure you can take care of yourself. Mathias may want to speak to each one independently."

Zilya's mouth tightened as if intolerant of anyone countering her orders. "As *I* am council to the Governing House, I *advise* you to bring the other two here for Mathias."

Some issue played out between them. Rayen didn't care about friction between those two so long as it had no negative bearing on her, Gabby, or Tony.

Callan turned and disappeared through the opening.

Rayen might as well start arguing in the defense of her group's position now. "You must believe *I'm* not a threat or you wouldn't send your . . . your guard away."

Zilya cocked her head at that, eyes cold and calculating. "I am hardly defenseless, and *he* is not my guard. I need no guard."

If she'd seen what Rayen had done to that croggle, she might rethink her statement, but bringing up the destroyed croggle would work against her goal of convincing someone in this place not to kill them. Before she could say anything else, another guy entered, striding so quickly the gold robe he wore whipped against his legs.

He stopped the minute he saw Rayen. "Who is this?

Zilya answered in a surprisingly humble tone. "One of the three captives, Mathias. I sent Callan for the other two."

Ah. So, this was their leader? As tall as Callan, this Mathias might not match Callan in muscle tone, but he carried himself as a king, shoulders back, eyes ahead. He had skin darker than hers. Reminded her of Nicholas from back at school, except Mathias had warm eyes that held a depth of understanding, giving him an approachable look. Strange for her to think that when he was in charge of the warriors who had captured her.

His eyes didn't fit his age. Not that he had lines or wrinkles, but he wore years of living in his gaze that said he'd seen far more than others with his seventeen or eighteen years. He asked, "What are you doing here?"

No matter where she went, she was doomed to be asked questions she couldn't answer. "I don't know."

Zilya interjected, "This is yet another tek trick, no doubt."

Mathias crossed his arms, irritation boiling in his face. "What new challenge have you brought to us?"

"None." Who did these people think they were? "We're not who you think we are."

Zilya answered, "In this sphere, you are either one of us or our enemy. There is no third option. So where does that leave you?"

The enemy.

Someone they claimed had killed children.

CHAPTER 13

MUFFLED FOOTSTEPS APPROACHED THE CHAMBER where Rayen stood. She turned as Gabby and Tony entered the feather-encased room ahead of Callan.

Mathias moved over to stand alongside Zilya where they both faced our group. Callan chose a position on the side where he could observe everyone.

And look foreboding.

Gabby had the same red vine wrapped around her wrist as Tony and Rayen had, but her forearms were now a deeper pink. Had the heat or humidity caused that, was it still a reaction to the fight with the killer-flower bush, or was her skin just extra sensitive? She stepped over to Rayen's right.

Tony stopped short behind them. "Your shirt's torn and you're bleeding. They stuck those spears in your back, didn't they?"

"It's okay, Tony," Rayen assured him.

He stepped up on her left, his dark eyes conveying rage at Callan. "She risks her *life* for your bunch of munchkin soldiers, or whatever those brats are out there, and you let them *stab* her?"

Callan might as well have been formed of granite, right down to his glare. Turning her into a sieve clearly didn't bother him at all.

Ignoring Tony's outburst, Zilya moved her head in tiny fractions as she considered the three of us, particularly Gabby.

That's when Tony noticed Zilya.

Rayen leaned over and whispered, "Shut your mouth, Jersey, unless you want to catch some demon fly in this place."

His mouth snapped shut and he speared her with a glare that felt more natural than his concern about her injured body.

Mathias addressed Callan. "Is it true we have a new portal site to watch?"

"Yes, in the area where we killed the croggle two months back."

By the subtle move of Mathias's head, Rayen had the feeling this was unwelcome news for some reason. Mathias spoke to Callan. "I understand these teks were trying to capture one of our new arrivals."

"Now wait a minute!" Rayen snapped. "I *saved* that little girl from that croggle monster."

Callan sliced a meaningful look at Mathias. "The child *was* unharmed when I arrived, but I still don't know where *they* came from. *And* she destroyed every piece of the croggle by torching it before we could harvest any of the parts."

The loathing Mathias swung at Rayen this time turned his eyes a brutal shade of purple, almost black. "That meat would have fed us for several weeks. The bones and skin offered additional shelter for those who cannot create their own."

She turned to Callan. "I had no idea that you intended to *eat* that thing." It sure hadn't looked appetizing. But Callan was doing his stone-faced warrior impression. No help there so she turned back to Mathias. "I only attacked the monster because I thought it was going to hurt the children fighting it."

A silent conversation seemed to flow across Mathias and Callan's hard gazes. Mathias finally nodded and said, "We haven't explored every inch of this realm. I will allow that there *could* be ... other captives."

Captives like them ... or did he mean *they* were captives?

Unconvinced, Callan crossed his arms, the muscles in his biceps clenching and unclenching. "They did not arrive in the area we normally monitor when the stripes appear in the sky, or we would have seen them when they ejected." He paused, his long fingers curled into fists, then he cast a suspicious look at her ankle. "What is that ring on your leg called?"

Rayen shrugged, trying to come up with a bland description that didn't scream criminal.

Unfortunately, Tony decided to help her out. "It's an electronic monitoring device." At the blank looks, he added, "You know. Remote surveillance via an electronic device attached to a person or vehicle." He winked at her. "That way their whereabouts can be monitored using GPS which reports their position via an electronic network back to a control center."

"To control a prisoner?" Zilya offered.

Thanks, Tony, she thought to herself. *Why not tell them I was suspected of theft and destruction while you're at it?*

Tony swallowed and avoided looking at Rayen. "No, it's a tracking device." He let out a dark chuckle. "But this place is kryptonite for technology."

"You think this is funny?" Zilya demanded, a frown creasing her face.

Tony raised his bound hands. "It was a joke, sister. Just a joke."

Zilya's frown deepened.

Where Rayen's actions had dug a pit for herself, Tony's words threatened to turn it into a bottomless hole. But before she could kick him into silence Zilya spoke to Mathias. "They do not dress as us so they could be high-ranking tecknati. They may wear strange uniforms thinking to confuse or trick us."

Were they were being judged by the clothes they wore? "What do our clothes have to do with anything? We're not tecknati, whatever they are. We're here by accident." She hoped to distance herself, Tony, and Gabby from whatever had killed children and the brother of somebody in this room. She felt certain the person those two boys had referenced as losing a brother was part of this discussion.

Would that be Mathias or Callan?

She also wanted to alert Tony and Gabby that being a tecknati was not a positive point, and even worse that Zilya inferred they might be high-ranking.

Callan's penetrating gaze cut across the room to Rayen with the precision of a honed knife and held the warmth of an ice storm. "Does SEOH think us so stupid as to believe this ruse? To send a bunch of vid players in here to *pretend* to be what you're not? To what purpose?"

Rayen lifted her hands, palms out, and shook her head. "I would love to know what someone in this place was talking about. I don't know what CO is. What does C and O stand for?"

Zilya's glower suggested she addressed a moron. "Is this the part in your script where I spell S-E-O-H and explain who that monster is? So sincere sounding. Save your effort for when you stand in front of a camera again, vid player."

"I'm *not* a player or a vid whatever." Wait, had Zilya said a *vid*? Rayen did know what a vid was–the short version of video–and that players performed in them. At last, a reference point for things that were coming back to her in bits and pieces.

"A great loss to young tecknati males, no doubt," Zilya sneered, then paused and said louder, "Our houses do not allow vids or fictitious tales shared. *We are* immune to your training."

Gabby piped up. "Sounds like a boring-ass house to grow up in, if you ask me."

Zilya scrutinized Gabby. After studying her closely, Zilya paused then her eyes flared with disbelief. "What house are you from?"

Why did she say *house* as if it was more than a dwelling?

Gabby gave a wry laugh, letting everyone know she found Zilya's question absurd. "This month? I'm stuck in a dorm room. No house, thanks to dear old dad."

Based upon Zilya's blistering scowl, that had been the wrong answer. "They think everything is funny, Mathias. Shall we see how much they laugh when they face death?"

His drawn-out sigh spoke of lost patience.

Rayen doubted his could equal hers, but she was making no headway with the current conversation. Time for a different approach. "This is the truth. We don't know where we are or how we got here. If you can tell us how to get back, we'll be on our way."

Zilya started to speak but fell silent when Mathias raised his hand. "We will not release you to report back to SEOH."

Gabby muttered low, but not low enough. "What exactly are you accusing us of?"

Zilya's attention returned to Gabby in a way that sent spikes of worry running along Rayen's spine, especially when Zilya demanded, "Look at me."

Gabby straightened her spine and leaned forward, only her eyes defying Zilya. "Get your fill."

"Your eyes do not match."

Irritation rushed out with Gabby's next breath. "Yeah, well. Some of us must rise above the mundane."

Reacting as if she'd been slapped, Zilya's fingers tightened on the folds of her tunic then opened slowly with a forced effort. She ordered Gabby, "Show me your ears."

Gabby raised an eyebrow at Tony then Rayen. He said nothing and she pushed up one shoulder, letting Gabby know that while she thought it sounded ridiculous it was not an unreasonable demand. She hoped Gabby wouldn't antagonize Zilya further.

Then she checked Callan for a barometer of the room. He'd unfolded his arms and now had one hand clutching his chin in a thoughtful pose. Darker blond than his hair, his eyebrows were tucked low over his unusual, yet always intense, gaze. The unguarded moment vanished when he shifted his attention and caught her staring at him. His arms folded back over his chest and his chin cocked up with arrogance.

Lifting her constrained hands, Gabby brushed back lavender-and-yellow strands of hair that had fallen loose around her face. When she did, she exposed first her left ear that had six earrings spiked through the outer curve, each one a similar thin silver ring except for the last yin-yang shape hanging from a tiny wire at the lobe of that ear. When Gabby turned her head to show the other side, only the matching half of the yin-yang earring dangled from her right ear.

Rayen tucked away the fact that she recognized the yin-yang design, intending to ask Gabby about it later. Whatever she could share about the design might trigger more memories.

To be honest, Rayen had found nothing notable about Gabby's ears or earrings if not for Zilya's sharp intake of air and Mathias's double blink in surprise.

Even Callan registered a moment of shock before hiding his reaction.

Gabby's ears seemed normal or average. What could be so significant about her jewelry?

Rayen studied Zilya closer this time, noting the delicate earring shaped as a swan inside a sliver of moon that dangled at the base of *her* right ear. She wore only one more earring inserted above that one. A small cut stone that blazed gold.

Mathias seemed to want all the information before making any decision, which gave her hope. As the leader, he might weigh what they had said and not be quick to order their deaths. When he spoke, he addressed all three of them. "Where are you from?"

Tony said, "A school in Albuquerque, New Mexico."

Mathias shook his head. "I know nothing of Albuquerque or New Mexico."

Great, talk about hitting a wall in the conversation. To be honest, beyond knowing the Sandia Mountains, Rayen had never heard of Albuquerque or New Mexico either before today, but she wasn't admitting that. Recalling how Etoi had treated her like an idiot when she'd suggested this was the girl's home, Rayen asked Mathias, "How did *you* come to be here?"

Zilya answered instead. "Stop the ridiculous questions. Do you really think to convince us you are not tecknati?"

"Not really."

Zilya's face brightened, Mathias looked disgusted, and Callan's countenance took a deadly shift.

Rayen explained, "If I knew what a tecknati was I could convince you we're not that, but I have no idea what those are or where we are or how we got here. That puts us at a huge disadvantage in trying to prove our innocence."

Tony interjected, "Look at us and look at you. We obviously come from somewhere different. Show us a picture of a tecknati that looks like us.

What else about us reminds you of them?"

Every time Zilya's attention landed on Tony her expression turned darker. "I would say you smell like them, but you wear a scent clearly meant to confuse us."

"You mean the cologne I'm wearing? That's Davidoff's Hot Water." Tony grinned. "It doesn't confuse women where I come from, babe. It attracts them."

"I admit that it does mask your stench."

"My what?"

Mathias had been studying Tony and angled his head, peering closer at him. "You have a mark on your neck. Explain it."

Tony gave him a frown that questioned his IQ. "My tattoo? The Blood Scorpions ... from Jersey."

Mathias did that visual exchange with Callan again then ordered Tony, "Uncover the entire marking."

"No problem, dude." Tony reached for his collar and pulled the material aside, turning his head to show off the image I'd noted earlier. A twisted, deadly looking thing with a claw. Rayen now recognized the art behind Tony's ear as a scorpion, with another claw in the fold of his neck and a swirled tail sneaking down Tony's back.

Tony grinned at Zilya with a wink. "Like it?"

"There is no family banner as yet," Mathias pointed out.

Tony rolled his eyes, insult sparking in his words. "What? The Blood Scorpions control the west side of Camden. That's all anyone needs to know about touching me or my family."

Where Mathias and Zilya had turned wary of Gabby, they were not the least cautious of Tony. In fact, Zilya's fingers quivered with a surge of anger. "Your arrogance knows no boundaries."

Gabby muttered, "She's got your number, Jersey boy."

Tony held his bound arms in front of him, hands up. "It ain't braggin' if you can do it."

"Then you admit you are one of the mighty teks?" Zilya quizzed Tony.

Rayen opened her mouth to object and Callan warned her, "Do not interfere or this discussion ends now."

Meaning things could deteriorate further. Not good.

Callan had kept any show of his emotions locked down tight, everywhere but his eyes. Fury stoked his gaze to the fiery shade of brown. She could swear the colors on his skin shifted a tiny bit. His markings *did* move. What caused that?

Mathias and Zilya hated tecknati, but Callan wanted blood.

Rayen clenched her jaw, forcing herself to remain silent when she sensed a trap being set for the Jersey Jerk.

Tony swelled with the implication that they thought he was special. He gifted Zilya with a beaming smile. "Nobody handles technology better than me back home. I *am* the man."

Smiles could say a lot of things.

Zilya's said she'd just heard the answer she wanted.

Mathias turned solemn, but pain and anger riddled his gaze. When he spoke to Tony, his words came out with quiet authority. "Enjoy your superiority for the short time you can. You shall be the first to pay for the transgressions of your people."

"What're you talkin' about?" With his forehead furrowed, Tony turned to me. "What's goin' on?"

She couldn't see a benefit in remaining silent at this point. "They think you're a tecknati, Tony. Something or someone they believe to be their enemy."

Tony's cockiness disappeared in a flash. "Whoa, everybody. That's not me." He swung a worried face to Mathias then Zilya. "I'm a geek guy. A babe magnet. A lover, not a fighter."

Zilya's posture stiffened. Anger spiked her breathing. "First you want us to believe you are a genius of technology. *Now* you want me to believe you are *not* tecknati?"

Rayen had a feeling the less this girl talked to Tony, the better off the three of them would be. And if this conversation didn't improve soon, they'd face a bloody resolution. Forcing a calm in her voice she hoped would hide the worry squeezing her chest, she asked Mathias, "What's it going to take to convince you we're not whatever this tek person is? A strong ruler would be sure before jumping to conclusions."

His eyebrows tightened in a brief flinch at her subtle strike to his leadership skills, but he lifted his hand and all conversation paused. "Fine. You want a fair judgment, even though your kind is not acquainted with such practice? How did you travel here?"

Tony jumped in, trying to be Mr. Helpful. "I can tell you that."

Rayen bumped Tony's leg with her foot, but he was undeterred. "Rayen here did some woo-woo with the computer and–"

Callan broke in. "*Computer?*"

Zilya froze.

Mathias opened his mouth but said nothing.

"Yeah, a computer. Never seen one?" Tony asked, his ego expanding by the second.

Mathias cut in. "Does this computer have a name?"

Tony made a half-laughing noise deep in his throat. "They all have names. Mac, Apple, IBM, Dell and a pile of others."

Once again, Mathias shared another of those looks with Callan that hinted of communicating, but Rayen read this one to mean the mention of a computer had been significant. If she tried to keep Tony quiet now Callan would think she had something to hide. She had a strong sense that he was the one they should worry about most.

Addressing Tony once more, Zilya said, "You were explaining how you traveled here."

"Right. Where was I?" Tony's eyes lit up again and he nodded in Rayen's direction. "She sticks her hand *into* the computer screen and the next thing we know, bam, we're sittin' in some pod that spits us out where that nuclear crocodile climbed out of the ground."

"Pod?" Mathias frowned.

"That thing that spins then vanishes."

"Ah, I see. You *did* travel to the sphere in a transender." Mathias's voice flattened, removing any hope of sympathy for Tony, Gabby, or Rayen. "Take them to the Isolation Unit, Callan."

Callan waved his hand at the three of them and ordered, "Follow me."

"You don't believe him?" Rayen asked Mathias, waving a hand at Tony.

He cocked his head as though he thought her question strange. "Of course, I believe him. I'm now *sure* he is a tecknati."

What had Tony said that ended all speculation on their part? Rayen demanded, "But why?"

Mathias spoke in the most matter of fact way. "Because tecknati are the only ones who can travel here voluntarily through the transenders. They are the only ones who can visit the sphere."

Tony sputtered a protest as he and Gabby were being herded toward the opening to the corridor.

Callan turned to her, no mercy in that face.

Rayen's hands were damp with a deep panic that their stay in this place had taken a disastrous turn. She made one last attempt to find out their future from Mathias. "What's the Isolation Unit?"

"Where we hold prisoners."

That might give them a chance to figure a way to escape. "How long will you keep us there?"

"For a short time."

"Then what?"

Thinking on that for a moment before answering, Mathias said, "I have not decided about you and the other girl."

Zilya finished the thought for him. "But *that* one–" She pointed at Tony. "–will be the first tecknati punished for the deaths of our children. He will pay with his life."

Tony's face washed clean of color.

Gabby's mouth dropped open.

Rayen felt the same way, but unlike Tony or Gabby, she knew she could stop these people. She wouldn't let them kill Tony.

Mathias glared at Zilya but didn't counter her claim.

Callan stepped toward Rayen in a threatening move.

She searched inside herself, calling upon the energy she'd experienced earlier, the power that could break the vines around her wrists and give her a fighting chance at getting all of them out of there alive.

Nothing happened.

Not even a flicker.

CHAPTER 14

RETURNING FROM THE ISOLATION UNIT, Callan padded down the walkway to Mathias's private domain and paused at the door when he saw Etoi and Zilya.

Some days, those two were almost as much trouble as the TecKnati and so caught up in their conversation that neither heard him approach. How many times had he drilled them in training that to be unaware is to welcome death?

Of course, a fully-grown prantheer hadn't heard him sneak up on her lair last week either, but she'd been caring for her cubs. Not gossiping.

Etoi worked on a basket of dried tullee pods for seasoning a stew and complained to Zilya, "The one who calls himself Tony is a TeK. He must die."

Zilya nodded. "Yes, I know." She sat on a separate mat spinning katoni threads into a skein the weavers used to embellish the hems of gilded tunics.

Poor use of labor. Had the decision been left to Callan, he'd have everyone train to fight and build defenses when not gathering food or hunting. Decorating clothes was a foolish use of time when faced with survival. But Mathias had pointed out that the simple task of sewing allowed those too young to hunt or gather food alone to have a feeling of worth.

That's why Mathias made an excellent leader.

But then there were *those* who felt that physical training was beneath their House level.

And Etoi and Zilya were not little children who needed to be coddled to have a sense of worth.

"Why does *he* still live?" Etoi's focus stayed locked on the topic of the TeK captive with the tenacity of a dugurat latched onto a last meal.

Zilya gave a dainty shrug. "I would use that Tony for croggle bait myself, but Mathias decides the fate of the prisoners."

"He is too soft. You should–"

"But he is our leader. I can only advise, not force his hand if he chooses to ignore my counsel."

"*You* should be leader here."

Callan almost stepped inside to let Etoi know he'd heard her traitorous comment, but he wanted to hear Zilya's reply.

"I will always regret having you with me the night I was captured, but I have to admit that I am selfish enough to be glad for your company. I am fortunate to have a champion such as you, Etoi, but to challenge Mathias for his position would be foolish on my part."

Callan agreed but didn't hear the outrage in her response that he'd expect from a Gild female, who should strike down impertinence against a leader, not preen under adulation.

Zilya added, "Let's finish here soon. I have much to worry over besides the prisoners."

Nodding her head in concession, Etoi still grumbled, "I just believe all TecKnati should be punished."

"As do I."

Callan could not listen to these two dribble on any longer. No one had more reason than him to feel deep hatred for the TecKnati who had killed his twin brother, but Mathias was the eldest of the Governing House and had studied MystiK law since taking his first steps. His word was final, and Callan would uphold the law here just as he would at home, even if it meant laying down his life to do so.

He'd failed once. That wouldn't happen again.

Making himself heard as he stepped in, Callan asked, "Where is Mathias?"

Zilya's surprised gaze shot up to his, then she calmly returned to winding her thread. "Checking on our new child."

Callan called to Mathias, mind to mind. *This is Callan. We need to talk.*

Mathias answered, *I'm on my way to my chamber. Meet me there.*

Speaking out loud, Callan said, "For one so busy as you claim, I would think you'd have more to do than sew, Zilya."

She tensed at realizing he'd overheard her conversation.

"What would you have her do?" Etoi argued in her usual surly tone. Her lack of respect knew no bounds.

"You could *both* use more training."

Etoi leaped to her feet, hands fisted and shoulders tight. "You wish you had more warriors like me."

"If you'd train as hard as you gossip, then I'd agree."

Growling, she lunged at Callan who only lifted a hand. Etoi smacked against the invisible surface of his power and bounced back, yelping and rubbing her nose that now trickled with blood.

He grinned. "You can put a bandage on your nose, but there's no cure for stupidity. On the positive side, those who act without thinking will eventually clean up the gene pool."

"Must you?" Zilya asked Callan.

"I did nothing except defend myself in the least painful way from someone who should take care whom she attacks."

Murder raged in Etoi's eyes. "In this Sphere, you are not of Gild or Rubio level. You are not your brother, only a second son who is unfit to rule the Warrior House."

Zilya went very still, her eyes raised watching Callan.

Etoi's words sliced through him back and forth, cleaving his heart with each reminder that he'd failed to protect his twin brother's back. Jornn should have been the next Warrior House ruler, but the TecKnati had murdered him. After torturing Jornn to the point of disembowelment, they'd cut a triangle where his heart had been and that was the last vision their mother had of her son's body.

Callan's last memory of his closest friend in the world.

But the TecKnati had not broken Callan, and neither would some spiteful elite-Gild-wannabe like Etoi. He forced a smile to his lips and told her, "You're right. I will not rule my House, but I never wanted to, where you will *always* lust after the life of a Gild female and the closest you will ever come is cleaning their hygiene facilities."

His strike slapped the arrogance off her bitter face and silenced her. He pointed at the door. "Go."

Wisely, Zilya stood and pushed a bowl at Etoi as though she had made the decision for them to leave. "Meet me in my chambers."

Etoi gripped the woven bowl with fingers so tight they turned white at the knuckles, but she left without another word.

Once Etoi was clearly out of earshot, Zilya whispered, "When did you realize you had *that* ability?"

"Stopping Etoi with my hand?"

"Yes."

"It's new and not of any significant use yet." Not that he'd let *her* know when any of his G'ortian gifts reached full potential. He could use those powers with fighting croggles if not for some defense mechanism the TeKs had put around the areas where the monsters lived.

Stepping up next to Callan, Zilya said in a sultry voice, "I'm *always* willing to train. When will you be available for a private session?"

Back home, men lost their wits when Zilya walked into a building. She was stunning and rare, and they all wanted her. *Not me.* He'd been interested, once, back when he was fifteen and before she'd been promised to his brother. Then Callan had investigated her as he would anyone who might have proven a threat at some point to his brother.

Beneath the layers of Zilya's beauty lay a deadly trap of deceit and a heart of ice. Sharing his opinion of Zilya with Jornn had caused an argument Callan didn't want to remember. He told her, "I'll let you know when I'm training grunts again."

Her eyes narrowed to angry slits. "Insulting me is dangerous."

"No, dangling you in front of a croggle is dangerous. Insulting you is rude."

"You can pretend the rules are different here, but nothing has changed at home."

Not having to deal with political issues at home was the only upside he'd found to being in this pit of death. "That's there. This is here."

Her chin lifted and her eyes flared with warning. "When we return–"

Mathias walked in. "Is there a problem?"

"Of course not. I was just leaving." Zilya's face glowed with a smile for the one person she believed would push Callan to do her bidding even here.

She was wrong.

If no one else had been able to force Callan to take Jornn's place as leader, what made her think she had any more power?

Still, he had to watch his back around Zilya. She'd proven more than once that she could be a dangerous adversary, and she'd never be more than that to him.

CHAPTER 15

RAYEN HATED TO ADMIT SHE had no idea how to escape this place. The Isolation Unit they were stuck in was some type of hut made of bright green reeds that vibrated with a low-level hum. Every time she approached the sides of the chamber, the reeds increased their vibration, which didn't reassure her.

But she kept that to herself.

She had failed Gabby and Tony. Where was that power in her chest when she needed it?

"That bitch blondie wants to kill me," Tony said as he paced ten steps across and back, for the umpteenth time.

"You mean the one with the white-blonde hair?" Rayen asked.

"Yeah, that one." Tony flapped his hand at me. "Point is we've gotta escape."

"Keep your voice down, would you?" She'd been trying to ignore him since the three of them had been thrust into this stagnant room except for an odd minty sweet smell.

That should be a refreshing scent, but it wasn't. Or maybe she was just suspicious of everything from flowers to children.

And why shouldn't she be? She was trapped in a hut constructed of a plant that she should be able to rip to shreds given what she'd done to that killer vine earlier. But her energy had abandoned her when they needed it most. The power humming in the walls keyed her senses that attacking the hut might have deadly consequences. No mercy anywhere in this place.

When Callan marched them here, not an ounce of sympathy had flickered in his eyes. He'd lifted his hand and an opening had appeared just long enough for Rayen, Gabby, and Tony to walk through, then the doorway disappeared.

No windows, no door.

No clue how to escape or how to help Gabby, for that matter.

Rayen walked over to where Gabby sat cross-legged, huddled in the center of the floor, her jaw clenched in pain. She rocked back and forth, cupping first one wrist then the other in her lap. Sweat beaded across her forehead.

"Any better?" Rayen asked, concerned about the deepening raw welts ringing Gabby's wrists. Red streaks had started running up her arms in jagged lines that indicated infection. Had it started earlier when Rayen had noticed pink on her wrists after the killer flower strapped her wrist to Tony? Or had the dull-red vines Callan's warrior used for constraint done this?

"I don't think I can use 'better' to describe the pain." Gabby spoke between her chattering teeth and tried to grit out a smile. "More like somewhere between having your appendix cut out without anesthesia and being burned to death."

All of their wrists were unbound now. Rayen's wrists and Tony's showed no skin reaction like Gabby's. They had to get her out of here, back to the school where someone could help her.

"I'm not stayin' here," Tony continued babbling and pacing. "These guys are serious whack jobs."

"We'll figure a way out of here as soon as we can," Rayen said, hoping to shut him up.

Nope. Tony pounded over to where she knelt next to Gabby but kept his focus only on Rayen. "'As soon as we can' is fine for you two. *I'm* on death row."

Fighting the urge to snap at him, she asked Gabby, "Please let me see your arms."

Lifing her chin, indecision playing hard through Gabby's flushed face.

Rayen understood her hesitation. Gabby shielded her secret gift by avoiding touch. Rayen offered quietly, "You can trust me when I say I'll not judge you or share anything about your gift."

Gabby must have decided she was telling the truth after seeing the things Rayen had done today, because air wheezed out of her with relief.

Rayen braced herself to touch the girl's skin, prepared for any image or sensation when she gently scooped Gabby's arm in her hand. Fragmented images scattered through Rayen's mind, mixed with burning pain and fear of dying. What she picked up came in pieces, meaning Gabby could hide her thoughts somewhat, but not very well while distracted by her body fighting an infection.

The red lines continued to crawl up Gabby's arms, raging hot looking as if acid etched deep into her skin.

Sniffing, Rayen detected an odor of something building that her mind labeled as gangrene. *Rotting flesh, right*? But this didn't fit with the vision of rotting flesh that followed that term. She didn't have time to question what she knew or how much she knew, but she was sure these streaks could kill Gabby if they didn't stop the strange infection.

"We'll be okay," she reassured Gabby and released her arm before Gabby could catch the desperation in Rayen's mind.

"Of course, *you two* will be fine," Tony continued ranting from where he'd paced to the other side of the room again. "Meanwhile I'll be sacrificed to the god of Loony Land. Or the goddess. But you don't care, which figures. Won't be the first time I end up thrown under the bus. The *last* time was by people I *thought* were friends."

Rayen understood Tony's fear of being put to death, especially for something he hadn't done. He should realize she wouldn't let this bunch harm him or Gabby without a fight, regardless of her sporadic superpower, but she didn't have the patience to figure out what Tony meant by a bus. She buried her need to strike at something out of frustration and told him, "No one is going to die. It's probably just a scare tactic." At least, she hoped so. "Put your mouth to some use for once. See if you can get us some health aid here."

"You mean medical attention?"

She shot him a look that had him backing up.

"You don't get it, Xena. They don't care if *any* of us lives or dies." Tony stomped back over and drew in a deep breath as if ready to unleash a snarl but stopped and whistled between his teeth on the next exhale. "Whoa, babe," he said, bending over to examine Gabby's arm more closely, really seeing her this time. "Daa-yum. That's bad."

"Not helping, Tony," Rayen snapped. "Need medicine."

"No problem. I'm on it." Tony spun around and got within a foot of the wall and yelled, "Hey, a-holes, you hear me?"

Diplomatic, Tony was not, but loud he was.

Someone should respond. Rayen had clearly been hearing noises on the other side of the reeds since they'd been deposited here. Mostly kid voices that sounded as though they were in a play area.

Laughable to think children played in this place.

Tony balled his fist and smacked it on the wall, only to earn a quick blast of energy zapping him. He jerked his hand back, yelping. "You sorry-sack-of-skunk-crap! Man, that stings."

"Try your feet?" Rayen suggested. "The soles might insulate you from the shock."

"Why don't *you* try, Xena?" Tony demanded, still shaking his hand, no humor anywhere in his voice. "Instead of givin' orders. Do somethin'."

"Fine." Rayen stood and approached the nearest wall, giving it a solid thwack with her sneaker-covered foot. That earned her a small tingle, but nothing like the static power that had surged when she'd hovered her palm near the reeds earlier. She raised her voice and shouted, "You? Out there. We need medical assistance. *Now!*"

"And *food*," Tony called from the other side of the cramped room before mumbling, "Who asks for 'medical assistance'? This isn't a five-star hotel." Then he put more force in his voice again. "More water, too."

But nothing happened.

Except the voices had quieted.

Rayen thought back on Zilya's reaction to Gabby. The blonde who acted like a queen had expected Gabby to know what she'd been talking about with houses. Zilya and Mathias had taken issue mostly with Tony, and maybe herself, but not Gabby. That gave her an idea.

She raised her voice even louder. "Tell Mathias the Gabby girl needs help. She could be dying."

Rayen looked over at Gabby quickly and mouthed the words, *Not true.*

Gabby, being the astute person she was, offered a tight, small nod.

At least, Rayen wished there hadn't been some truth in her claim. That Gabby didn't look as if she could get sicker, and die, if they didn't get help.

Tony and Rayen kept the shouting up, sometimes one at a time, sometimes both together, until their raw throats sounded hoarse.

Nothing.

In fact, even the scurrying noises around the chamber had diminished.

Maybe they *were* making some progress. But not much and not soon enough if the pain lines on Gabby's face were any indication. Sweat glistened everywhere. Blotchy pink patches covered her death-white skin.

Tony opened his mouth for another blast, but Rayen waved him off. "Save your energy. We have to find another way."

Gabby glanced at Rayen, fighting to sound strong, but coming out thin when she said, "What about what you did to the attack-vine earlier?"

Rayen had hoped that wouldn't come up for discussion again.

Tony glanced at her, his expression confused. "Yeah, how'd that vine just die, Xena?"

She crossed the room to squat by Gabby again, buying herself a few minutes. Gabby and Tony wanted answers. So did she, but she didn't have any. She offered what she could. "Let's say I didn't do anything consciously."

"So what? You were knocked out and somethin' happened?" Tony demanded, looking for a scientific answer he could wrap his head around.

"No, more like a thought."

"A get-us-out-of-this-mess thought?" Tony's tone made it clear he labeled that answer as woo-woo.

Too bad it was the truth, or as close to the truth as she could manage.

Gabby managed a weak smile of reassurance. "Whatever you did, you saved our lives, Rayen. Thanks."

Tony didn't share Gabby's appreciation. "She also managed to get us stuck here in the first place if her touch–as *you* pointed out–is doing these things." The stress of worrying about his life had brought back the abrasive Tony. He glared at Rayen as if she'd planned the trip through the computer. "That crazy girl wants me dead. If that happens, I let people down. If you don't get us out of this hellhole, I'm so going to kick somebody's ass."

"Mine?" Rayen shot back, tired of playing peacemaker.

Tony had a moment when she thought he'd say yes, but he shook his head. "I don't hit girls, but I wouldn't mind going a round with that Callan."

He gained a bit of respect from her for his personal code, but did Tony really think he could match up with Callan? He'd earn her appreciation if he'd just shut his broken trap. Her body ached from toe to head. She had no idea who she was or how she'd ended up in this mess. And she was tired to the bone, mostly of taking grief all day.

She suggested, "I'd take care threatening Callan."

Tony scoffed at her. "Where I come from, we'd eat a pretty boy like him for lunch."

When she didn't reply, Tony taunted, "What's the matter, Xena? No *come back*?"

Out of ideas and patience, she stood up, ready to give Tony the target he'd been wanting.

The changes in her stance should have warned him she had no tolerance for aggression right now.

He just kept on pushing her. "How'd you even end up in Suarez's class to begin with anyhow? That ain't a class for the short bus kids ... or criminals."

Whatever a bus was sounded even more insulting this time.

Ready to silence that mouth, she took one step forward then stopped. She suddenly sensed another presence inside the hut.

What the . . .?

The old man she'd seen back when she'd first opened her eyes in the desert took a filmy shape beside Gabby. Sitting with legs crossed, he hovered a foot or so above the ground again, speaking in that gravelly voice. "A warrior fights to defend others and for honor. A child strikes out in anger. There is no place for a child on this journey."

Easy for him to say. But as long as Ghost Man was back, she could use more information.

"Who am I?" she asked before the vision could vanish again. She might not make it back to the school to learn what had been discovered about her family. But here was a chance. Maybe her only one.

Tony stopped jawing and for a blessed moment went silent.

Gabby paused in rocking to look up at her with curiosity swimming through her mismatched eyes. She glanced next to her at the empty spot where Rayen stared then back up, whispering, "You okay, Rayen?"

Neither she nor Tony seemed able to see the old man.

How could Rayen answer that when even she questioned her sanity at the moment? She kept her eyes on the filmy figure. "Answer me."

The ghost with the weathered face had been staring off into the distance. His gaze shifted to meet hers. "You know what you need to know for now."

Fury boiled up her throat. "Who. Am. I? Either tell me or stay away from me you old goat."

Tony whistled behind him. "She's gone completely off the reservation, Gabby."

"Just shut up, would you," Gabby snapped, sounding weaker than before.

Rayen glanced away from the vision long enough to check on Gabby. When she looked back the old one was gone. Fine. Like she needed one more animal in this zoo?

"So now you're talking to invisible friends, Xena?"

Clenching her hands into tight knots of frustration, she stepped toward Tony, determined to shut that yapping trap.

Tony's eyes widened in surprised. His hands curled in reaction, and he came up on his toes, prepared to defend himself. "You gonna use your super juice on me?"

"Cut it out," Gabby grumbled. "We need to work together, not fight amongst ourselves. Doing that plays into their hands."

Rayen didn't want to listen. She wanted to do something to burn off the frustration churning her insides.

The old man's voice whispered in her mind. *Are you a warrior or a child?*

She stopped in the middle of the hut but couldn't say if it was out of deference to Gabby's words or the old man's taunts. "Gabby's right. If we allow them to divide us, they'll win."

Gabby groaned and bent over.

Rayen dropped down next to her. “What’s happening?”

“I can’t close my hands. My arms feel like ... the muscles are hardening.”

Tony squatted on the other side of her and carefully lifted hair from her neck then hissed and pointed to gain Rayen’s attention without speaking.

Leaning closer, she saw what he was trying to keep Gabby from knowing. The red lines were climbing up and around her neck. If the muscles in her neck hardened, she wouldn’t be able to breathe.

CHAPTER 16

ONCE ZILYA LEFT MATHIAS' PRIVATE quarters in a huff, Callan turned to his leader.

Mathias suggested, "You should try to get along with her."

Callan held up his hand. "Please, no lectures on Zilya today."

The weary sigh that escaped Mathias spoke of long days and nights trying to keep a band of children alive. At this moment, that meant providing for over sixty MystiK children stolen from the Ten Cities of the K'ryan Renaissance. Many of whom were barely past nine years old. Callan didn't envy him.

Mathias moved on. "In that case, tell me what you couldn't share about our captives when everyone was here."

"The girl with the long black hair who leads the trio is dangerous." Pretty, too, but then Zilya proved that physical attractiveness meant very little when it came to character.

"More dangerous than the TeK male?"

"Yes. Have you decided *she's* not TecKnati?" Callan didn't think she was, but he'd reserve final judgment until he had all the information. The fact that she'd been found in the company of his enemy and defended that same TeK counted against her. The TecKnati had cost him too much personally to allow anything to influence his judgment. Definitely not an unusual girl whose sharp eyes the color of turquoise had argued the innocence of her group.

What did her eye color have to do with anything? This was not the time to be distracted by any female.

"She doesn't appear to be TeK," Mathias agreed. "However, that doesn't clear up who or what she is." He waved toward the far wall for them to sit in two ocean-blue chairs he'd carved from the base of chopped-down terrian trees. "I'll have to ask V'ru, which reminds me. Would you spend some time with him?"

"*Train* V'ru?" Callan didn't even try to hide his shock.

"No, just talk to him. He's adjusting, but not as quickly as I'd hoped."

Words were not Callan's strength. He didn't know how to comfort anyone. "Can't Zilya talk to him?"

"V'ru tolerates Zilya, but he doesn't look up to her. He idolizes you."

That made it even worse. Callan wanted no one idolizing him, but he owed a debt to V'ru who had given Callan valuable information that helped in investigating Jornn's death. As a powerful G'ortian and a prodigy of the Records House, V'ru was better than any Cyberprocessor when it came to producing immediate information. And Callan wasn't entirely sure that V'ru hadn't been following him the night they were both captured. "I hate that he's here."

"I understand, but we lost a lot of children before V'ru arrived. I was barely keeping this village alive on what little we'd figured out was edible through trial and error."

"I'm glad we have V'ru's unlimited knowledge at hand, but he shouldn't be here."

"No MystiK should. He'll settle in."

Seemed like a good time to change the subject back to why Callan had stopped by. He told Mathias, "You need to train."

Mathias groaned. "I'm proficient with the spear. That's enough."

Not if Mathias intended to spend tonight in the woods alone, but Callan didn't want to add to his leader's worries by reminding him. "You missed the last two training sessions."

"I'll make you a deal."

Now Callan groaned, sure of what was coming. He pushed up from the chair and stepped over to where two shoulder-high spears were stabbed in the ground next to the feather wall. When Mathias stood, Callan lifted a spear and tossed it at him. "Fine. We both train."

Mathias grinned and caught the weapon with one hand then moved to the center of the room. He began stretching, using the staff for support. "If I must train to fight croggles, you must train to fight SEOH."

Here came one of Mathias's "leader" lessons.

Callan crossed his arms and spread his feet apart, ready to work Mathias to the point of distraction. "If you say so. I'm ready to meet him on the battlefield."

"That you are, but as leader of all the TecKnati, SEOH will never fight fairly, *or* on a physical battlefield."

"I have no intention of fighting fairly either. Not against someone who got away with killing three future MystiK leaders without sanction." Jornn had been one of those. "Our treaty isn't worth the spell that was cast on it."

Mathias paused from a contorted stretch and straightened. "Yes, it is. The sanction worked just as the spell on the treaty was intended. The moment each of those underage MystiKs were murdered, SEOH and two other TeK dignitaries lost their seventeen-year-old sons. An eye for an eye. A future leader for a future leader."

"But no one *knows* that's why those TeKs died. You want to know what really chafes my hide? The whole thing got covered up."

"I'll admit that SEOH is a genius when it comes to battle strategy."

Callan scowled at Mathias. "How can you praise him?"

"Do not misunderstand me. I do not praise him, but you were the one who taught me to thoroughly evaluate an enemy. I am only doing that."

"I said to look for an enemy's weak spot, because they always have one. Never underestimate an opponent."

Mathias nodded as he began moving through exercises while Callan gave hand signals of different attack and defense positions. Shove straight out, pull back to his chest, then a half spin to the right, another shove, a half spin left. Mathias said, "SEOH is a sociopath, and a clever one. My point was that he ran a brilliant damage control campaign to camouflage the deaths of the three TeK children who *appeared* to have collapsed from asphyxiation. Easy to accomplish with the technology at his fingertips."

"*Only* because idiots believed his lies," Callan ground out, disgusted. "I couldn't believe that even MystiKs bought into SEOH's claim." Callan dropped his voice to emulate SEOH's from the black-ban vid and struck a politician's pose with a hand over his chest. "Our planet has experienced a *rare* phenomenon."

Mathias snorted at the imitation. "Maybe we need a vid player as a ruler."

"That's the problem. Our citizens are lazy sheep. They accept anything spoken through a microphone or seen on a vid screen as truth."

"I concur, but no average person will dispute SEOH's statements when his claims are backed up by scientists."

Callan never understood how people could be so easy to trick. Couldn't they use their brains? "How stupid can anyone be to believe that fine particles from a meteor had passed through the atmosphere to cause the sudden deaths of three TeK boys?"

"Naïve, not stupid," Mathias corrected.

With one quick move, Callan struck unexpectedly and had Mathias on his back, the spear at Mathias's throat. "Never allow *anything* to distract you."

When Callan stepped away, Mathias climbed to his feet and snatched back the weapon, grumbling something about payback.

"You were saying?" Callan smiled.

"Just wait until I test you on MystiK law." Mathias nodded for Callan to resume, then stabbed and moved with the intense conviction that Callan had been looking for. Mathias continued, "All I'm saying is you must study the way SEOH handled that situation. Instead of allowing rumors of three mysterious TeK deaths to surface, he offered major credits to families who, quote, 'also had other children die of unexplained deaths' during that same time frame."

"I understand. With so many families coming forward whether they had an unexplained death or not, the three TeKs killed by our treaty were buried in the flood of reports."

Mathias nodded, lifting his arm to swipe sweat from his brow. "*That* is a TeK strength you must plan to confront when you return."

"I can't fight press conferences." If he could, Callan would have destroyed SEOH a long time ago.

"To be a strong leader, you must also learn how to fight political battles, Callan."

Callan ignored the comment about being a leader, determined not to argue with Mathias today of all days. He turned to find a water gourd near the chairs that he handed Mathias who upended it for a long drink then set it aside.

Mathias pressed on with his lesson. "When SEOH uses charm to sway the masses while he kills MystiKs, you must be just as creative when it comes to striking back."

"I'm the sword arm of Warrior House, not the mouth."

"And *that's* only one reason SEOH is successful."

Callan's entire body tightened at the insinuation that he was at fault for SEOH's success.

When Mathias noticed Callan's face, he stumbled in his movements and held the spear across his chest. "Save that look for a croggle or the enemy. I have enough nightmares."

Callan gained control of his anger and wiped all expression from his face.

Angling his head in a show of thanks, Mathias went on. "I meant no criticism of the Warrior House, but of the fact that none of our Houses work together. A sword arm alone will not save us. If we continue fighting the way we always have, we'll eventually lose everything."

Callan agreed about the lack of cohesion between Houses, but he *would* kill the man who took Jornn's life ... if he ever got out of this Sphere. The moment Jornn's soul had left his physical body, his brother's spirit had spoken in Callan's mind saying, "I'm sorry to leave you, brother. SEOH has murdered me. As decreed by the treaty, he's punished by the loss of his own son. But there will be more. Do *not* let him win."

SEOH may not have struck the killing blow with his hand, but he'd ordered the vicious attack. In one instant, Callan lost the equivalent of a limb and became the next in line to rule the Warrior House, except he wasn't ruler material.

But duty rarely took ability into account.

Callan would fulfill his brother's last command once he figured out how. "You're right. If our Houses weren't so competitive, secretive, and paranoid over protecting their powers they might communicate and know the treaty has been broken. As it is, the leaders of all seven Houses will not know that three MystiKs have been murdered by the TecKnati until our elders meet at the upcoming BIRG Con, expecting to indoctrinate new leaders and sign another worthless treaty. By that point, there may be no future generation to take the reins. What will our people do when they realize children from all Houses have gone missing? Will they figure out that the TecKnati have been capturing us? I tell you this as truth. The Warrior House will seek retribution, but will the other six make SEOH pay?"

"I don't know," Mathias admitted. "SEOH has to be expecting retaliation at the BIRG Con. I have to hope our leaders would put aside their differences and unite the minute they realize genocide is under way and, at that point, turn on the TeKs." Mathias paused, lowering his spear. "This could mean war."

"It should."

"But can we fight the TecKnati?"

"United, I believe we could, but not when our leaders only meet once every five years at the BIRG Con. SEOH has had the luxury of time for planning." Callan lifted his spear and gave a silent defensive order to Mathias to keep him training. Maybe when Mathias returned to his Governing House, he'd be able to show his elders that one could govern and protect at the same time.

Mathias agreed, "We have proven the power of shared knowledge and communication to survive in this Sphere. There is no value in hoarding information if the price is our future." Mathias made a difficult maneuver that included a back flip. He landed decisively, grinning.

"Well done." Callan could see a strong MystiK society if the Houses joined resources the way he, Mathias and other young MystiKs had done to survive this Sphere. But MystiKs didn't question the status quo, content to believe they were safe so long as they stayed inside the ten secured cities, secure to reside within their own corner of power. And the TecKnati population appeared as easily misled.

Both MystiKs and TecKnatis had lived in uneasy peace since the K'ryan Syndrome when an infection had wiped out ninety percent of civilization a hundred and six years ago.

But the peace would last no longer.

Callan changed up the training. "Now, without your hands."

Mathias balanced the spear on one arm and used his kinetic ability to roll the rod up his arm and dipped his head forward as it traveled across his shoulders. "Can you see the Warrior House ever being as forthcoming back home?"

"Security has always called for a certain amount of autonomy and maintaining classified information." Callan conceded the point though. "We have thick-headed seniors, too. The old ones have been in control for too long. They refuse to change the way things have always been done. Time for new blood, younger blood, but SEOH is wiping out our next generation before that can happen."

With a new hand signal from Callan, Mathias flipped the spear in the air, caught it and went into a series of attack positions. "No argument on that point. Sadly, the TecKnati's ability to communicate better than we do is why we're sitting in this Sphere."

Callan vowed, "One day I *will* prove that SEOH is a cold-blooded killer and see him sent to a cage worse than this place."

"That's probably one reason SEOH's glad to have you in here."

"I'm sure." Callan glanced up at the sky, always keeping an eye out for change. "Think this Sphere is the only world SEOH's created?"

"Quite possibly. According to V'ru, the engineering of an artificial planet such as this one takes an enormous number of credits that even SEOH's ANASKO Corporation would hesitate to spend twice. The media vids V'ru allowed me to review showed SEOH bragging about the plants and animals gathered as a result of his space exploration program. He touted the TeKs for donating generously to create a suitable host location for the study of adaptability."

"Adapt or die, in our case."

"Yes. Most people would assume SEOH meant the ability of his alien plant and animal specimens to adapt to *our* world, not that *we* would be doing the adapting." Mathias lifted the spear and began timed maneuvers that required rapid hand-over-hand defensive and offensive moves. “I think SEOH saw this as the perfect place to put captured MystiKs while justifying the expense of building this Sphere to his board of twelve. He probably convinced them this would be a sort of training area prior to relocating people–MystiKs–to other planets.”

Callan dodged forward with the speed of a striking snake and snatched the spear from Mathias, flipped it once into an attack pose, then handed the weapon back to a scowling Mathias.

Callan grinned, continuing. “I’ve heard that rumor about relocation. You think SEOH’s really going to try to wipe out MystiKs by shipping us off to another planet?”

“No.” Mathias paused, thinking as he cradled the spear. “I think his primary goal is to remove those of us approaching eighteen–take us out of circulation, especially G’ortians.”

Callan avoided discussing his G’ortian status since that was yet another reason his family had been disappointed when he refused to accept his role as a leader.

More powerful than other MystiKs, G’ortians only came along once every seven generations. Callan had experienced some gifts since birth, such as immediate telepathic ability that usually developed several years later. But his kinetics were a recent revelation and undependable as yet. He pushed the conversation back to SEOH. “I keep trying to figure out SEOH’s end game for putting us in here. What’s your guess?”

“To prevent us from taking our places as the next level of leaders within our Houses.”

“Sure, but SEOH’s also putting TeK children in jeopardy every time a MystiK child dies here. Even TeKs will eventually raise an alarm if they lose enough children.”

“I’ve thought on that quite a bit. I don’t believe the TeKs are losing children.” Mathias jabbed the spear into the ground and took a breath, wiping a sheen of sweat from above his mouth.

“Why not? The treaty decrees retribution.” Not that Callan wanted to see any child die, but without a consequence SEOH would continue capturing MystiKs.

“I believe this Sphere is their answer to neutralizing us.”

Callan argued, “But the treaty–”

“–stated that a TecKnati or a MystiK child would die in response to an intentional death caused by either group.” Mathias drew a couple of breaths. “SEOH probably thought little of that clause at the time it was written.

Rumors say he scoffed at the notion that anything supernatural would reach beyond our people to affect the TecKnati, and him, particular."

"SEOH was the fool there. Underestimating your opponent is shortsighted and dangerous." Callan had drummed that into his young warriors.

"Quite true, but when our MystiK forefathers negotiated the current treaty, the TeKs had never before experienced more than occasional interruptions in their technology caused by MystiK powers that they dismissed as coincidental. SEOH had no reason to believe our leaders could infuse any real power into that one retaliatory clause in the treaty. Not until he paid the price for ignorance and arrogance with his own son's death. Sending captured MystiKs to this Sphere is evidence that he's worried now."

Callan pondered on that, not liking the direction of his thoughts. "Are you saying SEOH has changed his tactics and there's no consequence?"

"He may not want to *believe* in our powers, but he has to know that MystiK power was behind the failure of ANASKO'S HERMES shuttle *and* the death of his son at the same moment your brother died." Mathias dropped his gaze to the ground. "My father and our House led the drive to stop that launch. As the Governing House, we should have been better prepared for the reaction. We anticipated a backlash, but no one expected SEOH to send an assassin after three of our future leaders or to orchestrate a plan for genocide."

There was little Callan could say to that admission, but Mathias did not deserve to carry the blame for those deaths. The only person responsible was SEOH. Callan walked over to lift the other spear and turned back. "Through resting?"

Once Mathias raised his weapon, Callan attacked. Strike, dodge, strike. Callan admitted, "Our elders must accept the need for change. Had all seven Houses worked together, my warriors would have been brought in to perform a covert attack on ANASKO's shuttle launch that no one could have pinned on the MystiKs. That being said, regardless of any mistakes, at least your father took an action when we had to do something. We can't allow SEOH to bring another deadly version of the K-Virus into our world again."

Mathias's father had led the charge against space exploration for years. Callan respected that. MystiKs believed the dangerous K-Virus that annihilated so much of the world's population five generations ago had originated in outer space. In his thinking, every effort SEOH took to expand space exploration placed the entire world's population at risk.

"The threat of the K-Virus won't stop SEOH from trying to ship us off planet," Mathias said, and shot forward, jabbing the spear.

Callan spun away from the sharp tip. He landed with his feet set to intercept a second attack, but Mathias was laughing too hard to follow through. Callan gave him his due and dipped his head slightly in a nod, the equivalent of high praise for getting that close to an elite warrior. "You're improving."

Shrugging, Mathias swung the spear up in front of his chest, holding it horizontally with two hands. Callan lifted his spear with two hands as if he wielded a sword, striking the wooden bar from different angles as Mathias blocked. Callan thought out loud. "With the threat of facing another K-Virus, does SEOH really think our Houses will go along with shipping MystiKs to a new planet?"

"Perhaps. There are MystiKs who believe in SEOH's relocation program as a chance for our people to rule their own world. I heard many excited about SEOH's announcement of his new HERMES shuttle plans. The ad campaign went viral within minutes. If I saw one more ad for Hermes, God of Travel, I threatened to destroy my Cyberprocessor."

"Foolish MystiKs and TeKs. Yet again, they hear only what they want to hear."

Mathias quipped, "I wonder if any of them realize Hermes was also the god of trickery and thieving."

Callan answered with a wry smile. Could Mathias be right about SEOH's reasoning behind using the Sphere as a cage for MystiK children?

After the K'ryan Syndrome wiped out billions of people, every generation of MystiKs since then had become more powerful in using their abilities. Gifts the MystiKs considered as natural as breathing, but TecKnati saw as supernatural freakishness. Now the G'ortians showed signs of unexpected levels of abilities that, if combined, threatened a power capable of impeding technological advancement the MystiKs deemed reckless.

Now that Callan thought on the specifics of the treaty–just as Mathias had intended during this training session–he realized Mathias hadn't answered his earlier question. "Why do you think no TeK children are dying at home?"

Swinging the spear tip up and down in fast arcs, Mathias blocked, breathing hard as he answered. "The treaty is written in such a way that if an underage MystiK dies by the hand of, or order of, a TeK as a premeditated act, a TeK child of equal rank will lose his or her life immediately. The idea was that no parent would willingly sacrifice his own child, and if someone who was not a parent killed a child, that the penalty would be great enough to force the people to revolt against the person responsible."

"But, still, the loophole in the treaty is *lack of knowledge* of this heinous act." Callan worked through the logic in his mind. "What about a *beast* that belongs to SEOH?" *If I'd studied with Jornn back when he went through government training, I'd know the terms of the treaty better.*

"I assume you don't mean sentient beasts, which were outlawed long ago and would still cause a TeK death if SEOH directed the animal to kill a MystiK child. Even SEOH wouldn't risk the death penalty that possessing one of those beasts carries."

"No, I mean what about a regular *living* animal?"

"If a TeK owns a living creature who attacks a MystiK who then dies, but the TeK did *not* train the animal to kill, that would be considered an accident, leaving TeK children safe."

"You think that's also true of things in here like croggles?" Callan started understanding where Mathias was going with his train of thought and put the blunt end of his spear on the ground.

A bit winded, Mathias lowered his spear as well. "SEOH did put the croggles and other deadly elements retrieved from planetary exploration into this Sphere, but those creatures are naturally hostile. SEOH isn't directing the plants, animals, or the poisoned liquids. So long as we die here, killed by natural events, he's found a way around the treaty language."

Callan's skin chilled at the possibility of what Mathias was saying. SEOH could capture thousands of children, ship them here to die, and get away with murder.

Again.

Footsteps approached at a fast clip from down the hall, then Etoi rushed into the room without requesting entrance, as always. "There's a corruption in the fog barrier."

Mathias frowned. "That might only be the atmospheric change we experienced a couple of months ago."

Callan snatched up his spear. "Or it might be something more significant."

Any change to the fog compromised the safety of the village. He ran out with Mathias and Etoi close behind.

CHAPTER 17

BRUSHING THE GAUZY, MOSS GREEN wisps from his hair, Callan warned Mathias, "If Etoi sends me on another fool's errand, she won't like the punishment."

"But you said it might have been a serious breach in our security."

"If the fog had truly *corrupted*, it would have been. She knows the difference between a hollow eucalypoon mist that's floated loose and a break in the fog curtain."

Mathias swatted a swatch of green off his shoulder. "They look similar, and it *was* quite a large mist cloud, taller than either of us and twice as wide. She can be annoying, but sometimes you just have to overlook it."

"And that is why you govern, and I protect," Callan pointed out. "I don't have your patience. Where'd you send her?"

"To check on the prisoners."

Callan chuckled. Etoi hated guard duty. She'd probably sneak off and find Zilya to gossip with, but he didn't care what those two did as long as they were out of his hair. "What are you going to do about the captives? We can't keep them without feeding them, and we don't have enough food to share."

"I don't know." Mathias sounded weary and not from just the trek to check on their defenses.

Callan offered, "In her usual bloodthirsty way, Zilya suggested we stake out that Tony as croggle bait."

Mathias's lips quirked at that. "She does have a homicidal streak."

"I do, too, when it comes to TecKnati," Callan admitted, though he'd never kill in cold blood. That would put him on the level with his enemy, lower than scum on the bottom of his boot.

"You would execute someone without a fair judgment?"

"No, but we're at war and many of ours have died. If you're right and there's no sanction happening back home, SEOH owes us TeK deaths in return for the children we've lost. It's the treaty. It's the *law*. Right?"

"Believe me, I'd like to personally enforce that law if we could use it specifically against SEOH," Mathias muttered.

The dire sound of his tone caused Callan to poke at him. "And here I thought only the Warrior House sought to solve issues with fighting first–as we're so often accused ..." He paused until Mathias swallowed a grin and added, "Rather than negotiate a problem to death like the Governing House. It's *your* House that preaches against vengeance."

"Living here has caused me to reevaluate many things, but I digress. We're agreed that the mouthy one with the skin ink mark is a TecKnati, right?"

Callan nodded. "He's the best candidate of the three. What about the girl with bi-colored eyes, excessive earrings that only the most powerful MystiKs are allowed to wear and ... did you sense anything from her?"

"Yes. She has a gift or gifts, but she clearly wasn't going to admit that to us. Not unusual for a Hy'bridt MystiK, the only explanation for those eyes. Except the colors she wore were all over the place ... but so were the clothes on the TeK one." Mathias paused. "And what was a Hy'bridt doing with *him*?"

"I don't know. I've never seen TeKs dressed that way. Based on what little we know, I'd say she's as MystiK as that Tony is TecKnati."

"We'll have to talk to the Hy'bridt some more and see if we can figure out what she's doing here. Makes no sense."

Callan swallowed a growl of irritation. Why would Mathias believe anything that Hy'bridt said? "I don't trust any MystiK that hangs out with a TecKnati. I told you when I first got here that I thought a MystiK traitor could be working with the TecKnati to help them trap us. Who's to say that person isn't a Hy'bridt?"

Mathias slowed next to the hut where several girls and a couple of young boys prepared food. He gave them a word of encouragement and snagged a bowl of buri berries, then continued to his chambers, not missing a beat in the conversation. "Hy'bridts are supposed to be as loyal as they are powerful."

"Maybe," Callan allowed, taking a handful of berries to refresh his dry throat. "But loyal to whom? And what about the other girl?" The taller one with midnight-black hair and skin the color of brewed tea. His mind fought to sum her up in one word but narrowed it down to two–deadly and attractive–much like some of the plants in this Sphere. She was a prime example of whatever group she belonged to, with her keen blue eyes, slashed cheekbones and a body that filled out her strange clothes nicely.

But anyone who associated with a TeK, even an exotic female, fell clearly within Callan's definition of enemy. Especially after watching her single-handedly annihilate a croggle.

"That one with the black hair throws me," Mathias admitted. "I didn't understand her name. Xena?"

"I don't think that's her real name. I heard both the TeK and the Hy'bridt call her Rayen, and she doesn't strike me as a TeK. Rayen has the skills of a Warrior. You know TeKs would rather push a button than dirty their hands fighting."

"Except for their Scouts." Mathias sounded resigned.

"They are the exception."

"But that Rayen has no TeK markings, nor does she have markings such as those of your Warrior House."

"I know," Callan admitted, trying to put the pieces together. "Plus, she has that device attached to her leg."

"Do you think she meant to destroy the croggle?"

Callan hated all things related to the TecKnati, but to falsely accuse anyone would be dishonorable. Without honor, a man was nothing. "Much as it still angers me that she destroyed our food, she did so with only one of our spears and the croggle *had* neutralized two of our hunters with its tail right before she attacked. That supports her claim that she thought children were in danger."

"How did she destroy the beast?"

"That was strange. Her power burned the croggle from the inside out. Blue flame, very hot. No TeK has ever been known to have our gifts, and few of our own have that level of power."

Mathias munched quietly on a mouthful of berries for a moment. "If she's not TeK and not MystiK, what then? Could she be a different type of G'ortian?"

Callan stared off, considering that possibility. "I don't know. What I do know is that she's the most dangerous of the three."

"But in spite of the power she displayed in battle, she didn't try to harm any of you on the way to the village?"

"No." Callan could see why Mathias hesitated to pass judgment on the two girls, but the mouthy male *was* a TeK.

And no TeK deserved to walk away free.

When Mathias looked up at the sky, Callan did as well, noting the subtle shift of color overhead that had begun undulating from the deep blue-purple shade toward a vibrant red purple. A hint of green stripes began appearing above the forest side of the village.

Mathias released a deep sigh heavy with the weight of responsibility on his shoulders. "We'll have to figure out what to do with those other two captives later, but the TeK does not spend the night in our village."

"Agreed but wait to deal with him until I return from checking the original transender site for new arrivals." Callan didn't want anyone at risk while he was gone.

"We need our strongest four to make that run and Jaxxson can't go. He has to watch the little girl we brought back for any signs of reaction to the Sphere."

True. They couldn't wait until Jaxxson declared the child stable or they might risk losing another one dumped in the Sphere with no defenses. Callan said, "I'll have to take just Etoi and Zilya."

"No." Mathias shook his head. "Not after losing Sebi. You can't go with fewer than four capable fighters and we have no one old enough or experienced enough yet to take Jaxxson's spot. I can't risk losing any of you, definitely not all of you. I'll go."

Callan understood the worry in Mathias's voice, but he couldn't include Mathias on this run even though he was capable in battle. Mathias had been too distracted lately with problems inside the village and now he had three captives to pass judgment on ...

The captives. That gave Callan an idea how to convince Mathias to stay behind. "You can't leave the village with those three in the Isolation Unit. That's a security risk."

Mathias lifted his large hand and rubbed his temple, thinking. "Are any of the younger hunters capable of joining you?"

"None are ready to face TecKnati Scouts. The captive, Rayen, easily disarmed two of my best-trained young hunters."

"That still leaves us with only three runners. We have to continue working four warriors in teams of two. Otherwise, it's too dangerous."

Callan suggested, "Maybe Zilya's idea about the TeK deserves consideration. If he dies, it's on the heads of the TeK Scouts."

"To use Tony as croggle bait?"

"Why not?"

Mathias laughed. "I'm not sure a croggle would have that one. Even if we did want to take the TeK with us, I sense that the dark-haired girl will not allow those other two to be harmed. That's why we have to be careful how we deal with this Tony."

Callan held up his hand. "I'm not concerned with any leniency for the TeK. And as for this Rayen, she may be strong, but she has *not* proven herself to be a MystiK as yet. If she is aligned with that Tony, it means she *has* to know a TeK will turn on his own mother to save his life."

"True. What're you suggesting?"

"With the right motivation," Callan said, weighing his words. "Rayen may not fight us to take Tony and, even if she does, she can't stop *both* of us."

"You would stake him like a sacrificial–"

Etoi came running up. "Mathias!"

Callan growled under his breath, but Etoi never gave him a chance to say a word.

"The girl captive with the strange eyes is very ill. The other two are yelling for help. They say she is dying."

Callan looked to Mathias, inspiration firing his smile. "Now we'll find out which one Rayen is willing to save."

CHAPTER 18

RAYEN PACED THE ISOLATION HUT, cursing Mathias and Zilya. She couldn't believe Mathias was going to let Gabby die.

Zilya might. She'd made it clear that Tony's life meant nothing to her. But Rayen had thought for sure that Mathias had shown an unusual interest in Gabby in a positive way earlier. So why hadn't they come to check on her by now?

"Come on, babe, keep your eyes open," Tony told Gabby in a concerned voice that Rayen wouldn't have thought possible at one time. Tony sat next to Gabby, using a strip of cloth Rayen had torn from the bottom of her shirt to brush sweat from Gabby's forehead.

For someone who could be so abrasive at times, Tony had shown another side by picking up quickly on Gabby's aversion to being touched. He'd been careful not to stress her additionally in any way.

Rayen could do no more than Tony right now since she had no idea how to help Gabby either. She'd taken turns calling for help again but hadn't heard a sound in a long while.

Gabby lifted her head. It wobbled a little as she leaned back against the covered arm and shoulder Tony had put behind her for a support. "Water. My throat's burning."

Tony looked at Rayen.

She fisted her hands and turned to beat against the wall of the hut regardless of what the energy sizzling through the structure did to her. It had hurt last time. Badly.

But a section the size of an opening started wavering.

She stepped back into a defensive position in front of Tony and Gabby.

When the opening finally appeared, Mathias entered first and stepped to the side. That allowed room for Callan to duck his head and walk in, a guarded expression in place. Mathias had a serene look, which Rayen trusted as much as she trusted anything else in this strange, hostile world.

Not one bit.

Mathias started to speak, but her frustration knew no limit right then.

"What's wrong with you people? You accuse us of being some murdering tecknati, but you place no higher value on life, do you?"

She'd expected Mathias to snap right back at her, not to turn rigid as a statue at her accusation as if she'd slapped him. Or maybe insulted him. She'd feel bad for yelling at him since he seemed to be the only calm one in the bunch, but Gabby had gotten worse during each minute that Mathias had ignored their calls for help.

He drew a breath and spoke with the authority she'd heard in their earlier meeting. "We have to make the run to check for new children dropped from the transenders."

Tony piped up. "What's that got to do with Gabby bein' sick?"

Callan's only reaction to Tony's words was a tightening of his jaw. His gaze moved to Rayen, and his words came out with a hard clip. "We need four who are experienced enough to do this. The young ones lack the strength and skill to face the challenges of this transender location."

"Still waitin' on the punch line, dude," Tony groused.

Callan turned on Tony. "Shut up, tecknati."

Rayen couldn't deal with those two at the same time. "Tony, please."

Gabby moaned and shivered.

When Mathias's attention shifted to Gabby, his face scrunched with concern. So now he finally noticed the puffy red skin on Gabby's arms? He demanded, "What's wrong with her?"

Shaking his head, Tony gave Mathias a look of rank disgust. "What the eff do you think we've been yellin' about for so long? She's having a very bad reaction. She needs a doctor. D-O-C-T-O-R. You got one?"

Dismissing him with a curt lift of his chin and speaking once again to Rayen, Mathias said, "We do have a healer–"

"Great." Her relief flooded out in that one word.

"But as I was explaining," he continued. "He is one of only four qualified to go on the observation run."

"Be serious," Tony argued. "You gonna send him out someplace to *maybe* find someone while Gabby gets worse?"

That stoked the fire that had simmered in Callan's eyes since he'd walked into the hut. He turned all that fury on Tony. "If not for *your* kind, we wouldn't have to go looking for children dumped in this place. If not for *your* kind, we wouldn't fear those children being eaten by a croggle or harmed by deadly plants. Don't lay her sickness or possible death at our feet when your SEOH is behind all this."

Tony looked at Rayen. "Who's he talkin' about?"

"I don't know, Tony." And right then, it didn't matter, because she was tired of waiting on help for Gabby. She also didn't want everyone to keep talking about Gabby dying in front of her. Rayen figured Callan wanted something and getting to that point sooner would be in Gabby's best interest, but she posed her question to both Callan and Mathias.

"What's it going to take for us to get help for Gabby?"

A vein in Callan's neck pulsed, restrained power waiting to be unleashed. Rayen sensed she wasn't going to like what he had to say. His lips parted to speak, but before he uttered a word his gaze drifted down to where she'd torn the bottom half of her shirt off for Gabby. He stared at her exposed skin as if he hadn't expected to see that and had lost track of the conversation.

Rayen shifted her stance, crossing her arms as she did.

He jerked his attention up. Rayen quirked an eyebrow to let him know she'd caught him studying her body. She might have found it flattering at another time, but she was too angry waiting on Gabby to receive help.

When Callan didn't answer her question of what they wanted, Mathias jumped in. "I have sent for our healer. We will see if he can do anything first."

Rayen hadn't heard Mathias request anyone to come to the hut, but in the next moment she heard a male voice outside announce, "Jaxxson coming in."

The opening appeared again. The guy who stepped forward had blond hair, a dark honey shade, and eyes so rich a brown and ringed by thick lashes that they appeared outlined in black. Naked chest showed above his skirt-like covering that reached his ankles. He was athletic looking, but had a lithe, sinewy build as compared to Callan's muscular physique. Between the two, she found Callan more attractive.

Not that her opinion would matter to either of them.

Callan's gaze tracked over to her. She merely lifted an eyebrow in response.

"Take a look at the girl's arms," Mathias directed the healer, his voice less hostile but no less authoritative.

As Jaxxson stepped past Rayen, he nodded once, either a sign of respect or just sizing up the stranger in their midst. Then he knelt on the opposite side of Gabby from Tony, keeping his movements slow, as if not to overwhelm or scare her.

Wise move. Even the most docile animal would attack when in pain.

Gabby pushed herself to sit up straight, wincing with the effort. She'd been so tough all day Rayen had come to understand that putting up a strong front was a matter of pride with her.

Jaxxson reached forward, then paused before touching her and asked, "May I?"

She shook her head and raised glazed eyes to me.

Rayen gave Jaxxson's back a don't-you-dare-try-anything threatening glare then explained, "She doesn't like to be touched."

"I'm a healer." Jaxxson spoke gently to Gabby, but hostility danced beneath his words as if coming here to care for a prisoner wasted his precious time. A possible tecknati prisoner.

"Can you open your arms just to show him," Rayen asked Gabby, wanting her to get the help she needed.

Gabby gritted her teeth, but she forced her arms to unbend halfway, which appeared to be all she could manage with her limbs swollen.

Jaxxson looked over his shoulder at Rayen and asked, "How'd this happen?"

Rayen flexed her fisted hands. "We had to fight off some monster plant that was trying to suck us inside a pink flower. Its vine wrapped her wrist." They weren't showing an appropriate amount of concern, so she glanced in Callan's direction and added, "Gabby's having a bad reaction to that ... *or* those red vines *your little warrior* wrapped around her wrists."

Mathias sent Callan a pointed look filled with silent questions. Callan asked, "Pink flower? Green spots? A frazzle vine with blossoms this big?" He used his palms to air sketch a shape. "And one huge flower head on the host bush?"

"Sounds like it." Rayen stepped toward Gabby. "Whatever it was, she's been the only one of us to react. I think your red restraint vines made things worse."

Mathias asked Jaxxson, "Can you do anything for her?"

"Yes, but I'll need to move her back to the healing hut."

Rayen immediately tensed. Last thing she wanted was to allow them to take Gabby anywhere alone. Especially if it meant Rayen's friend being isolated and vulnerable. "Why can't you help her here?"

Callan cut her off. "Because his supplies are in the healing hut, but that will have to wait until we get back. We need Jaxxson and have to leave soon."

Not good enough. Rayen stepped toward Callan. "She's getting sicker by the minute. She can't wait for later."

"She doesn't have a house," Mathias argued.

Was he serious? Rayen snarled, "I don't care if she doesn't have a tent, she could die from this. Are you willing to let that happen after we saved that little girl?"

Guilt slid through Callan's hard expression, but he looked as though he'd come to some conclusion. "I told you we have to run the transender lines then we *also* have to hunt for food."

Not my fault, she wanted to answer but instead said, "What do you mean by running these lines?"

He drew a deep breath as if just listening to her took all his patience. "Do not play games with me. The tek–"

"*I'm not a tecknati!*" Rayen roared. "I don't know who or what they are, but I'm starting to wonder about what kind of people *you* are if you're willing to leave her–" She pointed at Gabby. "–in pain."

"That is *your* problem," Callan charged. "Mine is saving our children." He paused as if wrestling his temper under control, then added in a calmer voice, "But we may be able to work out something favorable for everyone."

Finally. The trade she'd been expecting. "What do you want?"

"A fourth person to go with us who can ... help defend against a croggle. I will allow Jaxxson to remain and tend to the girl, but in exchange we need another person. We'll take the one who can't deny he is tek with us."

Rayen looked at Tony, easily reading the thoughts behind his ashen face. He believed once Callan and Mathias took him away from this hut he'd never return. He'd already said once that he expected to get thrown under a bus. Was this the bus?

Worse, the resigned look on his face said he thought Rayen would agree.

She didn't want to leave Gabby alone, but neither could she let Tony walk out of here with someone who'd marked him for death. Keeping her eyes on Tony, she announced, "No. I'll go instead."

A whole swarm of demon flies could have set up camp in Tony's open mouth before he recovered to shout, "Are you crazy?" He slapped his leg. "What am I sayin'? Of course, you're crazy. First you're talkin' to–"

"*Tony!*" She gave that warning in a voice that threatened serious harm if he said another word about her talking to someone he couldn't see earlier. She turned to Callan. "What's it going to be?"

He swung a stunned gaze at her. That had clearly not been the answer he'd been looking for, but that was the only one he was getting. She sensed a lot more not being said out loud between Callan and Mathias when they faced each other, the dilemma of what to do hanging between them.

Mathias started, "I don't know that we–"

Divide and conquer came to mind, but she didn't sense any real dissent between these two.

Cutting off Mathias, she swung to Callan, to get the terms straight. "Before I go, I want *your* word–as a warrior–that no harm will come to either of these two while I'm gone."

Something shifted in Callan's eyes that made her think he rarely had to put his word on the line. In that moment, she had a gut feeling that he took his honor to heart.

Then again, that perception might've been nothing more than the result of too many knocks to her head today.

Callan stepped in front of her, tight muscles in his face flexing as if fighting his temper again. When he spoke, each word had the bite of jagged ice. "And what if I choose not to agree to your terms?"

She crossed her arms and tilted her head up, their noses only inches apart. "Then prepare for things to get ugly. Because if you don't help Gabby, or if you try to take Tony out of here, it's going to get bloody, and I promise you there will not be four of you in shape to make the rescue run when I'm done."

Mathias asked Callan, "If there's a child to save, would we be better served to take a trained warrior than a ..."

Smooth approach on Mathias's part to give Callan an out by suggesting that someone who could fight would be of more benefit than a tecknati they only wanted to sacrifice.

While everyone waited in silence, Callan finally gave a single nod of agreement.

Rayen didn't want to admit it, but she admired the fact that Callan put the needs of the children ahead of his desire to punish a tecknati.

That was until he added, "If the sick girl is with Jaxxson until we return, there is no way for this one–" he bent his head toward Rayen.

If she told him her name, would he stop calling her *this one*?

"–to get to her if she escapes. If she runs or tries to interfere with us in any way–"

"I *won't*." She was tired of hearing threats. "I'm not going to abandon my friends or cause any problem ... as long as Jaxxson heals her. Are we through negotiating?"

Mathias didn't chuckle, but his eyes creased with an odd humor, as if stifling a half-smile at Callan.

Callan's eyes still seethed, probably from Rayen having demanded his word as a warrior again. "I have agreed but know this–if *any* of you try to escape while I'm outside the village, the other two will pay dearly."

"Understood," she said then turned and dropped down in front of Gabby. When she told Jaxxson, "I need a minute," she made it clear that was an order, not a request.

Jaxxson gave her a testy look but stood and moved to where Mathias and Callan waited.

Gabby still fought to hold herself upright. "Don't leave, Rayen. They can't be trusted."

Tony had recovered from his surprise and leaned in. "Look, Xena ... Rayen, I don't want–"

Rayen cut in, keeping her voice low. "Both of you listen up. Gabby, we need you healthy. Soon." She gave her a meaningful look she hoped Gabby understood – that they needed her to be in shape to run the minute they found a way out of here. When Gabby's infection-dulled eyes lit with understanding, she nodded. Rayen turned to Tony. "I don't know what a bus is, short or otherwise, but I'm not throwing you under anything. Take care of Gabby while I'm gone and ... be *ready* when I return."

As if the day hadn't been filled with enough surprises, for once Tony was not only speechless, but he nodded in agreement.

She then rose and strode over to the three waiting for her, turning toward Callan. "You ready?"

"Rayen!" Gabby pushed up to her knees, refusing Tony's offer to help her up, which would have meant his fingers touching her exposed arm.

Seeing her in such pain twisted Rayen's gut. "Yeah, Gabby?"

"Be safe." Her eyes said a whole lot more. "And come back."

"Plan on it." Rayen's gaze slid to Jaxxson who had waited next to the opening that had once again appeared in the wall. He didn't look any happier about the arrangement than she was, but she didn't care. Her words were as hard as stone when she warned the healer, "I promise you I *will* be back, and I had better find her safe and healthy."

She didn't wait for a reply as she turned, following Callan and Mathias out the door into the purple light that was becoming a noticeably darker reddish-purple.

Once outside and far enough away from the hut that neither Gabby nor Tony could easily hear them, Callan glanced over his shoulder at Rayen. "It's unwise to offer promises you have no way of knowing for sure you can fulfill."

"What? Telling Gabby and Tony that I was coming back?" She'd already fought one croggle practically alone, so how much harder could it be this time? If he hoped to rattle her confidence, he'd wasted his breath. She simply pointed out, "Croggles don't seem too hard to kill."

Callan's lips curved with a knowing smile when he cast another look at her. "The croggle you fought was a clumsy adolescent. The ones living around the transender site we go to now are full-grown creatures. Three times as large. Can't be stopped with a spear and not the least bit clumsy."

Now he tells her. "So how do we kill it?"

"That is the problem for the one keeping it busy if there is a child to save."

She didn't even waste her breath asking who he intended to send out to be croggle bait.

CHAPTER 19

IF I DIE HERE, HOW long will it take my dad to notice I'm missing if the school doesn't notify him?

Months. And Gabby considered that generous on her part.

One school hadn't noticed when she'd missed classes for two weeks.

She followed along behind Jaxxson, ignoring him since he ignored her. Outside the Isolation Unit, everything in the village was cast in intense reddish purples from that jacked up sky. Moving around had resulted in a small burst of energy, or maybe she was only experiencing an adrenaline spike over facing a new unknown. She kept forcing one foot in front of the other, struggling to catch her breath in the humidity that wrapped around her and squeezed, reminding her of childhood summers in Saigon, Bangkok, and Singapore. Mostly Singapore. Surviving that had been hard enough after her mom cashed out, but then her dad buried himself so deep in his work he'd forgotten he had a daughter.

A burden he'd pawned off on one private school after another since then.

She coughed and stumbled, catching her balance. Must not lag behind the grouchy healer from this weird world.

"Drink more of the water I gave you unless you enjoy coughing," Jaxxson said without turning around. The only words he'd spoken to her since leaving the neon-green hut this group used for a jail. "And keep up. You're not the only one who needs my attention."

She caught what his terse words hadn't said, that she imposed on his valuable time. Especially since he considered her an enemy, some freaky whatever they kept calling her, Tony and Rayen–techno-somethings. As if.

She had the brainpower to be a techno-whiz but lacked the passion for anything mechanical or electronic.

Numbers she loved. The rest? Bleh.

Jaxxson crossed into a less dense area. Not wide open like the grassy space where the metal pod had spit them out, more like trails wrapped in between trees where the underbrush had been cleared. Lots of trails, tons of big trees but no people, except for the sound of children, but she couldn't see any. The trees weren't brown or gray-skinned and the leaves weren't green. They were every color but. If not for working so hard to stay upright, she'd pause to admire the wicked colors, but not right now.

With Rayen dragged along on a hunting expedition that might involve killing croggles and Tony stuck in that prison unit, Gabby had to find out as much as she could while she was semi-free. Getting Jaxxson to talk at all would be tough, but he might if she started with a subject that interested him.

She asked in a scratchy voice, "How many kids are here in Camp Croggle?"

"Water," he ordered again.

Not a lively conversationalist.

She made a face at his back or tried to, but her face muscles weren't cooperating. Why should she be surprised at Jaxxson? He was just another self-consumed brainiac healer, like her father, right down to the bedside manners of a turnip. Only her dad *was* a physician, not some wannabe doc like Jaxxson.

A real doctor would have realized the reason she *hadn't* kept drinking was because she couldn't. Getting the lip of the water bag he'd hung around her neck up to her mouth became more impossible as her condition deteriorated.

Her swollen arms were so tight they didn't want to bend and neither did her puffed-up fingers that felt as though the skin would split any minute. But her throat ached with a dry, burning heat so she fumbled with the bag made of strange, aqua-colored leather hanging from a woven grass lanyard. She managed to lift the opening to her lips.

And pour *some* water in her mouth.

The rest ran down her chin and chest, dribbling over the front of her dress that was dirty from being dragged through the jungle. The multi-colored cloth would hide most of the wet stains. Dropping the water sack to lay against her chest again, she swiped a fat hand at her face and missed half the water still trickling down. Sort of like getting a shot of Novocain in her arms, hands and face ... but without the pain relief.

She focused on Jaxxson's back walking ahead of her and asked, "Where's this healing hut?"

"We're close."

"Where did Rayen, Mathias and Callan go?"

Not a word. The old silent treatment?

Being the new kid at a new school every six to eight months when her nanosurgeon-dad-turned-consultant accepted new contracts with different national and international medical programs meant a lot of stares and silence from her peers. You'd think after that and being ignored by her dad for the past six years, she'd have gotten used to being treated as an inanimate object. A useless dead weight.

But she hadn't.

On the other hand, she should be glad Jaxxson hadn't looked back at her the whole time she'd followed him since she could probably beat out the *Creature Of The Deep* for a scary-looking award. Her filthy arms and face were swollen and streaked with red lines, hair stuck out unintentionally all over the place and sweat glued her clothes to her body.

Not that she should care, but grouchy up ahead looked like he'd stepped out of a television ad for sexy shaving cream with that sarong wrapped around his waist, his nicely defined chest, smooth, olive-tone skin over an appealing masculine face and taut muscles that flexed across his back.

Wait. Back muscles?

That had nothing to do with shaving cream ads.

The infection must be frying her brain. Had to be the only reason she'd consider anyone who was even remotely related to medicine attractive. Underneath all that prime packaging lived the cold heart of an arrogant male with a God complex.

She'd met plenty over the years.

Sons of a few of her father's associates had taken an interest in her, until they clued into the fact that she wasn't her mother, the classic trophy wife.

Gabby had set her sights on being anything but. The more anti-trophy-worthy she could make herself, the better.

Jaxxson came to a sudden halt in front of a massive tree that reminded her of giant California redwoods you could drive a car through. Except this one's striped bark had a tiger-skin look to it and, way up high, polka-dotted yellow leaves flickered beneath that crimson-red daytime moon. But the moon had trekked some from one side of the sky to the other since she'd first seen it, like the arc of a sun going from horizon to horizon.

She kept plodding along to close the distance between her and Jaxxson. Why had he stopped here?

He turned with his arms crossed, as if waiting on an errant child. His dark-brown eyes swept up and down her, pausing on her face before he looked away.

I look that gross, huh?

Like she cared what he thought? But to be honest, the boys usually found her attractive, so on some what-the-hell-is-wrong-with-you level his action did sting.

When she finally reached him, he said, "Ready?"

"For what?"

"To enter the healing hut."

He was joking, right?

"I hate to point out the obvious, you being a medical professional and all," she said in a perky sarcastic voice she managed to dredge up in spite of the pain. "But it's a tree and I can't climb. I know, I'm self-diagnosing, something you doctors hate, but I'm just saving you from a possible malpractice suit." In case he needed a demonstration, she raised her sausage fingers and unbendable arms as high as she could, grimacing. The pain had increased as her heart rate picked up from walking and worrying.

He shook his head as if she were particularly slow or clueless. "Come on." He reached for her arm.

She flinched and stepped back, her voice coming out brisk, to make sure he understood. "Don't touch me."

"Don't give me orders," he warned. "I have enough to do without having to deal with someone like you."

"What do you mean 'someone like me'?"

"Think I haven't noticed you're a Hy'bridt?"

Did he mean hybrid? Like a mixed breed? A mongrel. "A what?"

"Mismatched eyes. Sign of a Hy'bridt."

Yeah, right. Everyone saw her different eyes before they saw her and marked her a freak without a single word of getting to know her. That's why she made a point of being the first one to put some distance between herself and strangers before someone had the opportunity to snub her. "I've been slammed by better than you, buster."

He jerked at her words. "I didn't touch you and I harm no one."

This whole conversation had gotten weirder than she could deal with until she found relief from this infection.

A battle of emotions warred through his gaze until he settled on irritated, his default emotion from what she could tell. He ground out his next words. "*You* wanted my help. If you don't go into the hut soon, that infection could reach your brain and, if it does, I won't be able to stop it from killing you."

Could reach her brain?

Was he telling her the truth or just trying to scare her? Either way, he was doing a damn good job of rattling her.

In fact, swallowing was becoming more difficult, especially getting past the lump of panic jamming her throat. "What do you want me to do? If your hut is inside this tree, show me the door."

"Door?"

She lifted her eyebrows. Was she speaking another language all of a sudden? "Yes. How else do you get in and out?"

"You have two different eye colors and *claim* to not be tecknati, yet you must be one or the other."

"One or the other what?"

"You waste my time!"

And you're making me crazy! She bared her clenched teeth. "I get it. You're important, but I'm not fluent in idiot and you're not making any sense. What does any of this one-kind-or-another thing have to do with getting inside this tree?"

"Tecknati can't enter this tree." His eyes flickered with a thought, something he battled about within himself until he looked up, whispering something silently that reminded her of her father when his patience ran out. Then he glanced back at her. "You have mixed eyes, yet you don't see the passage?"

One more snipe about her screwy colored eyes and he was going to end up seeing stars circling his head.

She took in the bark on the tree trunk, searching for a line or something that would indicate a doorway. Something that would prove she was *not* a tecknati. "Give me a hint."

"Put both hands up on the tree," he said, enunciating each word slowly.

She started to tell him she wasn't the moron here who thought she could walk through a tree. Giving him a sarcastic we'll-play-your-little-game glare, she gritted her teeth and moved right up against the bark, so she didn't have to reach far to touch it. She pushed her aching hands forward, past her hips, and then she paused, anticipating the pain of her over-sensitive palms hitting the striped bark.

But her hands touched nothing, kept moving as they disappeared into the tree that gave no more resistance than a cloud.

The unexpected lack of solidity startled her. She fell forward with no chance of getting her arms up to block her fall.

She squeezed her eyes closed and hunched her shoulders, preparing to hit face first.

And stopped in mid-air.

An arm scooped around her waist right before her face should have smashed into the ground.

She opened her eyes.

Yep, that smooth flat surface she stared at had to be the floor, because the two feet in odd sandals also in view matched the ones Jaxxson wore.

He hoisted her up to stand on her own and released her, stepping back with a strange expression. A mix of confusion and surprise.

Yeah, she was freaky, but this guy had no idea just how weird.

Want to talk freaky? Take a look at this place.

Awe stretched through her voice when she said, "This has got to be the most rockin' tree house I've ever seen." The room looked about fifteen feet across and more like an apartment than a doctor's office. Nothing cold and sterile here.

She sniffed. Eucalyptus? Sort of. And something else just as soothing. Sage? Or maybe lavender? It could be from the rough-hewn wood of the tree walls, toned down from the outside stripes. How cool was this to be inside the heart of a living, breathing tree?

Or were they? "Is this tree still alive?"

"Of course, it is." He strolled away.

She scrunched up her face and silently mimicked his words *Of course it is,* but he didn't see her.

Jaxxson stopped at a wall where an odd assortment of dried plants hung from a vine line. He pulled a wooden bowl off a crude shelf and sat it on a large slab table that was covered with a soft-looking gray skin of some kind. Reaching for several dried plants, he used a polished rock to crush the leaves into the bowl.

Definitely not like any kind of hospital or clinic that she'd ever seen.

Glancing up higher, there appeared to be another room accessed by a hand-hewn ladder, like a loft. She asked, "You live here?"

Putting down the bowl, he turned to her, a furrow between his brows as if he still tried to figure out something about her. "This is my temporary quarters until we find a way home."

So, he wasn't from here either.

"Where's home?" she asked, trying to figure out the emotion beneath his words. He'd gone from adversarial to quiet since she'd stepped inside this place. Maybe the scents in here had a calming effect on him, too.

He took his time answering. "Back through the transender."

"You mean that–" Just then she noticed something new about the table in front of him. No table legs. Nothing between the slab and the floor. "Is that, uh, floating on its own?"

He looked down at the space beneath the slab then back at her. "Of course, it is. I need you to sit on the surface so I can treat you."

She started to tell him the thing was too high when the slab suddenly levitated down low enough for her to easily slide onto it.

But she didn't move. Had that really happened or was this guy some kind of magician, which could mean he was fooling her about everything, even being a healer.

He ordered, "Sit."

Considering all the bizarre things she'd encountered since Rayen's hand had been sucked into that computer screen, Gabby decided to just roll with this for now. She inched herself onto the slab, waiting for it to slam to the floor at any second, Jaxxson reached for his bowl of ground-up leaf mixture. He grasped a handful that he let sift through his fingers as if checking to see if the texture suited him. Then he added some liquid from another bowl.

Was he a healer ... or a witchdoctor?

What if that evil-eyed girl with the sparkles on her face had convinced Mathias to do this as a set up?

Scary second thoughts bombarded Gabby. Her heart rate increased like a sprinter going for a record and her breathing shortened until it came in pants.

What exactly was that stuff Jaxxson held? Would it do more harm than the red vines? What if he'd brought her here to interrogate then kill? She knew nothing about tecknati. Would he believe her?

He paused, cocking his head to one side. "Why are you becoming more distressed?"

Had he read her thoughts? Without touching her? To hide her surprise at his question, she asked him one. "What kind of doctor are you?"

"Heal-er," he said in an exaggerated voice of laden with impatience. "Understand?"

She buried her worry under her temper. "Oh, I understand. Doc-tor A-hole. Got it."

If not for the dire circumstances, she'd get a laugh at the dumbfounded look on his face that said he had no idea what she'd just called him. And male ego, being what it was, meant he'd never admit to not knowing.

Instead, he frowned even more and reached for a basket on the floor. He pulled two puce-looking dried flowers out, tossed those in his bowl then continued crushing that with the leaves. He eyed her again, trying to decide something. When he finally made up his mind, he said, "I'm from the healing house. But I'm not called whatever you are calling me."

"Why not?"

He paused in thought. "There are many names for what I do, but I have not studied them all."

Odd answer. Who were these people? But no matter how much effort it took, she had to keep the conversation going, hoping to find out something useful. "I was born in China. Hong Kong, but we moved around a lot."

Digesting that for a moment, he asked, "*Your* home?"

"No." Her neck muscles ached, getting tight like her arms, but she didn't want to stop the tentative truce. That much she'd learned from her dad. The number of real discussions with him could be measured on the fingers of one hand, but if she did get him to talk, she made darn sure she kept him talking.

Jaxxson pondered a few seconds then asked, "If you're not tecknati, where *are* you from?"

Her heart did a double bounce at the word "if." Here was a chance to convince him she wasn't tecknati and open the door for his friends to consider that Tony and Rayen might not be either.

She carefully explained, "I live in Albuquerque, New Mexico for now, but my dad consults all over the world so I've lived everywhere–Berlin, Dubai, Singapore. What about you?"

The silence that met her words raised hairs along her neck. The intensity of his stillness sent her pulse skyrocketing and with each hard pump of her heart she could swear she felt the infection spread.

She started breathing in shorter, rougher gasps.

Jaxxson grabbed a handful of his mixture again, sandwiching it between his palms. He shook his head as if grappling with something he couldn't comprehend. "I live in City Four."

She shook her head. A city designated by a number? That couldn't be right. "Four?"

As if reading her mind again he explained, "Yes, YEG/4."

What was he talking about? Had she heard him correctly? Her eyes blurred then cleared. She wheezed a breath in and out.

He squatted down in front of her, real concern showing on his face for the first time. "I have to rub this on your wrists at the infection origin. Right now."

That meant touching her. She swallowed past her dry lips, and her fear. "No. Give me the bowl. I'll do it."

"How will you do that with fingers that refuse to work?"

She didn't have an answer for him. Her head was splitting, and it was getting harder and harder to swallow.

"This will not work without my touch," he added.

"Why?"

"You're serious? Were you born of this millennium?"

Pain blazed through her. She snapped at him. "Of course! I was born in ..." Her chest wouldn't expand. She forced out, "2002."

His eyes widened, as he whispered, "Not possible."

"Oh, really? When were you born ... uhggg ..." She flailed her arms at her neck, her hands unable to reach her throat.

Jaxxson reached for her, his face etched with anxiety and anger. "*You lie. Who are you? Don't close your eyes!*"

His fingers latched tight onto one of her wrists.

She tried to protest but couldn't. Words snagged in her closing throat. Her vision blurred. Pain raged through her wrist, her whole body. She jerked her arm, but couldn't pull away and started falling back, back, back into a bottomless void.

Jaxxson's bewildered thoughts burst into her mind.

She lies. 2002 is impossible. I was born in 2162.

CHAPTER 20

RAYEN STALKED BEHIND ZILYA WHO followed Etoi as Callan led all of them through another tunnel in the green fog that protected the village. The air seemed to have thickened, clawing at her skin and making each breath labored, even though they were not yet in the jungle.

Zilya had traded her queenly robes for a leaner, two-piece attire similar to Etoi's. The tops covered their breasts and tied at the necks. The bottom parts stopped mid-thigh. Pants ... no, Rayen had heard them called shorts.

Where? At the school? Or somewhere else?

The material hugged their bodies like soft deerskin.

But deerskin was tan colored. Not spotted like a leopard.

Leopards have spots. If that was correct, more fragmented memories and knowledge were sifting through the black hole in her mind.

They exited on the opposite side of the village from where she'd originally entered. She set her bearings according to the red moon–as Gabby had labeled it–that had moved halfway across the sky. Hard to believe that a full day hadn't passed yet since they'd arrived here.

Or had it?

Callan picked up his near-silent pace, moving them quickly over a narrow strip of open land, through dead grayish and yellow-orange vegetation to a copse of trees that looked more like forest than jungle. The minute the four of them reached the first tall trees with ghost branches, gnarled and white, Callan swung around and said, "This is good."

Etoi carried two spears and whispered something to Zilya as they both stopped.

When Zilya's gaze intercepted Rayen's, she lost her chuckle and fumbled with the short spear Etoi handed her. Could the delicate Zilya handle that weapon and hold her own? Guess she'd find out soon.

Callan ordered, "Etoi will lead, then Zilya, me, then her."

Her? "My name's Rayen."

Etoi protested, "I won't have *her* behind Zilya."

So much for trying to get on a first-name basis. Rayen felt a smidgen of sympathy for Callan who always seemed one word from losing his patience with Etoi.

Zilya didn't interfere, other than allowing Callan to see that she, too, wasn't comfortable with Rayen following her.

Callan's skin deepened in hue when he drew a long breath as if that would wash away his frustration with outspoken Etoi. "If the three of us don't return to the village, the other two prisoners will be executed. She–" Callan nodded at her. "–knows this and won't try to escape or harm one of us. And since you *should* know the most vulnerable position is the last in line, does that mean you wish to take her place?"

Understanding brightened Zilya's eyes once she grasped Callan's logic. "Good plan. How do you want to split up?"

Etoi opened her mouth to voice her opinion and Callan glared her into silence. "You take Etoi, Zilya, and I'll take ... *her*."

"Why?" Zilya demanded.

That snapped the latch on Callan's temper. He stepped over to her, his body swelled with restrained fury, his color one shade now–deep violet. "Etoi is too impulsive to be put with her and heeds only you. I'm the best one to deal with the captive if she creates a problem. We don't have the time to argue with a child's life potentially depending on us. You're of the Governing House, not the Warrior House. Need I remind you who is in charge out here? Force me to waste another breath explaining and you'll regret it."

"We'll discuss this further with Mathias when we return." Zilya stood firm and spoke with authority, but everything else about her seemed to shrink back from his anger. Flags of embarrassment waved in her cheeks. She didn't wilt like a flower that had been trampled but withdrew in respect of the foot that could smash her.

Interesting dynamics. Now if only Rayen could use that tension to her advantage to get herself, Gabby and Tony free.

Callan sent Rayen a look of discomfort at having his group's flaws laid out in front of a stranger, but when he spoke to Etoi, his voice was that of a leader. "Are we clear?"

"Of course."

She'd answered in a respectful tone that Rayen didn't believe for a minute, but it seemed to mollify everyone's temper.

Rayen didn't know why she wanted to do it, but she decided to help out

Callan by distracting his attention from the other two. "How long is it going to take to get where we're going?"

"Not long. Let's get moving."

Etoi took off into the undergrowth with Zilya right behind. Zilya's white-blond spikes of hair bounced above the vegetation, keeping her visible.

Callan stepped away and tossed over his shoulder, "Keep up."

Rayen smiled and waved her hand in a keep-moving motion. "I won't lose you."

He headed into the forest at a brisk pace, slapping chocolate-hued branches out of his way with sharp swings of his spear. She noticed which plants he tended to sidestep—orangish pink, and deep blue ones. Some were spiky and others furry like soft chick-down. Huh. So, she knew what chick-down was?

A loud caw overhead alerted her to a gray-yellow bird. At least she thought it was a bird, except for the long scaly tail that drooped behind it. The tail broke off into four individual lengths, like different sized whips.

"Watch that," Callan ordered, halting her in midstride.

She shoved her gaze in the direction he pointed and saw a very small bear-type animal, all fluffy and furry until the critter's neck extended once again as long as its body. Half its head split apart to expose three rows of lethal, slicing fangs that were almost as large as the animal's wide paws.

"What is that?" She didn't realize she'd spoken out loud until Callan made a snort sound.

"It's called a muttrapper."

"Is it as lethal as it looks?"

"Worse. Each of those teeth is tipped in poison."

"Nice mutt-whatever. Be a nice mutt-rapper," she murmured as she sidestepped around the critter. "Guess this means you're saving me for the croggle."

He glanced at me, puzzlement staining his expression. "If I wanted to feed you to something, I'd have told you to pet the muttrapper."

He'd sounded insulted. What had she said wrong? "Just joking. I appreciate the warning," she said to his back as he marched ahead. This bunch didn't have much sense of humor.

Fine by her. Now, she could drop her mask of subservient prisoner and focus on the important things, like keeping track of where she was in relation to the village.

Callan followed a trail deeper into landscape thick with vines as large as her legs, leaves of yellow, red and rust.

She tried to memorize as many landmarks as possible in order to return on her own if she needed to, but the trees were so huge they blocked out any distant view. She started noting shapes of trees like the one she'd just passed that hunched over like an ancient elder. Another towering one dead ahead split into five arms, with long, thin branches like fingers reaching toward the changing sky. Everything in this place seemed oversized, twisted, and lethal.

What made this place a sphere? That's what Zilya and Mathias had called it. Who *were* Callan, Mathias, Zilya and the others, and where had they come from if this was not their home?

They clearly weren't happy about being here and it wasn't by choice, so what had happened? Were they prisoners, too? Maybe Rayen could convince them to work with her group and find a way home ... but where was *their* home?

And what was the possibility of Callan working with Tony–the one he'd deemed an enemy tecknati beyond any doubt–in any lifetime? Zero.

That put her back to where she'd started, which wasn't much of a place to be, considering she had no idea what the word "home" meant to her either. And if she didn't get back to the Institute, she wouldn't find out what information her fingerprints had revealed.

Even if she did, would that return her memory?

What about that healer who was hopefully taking care of Gabby? Could he heal more than the body? Like finding Rayen's lost memories? She asked, "Can your healer work on any part of the body?"

Callan snapped at her, "Are you feeling ill?"

"No."

"Then be quiet and keep up."

So much for a friendly conversation.

She managed to stay on pace just fine and, like Callan, she moved ghost-quiet in this setting, which made her wonder again if being in the wild was familiar to her. Had she hunted at one time?

Slipping up close to him, she whispered, "Right behind you."

Smooth muscles flexed with his fluid movements. The mottled colors on his skin shifted a tiny bit. Did emotion affect the change? He'd never admit she'd surprised him.

With Etoi and Zilya moving along seven to eight steps ahead of Callan, she tried once more to engage the hard-nosed warrior in a conversation. "Why are you here?"

He wouldn't answer.

"What is this place? Did you get into trouble to be sent here?"

He sent an implacable expression over his shoulder that should unnerve her if she had that kind of temperament, but she was finding she didn't have many docile bones in her body.

She kept verbally poking at him, telling herself it was only to get information. Not because she wanted to break through that stony wall and make him interact with her as someone other than a prisoner. "How long have you been here?"

"Be quiet, tecknati," he growled.

"Thought I made it clear that I am not a tecknati."

"Anyone who walks with the enemy and protects the enemy *is* the enemy."

That told her the cost of defending Tony and stepping in to take his place. "You going to tell me what a tecknati is?"

"Vermin. You're all vermin." He spat the words.

Vermin? That sounded familiar. "You think I'm a ... rodent? A rat?"

He shook his head as if to himself and muttered something that would be dark if it had color. "Calling you a rat would be unkind–"

There was hope for this conversation.

"–to rats. Tecknati are more like cockroaches. Single-minded, stupid insects with no regard for what's decent. No other creature than the cockroach has survived every devastation in our world."

His attitude annoyed her on a level she couldn't explain. More than feeling irritated. He compared her to something disgusting. That cut her when she shouldn't care what this stranger thought.

She changed the direction of her next question. "So where do the tecknati stay in this place?"

He swung around so fast she almost ran into him and had to throw her hands against his chest to stop herself.

Her pulse pounded at touching him.

He stood there for a second, long enough for her to feel his heart thrumming a fast beat. His eyes held her captive, unable to move though her mind warned her to back away.

He backed away first with a frown on his face.

She dropped her hands, fighting an awkward feeling at the way he made it clear how much he detested being touched by her.

He kept walking backward, so she had to follow, but not as close as before.

After a silent couple of steps, he said, "You *know* tecknati only visit this world to drop off incoming mystik passengers or spy on those of us who still live. Why do you ask these questions?"

She juggled what she knew to this point. She could understand his hostility if the tecknati forced kids into this scary place and killed them, but she still didn't understand why he seemed convinced that she was one. She had no mark on her neck like the one on Tony that had created a stir with them.

"You're an intelligent person, Callan. Think this through. You have no solid proof that I'm a tecknati. If you could open your mind to the idea that I might *not* be your enemy, then maybe we could help each other."

To be fair, there was some chance she could be a tecknati since she had no memory prior to this morning, but she would not harm a child. Without any real proof, she refused to be marked as a child killer.

Callan turned around and picked his sure-footed way through an undulating area of roots. Rayen took a second look at one. Had that root just moved? No time to study it, she continued across uneven, hard-packed red dirt until the path leveled out.

Callan remained quiet. Was he actually entertaining the possibility of what she suggested?

She thought so until he muttered, "I will *not* be tricked again by a tecknati." He turned to her once more and jabbed the spear at her chest, point first, but stopped short of breaking skin.

Furious at the mere threat of attack, she caught the shaft before the tip had any chance of doing damage. Yanking the end up and toward her, she brought them face-to-face, feeling smug when they stood so close that she could see sparks of red firing through his eyes that were now a somber brown in this shadowed light.

His nose flared as if he'd caught a wild scent and his gaze dropped to her mouth.

Her thoughts skidded to a halt, long enough for the anger to bleed out of her. She had the craziest thought of wanting to run her finger across that sculpted mouth to force a smile, just to see what he looked like happy.

A flash of movement drew her eyes to a flutter of rainbow-colored wings the size of her two hands spread open. Four flapping wings on a furry body that had a chipmunk-looking head, beady black eyes and small legs with claws now extended as it flew towards Callan.

Large and lethal claws.

Shaking himself from whatever had happened for those few seconds, he snarled at me. "Don't think to use your powers on me without suffering repercussion."

She ignored his words, too focused on the threat. She spun away and broke a dead limb thick as her thumb from a tree and leaned back, prepared to throw her make-do spear at the attacking bird.

Callan took one look over his shoulder and dove at her, grabbing her arm. "No!"

They both lost their balance. She toppled backwards, landing hard against the ground, one shoulder scraping a tree. He came down on her chest with a thunk, knocking the breath from her. She groaned, but kept her eyes open, searching for the threatening bird thing.

The flying critter had landed on a small sapling at Callan's feet but now flew back up into the tree, squeaking in terror the whole way.

The little bird animal landed on a branch and turned to keep an eye on her as if *she* presented the real threat.

Rayen let out a pained breath and relaxed her guard. The minute she did, she noticed every curved muscle draped over her. A distinct masculine scent tangled up her next breath.

The heat she felt building inside this time had nothing to do with preparing to fight a battle.

Callan pushed up on his arms, sharp breaths squeezing out between clenched jaws. She could swear embarrassment skittered across his face before his eyes hardened and he snapped, "Have you no brain?"

"Evidently not, because I try to save you from being attacked and end up catching the devil for it."

The surprise on his face was comical. "Save me? From a dallymoth?"

"Moth? Aren't those like butterflies? That thing's no moth. I saw teeth and claws."

He growled another dark word she didn't catch. "Teeth for eating insects with hard shells and claws for grabbing branches as it flies around spinning thread ... which we use for weaving. You frightened it so badly I bet the thing doesn't make a strand of thread to harvest for another week. Do you have to kill *everything* that helps us survive?"

Her face heated so fast she had to be glowing red with humiliation. She shot back at him, "I only meant to protect you. Wasted energy on my part."

Her answer must have stalled his brain because he stared at her slack jawed.

She'd have laughed at his expression if she could find one thing funny about this situation. "Get off me."

Now he looked embarrassed. Good.

He shoved up to his feet, stood there a minute debating something, then offered his hand.

She slapped it away and struggled to a standing position. "How am I to know what's dangerous or not in this place? You got a book or a list of things not to kill?"

Callan had no answer to that. He just stared at her for several long seconds then lifted the spear and turned back to whatever trail he followed.

"Is there a problem?" Zilya called out, coming back to them, her eyes a deep purple with intensity.

Rayen watched Callan's face for a sign of how he'd explain this. Depending on the way he answered, she could end up with her wrists bound again ... or worse.

He waved off Zilya. "A dallymoth frightened her."

Etoi roared with laughter. "Our youngest children don't fear dallymoths."

Rayen narrowed her eyes at Callan who ignored her, his don't-cross-me mask back in place. By the time she'd dusted herself off, Zilya and Etoi were waiting for them.

Etoi kept a sly eye on Callan, whose curt voice made it clear he blamed Rayen for this delay, which improved Etoi's mood significantly. Especially when Callan stepped over to Rayen and dropped his voice to a menacing level. "The sky is changing faster. Hold us up again and I'll leave you staked until we return."

She held up her hands. "Just a mistake."

"Don't make one when we reach the transender," he warned. "If you cause us to lose a child, I'll kill you myself and leave what's left for the croggle."

Just when she thought they might have reached a friendly understanding, but no. "I won't allow anything to harm a child."

Whether Callan believed her or not was yet to be seen, but she saw something in his gaze that hinted at a change despite his cold voice.

That he might truly believe she'd tried to protect him.

If so, that had to fly in the face of her being a tecknati. Didn't it? But it probably also rubbed for any girl to protect a warrior such as Callan.

What had he said? That he wouldn't allow an enemy to trick him again. In that case, she might be reading more into his reactions than was there.

This time, Callan set a faster pace.

She jogged in step behind him, waiting for Etoi and Zilya to pull ahead once more as they had last time. Over roots, around trees growing thicker, beneath leaves everywhere. Easy to get lost in a matter of minutes.

When Callan gave a hand signal with two fingers, Zilya split off to the left with Etoi. Callan spoke over his shoulder to Rayen in a whisper. "Follow me. Do *not* make noise."

"What's happening?"

"Do not make noise means to keep your mouth closed."

She mimicked his snippy attitude silently behind his back and whispered, "I can't help you unless I understand what's going on."

He looked up at the changing sky for answers to his silent questions and hissed.

She started to ask what had happened now but saw the green stripes whipping across the sky like giant brush strokes.

Callan started running. "The sky's changing faster than before."

"What does that mean?" She jumped over downed trees, chasing after him. "Why'd you split up from the others?"

He answered in a low voice sharp with impatience. "The sky stripes when the transender arrives to deliver children and sometimes scouts. Our teams divide as we approach ..." He must have decided she really was confused because he kept explaining. "That way, if one team is penned in by a croggle or a different threat, the other team can help the child. We may be too late."

"What if—"

"Shhh," he snarled. "When a child is delivered, Zilya and Etoi will distract the threat. I'll hand off the child to you to protect then I'll draw the croggle away so they can escape. Each team knows their duty. No arguments."

That sounded like Callan had to be the last one to escape the croggle. Wouldn't that be harder to do alone? When the forest started to open up ahead, Callan stopped abruptly and dropped into a crouch behind paper-thin bushes that barely hid anything.

Rayen dropped into a crouch beside him. She studied the quiet area, thinking this might be the wrong place when she heard his sudden growl of anger.

Something was up.

Searching further to her left, she spied Zilya and Etoi hunkered down, too.

She could feel the double beat of her heart racing as she inhaled the acrid scent of the blood-colored earth. Sweat ran down her face and dripped into her eyes.

Leaning her mouth near Callan's ear, she noted how he forced himself to remain still when he obviously was bothered by her being so close. Could she use that to her advantage at some point?

She asked, "What's the problem?"

"Tecknati scouts."

Lifting up, inch-by-inch, she braced herself on her arms and managed to see through a gap in the intense orange-and-black leaves. An area that looked similar to the same grassy field where she'd fought the croggle monster earlier fanned out before them. The trampled rubbery grass here had gray-blue bloodstains darkening the ground.

But she saw no dead monster carcass. Was this the right field?

What happened to the croggle? Or were those bloodstains from something else?

A sudden movement to the left snagged her attention.

No monster, but two people. The tecknati scouts? Both males in their early twenties, each holding the arm of a little boy, a toddler, no older than three or four, with bright red hair and horror etched in his tear-streaked face.

The two guys wore shiny, metallic gray one-piece clothing that covered them from neck to boots. The way they carried themselves, their demeanor reminded her of the people in uniforms who'd arrested her near the Sandia Mountains this morning. That seemed forever ago. These two scouts were far more lethal looking than the elders who'd carted her to the Institute. Dark, short-cropped hair gave these two young men an aggressive and harsh appearance. Unmerciful.

And they both had menacing designs painted in black on their exposed forearms. Like the scorpion on Tony's neck.

So those were tecknati, huh?

Now she understood why Mathias thought Tony was one since he had that same short hair with an arrogant cut to his chin, a scorpion tattoo, and he strutted with attitude the way those two moved.

One scout clutched a metal instrument. A flint-gray box that fit in the hand he raised and pointed at the child.

The other scout, with a wide forehead and dull eyes, shook his head. "You know we can't kill any of them unless you want to explain a tek death back home."

The first male laughed, a cold chilling sound, eyes trained on the small boy stumbling between them. "Don't be so serious, Phen. I won't kill the package. But I can play with the furkken brat."

She wanted to ask Callan what furkken meant, but from the way a muscle jumped in his jaw she took it as a curse or derogatory term.

The scout who had warned his partner about killing the child argued, "You're not torturing that kid with me here, Phen. Do it on your own time so I don't get charged with misconduct. SEOH could have vids in this area. Let's get our surveillance done and go home. This is as good a place as any to dump the incomer."

Phen waved the gray box in his hand toward another spot. "Not here. Further in the middle. That way the croggle has a better chance of catching dinner. Need to keep the livestock fed, plus feeding him there means we won't have to walk through blood to reach the transender to leave."

She couldn't find words. Were those two really going to feed that child to a croggle?

Not while she was here.

The little boy cried out, startling Phen, the guy with the gray box.

His hand twitched, or he must have hit a button, and the child screamed in pain. A single burst of terror.

Rayen launched forward.

Callan shouted something at Zilya, but Rayen had already exploded from cover, racing toward the little boy.

The scouts were so surprised by the toddler's sudden wailing they weren't looking up as Rayen charged them.

The guy holding the box lifted his head a second before she reached him. She took advantage of the shock on his face. Moving fast and hard, she hooked an arm around his neck, slamming him to the ground.

The small box dropped from his fingertips.

She punted the strange weapon further away and spun to meet the second scout who'd abandoned the child to jump in.

Then the battle really started.

The second guy attacked her. A child's terror-filled cries clawed the air.

Hurt a child? Pay the price.

She drove jabs at him over and over, not sure how she knew to fight this way but going on instinct. Connected with soft flesh a few times, hard bone more. Callan had joined the fray with Etoi standing back, her spear pointed at all of them.

Rayen lost her balance. The ground had shifted beneath her. Was it from one too many hits to her head?

Her gaze strayed to the child just as Zilya snatched him up and rushed away from the battle.

The distraction cost Rayen a rock-hard fist in her ribs. She sucked air at the blow, the only pause she took before immediately returning the favor with a brutal right cut to the scout's face.

Cartilage shattered. Blood geysered from a broken nose.

That was worth the ache in her knuckles.

But the tek scouts were well trained. They didn't back down. They continued to rain hammering blows just as punishing and with vicious precision.

Staggering back, she stumbled, then caught her balance in time to see that the scout she'd been fighting now staring past her, toward the trees.

Where Zilya held the child.

The scout sneered at Rayen and moved toward Zilya.

Protect the child.

A blazing haze of fury clouded her vision. Hot energy started building inside her.

She yanked the scout back around. The tecknati only laughed, fists up and moving like lightning, raining hits over her again and again, the strikes pummeling her shoulders and head.

Anger so molten it threatened to sear her insides whipped through her. Strong enough that she wouldn't back down either. Instead, she fought the scout harder, forcing him away from Zilya and the boy.

Over the grunts of the attackers, she heard Callan shouting at Zilya and Etoi to run.

With one last surge, she knocked the scout backwards ten feet, rolling over and over, with her right after him.

The scout landed on his feet, spotted the gray box, and scooped it up. He swung around, pointing it at Zilya.

Rayen ignored everything except charging forward and knocking the scout's hand away just as the box buzzed.

The gray box went flying another thirty feet away from the tecknati. Her next punch landed under his jaw, snapping his head back and causing him to stumble around, arms flailing to keep his balance.

But then she stumbled sideways, too, trying to keep her own feet stable again.

That's when she realized knocks to her head were not the issue. The ground was shifting back and forth beneath. Her feet flew out from under her. She hit hard at the same time the scout went down.

Callan and the other grappling scout hit the ground as the earthquake erupted.

Not an earthquake, but a violent tremor. One she recognized. If she was right, that shaking announced a greater threat.

Croggle.

Rolling to her knees, then her feet, breathing hard, she glanced around. Callan and both of the scouts had broken apart, jumping to their feet, but still shuffling with their arms stretched out to keep upright. Dirt and rocks exploded into the air when the croggle burst from beneath the ground.

Callan hadn't been joking about this beast being larger than the one she'd killed earlier.

This one could kill all of them with the swipe of one claw.

Struggling to keep Etoi on her feet and moving the child deeper toward the tree line, Zilya looked back first at Rayen then at Callan who yelled, "Protect him!"

Then Callen turned back to face the croggle.

Zilya stared at Rayen as if she couldn't believe their prisoner would stand next to Callan and fight the croggle.

Callan glanced at Rayen and shouted, "*Go!*"

She shook her head. Seeing Callan's eyes warm, even for a fleeting second, sent her heartbeat thudding at a crazy speed.

The trembling stopped. Everything went deathly silent.

Callan raised his spear toward the monster, as if one weapon was going to stop that thing.

A toothpick against a mountain.

With the scouts stunned, watching the greater threat, Rayen inched slowly over to stand within a few steps of Callan, her voice soft. "Got a plan?"

"Stay alive?"

"Good as anything I have."

He spared her a quick glance. In that moment, she saw something she wanted to call respect in his gaze. Probably her imagination, but it gave her a warm feeling she needed right then.

If she ran now, she'd have no chance to prove she was not tecknati. If she fought alongside him and convinced him she wasn't his enemy, she had a chance to save herself and her friends.

The scout who'd zapped the little boy turned to run toward a spot where the transender pod had beaten down the grass.

The second guy held his ground. No, he stood locked in fear, his face pale beneath blood dripping from where she'd damaged skin and bone. Callan had pummeled the other guy worse.

That meant three against one giant beast. Not favorable odds.

Didn't matter. They'd never make the woods before the thing reached them. Facing the beast gave them a better chance than being caught from behind.

The fleeing scout stopped before he reached the transender landing spot, searching the ground for something.

The box.

He dove for it, grasping in a smooth somersault move that landed him back on his feet in position to aim the device at the monster.

Callan and the second scout both shouted, "*Nooo!*"

The tecknati with the metal box paid no heed to their warning yells. He hit the button.

Must have been a stronger charge than what he'd used on the child. Blue bolts of electricity arced all over the croggle's head, lighting up his skin where it shocked him. But whatever zap that little box had spewed out meant nothing more than spitting in the eye of a wild beast.

The croggle stood up on its two hind legs, tall as a five-level building, and roared so loud Rayen thought her eardrums would burst. It lunged forward, pounding the ground when it hit, tossing all of them off their feet again.

Enraging the croggle with an electric charge had accomplished only one thing–to zero the monster in on the person who'd zapped him. The idiot scout had no chance to move before the croggle swung its massive jaws at him.

The first bite cut him in half at the waist, leaving two legs standing. The rest of him disappeared between churning earth, spewing blood and severed body parts.

With the croggle distracted, Callan shouted, "*Runnn!*"

Sounded good to her. She scrambled to her feet, ready to sprint toward the forest cover.

She caught sight of the other scout, paralyzed with fear.

"Get out of here," she called, but the guy either couldn't hear her, or was so petrified nothing registered. If the fool stayed where he was, he'd be dead in moments. The croggle was already shifting its ungainly size around, seeking new prey.

Leave the guy? He'd die for sure.

"Let the croggle have him," Callan yelled at her as he dashed toward safety.

At that moment, the croggle's bulging black eyes streaked with yellow veins flared wildly in the direction of the tecknati and roared, ready to kill.

CHAPTER 21

REARING UP AGAIN, THE CROGGLE prepared to lunge in another attack.

Rayen screamed again at the scout. "*Runnn!*"

He stayed frozen in place between the croggle and her.

As the monster arched forward then plunged down, she ran full out, smashing into the scout, her body throttling them both forward. The monster's hot breath rushed past them ahead of its jaws slamming the empty space where the scout had stood seconds ago.

The scout rolled twice with the momentum from her blow, which must have shaken him out of his stupor. Jumping up, he yelled something at her that she couldn't hear over a loud whine.

She was too busy scrambling away from the monster now that the scout could save himself. When she turned to see the beast's position, a massive claw swung toward her at hyper-speed.

She twisted to dive away but didn't move fast enough to dodge the sharp tip of a claw the size of her forearm. It raked a burning slash across her stomach and side. Arching in pain, she forced herself to keep scrambling, barely avoiding the solid thump of a foot pummeling the ground where her head had just been.

"*Ayeeee! Here! Here!*" she heard Callan shouting somewhere nearby. "Croggle. This way."

Smart guy. Taunt the monster away. Then what?

Rolling her head to the side, she saw the scout sprawled on the ground with Etoi on top of him, a spear at his chest.

The tecknati yelled up at her, veins in his throat standing out.

Rayen couldn't make out anything he said.

Etoi pushed the tip of the spear into the scout's chest and yelled right back. That shut him down.

Scary girl.

Farther away, Callan kept distracting the monster as he shot back and forth so fast in front of the creature that Rayen could barely see his legs move. But a person could only do that for so long before he gave out or made a mistake and got caught.

She couldn't leave him to deal with the croggle alone, not when he could've gotten away with the others if she hadn't stayed to save the scout. Callan's enemy.

Clenching her teeth, she clamped a hand on the wound gouged deepest at her side and struggled to her feet. Where had the power within her gone? What had brought it on?

Then it dawned on her that the energy had powered up when that scout headed toward the child.

If that's what it took to bring on the energy, she imagined the croggle turning on that little boy after it killed her and Callan.

At once, heat churned in her middle. She staggered toward the croggle now down on all its limbs, pounding the ground and snorting, snapping at Callan. Power swirled inside her, building. She started jogging.

Callan split his attention for a second, glancing her way, and roared, "Stop. *Nooo!*"

She couldn't look. No distractions. It took all her attention to stay upright. Moving her feet faster forced blood to gush around her fingers. She felt dizzy and shook it off, growling. The power coiled tight inside her then expanded. She yelled at Callan. "*A spear!*"

Fury made the veins stand out on his forehead.

Two more steps and she'd reach the croggle.

She jumped on the monster's tail that was taller than her at its thickest part.

And almost fell off.

Grabbing a scale, she hoisted herself back to her feet. Would the monster notice something that weighed little more than one of its scales? She climbed toward the air flap that moved in and out, just as it had on the smaller croggle, only this time it was like climbing a mountain, not a hill.

Callan dodged right and left, keeping the monster confused as he worked his way around to the monster's side. He yelled at her, "*Catch!*"

She braced her feet to free one hand. If she moved her other hand from the gash, she'd bleed out faster. When Callan threw the spear, she caught it and flipped the spear around, ready to stab the monster the second its breathing hole flapped open again.

The beast howled, shaking its bulk and snapping its jaws, the sound of giant teeth grinding. Massive feet stomped and the smell of raw sewage reeked in the air. Its twenty-foot tail lashed back and forth then curved, the tip swatting her off like an annoying fly.

She cartwheeled in the air and landed on her back with a dull thud when she hit the ground, her fingers still clutching the spear.

Callan had raced away, yelling and waving his hands to hold the monster's attention. Even with his speed, he was too far away to reach her in time to offer any help.

Jaws as wide as the transender pod swung around to her. Black eyes streaked with yellow rage turned on her.

Callan's voice reached her above all the noise. "*Rayen!*"

He said my name.

A small thing but hearing that gave her a renewed surge to fight. She had to tap the red-hot energy she felt spinning inside her, but how?

Callan bellowed at the top of his lungs, running straight at the monster.

The croggle paused, head swinging over to Callan for just an instant before whipping back around to lunge at her. Razor-teethed jaws opened to cut her in half.

That was the extra second she needed.

Power detonated inside her once more. She knew it wouldn't last.

Rolling to her feet with pain lashing her middle, the world spun around. She yelled, "*Tenadori!*" and grasped the spear with both hands, ramming the lethal point into the croggle's massive foot.

Reaching deep, she focused all her thoughts on *die and burn!*

An inferno of heat pulsed through her into the spear and blasted into the massive foot. Blue flames and smoke shot from the monster's air flap. It bellowed in anguish. Scales glowed fiery red.

She released the spear and fell backward. Warm liquid gushed from her wound and ran across her stomach. Her heart thumped slower and slower.

The croggle kicked its legs then crashed over on its side, shaking and emitting a screech that rattled the trees.

Closing her eyes, she drew a gurgly breath, sick of smelling the stench of death.

What about Callan and the others?

Footsteps pounded up. She peeled her eyes open.

Callan walked up to her, chest heaving for air. He dropped down beside her, his eyes now reddish-golden. "You look worse than the croggle."

"I don't want ... to hear grief ... for killing it."

Shaking his head, he released a breath that almost sounded like a chuckle, but raspy as if he hadn't done it in a while. Warm hands covered her stomach.

She gasped and jerked at the pain racking her body.

What humor she'd seen in Callan's face a moment ago fled quickly beneath a grim mask, the severity of her injuries written in the worry lines creasing his forehead. "Got to get you out of here before that thing bleeds out and you drown in croggle blood."

"Doubt I'll make it. Go. Save the child. But—" She drew another rattling breath. "Please ... let my friends go."

Zilya's face popped into view. Confusion scrambled the color in her eyes. "You should have let that scout die."

Rayen breathed out, "Couldn't let that beast ... kill anyone."

"He's an *enemy*." She placed her hands on her hips. "Why would you help a tek? Protecting your own?"

"No." Rayen scowled at her, gritting her teeth when Callan pressed harder. "Can I just die . . . in peace?"

Callan's gaze never left Rayen's when he said, "Leave her alone, Zilya." Then he told me, "You will not die ... yet."

Now that Zilya had pointed out how Rayen had, once again, protected their enemy, she wondered if Callan wanted the honor of killing her himself.

She closed her eyes, trying to separate herself from the pain snaking through every inch of her body.

The cries of a child approaching forced her eyes open to find Etoi hovering in her line of sight. Etoi told Zilya, "I think this little one is reacting to the Sphere. He already has a rash on his arms and legs."

Callan kept his hands in place, applying pressure that tortured her as he turned to address Zilya over his shoulder. "Where's the prisoner?"

"Tied to a tree."

"Take the child to Jaxxson."

"What about *her*?"

Now I'm her *again?* Rayen fought to stay alert when all she wanted to do was close her eyes and withdraw from the jagged ache clawing her stomach. Had Callan been telling the truth that she wouldn't die?

Callan shook his head as if debating with himself. "Leave her with me. We'll follow once she can walk."

He expects me to get up and walk? After losing a couple of quarts of blood and with a gaping wound?

As usual, Etoi had an opinion. "This one killed a fully grown croggle. She protected a tek. Why save her?"

Hmph. I'd graduated to 'her' then back to 'this one.' At this rate, I'd be 'it' next.

Callan still pressed on the wound.

Rayen hissed, nauseous from the streaking pain.

The struggle to figure out something warred in Callan's face. "How'd you kill these croggles? Our spears can't pierce the hide of a grown one, but you stab him in the foot, and he dies."

Something she could do better than warrior-guy? *Sweet*, as Tony would say.

Throat dry and fighting dizziness, she opened her hands but couldn't lift them from where her arms had flopped down beside her body. "With these. Not sure how it works." She took short breaths, which was all she could handle. "I feel an energy … then I think about ... what I want to happen. That's how I killed the flower vine that ... attacked Tony. Just worked." Her eyes fluttered closed. Too much effort to keep them open.

No doubt they'd think she was insane and lock her away in that isolation hut forever ... if she lived.

"Wake up," he ordered.

She didn't want to, but forced her lids halfway open, just enough to see the blurry image of Callan still kneeling next to her and arguing with Zilya. "She doesn't wear her hair like the tecknati females and no obvious marks on her body."

Zilya glared an easy message to interpret. She didn't want Callan discounting her theory that Rayen was the enemy. "We'll discuss this later, but no matter how great a warrior you are, you risk someone like her using that power to kill you."

Looking up at Callan, Rayen tried to speak, but it came out as a whisper.

He leaned closer to her. "What?"

Licking dry lips, she whispered, "My word ... as a warrior. I will not use my power against you."

The respect that had shined in Callan's eyes earlier took on new meaning now. He believed she was not tecknati or at least he had reservations about condemning her. She could see it in his face.

He said nothing to her, but he told Zilya, "Get moving. The child needs Jaxxson. I'll deal with this. That's final."

Did she have the beginning of an ally in Callan? An alliance that might help Gabby and Tony once she made it back to the village.

If she made it back.

"The blood still flows too fast," Etoi pointed out in a smug tone. "The decision of her fate may no longer rest in your hands. Staying here may draw another croggle."

He snarled something at Etoi that Rayen didn't get then he scooped her into his arms.

Bad move. Pain ripped through Rayen's chest. Felt as though the croggle chewed on her. She'd lost too much blood. Licking her dry lips, she tried again to say, "Please don't hurt Gabby and Tony," but nothing came out.

Darkness closed over her.

CHAPTER 22

COLD. HER TEETH CHATTERED.

Gabby hated the cold. She wanted out of here. But where was here? She fought, clawing her way out of this frigid hole.

"Can you hear me?" a deep male voice asked.

Sure, I can hear you, she replied mentally. *That means there are two of us stuck in this dark place. Got any idea how to get out*?

No one answered her.

Too bad. He had a nice voice. She'd like to see the body and face attached to it. But like everyone else in her world, he seemed to have walked away from her.

As usual, she'd have to find her own way out of hell.

First, she had to figure out what kind of place her father had dumped her into this time. Her teeth chattered more.

Something heavy covered her, taking the edge off her chill, but not by much.

Why couldn't her dad find a private school near a beach? She might consider applying herself and sticking around if she had sand, water, and tanned guys in board shorts.

She wouldn't be freezing to death right now.

Had she been sent to Antarctica?

I've gotten out of worse places. I think.

Drawing on all the physical energy she could muster, she ordered her eyes to open. Her lids weren't cooperating. Like they were glued shut.

The weight over her body increased, the new layer tucked against her. Which helped. A lot. The shivering slowed. Her arms and legs felt heavier.

Fine. She could sleep now that she was warm again.

"Come on, wake up," the male voice ordered.

She really would like to see who she had as a hell-mate. Giving it one more try, she pried open her eyes and stared up at a guy with a naked chest. A very nice naked chest and beautiful dark, sinfully delicious eyes. "Aren't you cold?"

He chuckled. Had a nice smile on his oh-so-nice face. "No, I'm not the one fighting off a fever."

Fever? She stared at him, trying to decide if she was truly awake then turned her head, taking in her surroundings. Dried weeds hung from vines. Ladder over there that went up to a loft. Odd-shaped walls of wood.

A deep breath of lavender eucalyptus snapped her jumbled thoughts into order.

I get it. She was still in this freaky world with ... her eyes shifted back to hot, bare-chest guy ... medicine man. Jaxxson, aka the healer, and not naked, unless he'd ditched the sarong.

He must have levitated the slab table she was stretched out on because she could only see from the middle of his abs up. He didn't have a body all cut with muscle like that guy Callan, but she found she liked Jaxxson's lean physique. More her style. Her gaze kept climbing higher up his tanned skin, up to the stern chin, up to the sharp cheeks and ... smack, back to the dark brown eyes observing her with wary caution.

What had she done or said to get that look? Had the mixture he'd crushed in that bowl caused her to babble something about her ability to hear other people's thoughts? "What happened to me?"

"The infection accelerated when you got upset. It spiked sharply, cutting off your air supply. You started suffocating. I treated you, then checked on the new child brought into our village."

Infection. From the vines. Right.

But he wasn't telling her something. She'd been burning up and in pain. He'd mixed a poultice of some type in a bowl then she started getting worse to the point that ...

Glaring at him with unveiled accusation, she asked, "Did you touch me?"

"Yes."

"I told you not to." She dug those last moments of lucidity up from the dregs of her mind, recalled him grabbing her wrist. She'd heard a thought just as she'd lost consciousness.

What had he been thinking?

What had they been talking about?

Irritation migrated back into Jaxxson's face. "If I *hadn't* touched you, you wouldn't be here to berate me for executing the duty I'm sworn to perform, which is saving a life if I can. Even one who lacks appreciation."

She thumped her fingers against the table slab, accepting that she owed him and was behaving like a wounded animal. "Thank you."

"You're welcome."

They stared at each other, a visual stand off until he lifted two fingers to graze his chin as he speculated on something. "About touching you."

Here it comes. *What's wrong with you? Why won't you let anyone touch you? That's not normal.* "Go ahead. Ask."

"Why do you fear touch? How have you survived to this age without allowing any physical contact?"

She hadn't expected that second question.

No one had cared that she hadn't been embraced in years, not after she'd convinced her father and the staffs at multiple schools that she had very sensitive skin and touching caused her actual pain. It hadn't taken long for word to get around that she was the weird kid to be avoided. She'd never so much as held hands with a boy much less kissed one.

If a brief touch opened the path to another person's mind, the idea of an intimate contact such as kissing terrified her.

She didn't want inside anyone else's mind again.

She never wanted to cause another death.

Jaxxson waited quietly for her answer, showing patience she hadn't thought he possessed when she'd first followed him from the Isolation Unit. People never believed the truth. So she gave him the same patent answer she handed to everyone who asked about her phobia.

"No big deal. My skin is sensitive, so I don't like to be manhandled. That's it." With her reaction to the vine, that should be an easy sale this time.

"Why are you lying?"

How had he known that? "Are you a mind reader?"

He studied her with narrowed eyes. "Mind *reader*?" Then he stared straight ahead, thinking. "An outdated term, but that would make sense."

Awestruck at what he was admitting, she whispered, "You *did* hear my thoughts didn't you?"

"No. That would be inappropriate to enter your mind without an invitation." His shoulders lifted in dismissal. "It was simple to see that you lied. I used my empathic ability to read the changes in your body."

Good grief. *Someone weirder than me.*

He reminded her, "You still haven't answered my question. Why did you lie when you are clearly disturbed by being touched? I'll grant that you did have a reaction to the vine, but I don't believe that's the reason you avoid contact."

Something he'd said a moment ago struck her. "Did you say it would be inappropriate to enter a mind uninvited?"

"Yes."

"Ah, so, you can enter someone else's mind if they invite you?"

"Yes, of course. Why is that surprising? It's a simple matter of training for some and bonding for others."

"Huh. I'm not the only one," she murmured to herself.

"You try to hide this ability by not touching? Why?"

This had to be the most bizarre conversation she'd ever had. How could he act as though picking up thoughts was as natural as breathing? What would be the point in trying to lie again with someone like him? She admitted, "You're right. I hear thoughts through touch, but I hate it."

She especially hated the day she'd heard her mother's thoughts about sleeping with another man who wasn't Gabby's dad. Barely ten years old, Gabby had blurted out, "Why were you in bed with that man?"

"What man?" her mom had stammered, squeezing Gabby's hand harder.

"The yellow-haired one. At the Four Seasons where we've had tea. The hotel."

Her mother had backed up from her, demanding in a frightened voice, "How'd you know?"

Gabby told the truth. "I saw it in your mind." She raised their joined hands and looked at them, whispering, "I see things when I touch you."

That was the day her mother backed away from Gabby with a look of horror on her face. Her mom normally only drank at home, but she grabbed a bottle of liquor and jumped in her convertible Mercedes, squealing tires when she tore away from their home. Hours later, the police arrived to inform Gabby's father that her mother had died in a single car collision. She'd been ejected when she lost control and the car rolled down an embankment.

Gabby developed her skin phobia the day she killed her mother.

"Did you hear me?" Jaxxson said, snapping his fingers in front of her face.

"No. What?"

"I asked why you listen to other people's thoughts via touch if it bothers you? And to do so is wrong anyhow."

Her temper came back with a vengeance. "I hate to point out the obvious, but *if* I could prevent hearing them, don't you think I would?"

Jaxxson dropped his arms to his side, angling his head and frowning with exasperation. "Our children learn to shield their minds by the time they can write their names."

"You can do this, too?"

"Of course."

Pushing herself up, she scooted back to sit up. To get out of a vulnerable position. Lying down reminded her of too many visits with mental health professionals. She lifted her wrists to find the swelling had gone down, her hands flexed normally again. So Jaxxson was some kind of doctor after all, but he'd also been able to access her thoughts while she was out of it.

She asked point blank, "I'm having a hard time accepting that you didn't listen to my thoughts."

"Entering someone's mind when they are defenseless is no different than entering someone's home uninvited. I am not an intruder."

Where were these people from? "I've never met anyone else who can do this."

"So, you were telling the truth."

"About what?" She had the feeling she was about to find out what had caused that wariness still hanging in his gaze.

"That you were born in 2002."

"Oh, that. Well, of course, it's the truth." Her whole body relaxed. "Look at me. Don't I *look* sixteen?"

She might have gotten an early gift from the booby fairy, but she had a baby face that had never been mistaken for being older.

What was the big deal about her age?

Then out of nowhere, the thoughts she'd heard from Jaxxson's mind a second before she'd lost consciousness rushed forward.

She lies. . . impossible. . .I was born in–.

Her jaw dropped. "Now I remember. I had no way to stop myself from hearing *your* thoughts. You were thinking about being born in ... 2162." No way. No freakin' way. Unless … "What planet are you from?"

"It's known as Earth."

"That can't be possible. I'm from Earth, too, and 2162 hasn't happened yet."

But he was shaking his head. "I don't understand. How can you be here?"

"Right back at ya."

"What?"

She gave him a half grin, feeling it wobble around the edges as she grappled with what she was saying. "It means I'm asking you the same question. Really? Seriously? If you were born in 2162 then what year do *you* live in?"

"2179."

No way. "Are we in some kind of weird time travel warp?"

"No, the tecknati would never risk sending one of *us back* in time."

This conversation got stranger by the minute. If not for seeing purple and green striped skies, having traveled here through a computer, fought killer flowers, and watched giant croco-monsters climb out of the ground, Gabby might be surprised by meeting someone from the future.

She reminded herself to roll with it. "What are these tecknati? Bad boy teckies or what? Sounds like naughty techs."

After a long moment, the suspicion and irritation that had held his face hostage disappeared. He smiled, surprising her. Then he folded his arms, starting off his explanation by spelling MystiK and TecKnati. "Many years ago, civilization divided up between the MystiKs and the TecKnati. The TecKnati excelled in science and technology while our MystiKs developed gifted skills and supernatural powers with each generation becoming stronger."

"Why'd the TeK dudes put you in this place? And if this isn't a time warp, where am I?"

"V'ru says this Sphere is an artificial planet. A satellite."

"V'ru? Is that a guy or a girl? A MystiK or a TecKnati?"

Jaxxson looked as if he couldn't decide if she was joking. "A male MystiK. V'ru is from the Records House, a rare G'ortian no less."

"Does that mean he keeps journals for you?"

"His gift is much more sophisticated than that. Upon being captured and arriving here, he assessed the contents of this Sphere and began identifying the plants and animals that are from other planets the TecKnati have been exploring and placing in this Sphere. The TecKnati are capturing young MystiKs and sending us here, using this as a holding facility."

Was this Jaxxson for real? "Why?"

"We're in constant conflict with the TecKnati. They see our gifts and powers as impeding research and expansion plans in space that they feel will assure us natural resources and a better way of life as our world rebuilds. We see their technology as exposing us to greater risks outside of earth and threatening our ability to continue developing powers due to health risks caused by technology."

"Who'd have thought?" she murmured.

"The TecKnati are at heart fearful of any threat against their supremacy. We now believe SEOH, their leader, plans to rid our world of powerful MystiK rulers who pose a greater threat to TecKnati than before, even though the TecKnati claim no respect for our powers."

"So, the TeK guys want to get rid of you and have all of earth for themselves?"

Jaxxson nodded. "Currently they control the ten cities, but that's not enough for them."

"Your whole world is limited to only ten cities?"

"Yes. Our records indicate that once there were many more, but now..." He shrugged and glanced away.

"What happened?"

"The K'ryan Syndrome wiped out populated areas around the world, including North America, leaving small groups of people in isolated outposts. As the survivors joined up, they made their way to ten cities that were still physically intact and capable of sustaining a sizable population."

Unfreakingbelievable. Gabby couldn't form a thought, but Jaxxson didn't seem to notice and kept talking.

"The great TecKnati minds came from those sequestered in remote research locations and labs. Powerful MystiKs developed from those who had chosen a more simplistic way of life, living in areas away from any civilization. Each of the cities in the new world is encircled by an energy field that is controlled by the TecKnati, as is all travel between cities."

"Why do you need an energy field?"

"For protection. The virus didn't kill everyone. One particular group became rabid and, even though they were destroyed, there is fear that other infected humans might come to the cities. I admit the energy field keeps us safe, but there is a price to pay for giving TecKnati that power over us."

"So that's what's going on in the future." She didn't want to tell him his world sounded like it sucked, big time, and she had another burning question. "How did we end up here? In this Sphere place?" she wondered aloud.

"Wait a moment." Jaxxson walked away and lifted a stump that had been cut from the middle of a tree trunk and brought it over to place next to her.

Gabby enjoyed the rare opportunity of admiring a male up close while he was unaware that she checked him out. Jaxxson's lean body flexed with hidden strength. She'd never spent time with someone who looked like him.

Get real. She'd never spent time up close with any guys.

He sat down, now on eye level with her, which she appreciated. He admitted, "I don't understand how or why the three of you arrived ... if you are not TecKnati."

"There's not much else I can say other than we're not. At some point, you have to decide to believe me or not." She hoped he took that in the spirit it was offered.

He nodded. "Until I see differently, I accept that you were not sent by SEOH. As for your being here, I can only think that the TecKnati made some error to bring someone into this Sphere from the past. V'ru says there is evidence of TeK time-travel research, but every confirmed report indicates that as yet they can only send a person into the past, not bring one forward."

She was so going to blow Tony's mind when she told him all this. *If* she told him. "You said the TecKnati never send someone like *you* back. What did you mean?"

"TecKnati would never send a MystiK into the past and risk MystiKs alerting the world to the strategies of TecKnati in the future, otherwise MystiKs would become even more powerful over time. A bigger threat to TeKs. TeKs send only their own kind into the past."

"Time travel," she whispered, marveling at what was going on in the future one minute and still in shock the next.

"But we have no report of this being successful so they may have killed everyone they experimented on. They don't value life as we do so we think they are only sending those they consider disposable on missions to the past."

"How would they know if they were successful?"

"I don't know for sure. Our reports confirm that the TecKnati have not found a way to communicate with someone once that person enters their time travel portal. And since the TecKnati are very good about shouting their accomplishments to all the cities, I trust we would've heard if they'd succeeded in teleporting to the past and returning. At least, that's our most recent news."

"How would you know in this place?"

"MystiK children are dropped here fairly regularly. The older ones arriving bring reports from home."

"Wow, this is over-the-top crazy," she murmured. "And people think *I'm* a freak."

"Why?"

She gave him her best duh look. "Because I hear thoughts. Where I come from that sort of thing brands you as strange, a sideshow act, to be avoided at all costs."

Jaxxson's face tightened, and his eyes darkened. Why did that make him angry?

Shaking his head as though what she'd shared was irrational, he said, "Although I've not studied all ancient worlds, I knew our gifts were not once celebrated and appreciated as they are now. But I had no idea those with our abilities who lived two centuries back were persecuted."

"Persecuted is a strong word," she argued, thinking of entire civilizations lost or abused at the hands of evil people.

"It's not strong enough if you've spent your life without basic human comfort because of being born with a gift. To treat one as that in our MystiK world is to face punishment, because the gifted are rebuilding our world and protecting our future."

Good grief. He made her sound like something special.

Valued.

She couldn't wrap her head around that.

Or that he came from the future.

If not for having Rayen and Tony on this whacked-out trip, she'd think this was all some insomnia-induced dream. Speaking of Rayen and Tony, she had to do her part and get as much information as possible on how to get out of this place. She'd been so engrossed by talk of the future– could that all be true? –she didn't know where to start. Since Jaxxson claimed to be a captive as well, she led with that.

"I've figured out that none of you want to be here," Gabby began. "Can't you escape?"

"No. Only TecKnati scouts can operate the transenders."

"That metal thing that spit us out here?" She described it further.

"Yes."

If only TecKnati could operate the pods, what did that say about going home to Albuquerque? Had that little girl Rayen rescued traveled in their same pod since she was dumped in the clearing they'd been ejected into?

What a weird place, but one where her strange ability was accepted. No, celebrated as special. And Jaxxson could teach her so much.

Staying here had huge benefits, for a short time anyway, while she learned from Jaxxson, but she had to help Tony and Rayen find a way home. This was a dangerous place where people with abilities were held as prisoners.

And too easily died.

She could see why everyone had reacted so strongly to her, Tony and Rayen.

Still, where had Jaxxson's antagonism from earlier gone when he'd seen her as a hybrid or whatever that word was? "I appreciate that you're no longer looking at me like I'm a devil spawn, but what changed your mind about 'my kind' as you called me?"

He took a moment to answer, looking chagrined. "In my world, one with your unusual eyes is called a Hy'bridt, and is revered above all other MystiKs. The majority are women, who are allowed choices other MystiKs are not."

Revered? *Fat chance that'd ever happen back home.* "What kind of choices?"

A muscle twitched in his jaw and his words came out loaded with resentment. "Such as the one in my family who *should* have been the next healer sent to YEG/4. City Four. But it would have meant traveling from ORD/1 where we both lived."

"What's city one and four?"

He thought on that a moment then lifted a finger. "I understand what you're asking. Where would these cities be in your world?" When she nodded, he explained, "Due to my need to understand medicinal resources available in each of our ten cities, I had to study the development of different lands. At one time ORD/1, or City One, was known as Chicago and YEG/4, or City Four, was called Edmonton."

"Those are definitely in North America," she acknowledged. "What happened with this Hy'bridt girl? How old was she?"

"She'd reached eighteen, her age of maturity, and chose not to leave home. I was sent instead."

"How old were you?"

"Thirteen."

Outrage surged through her on his behalf. She'd been sent here and shuttled there since an early age with no regard to how difficult the changes had been on her. "That's so wrong. How could they do that to you? You were just a kid."

"MystiKs are considered mature at eighteen and expected to take their respective places in society at that moment. Thirteen is not a child in our world. Healers are rare. Except for Hy'bridts, few are female. For that reason, we're trained from birth, prepared to go anywhere at any time."

She waved off that comment, refusing to accept that it was okay to do that to an adolescent. "Regardless. You deserve to feel ticked off about being screwed."

He smiled. "Ticked off? Screwed?"

"Ticked off means angry, po'd, really, really frustrated," she clarified. "And screwed is, well, it means that no one considered what it meant for you to be yanked out of your home and shipped across your world."

"Ah. Interesting terms, yet accurate assessments."

"Sounds like the world hasn't improved since my time." She put her hand on her forehead. "I can't believe I'm sitting here talking to someone from the future. Tony would go bat-crazy if he was here."

"Why?"

"He'd kill to find out what happens with technology and science in the future." At Jaxxson's look of horror, she said, "Wait, I don't really mean 'kill' as in bloodshed. Just another slang word that means he'd really like to know all this. That'd give him an edge in a special school project. I think Tony believes he's the next Steve Jobs."

"Who?"

Now *that* was funny. "Never mind."

Jaxxson stood. "I'd like to continue our conversation, but I must check on the little girl who arrived today."

The one Rayen saved. Pushing away the paper-thin coverings that appeared to be made of pounded leaves, Gabby swung her feet around, dangling them off the side. "Is the little girl sick?"

"I don't know yet. I'm watching for a reaction."

"To what?"

"The Sphere. MystiK gifts and powers are drawn from natural elements in their surroundings. When new MystiKs arrive here we have to observe them constantly. Some react negatively to the elements in the Sphere right away, some later on, and some not at all. We've lost children early on by not recognizing the signs. I must return you to the unit before I can see the child."

She didn't want to go back to jail. "I'll go with you."

"Callan, who oversees our security, would *not* be happy with that decision."

"Because he thinks I'll try to escape. I won't." Before he could argue further, she raised a hand, palm out to stall him. "And you *know* I'm telling the truth."

Sighing, he ran his hand over his sandy-blond hair, considering what she said and clearly in a hurry to get moving.

Gabby wouldn't lose this opportunity. "I'd like to ask you questions about how to block other people's thoughts. I'm tired of constantly worrying over being touched."

The healer in him considered her request, but he shook his head. "If you did try to leave, which I'd understand, I'd be forced to contain you and would rather not harm you."

Bottom line? He had powers he had yet to reveal. She got it and let her hand fall to her side. "I promise to be your shadow and follow orders."

"I'm sorry, but I can't do this." He looked at the table and it floated down until her feet reached the floor.

He suddenly became very still. His eyes stared vacantly but concern gripped his face.

Gabby held her breath.

When his eyes focused on her again, he said, "I'm being summoned for the little girl. There's a problem."

"We helped save that child. Take me with you. I'll help."

He hesitated and then seemed to make up his mind. "Fine. But know that even though I believe you're not TecKnati, Mathias believes you are one. As the leader of the Governing House here, his word is final. If you make any unauthorized move, I *will* stop you."

Hair danced on Gabby's arms at the threat in his tone. This was not the guy who had patiently explained his world to her. She swallowed as she said, "I understand."

Following him to where she'd have to pass through the wall of the tree again, she rationalized that she'd only agreed to not try to escape. She'd said nothing about using this opportunity to find a way out of the village and the trick for passing through the wall of fog. There had to be a plan for emergency exits with all these children in one place.

What if Jaxxson *thought* there was an emergency?

Would he and the others herd the younger children out of the village?

Gabby had activated a few alarms in her past. Could she get away with it here?

CHAPTER 23

WHEN RAYEN OPENED HER EYES again, she was propped up against something that sloped back.

She saw soft golden-brown hair that fell across Callan's head and touched his shoulders.

He knelt beside me, bent over, muttering more of those strange, vicious words sounding as if they belonged only to him. She enjoyed a moment of studying the strong muscles in his neck and the way his shoulders flexed when he moved. He muttered some more. "... stupid to keep a furkken tek alive ... they don't have powers ... how could Rayen kill the ... no other explanation ..."

She smiled at overhearing her name again and moved her hand to grasp his arm with a weak grip.

He stilled, lifting his head slowly until molten brown eyes met hers. "About time you're awake."

Sort of awake. Her head floated in a fog, but she did feel alive. The pulse in his wrist raced beneath her fingers. She had the strangest impulse to put her hand over his heart and feel each beat.

But she didn't want to bring back his stony face.

She tried to speak and managed only a growl from her dry throat.

Slowly, he tugged his arm away from her hold.

He reached for a furry round shape the size of a large coconut cut in half, but she didn't think coconuts came in shades of dark pink or had furry hides. Come to think of it, was she even sure what a coconut was? Too much to still grapple with. After he gave her a drink that had a tart and sweet taste, he put the container down and touched a finger to her stomach.

She flinched at the sharp ache, but the killer pain from before had worn itself down to a constant throb. Somewhere between close to dying and now, she must have passed out. How could she still be alive?

"What'd you do to me?" she asked.

"I closed your wounds."

"Really?" Rayen stretched her neck forward to see her abdomen below her half shirt, all that was left after ripping off a cloth for Gabby. The gash from the croggle's claw was now a red welt that ran in a wide line from her left side across her stomach. Her arms had several similar welts.

Something tickled her memory about healing, but she couldn't put a finger on it. "What'd you use to close the gashes?"

Studying on his answer, he finally said, "My hands. How would you repair a wound?"

"I don't know. No wonder you thought I'd be able to walk back to the village."

"You can't yet. Not until your internal organs heal."

"Can you fix those, too?"

Confusion fed through his voice. "I can help ... but I don't have Jaxxson's skills. Plus, I've drained my power getting your wound closed. You have to complete your healing."

"I don't know how to heal anything." Or could she? "Can you show me?" Adding mentally, *Since, you have magic hands.*

Things had been going along so well, but that question rallied his suspicions. "TecKnati can't heal with hands either."

"Then wouldn't this be a good test if you'd show me what I need to do and let me try?" Unless she failed, which would give him the proof he needed that she was a tecknati. But would he kill her after keeping her alive? Only one way to find out.

Still, he hesitated to make a move.

"Afraid I'm telling the truth, Callan?"

"*Fear* a tek?"

Now she'd insulted him. "I meant, are you willing to take the risk that I might not be one? Me? I'd take that challenge, but you might not–"

He leaned forward, some decision made, and ordered, "Spread your hands over your wound."

She moved her arms that were still heavy with weakness. Once she got her hands settled over the scar on her stomach, he spread his fingers and covered her hands with his.

A tingle of energy vibrated where he touched her, but she felt nothing changing inside her abdomen. "What else?"

"You have to see the injuries in your mind and focus on repairing the organs."

This would not be the time to admit she didn't see anything in her mind. "I've got a headache like you can't imagine. Think it's interfering with my vision." His expression became even more suspicious if anything. She had to make this work. "I'm asking for a little help to get me started, that's all."

His sigh came out weighted with irritation then he said, "Lift your hands."

When she did, he slid his beneath hers and spread his fingers over her skin.

The minute she placed her hands over his, she felt warm energy flooding her body. The weight of his touch didn't hurt as she'd expected after having suffered earlier when he'd touched her wound. His touch felt right, comforting.

For the first time since coming awake in the desert, she didn't feel so alone.

Closing her eyes, she opened her mind as if she'd done this before. This time, she did see something. A healing river of heat traveled from her hands down through his and inside her. She saw the shredded damage inside her belly ... but how?

Was she seeing it through his eyes?

She pushed the swirling energy like a tidal wave from ravaged organs to torn veins and arteries, amazed at the way her body responded as it began to heal.

Renewed strength poured through her. Ready to be whole again, she shoved the energy hard throughout her belly and side so quickly it ricocheted back to her hands.

He grunted in surprise, having been the conduit between her hands and body.

She opened her eyes and closed her fingers around his. He had large hands, calloused fingers. She felt a pulse beating through his hands, pumping harder the longer he stayed still.

His face was so close to hers she could see each long brown eyelash around his intense eyes. Was he breathing faster?

From the effect of healing her ... or being so close?

She was breathing pretty quickly herself.

As for her organs, her heart functioned just fine, pumping with the speed of a cougar running across an open field. She was afraid to move and break whatever spell had wound around them.

Her gaze moved to his lips, so firm and masculine.

That pushed everything out of her mind except one strumming thought. *I wish he'd kiss me.*

He leaned toward her as if drawn by her thought.

Her heartbeat raced out of control. Their faces were inches apart. She could smell his warm skin, a musky scent heated from battling the croggle.

Movement drew her eyes to his chest where the strange colors on his skin shifted, a lot, morphing in hue and shape. She whispered, "Why does your skin change?"

He jerked back, withdrew his hands, and stood. The shapes on his skin became fixed again. "Are you healed?"

What happened? Did his strange skin embarrass him?

She didn't think so. No, she sensed anger, but why?

"Are you healed or not?" he repeated, snapping out the words as if she was taking a long time to decide if she wanted to live or not.

She surveyed her stomach. Where she'd had a long welt before there was now a smaller scar line. Looking up at him, she said, "Looks like it. Thank you for saving my life."

It took him a few minutes to decide on a reply. "You're welcome."

Accepting her appreciation hadn't been easy for him, especially from someone he believed to be his enemy.

But joining hands with him to heal herself must have cracked his conviction. "Sooo, we're clear now that I'm not a tecknati, right?"

"I haven't decided. How'd you make the croggle burn?"

So much for *no tecknati can heal himself.* She had no better answer about the croggle now than the one she'd given him earlier. "I wish I knew."

"Let me know when *you're* ready to risk the truth." Disgusted, he turned, searching the distance. "Time to go."

She uncurled her fingers, regretting the loss of touching him. Even without her memory, she knew on a deep level that she had never met a boy like him, and yet the word boy just didn't fit in the same sentence with Callan. Besides being ripped with muscle, he had an air of maturity that came from carrying responsibility for many lives.

Warrior, through and through.

She still wanted him to kiss her.

A sure sign that she'd taken too many hits to her head today. Twisting, she pushed up to her feet.

And caught his gaze whip to her chest. Her half shirt had ridden up dangerously high but still protected her modesty, though barely. She gave a little tug on the torn edge and heat ignited in his eyes, simmering beneath a barrier of strong will.

Snapping up the spear that had been stabbed in the ground, he turned to walk. "Keep up."

She tried out a few steps and suffered no sharp pains so she hurried to catch up, striding beside him as much as she could along the narrow path. The area around them confused her.

"This looks different than where we passed through earlier on our way here."

"It is," he said, not slowing or looking at her.

She took in their surroundings that seemed more open, less thick brush and lush vegetation than before. She couldn't help but point out, "Seems like it'd be easier to have your village in this terrain. Less lethal than near the jungle."

He made a scoffing sound that ended with him saying, "Think we're stupid as dugurats?"

What had Tony said that sounded like? A moron? "I have a great deal of respect for all of you who have survived living here. I'm sincerely interested in knowing how all this works."

Still no answer from him. "Can't you, for one minute, accept that I really don't know what's going on? If I did, would I be fighting croggles and staying captive if I was with those scouts?"

Ten more steps then Callan said, "SEOH built the framework of the village where it is. We've been too busy surviving to spend time and resources on creating a new habitat, though we may have to as more and more children are being sent here. Besides. . ." He swept a look from side to side. "This area has its own threats, different than the jungle and the denser forest, but just as lethal."

She had so many questions to ask, it was hard to figure out where to begin. But she didn't want to lose the chance to learn more with him willing to share.

"Tell me what qualifies as a tecknati?" When he made a grumbling sound at that, she added, "Please. If you'll answer my questions, I'll answer yours."

Either her offer, or her tone, must have gotten through to him. Tension loosened in his shoulders.

"Tecknati seek to control, and destroy, the world through technology."

"That leaves me out then." She pushed a mottled green leaf the size of her head out of the way of her face and admitted, "I don't care one way or the other about technology. How else are you different from them?"

Fine lines formed in his face when he frowned. "Tecknati have no gifts and don't believe in ours."

"Gifts? Such as?"

"Healing with hands or divination ... via scrying, to name a couple of simple ones. I'll not share all our abilities."

She didn't blame him. Never give an enemy that kind of information and she was still marked as enemy. Gabby had just such an ability, or a gift.

But Rayen wouldn't expose her friend's secret.

Callan called healing with hands a simple ability. Hadn't they just done that very thing? But what about the internal power she'd used to kill the vine and the croggles?

Would he consider *that* a gift?

"You asked me to explain healing. Now, how did you kill that croggle?" Callan asked again, as though *he'd* lifted her thoughts.

"I was just thinking about that myself. Can you hear my thoughts?"

"No. We have no bond."

She didn't know what he meant by a bond, but let it go to answer his question. "You felt energy when you helped me heal, right?"

He nodded, albeit reluctantly.

She explained the only way she could. "I start feeling this thing inside me, an energy, something stronger than just being a human. That's as good as I can describe it. Anyhow, that energy starts building and releases when I need it ... like when I had to kill the flower vine and the croggles."

He didn't need to know that she'd tried and failed to call up the energy a couple of times today. Sharing that would make her, and Gabby and Tony, too vulnerable. Better to let Callan think she had a weapon she could use against his group should her group need one. Though she'd given her word she wouldn't use her power against Callan, neither could she allow him or his people to kill her friends. If it came to that, she'd have to figure out something.

Muscles in his jaw pulsed as he thought deeply. "How long have you had this power?"

"I don't know." Seeing his quick temper flare, she held up her hands. "Before you get angry, give me a minute to explain."

He sent a curt glance her way which warned he was losing patience. "I'm listening."

"I woke up this morning in the middle of a desert with no memory of who I am or where I came from."

That surprised him. "What desert? And how can you not know?"

"I might have hit my head. I don't know, but when I came to, a beast was chasing me and I ended up getting caught by people I didn't know, then taken to a school I'd never seen."

"You recognized nothing?"

Hearing interest in his question, she rushed on. "No, well, that's not true.

I did recognize the land and the mountains but had never heard of the place where the school was located called Albuquerque."

"I don't know Albuquerque."

"What about the Sandia Mountains?"

"No."

"Then you probably won't know The Byzantine Institute of Excellence that we came from."

"No. Is this the school where your *friend* Tony said the computer sent you here?"

She was encouraged to see him considering everything they had told him even if he had slurred the word friend to remind her of her association with his perceived enemy. "Yes, but the computer didn't really send us here so much as we got sucked into it and landed in what you call a transender."

"Are you sure someone was not playing a prank on you? Could this computer be an advanced Cyberprocessor?"

Colors flashed behind her eyes and alarms went off in her head. She'd heard that term. "I don't think we were tricked since there were only three of us in an enclosed room when it happened. And the computer we got sucked into was one that had been discarded. All of them in the room looked as if they were useless or old."

Stopping in mid-stride, he reached for her arm. "There were *more* computers?"

"Sure. Remember Tony said all those names like Mac, Dell, whatever?"

His mouth tightened at the mention of Tony's name.

She made a mental note not to bring up Tony again until after she convinced Callan that *none* of them were tecknati. She pushed the conversation back to what had spurred his interest.

"There were a bunch of old-looking computers in that one room, but I saw some newer ones in several classrooms." She didn't pay attention to his hand, hoping he'd leave his fingers where they held her arm. She liked the warm feeling of his skin touching hers and picked up a low vibration, as if the energy lying dormant inside her recognized him.

"I don't understand," he said. "Is this a tecknati school? Or a museum?"

"I have no idea. Don't even know how to spell tecknati."

He rattled it off without thinking, his eyes staring into the distance. "You would know if this school was TecKnati owned. They mark all their possessions with the ANASKO triangle emblem."

"What's that look like?"

"Three circles and an A." He released her and started walking again, lost in thought. "This makes no sense, but if you truly came here on your own ..."

With Callan sounding open-minded about what she'd told him, she decided to jump on this opportunity to make him an offer. "If you'll let the three of us–me, Tony, and Gabby–leave, we'll take you and the others back with us. We'll show you the school and the computers. We'll get you out of here. Then we'll figure out how to get you back to your world."

He turned to her, hope and excitement flickering in his eyes for a moment, until they dimmed, and he shook his head. "You arrived in a different transender than I did. We *must* travel back through the same one we came here in. The scouts made it clear that to return any other way would result in death."

"Why would you believe them? How can using a different one matter?"

He smiled as if she'd asked a foolish question. "As MystiKs, we may not have entire cities devoted to science and space exploration, but neither are we ignorant of the laws of transitional travel. If we don't return to our world through the same path, our molecules would rearrange. We might either die slowly or explode upon arriving."

Not good.

Transitional travel sounded strange, but not wholly unfamiliar. She'd leave all the technical and scientific discussion for Tony. Right now, she wanted to keep Callan talking and find mutual ground for them to work out an agreement. She had to offer him something worth their freedom. "*If* we can get back the way we came, then I give you my word I'll find a way to help you escape this place."

"You make it sound possible."

She heard hope in his voice along with disappointment. She understood. From the minute her eyes opened in that desert, she'd longed to find out who she was and where she belonged. A sick worry crawled around inside her, warning that she would never get those answers if she didn't return to the Institute.

He asked, "How can you help us go home without SEOH's permission?"

"I don't know what this SEOH is."

"He's the leader of the TecKnati. Each City has its own SEOH, but one is superior to all others. He created the Sphere. He sent us here. He's the one responsible for the deaths of our children."

"Sounds inhuman."

"He *is* human. And he *will* die." The brutal chill in Callan's words told her he would fight for the honor of killing this SEOH himself. He seemed to shake the emotion off and asked, "Something else doesn't make sense. Explain about this school in Albuquerque. Tell me more about where you come from, something that might allow V'ru to fill in what you do not know."

"Who's V'ru?"

"He's an elite member of the records house, revered for his abilities. He has access to all known history. If there is information on your world and this school, he may have it. But he will need the date the school was opened or something more than just a name."

Why hadn't Callan taken this V'ru to check the transender area? Maybe V'ru wasn't cut out for fighting croggles.

Callan wanted information on the school. She dug up what she remembered from her conversation with Hannah on the way to Suarez's class. That and the green book she'd read in a matter of seconds. "I only know what I've learned since waking up today, but Albuquerque is in New Mexico and that's part of America."

His face went still as stone. "America?"

"I might have that wrong. Someone mentioned New Mexico was a state ... that's it. One of a united states."

"United States," he whispered. "I have heard of the United States ... in my world ..."

She wanted to shout with joy. This had potential. "Really? Where do you live?"

He snapped out of whatever had distracted him. "I live in ATL/5, one of the ten cities."

She read somewhere in Hannah's book that there were fifty united states. Wouldn't that mean there were at least that many cities? "What ten cities? Aren't there more?"

"No." He shook his head, his tone solemn. "Life outside the renaissance cities is too dangerous." His words drifted off with his straying gaze that focused on nothing. He murmured to himself, "How can ... ancient ... I don't understand."

"What? Ask me, Callan. I want to work together. I'll tell you anything I can."

"Give me more information."

"Like what?"

"About the school. How old it is, anything. As I said, the more information I have to give V'ru the better he will be able to answer my questions."

If this V'ru was all that good, he should be able to confirm whatever she told Callan. "I read a book that said the Institute has been there for four years, so that would mean they opened it ..." She paused, calculating the current year based on the date Suarez had written on his board in class. "They opened it in 2014."

Callan stopped dead in his path then stepped away from her as if too close to a poisonous snake. "The *year* 2014?"

"Yes." Had she said something wrong? "I saw 2018 written by an instructor as part of today's date on his board, so I'm pretty sure 2014 is correct." Had she screwed up simple math? "I'm telling you the truth, but you can ask Gabby if you don't believe me." She tried to reassure him. "Regardless of the date, believe me when I say I *will* help you leave here."

"You can't." Horror spread across his face.

"Why not? What's wrong?"

"Because, if what you say is true ... that's not my world."

"I don't understand. You said you know of America."

Disbelief rocked his expression. "I do, but I don't exist there."

How could that be? "Now I don't understand."

"I live in the year 2179. The United States did exist in 2014, long before the K'ryan Syndrome. Even if I could travel in your transender, I wouldn't survive in a world where I haven't yet been born."

She thought she couldn't be shocked any more today. Her heart pounded faster as what he said settled into her mind.

He came from the future?

If so, that meant ...

The significance of his words hit her like a fist to the middle, raising an even greater concern. If his words were true, she, Gabby, and Tony were from the past ... and would die if they tried to return to their world in the wrong transender pod and arrived in the wrong year.

Even if she convinced Callan that they weren't TecKnati, how could they be sure which pod they traveled here in?

How were they going to get back to their world?

CHAPTER 24

2179 ACE, in ORD/City One

THERE MUST BE A FASTER way to exterminate MystiK brats.

SEOH ANASKO stepped away from his floor-to-ceiling window view of Lake Michigan, a swatch of blue a hundred and seventy floors below his penthouse office in ANASKO Central Tower. His image reflected from the glass–his face cosmetically altered to allow little room for emotions to show, his hair surgically implanted and a bull of a body even if he wasn't tall–all tools to rule the furkken unwashed masses.

He turned to face Vice Rustaad, his second in command and most trusted confidant ...who was pissing him off right now.

Rustaad watched him through the icy gaze of a forty-six-year-old man with the soul of an AI. He wore his short, sealskin-brown hair slicked back in a take-no-prisoners look. A mimic of SEOH's own head of thick, dark hair. A former competitive swimmer, Rustaad's discipline was evident in the way he maintained muscle definition at his age, and a competitive edge second only to SEOH's. "I understand your frustration, SEOH, but the fact remains that we have a potential problem."

SEOH had chosen Rustaad years ago because nothing stood in Rustaad's way once he was committed to a goal such as winning a gold medal in the International Alliance Games that had replaced the Olympics after the K'ryan Syndrome. SEOH would love to know if Rustaad really had anything to do with the "accidental" death of his closest friend–another gifted swimmer—as the rumors suggested. According to the media, Rustaad's childhood friend had posed the only threat to Rustaad's winning his last two titanium medals in swimming.

My kind of man.

Undeterred by SEOH's foul mood, Rustaad went on to say, "With the threat against TecKnati children–"

"I still don't totally accept that our children died from some *power* woven into the treaty." SEOH could only admit that brutal truth within the soundproof walls of his private sanctum, and even here he resented the need to speak of the unspeakable.

"But the evidence shows–"

SEOH held up his hand, cutting off Rustaad. "That our three TecKnati children died as a result of vengeance and a traitor inside our group. Has to be someone who alerted the MystiKs of our complicity in the deaths of *their* three children, then assassinated ours."

SEOH's opinion hadn't changed in the past thirteen months that Rustaad had wisely not brought up the topic again, until now. Damn him for his persistence. SEOH understood collateral damage in any war–and make no mistake about it, he was at war with MystiKs–but he hated losing those three TecKnati teens who'd shown such brilliant potential.

No loss being greater than the death of his oldest son, one of his three most prized possessions. SEOH still couldn't believe his perfectly healthy seventeen-year-old boy had clutched his throat, gasping for air as he'd played his holo games. The security vids in SEOH's home had recorded the entire event.

Screw the furkken treaty.

If not for Furk, the decrepit TecKnati who'd been the tiebreaker on the board of twelve before he'd finally died, there wouldn't have been a treaty. Furk had wanted to leave a legacy, and he had, in a way. His name had morphed into a curse used by TecKnati and MystiKs. Fitting.

Rustaad still had the stubborn jut to his chin he'd walked in with this morning and continued. "My investigation has been thorough, and the results speak for themselves, SEOH. There's no way the MystiKs could have known fast enough about the deaths of their children–that I personally eliminated–for them to retaliate so quickly. Each of our three teens collapsed in identical manners. Asphyxiated. No weapons involved, as stated in the penalty clause the MystiKs added to the treaty."

"Words on a vid screen."

"Words written by the hand of a Hy'bridt, initially on lambskin that was blessed by the rulers of all seven Houses and ratified by you," Rustaad amended, bowing his head to remove some of the sting of his words. He added, "Your media campaign was exceptionally successful, but some MystiKs continue to circulate word that they warned us this was how the Damian Prophecy would come to pass. They claim the prophecy begins with the deaths of three children on each side of a battle line."

Prophecy garbage.

But after losing his oldest son, SEOH had taken measures to protect his youngest, the fourteen-year-old future TecKnati prodigy who would follow in SEOH's footsteps. Until the BIRG Con meeting with the MystiKs, Bernardo would be kept under heavy guard with a medical team on hand. His son might be unhappy, but no one, not even a prophecy, was touching one of his only two remaining male children.

As for his middle son, well, the less thought about him, the better.

Rustaad pressed on. "Much as I hate to give them credit, the MystiKs *can* stand in the way of our future." He clasped his hands behind his back, tone even and dry as old bones, an influence of being raised in a TecKnati boarding school with AI instructors. "Twenty years ago, I wouldn't have thought the MystiKs could become this dangerous, but I have disturbing reports that confirm what we only suspected months ago."

"Go on."

"The young MystiK G'ortians, some of whom are in line to be the next leaders, intend to unite the Houses and, when they do, the MystiK power is purported to become ten times stronger when joined together against one target."

"Damned new generation." Accepting that supernatural abilities could interfere with science went against everything SEOH believed, everything he'd been taught.

He grunted, glancing again out the window at the crisp sky, one that was pollution free, thanks to ANASKO. How could intelligent humans believe in the 'abilities' of these MystiK wackos?

Easily. Most of mankind were lemmings, willing to follow anyone even if they were being led off a cliff. "Have people forgotten that *technology* rebuilt civilization from the K'ryan devastation and has handed them a world they enjoy today where the climate no longer destroys the earth? Where hunger is a choice?"

Before Rustaad could respond, SEOH corrected himself.

"No, *not* technology. *TecKnati.*" He thumped his chest with his thumb. "*We* created this ideal environment that the MystiKs benefit from as well. *We* have placed the protection of the laser curtains around the Ten Cities. *We* prevent the rabid humans from entering our cities. The MystiKs should be on their knees thanking us for dealing with the feral C'raydonians."

But SEOH would never admit *some* things that had happened to the C'raydonians, not even to Rustaad. No shared secret was safe, and this could not be found out.

"Quite true," Rustaad agreed, his nod from across the room reflected in the window facing SEOH. "And all of this progress has come about due to your recruiting the most brilliant TecKnati to work here at ANASKO, because ... you set the bar for thinking beyond the box."

SEOH looked over his shoulder, eyeing Rustaad who didn't have the genetic makeup to suck up. Still, a wary man was a wise one. SEOH understood the point Rustaad made, that ANASKO had attained this pinnacle of success because SEOH not only pushed the greatest minds to reach new heights, but also because he considered the impossible to be possible.

That, in fact, had been a direct quote from the media about his HERMES space program after ANASKO transported plants and animal life from Jupiter's second Galilean moon back to earth. SEOH missed the days of unrestricted development. But the weak stomachs of today's world had outlawed so much, even importing or building sentient predator guardians that could morph from shape to shape as needed. Manufacturing one now would land him in prison, a cage the most hardened criminals feared. Gone were the glory days where he could take whatever action needed to protect what remained of the world.

Guard and preserve the TecKnati.

He turned all the way around, ready to solve the problem digging under Rustaad's skin and move forward. "If the G'ortians are the issue then we simply capture the rest of them. That will clear the way for the return to unfettered domination of technology in this world." *My domination.*

"I agree, but we're running short on time with the MystiK's BIRG Con coming up. If plan B has a hitch–"

"It *won't.*" SEOH let Rustaad see the truth in his eyes. "Neither of us can afford to allow Plan B to fail under *any* circumstances. Even if I would consider signing the Amity Treaty again at this BIRG Con, the minute the reclusive MystiK leaders walk into the same room with each other they'll realize they're all missing children from their ruling families. That would be enough for them to join forces and turn their powers on us ... *if* they really can do what your reports claim."

Holding his thoughts silent for a long moment, though a deep furrow formed between his eyebrows, Rustaad calmly said, "You've never allowed arrogance to influence strategic planning. Why now?"

"A warning, Rustaad–take care how you choose your words."

"I'm the last person who wants to be on the receiving end of your wrath, but you brought me on twenty-four years ago with the specific orders to watch your back. I intend to fulfill my duty even at the risk to my person." Not missing a beat, he continued. "Our analysts have not come up with a viable scientific explanation for the interference with our last two HERMES shuttle launches. Have they?"

SEOH ground his back teeth, sure that there *was* a scientific answer, but since none had been discovered he had to admit, "No, they haven't."

"Then you must consider my intel that the leader of the Governing House did in fact combine powers within his house to interfere with those two launches to show us he was serious about stopping our space program and he isn't even G'ortian. Can you only imagine what might be possible if the G'ortians succeed in uniting the Houses?"

If not for losing his son, SEOH would be glad he'd had the next in line for the Warrior House eliminated. "I'm not convinced they're capable of the damage incurred in those two aborted launches. Not without help. Logic says we have a traitor, which is why I retaliated." He paused, giving that statement weight. "Someone inside our program who sabotaged the HERMES system only to give substance to the MystiK claims of power."

Rustaad pressed his opinion in a stronger voice. "We erred once in underestimating the MystiK abilities and lost three geniuses–future TecKnati leaders–as a result."

Rage bunched in SEOH's chest and rolled down to his fingers that fisted, searching for a target to crush. "Do you think *I* need to constantly be reminded of their deaths?"

"Of course not, and I don't like bringing up the subject. But–"

"That's why we're capturing their prodigies instead of killing them, so what's your point?"

The dark silk suit covering Rustaad's chest rose and fell with a soft sigh, the most reaction anyone would see from the man. The gunmetal greenish-gray uniform appeared at first glance to be the same all TecKnati wore, but was very, very different. The color a shade darker, the texture richer, the construction handmade. Plus, Rustaad wore the ANASKO tri-circle insignia, awarded to only the most deserving, the most loyal of TecKnati.

Rustaad cleared his throat and continued. "My point is this. We did not expect captives no older than seventeen, with many much younger, to prove exceptional at surviving in the deadliest part of the Sphere."

That did give SEOH pause, but not much. So long as the brats were isolated from this world and their families, they were not a problem. He couldn't expend energy on something that didn't deserve his time. Especially not right this minute. He had an impending meeting with his damn board of twelve. They were waiting to be updated on the Sphere.

Eleven now, he corrected himself. "I know you're not here just to debate the power of the MystiKs again, Rustaad. What is it you want?"

"I want you to put aside your prejudice against the supernatural and open your mind to the possibility that if we underestimate MystiKs we risk making a major mistake, one that may end with them ruling this world if they unite."

Rustaad had a way of presenting the inconceivable in a deadly tone that warranted credibility. SEOH tossed back, "I think spending ten million credits out of my own pocket to build a laser grid says I'm giving serious consideration to their power potential."

"I'm not discounting what you've invested in this project, but your primary reason for building that grid originally was to allow you control over all Ten Cities. Control over TecKnati and MystiKs that depended upon TecKnati resources. Finding out the laser grid harmed MystiK powers was a bonus."

"Point taken." In the interest of getting this behind them, SEOH finally let go of his irritation long enough to give Rustaad's point the respect that his second in command was asking for and deserved. In a more thoughtful tone, SEOH said, "I don't see how MystiKs can join up as one group if they're as untrusting of each other as we've been informed. Their lack of unity is one of our best weapons against them. Seems like that alone should be enough to undermine the prophecy you keep nattering about."

"We have to expect the unexpected. *You* taught me that."

"I've allowed you resources to analyze that furkken prophecy, and for what? You said we only needed to grab those two G'ortians ..."

"Callan and V'ru."

"Right. Now you say we need more. We can't succeed by chasing invisible threats."

"I understand, but the prophecy is written as a puzzle we're using Cyberprocessing and scientific expertise to unravel. Based on what I learned this morning, I now believe we should locate and confine the five remaining G'ortians we know of."

SEOH missed the days when technology ruled and the MystiKs were nothing more than a group of harmless spiritualists. How had things gotten so out of control? But Rustaad *was* a brilliant strategist whom SEOH trusted, an allowance he rarely granted anyone. "Why?"

"Because at first we believed the prophecy meant the final step would require the G'ortians to join as one. But as we're unraveling the meaning, we now believe that one specific G'ortian will unite all, and we have no way of knowing which one."

SEOH raised a hand in deference. "Then do it. Grab them."

"We will, but we can't move too quickly. G'ortians disappearing will draw more attention than losing the other MystiK adolescents. And still, capturing those other five may not be enough."

SEOH breathed through clenched teeth for a moment, determined not to lose his patience. "Now what do you want?"

"To prevent the MystiKs any chance of outplaying us. I'm concerned about the unknown element in this plan, which could jeopardize everything we've worked toward. To win this war for domination, I believe we must strike from *all* sides at once."

Now Rustaad was talking SEOH's language. "I'm listening."

"First we capture the other five G'ortians, all of whom are future MystiK rulers, and take them out of play, which will prevent their prophecy from coming to fruition."

"You're sure."

"As sure as I can be. We interpret the prophecy to mean that a specific G'ortian will guide the future of the world."

I hate that mumbo jumbo crap. But SEOH believed in TecKnati analysts, the ones he'd hand selected from the best to work on his secret project. "Go on."

Rustaad lifted his hand, two fingers unfolded as he counted. "Next, we need a successful activation *on time* of the laser grid to neutralize *all* MystiK power before the leaders meet. But to ensure our final step in this plan, we must have number three–to locate the sentient computer before the MystiKs do and perfect time travel in both directions, not just into the past."

"I do want that computer for many reasons, starting with keeping those crazy MystiKs from destroying it. But even if we don't get our hands on it before the BIRG Con, we have confirmation that our people in the past are on track with DNA testing and inoculations. While we maintain the ability to travel back in time, we're still good."

Rustaad stared unfocused for a moment then said, "True. But gaining that computer would be a game changer, even more so than the grid system."

SEOH sighed, wishing he could just blast the MystiKs to hell and back with a T-970 missile. "Speaking of the laser grid, is everything still on schedule?"

"Yes, but I'd prefer another test before the BIRG Con–"

"No. We can't risk the MystiKs figuring out what we're doing. If we didn't have that idiot Troade in our pocket, the head of his House would have found out about the test we ran in City Three that caused their MystiKs to get sick." SEOH would never allow someone with so little loyalty and backbone to remain in his camp, but MystiKs obviously didn't demand the level of loyalty that TecKnati expected. Creature comforts were Troade's addiction and SEOH made sure the weasel MystiK got everything he wanted.

For now.

Rustaad shifted his pose, slightly, not enough to indicate any change in his non-existent emotion. "We've taken some large risks over the years, but this one is huge. With such a tiny window of time to activate the grid before the MystiK leaders meet the first day of the BIRG Con, we should have a contingency plan."

"No. You've convinced me to treat their powers like any other dangerous weapon. That damn grid must work, and *when* I want it to work, so we can shut down these invisible powers for-*ever*. Our engineers have confirmed the grid will function exactly as intended. All you have to do is make sure the final grid connections between cities are completed during the twenty-four hours the leaders are between cities traveling, when they are unable to communicate with anyone from a distance. If that doesn't happen, there's no contingency plan that will save us from the fallout."

Rustaad's chest hardly moved with his shallow breaths as if he wasn't alive. "You're right."

"Of course, I am. And I'll remove *any* obstacle, human or otherwise, that gets in my way."

Inclining his head in agreement, Rustaad spoke with the quiet strength of an eagle in flight. Silent, but deadly. "We *will* be prepared for anything and everything."

Scratching his neck, SEOH slowed his pacing, a new idea forming. He'd never been half in on anything and certainly not now. "We need to combat the prophecy crap they're spewing with a counter-campaign that sways public opinion, even for those of the MystiKs like Troade who enjoy life through technological advantages. That way, when we take control through the grid and/or the computer, the majority will not buck us. Lemmings do not fight."

"What are you thinking?"

"We launch a massive campaign to remind the world that it's TecKnati scientific and technological advances that brought us back to a civilized existence after the K'ryan Syndrome. Get a marketing team working on feel-good initiatives. I want to see a presentation by tomorrow."

A musical hum turned SEOH's attention to a holographic image of his AI female assistant. He said, "Yes, Leesa?"

Her soft voice floated into the room. "The ANASKO Board is assembled for your meeting."

"Thank you." When the image disappeared, SEOH pinched the bridge of his nose. "I wish I knew who was stirring up the board this time." SEOH would eliminate that headache just as he had Komaen and Furk. A fitting end for Komaen, a man whose name translated as "being sent to eternal sleep."

"They are old, SEOH. With Komaen himself gone, the rest are more cranky than actually problematic as long as–"

"I keep them content about the Sphere?" SEOH finished.

"Exactly."

"Let's go." SEOH led the way to his private interoffice shuttle. It whisked him and Rustaad away at a speed that would blur the eyes, but which the human body hardly felt. Another technological breakthrough thanks to ANASKO's efforts.

ANASKO headquarters had been built as an octopus-like structure, with arms spreading from the main building that supported entire divisions and landing pads, the interoffice transport shuttle capable of moving in any direction.

They stepped out of the shuttle into a circular conference room protected by hyper-glass that only a quad-laser could penetrate. Turbo-projectiles were mounted within the infrastructure of the compound that could be launched within two seconds if the ANASKO defense system picked up an approaching threat that could not be otherwise contained.

A paranoid man worried about threats.

A powerful man prepared for an attack.

Once inside the spacious room, Rustaad marched to a titanium antigravity podium positioned on the side of the massive circular table where he would perform vid relays as SEOH directed him.

SEOH sauntered to his spot at the table where he stood between AB One, or ANASKO Board member One, and AB Twelve. The seat for AB Seven remained empty, waiting for the board to replace Komaen. The board would decide soon, once the four most qualified candidates completed the complex steps of high-level clearance. It had already been over a year and a half since Komaen met his demise, but one could not rush some procedures, especially those written by his own father.

Names were not used in meetings to limit any social intrusion on business. SEOH had no choice but to use Komaen's *now* after SEOH had awarded a special tribute to show his deepest respect for the man he'd quietly eliminated. "Good morning, ANASKO Board. I have the quarterly progress report on the newly christened Komaen Sphere that you requested."

He nodded at Rustaad who moved his fingers silently at the podium control panel. Individual holo-vid screens appeared immediately in front of each seated board member.

SEOH continued. "This is a short vid showing the adaptability of the MystiK children in the current trial Sphere." He waited as several scenes scrolled by with images of happy children living in stylized cabins built from natural sphere materials. Next to the lush setting landscaped with exotic plants and welcoming grass, some of the children splashed in a man-made lake while others played games. All were dressed in simple, but colorful, tunics also made of natural materials that looked as though they were found within the Sphere.

Well, materials found within *one* part of the Sphere.

AB Five lifted his wrinkled gaze to SEOH. "I see only one who could be close to maturity age. Your original report indicated a number of sixteen and seventeen-year-old MystiKs captured."

SEOH had no intention of telling this bunch just how many kids, or which ones, he'd captured. The board of twelve only needed enough information to keep them content that the children were safe and happy.

All eyes lifted to SEOH when he opened his arms, palms out, the expression of an indulgent father on his face. "As many of you pointed out when we first discussed this, the MystiK teens are no different from our own and had to be given the same consideration as our children in this situation. Because certain children are not in view does not mean they're not within the Sphere. When have we ever been able to control youth when they were out of our sight?"

Most of the men chuckled agreeably with knowing looks, having dealt with errant teens in their own lives, even if the experience was decades ago and more memory than reality.

SEOH gave them a smile in commiseration. "We do have Mathias of the Governing House and Callan of the Warrior House. In fact, we even have V'ru of the Records House."

That snagged their attention. Approval murmured through the room.

Capturing V'ru had been an accident, but a providential one since the boy rarely left his family home. V'ru had been near Callan, an unexpected double trophy that SEOH had no problem taking credit for capturing.

AB Five thumped the table, shoving his frown at SEOH. "But where *are* Callan, Zilya, V'ru and Mathias? Are they adjusting well or not?"

Once the room quieted again, SEOH explained in a patient voice he had to dig deep for. "All the children are doing fine, better than fine. Our scouts informed each of the captives that they would only be in the Sphere while the MystiKs and TecKnati work out our differences for the joint benefits of our children. Mathias and Callan are future leaders of their respective Houses, headstrong teens. I doubt any of you will be surprised to learn that those two took a few of the more adventurous children with them and went exploring. I find that to be a positive sign."

"How so?" AB One asked from his left.

"The Sphere was originally created to test the adaptability of plants and animals," SEOH said, just getting warmed up for his speech. Discovering life on a planet previously thought of as only a subsidiary moon had been significant and eye-opening. And the timing could not have been better as he'd already envisioned a way to use the fact that life could exist elsewhere as a strong reason to eliminate the MystiK vermin once and for all, without damage to TecKnati.

MystiKs should jump at the chance to rule their own planet once he took away their power in this world.

He could feel the anticipation in the room and launched into his presentation. "When we faced the possibility that the next transfer of MystiK power to the new rulers coming of age might interfere with our HERMES Intraspace plans …" He paused for effect, adding, "The greatest program in the history of mankind," then continued.

"The Komaen Sphere offered a second value for our investment by becoming a holding facility for these teens while we negotiate with the MystiKs. Their families must meet us halfway and agree that the only way we will continue to survive and thrive as a civilization is through a joint effort."

Wrinkled necks wobbled with heads nodding. Thumps from fisted hands on the table drummed three times around the room, the premier sign of agreement.

He had them. "The exciting thing about how these children are adapting so quickly and clearly enjoying the Sphere is that first of all they're secure and content. Number two is that this is a longer-term peaceful option for the MystiKs who do not want to ... work with us."

AB Five had taken Komaen's place as SEOH's most annoying board member. He sat back, fingers tapping silently on the table. "Are you suggesting that all of the MystiKs would consider *living* in the Sphere? It's only slightly larger than the ten cities."

So, AB Five believed.

"Putting them in the Sphere would be better than what happened to the C'raydonians when they refused to cooperate and threatened the TecKnati," AB Four muttered.

SEOH withheld a smile at the single board member he could always count on. One of the TecKnati children who'd died of asphyxiation on the heels of the first MystiK child Rustaad eliminated had been AB Four's only son. That board member would enjoy seeing where Callan and Mathias were really living in the Sphere.

But no one other than SEOH and Rustaad could be privy to *all* the activities that went on in the Komaen Sphere.

Rumbling conversation swept around the table until SEOH answered AB Five. "The entire MystiK population would clearly not fit in the Sphere. But if we can't come to an agreement with them before the MystiKs hand over power to their next generation of leaders, who are consistently showing more abilities and less willingness to work with TecKnati, we have to accept the possibility of significant technological and scientific destruction at their hands."

The room erupted with a clash of opinions, arguing with each other whether this level of power was even possible and, if so, would the MystiKs risk destroying their own world?

The majority feared MystiKs. Which worked in SEOH's favor.

SEOH might not believe the MystiK power to be indefensible, but many of these old bastards had lived during the first effects of the fallout from the K'ryan Syndrome and still shuddered over several unexplained phenomenon that had occurred since then.

Catching Rustaad's eye, SEOH nodded, ready to add fuel to SEOH's self-made fire.

Screams spewed from the vids, drawing silence in the room when every set of eyes watched in horror as the last space launch ended in disaster with flaming metal debris slicing through people racing from the observation stands. TecKnati friends and family were lost that day.

The downside of living to an old age, as these board members had, was that every one of them had been affected by disasters such as this one.

And every board member believed the MystiKs had been behind the destruction. SEOH had made sure they believed.

"Gentlemen," he said, softly this time, addressing them as human beings instead of numbers. "We owe it to the future of this world to stop the insanity. What I'm suggesting is that if the MystiKs refuse to join us in developing and protecting this fragile world we call home, that we protect our future by gifting them with a planet to make their own. We start by taking their next most powerful generation of leaders and sending them to the planetary outpost first."

SEOH silently amended his words. *That is, if we don't manage to eradicate the entire bunch by sending the K-Virus back into the past once the inoculations for the chosen few to survive are completed at the Institutes.*

CHAPTER 25

TONY PACED ALONG THE GROOVE he'd worn in the hard-packed, green dirt floor of the crappy isolation hut. The hum of energy circulating through the walls taunted him.

No way out of here. Not alive.

Where was Rayen? Had they killed her and Gabby by now?

When the humming sound stopped all at once, the change was chilling. He moved to the center where he could turn in any direction, prepared for the worst.

An opening appeared, then a young girl stood there holding a gourd-like flask and a bowl. When she stepped inside, Tony looked past her shoulder until she said, "There are guards outside."

"Figures." He swung his gaze back to her. She might be a little younger than him, but she didn't look like she'd survive more than a day on the streets of Camden where he'd grown up in Jersey. Slender, fine-boned, her hair in strawberry-colored cornrows, her tunic some shade of red. She didn't look too threatening, but you never knew. Sure, he could probably overpower her and figure a way to use her to get past the guards, but that wouldn't help Gabby or Rayen and right now he was tired of being alone. "What's your name?"

"Neelah." Her voice fluttered when she spoke and gave him the impression she might talk. Which surprised him. It was kind of nice not to be treated like evil incarnate the way Sparkle Face treated him. Neelah extended the flask and bowl. "Here's some water and fruit."

"Thanks." No chance to make a run for it, so Tony accepted the food, trying not to act too grateful, even if he was. He took a deep swig of ... water? The stuff smelled like perfume and had an oily aftertaste.

Feeling her eyes on him, he managed to look as though he liked the water. "My friends, okay?"

Her face brightened with interest that found its way into her pleasant tone. "One is still with the healer and the hunting party hasn't returned."

She didn't seem to be in a hurry to leave, so he decided to make a stab at getting information. Plus, he liked the sound of her voice. "How old are you?"

"Sixteen. How old are you?"

"Seventeen." He squatted down to put the bowl on the floor then took another long drink from the flask. Once he got past the weird taste, the water refreshed his raw throat. "What's with all this House talk? You from the same place as what's her name? Zilya?"

She glanced over her shoulder and when she looked at him again her eyes had lost the happy creases. She moved forward, squatting down to his level. "No. She's of the Governing House, as is Mathias."

Neelah said that with a load of disdain.

Discontent among the natives? That could be useful.

Wouldn't Rayen get her panties in a twist if Tony figured out how to get the three of them out of here first?

He hadn't found a reason to smile since walking into Suarez's classroom this morning and getting tied to Rayen, but he beamed one now. All girls liked to be appreciated. He'd learned that about the same time he learned to walk. "What's so special about Zilya? I mean, can't be looks 'cause you're gorgeous."

That hit the mark with Neelah. Her face visibly relaxed and a shy smile touched her lips. "All who come from the Governing House believe they are above the rest of us, even Etoi."

"You talkin' about Zilya's prune-faced girlfriend?" He lifted a handful of fruit, tasted a piece after deciding that if they wanted to kill him, they wouldn't waste food by lacing it with poison.

Not when they could use spears to turn him into a human pincushion.

Neelah nodded, her lips now curling in a sneer. "Etoi is a Rubio level servant. The very highest of rank for her position, but she is still just a servant. Nothing more."

"What's the deal between your group and the tecknati?"

"You're our enemy."

"Not me, babe. I'm not one of them. Don't even know what that is or what you guys are." Tony had an idea. "Can you write those names on something?"

She cocked her head at his request then swirled her finger above the ground and the letters carved into the surface even though she never touched the dirt.

"Awesome! How'd you do that?"

Neelah grinned, dark brown eyes shining at the compliment in his tone. "I have *other* gifts."

Tony had never been slow to understand when a girl was coming on to him. "I have no doubt, babe." He straightened his shoulders even as his mind raced with conflicting thoughts. He wanted to encourage a possible ally, but she could just be jerking his chain, so he kept her talking. "How'd you end up here?"

"I was in the wrong place at the wrong time, like Etoi, except that she's glad to be here with Zilya. Etoi believes she will be treated as more once we return, if we ever see home again, but she's wrong."

"I still don't understand." He shook his head. "Who were the TecKnati trying to catch if you were grabbed by accident?"

"It appears that the TecKnati have devised this plan to prevent Zilya and the other future rulers from attending the BIRG Con or taking over their respective Houses afterwards."

"Taking over? Like becoming crowned or something?"

She shrugged. "I don't know this crowning, but once a MystiK is presented at the BIRG Con, they're acknowledged as leaders in training. They begin their official duties as they will assume the role of House leaders within ten years, or upon the sudden death of the existing leaders."

"So, these TecKnati people grabbed you instead of the MystiKs they wanted. Yeah?"

She gave a sad nod.

"That sucks."

Her smile peeked out again. "You speak in the strangest way. I must go. But I will return if I can."

"Hey, you sayin' you don't think I'm a TecKnati?" he asked.

"Oh, I'm hoping you *are* one."

That made no sense. Did she want a TecKnati ally? "Don't take this wrong, babe, because I'd love to have you come back to visit, but if ya think I'm your enemy, why you wanna be friends with me?"

She stood to leave. "I'd befriend the devil himself to get out of this place." She paused. Her face shifted to determined. "And I'm not the only one."

In the next instant she was gone, and the walls buzzed again, but Tony felt better after the water and fruit. And Neelah's information. He shifted the fruit bowl and flask near a wall so he could pace. The longer he walked in circles and crisscross patterns the more frustrated he got at being stuck in this place when Mathias had no reason to lock him up.

Or kill him.

He slammed his fist into his palm over and over, ready for a target. How could everything he'd worked for at the Byzantine Institute disintegrate in the blink of an eye *because* of a computer?

Until now, he'd believed his skill with computers would rule the day. That his natural abilities with technology would afford him control over his future and, most important, the chance to find his little bro.

He'd never get Vinny back if Tony had to depend on other people. Gram had done all she could when Tony and Vinny got dropped in her lap as small boys. She'd held off child services for as long as possible, but the day had come when the social worker put Gram in the position of losing one or both, forced to admit she couldn't afford to care for two children.

At eight years old, Tony had begged the don't-give-a-damn social worker to take him and leave his little brother who'd only been four at the time.

That's when he was given his first lesson in logic.

Younger children were easier to place, sort of like mutt puppies were cuter as puppies.

Tony squeezed his eyes shut, fighting off the misery of thinking about Vinny. Gram was too old to fight the authorities. She barely managed to keep her and Tony alive, even with him working every minute he wasn't in school.

The day she told him only wealthy and powerful people got to choose their futures, Tony chose his and studied nonstop.

He'd jumped at the opportunity to be tested as a candidate for the Institute three months ago. Money and age didn't matter to the Browns. If he made the grades, he got a full ride to a prestigious university. But the Top Ten Project meant going to MIT a year early if he won the competition.

No. Not if, but when.

That was a year closer to finding Vinny.

First, he had to get out of this freakin' prison hut ... and this nightmare.

If Neelah came back, he'd find out just how willing she was to go against Zilya and maybe Mathias. He should've asked her to go find out what was happening at the healing hut.

Gabby could be dead from her reaction to the vine if that goofball healer in the skirt didn't kill her. And Rayen had beaten one croggle, but that Callan couldn't be trusted. He might spear Rayen and serve her up to the croggle.

Even if Mathias has any doubts about Rayen and Gabby, he's still convinced that I'm the devil's spawn.

He hoped Gabby and Rayen were having better luck.

If they survived.

He swiped a layer of sweat off his forehead with the back of his hand.

Friction sparked in the air, alerting him to potential company again. Good. *Just give me someone who isn't a kid, or a girl.* Someone he could pound out his frustration on if they refused to let him out.

Stepping to the middle again, he faced the blurry change in the wall where everyone had entered so far. Fists raised to defend himself, he shifted his body into a fighting stance.

When the opening finally appeared, a tall guy stood there in a metallic jumpsuit that Tony couldn't decide if it was green or gray. Dark, short-cropped hair and a sick-looking tattoo on his exposed neck. Dude made a good candidate for the Scorpion gang from Tony's old hood. The guy was shoved inside so hard he fell flat on his face at Tony's feet.

Looking over at the opening, Tony found Etoi standing half inside the hut with her spear propped on the ground.

She sneered at the guy on the floor. "You two should get along fine, TeK scum." When her gaze jumped up to Tony, she took in his raised fists and rolled her eyes then disappeared as the opening vanished.

The guy on the ground let out a painful groan. The tat snaking around his neck was a cobra, which writhed as he moved. Tony was so gonna have to get one of them. Floor guy bent his elbows and pushed, trying to get up.

Ah, crap. Tony dropped his fists and hooked one of the guy's arms, giving him a tug.

Once Cobra guy was on his feet, he dusted his hands then wiped green off his face and stretched his jaw back and forth. "Not broken."

"Who are you?" Tony asked.

"A scout of course. Phen. You're?"

"Tony." *That's all this guy needs to know.* "You're a TecKnati?" Tony asked just to be clear.

"Course I am." Phen eyed Tony. "Where'd you come from?"

"One of those pod things. Transender."

"What TecKnati brought you here?"

Shoving his bottom lip up, Tony shook his head. "Don't know any TecKnati, except you. I traveled here with friends."

"Not possible."

"Why?"

"MystiKs can't travel in a transender without an escort."

Tony tossed his hands up in the air and walked away then swung around. "I'm *not* a MystiK or a TecKnati. Got a third choice?"

"C'raydonian, but you couldn't be one of those."

Based upon Phen's dark tone, Tony didn't want to be one of those either. "What's going on between you guys and the MystiKs anyhow? You have a throw down?"

Phen's forehead wrinkled. He stared harder. "Your clothes and speech ... I've never seen or heard anyone like you."

Making a chuffing noise, Tony gave him a wry smile. "Not surprised. There's only one o'me."

"You say that as if it is a positive."

Tony caught the insult and considered popping the mouth that uttered it, but he had a chance to find out how to get out of here if this guy played 'escort' in the pods. "Where's home for you?"

"TeK City Two."

"What planet, dude?"

Phen's eyebrows lifted in amusement. "Earth. What planet are you from ... *dude*?"

Earth. No way. Unless this was some military experiment gone bad. But that didn't explain getting pulled into a computer. Would Phen tell him anything if this was some whacked out military program? Nah.

Back to Tony's immediate problem–finding a way home. "Do those transenders return to their original destination?"

Eyeing Tony with wary observation, Phen answered with a superior attitude. "Yes. They can only return to where they were initiated, but don't get any foolish ideas about hijacking one. I told you. A MystiK can't travel in one without an escort."

The way Tony saw it, this was outstanding news since neither he, Gabby nor Rayen were MystiKs, and they hadn't needed an escort the first time here. But he'd have to figure a way out of this prison hut first. "I'll make you a deal."

Phen listened silently, his stance noncommittal.

"Let's work together to get outta here. In return, I only want to know how to call up and operate a transender."

Phen smiled at some inner thought. "I *will* escape and without your help. I'm not telling you anything about a transender."

"How can you be so sure you can–"

The power that constantly hummed through the walls went silent.

"See you on the next trip," Phen whispered and put his palms together. He shoved them between the vertical reeds that made up the walls and pushed his hands wide, creating an opening he stepped through.

Tony hesitated only a second then jammed his way out of the hut, too.

Power hummed behind him the minute he stepped clear.

His knees went weak.

That was a close call. *I coulda been a fried Italian.*

Taking in his surroundings, Tony caught sight of Phen who'd run thirty paces away and stopped, swinging his head as he looked for something. Two more steps past a wide thatch of inky black plants twice as tall as Tony that reminded him of bamboo, and Phen halted, his attention drawn to his right. A smile appeared on his profile, as if he'd hit the Jersey Lotto.

When Phen paused, a small-sized hand appeared from behind the bamboo stalks and passed Phen something he shoved in his pants pocket. Then he nodded and snuck off down a path that had been cleared through the trees dotting the village.

Tony followed, trying to keep his footsteps soft. He slowed next to the stand of bamboo and leaned forward to see who was there. No one.

When he caught up to Phen, the scout had reached the fog wall surrounding the village.

The guy was running straight for the deadly haze.

Tony called out, "Stop! The fog'll kill ya!"

Phen spared a quick glance over his shoulder but didn't slow down, rushing headlong into the puke-colored mist.

Tony tensed, ready for the blood-curdling scream ... that never came. What happened?

Crap. He couldn't lose that TecKnati.

Besides Rayen had stepped in to keep the crazies from executing Tony and had saved the three of them from a killer plant. And Gabby had tried to help Tony when the vine first attacked him. This was Tony's chance to do something to help them get out of here.

He ran five strides and reached the fog where he realized how Phen had gotten through.

The angle of Tony's approach hadn't allowed him to see that someone–probably the person who helped Phen escape–had cleared a narrow path through the protective wall.

And that tunnel was squeezing closed.

No time to lose.

Plunging ahead, Tony lifted his St. C medal and kissed it. "Please don't let me die now." Then added, "Not 'til I get laid ... at least once."

CHAPTER 26

GABBY REALIZED HER MISTAKE TOO late. She stared at the little girl Rayen had risked her life to protect from a croggle. "Can't I just, like, hand you stuff when you need it, Jaxxson?"

He paused from what appeared to be him checking the child's pulse. Her skin had turned too bright a pink to be healthy. Jaxxson said, "I need to get her blood pressure calmed down. She's having a reaction to the Sphere. You said you wanted to help."

But she hadn't thought that would entail putting her hands on the child. And Gabby had also thought she'd have a chance to search for a way out of the village if she tagged along with Jaxxson.

Not going to happen from inside this dome thing surrounding all three of them.

Jaxxson had walked her through a canopied area where two girls who looked about twelve were making aqua-blue orbs appear and disappear for a group of very young children who ooohhed and awwwed. They were inside a woven pavilion type of enclosure. Sort of like a tent only in ratty shape and held together with vines and patched with leaves, but since the leaves were all different colors it had a kaleidoscope look to it. Different but cool.

Jaxxson had walked over to a luminous white bubble that hovered on one side of the kiddie area. The bubble looked about the size of a small bedroom. He'd placed his hands on the outside of the dome and murmured words until the opal glow shimmered in front of him and a section opened up that allowed him to enter without bending over.

He had told Gabby to follow him.

She hadn't seen much choice.

The wall returned to its original form as soon as she'd stepped inside and thankfully found the floor to be flat. She'd tentatively pressed a finger against the dome wall. Her finger sank into the strange surface then stopped as if hitting a solid material.

That had curtailed any hope of her wandering around and snooping for exit points in the village.

"Gabby?" Jaxxson drew her attention back to the child who was lying on a pillowy cloud-type of bed that hovered about three feet off the floor.

She backed up a step. "You know why I don't want to put my hands on her."

The little girl raised a timid, silver-eyed gaze to Gabby. Her tiny bottom lip quivered.

Turning her guilt-ridden anxiety on Jaxxson, Gabby snapped, "Just great. Look what you made me do."

"Nobody's making you do anything. Refusing to offer comfort is your choice."

Now she sounded like an ogre. She inhaled a breath and flexed her fingers, determined to keep the unspoken truce intact between her and Jaxxson, who stared up at her from where he knelt beside the girl. One of his hands had moved from the child's wrist to above her elbow.

Gabby stepped back to the bed and squatted down beside Jaxxson. She'd never been able to walk away from a kid in need, not after spending her life being ignored by everyone around her.

"If you can tell me how to shield thoughts from my mind ... I'll try," she implored Jaxxson with a soft voice to keep from upsetting the little girl.

Maybe a child's thoughts wouldn't be as abrasive as an adult's. Thoughts that could be so negative or hateful they had sent Gabby to her knees in the past, leaving her emotionally shredded.

Jaxxson answered her in an equally calming voice without looking at her. "Your body is still healing from the vine infection, but the weave I placed on your wrist will also prevent anyone's thoughts you don't want to hear from impacting you. Unless the other person is so powerful a telepath that they could force their thoughts on you. I doubt Be'tallia is such a threat."

Gabby exhaled a breath, still trying to accept everything in this place. The twinkle in his eyes made it easy for her to joke. "Oh. So, I'm wearing the equivalent of a Batman wristwatch for telepaths, huh?"

He chuckled and said, "I have no idea what you're talking about."

"Never mind. But why didn't you tell me about this wristband sooner?" Gabby crabbed at him.

"Because you must learn to trust touch, even when you lack external protection. Place your hand on Be'tallia's forehead to soothe her." He returned to treating the child, moving his palms to cover the girl's abdomen while smiling at her.

Gabby lifted her hand and slowly extended it, fingers trembling.

Be'tallia's gaze jumped from Jaxxson to Gabby, watching with huge silver-gray eyes, several shades darker than the party dress she wore.

Breathing hard, Gabby finally lowered her hand to the child's forehead and braced herself.

No thoughts came crashing into her mind.

Jaxxson hadn't lied. Call her paranoid, but she'd been tricked in the past and hadn't liked it one bit.

But here she was, touching another person who actually smiled at her.

Gabby started laughing, not a loud sound but a private little *hot-dang* one.

Jaxxson gave her a way-to-go glance then returned to whatever he was doing to heal the little girl.

Giddy with having accomplished something she'd been denied for so many years, Gabby used her other hand to hold the child's miniature fingers. "You have pretty hands and long fingers. Bet you could play a piano."

Be'tallia's gaze moved from Gabby to Jaxxson who seemed intent on something then chuckled. His beautiful brown eyes twinkled at the child who nodded, lips curling into a half-smile.

Gabby felt like an outsider. Again. But were those two really communicating telepathically? "Did you just talk to her mind-to-mind?"

"Yes. Why?" He seemed perplexed by her tone.

Refusing to sound like the terminally uninformed, she just said, "Isn't that rude to do with me sitting here?"

"No. It's no different than if you were to ask for a word in private with me."

How could she argue with that? "Wouldn't it be nicer for the three of us to talk?"

Jaxxson kept working some sort of magic with his long-fingered hands, moving them up to the child's neck as he spoke. "Be'tallia isn't ready to talk. Her throat's still raw from screaming when they kidnapped her. Speak to her with your mind if you want to communicate with her. It will help her relax around you."

Oh. Dang. Gabby flushed with embarrassment over not realizing the little girl might be in worse shape than just having a skin reaction. Poor thing had been ripped from everything she knew.

But talk to her mind to mind? Be serious. "I don't know ... I, uh, that wouldn't be a good idea."

"Why not?"

Her temper lived just below the surface on most days and the only thing stopping Gabby from yelling at Jaxxson right now was that she didn't want to upset Be'tallia. But her words came through clenched teeth. "Because I don't know how to communicate that way and I'm not messing around with anyone else's mind."

"You can't harm Be'tallia's mind. She's the second born of the ruling family over the House of Developers. She's been trained since birth, how to both use *and* protect her mind. You could choose no better person with whom to test your skills the first time."

Could she do that? Gabby swallowed hard at the idea of attempting to intentionally use her mental ability instead of avoiding mishaps with it. Then she remembered the weave on her wrist. "What about the bracelet you put on me?"

"It'll only reinforce what you want. You did *not* want to hear Be'tallia's thoughts, so the bracelet helped you avoid that. If you *choose* to communicate then the bracelet will also help."

Could she control mental contact and speak to Be'tallia with her mind?

Was she really going to give this a try? Maybe. "You said it was wrong to enter another person's mind so how do I talk to her without forcing myself into her mind?"

Jaxxson nodded, as if she'd earned points with him. "Give me a moment to explain to her."

While he was silent, Gabby watched the interplay between him and the child. Be'tallia concentrated as she listened to something he told her telepathically then her eyes widened as if surprised. She finally nodded with a serious expression Gabby wouldn't have expected on the face of a five-year old.

Jaxxson explained, "I had to tell her that you'd never been trained to speak with your mind."

"That jolted her?"

"Yes, but not in a bad way. It's as much a part of our culture as learning how to levitate."

Of course, he'd say that. Why had I been expecting him to say that telepathy was as much of his culture as something like learning to ride a bicycle? Did they even have bicycles? "Are you sure I can't hurt Be'tallia?"

"Yes."

"Okay, then tell me how to do this."

"I'll first have her reach out to you so that you can feel her tap on your mind. When you do, allow yourself to relax and stop worrying about hearing someone else's thoughts. You'll hear her."

Gabby took a deep breath and relaxed her hands then nodded at Be'tallia.

In the next moment she felt a light bump, bump, bump in her mind, just as if Be'tallia had used one of her tiny fingers to tap against Gabby's forehead. Heart thumping wildly, Gabby slowly released her fear and opened her mind. She heard, *Hello. Who are you?*

Goosebumps raced up Gabby's arm at the sensation of hearing Be'tallia's sweet voice really inside her mind. Tears pooled in her eyes. She'd never experienced anything so wonderful.

Gabby replied, *Hello to you, too. I'm Gabby. Thanks for letting me try this with you.*

Your parents have gifts?

No.

Be'tallia's smooth forehead creased. *You talk to friends? Yes?*

The child really couldn't fathom that Gabby wasn't communicating with others this way already. She shook her head. *Nope. Never met anyone who could do this until now.*

Be'tallia screwed up her face in that funny frown that kids had when they thought an adult was trying to joke with them.

Gabby couldn't stop grinning. She'd never been so happy as in this moment. *Do you talk to your friends this way?*

Yes. Be'tallia looked away, sad. *But not here. I call out, but no one answers. I miss them ... and my mother.*

Gabby felt moisture pool in her eyes. Be'tallia sounded so lost.

Having spent most of her life feeling lost herself, Gabby wished she could fix this for the little girl.

And Gabby yearned for the world Be'tallia lived in ... until she realized this child hadn't lived in a perfect world. Certainly not a safe world.

Be'tallia's gray gaze lifted to peer at the top of Gabby's head. *So many hair spools.*

Out of knee jerk reaction, Gabby lifted her hands to her hair where she'd fixed her ponytails as well as she could and retied the ribbons. She grinned. *I know it looks pretty funky, huh?*

Funky?

Strange, Gabby explained.

Not strange. Beautiful. Be'tallia's awe brushed across Gabby's mind like a gentle breeze. The child had a cherub's face and innocent mind filled with tranquility.

Gabby wiped a watery eye and said, *Thank you. I've never been called beautiful.*

Jaxxson looked over at her for a moment, a small frown creasing his brow, but he said nothing.

Be'tallia's eyes crinkled with humor. *Do they not see you?*

From the mouths of babes, as the old saying went. *People are different where I come from. None are special like you.*

Be'tallia's mouth spread wide in happiness.

Gabby had no way to thank this wonderful child who'd allowed a perfect stranger to speak to her telepathically. If she could do this with a child, maybe she really could train herself to the point of touching others.

And have a normal life.

Wait a minute. Gabby wasn't touching Be'tallia.

Sometime while she'd been fixated on talking with Be'tallia, Gabby had moved her hands to her lap where she now yanked them up in front of her face. Then she looked at Be'tallia and sent her a thought. *I'm not touching you.*

The little girl shook her head.

How can we still be talking without touching?

Babies touch. Big girls don't have to, Be'tallia explained, her telepathic voice sounding wry.

Unbelievable.

Then Be'tallia added, *You made my head better.*

Did this child mean what Gabby thought she meant? Turning to Jaxxson, she said out loud, "Be'tallia said I helped her head to feel better."

"Uh huh."

"I'm not a healer."

"You sure?"

How could she answer that? "I don't ... can't ... never have ..."

Jackson patted Be'tallia's cheek, making her giggle. He told her, "Your skin is no longer red. You'll be fine and you *will* be safe with us." Then he sat back on his knees and crossed his arms, facing Gabby. "You work very hard at proving you can't do something. Perhaps you should try figuring out what you *can* do."

She didn't react to Jaxxson's not-so-gentle verbal smack about putting more effort into figuring out what unusual skill she might possess. She'd heard that often from instructors, psychologists, *and* her father ... *you don't try hard enough.*

Jaxxson hadn't meant his words as a criticism so much as an observation. But he was certifiable if he thought she could heal anybody. She could accept the telepathy part only because she'd struggled her whole life with hearing other people's thoughts. And even now she had a hard time believing she'd just spoken to someone mind-to-mind.

But a healer?

If she'd been a healer, she could have saved her mother from being a destructive alcoholic. Or healed her own wrists. "I think Be'tallia was confused because *you* were working on her the whole time we were talking."

"Perhaps." He shrugged. "Now for the next stage of healing."

"Why? Isn't she better?"

"She'll be fine. In fact, her throat is healed."

Gabby glanced over at Be'tallia who had the sly I'm-hiding-a-secret-from-you look. "So now you can talk?"

"Yes." Be'tallia's grin exposed a gap in her teeth.

Nice to see that children in other worlds still grew up with some of the same issues those in her world such as losing front teeth.

Returning to Jaxxson, Gabby opened her hands. "I'm confused. What's this next step?"

Holding her gaze with his steady, dark-eyed one, she felt a stronger thump on her mind this time and realized Jaxxson wanted to speak to her silently.

She panicked for a moment as he waited patiently then slowly opened her mind. Trusting a child was very different than trusting someone who said he was her enemy. When she didn't hear anything, she asked him, *Can you hear me?*

Yes. When we bring Be'tallia out of this protective dome, she will lose the soothing effect I infused in the bed beneath her. She'll begin to remember that she's been torn from her family. I've found one thing that seems to help ease the children through this difficult time.

You mean separation anxiety? Gabby asked.

We have other terms, but yes, that's correct.

What do you do?

I'll show you.

After telling Be'tallia that she was going to leave the dome and that she might feel different but to remember that she was safe, Jaxxson lifted her into his arms and stood. When Gabby popped up next to him, Jaxxson wrapped his fingers around her wrist before she could stop him.

He murmured a brief string of strange words.

In the next moment, all three of them stood outside the dome in the canopied area with the other children.

She withdrew her wrist from Jaxxson. "Why'd you do it differently this time?"

"Before, you'd have become upset if I'd touched you. You now know you're not controlled by your gift, but that you're in charge. You knew I wouldn't force my mind on you and that you were safe with my touch. Another step in developing your gift."

He was right about one thing.

She'd never trusted contact with another person since losing her mother, but she did believe that Jaxxson wouldn't harm her.

She wasn't sure she liked that knowledge, after all Tony was still stuck back in the prisoner hut. So, until all of them were free, none of them were free. She might trust Jaxxson now, but could she trust him if that Zilya chick and Mathias wanted her dead?

Jaxxson carried Be'tallia to where a group of children huddled together on the ground giggling over something. When he asked them to make a space, the children parted, revealing a pile of odd little puffy animals that squirmed and crawled all over each other.

The critters reminded Gabby of furry four-legged troll dolls with large blue-green eyes, fat lips and a pug nose. Their ears sat up like a horse's and short, thick, multi-colored hair sprouted out the tops of their heads. They had plush cinnamon-colored coats except for the same poofs of rainbow hair sticking out around their paws and at the ends of their long rat-like tails that dragged behind them.

"What are those?" Gabby asked, grinning at the funny creatures.

"Pupples." Jaxxson sat Be'tallia down on a woven mat covering the ground and petted one of the little animals. "They're the dugurat offspring."

"They look too young to be weaned from their mothers."

"They are. We rescue as many as we can and bring them in for the children. The dugurats breed constantly but are easy prey. They'll defend their young, even attacking viciously to protect their pupples when threatened, but are otherwise docile. They have a low percentage rate of survival, because a dugurat brain never grows much beyond the size it is at birth."

"Never heard of a dugurat before." *Well, except for Etoi using that term to basically call Rayen an idiot.*

"I hadn't either prior to coming here, but we have V'ru of the Records House with us. He knows just about everything there is to know about all things."

"V'ru? That's a strange name."

"He was named after an ancestor and is a rare MystiK who was gifted with the knowledge of all his ancestors upon his birth."

"Shut the front door."

"What?" Jaxxson stopped moving his hands. "What door?"

She lifted a hand, waving her fingers. “Sorry. It’s an expression from my time we say when we hear something phenomenal. If this V’ru came to life with all that knowledge, did he still have to study?”

“Oh, yes. His has been a life of continuous study, but that’s expected of a gifted one such as he, to whom current leaders turn for valued information.”

Poor guy. She thought her life sucked, but she wouldn’t want his job. Gabby took in Be’tallia who’d sat quietly, now looking like a ragged princess doll that had been dragged through the dirt. Her face was starting to show the stress of her thoughts. A tear slipped from her eye.

Gabby squatted beside her. “Be’tallia?”

The child turned to her and whispered, “Yes.”

“These pupples are all alone, away from home. They need someone to hold them, so they know they’re loved.”

Be’tallia glanced at the pupples, still not reaching for one.

Gabby looked up at Jaxxson who was watching Gabby with the strangest expression on his face. She started to ask what bothered him, but Be’tallia was her first concern. “You may need to take her back to the dome.”

He shook his head. “She must be given a chance to adjust. Keeping her in the dome will only delay what she must come to understand. I see you’re not pleased, but my powers can only heal the body, not the mind or the emotions.”

She supposed he was right. Gabby’s father had always provided the best in medical care for her mother, but no one had been able to heal her mother’s damaged psyche when rumors of her father’s affairs with younger women had surfaced.

Jaxxson reached over the children and lifted two pupples that made weird little grunts and growls, sounding like pig-puppy chatter. He placed one in Be’tallia’s lap where the pupple started licking the little girl’s fingers then pawing the front of her dress.

Gabby wanted to encourage Be’tallia, but she knew what it felt like to have everyone trying to make you “be better right now.” When the little girl picked up the pupple and held it against her cheek, Gabby stood and turned a thrilled smile on Jaxxson.

He then handed her the other pupple.

She’d been itching to hold one and didn’t hesitate to take the ball of fluff, running a finger over its salmon pink, aqua and butter yellow tufts of hair sprouting everywhere. Bringing the bundle of nipping, licking, squirming energy to her face, she laughed when it yipped at her.

She sensed a deep curiosity coming from Jaxxson.

Letting her gaze wander over to him, she found his eyes concentrating intently. As if he knew that she'd never held a pet because of her fear of touch. True, but another reason had been the constant moving from one city or country to another.

Pets were like children. Both deserved a stable home.

After a long moment, he said, "We can only heal others if we understand how to first heal ourselves."

She started to explain, once more, that she wasn't a healer, but just then Zilya came rushing up with a little boy in her arms. A toddler. She thrust the child at Jaxxson. "He's stable for now, but he started reacting right away."

For the first time, Jaxxson appeared worried. "How bad?"

"I had to resuscitate him twice on the way here."

"Where's Callan? I may need his help."

"He should arrive soon, but I don't know how drained he'll be from healing another."

Gabby tried not to feel hurt over having just been bumped as Jaxxson's assistant, but she dismissed the petty reaction with a child's welfare on the line. "Callan's a healer, too?"

Jaxxson swung his attention to Gabby just long enough to answer her. "Many of us can heal minor wounds and cuts, but he is a G'ortian, whose powers are still developing and can manifest in many different ways. He has proven to be skilled in healing mortal wounds even though he's not from the Healing House."

Zilya told Jaxxson, "We captured a TecKnati scout Etoi is delivering to the Isolation Unit. Do what you can for the child. Callan may or may not have the strength to help you after tending to serious wounds."

Gabby did the math and came up with who'd been injured. Sudden fear made her voice sharp. "Rayen! What happened to her?"

Zilya kept her voice even and calm. "She was struck by a croggle, but she'll survive."

That flew all over Gabby. "Why'd you let that happen?"

Glowering at her, Zilya explained, "She wouldn't have been harmed if she'd not chosen to protect a TecKnati. You should be thankful Callan deigned to repair her after she saved our enemy."

Oh, boy. That wasn't going to win Rayen any points. Or any of them for that matter.

The toddler started jerking spasmodically. Jaxxson snapped into all business mode. "He's stressing. We have to go."

Gabby was right behind Jaxxson when he reached the dome, but she still held the pupple in her hand. She deposited the small critter into a dress pocket and announced, “I’ll help.”

His answer was to grab her arm, getting them inside the hut with lightning speed.

She’d just dropped down on one side of the cloud bed and had placed one hand on the new child’s head when she heard the little boy’s internal screams of fear and pain.

He was in a comatose state. His mind locked tightly with hers. She had to break away, but she couldn’t. Put up a wall. Not happening. What about her Batman vine watch? Why wasn’t that working?

She snatched her hands away and covered her ears, but the screaming wouldn’t stop. She fought against the chaos. Losing.

Jaxxson was saying something, shouting at her. But the words weren’t clear.

Her brain felt like it was exploding.

He swung away from the child and grabbed both of her arms, his voice shouting in her head. *Stop it! You’re killing him!*

CHAPTER 27

RAYEN SCRATCHED AT THE WOUND on her stomach that itched as it continued to heal, still not clear on how she'd survived a mortal wound from the croggle.

"Leave the scab alone," Callan admonished.

How had he known what she was doing when he walked ahead of her, navigating their way through the woods toward the village?

"Itches," she grumbled.

"Of course. The skin is repairing."

She kept pace close behind. Following him had been no hardship since she had an unobstructed view of all that toned body. "I still don't understand how you healed me."

He tossed her another of his speculative glances, as if he just couldn't make up his mind if she was telling the truth about landing here by accident in the pod without a TeK scout. "I did not heal you alone."

"Don't look at me as if I'm hiding something from you," she reprimanded. "I told you I don't know how this power inside me works. I'm pretty sure I couldn't have fixed my insides without your hands involved."

Pondering silently, he led them through the last fringe of woods before they reached the green fog wall coming into view. "Have to talk to V'ru. This is confusing."

V'ru, whose mind worked better than a Cyberprocessor. Was he Artificial Intelligence? Some kind of computer? That reminded her about another thing. "What's the big deal about computers?"

Callan slowed until she reached his side and turned to her. "There's a myth about the very first computer from over two thousand years ago. A technological creation with supernatural power that MystiKs and TecKnati are searching for."

"Why? I thought MystiKs didn't like technology."

"We don't," Callan admitted. "We just want to keep it out of SEOH's hands, because he'll use it to destroy all the MystiKs."

A computer with that kind of power was hard to imagine. Maybe it was an AI unit. "Is SEOH planning to use it here?"

"If this computer truly exists and he gets his hands on it, I doubt it will matter where we are when he hits the destruct button. Let's keep moving." Callan led the way to the green fog, then he opened the tunnel through it.

She stayed tight on his tracks, not touching the fog.

The minute Callan stepped inside the compound and closed the fog tunnel, he stopped suddenly, staring straight ahead, eyes unfocused. One blink and he dashed forward.

She caught up to him, striding step for step. "What's wrong?"

"The new boy we saved is reacting violently." He gave her a sharp look. "Your friend is killing him."

"Who?"

"The Hy'bridt."

"*Who?*" She was panting.

"The one with two eye colors."

"Gabby?" Not possible. "Hurt a child? You've got to be kidding."

Racing past a murky puddle of gray sludge and through hanging moss he slapped away from their faces, he said, "Do you hear humor in my words?"

Annoyed-distrustful-stone-face Callan was back.

When they entered deeper into the village, into a tented area she hadn't seen before, Callan continued all the way to a pearl-white dome.

Zilya stood in front of the dome, pounding on the curved wall that surprisingly did not budge. "Let me inside. I'll stop her."

Rayen guessed Zilya meant Gabby. But how would she stop her?

Callan raced up to the dome. "Why can't you enter?"

Zilya stopped pounding. "I don't know. Jaxxson called out that the child was dying, and he had to stop Gabby from ... something. That's all I got. I can't pass through the protective wall."

Rayen placed her hand on the smooth, but shifting, surface that never appeared quite solid. The outer shell really didn't give when she pushed on it. "What is this thing?"

Frantic to get inside, Zilya gave her a straight answer for once. "A personal space some of us can create. This one's for isolating new arrivals." She grabbed a fist of Rayen's shirt. "Stop that girl."

Rayen yanked out of her grasp. "Gabby wouldn't hurt a child. But I can't do anything unless you get me inside."

Without another word, Callan grabbed Rayen's wrist then put his hand on the wall. Nothing happened. He slapped the wall and growled through clenched teeth. "What's she doing to bar us from entering?"

Rayen didn't know what made her do it, but she put her hand over the one Callan still pressed on the dome.

He looked over at her with suspicion.

She told him, "Try again. Both hands."

When he slapped his other palm on the wall, she covered both of his hands with hers and closed her eyes, searching inside herself for the swirling heat. Her muscles tensed with the effort.

She didn't feel anything like the power that surged when she'd fought the croggles and the flower, but her chest heated with warmth that reminded her of when they'd healed her wound.

A second later, Callan said in a hushed voice flooded with surprise, "You did it. We're in."

She opened her eyes to find they were inside a giant white bubble…and she still held his hands.

Suddenly embarrassed to be caught holding Callan's hands, she dropped them. She glanced around and found the little boy from the croggle field stretched out on a puffy bed of air. His lips and fingers were a chilling color of blue.

Jaxxson had one hand on the child's head and the other around Gabby's throat. Her eyes were rolled back in her head.

Rayen lunged at the healer, ripping his hand away from Gabby. She fell back and slumped on the floor. When Rayen swung around to deal with Jaxxson, Callan shouted at me, "Do not touch him!"

Jaxxson turned on them and ground out his words through clenched teeth. "Silence everyone! This child's barely alive."

Rayen shook with the anger of finding Gabby being attacked. If not for holding a child's life in his hands, this healer would be laid out flat. She'd been led to believe this guy would take care of Gabby. Dropping down on one knee, Rayen checked her friend's pulse. Lucky for the healer, she found one. With a look over her shoulder, she demanded, "Why were you trying to kill her?"

Callan broke in. "I told you–"

Rayen snarled, "*No!*" and speared the healer with the bulk of her fury.

Jaxxson's hand never left the child's head. "Gabby helped me heal the little girl from this morning."

"Really?" Callan asked, sounding just as confused as Rayen felt. "Then why were you choking her?"

She glared at him. *Oh, he can ask questions, but I can't? I don't think so.*

"I'll explain later, Callan, but Gabby is truly a Hy'bridt. She has to be. Anyhow, she helped with that one, which was good, because I was drained from healing Gabby of the vine reaction."

It took Rayen a minute to realize that the healer was using his voice to soothe tempers in the room. Even hers had dropped a notch, but she still noted that there was a limit to what this group could do with their powers at any one time. That might work in her favor when she found a chance to escape with Tony and Gabby. And they would, as soon as she convinced Callan and Mathias to release Tony.

Turning halfway around, she took in the return of Gabby's healthy color and that her arms were no longer swollen or streaked with infection. The healer *had* done some good. Gabby stirred, lifting her hands to her neck.

Not understanding any of what was happening, Rayen turned back to Jaxxson. "Why'd you heal her then try to kill her?"

Gabby coughed and sputtered, struggling to sit up at that point. She whispered, "He wasn't choking me. He had his finger on my carotid artery to slow the blood flow, which saved me from imploding mentally."

Rayen didn't have a clue what Gabby was talking about, but she seemed fine now. Reaching out a hand to help her up, Rayen snatched it back quickly before making contact.

Gabby smiled. "It's okay. Jaxxson has been teaching me how to deal with casual contact. He believes I can help heal others, but when I touched this little boy, he was screaming so loud inside his head and in such pain that I lost control and couldn't disconnect from him."

Jaxxson finished explaining, his voice still calm and soothing, not looking at anyone except the little boy he hovered over. "By staying attached mentally to the child when she went into distress, Gabby was actually harming him ... and herself."

Gabby gulped. "I'm so sorry, Jaxxson."

"No, that was my mistake. I didn't consider that a child in this much anguish would overwhelm you, but once I intervened, you were actually healing him with me as a conduit between you."

Callan glared at Rayen, still angry from their shouting match. She put her hands on her hips and gave him back a glare of equal fury for his part in the confusion. He narrowed his eyes then turned to Jaxxson. "How is the boy now?"

"Still not stable. Gabby doesn't have training. I need your help."

"I'll try, but I may not be able to do much for another hour or two." Callan's gaze strayed to Rayen for a moment, letting her know he'd depleted his healing energy on *her* wounds.

Gabby butted in. "I'm not sure I can really help you, but now that I know to be careful, I'm willing to try again."

Jaxxson nodded at a spot on the far side of the boy and waited for Gabby to get settled before he sank down next to her. "You and I will work together."

Rayen wasn't sure she liked how easily those two seemed to mesh. Just what all had happened while she'd been out fighting croggles? Gone was the girl who normally panicked at the idea of being touched.

Callan dropped to his knees on this side of the child, eyes on Jaxxson who lifted Gabby's hands and slowly placed one on the child's arm and her other palm on the boy's pale forehead.

Gabby flinched at first then nodded a few seconds later, acknowledging that she could handle whatever she was feeling through the touch.

Callan moved to place his hands on the child when Rayen interjected, "Thought you couldn't help for another hour?"

"I can't heal but I can assess how he is and maybe help that way."

Rayen held her tongue, surprised she worried about Callan as she watched him place both of his hands on the little boy's chest. He let out a guttural groan of misery.

Kneeling beside him, she asked, "What's wrong?"

"This child has a damaged heart. We've lost others who had pre-existing physical problems, then reacted to the Sphere once they got here. None of those had as severe damage as this one." He closed his eyes, gritting his teeth for several moments then looked over at Jaxxson and shook his head. "His life force is down to a whisper. I tried to reach the heart, but his pain blocks access from me."

Gabby raised a desperate gaze to me.

Rayen was not a healer, but Callan had proven his skill by healing her ... after she put her hands over his. What kind of power did she possess? What was the chance she could help him now?

Or what was the chance she might do this child harm with uncontrolled power?

Callan let out a slow breath that carried heavy disappointment, ending her debate.

She covered his hands again, murmuring. "Don't give up yet."

Heat swelled where their skin connected.

He looked at her sharply but didn't move his hands.

Jaxxson spoke in an excited whisper. "I felt a pulse in the boy's life force, but it's not strong. Everyone must continue doing what you're doing."

Rayen closed her eyes and hoped she was doing the right thing when she searched for the power coiled inside her, waiting to be released. What if she released too much?

This time, she used what she'd learned when Callan healed her. Fearful of endangering the child further, she drew slowly. Energy snaked through her arms and spread out from her hands. When the blur in her mind cleared, she realized she was seeing through Callan's eyes. She watched, amazed as he began working frantically to repair the child's heart. With him taking care of the little boy, curiosity pushed her to ease back from watching the organ repair and open herself more to him.

She saw a warm glow deep inside him that drew her closer.

Noises faded away until all she could hear was Callan's rhythmic inhale and exhale. A peaceful place she hadn't known existed. Was this what home felt like? Safe. Welcoming. Intimate. She wanted to stay.

Warmth radiated inside him while he centered his energy on the boy. Gone was the fierce warrior ready to battle and the hard exterior he'd shown her all day. Here was a heart that beat strong and cared for others.

The minute he released that focus, she brushed up against grief ... heartache ... despair that he'd kept hidden and buried deep.

"Rayen?"

Hearing her name from a distance yanked her back toward consciousness. She struggled, not wanting to leave this peaceful place, but the voice insisted. She opened her eyes to find Callan, Gabby and Jaxxson staring at her.

Their faces were a mixed bag of relief.

That's when she glanced down to find the little boy no longer blue around his lips and fingers. He was sleeping soundly, and his skin was flush with natural color. "Is he better?"

Jaxxson stood, helping Gabby to her feet. "He's healed. Callan repaired his heart and we infused so much healing energy into him that I believe he's over his initial negative reaction to the Sphere."

But instead of a smile Gabby shot Callan a look that threatened harm.

Callan's lifted eyebrow smirked at Gabby for daring to think she could.

Rayen had no idea what was going on between those two, but Jaxxson must have. He nodded at her. "And we have you to thank for lending Callan the power he needed. I was quite impressed by what I felt circulate in the child's body."

All eyes went to Callan to see what he'd say about Rayen's help.

Would he send her back to isolation even after what had happened here?

When Callan turned to her, he avoided her gaze and admitted, "We owe you a great debt for saving this child. We probably would have lost him without your aid." He bowed his head an inch. "Thank you."

That must have been what Gabby had wanted, because now her face had a cat-sly, cocked eyebrow and smile.

"You're welcome," Rayen told Callan, aware of how he could hardly now accuse her of being an enemy if she'd saved this child. Twice. But would this momentary camaraderie bode well for getting Callan to lighten up on Tony?

Jaxxson stepped toward the wall they'd entered through. "The child is safe here. We'll allow him to rest."

Once they were outside in the tented area again, Jaxxson walked over to a concerned Zilya and Mathias, quickly explaining what had happened.

Rayen caught Callan before he could put her and Gabby back in the Isolation Unit. "We've proven we're not here to harm you and that we'll help you. Tony's not a danger to your village. I promise if you release him, he'll not hurt anyone."

Callan's hard expression had returned. He clearly didn't want to agree, but this time he at least seemed to struggle with the decision. "I'll admit that you and Gabby have proven yourselves to not be a threat." Rayen noticed he didn't say we were safe from retribution, but he was still talking. "But we knew with Gabby's eye colors that she had to be MystiK."

Rayen turned to Gabby. "Really? I'm thinking that's good, right?"

She shrugged in a self-conscious way.

If that made Callan happy with Gabby, Rayen wouldn't argue. One down, two to go. "And what about me?"

"I have no idea."

Not what Rayen was hoping for on several levels. She muttered, "At least you're honest."

Callan added, "But V'ru will know."

Mathias joined their group, asking what Callan was talking about. Callan explained what had transpired and Mathias agreed that V'ru would be the final word.

The infamous, all-knowing, all-seeing elite V'ru. Rayen disliked him without even meeting the guy just because of the reverence in Callan's voice when he talked about V'ru. How could any one of them hold so much power? Where was this infallible center of knowledge? Probably being worshipped somewhere. "What about Tony?"

Callan held up a hand, stalling me. "First, I want to interrogate the scout we captured. If he doesn't give me reason to believe your friend is TecKnati then–" Pausing, he looked at Mathias who said, "I'll consider releasing him."

Rayen would like to take Callan's willingness to talk with Tony as a positive indication, but Mathias had stopped before sharing his entire thought and she wanted more. "What if you still believe Tony is TecKnati?"

Mathias didn't hesitate when he said, "Then he and the scout will face punishment for the premature deaths of MystiK children who have perished here."

She knew that would likely be his answer, but still pushed for clarification. "What's the punishment?"

"We'll give them the same chance they gave these children. The guilty TecKnati will be placed in the middle of a transender docking location where they can pit their skills against a croggle. I understand from Zilya that I have you to thank for giving us the gray box we can now use to call up a croggle without endangering our own."

Tony would never survive against a croggle. Neither would that scout. Rayen had to find a way to sway Mathias and Callan from doing this even if they did find Tony guilty according to the rules of their world.

She didn't know the rules of anyone's world, hers included, but she did know she couldn't stand by and watch anyone sacrificed to a deadly croggle. Then again, she had not been forced to witness the brutal killing of innocent children either.

Before she had a chance to convince Mathias that killing TecKnati wouldn't solve their problems, Etoi and several of their half-sized warriors came pounding into the village proper, the cleared area where the four of them stood.

"They escaped," Etoi cried out.

Callan stepped to the center of the group. "The prisoners?"

"Yes."

Rayen couldn't believe Tony would leave Gabby and her to find a way home on his own. Or had something else happened to him? She wouldn't put it past Etoi to vent her hatred of TecKnati on a hapless prisoner and dispose of Tony's body. Or had the scout taken Tony hostage? That had to be what happened, but what was the chance of convincing Callan or Mathias of that possibility?

Zero.

Mathias pushed forward, demanding. "How did the TecKnati get out of the Isolation Unit without being burned to death by the energy enclosing the hut?"

"I don't know." Etoi's dark eyes swung to Rayen, accusing. "The scout was searched before being put inside the unit. He had nothing on him. We didn't search these *others* for weapons or hidden technology."

Callan raised his hand. "Neither of these two—" He nodded at Gabby and me. "Could've done it. They've been with Jaxxson or me the whole time." He turned to Mathias and lowered his voice, though Rayen could still hear due to standing so close. "There's only one way to leave the Isolation Unit and that's by the hand of a MystiK in this village."

She caught the meaning beneath Callan's words. He thought one of his own had released the prisoners.

A traitor?

Someone working with the TecKnati?

Mathias merely nodded. His mouth pressed into a firm line. He ordered Zilya, "Organize a hunt. Find them."

Zilya started issuing orders to Etoi and her small band of warriors. Within minutes, another thirty children around ten to fifteen in age flooded into the area, all carrying weapons capable of deadly harm. Some looked fragile and all were dressed in ragtag outfits, but their expressions were determined. A sort of stab-first-and-ask-questions-later bunch, which wasn't looking good for Tony.

Rayen stepped up. "I'll go."

At the same time, Callan and Mathias said, "No."

Then Callan added, "I can't allow you to help your friend." His next thought trailed off in his eyes.

With one look at him, she knew what he was thinking. If she interfered, he'd have no choice but to use deadly force against her. Her dying wouldn't help Tony, or Gabby either, but that didn't mean she liked the implied threat in Callan's gaze.

Gabby moved close to her and whispered, "You think Tony abandoned us?"

"No."

"Strangely, I don't either." She glanced around before adding, "But I don't trust that Etoi not to hurt him if she can catch him alone."

Rayen nodded, but she couldn't stop Mathias and what had grown to be a formidable hunting party of armed warriors.

When Mathias made a motion with his hand for his hunters to head out, Callan stopped him. "I'll go with them, Mathias. Take Rayen to see V'ru."

"No." Mathias spoke just as softly, but Rayen heard him. "I can use the exercise and you take her to V'ru. While you're at it, do me a favor and check on the preparations for the BIRG Day celebration. I know it sounds trivial at this moment, but we promised that to the children and those putting it together don't want me to see what they are creating."

Mathias rubbed his head, giving Rayen the impression he found something tedious about this celebration.

Callan offered, "Sure you don't want to delay it until tomorrow?"

"No. This is the first tradition we've upheld here. I'm not much for parties, but I'll do it for the children. This Tony will be easy to track. Tell them to have the party ready to go as soon as I return."

Callan gave him a long, concerned look.

The grim set of Mathias's jaw softened. "Remember, our first responsibility after keeping these children safe is to give them hope. No matter what it takes to do that. It doesn't matter if celebrating is the last thing we feel like doing, always think of them first." He offered a tight, half-smile. "The scout may know this land, but the other captive doesn't. If I find Tony first, I'll return with him, or his body, in time for the celebration. Find out who *she* is before I return. I *must* know."

Then he pivoted away and took off running.

Rayen had to be the "she" Mathias ordered Callan to find out about. But the dire warning in Mathias's voice worried her. Something had changed in the way Mathias viewed her and she had no reason to believe it was a positive change.

Callan snapped around, pointing at Gabby. "You, stay with Jaxxson. A warning. When I'm in the village, he can reach me telepathically if he needs me."

So that's what had been happening when Callan exchanged looks with Mathias and that's how Callan had heard about the little boy being in distress.

Rayen asked Gabby, "You sure you're okay with Jaxxson?"

"Yes."

That left no room for question. Gabby didn't have that empty, don't-step-too-close look in her face she'd worn when Rayen first met her. Something profound had happened while Gabby had worked with the children and the healer.

Or because of something Jaxxson had done to her.

"You." Callan speared his finger at me.

How had she ended up as 'you' again with Callan after all they'd done together? "You forget my name?"

He ignored her sarcasm. "The girl is Hy'bridt and the escaped prisoner you call a friend is TecKnati. That leaves the mystery of who you are. I'm tired of guessing. You will answer V'ru's questions. He can discover who or what you are. Follow me."

Her heart hammered her chest with two fists. He hadn't even suggested that she might be MystiK. Not that she wanted to be, but right now that was the only winning side in the war these kids waged with the TecKnati.

On the other hand, wasn't that what she wanted? To find out who she really was? Could this V'ru know her history, know who she was? And where she came from?

If these children were from the future, maybe V'ru had information on the past.

On the surface, that sounded somewhat encouraging, until she considered the alternative.

What if this elite MystiK V'ru decided she had some type of connection to the TecKnati? Callan spoke of him in reverence and Mathias would make his final decision based upon what V'ru alone revealed.

What would Callan vote to do with her if V'ru declared her the enemy?

CHAPTER 28

WHAT HAD HAPPENED TO THE jungle?

Tony kept taking in this forest, trying to figure out where that TeK scout was going. This place was just as funky looking, but not as dense as the jungle Tony had traveled through right after being dumped out of the pod. He doubted the thickly wooded, tree-looking growths that towered overhead, or the more open terrain at the base of the trees offered any more safety.

'Specially for a Camden-raised dude.

Eyeing the red moon through the canopy of branches, he used that marker to keep track of his direction since leaving the village. That moon kept sliding down.

What happened in this place when the moon sets?

He swatted low-hanging branches that smelled like petro-chemicals out of the way and kept that scout, Phen, in sight. The Tek guy wound through knee-high, berry-covered bushes and trees with twisted limbs. If you could call these things he ran past trees.

Trees were supposed to have brown or gray bark, not chartreuse stripes and tubular leaves. Not puffy and corkscrew shaped things in shades of black, pink and purple.

Tony stumbled over jagged breaks in the ground that could be roots and pushed through a clump of spiky bushes that looked like the barbed wire on top of prison fences. Sweat stung his eyes, streamed down his neck and soaked his shirt.

Where was this scout going? Why hadn't he headed the other way through the jungle? Didn't he want to snag a pod, or transender as Mathias had called it, and fly home? The guy moved through this big-ass forest as though he had a specific direction in mind but kept looking around as if he watched for someone. Or wanted to avoid someone. Who?

Don't let there be any other crazies out here running loose.

What if this guy stayed somewhere in this place, like in a guard shack, and was heading there instead of back to a transender pod?

Don't think that way.

This whole place was jacked-up crazy enough.

Tony had never touched anything that could screw with his brain, but just this once, he almost wished he was tripping on acid. That'd mean there was an end to this nightmare. But no, he was lucid and breathing hard from more exercise than a Jersey boy needed to work on computers. The muggy air he slogged through reminded him of a heat wave in Camden last summer.

Xena is cut out for this native crap. Not me.

But Tony wouldn't admit that to anyone.

Once he found a way home, he'd prove who'd had the skills for getting away from here.

The scout slowed down just before the woods thinned ahead.

Tony hurried, closing the distance to fifteen feet and tucking in behind a sprawling tree. He scanned the wide-open space beyond the tree line.

No towering pod, transender or other transport unit out there. Crapola. This might've been a big mistake.

Phen stood in knee-high, weedy grass, clearly looking for something, then must have found it. He ran two steps and shoved his hand into a ... pink flower!

Tony had no time to yell a warning.

But even though the flower looked just like the one that had attacked him earlier, it made no threatening move toward Phen.

In fact, in the next five seconds, a holographic screen appeared chest high in the air near the scout who stood up, withdrawing his hand from the flower.

The screen lit up and a hot feminine voice announced, "*One hour, twenty-eight minutes left to request transender return from Sphere.*"

Tony's heart rate soared. There was a time limit for calling up a transender. He had to find Gabby and Rayen fast.

Lifting his hand, Phen placed his right palm against the translucent screen. A red line streaked around the outline of his hand then started blinking until it turned bright green. The minute that happened, the scout yanked his hand back and the woman said, "*Request acknowledged.*"

Then the screen vanished without a sound.

When Phen hurried toward the open space, Tony took off right behind him. Cobra dude was going nowhere until he told Tony how to get out of this hellhole.

A high-pitched whining started.

He knew that sound and increased his speed.

Bursting from the trees, he noticed a gigantic burned croggle lying dead fifty yards away. Had Rayen fought *that*? Tony closed to within three steps behind Phen who'd been jogging along. Phen must have heard Tony's footsteps. He cast a ragged glance over his shoulder. "What the–"

Phen kicked up his speed.

You don't grow up on the streets of south Jersey and not be fast in a sprint.

Tony raced ahead, cringing as the whining grew louder.

On the far side of the clearing, dirt and other particles spun an orange-red tornado in one spot. The whirling image of a huge bullet-shaped metallic object started taking shape.

The spinning stopped at once. There stood the pod again.

Busting a gut, Tony growled and powered forward with everything he had. He went airborne, body tackling Phen, taking them both down hard and rolling.

Just like back home when an a-hole kid had pushed over Tony's little brother and tried to run.

Sucking gulps of thick air, Tony jumped on Phen's back while he was still face down. He shoved his knee hard and wrenched one of the guy's arms behind his back. That move exposed the rest of the guy's cobra tattoo that wrapped around a triangular shape like an A with three circles worked into the design. It had a small barcode beneath it.

"Let me go!" Phen yelled, pounding the dirt.

"Not gonna happen until you tell me what I want to know. Asked you nice back in that hut. Not askin' this time."

"I've only got minutes to embark since the transender is here. Or it returns without me."

Good to know. But even better was the panic in Phen's voice.

Tony growled, "Then time is of the essence, right, buddy? Stop wasting seconds. What happens if you don't get inside in time?"

Phen slapped his free hand on the ground again. "*You* can't make it work."

"Pay attention, dweeb. I'm not a MystiK and I can sit here for hours. Won't take the others long to figure out we both escaped. They'll be here soon." And Tony had to have information before that happened.

"Okay. I'll tell. I'll tell."

Tony loosened his grip, but only a bit.

Phen continued, "Doesn't matter anyhow since you can't travel without an authorized scout. Once a transender is called up, you have only three minutes to get inside, or it leaves without you."

Tony leaned down close. "Letting you go depends on how well you convince me that you are tellin' the truth. I'll know the second you start lyin'. One lie and you're stayin' here with me. Understand?"

"Yes. Just hurry. What do you want?"

Nothing like fear to loosen a tongue. Another Jersey lesson learned early and well. Tony started firing questions. "Saw you call it up with your hand on a screen. I'm guessin' it works for more than one handprint."

Phen expelled a pained noise as if he'd made a grave error by allowing Tony to see him activate the holographic panel, but he kept answering as fast as he could spit the words out. "My palm print calls up the transender that brought me here. No one can call that one but me during a moon cycle."

"What?"

"Transenders can only travel to and from this Sphere while the red moon is in view overhead. Once the moon sets, the lunar surface energy diminishes to the point that it's too dangerous to risk coming or going." Phen continued without needing a nudge. "Human molecules have to be suspended while the unit transcends from one dimension to another. We still have a few flaws that haven't been worked out yet."

Oh, man, why can't I have an hour with this guy? Tony asked, "What happens if you miss *this* transender?"

"You can't do that to me," Phen pleaded in a voice pitched high with hysteria. "Transenders are reprogrammed daily. I can't call up another one once I've activated this one. And if the MystiKs find me again they'll torture then kill me."

"Then talk faster. What happens if a MystiK takes a transender without an escort?" If Tony had something to offer Mathias that his group could use to escape this place, he might be willing to let him, Rayen and Gabby leave.

"Not possible," Phen whined, stomping on Tony's hope. "The palm screen is programmed not to work for a MystiK. Even if they could call a transender, they'd die of asphyxiation once the transender returned if they didn't have the daily exit code entered as a secondary security."

That's no use. If he, Gabby and Rayen found a way to the transender that brought them, would a return trip suffocate all of them? But he doubted this guy would know that answer.

Phen drew a quick breath. "I've got to go in the next thirty seconds. Have to take this one. Let me go ... or be responsible for my death."

Decision made. Tony had no reason to cause Phen's death and he wouldn't trust Zilya not to kill this guy.

Getting up, he helped Phen off the ground for the second time today and told him, "You better hope I find a way home. If not, I'm gonna be your worst enemy if you come back and hurt any of those kids."

Of all the things Tony expected Phen to say, "Thanks," had not been on the list.

A whirring noise started again.

Phen rushed to the transender and put his hands on the side. He swung his head around and yelled, "Same person has to palm the outside of the transender to open it."

Freebie intel. Sweet.

Two of the tall panels covering the exterior slid apart.

Phen dove inside as the panels snapped shut and the pod started spinning ... then poof, it vanished.

Dusting off as much of the red clay as possible, Tony strode back to the trees to find that flower. When he did, he couldn't convince himself to stick his hand down into those pink petals. But the longer he studied the plant, the more he became convinced it was one heck of a reproduction.

Nothing moved. No breathing in and out like the killer flower had done. But now that he thought about it, there had been *other* big-ass pink flowers around. While hiking through the jungle, Rayen had told him about watching for the flower breathing.

This one acted dead as a corpse.

Good camouflage for a TecKnati transender call panel.

As much as hesitating put him at risk of being discovered, Tony couldn't go back without knowing for sure that he could find this panel again. When he convinced himself to walk all the way up to the plant, and after he'd left his phone several yards away, he thought he'd beaten his nerves. But his fingers shook like old Mr. Belokov waiting for Sol's bar to open. When Tony stuck his arm toward the pink petals they might as well have been shark jaws.

Sweat broke out on his forehead. He leaned over, looking inside the opening that was wide enough for two arms. But he couldn't see all the way to the bottom of the dark hole.

Just do it.

But Phen and these crazy MystiKs were from another world even if Phen had called it Earth.

Time was of the essence.

Ah, hell. Tony took one for the team and jabbed his hand down into the hole. His fingers reached tentatively further ... more ... until he touched a round knob. Okay, good sign. Breathing hard, he pushed the knob.

Nothing happened.

Curling his fingers around it, he tried twisting one way then the other.

That's when the knob turned, and he heard a loud *click*.

A holographic screen came alive just out from his left shoulder and that killer female voice announced, "*One hour, twenty minutes left to request transender return from Sphere.*"

So this place was a Sphere? More to figure out later. His ticket home was calling.

Looking around to assure no one was sneaking up on him, Tony lifted his hand to the screen. The same red line traced around his palm, blinking, then stayed solid red.

The female voice came on again. "*Request denied.*"

Compatibility bitch!

Tony knew, now, that this was not the same location where he, Rayen and Gabby had exited the transender. Would this work for *Rayen* if Tony could find a similar holographic screen near where the three of them had arrived in this place? Rayen's hand had started the computer freaking out back at the lab. So maybe that's what was needed here.

He wouldn't find out if he didn't get back to the village and figure out a way to break out the other two in the next eighty minutes. Based on what Phen had said, if they didn't find their original pod, they might not be able to return at all. And they couldn't get the transender activated unless they found the right panel.

Damn.

Blowing out a breath and cracking his knuckles, Tony looked skyward until he had a bead on the moon position that he'd noted on the way here. Using that, he started double-timing it back to the village.

Now all he had to do was find his way without getting lost. Not get killed or eaten by vines. Not become dinner for some weird-ass animal. Not get stopped or caught by some of the village gang.

If he managed all that, and survived, he still had to pass through the skin-peeling fog around the village.

And he'd thought growing up in Jersey was rough.

Tony found a stick that had a velvet-like bark and started thrashing his way back. He kept checking the moon through the speckled leaves and could swear that orb had picked up speed on its downward slide to the horizon.

Unless the moon was moving around, it should stay on his left all the way back. Simple astronomy.

Between keeping up with the moon's movement and trying to find his way back, he started sensing he was lost. His cell phone was stuck on the time displayed when he'd entered this place. Who knew technology could backfire? His best guess was that he'd been walking for about fifteen, maybe twenty minutes. That meant he had somewhere around an hour to find Rayen and Gabby, figure a way out of the village and call up the transender.

And what if I can't find a freakin' fake pink flower at our transender site?

Or if Rayen's palm wouldn't activate the holographic screen?

Or if Rayen hadn't returned to the village and still wandered around this godforsaken jungle with that crazy warrior and his friends?

If any of the boys from back home were in his shoes and had his computer skills, they'd just skip the village, find their way back to the right transender location and take their chances with the holographic panel to access the pod.

But Tony didn't throw *his* friends under the bus. No way.

Rayen might be clueless about technology, but she was turning out to be tough and decent.

And Gabby had paid for helping him fight the flower vine by getting an infection he hoped hadn't killed her.

Tony couldn't name one person who'd do what either of those two had for him.

Bottom line, he was going nowhere without Xena and Psycho Babe.

A wisp of movement caught his eye.

He shifted right and hunkered down behind a bush with feathery leaves that smelled like Mrs. Wolsinski's cabbage soup she cooked every Thursday. Easing up to watch, he listened for the crackle of feet snapping twigs and branches.

Of course, these people were like Rayen who could move through a jungle or forest like a shadow.

There it was.

One of the pint-size warriors about twelve years old popped into view at a distance. One of those kids with the freaky purple eyes marched calmly through the woods, not sneaking as though they were trying to catch someone.

Tony could hide from them and try to make his way back, but even if he did find the village, he still faced having to get through the fog wall.

And he was running out of time.

He stood up and moved into a clear area, waving his hands. "Hey, guys. Over here. Glad to see ya."

Etoi popped into view between him and the kids. She took one look at him and came flying at him, drawing back her arm to throw her spear.

"*Whoa! Hold it!*" Tony yanked his head down. The whistle of the weapon reached him just as it missed him. He dove sideways, crashing into a sticky bush, kicking his legs to get free.

Were all the girls in this place insane? The sound of someone running all out in his direction got him moving. He pushed to his feet, pulse pounding with adrenaline. Had to get away from Godzilla's bride.

Wheeling around quickly, he spied her.

She yanked her spear from the ground and hoisted it, spinning to face him from no more than ten feet away. Close enough for her to make him into a shish kebab.

Tony raised his hands above his head. "Wait a minute, babe. I was comin' in. Givin' myself up."

Out of nowhere, Mathias stepped in front of him.

Tony had never been so glad to see someone. Not that he wanted the crazy witch to skewer anyone else, but he doubted she'd make the mistake of attacking her boss.

Mathias ordered, "Put down your spear."

Etoi lowered her weapon but pointed a finger at Tony. "He released the prisoner. The scout will report to SEOH."

"We'll deal with that *if* it happens. We don't know that the scout isn't still wandering around in the Sphere."

Tony mumbled, "Glad *someone* in charge isn't hormonal."

Muscles bunched from exertion, Mathias turned on Tony, snarling, "Shut up. You've caused us enough trouble." With a flick of his hand, Mathias called up his boys. "Restrain him."

"Hey, I was wavin' my hands, coming to you," Tony complained. "That's a sign of surrender." Granted he'd had no white flag, but still. "Where I come from, we talk after someone gives up."

Sometimes. Other times, they beat the crap out of you for being stupid enough to get caught, but he figured these guys wouldn't know Jersey rules.

He *hoped* they didn't know them. "I've been tryin' to find my way back. You found me headin' *toward* the village, not away. Doesn't that count for somethin'?"

Mathias vibrated with anger. "You've released the TecKnati scout we captured. Nothing will save you from judgment now."

"No, no. You got that all wrong." Tony backed up, but two boys moved forward, spears jabbing at his neck. A third one stepped in front of him, wrapping Tony's hands and arms to his body then winding those crazy red vines around his legs. He protested the whole time, "Listen to me. I didn't break us out. The other guy did."

Someone slapped a wide, flat leaf over his mouth then wound a vine around that twice. No matter how hard he tried, all the sound he could make was a muted mumble. Then they tied him to a long pole that two of the taller kids hoisted over their shoulders and carried him back toward the village like a pig on the way to being roasted.

Now he couldn't even yell the information to Rayen and Gabby so they could get to a transender on their own.

Mathias might not let them go either if he thought they had any part in Tony escaping.

We're so screwed.

CHAPTER 29

WHY IS RAYEN LOOKING AT me as if I've wronged her?

Callan kept his chin up, refusing to allow Rayen's brooding silence to bother him. She kept pace with his fast stride toward the Governing chamber. Anger burrowed deep in her gaze during the brief moments she flicked a look his way.

He had not put her in this position.

She was a prisoner. Even if V'ru cleared her from being TecKnati, Rayen was still in league with his enemy otherwise why had she helped the scout earlier and called Tony a friend?

Callan refused to believe he'd seen hurt in her face when he'd ordered her to meet with V'ru. *Never allow an enemy to get close.* Something he should have been thinking about when he'd almost kissed her in the woods.

Did she wield some power over him?

No. Even he could not accuse her of that. He'd know if anyone used power against him. The only times he'd witnessed her tapping an energy force had been to kill croggles, twice, and to help save that little boy.

She confused him.

Maybe that was her game, to confuse him and Mathias while her friend, Tony, the without-question TecKnati, had aided the scout in fleeing.

But that left Rayen and Gabby to fend for themselves, which would fit the selfish mentality of a TecKnati like Tony. So why would Rayen do anything to help him? Or continue to defend him?

Was she thinking the same thing right now? That her so-called friend had abandoned her and the Hy'bridt?

Betrayal cut. Callan knew that firsthand.

Why should I care? He had a duty to his people and these three strangers were creating problems he didn't have time to deal with today, not with the stupid celebration for Mathias's turning eighteen before the moon set in less than an hour. He was no longer in a hurry to enforce a judgment against Rayen's friend.

A TecKnati, he reminded himself.

But Rayen would not look at him the way she had in the forest if he sent Tony to his death. *Why did that matter?*

Callan lifted his hand to his neck and rubbed the tight muscles, cursing himself for whatever had gotten under his skin. He never vacillated on decisions and couldn't now.

Rayen broke into his jumbled thoughts when she leaned close to say, "Callan?"

Her rich voice rushed over his skin with the edgy feel of a vibration. A confused part of his brain was cheered over her finally speaking to him and in a non-angry tone. But he must remember he still dealt with an enemy.

He intended to answer with a sharp, "Yes," but the single word came out gentle.

"Will they bring Tony back alive?"

Of course. She only wanted to know about the TecKnati. "Maybe."

"What kind of answer is that?" she demanded, her brisk tone irritating him.

Maybe a little irritation was just what he needed to shut down any stupid reactions he had when she got near him. "That's the best answer I can give. If he doesn't harm one of our own, then Mathias will very likely bring him back alive. If not, Mathias knows his first duty is to protect MystiKs, especially the next generation."

"Tony won't harm a child."

Callan stopped and faced her, his voice whipcord hard. "You told me you have no knowledge of anything before today when you opened your eyes in a strange desert, but you speak of this Tony as if you've known him your whole life. How can you make *any* claim as to his character or be so sure he's not TecKnati? Especially after he left you and Gabby to face the result of his escape."

"I may not have known him long, but I know Tony would never harm a child and I *don't* believe he'd leave us by choice. The scout might have taken him as a hostage."

He didn't want to admire Rayen's sense of loyalty to someone she claimed she hardly knew. In her position, he'd be furious with Tony. No TecKnati deserved this type of unquestioned support or the earlier sacrifice Rayen had made to step in, taking Tony's place as the fourth person to check the transender lines.

And how had Tony thanked her?

By disappearing without a word.

How could someone as selfless as Rayen appeared befriend a soulless TecKnati?

And why was Callan so furious on her behalf?

Because her commitment to Tony and constant arguing on his behalf chipped away at Callan's conviction that Tony was TecKnati.

Made him doubt himself.

That was the quickest way to wake the bear inside him and bring out the raging warrior, because warriors could not afford to doubt their decisions.

Standing firm on his opinion, he crossed his arms and gave his answer in a voice meant to quell an enemy. "Believe what you will. But the question is, what will *you* do when your friend is brought back by Mathias, proving Tony did not return on his own?"

Pain eased into Rayen's gaze over the long moment she spent thinking before quietly admitting, "I don't know."

Callan should enjoy his moment of triumph, but the disappointment riding alongside Rayen's doubt made him feel like he'd been cruel to a pupple.

Why did she cause him to question everything he did, every word he spoke ... and stir up the urge to protect her from being harmed?

With her standing so close, he battled to keep his hands to himself.

Rayen might handle herself as a warrior, but she was feminine in a strong way he found attractive. And sexy. He couldn't keep his eyes off the exposed skin below what was left of her shirt. That sliver of cloth barely covered shapely breasts.

His thoughts skidded to a halt. *Wrong direction. Think enemy.*

Rayen's gaze had wandered past Callan.

He turned to find out what held her interest.

Three girls ranging from thirteen to fifteen created decorations for Mathias's celebration. They were watching him and Rayen with guarded glances. He knew nothing about decorating for a party and felt sure Mathias had raced off to hunt Tony just to dump a "leader" duty on Callan. He told Rayen, "Stay here. I'll be right back."

Striding over to the girls without a look back at Rayen, Callan searched for the right thing to say. "Are you almost done?"

All three girls turned looks of panic on him. Guess that was not the right leader thing to say.

Rayen appeared at his side, ignoring his glare at blatantly disregarding his order for her to stay put. She smiled at the girls. "Those are beautiful."

As if someone had released the air in a taut balloon, the girls all let out a breath at the same time and became active again.

Phoebe, the one in charge, lifted a pango orb made of the brightly colored feathers from little pik-pik birds and answered, "Oh, thank you." She peeked up at Callan. "We have only to hang these along the vines and cover the floor with tullee petals."

When his gaze landed on the pile of hōzuki lantern flowers with their orange coloring and transparent skins, he followed Rayen's example and smiled. "Those are pretty."

All three girls turned adoring eyes up at him as if some mythical god had spoken to them.

Rayen angled her head at him in a way that made him want to say, "What?" The universal word every male spouted when faced with silent female accusation.

Rayen asked the girls, "What do you call those?"

Swapping shy looks between them, Phoebe once again played spokesperson. "Our version of a Physalis alkekengi wreath, which is meant for many years of happiness and health. The *real* ones are made of blown glass ... at home."

No one could have missed the misery in Phoebe's mention of home.

Once again, Callan had no idea what to say that would lessen the hurt in Phoebe's voice. Mathias could always find the right words at a time like this, but he was not here. *And he shouldn't have stuck me with this.*

Wait until the next training. Mathias would pay for putting Callan in this position.

Rayen scrunched her eyebrows together in thought, glanced from Callan's face to the girls, trying to figure out something. When she spoke to the three girls, her voice carried a sincerity that reached out and touched anyone close. "But these decorations are more delicate than anyone could craft from glass. When you go home, you may become famous for creating these and be sought after to teach others this art."

"Art? You really think so?" Phoebe asked, glancing up through silver bangs at Rayen.

"Of course. Change is good." Callan caught on quickly and added, "Every generation should leave its own mark."

All three girls' faces lit with enthusiasm, then Rayen said, "Artists capture moments in history for others to enjoy over a lifetime."

The girls started chattering amongst themselves about different ways to customize the Physalis alkekengi. Phoebe paused and looked up with brighter eyes at Rayen first then Callan. "Thank you."

The other two chimed in their appreciation right behind her then went back to discussing their new possibilities. Callan experienced something he hadn't felt in a long while. Making someone happy warmed his heart. A moment ago, those three had only been doing their duty, but now they had a calling as artists, even though none of them came from the Creativity House.

What would Rayen do next?

He had to get to the bottom of just who she was before this got any more complicated. He stepped away, ordering her, "Follow me and do not stray."

"I wasn't the one who took this detour," she reminded him.

He clamped his jaws shut, unwilling to say another word that would give her an opening to cloud his judgment further.

A wise plan that would have worked if Rayen had complied by not asking, "What're you celebrating?"

Ignoring her might send the message that she made him uncomfortable. A warrior never appeared weak or unsure. "Mathias will reach the age of maturity prior to moonset. In my world, reaching one's eighteenth BIRG Day marks the end of childhood."

"What is a BIRG Day?"

"It's the annual celebration of one's birth. We have a BIRG Day each year and a BIRG Con once every five years where those who have reached eighteen since the last BIRG Con are honored before representatives from all the Houses."

"So, the BIRG Con is a big deal?"

He shrugged. "One may have a BIRG Day every year, but a BIRG Con only once in a lifetime."

"Must be hard for you and Mathias to keep everyone's spirits up with no idea when you're going home."

Her unexpected compassion chipped at his hard shell and struck close to his heart. She saw past the decorations and celebrating to the plight of the MystiKs in the Sphere. She'd understood more than he'd given her credit for. She'd understood the need to care about tomorrow as much as today.

Mathias would tell Callan to welcome any opportunity to improve the morale of the village, even if the encouragement came from a stranger.

He had taught Callan that part of his duty while in the Sphere was to smile in the face of disaster and on his worst days. Just like a warrior, leaders did not show weakness.

For that reason, Callan would smile during the celebration of Mathias's BIRG Day despite it being a huge nuisance and waste of time. In truth, Callan didn't really mind because Mathias deserved a special celebration after having spent the last year in here instead of a final adolescent year of carefree time most in his position enjoyed.

This would not be the extravagant production Mathias would receive at home, or at this year's BIRG Con, the symbolic–and often too realistic–end of childhood. As a Gild Level, Mathias would be first in line to the next Governing House leader. Mathias deserved to lead the Governing House and Callan would do everything in his power to make sure his friend got that chance.

Mathias was built of integrity, but he also understood when he had to be sly, like turning TecKnati lies into a morale booster by leaving the party tonight. Knowing Mathias, he would not lounge around and use the time to rest. He'd show up tomorrow evening with something for dinner. And truth be told, he would probably enjoy a night alone without sixty kids looking to him for guidance.

But Callan couldn't watch his friend's back if Mathias was outside the village and Callan was stuck inside here babysitting. TeK Scouts had told all the MystiKs they would only be here until they were eighteen. Only someone who drank shroom juice would believe that, but Mathias had been adamant about using that story to keep hope alive in the hearts of the children. Callan and Mathias had created a plan to make it appear as though Mathias did leave this evening.

A plan that Etoi or Zilya could not know about since Etoi had no leash on her tongue and Callan didn't trust Zilya.

A night of solitude might be the best gift of all for Mathias.

Callan entered the common area where a thirteen-year-old boy supervised the food being prepared for the feast. He used the word "feast" loosely. They'd been anticipating preparing fresh roasted croggle meat for this evening's celebration, but now they were reduced to tullee pods and dried banban seeds.

Rayen's gaze swept over everyone, her face closed off as she kept her thoughts to herself while matching Callan step for step.

Crossing the open area to reach the Governing chamber, Callan returned polite smiles to all the excited faces turning toward him ... all but one.

Neelah rarely had a smile for anyone these days, every glare blaming the Warrior House and Governing House for pulling her away from her betrothed. Callan might feel some sympathy for the girl if she'd direct her anger at the TecKnati, not other MystiKs who suffered alongside her. Neelah was not the first, nor probably the last to leave a betrothed behind.

Entering the Governing Chamber, Callan crossed the room to one of the carved chairs and sat down, weary from using so much energy to heal.

He waited to see if Rayen would take the other one, but she'd paused just inside the door, thumbs hooked in the top of her blue pants.

Did she have to draw his attention to her narrow waist like that? "Have a seat."

"I'll stand."

So be it. Best way to put himself back on firm footing with her was by not treating her as a guest. That might also help toss a wet rag on this strange awareness of her that kept his thoughts in turmoil.

Rayen took one look around and moved further inside the doorway then crossed her arms. "Where's V'ru and what makes him so special?"

Callan wanted to slap himself. He'd forgotten to tell V'ru to meet him. Holding up his hand in a sign for Rayen to wait, he sent a brief telepathic call to V'ru, asking him to join Callan to interrogate a prisoner.

Finally, he answered, "He's a G'ortian, a rare descendant of the Records House. He's on the way."

"Did you just call him telepathically?"

"Yes."

Even motionless, Rayen emitted a silent power. "What's a G'ortian?"

"Someone of unusual gifts and powers that develop very young." That's how he saw V'ru, but not himself. When he looked in the mirror, he saw a waste of power that should have gone to someone else, someone like his twin brother who would have used it to lead. G'ortian abilities were too unknown, too unpredictable to be used by a warrior.

Rayen asked, "Are you going to give Tony a real chance to tell his side of what happened today?"

That again? "What is it you think he can explain about escaping that's not obvious? At least, to everyone else but you."

"I told you. Maybe he had no choice and was taken as a hostage." Her words were given in an even tone, but there was nothing easygoing about the snap of her dark eyes.

"If your friend was taken hostage then the decision will be simple."

Rayen's body relaxed, the combative edge leaving her gaze and tone. "Good. I was worried you'd just find him guilty no matter what."

He hated to destroy Rayen's moment of relief, but she had misunderstood him. "If your friend *was* taken hostage, Mathias won't have to make any decision, because the TecKnati do not take hostages. If the scout does not recognize your friend, he will assume Tony is a TecKnati traitor who has gained unauthorized access to the Sphere and kill him."

Rayen looked away, her face schooled to reveal nothing when she turned to him again. "Having Tony end up dead would suit you just fine, wouldn't it?"

She made him sound heartless. He hadn't ordered her friend's death. Yet. What would she do in his place? "I only told you the truth."

"Then here's the truth, too. I hope Tony did manage to escape on his own, because I don't want him to die. He's not a traitor or anything else and hasn't harmed any of you."

"He *is* a–"

"TecKnati. I get it. You *hate* TecKnati and you *think* Tony is one therefore you're justified in hating him."

When she put it that way, the correlation sounded completely irrational, but he'd already figured out that she had a way with words. A skill he had never developed.

With no better argument, he waved a hand at her. "I don't play word games."

She moved so quickly he couldn't get up before she towered over him, an avenging angel with her hands gripping each corner of the chair back at his shoulders, locking him into place. Yes, he could shove her across the room. She'd sworn to not use her powers against him, but he was bigger, and physically, he was stronger, and he had kinetic powers she didn't know about yet, though that gift was still evolving. The bottom line was that he didn't want to harm her.

On the other hand, maybe she'd like a little sparring match. Talking to her might be easier if he let her work off some of that bottled-up fury.

She leaned her head down. "Word games? I'm *not* playing games with someone's life. You can't just declare someone an enemy without reason. As a leader, you're expected to be fair and consider all possibilities."

What had been *fair* about killing MystiK children?

"Mathias is the leader. I'm his sword arm." He angled his head back, trying not to be distracted by the sizzle of her emotions roiling through the air. "Regardless, do *not* think to tell me my duty. Every person here is my responsibility. And everyone here *has* been harmed by TecKnati. Do not dare to tell me how to handle the travesties committed by our enemy. Crimes they must be punished for."

"I'd understand your punishing a crime committed here, but you blame Tony for crimes he hasn't committed. That's wrong!"

He lifted a hand to cup her face and stopped himself, folding all his fingers until only his index finger stood. "Here's what's wrong–TecKnati using their advanced technology to commit heinous crimes with no chance of being caught."

"You're okay with holding anyone you merely *suspect* of being TecKnati accountable for a death?" Rayen's low voice bubbled with fierce determination. "How is that right? Or fair?"

"You want to talk fair? They murdered Jornn, my twin brother and sent his body home for my mother to see, his bowels hanging out and a triangle hole where his heart had once been." Callan grabbed the sides of his chair in death grips and pushed up into her face. "They tortured him, brutalizing every inch of his body except his face. TecKnati wanted that to be my mother's last vision of her oldest son."

Rayen stared open mouthed then dropped her head, her shoulders easing, her voice lowered. "I'm sorry. I didn't mean …"

He hadn't meant to talk about Jornn. He'd kept that pain locked behind a strong wall, hidden from the world. Grief welled up in his throat until he couldn't breathe.

His amazing, gifted brother, the one expected to take over the Warrior House. The one who possessed all the attributes of a leader his people would follow.

Not me. But Callan would do whatever it took to protect these children and find a way home. Too many had died. No more.

"Callan."

When he shook off the suffocating grief, he found Rayen squatting in front of him.

For the past year, he'd worked himself twice as hard as any other warrior he trained for the simple reason that it kept him from thinking. And feeling.

This strange girl had done this to him. Made him feel.

He lifted a calloused thumb to stroke the soft skin on her cheek.

The sound of her voice soothed the beast that wanted out to rampage and kill his enemies. She whispered, "I understand your pain. I'd probably feel the same way if I lost a brother or sister that way." She lifted her hand and touched his arm. "I'm not judging you. I only wanted you to think twice before condemning an innocent person."

Callan lifted his other hand to her face, holding it there in indecision. He wanted to touch his lips to hers, to feel the warmth radiating from her.

"Are you at a disadvantage, Callan?" a young voice called from the doorway.

Rayen stood quickly and backed away.

Callan took a breath, shaking off the strange feeling that had come over him and called out, "No, I'm ready to meet." He stood, angling his head toward the door, and said, "This is V'ru of the Records House. He'll tell me who you are."

CHAPTER 30

STARING AT WONDER BOY V'RU, Rayen wanted to ask Callan if he was the one playing games now. Was he serious about taking advice from some boy whose head didn't reach her shoulder and who wasn't even in his teens yet?

V'ru had gangly stick arms and legs, huge brown eyes, and a toothy smile that fell away the minute he stared up at her. He wore a cloth wound around him that brought the word "toga" to mind for some reason, but he was so skinny the loose clothing looked as though someone had wrapped a toothpick with a napkin. His thick black hair fell mop-like into his face as one small hand kept shoving it out of his eyes.

This was the all-knowing wise one?

"V'ru, this person is known as Rayen," Callan said, by way of finishing introductions.

"How old is he?" she muttered, seeing her fate in the hands of a kid who would topple over if she blew on him. Not just her fate, but Tony's, too, if Mathias showed up with the Jersey Jerk captured.

"*He* is eleven years of age and prefers to be spoken to directly rather than treated as though he does not hear you," V'ru said, as though admonishing a small child.

Rayen lifted her hands and struggled to keep a straight face. "No insult meant."

V'ru merely dipped his head slightly, accepting the apology, which caused his hair to slip into his eyes again, then stepped forward to ask Callan, "How may I assist you?"

"We found Rayen and two other unknowns at a new transender location today. We have determined the other female in the trio to be Hy'bridt."

That garnered a slight slant of V'ru's eyebrows in surprise before Callan continued. "We *suspect* the male with them to be TecKnati." Callan glanced at Rayen as if to say, *See? I can be fair, too.*

Even though she now better understood his rabid hatred of his enemies, she still couldn't allow anyone to take the life of someone who had not personally caused harm, or judge Tony based on what others had done. She was betting her life that Tony was not TecKnati. Sure, the Jersey Jerk could be a pain, but that didn't warrant a death sentence.

She considered it a move in the right direction that Callan had used the word "suspect," but that may only have been to prevent her from protesting further.

V'ru held himself very straight, his fragile hands now clasped behind his back. He spoke as if he stood before elders six times his age. "And what do you know of this one?"

This one? She lifted a hand. "Stop right there. I'm not *this one*. If you don't want me to refer to you as if you aren't here, then call me by my name. Rayen."

V'ru's eyes rounded even more at the order. "I see what you have had to suffer, Callan."

What did that mean?

Callan gave V'ru a friendly look unlike anything she'd seen cross his face since meeting him. He clearly had a fondness for this kid. "It's not so bad, V'ru, but I need your answers to help Mathias make a decision on what to do with the three of them."

How could anyone make a life-and-death decision based on a conversation with an eleven-year-old boy?

V'ru made a quarter turn with his body as if he were on a spindle and addressed her. "State your family history."

Spearing Callan with an impatient glance, she summarized what she knew quickly. "I don't know my family history. I woke up this morning in the middle of the desert near the Sandia Mountains with a beast chasing me and with no idea who I am or where I'm from. Some people picked me up in a transport unit with wheels and took me to a school."

"Wheels?"

She nodded, noting that she wasn't the only one who thought that odd.

"Intriguing. How do you know your name is Rayen if you do not know who you are?"

This kid *would* ask that. "I ... uhm, let's just say I do have some innate knowledge, like the fact that I'm seventeen." No point in mentioning the ghost or that she was allergic to peanuts.

Time stretched from one long second to the next as V'ru appeared to study on something before asking another question. "Why did you come here?"

"To this Sphere?"

"Yes." The word might have been short, but V'ru loaded it with serious *of-course* attitude.

"I didn't have a choice. I was in an equipment room at the school with Tony and Gabby, looking for a computer when I turned one on and got sucked into it."

"Computer?" V'ru looked from her to Callan. "That is ... not possible."

Callan interjected, "I thought the same thing, but I believe she *is* telling the truth." He paused, then added, "About the computer."

Meaning I might be lying about everything else? Rayen kept her thought to herself and let that go, speaking to V'ru again. "Anyhow, Tony and Gabby grabbed my arm to keep me from disappearing, but they got pulled in, too. Next thing we know we're in a metal room you call a transender, then spit out here where we end up fighting for our lives *and* saving little kids."

She sent that last comment in Callan's direction to remind him that two children were alive right now because of what she had done as well as the efforts of Gabby and Tony.

His eyes wouldn't meet hers, but she could tell she'd hit the mark by the way his fingers curled into fists and uncurled.

V'ru cocked his head at her. "What year were you born?"

"I don't know, but I'm guessing if I'm seventeen that I was born about 1999 or 2000."

That answer turned V'ru into a statue, staring at her as if she weren't human. When the kid did speak it was with a hushed awe. "No one has ever perfected forward travel through time. Not even the TecKnati."

Callan nodded, "Exactly, so how can this be?"

"Either she lies–"

Rayen snapped, "It's not a lie."

"–or the TecKnati have developed technology I cannot access." V'ru sounded as though that was beyond improbable. He looked right at her when he said, "Give me your blood."

"What?"

"I said–"

Rayen waved him off with her hand. "I know what you said, but I've given up enough blood today."

"Why do you fear me?" V'ru appeared completely baffled.

Fear a skinny eleven-year-old? Insulting. "I'm not afraid of you."

"Then hold out your hand."

Callan explained, "V'ru needs a sample of your blood to process."

She could accept that, though she didn't like getting jabbed with another needle. The Institute had already taken blood samples and fingerprints. With V'ru stuck in this Sphere, she doubted the kid would get results back faster than the school.

Still, to show good faith, she extended her hand with the palm up. V'ru nodded at Callan who produced a short blade from where it had hung in a loop on the belt slung around his waist. She breathed a sigh of relief that he hadn't cut her throat when she'd stood over him earlier. Now he just pricked her finger then backed away as she offered the bubble of blood to V'ru.

What exactly would this kid do with the blood?

Reaching out with two narrow fingers, V'ru carefully lifted a smudge of blood between his thumb and forefinger. He swirled the drop for a minute between his fingers then took a deep breath and closed his eyes.

She watched Callan for his reaction, but he seemed content to wait on whatever V'ru was doing.

When V'ru opened his eyes again, he reached into a pocket on his toga outfit and produced a small cloth to wipe his fingers clean, then put the cloth back. With his arms shoulder-width apart, he lifted his hands, palms facing out.

A bright, translucent image in the shape of a rectangle came to life in midair, like the computer screens that she'd seen in Mr. Suarez's classroom. But this one had no structure holding the floating image in the air. It wasn't even solid.

She pointed. "That's–"

Callan answered, "–a holographic monitor. Shhh. We have to be quiet while V'ru uses his gift to analyze."

V'ru moved his hands back and forth in front of the monitor, tapping in places and pausing images that streamed past faster than she could process. When the kid slowed down, the screen image coalesced into one of a stark, light-filled landscape and a cliff-dwelling abode that brought up the word "home" in her mind.

Were more memories surfacing?

Could this kid truly figure out who she was? Her heart started beating faster. She sucked in a sharp breath, excited. *Home!*

V'ru pushed the screen to his left as if it slid on a track and she felt as though something vital to her disappeared.

She spoke first, aware of half-formed thoughts pushing at her. "I've seen a projection like that before. That's driven by a Cyberprocessor, isn't it?"

"Some are," V'ru allowed, considering her with a curious expression.

"MystiKs do not utilize Cyberprocessors, but you are not MystiK."

She'd survived deadly beasts, a trip through a computer, and spear tips to face this judgment-by-child without trial? *I don't think so.* "I'm getting tired of saying this, but I am *not* TecKnati."

"I believe you."

Callan said, "What?" as she said, "Really?"

Addressing Callan first, V'ru explained, "I must have more time for a complete analysis, but this one–Rayen–has no residue of the K-enzyme, the metallic ink in her system. This ink is what all TecKnati use to mark their human population."

She gave Callan a victorious smirk. "See?"

"However," V'ru continued. "As I said, I need more time to study on this. Your physiology is not of the ancient times that you claim."

Callan returned the smirk but added a dose of suspicion. "So, you *did* lie about coming from the year 2018."

"No, I didn't, but if your boy recorder here is so smart what year am I from?"

She and Callen turned to V'ru who said, "If you know what a Cyberprocessor is then you cannot be from the year 2018 as it was not created until the year 2129, month July, the day 17, time–"

Rayen cut in, "Okay, I get your point and I don't know how I know about Cyberprocessors, only that I do. Just like I know I traveled here from 2018."

No judgment showed in V'ru's expression, in fact nothing crossed that blank little face. He said, "What else can you tell me about when you woke up in the desert?"

"Nothing except that I did recognize the mountains I saw in the desert, but then they took me to the city called Albuquerque."

With a touch of his finger, V'ru slid the floating monitor back in front of his face again, tapping several times before the image returned to the scene with the strange house. "As one of the ten MystiK cities, Albuquerque did exist–"

Callan's eyes rounded. "Really? I've never heard of that."

V'ru paused with a look of strained patience on his face. "That is because you are not a historian. Albuquerque is the city you know as ABQ/City Seven."

"Oh."

"As I was saying, Albuquerque existed in a territory once known as the state of New Mexico during the year 2018, established in 1706 by–"

"That's all we need on Albuquerque, V'ru," Callan said with heavy politeness to smooth over his interruption.

Good thing to know she wasn't the only one anxiously waiting for some concrete information.

"I don't know about it being MystiK or not," Rayen said, wondering if that would work in her favor or against her group. "But since Gabby and Tony *are* familiar with that area, yet aren't familiar with MystiKs, I'm not sure we're talking about the same place."

V'ru opened his thin lips to speak, but Etoi raced into the room, announcing, "We caught the TecKnati."

Rayen turned to face her. "Tony?"

Etoi ignored me, only speaking to Callan. "The one who released the scout. Mathias sends for you."

"I'll speak to Mathias about the recaptured prisoner, but we are almost at the time for celebrating his BIRG Day. Go oversee the final preparations."

"I should help with guarding the TecKnati." Etoi was clearly annoyed at Callan sending her to do a mundane job of preparing a celebration, even one for Mathias. Or maybe especially because it was for him.

V'ru seemed perplexed. "Should we not postpone the BIRG Day so there is no rush, Callan?"

"No. It's important to hold true to our customs, even here. Mathias and I both believe we must not become lax with rituals that are significant to our Houses."

"Mathias will be eighteen. Do you believe what the scouts told us about leaving here at eighteen?" V'ru asked with the first emotion Rayen had heard in his voice. The boy yearned for home, as did all the other children. On top of that, he clearly feared being left.

This new information confused her. "You get to *leave* here at eighteen?"

Callan only said, "That's what the TecKnati scouts told us when we were dropped here."

She'd think that good news, if not for the way his gaze had shifted away when he'd explained the statement. She didn't know that he lied, exactly, but he hid something.

But why would the TecKnati release one of their MystiK captives? Surely, they realized Mathias would go straight to his people and bring the wrath of the MystiKs down on the TecKnati.

Anyone would declare war to regain stolen children.

If she'd thought it was hard to understand the world she'd fallen into earlier in the day, that was nothing compared to the world in this Sphere.

Callan's smile expanded, but with a forced effort. "Of course, I believe we'll leave here at eighteen. My guess is that the TecKnati will use each leader they return as a pawn in negotiating with our Houses. This is clearly about the HERMES space launches that our leaders interrupted. The sooner our Houses know where we are, the quicker they will find a way to return us home."

"That will be soon?" V'ru asked, sounding more like a boy of his age and less like a stuffy know-it-all.

"Yes." Callan nodded with conviction. "Once our Houses and the TecKnati come to an agreement this will all be over. I want you to continue analyzing the information on Rayen while I speak with Mathias." Callan turned to Etoi. "Go now and check on the preparations."

Rayen watched as those two marched out with their orders, fairly sure that she was the only one who realized Callan had not told V'ru and Etoi the whole truth. She didn't know how she knew, but she did.

Why?

She had to reevaluate Callan and didn't like what she suspected.

Anyone who would mislead these kids and raise their hopes only to have those hopes crushed when Mathias didn't leave could be capable of ordering the death of a stranger just because of a scorpion tattoo and an attitude.

Callan couldn't see beyond his grief to pass up a chance for vengeance.

When he dipped his chin, ordering her to follow, then stepped out of the chamber, she rushed to catch up.

If he was willing to kill Tony, he'd better be prepared to kill her as well.

And that meant she had to be prepared to do whatever it took to stop him.

CHAPTER 31

HANGING VERTICALLY FROM THE POLE that was more rigid than it first looked, Tony struggled against the vines, but nothing gave. He sucked air through the slim opening allowed by the leaf covering his mouth. Smelled like one of those cinnamon candies cheap restaurants had on their counters.

He wasn't sucking any mints ever again.

When the kiddie army stopped, someone cut the vines wrapping him and he hit the ground as hard as a bag of cement. That hurt.

Mathias stepped into view, found a handhold between the red vines still wrapping Tony like a neon-red mummy and hoisted him to his feet.

For a second, he thought he was in a different village. This place looked like Party Central with hanging strings of multi-colored flowers, twined vines and a whole bunch of globe plants that reminded Tony of Mr. Tan's Japanese lantern flowers.

Did this bunch celebrate executions?

Gabby walked into view. She shadowed the healer, Jaxxson, who was no longer looking at her as if she topped his list of inconvenient chores. What had happened for him to be giving her the eye, the guy look that said he was interested and waiting to pick the best time to make his move?

Gabby would shut him down in a heartbeat. If Rayen didn't get to him first.

But at least Gabby looked healthy again. When her gaze danced over the crowd and landed on Tony, she broke into a run.

Never thought he'd be so happy to see Psycho Babe.

Mathias put his arm up to stop her from getting close.

Instead, she leaned her head past Mathias. "You okay, Tony?"

Do I look okay, babe? He shook his head, trying to talk, but the only sounds that came out were garbled noises.

"Uncover his mouth," Gabby demanded of Mathias.

You tell him Gab!

"No."

Well, at least she tried.

When Gabby's attention shifted past Mathias, Tony followed her line of sight and, halle-freakin-lujah, Rayen stepped out of that feather structure with Callan, Etoi and some skinny punk kid. Rayen would find a way to get this leaf off Tony's mouth so he could tell Rayen and Gabby he'd found their way home.

But that red moon had dropped pretty low by the time this bunch of munchkins had carried Tony through the fog wall around the village. By his estimate, they had something like forty-five minutes left to call up the transender.

Maybe less. *Cuttin' it short here, people.*

Etoi peeled off from Callan, heading over to where Zilya spoke to Neelah and some other girls who were busy hanging a bunch of feather balls from vines looped between tree limbs overhanging the area. Like the old ladies in Camden draped green, red and white bunting to celebrate St. Anthony's day. Except these colors were weird–purple, oranges and some crazy green blue. Etoi did spare the time to send Tony one more death glare on her way.

"Where did you find him?" Callan asked Mathias when he reached Tony.

Mathias pointed toward the forest area. "On that side of the village. We flushed him from where he hid. Alone. There's no sign of the TecKnati, but I doubt the scout's still here."

Callan nodded. "Take this one to the Isolation Unit."

Tony started shaking his head and grunting noises in Rayen's direction.

Rayen stepped forward. "I want to talk to him."

Callan turned on her. "He has proven himself TecKnati."

"Just give me a moment. Please."

He worked his jaw back and forth then rolled his eyes and said, "And you'll believe what he says?"

Rayen's gaze shifted to Callan. She stared hard into the badass dude's eyes before saying, "Sometimes you just have to look a man in the eye and take his measure to decide if he's telling the truth."

Was that some kind of jungle alpha talk?

Callan didn't speak for or against Tony, but he shifted his gaze to Mathias who granted Callan's silent request by giving a jerky nod of his head. "Do it quickly."

Rayen turned to Tony. "Were you leaving me and Gabby?"

Tony shook his head, hoping Rayen would believe him, but why should she, just based on Mathias bringing Tony back strung up as if he'd abandoned his friends?

Rayen studied on it a moment then asked Callan, "Will you loan me your blade?"

No, Rayen. *I swear I wasn't leaving!* But Tony had no way to shout beyond making panicky sounds.

Accepting the knife, Rayen reached for Tony's hand that was pegged against his thigh by the vines. But instead of a slice, Tony felt a prick at the end of his finger. What the heck?

Rayen lifted the blade point with a drop of blood perched on it. She turned to the little guy who had followed Callan here, but Rayen spoke to Callan. "If you're so certain Tony is TecKnati, then ask V'ru to test this blood for the K-whatever ink."

What? Tony watched as Callan gave V'ru a hand sign to call him forward. The kid touched the blood and rolled it between his fingers.

Just great. Now my life depends on some kid in middle school playing chemist with my blood.

After cleaning his fingers, this V'ru character lifted his palms and a holographic screen appeared, Tony forgot about blood, MystiKs and TecKnati. How had junior pulled up that wicked screen from nothing but thin air? *So* frickin' awesome.

Lowering his hands after a moment, the kid announced, "There are no trace elements of the K-enzyme metallic ink in his blood."

What did that mean? Was it good news? Or bad?

Rayen lifted her fist and gave it a short pump. "All right." She swung around to Callan. "There's your proof."

This was looking good.

"However," the pipsqueak kid added. "I must complete a full analysis for a final determination."

"Now wait a minute," Rayen groused. "You have your proof."

Callan shook his head. "That's one marker, a simple one. We'll give V'ru time to be thorough." That forced smile popped up on his face again. "Send the prisoner to the unit. It's time to start the celebration."

Rayen took one look at Tony and suggested to Callan, "Why do that when he escaped from there once? Wouldn't you prefer to keep him within sight until you make a final decision? Besides, don't you want everyone here for your party?"

Mathias considered this. "The prisoner can't break the bindings." Appearing ready to agree to anything to get this celebration moving, Mathias snapped fingers at two of his hunters and pointed. "Seat him there."

Gabby followed Tony and sat down next to him. She leaned close, whispering, "Rayen and I believe you. We'll figure a way to get you out of here."

He owed Psycho Babe a hug … and to stop calling her Psycho Babe. He nodded and made a grumbling noise.

Gabby whispered, "I don't know what you're saying, but I have a way to find out ... if you're game?"

He nodded. At this point, he'd play Ouija Board with his nose if she could figure out what he needed to tell her and Rayen.

"It means having to speak to you mind-to-mind," she explained.

He rolled his eyes. Just when he was ready to kick her nickname to the curb, she said something like that. It was a good thing he couldn't speak right now because he was sure she wouldn't want to hear what he thought of her crazy solution.

Mathias stepped up and told Gabby, "Move away from the prisoner."

Instead of blindly jumping, she held up her hands. "I don't have a knife."

"Now."

She stood, but growled her discontent, making sure anyone close by knew she thought Mathias was a tyrant.

Now Tony wished she could've at least tried the Vulcan mind meld or whatever she was talking about.

The celebration turned out to be what looked like a birthday party. Tony couldn't believe while the time for calling up a transender ticked off the red moon clock, this bunch was serving some kind of fruit cocktail like it was a birthday cake and each one coming by to hug Mathias and saying goodbye.

Was this a farewell party?

Where'd they think Mathias was going?

Some kids beat gourds and blew through reeds, while others twirled and danced with orange and yellow vine streamers. The littlest ones clapped their hands and threw flower petals into the air like confetti, then they'd stare at them for a second and the petals would remain suspended. Several others were concentrating, and around them spun vine streamers and whole flowers as if they were mind activated. Everything seemed frenzied though, as if they were forcing happiness.

Finally, the main whoop de doo ended, with Zilya saying a few words, holding a politician's smile in place. Her eyes held a boat load of denial, not believing something about this party.

Mathias took time with each of the kids, praising them for the decorations and laughing at their antics.

When Gabby had left Tony's side, she'd passed by the healer who frowned when she bypassed a seat next to him.

She'd planted herself shoulder-to-shoulder with Rayen.

She and Rayen had both kept visual tabs on Tony throughout the party.

Like I can go anywhere being wrapped up this way?

Rayen whispered something to Gabby who nodded, then winked at Tony as if she sent a message.

If I get out of this, I'm going to teach Xena and Psycho Babe some useful hand signals.

Mathias finally stood and everyone applauded. He lifted his hands for silence. "Thank you for a BIRG Day celebration that exceeded my greatest expectation."

You got some low expectations there, buddy.

Mathias continued, "I must go now, but if I'm given a choice know that I will return. However, until that happens you must stay united and follow Callan's leadership."

Zilya spoke up at that. "I am the next highest in rank from the Governing House."

"That is true," Mathias agreed. "But I am designating Callan who is better prepared to lead our group in this Sphere. As you well know, I hold the power to make that decision at any time our people are under threat such as we are here."

"As you wish." Zilya shrugged as if she couldn't be bothered. The minute Mathias turned from her, Zilya whispered something to Etoi who chuckled, as if they both thought this whole production was funny. Maybe they didn't expect Mathias to leave at all. That would be a mean trick to play on these little kids. Tony wished he could hear what Zilya and Etoi were whispering, but Mathias kept talking.

"Protect and watch over each other. Never give up hope of leaving. We will win this war. Our families *will* find us. This I believe with all my being."

Mathias gave a pointed look at Callan who came to his feet and offered, "I will join you on the walk."

What walk? And would that be the time to make a run for the transender? But how could they when he couldn't even talk to Gabby or Rayen?

Giving Callan a quick head dip, Mathias added, "I ask Rayen to join us as well."

Nooooooo. This was a bad time for Rayen to leave. *We probably got less than twenty minutes now.*

Mathias's statement also startled Zilya and Etoi whose confused gazes darted from Mathias to Callan to Rayen. Zilya jumped to her feet, mouth open to protest.

With a lift of his hand, Mathias cut her off. "This is my choice."

Rayen didn't stand, but she did say, "I want to know that Tony and Gabby will be safe while I'm gone if I agree to go."

You tell 'em, Rayen. But don't go.

Callan addressed Zilya and Etoi. "As long as those two don't attempt to escape, they're not to be harmed. To do so will result in painful punishment."

Etoi blanched at whatever Callan alluded to, which gave Tony a moment of relief about being left tied up.

With that settled, Rayen spoke quietly to Gabby then stood and followed Callan and Mathias from the common area.

Gabby got up and crossed to Tony. She squatted down and reached up to pull the gag off his mouth.

When she did, Etoi shouted, "Do *not* touch him!"

Gabby didn't even look back when she answered, "Chill. I'm only letting him breathe."

Go Gabby!

Etoi grabbed her spear and rushed over to point it at Gabby's back.

Tony shook his head. Much as he wanted to tell Gabby what he'd found out, he didn't want her hurt.

Gabby shoved up to her feet and pivoted to face the spear, looking down as she scoffed. She slapped aside the tip. "Everyone has the right to be stupid, but you're abusing the privilege. Taking his gag off doesn't constitute trying to escape. But if you want to stab me then argue that point with Callan, I'm game as long as I get to watch *you* being punished."

Careful, Psycho Babe, but man that is so hot. Tony let out a muffled chuckle when Etoi backed down.

Sulking, Zilya stood off to the side, not offering an opinion.

Jaxxson strolled up. "There are better uses for your energy, Etoi. Such as helping the others clean up and making sure the smallest children retreat to their chambers before moonset." When she turned away sharply from him, he added, in a lower, tighter voice, "Please follow Mathias's example by giving the children encouragement. Do not spew venom when they face enough hardship."

Etoi stomped off without agreeing or spouting another snotty comment.

Jaxxson's serious gaze bounced from Tony to Gabby. "Do you give your word you'll not attempt to escape or help him escape, Gabby?"

"Yes."

"Then you may remove his mouth covering." The healer moved on to each group of children, touching their heads lightly and issuing compliments on the decorations and food.

When Gabby sat back down, Tony noticed her hands had been clenched, ready to fight.

He had a whole new respect for Psycho Babe.

She slipped her fingers inside the leaf across his mouth and started tugging it down, whispering to Tony as she did. "If Rayen can't talk sense into Callan then maybe Jaxxson can. I've gotten to know him today."

Tony sucked in a deep breath of air and sighed. "Finally. We don't have much time."

"What're you talking about?"

"I followed the scout back to his transender location."

"You *did* break him out of the prison hut?"

Tony didn't know whether to be impressed that she thought he was capable of that or insulted at her you-did-try-to-leave-us tone. "No, someone here shut down the power. When the scout jumped out, I did, too. Barely made it before the power zapped back up. Has to be someone in this village who helped him, but that's their problem."

"We have to tell Jaxxson."

"We can tell him on the way *out*, but right now we need to grab Rayen, because I've found our ticket home."

Gabby's lips parted. "What are you talking about?"

"I saw how the scout called up the pod. Then I tackled him and made him tell me everything about how to get into one. I think we have to call up our original transender to go home, but we have to do it before that red moon sets." He nodded to the darkening horizon. "I'm guessin' we don't have more than twenty minutes, tops."

"But ... I don't want to go home. I'm staying here."

CHAPTER 32

WORRY TIGHTENED THE MUSCLES IN Rayen's shoulders. Where were Mathias and Callan going? Did this walk mean Mathias really intended to abandon his own people? How could he leave Callan alone to deal with that hateful witch Zilya and her annoying shadow Etoi plus a village full of small children?

Something didn't fit here.

Callan followed Mathias with his head held high, but anxiety radiated from Callan's every move and tensed neck muscles.

Rayen fought the urge to put her arm around him, doubting he'd welcome her comfort right now. He still hadn't decided if she was his enemy or not.

She couldn't let this go any longer. "Are you really going to do this, Mathias?"

Callan answered instead. "This is not your concern."

"Then why am I going with you?"

Before Callan could say another word, Mathias cleared his throat as if he had something blocking his words. "Let me explain, Callan." Then he addressed Rayen. "The TecKnati scouts told us we would not stay here past turning eighteen, but Callan and I have figured out that this is only to demoralize our group when it doesn't happen. So, we're pretending I am leaving, then I will come back tomorrow, explaining that the TeKs gave me the choice to be locked up back home or to stay here."

Now she understood. What a nice thing to do for everyone considering how dangerous it was out in these woods. "Exactly how long are you going to be gone?"

Callan had given Mathias a questioning look, then must have decided there was no point in keeping the rest secret. "Just twenty-four hours. Mathias will enjoy a much-deserved break."

She asked, "But why did you bring me instead of one of your people, Mathias?"

"Callan has shared with me about how you battled two croggles and how you fought to rescue the little boy then helped heal him."

That didn't really explain why she was walking with them, but she let it go since it sounded as though Mathias had a more favorable opinion of her now.

Mathias had entered the forest and stopped in a small clearing, evening twilight feathering through branches and leaves, slanting cold fingers of darkness, and quieting all bird sounds. He turned to Callan with a look in his eyes that gave her chills.

When Mathias spoke, his voice sounded raw. "It's time for you to know everything, my friend."

So, this is where all her bad feelings were coming from.

Callan's face fell at hearing that *he* didn't know everything. "What do you mean?"

Callan hadn't shown even the slightest indication of fear while facing the croggle, but some worry shadowed his eyes now, and darkened his skin. The pattern on his skin began changing rapidly, a physical action that she'd decided was tied to his emotions. What would cause such a severe emotional reaction in Callan?

Mathias looked resigned as he glanced over his shoulder where she saw a glimpse of the red moon low in the purple sky, but no green stripes.

Were the TecKnati really coming for him? Had one arrived during the ceremony and everyone missed the signs but Mathias?

That couldn't be. Callan missed nothing, and should have seen an intruder, too.

Mathias scrubbed his hands over his face then told Callan, "We don't have much time."

"What have you kept from me?" Bitter disappointment seeped into Callan's voice.

She wished for some way to figure out exactly what had Mathias acting so spooky.

Mathias drew a deep breath that shuddered through him, then he told Callan, "I had you bring Rayen for a reason. V'ru told me what he'd learned so far."

Callan's stony silence weighed heavier than the humidity clinging to her arms.

She couldn't stand the tension between these two. "Do you believe what I've told you, Mathias?"

"Yes."

Chill bumps raced up her arm at finally hearing the right answer. "Then you'll tell Callan to release us?"

"He can release you, but only if you promise to help them find a way out of the Sphere."

That got a reaction out of Callan. "What can she do?"

Rayen had no idea, but she told Mathias, "You have my word."

For the first time since meeting Callan, she heard true worry enter his voice when he asked Mathias, "You're still only going away for a day, right?"

Mathias took another look up at the sky. "No, I'm disappearing. For good. There'll be no coming back."

"*What?*" Callan's golden-brown hair turned bright blond and the splattered aqua shapes on his skin darkened into blackish-blue storm clouds. "You've been holding out on me?"

Mathias kept speaking quietly, every word forced from deep inside. "Yes, I haven't been completely honest, but you'll soon understand why I had to do this. And just as I have lied to you, you will lie to the others as well when the time comes."

"No, I will *not.*" Callan quivered with anger. "*You* said we are to be leaders. Leaders do *not* lie to their people."

Mathias grimaced as if Callan had cut him with his blade. "Listen. I could not tell you what would happen before now, or you would have focused on the wrong things. Your duty is to keep their spirits up and convince those children they are going home. If not, they *will not* survive. I was here for eight months longer than you. I watched our children lose their will to live without hope and they died."

Rayen heard things in Mathias's voice that weren't coming out in his words. He still hid something from Callan.

Crossing his arms, Callan snarled, "I have *believed* you, trusted you. And now ... *now* you tell me you won't come back? Tell me the truth, all of it."

"I always did tell you to be prepared for anything, including my not being around to help."

Walking several steps away, Callan muttered, "But I thought you meant if a croggle killed you. I would never have let that happen."

"I–" Mathias choked on the word and his shoulders jerked straight as if he stood at attention, muscles clenching. Sweat broke out on his skin.

Callan spun around and stared at him, lips moving but no words coming out.

Rayen lifted a hand toward Mathias, and he shot her a warning look. "I did not bring you to interfere."

"Why did you bring me?" she pleaded.

"To understand why you must *not* break your word."

Callan took a step toward Mathias who shouted, "*Don't touch me!*"

"Why?" Callan shouted back and took another step toward him, a cautious one. "What's happening? Talk to me."

Mathias gritted out his next words. "I am not the first to turn eighteen in the Sphere. Anatoli arrived with me."

Callan looked bewildered. "I know that name. He's of the Cultivation House."

"Yes," Mathias continued. "And he reached his BIRG Day a month before you arrived."

Callan's eyes opened wide. "Where is he? He should have told the House leaders about us or stayed here to help everyone."

"He's not to be blamed for anything, Callan, and you will not tell the children where I've gone when you return to the village."

"Anatoli left and ..." The struggle to understand what was going on carved anxiety in Callan's face. "Did SEOH send Anatoli to a prison a telepath can't reach into? Being G'ortian, maybe I can help. Tell them to take me."

"No, SEOH hasn't figured out how to do that, but he has proven to be far slyer than any of us anticipated." Mathias's body jerked with a spasm. Sweat now dripped from his forehead and arms, as if his body wrestled with something internally. He groaned.

Callan rushed forward, but at that moment, Mathias flew up ten feet off the ground with his arms stretched above his head like a puppet whose master had yanked the strings. He hung there in midair.

Callan roared, "*Mathias!*"

Rayen reached for the heat within her to do battle and called out, "What holds you? How can I kill it?"

Sweat poured down Mathias's face when he lowered his chin, speaking through gritted teeth. "I'm sorry I lied, Callan. You've been a brother to me, but now you'll know why I could not tell you. I did what you must do. Lie to protect the others."

A howling noise started deep in the forest and gained volume. Like a killer wind bent on destruction. But what was it?

Callan shouted, "What are we fighting?"

Mathias looked right and left, terror riding his gaze. His body shook. He yelled back, "Give Rayen her freedom. Trust her to use it wisely."

Streaming bands of black energy shot through the opening, whipping past Rayen. Heat built inside her chest, rolling through her body. She lifted her arms into the energy shooting around them on the ground. Sparks crackled with contact between her power and the attacking energy. Something clasped her wrist and yanked her up a foot off the ground.

Mathias screamed.

Steel bands of strength latched onto her waist, pulling her body backwards. The force holding her arm drew her up, threatening to rip her body in half.

Mathias shouted, "Noooo, Rayen. Your word."

Her heart thundered in her chest. She fought tears over the pain tearing through her.

Callan yanked on her body, shouting, "*Let go!*"

She couldn't.

But whatever had her wrist released her and whispered in her mind, *Next time.*

She fell backwards, landing against something hard and warm. Callan.

The energy still swarmed, alive with distorted faces and glowing yellow eyes, but none of it touched her again or Callan. A dozen or more black spirits howled through the clearing.

Wind blasted branches and scoured leaves across her face and body, held wrapped in Callan's arms. His shouts were nothing more than hoarse noises filled with raw pain. She looked up as the horde of black ghostly bands whipped around Mathias one at a time, round and round until the only part left in view was his agony-filled gaze, staring at nothing.

All at once, the howling ended.

And Mathias was gone.

An unearthly silence reigned.

She couldn't stop shaking. That was what the TecKnati meant by the MystiKs leaving here at eighteen?

How hideous.

Somehow, Callan managed to get to his feet with her still clutched against him. He turned her to face him.

She wanted to cry over the misery in his eyes.

Instead, she wrapped her arms around him and held on. He pulled her tight into his embrace, his breaths coming in ragged shudders. She wanted to comfort him, but his strength comforted her. Rayen's mind raced to understand what had happened. These deadly spirits had to be something created by the TecKnati for them to attack at moonset on the day a captive reached eighteen. That made MystiKs fair game when they were no longer technically children.

Demonically brilliant.

Mathias had spent all these months knowing he faced this end to his life.

Only a truly cruel person could come up with that kind of torture.

Mathias was right. Those children in the village couldn't know what had happened to him, or that the same fate waited for anyone else they depended on. Or for them.

She pressed her lips against Callan's chest, tasting the salt of his skin. He tucked her head against his shoulder, unwilling to give her up and she didn't try to push away.

Mathias's message was clearer now. He hoped that she wouldn't abandon Callan once she knew that there was no way for Mathias to return to the village.

He was right.

Callan finally drew a breath that had a sound of finality to it. He eased his hold on her.

She placed a hand on his chest and took a step back. "I, uh," she mumbled, at a loss for what to say. Saying sorry he'd lost his friend didn't begin to cover Callan's loss.

He touched her chin with his fingers, lifting her face to meet the eyes of a warrior, but he had to swallow before he could speak. His voice came out hoarse, yet strong. "Mathias is right. You can't tell anyone about this."

Nodding, she added, "My word."

She still had to get Gabby and Tony back to the safety of Albuquerque. An hour ago, she would've had no problem abandoning this place. Lifting her fingers to brush Callan's cheek, she made him an offer. "I'll stay to help you protect these kids and search for a way out of here, but I want you to free Tony and Gabby to leave if we can find a way to get them home."

He didn't answer at first. Lines formed at the bridge of his nose in a sign that he struggled with a decision. "You would stay?"

Looking deep into that haunted, brown-eyed gaze, she realized she'd do far more than that for him. "Yes."

"And you're certain that Tony is not TecKnati?"

"Yes. He's from over a hundred and sixty years in the past, not your world."

He took her measure with his next look. "Then I'll free him. He and Gabby will be allowed to return to their home."

CHAPTER 33

RAYEN HOPED GABBY AND TONY would understand about her staying, but Callan and his band of young warriors needed someone with her strange superpower to fight monsters. Someone more than Etoi, Zilya and matchstick V'ru.

The upside of staying would be spending time with V'ru who might shed some light on where she'd come from if her blood wasn't as old as that of Tony and Gabby. Maybe, if she survived all this, she'd get a chance to search out her family, wherever they might be.

When she returned to the village and entered the common area, she was a step behind Callan who'd shed any grief during the walk, at least grief that someone could see in his face. She knew his insides were shredded from watching what had happened to Mathias.

She felt nauseous and would have nightmares over seeing Mathias in his last minute of life. No one should have to face that destiny. Callan had a heartwrenching future of keeping this village full of hope while hiding this devastating loss.

A commotion erupted in the village.

Callan stopped short in front of her and called out in a voice that belonged to a leader, "What's happening?"

As usual, Etoi jumped in first. "V'ru has completed his analysis of the TecKnati's blood."

Just the way she put that raised the hairs on Rayen's neck. She saw Gabby standing next to Tony, who was still wrapped in vines, but now had his mouth uncovered and a scowl on his face.

Rayen stepped forward, speaking directly to V'ru, "What'd you find out?"

Lifting his narrow chin, V'ru pointed a finger at Tony. "That one has a genetic marker of the TecKnati–"

"An *enemy!*" Etoi shouted. "The lack of K-enzyme ink means nothing!"

Tony spoke up, "We got bigger problems, Rayen. Need to move this along so you and I can talk."

She lifted a hand to let Tony know she understood and to wait a second then she turned to Callan. “Can you shut up Etoi for a moment so we can get to the bottom of this?”

Callan shoved a dark look at Etoi that would have silenced a croggle. “Not another word unless I ask you a direct question.”

For once, Etoi clammed up and nodded respectfully.

Rayen asked V’ru, “What does this genetic marker mean?”

“That he is of the TecKnati lineage.”

“I still don’t understand. Tony’s not from your world.”

“I did not make that claim.”

At the eternal end of her rope, she asked bluntly, “Callan needs to know if Tony *is* or is *not* a TecKnati from your world.”

V’ru turned to Callan. “No, this one’s blood is older, from the year 2018, born in 1999, the month of–”

“Got it.” Rayen stopped V’ru from rambling on then added, “Thank you,” before reminding Callan, “You agreed to free Tony.”

“I did.” He called out, “Jaxxson, release him.”

With Gabby and Jaxxson’s help, Tony was shaking off vines and stretching stiff limbs before hurrying over to Rayen. He said, “I know how to call up the transender, but we’ve got maybe ten minutes to get back to where we first arrived.”

What … he wanted to do this now?

Gabby strode right behind him, a determined look in her eye. “I’m not going.”

“You want to stay?” Rayen asked, taken aback by her words.

“Yes. This is the first place I’ve ever felt ... normal.”

Tony released a tired exhale. “What about your family, Gabby?”

“I doubt my dad’ll even notice I’m missing.”

“That can’t be true, Gabby.” Tony looked to Rayen, but she wasn’t the one to convince her to go.

“If you’re sure,” Rayen said to her. “I plan to stay, too.”

Tony raised his hands. “Whoa. Listen up, you two. We *all* gotta go together, because we need Rayen’s handprint to call up the transender and to make it function. And two may not be able to return without the third one. We’re all in this together. And if we don’t get into the right transender before that moon sets ... there may not be any other way home.”

Rayen’s chest hurt from the sudden pounding of her heart. She’d promised Callan she would stay. Given her word. But she couldn’t condemn Tony to being trapped in this dangerous place.

Taking in Gabby's mutinous face and Tony's worried one, Rayen ran her hands through her hair, needing a way out of this.

Jaxxson stepped forward and spoke to Gabby. "You can't go with us to our world once we find a way out of here. I'd rather you go home because I would not leave you here."

From the softening of Gabby's face, Rayen figured her friend had caught Jaxxson's meaning, too. The healer was saying if he got the chance to return to his home, he wouldn't leave if it meant Gabby would remain alone in the Sphere.

That was, if Jaxxson didn't turn eighteen here first and leave a different way, as Mathias had.

What about Gabby? Would the same thing happen to her if she turned eighteen? Granted, she was only sixteen, but Rayen couldn't let her stay and not know what risk she faced, but neither could she share what had happened to Mathias.

And Tony would turn eighteen if they got trapped here for any length of time.

Which left Rayen with having to leave the Sphere to get Gabby *and* Tony out of here.

Something silent passed between Gabby and Jaxxson that brought a watery smile to her face. She turned to Rayen. "I'll return with you."

Tony muttered, "Halle-freakin-lujah."

That left the final decision to Rayen, who Tony believed was the only one who could call up his ride home. But she'd promised Callan ...

V'ru spoke up. "I have the results of Rayen's blood analysis as well."

All commotion ceased.

Rayen asked, "What'd you find out?"

"First, tell me what beast chased you in the desert?"

"I don't know, some strange thing that could change shape."

Callan's eyes widened at that then he sent a stern look to V'ru, one that questioned where the young boy was going with his question.

V'ru nodded, as if puzzle pieces slipped into place. "That confirms what I have determined. You are of C'raydonian descent—"

Every child in the common area gasped.

Rayen had no idea who or what a C'raydonian was, but it sure didn't sound good.

"That is all they have time for," Callan snapped, grasping her hand, a serious edge to his words. "You must go. *Now!*"

"Wait. I need to hear more from V'ru, plus I said I'd stay. I don't want to leave you and the children here alone."

"I'll tell you what you need to know on the way, but ... you'll never be able to live with yourself if you fail to take your friends home."

She didn't think that was the real reason Callan had decided she had to leave right this minute.

He squeezed her arm, letting her know he was sincere and not just trying to get rid of her. "Go home with them. That may be the only place to find a way to free us."

There was something he wasn't saying. But what? And what was a C'raydonian? She thought there were only MystiKs and TecKnati.

Callan started barking orders at the children. "You three finish getting the young ones to their chambers. Etoi, pull together ten hunters who can travel to the transender location where we originally found these three. Get moving."

Rayen grabbed Callan by the arm. "I can't do this."

He stepped close to her. "Yes, you can, just as I can, and *will*, take care of this village ... until you return."

The faith he showed in her was humbling. She put her palm on his cheek. He was right. She had to take Tony and Gabby home, but could she really find a way back here?

She had to. For him. For all of them. And what if V'ru could share more about her background? She vowed, "I *will* return as soon as I can. Just as soon as I get those two back to the school."

"I know. But we need to move out. The moon is close to setting."

When she turned to leave, she noticed one person who wasn't joining them. Zilya had watched the entire exchange through eyes flashing dangerous thoughts. Rayen didn't have time to waste wondering what was going on between Zilya and Callan.

After giving Rayen a wide berth as if she were a threat, Etoi whipped together a band of young hunters, all the while her expression saying she didn't like doing it.

Callan led the march through the fog wall, out to the jungle side of the village. Once the kids entered the dense foliage made darker by the setting moon, every fourth child lifted his or her hands in the air and light glowed from their palms. At that point, they raced forward, beating a path to the transender, and making it impossible to talk.

Rayen took the last position, watching over all of them and trying to convince herself she wasn't doing the wrong thing and that Callan was right.

Tony and Gabby had ended up in this dangerous place because of her. She owed them and the best payback would be to take them home.

When their group reached the edge of the jungle next to the transender landing spot, Rayen searched beyond the thick leaves for croggles.

Callan stepped up to her, barely winded from the run. He said, "Hurry. Giant croggles only come after a transender lands, but the baby croggles are more active and appear unexpectedly sometimes. If you go quickly, you should be safe."

"What did V'ru–" She started to ask when Gabby yelled, "*No, Tony!*"

Rayen turn to Gabby who rushed toward Tony. He knelt next to a pink bloom identical to the attack flower and stuck his arm into the center of it.

Was the guy suicidal?

Running over to him, Rayen got there first and grabbed Tony's free arm.

"Let go, Rayen. I got this. It's not a real flower."

When a holographic panel like the one V'ru had used appeared next to Tony, he stood up, pulling his arm free, grinning his who's-the-boss-now grin he'd had when she first saw him enter Mr. Suarez's classroom.

A female voice from the panel announced, "*Four minutes left to request transender return from Sphere.*"

Tony told her in a rush, "Put your palm here." He pointed to the panel. "And hold it there until you get a red outline."

She hadn't gotten the information she wanted from Callan, but with minutes counting down, she did as Tony instructed. A red line traced her palm then started blinking, and finally the outline glowed green. The voice said, *Request acknowledged.*

"That's it!" Tony shouted. "You *did it*, babe."

A whirring sound began out in the open space.

Rayen turned, searching for Callan who was right behind her. She grasped his shoulders. "What was V'ru saying about C'raydonians?"

Tony stuck his face next to Callan's. "We gotta go. That thing takes off in three minutes whether we're in it or not."

"Move." Her one word shoved Tony out of the way. She pleaded with Callan, "I have to know."

He lifted his hands, cupping her shoulders, disappointment rippling through his voice. "C'raydonians lived in our world at one time."

Lived? That did not sound good. "And?"

"They were ... after the K-Virus ... they ..."

"Say it!"

"They were rabid. Dangerous to the rest of the survivors." He sounded guilty having to admit that. "C'raydonians were hunted to extinction by sentient beasts fifty years ago because everyone feared them breaking through the laser curtains protecting our cities. The last ones disappeared forty-five years before I was born."

"What?" She felt lightheaded. "That means–"

"That you shouldn't be alive."

"Why ... how could I end up in 2018?"

Tony yelled, "*Come. On. Rayen!*"

The whining noise screeched louder. Wind swept from the open space and into the jungle around us, rattling through the dense foliage, whipping the blood-red earth into a frenzied, dense funnel cloud.

Callan shouted down the wind. "The C'raydonians could have had time travel to the past. You may have been thrown into a portal to spare your life and have been bouncing your way back in time. The beast that chased you is a sentient machine built to track and kill C'raydonians. It may have followed you into the same time travel portal."

She trembled at this news. Her people were dead. Her family. She should be dead.

We were hunted ... as dangerous beasts.

Callan sucked in a quick breath and rushed on. "V'ru spoke to me in my mind before I left. He said many young people were lost in the C'raydonian Siege. He warned that the TecKnati would be thrilled to discover a living C'raydonian to imprison and run tests on ..." Callan's fingers tightened on her shoulders, demanding she heed his words. "Staying here puts you, and us, at risk. You *must* go."

She didn't believe he really thought she was a risk to him if she remained. Not the way he added "and us" almost as an after thought. Shaking her head, she admitted, "I don't understand."

"I'm telling you to stay in the past. Where you're safe, Rayen. If the TecKnati find you here, they'll take you to SEOH and he'll kill you." He whispered, "Don't come back for any reason. I don't want you to die."

Tony grabbed Rayen's arm, pulling her around. "Now means *now!* The pod's spinnin' into view."

Out in the field beyond the jungle, a whirling circular mass of gray metal emerged.

She let Tony pull her away to where Gabby stood looking as if she was going to bolt in some direction, but Rayen wasn't sure whether Gabby would head for the transender or back to the village.

When Tony released Rayen and pulled Gabby's arm, she followed him. Rayen fell into step behind them, ducking her head so she wouldn't be swallowed by the winds.

Her insides were ripping apart.

She didn't care if she was C'raydonian. She couldn't be rabid. Just couldn't.

At the edge of the field, she stopped and turned. Callan stood two steps behind Rayen, as if determined to protect her to the last second.

She would never see him again. She closed the distance between them and reached for him.

He yanked her into his arms, kissing her and letting her know in the most honest way he could that he didn't want her to go. His lips embraced hers with fierce determination, just as he did everything else. His arms banded her back and hugged her close. All the turmoil and chaos disappeared.

Nothing existed except this moment.

A life she had more questions about than answers.

But nothing could make her question what she felt for Callan. She might not fully understand it, but she knew no one would ever mean as much to her.

Warmth burst inside her, but not like it had before. This time the heat that rushed through her body held the power of a tidal surge, threatening to consume everything in its path.

Just as his lips were consuming her with every touch.

Tony yelled, "*Raaayen!*"

She broke away, regretting the separation as if she'd lost an arm or leg. She would not accept this as the last time with Callan. "I *will* return. Don't even waste your breath arguing. I'm coming back. That's a promise."

She kissed him quickly once more and swung around, running across the field where Tony stood with his mouth gaped open and Gabby grinning. When Rayen reached the transender, she looked at Tony. "What now, Jersey?"

"Oh, uh, put your hands up on the pod."

She did, joining her hands with his and Gabby's.

Two panels slid open. Tony scrambled in, pulling Gabby in right behind him.

Turning for a last look, she saw a sad smile on Callan's face. He didn't think he'd see her again. She just knew it. Leaving him was killing her, but she would come back. She waved and dove inside as the panels started sliding shut. Then something she hadn't thought of earlier slammed into her brain.

She shouted at Callan, "When are you eighteen?"

For a second, she thought he hadn't heard her.

He hesitated then called out, "Not soon."

Those were the last words she heard as the panels snapped closed.

Her next breath came out harsh and shaky. She couldn't breathe when she realized Callan had already started fulfilling the role Mathias had just vacated.

He'd just lied to her.

CHAPTER 34

2179 ACE, in ORD/City One

SEOH LOOKED UP FROM HIS rare wood desk–real mahogany wood –where he'd been scanning the latest hologram report on production in City Three as Rustaad entered his office. "Your message said there'd been developments in the Sphere."

"Odd ones."

Pushing back in his chair, SEOH rested his elbows on the chair arms. "Vid report or a Scout report?"

"Scout. We lost one today. A croggle attack."

"How could that happen when they have full control over summoning the beasts?"

"Phen T-112 said his Scout partner accidentally hit the button while they were in the middle of transender landing space Zulu."

"Accidentally? No TecKnati can be that stupid."

"T-112 explained it as the other Scout 'fooling around' with the MystiK child they were delivering."

Idiot. "In that case, the croggle did us a favor by eliminating a waste product." He turned back to his hologram.

Rustaad gave a mild smile of agreement. "I've called for an immediate review of all Scouts being sent into the Sphere to determine future suitability."

"How did Phen T-112 stop a croggle with the stun unit?"

"He didn't. A foursome of the older MystiKs attacked the croggle and took T-112 captive."

SEOH slammed his fist down on the chair arm. "Did they get any information out of him?"

"No. Fortunately, this worked in our favor. The MystiK we planted in the Sphere freed T-112 and sent information with him."

Easing back against the plush leather only the elite TecKnati enjoyed, SEOH chuckled. "They're too stupid to realize we'd put one loyal to us among them."

"Perhaps, but that's not the odd part of the report. He claims there are interlopers in the Sphere."

Too impossible to consider. "Were there any unauthorized transender trips to Komaen?"

"Not from here. Our security system released no alert of a transender traveling from here to the Sphere or back without authorized hand recognition. But when I looked closely, our system picked up a transender landing in the Sphere that did not originate here."

"What? Did someone hijack one of ours?"

"I don't know. Every person is scanned for identification when they leave home base and when they exit a transender upon return to home base. I ran a thorough check on the systems. Nothing shows up."

SEOH pounded his desk. "If it's a closed world–and it damn well better still be–where did interlopers come from ... and are they MystiK?"

"Two questions I can't answer yet, but I will very soon. The Scout said one of the strangers that fought the croggle killed it on her own, with nothing more than stabbing a stick into the beast. Next thing the beast exploded into flames. That's far more powerful than anyone we anticipated having in the Sphere."

"Her?"

"Yes, her."

SEOH mulled over everything Rustaad had shared and decided he'd been too lenient with this program. "These brats are more versatile and adaptable than we anticipated. It's time we changed the plan."

"To what?"

"They've had it too easy playing in their village that *we* set up for them with no real trials. I have something in mind that'll test the best from their Warrior House." He paused, then added, "Mathias should be out of the equation by now, right?"

"Yes."

"Then what I have in mind will be quite entertaining and even more of a challenge. Call a meeting of the Sphere engineers for tonight. I want changes made. Now."

"Is it worth another meeting with the board to approve the expense?"

SEOH hadn't reached this point to lose. He could not allow anyone to come and go into that Sphere who could put everything at risk. "I'd pay out of my pocket to see the face of the one called Callan confront what I have in mind. His Warrior House is a bigger worry than those blasted Governing

MystiKs. They're enough of a pain in my side, but Callan has some paying up to do."

Rustaad moved to leave.

SEOH's voice stopped him. "Plus, I want those Sphere interlopers caught and brought to me. I can't imagine a MystiK figuring out how to get inside the Sphere but let me find out the intruders are TecKnati ... and blood will run."

"Very well. I'll arrange the meeting in the battle room." Rustaad indicated the soundproof room where SEOH brought his most loyal and brightest minds to discuss things the board would never know about.

When Rustaad turned to leave again, SEOH added, "Wait. I have good news."

"Oh?" Rustaad paused, completely still. At times it appeared the man didn't breathe.

"Another sign that the Byzantine Institute in the past is on track."

"Do we know if they found the Genera-Y computer?"

"Unfortunately, not yet. If only we could communicate directly with them." SEOH shook his head at the frustration of having operatives who were assigned a mission where they were sent to the past and unable to contact anyone in the future. "But no matter, we did receive verification that the genetic monitoring program is performing just the way we intended. They've clearly begun to identify MystiK ancestors and have the female Bio-Genetics Research Center up and running at the Institute."

He smiled at Rustaad's raised brows, adding, "It's true. I received a report today that several entire families of MystiKs in three cities disappeared. These must be descendants of females going through the Bio-Genetic program in the past."

"No TecKnati children missing?"

"Not a one."

Rustaad grinned. "My admiration SEOH, the egg removal program works."

"Absolutely. I wish there was a way to communicate with the agents we sent back to the year 2014 to let them know the eggs they've removed from MystiK ancestors have wiped out entire lines."

"The agents we sent are exceptional scientists and well-trained TecKnati who'll continue to perform their jobs regardless, even if they never learn of the results. This is outstanding. And neutralizing MystiKs this way defies their power, because the treaty's specific words were 'no TecKnati shall kill a MystiK child born since A.C.E. 2127.' Fools weren't bright enough to consider that the treaty did not prevent sending someone into the past to prevent a MystiK birth." His grin deepened.

Caught up in Rustaad's unusual show of emotion, SEOH even chuckled, more than pleased with the results of his plan. "Our agents in the Byzantine Institute have clearly reproduced ANASKO technology for engineering the removal of eggs from a female without leaving a mark on her body."

"MystiK female ancestors will not suspect they've been sterilized. Excellent."

CHAPTER 35

WHEN THE PANELS ON THE transender pod slammed shut trapping Rayen inside, she froze with shock, digesting Callan's last words.

C'raydonians were hunted as a rabid race.

All her people were dead.

And Callan would turn eighteen soon.

Gabby shook her loose from her stalled mental state when she asked Tony, "What now?"

"Don't know. This was all I found out."

A low hum started again, picking up volume until the sound screeched.

Gabby dug her fingers into Rayen's arm and yelled at Tony, "Grab Rayen's other arm."

"Why?" Tony acted appalled that she thought he should cling to a girl.

"Don't go back to being a jerk just when you've shown signs of evolving into an intelligent life form," Gabby shot at him, raising her voice over the increasing whine. "You're the one who wanted to do this. You're the one who said it took all three of us, so either grab her arm or say goodbye."

Rayen didn't know whether Gabby was right or not, but just as her body felt pulled in multiple directions and everything blurred, Tony's hand latched onto her other arm.

She clenched from head to toe against the sensation of being warped while suspended in a spinning free fall. Her body turned into a human bungee cord, stretched thin and sucked forward.

Her arms slapped against her body. She shot through a rotating tunnel of blurry muted colors ... toward a flat surface.

The equipment room floor came at her fast.

Tucking at the last minute before she hit, she slammed the concrete floor and rolled.

Gabby slapped down next. "Ouch."

Rayen pushed Gabby out of the way just before ...

Thump!

"Ah, man, that sucks." Laid out flat on his back, Tony dropped his arms and groaned.

Gabby muttered, "Are we really back?"

Forcing herself to sit up, Rayen gripped her dizzy head. "Think so."

"Think I'm gonna be sick," Tony grumbled.

"Do it and *you* clean up." Gabby pushed herself up, holding her head, too.

A ding sounded three times out in the hallway.

Doors opened. Voices filled the silence along with hundreds of footsteps pounding through the halls.

Tony shot upright, fingers clutching his forehead. "What time is it?"

They all turned to the black-and-white school clock hanging on the wall.

"5:00!" Rayen shouted, shoving to her feet. "I'm late for a meeting in Maxwell's office."

Tony struggled to stand then offered a hand to Gabby, giving her a tug up. "Don't panic. Maxwell knows it takes five minutes to get from most classes to his office. I hope Suarez didn't send anyone here to check on us. We were supposed to report to him by now."

Would Rayen's fingerprints reveal anything?

Was she really a C'raydonian? That would be putting a lot of trust in an eleven-year-old boy living in a strange Sphere. She had to know what they found out in *this* world from her prints. As much as she wanted to tear out of here and go see Maxwell, she also needed to keep Mr. Suarez happy for any chance of staying in this school.

Leaving would mean losing her one shot at getting back to Callan. Every minute of waiting to return was already driving her crazy. "What're we going to do about the computer?"

Tony and Gabby both looked over where three circles spiraled on the computer screen that she'd touched to send them on that trip.

Gabby spoke first, echoing her thoughts. "We can't lose it."

"No," Tony agreed, picking up the laptop and folding the case shut like a book then shoving it under his arm and wrapping up the power cord. "No one's touchin' this but us." Then he turned to Rayen with a cocky grin. "You go see Maxwell. I'll explain to Suarez that we got so involved working on this that we lost track of time."

She hesitated, not ready to leave these two with so many questions still raging in her mind about what had happened in the Sphere.

Gabby brushed a wrecked mass of ponytails back from her face. "I was dodging the front office when I came here to hide. Guess I better swing by and see if I'm in any deeper hot water than what I usually trudge through." She smiled up at Rayen then Tony. "Can't be any worse than facing croggles, huh?"

Tony snorted. "Guess not, sweet cakes."

Rayen even smiled, but the mention of croggles brought another beast to mind.

She held up her hand to stop them from leaving the room. It was time to come clean. "I need to tell you this, even though you've probably gotten pieces of it in the last few hours. I came to in the desert this morning with some big hairy beast chasing me that morphed into a more streamlined shape when I climbed into the rocks. I saw it again, outside this room, right before we got sucked into the computer. This time it was a black bird."

"Like a crow? Or a vulture?" Gabby asked.

"Maybe a raven, but who knows with my memory holes. All I know is that it was here for me, and I'm concerned about who else it'd hurt trying to get to me."

Gabby and Tony shot quick glances at each other then back at her.

Maybe she should've kept that to herself since V'ru's information *had* confirmed her first suspicion that the beast was after her. But she didn't want to hide this from them after all they'd been through.

Gabby spoke first. "Do you think it'll attack just anyone here?"

"I don't know. The minute I was around other people, it stopped chasing me. And, I'll explain later, but V'ru said they were created to track people like me ... C'raydonians."

"When'd he tell you that?" Tony asked.

"V'ru spoke to Callan mind-to-mind, telling him my history. Callan told me as we were running for the pod."

Tony chuckled. "Didn't look like no *talkin'* goin' on to me during that liplock." He shrugged, and added, "Don't give me that look, Xena. I'm not insulting him." He scratched his head. "Morphing animal-to-bird things, huh? Just try not to burn down the school if you have to kill the thing."

For lack of a better description when Rayen had first entered the Sphere and spoke to the MystiKs, she had called these two friends.

Now, she found that word lacking when she considered the value she placed on both of them. But she couldn't waste another minute. "Where can we meet up again?"

"If you're going to Maxwell's, we can wait for you in the hall outside the front office," Gabby suggested.

"Good by me," Tony agreed.

Sticking her head into the hallway first, Rayen sniffed for the stench of the predator and smelled a faint residue. But nothing strong enough to indicate the thing was nearby. At least, for now, she wouldn't be as concerned over this beast.

Could she draw on her power to destroy the thing if it attacked her? Would her power even work outside the Sphere?

She could only imagine how a display of power like that would go over in this world or with the Browns. That'd probably get her in worse trouble than kicked out.

She had to stay here, no matter what.

Signaling to Gabby and Tony that all was clear, Rayen took off for Maxwell's office, rushing through clumps of students gathered around lockers. When she reached the office, she looked down at her clothes that were torn and dirty. And her shirt was half as long as it had been this morning.

Running nervous hands over her hair, she smoothed it back from her face, which she hoped was not filthy.

She made a quick knock on the door and was called inside where she found Dr. Maxwell sitting at his desk. Mr. Brown stood off to one side again and Mrs. Brown was perched on one of the two chairs facing the desk.

"You're late," Mr. Brown announced. "What happened to your clothes? Did you try to leave the Institute?"

"Uh, no." She looked down again as if she'd forgotten the shape she was in, and the instrument attached to her leg. Guess one of her questions had been answered. Traveling to the Sphere hadn't activated it. She actually smiled as she answered, "Mr. Suarez assigned me to work with another student on the Top Ten Project together. We had to dig through a bunch of old, dusty computers and stuff. Some of them snagged on my clothes."

"Something snagged and ripped off the bottom half of your T-shirt?"

"I should have been paying better attention. I will from now on." In other words, she wanted to stay. "Sorry. We got ... sucked in so deep with the computers we lost track of time."

Mrs. Brown brightened. "Getting involved in a project and working as a team is encouraging."

Dr. Maxwell pointed at the empty chair. "Have a seat, Rayen."

Sitting quickly, she took in Mr. Brown who stood with feet shoulder-width apart and arms crossed, creasing his crisp gray suit at the elbows. Questions hovered in the man's intense eyes, shadowed beneath his furrowed brow, but he seemed in no hurry to ask them. Had Nick told him about her head injury?

If he had, they would be shipping her off already, right?

Lifting a paper, Dr. Maxwell said, "We have the report from running your fingerprints. You don't show up in any criminal databases."

Leaning forward with hands gripping the arms of her chair, she asked, "What does that mean? I don't ... exist?"

As that question fell from her lips, she realized she'd been hoping that V'ru had been wrong. That she did belong in this time frame. That she did have people . . . family looking for her.

Dr. Maxwell answered, "Oh, yes, everyone exists, even if they are only a cog in a wheel. But without knowing where you came from or who your family is, we can't generate documentation, which means we'll have to hand you over to social services. We can't take the liability of keeping you here."

Her mouth went dry. She couldn't get separated from Tony and Gabby. Or that computer. She needed to get back to help Callan. "Social Services? Are they here in the school?"

"No, their office is downtown, about thirty miles away."

Thirty miles might as well be another world away. She was emphatic when she told Dr. Maxwell, "No. I want to stay."

"You don't have a choice." Dr. Maxwell leaned back, looking extremely content with this news. Maybe even pleased.

Sweat formed on her palms. She couldn't go somewhere else where no one knew her, and somewhere far away from the computer Tony carried with him. She turned to Mrs. Brown who had championed her earlier and seemed no happier than Rayen about this. "I really want to stay."

Mrs. Brown asked, "Have you remembered anything about your home, Rayen?"

"I know the Sandia Mountains. That's my home." The words were out of Rayen's mouth before she realized the truth behind them. Those mountains did feel like home.

But at what point in time?

"Really?" Mrs. Brown's face lit up. She turned to Mr. Brown. "I've got an idea. Rayen might not be in law enforcement data files for fingerprints, but she's clearly Native American at least on one side of her family. She might be in the BIA records."

Rayen asked, "What's BIA?"

"Bureau of Indian Affairs." Mrs. Brown's enthusiasm picked up momentum. "She *could* be listed in local tribal records. If so, Takoda would be able to tell us."

Who could this Takoda be? Rayen frowned. And could he really help?

She watched anxiously at the interplay between the Browns, pinning her hope on Mrs. Brown. The husband and wife exchanged some silent looks until Mr. Brown's face shifted from rock hard determination to something less resistant.

That gave her hope that Nick hadn't said anything. Yet. She asked Mrs. Brown, "Does that mean I can stay?"

The uncertainty of this moment sent terror through her, which seemed ridiculous after facing deadly creatures and carnivorous plants in a strange Sphere.

But she had nothing if she got kicked out of this Institute. She'd lose the only friends she had plus any chance of returning to the Sphere–and Callan.

Mr. Brown unfolded his arms and shoved his hands in his pockets. "You can stay while Takoda researches the Tribal Records–"

What had Tony said today? *Halle-freakin-lujah!*

"–but it's a long shot so don't hold your breath."

Rayen *had* been holding her breath and let it out now that she had a reprieve, even if only a temporary one. "When will you have this information?"

Mrs. Brown said, "Probably within a day or so."

Not much of a reprieve.

Dr. Maxwell had been scribbling notes the whole time and stopped writing. His jaw rigid, he forced his flattened lips to lift with a polite smile that failed to hide his lack of support for this plan. "You can sleep in dorm eight. Mrs. Brown provided a duffle of clothes and personal items for you on the chance that you could stay." He sent a scathing look up and down Rayen. "Try to do a better job taking care of those items than the ones you're currently wearing."

"I will." Rayen stood, turning to add, "Thank you, Mrs. Brown." She gave a nod to Mr. Brown who made no move to acknowledge it.

Outside the administrative offices, Rayen searched until she found Tony, who was reading a paper posted on a glass window to the administrative offices.

"Where's Gabby?" Rayen asked, walking up to him.

"Down the hall." Tony pointed to his right without taking his eyes off the paper. He mumbled, "She had to go somewhere."

Rayen searched the hall. There went Gabby, the prancing rainbow with bouncing ponytails, alongside Hannah who had guided Rayen through the building this morning. Had it only been hours since she woke up in the desert?

She gave another look down the hall, concerned about Gabby leaving them. Hannah had no reason to harm Gabby. Right? But after having fought their way through one battle after another today, Rayen had the urge to grab Tony and follow Gabby to make sure she was safe.

"Oh, man!" Tony slapped the wall beside the window. "I can't believe he's doin' that to me."

"What?"

"Suarez said he posted a roster for the Top Ten Project and that he made a few adjustments." Tony wheeled around, snapping his knuckles. "He's teamed me up with Nicholas Brown."

Had Suarez also put her with someone else or assumed she was leaving? She searched the list and found her name matched up with Hannah. Annoying, but not so bad.

But Tony still stomped around.

Rayen didn't understand the problem. "I thought you wanted someone good at computers." Lowering her voice, she said, "Maybe someone who can work *on* them ... and not inside one."

"Very funny, Xena," Tony said, not smiling. "You don't understand. There can only be *one* Top Ten winner sent to MIT, the second member of the team can have another school, but both can't go to MIT."

"And that means what?"

"Nicholas is no slack, but he knows I'm better with computers, which is why he probably pulled rank and got himself teamed up with me. We have to choose a team leader. There's no way Nicholas will agree to me runnin' our project, which means when we win that he'll get first choice and walk away with MIT a year early. I'm so screwed."

She had yet to figure out what this MIT thing was, but clearly Tony wanted it badly. "Is this another one of those bus situations?"

"This is a fleet of buses."

"Can we fix it?"

Tony's voice bottomed out. "I don't know."

She spoke even softer, glancing over her shoulder to make sure no one else was near before saying, "We traveled through a computer to another world, fought giant monsters and attack flowers then found our way back. Nicholas can't be as difficult to deal with."

Not as difficult as her trying to figure out how to stay after tomorrow if this Takoda person didn't supply documentation that couldn't possibly exist if she was C'raydonian ... and from the future. But Tony didn't need any more bad news at this moment.

"I suppose," Tony grumbled. "Let's get something to eat. I'm starved."

"What about Gabby? Where did she go?"

Tony waved that off with his hand. "Hannah said Gabby had been scheduled for testing at the Bio-Genetic Research Center division of the hospital."

A frisson of worry fingered across Rayen's neck at the word hospital. Nicholas had warned her about staying away from there, but he'd been toying with her earlier.

Still the worry remained. Rayen whispered, "Will Gabby be safe?"

"Of course. It's a women's center for cryin' out loud, Xena. What could happen to her there?"

She looked down the hallway as students streamed past them and scratched her head. "I don't know. What could happen to three students in a school equipment room ... with a computer?"

Her eyes tracked over to a boy who seemed familiar from the back. She would have dismissed it if not for catching a glimpse of a snake image on his neck.

Had that been a cobra tattoo? Like the one on the TecKnati scout, Phen?

The boy disappeared into a sea of students.

She shook her head at her runaway imagination and followed Tony. No way could Phen be here.

TIMERETURN

RED MOON TRILOGY

SCIENCE FICTION TIME TRAVEL BOOK 2

DIANNA LOVE & MARY BUCKHAM
WRITING AS
MICAH CAIDA

CHAPTER 1

HELP ME! GET ME OUT of here before –

Gabby's screaming voice woke Rayen from a deep sleep, chilling as getting hit in the face with ice water. She sat up in bed, panting and clutching the sheets. Her heart tried to beat a hole in her chest.

Just a nightmare. But it felt real. Sounded terrifying.

She looked around the dark room as her eyes slowly adjusted to the dim light offered by the first hint of dawn. It peeked through the horizontal window coverings.

Blinds. Someone had called the coverings *blinds*. A strange term that didn't ping any new memory for her.

Surely, she'd had some type of window shield in her life.

She thought on it, willing to take any memory of her past that her mind would offer, no matter how insignificant. Nope. Still stuck with a big gaping void when it came to anything about her, possible family, or even the place she must have called home before yesterday. All she knew right now was life in this isolated school in a land called Albuquerque.

Home … until she found hers.

As her eyes adjusted to the dim light, sparse furnishings took shape around her room. A wall lamp hung over a small table next to her narrow bed. Across the room, a spotless wooden desk had a stiff chair and matching lamp. Other than that, just two metal doors the color of an early morning fog.

She closed her eyes, thinking of what stood on the other side of those doors. One opened to a bathroom with shelves and drawers for clothes. All her storage space was empty. She had no clothes or personal things of her own, only what had been given to her yesterday.

Good to know her recent memory still worked.

The second door led to a hallway with other rooms. More female students sleeping in this area. Boys had their own section. Did any of the others feel as confused and alone as she did?

Rubbing the heels of her hands over her eyes, she blinked to clear them better. Her scrambled thoughts began to separate and focus with details of what she did know. She was still at the Byzantine Institute of Excellence, a school filled with a mix of unusual and brilliant teens. She still didn't know who she was beyond the name Rayen–which was suspect at best. She'd gotten that information from a ghost–and that she was seventeen, another nugget from her grumpy specter.

Basically, she *still* had no memory beyond when she woke up in the desert yesterday with a sentient beast chasing her.

Rayen couldn't get past the sound of Gabby's frantic voice in her mind. Had that been real or just a bad dream? Gabby's words bounced around, slowly vanishing like a lost echo in a deep canyon.

Where *was* Gabby?

The women's center in the school hospital.

Gabby was supposed to be doing something basic. Tests of some kind. Rayen hadn't been sent there yet so she had no idea of what went on in the hospital. Her other friend, Tony, had told her not to worry about Gabby, but Tony didn't have the ability to hear voices in his head.

Not that Rayen really possessed that gift.

Gabby was the one who could hear thoughts, but Rayen *had* heard Gabby's yesterday at one point.

That had been accidental.

Not like this, where they weren't even in the same room.

Could Gabby be projecting?

Tony would roll his eyes at Rayen and tell her to stop imagining things. He knew more about this place than her … *and* he knew the girl who had led Gabby to her clinic meeting.

Still, Rayen kept thinking about how Gabby hadn't wanted anyone to know she heard other people's thoughts. All of that changed in the matter of a few hours in a strange world.

A lot of things changed yesterday.

Rayen couldn't stop worrying. Gabby and Tony were her only friends in this place.

She'd known them for just a short time, but the three of them now shared a huge secret. They depended on each other. She couldn't lose either one of them.

Rayen scrubbed a hand over her face. Maybe her nightmare about Gabby was nothing more than a reaction to the bizarre time travel they'd experienced yesterday.

Rayen grabbed her head and pulled her thoughts together.

Tony had assured her Gabby was fine. Might as well get dressed and track him down to come up with a plan for today.

Children were depending on her.

Climbing out of bed, Rayen hissed at the cold floor beneath her feet. She'd slept in a short-sleeved shirt and underwear. She made her way to the bathroom and flipped on the light, squinting.

The reflection in the mirror taunted her.

She didn't recognize that girl with the long, black hair mussed from sleeping, or eyes a light blue-green color she'd seen on no others yesterday. She splashed water on her face just to look away. While she and Tony had eaten dinner in the school cafeteria last night, he'd asked if she wore aqua contacts and explained how the thin eye covering corrected vision or changed eye color.

When she'd said no, he'd warned, "You tell anyone who asks that you're wearing contacts or they're gonna know you're not from this world. I've never seen natural eyes that color."

To be honest, her eyes looked strange to her, too, but her eye color could be normal for C'raydonians. Based on what V'ru had told her yesterday, those were her people. They'd existed over a hundred years into the future from the world in which she stood.

The head of this Byzantine Institute thought she was a Native American, someone from a local tribe she'd never heard of before or met.

Any family she might have once had no longer existed. She didn't even know who they were to mourn them.

A wave of sadness pushed her off center. She missed ... she slapped the sink counter, frustrated at not even knowing who she missed.

She wasn't from this time.

She didn't belong to anyone in this world. Based upon what she'd learned yesterday, she hadn't been born yet in this world.

And the one she had been born into had eventually been destroyed.

If she focused too hard on what little she *had* learned about herself yesterday, it would cripple her.

Hissing out a long sigh, she finished up in the bathroom. Maybe her brain would yield its secrets today. Turning the lamp on in the bedroom, she found the bag of used clothes that had been dropped off in her room. Good thing she was a quick study since everything from speech to paper books to the location of this school had tested her yesterday. She pulled a T-shirt over her head.

Lifting jeans from the bag, she stepped into each leg and fumbled with the zipper thing.

She had to let go of the family and life she'd lost. Just stick with living in the moment.

First thing, she needed to make sure Gabby was safe, then track down Tony. Once the three of them were together again, they could travel through the computer time portal back to the Sphere. She had to help save children imprisoned on that artificial planet.

Sitting on the edge of the bed, she shoved her feet into socks, sliding the metal ankle cuff over the sock to keep it from chafing her skin. The security device had shocked her when she'd tried to run past the front gates of the school. She had no idea if it would shock her if she entered an area of the school where she was not allowed. Thankfully, it hadn't functioned in the Sphere. She struggled to tie the strings on her sneakers, ready to get moving.

She wanted to return to the sphere this minute.

More than that, she *had* to go back. She'd made a commitment to Callan.

His strong face formed in her mind's eye and the pressure on her chest of being alone lifted. He was a healing light that she longed desperately to see and feel again.

She touched her lips and replayed his kiss for the hundredth time. Had that been her first kiss? How would she know with no memories? It had felt like what should be a first time. Chuckling at herself, she murmured, "I'm pretty sure I would have remembered experiencing something that spectacular."

Rayen! They want to ... STR ... V.

Rayen jumped at the ragged cry in her head.

Gabby called her by name. Her heart pounded wildly. That was so real this time that bumps pebbled across her skin at Gabby's terrified voice.

Rayen tried to reach out to her mind-to-mind. *Gabby?*

Nothing.

Time to go find her. Rayen hurried to the exit door and eased from the room.

No alarm went off.

Two young girls stood talking at the end of the hall. Taking a deep breath, Rayen headed out, moving as quickly as she could without running.

Once out of the sleeping areas, she navigated a series of halls and reached the office for the women's center of the hospital. She tapped on a small window.

A short woman twice her age dressed in loose blue pants and a matching shirt sat at a desk with a computer in front of her.

She slid the window open. "Can I help you?"

"I'd like to talk to Gabby Lin for a moment."

The woman typed on her keyboard, read something, then her face turned sharp and serious before she wiped that look away and presented a false smile. "I'm sorry, but Miss Lin is indisposed right now and isn't scheduled to be released until tomorrow. Come back then."

Rayen's skin tingled with worry.

This woman was hiding something. Rayen had nothing to base that on, but she knew. Just a feeling. With no argument to offer the woman that wouldn't sound as if she were making trouble, she mumbled, "Thank you," and backed away.

Why can't you hear me, Rayen? Gabby pleaded in her mind.

I do hear you, Gabby. Rayen listened for a reply, but Gabby didn't respond, which meant she couldn't hear Rayen. Gabby had that exceptional gift of talking in Rayen's mind, but she was clearly still learning how to use it. Evidently, telepathy wouldn't help Gabby escape her situation.

Rayen couldn't stand here doing nothing so she headed for the one person who could find out what was going on with Gabby.

As she turned to leave, she caught sight of a familiar shape moving through a cluster of students. A boy who reminded her of someone she'd encountered yesterday in the Sphere, but everyone there was from over a hundred years in the future.

That boy couldn't be Phen, could he? He had not traveled back to the school with the three of them.

She stilled at catching a whiff of a nasty smell. It belonged to the deadly, sentient beast that had chased her in the desert yesterday and shown up in the school as a bird.

Bad sign.

Worming her way through groups of students starting to congregate in the halls, she kept the boy in view. If that was Phen, they had to find out what he was doing here, and it could only mean trouble since Phen was a TecKnati scout, enemy of the MystiKs.

The boy she followed looked to be an older teen, which fit, because Phen had seemed closer to twenty. He managed to stay several steps ahead of her before he disappeared around a corner.

She rushed forward and stopped when she saw him thirty feet away where he paused next to a door that led outside. She looked around to see if anyone was close to her.

Not this early. Most students were heading to the cafeteria.

When she looked back at the boy, he pulled a small creature out of his pocket. A rat that jumped from his hand and changed shape in mid-fall on its way to the floor. The animal was now a tall black dog with a thick, muscular build and wide jaws. Its coat was black marked with brown highlights.

And it stank like the sentient beast.

Rayen's heart skipped a beat as she realized that dog was the beast that had hunted her yesterday. The boy had control of it. He looked over his shoulder, met her gaze, and boldly smiled in recognition.

It *was* Phen.

Had the TecKnati leader from the future sent him here? Had he traveled back to this time? From what Callan had told her, the TecKnati had developed time travel, but only to the past.

She started forward, but Phen and the creature ran out the door. They'd disappeared by the time she reached it and looked outside.

She'd deal with Phen as soon as Gabby was safe.

Working her way back through the halls, she passed a few students meandering around. School didn't officially start for another hour. When she reached the double door entrance to the boys' sleeping area, she paused at the "No Female Students Allowed Past This Point" sign.

What would be the penalty for getting caught in the wrong place?

Would her ankle cuff set off an alarm or try to electrocute her again if she entered this area?

"Who you looking for?" a squeaky male voice asked.

She turned to look down at a boy who was two or three years younger than her. He had freckles, bright red hair, and a crooked front tooth.

Rayen smiled at him, hoping he didn't report her. "Tony."

"What's his last name?"

Once again, the questions she can't answer starts. "I don't know."

"What's he look like?"

She searched for the right words to describe Tony, so she didn't sound strange. "He's my height, kind of strong looking, and has short black hair."

The boy thought on that and asked, "Is he a senior?"

"Senior what?"

He gave her a look that questioned her intelligence. Great. What did senior mean at this school? Something dawned on her that might be helpful. She remembered Tony telling a teacher that his name started with an S. "Tony's last name is S something."

"Like Smith or Stevens?"

How would she know? She lifted her shoulders. "All I know is he's from a place called Jersey." One more thing hit her. "He's in some Top Ten contest."

He snapped his fingers. "That's gotta be Tony Scolerio. He's sick on computers."

Searching her mind for the word "sick," she recalled Gabby explaining that it meant good. "Yes! That's him." Rayen let out a gust of relief. "Do you know where he is?"

The young one gave her a head nod for that.

"Where? I need to get to him right away."

The boy's red eyebrows lifted high, and his eyes rounded in horror. "If you get caught in our dorm, you'll get suspended. Maybe worse."

Suspended? Did that mean she'd end up hung in the air? She didn't have time to figure out a new term. "Tony and I have a friend who is, uh, not doing well. It's very important. If I get in trouble, then I do."

"Really?" He stared at her, his surprise telling her he didn't believe her. Shaking his head, he said, "We're all competing here. No one sticks his neck out for someone else. Why take that risk?"

"My friends are worth any risk," she stated firmly.

"You're not like the other girls here," he mumbled with a touch of awe she didn't understand.

She tried to decide if that was good or bad, but this was taking too long so she ignored it and pressed on. "Please tell me if you know where Tony's room is. I'm in a hurry."

He looked around then back at her and whispered, "It'll be faster if I show you, but if you get caught anywhere in the boys' dorm, I don't know anything about it. Got it?"

She swallowed her excitement. "Got it. I promise not to tell anyone you helped me."

Pulling one of the doors open, he led the way down a beige hall that mimicked the one in the girls' dorm.

She held her breath as she followed, hoping her ankle cuff didn't set off any alarms. When everything remained silent, she let out that breath and hurried to keep up with her guide. He turned a corner at the end of the hall. She was right behind him and barely missed getting hit by a door that opened as they scooted past.

After another two turns, he stopped at the first door on his right and pointed. "That's Tony's room. Don't get caught."

"Thank you."

He'd already backed away and took off, disappearing around the corner.

She knocked on the door and heard, "*What?*"

"It's me, Rayen." She kept her voice low.

Grumbling noises came through next, then he called out, "*Come in.*"

Turning the knob, she pushed the door open and closed it just as quickly.

Tony's room was a lot like hers except his bed was neat where she'd left hers in an unmade pile. He sat at his small desk, tapping quickly on a computer that was much newer looking than the one they had used to time travel.

No one from this time would believe them if they told anyone here about yesterday, but the portal to the other world really had been through the monitor of an abused computer that folded up. A laptop.

Tony flicked a look her way just long enough to scowl at her and kept typing as he asked, "What the 'ell you doin' over in the boys' dorm? Want to get thrown outta this place?"

"Gabby's in trouble."

Tony's fingers flew over the keys, tapping rapidly. His eyes never moved from the screen. "What kinda trouble?"

"In the hospital."

"Be specific."

The snarly, impatient Tony was back. The one she'd first met yesterday, before their little trip had taken the edge off his attitude. Traveling to another time with deadly flowering vines and unusual-looking kids trying to kill them had brought a change in him.

Tony was showing no signs of budging.

He'd proven he could be compassionate and loyal when things got tough, but this was the other side of him–belligerent, hardheaded and sarcastic–none of which she had any patience for with Gabby in danger and Phen running around the school.

Tony's foul mood would be nothing compared to hers if he didn't start paying attention so they could get moving. She tried for easy by sticking with the most important issue at this moment, which was getting him to realize Gabby was in trouble.

"I woke up with Gabby screaming for help in my mind." She expected him to be as shocked as her, but no.

"Oh, man, are you kidding me?" He leaned forward, paused then tapped keys harder. "I don't have time for your woo-woo stuff right now, Xena. You had a nightmare. That's all."

There were times he called her that weird Xena name when it sounded friendly.

This wasn't one of them.

She walked toward his desk where she watched little animated caricatures on his monitor attack each other. Buildings were blowing up. He was grinding her patience to a fine dust that would evaporate any minute.

What was so special about pretend fighting? "I thought it was a nightmare, too, Tony, but not anymore. I'm telling you I hear her in my head, and she's scared of something." When he continued to ignore her, she gave up on patience. "What *are* you doing?"

"I'm just about to win a game against the champion–"

"A *game*? Gabby's in trouble and you're ignoring me for a game?"

He muttered, "Not just any game."

Rayen! Please, please help me! Gabby cried out in Rayen's mind.

Rayen's heart raced at her terror. "Listen to me, Tony."

"Not. Now." He was hunched over the computer, intent on that ridiculous game.

Gabby's voice shouted, *Raayeeen!*

Energy swam through Rayen in a rush and heated her hands. She slapped a hand down on top of Tony's fingers.

His keyboard glowed red.

CHAPTER 2

WHITE LIGHT BURST FROM TONY'S monitor then it blanked out.

Rayen snatched her hand back. Uh oh.

He swung around, his face wearing shock for a second then he shoved up from his chair, yelling, "Do you realize what you just did? I'm gonna kill you!"

"I'm sorry. I – " she mumbled.

His chair flew backwards. He ignored it, hands fisted and his brown eyes glittering with rage.

Rayen took a step back to give him space. She wasn't afraid of Tony. They both knew what she was capable of, especially if she drew on that strange power inside her.

Besides, Tony wouldn't hit her.

He had a personal code he followed that included not harming a female, but he was vibrating with the need to crush something right now. She didn't want anyone to come running at the sound of furniture breaking.

"Are you out of your freakin' mind?" Tony roared at her.

She didn't think so. With no idea who she was, that might be open for debate. "I'm trying to tell you about Gabby."

"I've been at that game for over two hours. *Two! Hours!* I was six points from ripping the Dragon Goddess to pieces for the first time and you screwed it."

How could he be so angry? "What's so important about a stupid game when your friend is in danger?"

He closed his eyes and drew a hard breath. His jaw clenched and unclenched, then he opened eyes that still promised retribution. "This is *not* about a game. There's an online trading post where players offer prizes like electronics, jewelry, whatever. You put your prize up against theirs then you play a game to see who wins and who has to forfeit."

"What did you lose?"

"A half hour of electronic diagnostics, which I don't care jack about. You just cost me a win I had to have."

"What were you playing for?"

Disappointment washed through his gaze then it vanished as if he'd ordered his face to hide any emotions. "A 1968 *Captain America* comic book. It was for my little brother's birthday next month."

She had no idea what a comic book was or who Captain America was, but it didn't take much to figure out that she'd just ruined something that meant a great deal to Tony.

"I'm sorry, Tony." That sounded lame and useless, but it was honest and all she could offer. "I'm just worried about Gabby, and I don't know how to get to her. I went to the clinic. They wouldn't let me see her. I keep hearing her voice in my head, screaming for me to come help her before they do something. She'd probably be in your head, too, if she knew how to reach you."

He scrubbed his hands over his face, still pumped up and angry, but he pulled himself together to ask, "What exactly is goin' on with Gabby?"

"I don't know."

"You screw up my game and that's all you got?"

"No." Wasn't what she'd told him enough? Now she was fuming and let him hear it in her voice. "Gabby keeps saying she wants out before they do something, but I never hear what it is. Gabby says things like 'They want to' then her voice trails off. The last time her voice came back, she said 'STR' and 'V'. What do those letters stand for?"

"How should I know?" He sounded appalled. "That's women's center stuff." He stomped around for a moment, then picked up his chair and sat back down at his computer, grumbling, "This better power on again." The minute the monitor came to life, he grew quiet and started typing.

Now that he was calm, Rayen moved to watch over his shoulder. His fingers flew lightning fast over keys for a few seconds, then he paused to read text that meant nothing to her. He kept that up, typing and reading, for several minutes until he frowned at the monitor. "What the 'ell?"

She leaned down but couldn't decipher anything. "What does it say?"

"That's just it. I've hacked into the patient records, but I got stopped cold at one area where I can't get past the firewalls." He swung around to look at her. "What did you say those letters were?"

"STR and V."

"STR-V is the name of the patient files I can't access."

Rayen straightened up and crossed her arms. "*Now* do you believe me?"

Tony scanned his monitor again then pushed his chair back and stood, nibbling on his thumbnail as he thought. He leaned over and tapped the keys again, scrolled down the page and made an angry sound. When he lifted up and turned to her, he said "They have a level of security on that one area that's like nothing I've ever seen."

"Why would they do that if it was just some basic test?"

"Makes no sense. This whole deal is too weird a coincidence even for you and Psycho Babe." He stared off at nothing, eyebrows dropping low over his narrowed gaze. "I *might* be able to get into their system from inside the clinic."

"I told you, I already tried to see Gabby and they wouldn't let me in."

Tony found that amusing. "That's because you asked."

"How do *you* plan to get inside?"

He cracked his knuckles. "By using the 'ask for forgiveness instead of permission' rule."

Tony pulled a gray hooded jacket over his head. It had a black scorpion image sewn on the chest that matched the design inked on his neck. He scooped his dark brown backpack off his bed, slid his arms into the straps and started for the door. "Let's go."

She stood firm.

He did a double take. "Thought you wanted to help Gabby."

"I do, but if I get caught in this area and you're seen with me, they may suspend you, too." She envisioned both of them hung from the ceiling like dead game. *Hmm. So, I know about hanging animals from a hunt?*

He waved off her concern. "We won't get caught. No one on the staff is coming here today."

Mr. I Know Everything was back in full force. "How can you be so sure, Tony?"

"It's a teacher's PPA day."

"What's *that*?" She was beyond tired of phrases she didn't know.

Shaking his head, he turned back. "I forget that you don't know this stuff. Every six weeks the teachers have a Preparation, Planning, and Assessment Day to catch up on their work. We're supposed to spend our time studying or working on whatever we've been assigned."

That meant Rayen should be helping a girl named Hannah work on the special Top Ten computer project for Mr. Suarez's class. She had originally been assigned to Tony, but Mr. Suarez changed up the partners yesterday. Tony was no happier about his new partner than when he'd been stuck with Rayen.

She wasn't thrilled about Hannah since that girl barely tolerated Rayen being in her presence. But with no memory, Gabby in trouble, and Callan waiting for her to return to the Sphere, school was low on her worry list right now.

Speaking of concerns, why hadn't Tony mentioned this PPA yesterday while the three of them were still together? They might have gone back to the Sphere right away. She put a hand on her hip and frowned. "It would have been nice to know about this teacher's day off last night. Why didn't you tell me and remind Gabby before we split up?"

"Oh, I don't know," he snapped with a sarcastic edge. "Maybe because it wasn't the first thing on my mind after getting sucked into a time-travel portal in a computer, meeting a bunch of crazy teens with graffiti skin, and fightin' everything from freakin' plants to croggle monsters in that screwed up world."

He had a point.

Tony added, "What really sucked was coming back to find out I got stuck with the Browns' kid as my Top Ten Project partner. Call me distracted at that point."

The Browns had built this school, and Nicholas, or Nick as he'd told Rayen to call him, was their only child. "Have you talked to Nick? Maybe that won't be as bad as you think."

"You don't understand." He grabbed a strap on his backpack, squeezing it. "I need to go to MIT now, not next year, but *now*."

"What is so important about going there right now?"

Tony took his time replying. "My little brother is in foster care. That's a place kids go without a parent. It's a long story, but Vinny isn't doing too good without me. I need to get into a top college and land a decent job, one good enough that they'll let me raise him. I can't afford to lose any time."

Rayen's chest hurt just listening to Tony, who explained, "I need to ace this competition. Nick doesn't. His parents can send him anywhere at any time. I need the full ride, which means the college covers the cost, and if I go a year early I can–" He stopped, sadness invading his eyes before he looked away then back.

"Save your little brother?" she finished.

He swallowed. "Right."

Rayen held up her hands to pacify him. "I'm not here to argue about Nick and I'll do anything I can to help you figure a way to win. Right now, we have to save Gabby. If you think you can find her, please lead the way. The minute we get her out of wherever they have her locked up, the sooner we can head back to the Sphere. The sooner we can help you with the competition."

Tony didn't say anything to that, but he tensed up, which bothered her more than his usual mouthy posturing.

She waited for him to snap at her again.

He just shook his head at some silent thought, walked out the door, and took off in the opposite direction from the way she'd come. He led them to another hallway that ended at a locked door with an illuminated security panel on the right. The 12-button keyboard mounted shoulder high had a message warning all but service personnel to stay out.

Rayen kept her voice soft. "Where does this go?"

"While I was searchin' the clinic's electronic files on Gabby, I found the staff access codes to their behind-the-scenes work locations and a schematic of the clinic. This door goes to a hall that connects with the clinic. Like a service hallway." He raised his fingers to press buttons and looked over at me. "No one comes to our dorms on a teacher's day off, but the clinic is always staffed. We might run into someone on the other side of this door."

"Can't be any worse than facing a carnivorous plant with teeth the size of my fingers." She went for levity in reminding Tony about getting attacked in the Sphere yesterday, but he didn't find it funny.

In fact, he looked away quickly. Like a guilty reaction.

What could he possibly feel guilty about?

He punched in a series of numbers. The text on the panel showed "Access approved," and the door lock made a *click* sound. Tony entered with her at his heels. They shuffled quietly along a shadowy hall. A row of tiny white lights ran low along the floor. This corridor had no doors.

At the first corner, Tony slowed and peeked around to the left then waved her to follow him into another barely lit hallway.

She had the feeling that few came this way without a specific reason.

Four doors down, he stopped at a room with two huge glass windows, one on each side of the metal-and-glass door. Lights blinked and glowed on walls of equipment inside.

But there was no security panel next to the door.

Tony tried the doorknob. Locked.

He breathed out a labored sigh and kept his voice low. "This is the power and electronic control center for the clinic. I need to get in here to access the internal computer systems. We'll have to find a key."

He didn't sound enthusiastic. She asked, "How difficult will that be?"

Tony shook his head. "The minute we enter the populated areas of the clinic, we run the chance of getting caught. I could get us in here if I had something to pick the lock with."

"Explain picking a lock." She had a feeling it was a simple process, but she didn't recognize the terms or meanings.

Tony's face cramped like he was going to snap at her for asking a stupid question, but he explained, "The inside of a lock has pins that a key lifts to allow the plug to turn. The more pins, the more secure, in theory. Lock picks are metal sticks you use to move those pins just like a key would."

That didn't make a lot of sense to her, but it gave her an idea. "Do you know what the inside of a lock looks like?"

"Of course."

She'd helped Callan heal an injury because he'd known what the inside of a body looked like when she hadn't, or couldn't recall if she'd known at one time. She had no clue where her superpower came from, how to call it up–or how to control it sometimes–but if she could find it this time, she had something in mind that might work.

She told Tony, "Put your hand on the doorknob."

He arched an eyebrow. "What've you got in mind, Xena?"

"I know you don't understand Gabby's mental communication gifts or my powers, but you've seen me use my power. Put your hand on the knob and give my idea a chance."

That got her an I-can't-believe-I'm-doing-this groan, but he curled his fingers around the doorknob.

She placed her hand over his and said, "Envision the parts in the lock and show a little faith while you're at it."

Tony growled something about crazy women.

Nothing happened. She felt no push of energy coming up through her center.

"What's happening, Xena?"

"I don't know. It isn't working. When I did this yesterday, my power just seemed to show up." She pulled her hand back. "This is so frustrating. What use is that kind of power if you can't find it when you need it?"

"Take it easy, Xena," Tony said gently. "Think what caused it to work the last time you tried this."

"Callan needed my help to heal a child who was dying."

Tony's eyebrows cinched together. He was showing a rare moment of tolerance and seemed to be trying to help. He pointed out, "Back in my room, you used your power on my computer to kill the game, right?"

Did he have to bring that up again? "Yes, but that wasn't intentional."

"How'd you do it then?"

How had she tapped her power then? She realized where he was going with his questions and searched her mind for what happened right before she slapped her hand down on his keyboard. "Gabby had just yelled in my head. I was worried about her and angry that you were ignoring me. I just wanted you to stop playing that game."

"You stopped it all right," he groaned.

"I said it was an *accident*." Tony just couldn't let one little mistake go.

He raised his free hand. "Whatever. Back to the problem before we get caught." He looked around then returned to her. "Think. You were worried and angry. Aren't you at least worried about Gabby right now?"

"Of course, I am."

He made a snorting sound. "Don't look like it to me. If we don't get in this room, we might as well go back to the dorms."

No. Something bad was going to happen to Gabby and soon. If not already.

She put her hand back on Tony's.

He tried to pull away from the doorknob. "Forget this. I'm outta here."

She clamped her fingers hard, holding his in place. "*No!* We can't walk away."

"Gabby's resourceful. She'll figure a way out."

Rayen dropped her voice to a threatening level. "If she could have left on her own, she wouldn't be screaming in my head. She needs us."

"Give up, Xena. We'll check on her later."

"No!" She tightened her grip on his hand.

All at once, her arm heated, and the power flowed to her fingers.

He hissed and tried to pull back. "Whoa, Xena, I was only trying to get you worked up to do something, but your freakin' hand's hot."

Had he been intentionally tricking her? She told him, "That's the power. Use it."

"Are you nuts? How am I supposed to use *that*?"

She should have fed him to that monstrous croggle when she had the chance. Rayen forced her answer past clenched teeth. "Think about the lock, Tony. See the pins or whatever parts moving in your mind. Once you see them, make them move until it unlocks."

"I don't think–"

"Stop talking, Jersey, and start doing. Close your eyes and see the inside of that lock or I'm going to keep my hand here until your arm burns to a crisp and falls off." Empty threat.

Or not.

She *had* burned a gigantic croggle from the inside out, but she wouldn't harm Tony.

He must have believed her though. He slammed his eyes shut. His neck muscles tensed and flexed ... then she heard a click. And another click. His face relaxed then his eyebrows drew tight as he concentrated.

Three more metallic noises happened then the doorknob turned freely.

She released his hand.

Tony blinked, slowly swinging a wide-eyed expression at her. "That was crazy. Freakin' crazy. Man, I wonder if you could do that with a computer and–"

"Find Gabby first. Talk later." Something had been bugging her since seeing the Browns yesterday that now had her wondering if there was a relation between that and why they had Gabby in the clinic. She told Tony, "When you get in the files see what it says about my blood. When I first got here, I heard Dr. Maxwell saying something about markers in my blood and the Browns got excited, but by the time we met yesterday Mr. Brown and Dr. Maxwell were ready to boot me."

"We don't have all day, Xena." Grumbling the whole way, Tony entered the dark room, but didn't turn on any lights. There were enough scattered lights glowing on the equipment to allow them to move around safely.

She left him alone as he studied panel after panel. He stopped in front of one and put his backpack down. Next, he pulled out his phone and a thin white cord. He connected the cord between his phone and a machine. This machine had a screen similar to a larger one in the cafeteria that flashed with information on classes and events.

If she thought Tony had typed fast with all his fingers on a computer keyboard, that was nothing compared to the way his thumbs tapped the screen of his phone.

Tony paused, reading. "Says your blood test was corrupted and they have you listed to schedule for a new test depending on your meeting with Takoda."

She'd worry about that when the time came. "Okay. What about Gabby?" The air was chilly in there. She rubbed her arms, looking around, feeling as out of place as she had everywhere else since opening her eyes yesterday. What could they be doing to Gabby in this clinic? Why hadn't she heard Gabby again in her mind?

"I found her," Tony announced softly. He leaned in reading intently.

Moving close, Rayen studied a screen that listed names with last one first. Lin, Gabby was the third name down. "Great. How do we get to her?"

"I don't know."

"What do you mean?"

"She's been flagged for pre-op. They're getting ready to do some kind of surgery on her." He turned to Rayen with the first real worry showing in his face. "I found out what STR-V stands for. I think they're going to sterilize Gabby."

CHAPTER 3

GABBY FOUGHT THROUGH LAYERS OF drowsiness. She wanted to sleep but had to stay awake because ... she forgot why.

The drugs were making her loopy.

Drugs? She didn't take chemicals for many reasons, but an important one was so that she wouldn't lose control and slip.

Say the wrong thing and everyone would know her secret.

That would give them even more reason to call her a weirdo and put her back in a mental health ward. Only crazy people heard voices, right? She didn't hear just *any* voices. She heard a person's thoughts if she touched their skin. That was how she'd killed her mother.

The police report pointed to alcohol as the reason her mother's car had left the highway at over a hundred miles an hour and rolled down a steep drop.

Gabby knew the truth. Her mother had run from the freak she'd birthed.

That day had changed Gabby's life forever.

No touching anyone. No drugs. Never lose control.

That woozy feeling came back. The nurses wanted her calm for ... surgery.

Surgery?

She jolted awake, forcing her heavy eyelids to stay open this time. She was flat on her back in a bed and swung her head to the side to look around. Big mistake. The room spun. Lights blurred on the monitor hanging next to her bed. Okay, no fast movements. When everything settled back into place, she recognized the hospital room. Not a hospital.

The women's clinic in the Byzantine Institute.

She was a patient.

Thinking was harder than trying to run through waist-deep mud, but she had to clear out the cobwebs. Her mouth was dry as the desert sand surrounding the school. Water would help her thirst and maybe dilute whatever drug she'd been given.

Looking to her right, there was a half-filled plastic pitcher sitting with a glass on the nightstand next to her.

She went to reach for it and couldn't.

Her arm was caught.

Someone had strapped her to this bed. She jerked both her arms and legs. Trapped. Why had they tied her down?

Panic set in, shoving some of the wooziness from her head. Her heart hammered into overdrive despite whatever drug they'd given her. She yanked on the wrist restraints again. Tears burned her eyes.

What had she done to end up here?

All these years, she'd kept to herself, touching no one, not even a hug. Nothing that would expose her to thoughts she couldn't handle hearing. She'd been barely ten years old when she revealed that she could hear others and that had ended badly the night her mother died. Screaming that she was sorry she'd heard her mother's thoughts and begging her father to forgive her for killing her mother had landed Gabby in a hospital room, strapped to a bed so she wouldn't hurt herself.

All for her own good.

Her father liked to say that, but the truth was that he didn't want to deal with a crazy child. What surgeon with his reputation would?

She'd kept everything to herself all this time, eventually convincing everyone she had a painful reaction to being touched.

So why was she strapped down now?

The nurse's thoughts trickled through Gabby's mind. Last night, or maybe early this morning, was coming back to her now. Gabby had awakened groggy once before to find a nurse holding her wrist. She'd been unable to prevent hearing the nurse's thoughts ... about a surgery.

These people didn't think Gabby was going to hurt herself.

They were going to do something *to* her.

Some procedure ... the nurse had been keeping Gabby sedated until it was time for some STR-V laser surgery.

What kind of surgery was that? Did she really care? No. She just wanted to get out of here.

Rayen and Tony would help her if she could reach them.

But Rayen hadn't answered Gabby's mental calls. So much for being a powerful Hy'bridt. That's what they'd called her in the Sphere.

Had that really happened yesterday? Maybe she'd dreamed the entire trip, the TecKnati scouts and the MystiK kids imprisoned there.

If it were only a dream, that would mean she hadn't met Jaxxson, Mr. Hotbody healer.

That would suck.

She pushed at the sheet with her fingers until she could see her hand, then flipped it over. Yep, there were the scratches she'd gotten in the jungle.

That meant Jaxxson *was* real, just as running around a strange jungle with Rayen and Tony had been. She had even more evidence. Random voices no longer barged into her mind. Jaxxson had taught her how to shield her mind and control her telepathy.

But right now, she wanted to hear one telepathic voice answer her. Rayen's.

Why can't I reach her?

If Jaxxson was here, Gabby was sure he would hear her, and he wouldn't allow a bunch of strangers to operate on her for no reason. What was STR-V? The nurses hadn't informed her yet of any such procedure. If this bunch was performing the surgery without the permission of Gabby's father, then there was something illegal and just plain wrong about all of this.

She had to escape. But how? She wasn't a warrior like Rayen. Gabby had mad skills when it came to irritating people and power that allowed her to heal someone yesterday, but nothing that would unlock her wrist and ankle restraints. Her gaze landed on the monitor hanging beside her.

A digital clock blinked red numbers that changed.

Wait a minute. A clock should *gain* time, not lose it. That was no clock, but a countdown timer.

Was it counting down to give her more drugs or to take her away?

Either way, she wanted out of here.

She started to yell for Rayen again in her mind when the door to her room opened and two orderlies came in rolling a gurney. They both wore blue scrubs, facemasks and scrub caps on their heads that were worn for surgery.

They were coming to take her away now.

Her skin chilled and she felt lightheaded. She couldn't faint now. Not when she'd need to fight. They were not operating on her, laser or otherwise.

She shouted one more time in her mind. *Raaay-en!*

One of the orderlies stopped pushing and clamped his hands over his ears. "Stop that!"

He sounded like ... *Rayen?*

Gabby whispered, "Is that you, Rayen?"

"Yes. You're giving me a headache yelling in my head." Rayen stood upright and unclipped a facemask she let dangle from one ear. She was grinning, then her blue-green eyes turned serious when she said, "We're getting you out of here."

Gabby could breathe again. "I don't think I have much time. They have me scheduled for some STR-V surgery."

"We know," a husky male voice replied. The other orderly turned around. Tony's dark eyes stared out above the mask then shifted to take in the monitor. "It's a sterilization procedure."

Gabby saw dots in her vision. "No."

"Yes," Tony argued. "Get your butt moving or we're all gonna end up in deep crap."

"I can't. I'm strapped down."

Tony and Rayen hurried over to Gabby's bed.

Rayen asked Tony, "Do you need my power to unlock it?"

"No, I got this." He unsnapped the latches on Gabby's arms. She noticed that Tony was careful not to touch her even though Jaxxson had taught her how to block the thoughts of others.

Tony could be a roaring pain at times, but he *did* have the ability to be nice if he wanted to be.

Gabby rubbed her wrists then swung her legs around and dropped her feet to the floor, groaning at the muscle ache from being in that bed for hours. She wobbled to the left.

Rayen reached out. "You need help."

Gabby grabbed the bed and her head. "No, but I need my clothes and some water."

"We got less than four minutes," Tony warned.

"I only need one if you'll get my clothes," Gabby crabbed at him. "I hid them in the bottom drawer. Don't unwrap them."

Ignoring Tony's growl of impatience, Gabby turned to the nightstand and poured a half glass of water while Rayen helped Tony get the clothes. When Gabby picked up the plastic cup, the plastic changed shape in her hand, morphing into a curvy piece of art. The water ran up one side, paused as if held there, then dropped back into the cup.

O. Kay. She drank quickly and tossed the cup into the waste can, so no one saw it. "I'm ready."

"Don't rush on my account. I'm only going to get tossed out on my butt if I'm caught in here," Tony snarled.

There was the Tony she knew. Gabby climbed up on the bed.

Rayen handed her the dress that Gabby had wadded up in a very careful way. She put the blob of material next to her on the gurney. "How did you two get in here?"

Hurrying back to the foot of the gurney, Rayen said, "Tony found the central computer for the clinic. He changed those numbers on your monitor or you'd already be gone. Then he sent an alert to the nurses' station that there was a gas leak on the far side of the building."

See? The Jersey Jerk had his moments.

"Thank you, Tony." Gabby turned to Rayen. "You, too. I didn't think you could hear me."

"Trust me. You were loud and clear," Rayen confirmed, but with a smile in her voice. "I just couldn't reach you the same way."

"Put your mask back on, Xena," Tony ordered, his abrupt tone making it clear that he wasn't waiting another minute to escape. "Lay down and look out of it, Gabby."

"That shouldn't be too hard," she muttered.

Gabby watched all around her as the gurney started moving.

Tony whispered, "Close your eyes so they think you're knocked out for surgery."

She did, but all the movement was making her feel nauseous. It seemed forever until the gurney finally stopped. She'd spent the entire ride expecting someone to come running down the hall shouting to bring her back.

When Gabby opened her eyes, she was in a dark room with a humming noise and illuminated panels on some kind of equipment.

"Let's go, sweet cheeks." Tony stood over by the door, taking a position to keep watch.

Rayen helped Gabby off the gurney and held her arm. She leaned down to ask, "Are you okay with me touching you?"

"Yes. I can still block your thoughts."

"Jaxxson was a good person for you to meet."

In more ways than one. Gabby nodded. "I'm ready to see him again."

"Are you two through having girly time?" Tony complained.

"Turn your back and stay that way until I tell you it's okay to turn around."

"Whatever, sweet cheeks."

Gabby shrugged out of the hospital gown and put on her dress that had been battered in the Sphere. It smelled nasty and felt just as yucky, but she smiled when her pocket moved.

Rayen noticed the movement. "What's in there?"

Reaching into her pocket, Gabby pulled out the pupple that was an offspring of a Sphere animal called a dugurat. It reminded her of a cross between a puppy and a soft troll doll. Her heart hit her toes when she saw how lethargic the poor thing appeared.

She whispered, "It's sick."

"You brought a pupple back?"

Gabby flinched at the censure in Rayen's voice. "I didn't mean to. It was in my pocket when we ran for the transender. I think it's dying."

Tony swung around. "Oh, man, you didn't."

Giving Tony a dark look, Gabby said, "I clearly did."

"That thing probably won't survive here."

"Thanks for the encouragement," Gabby snapped. "You have the bedside manner of the Grim Reaper."

Rayen raised a hand. "Let's not fight while we still have to escape without being seen. Jaxxson can probably fix the pupple when we return to the Sphere."

"Good point." Gabby eased the little guy back into her pocket. "I need clean clothes then I'm ready to go." She turned to Tony. "Have you got the computer?"

There was no question that she referenced the laptop with the time travel portal.

"I've got it."

That had come out of Tony with the gloominess of a man on death row. What was his problem?

Terminal PIA evidently, but she and Rayen couldn't open the portal for time travel without him. For that, she'd put up with the devil himself. Gabby shoved her hair back over her shoulder, ready to wash the icky mess that she normally kept in multiple ponytails because it was so thick and fell to the middle of her back. "Let's just go so I can shower and change."

Tony led them out through a series of dark corridors illuminated by ankle-high lights. When they got outside the last door, Tony punched buttons on the security panel then turned and fell silent.

His shoulders were hunched. He couldn't meet her eyes or Rayen's.

Rayen took over, the desire to get moving as strong in her face as Gabby felt it in her bones. "I'll go with Gabby to her room and help shield her from view on the way. As soon as she's done, we meet to power up the computer and head back to the Sphere."

Gabby nodded. "Sounds good. I only need about twenty minutes tops."

Tony lifted his phone from where he'd clipped it on his belt and tapped it, reading something.

"What's up?" Gabby asked, anxious to go.

He shoved the phone back on his hip. "A text from Hannah."

Gabby asked, "Was it about me?"

"No."

She let out a tight breath. "Even more reason we need to hurry up before Hannah shows up with something from the front office saying I'm AWOL. They may be looking for me already. Where do you want to meet, Tony?"

His gaze moved to the side, looking anywhere but at Gabby or Rayen's face. After a long second, he swung his backpack off his shoulder and pulled out the beat-up laptop that had activated a time-travel portal yesterday.

The portal that would send her back to Jaxxson.

Tony dug out the power cord, paused a moment then said, "Traveling to the Sphere yesterday happened by accident. I've had time to think about a few things. If I don't win the Top Ten Competition and get into MIT now, it'll be another year before I'm accepted by a major school."

"Why are you in such a hurry?"

Tony's mouth flattened and his face looked like he was about to blow a mental gasket

Rayen held up a hand as if to calm him and quickly explained to Gabby about Tony's little brother being in foster care.

Nodding, Tony jumped in. "See? That's another year farther away from getting my little brother back and being able to provide a stable life for him. He can't wait forever."

Gabby felt another twitch coming on. "What are you saying, Tony?"

Tony held the computer and cord out to Rayen. "I'm not going with you two."

CHAPTER 4

"RAYEN?" GABBY SAID TO HER as if she could fix this somehow.

"What do you want me to say, Gabby? I'm not going to force anyone to go back to the Sphere." Rayen accepted the computer and cord from Tony. She tried to understand his dilemma, but all she could think about was Callan and a village full of small children that he would die for to keep safe.

She'd also seen what happened to any MystiK who turned eighteen in the Sphere.

There was normal death, then there was what happened to Mathias, who had led the MystiKs before Callan. No person deserved the hideous death Mathias had suffered, except maybe that SEOH guy who captured the MystiKs and sent them to the Sphere.

Rayen wanted to help Callan and the rest of the trapped MystiKs figure out how to go home before anyone else died, even though it meant her never seeing Callan again. But how could she ask Tony to turn his back on his family?

She couldn't.

Their nothing-bothers-me Gabby disappeared as she wilted before Rayen's eyes. Gabby's lavender-and-yellow hair hung limp around her shoulders instead of twisted up in her usual happy look of ponytails sticking out everywhere. She swung a load of disappointment and hurt in Tony's direction. "You know it takes all three of us to make the portal work."

"No, I don't know that and neither do you," Tony shot right back at her. He ran a hand over his short hair, rubbing it back and forth. "I don't think you should go either, if you want to know the truth."

Gabby made a chuffing sound. "Oh, please. Deal with your guilt some other way than trying to convince us you're worried about our welfare."

"I am worried, Gab."

Tony never used Gabby's name. Rayen believed he was sincere, but she'd made her decision yesterday and this argument wasn't getting the two of them any closer to the Sphere. "We'll go by ourselves, Gabby. We shouldn't pressure Tony into doing something he doesn't want to do, especially when it's traveling to a place like the Sphere."

Gabby argued, "But what if the portal won't work with just two of us? Or what if we get stuck halfway there?"

"I don't know," she admitted and turned to Tony. "I really do understand why you aren't going. Thanks for helping me find Gabby."

"No problem, Xena. If you need help with the computer, let me know." He sounded low about not joining them, but he wasn't changing his mind. "Be careful, you two. That place is wicked dangerous and those scouts ain't playin' around."

Rayen slapped her forehead. "I forgot to tell you."

"What?"

"I saw Phen."

"*Where?*" Gabby and Tony asked together.

"Here at the school. I thought I saw him last night when we got back, but I figured I was imagining things. Then I saw Phen again on my way to find Tony this morning and followed him. I lost him when he ran outside, but he has control of the sentient beast that was hunting me."

Pinching the bridge of his nose, Tony muttered, "Unfreakinbelievable." He dropped his hand. "What could he be doin' here?"

Rayen shook her head. "Don't know, but that SEOH guy must have sent him back in time. Callan told me the TecKnati had figured out time travel to the past, but they didn't know how to communicate with anyone sent back and they couldn't bring anyone forward again."

"They didn't just ship him back a hundred and sixty some odd years for no reason," Tony bit out, frowning. "That must mean somethin' is going on here and now."

Rayen agreed but had no idea what was happening here or in the time when she was born, years in the future. If she was honest with herself, she'd want to be in Callan's world, but his people had hunted her people to extinction by the time Callan was born. She should hold that against him, but she couldn't. Callan hadn't personally killed C'raydonians. Her people had been terminated to stop the spread of the disease that had driven them rabid.

Yet again, she was reminded that she didn't belong here, there, or anywhere. That dark place inside her threatened to steal her breath. She shook it off and kept her mind on returning to Callan.

Rayen told Tony, "Just be careful here, too."

"I will." He glanced over at Gabby, who pulled the pupple out of her pocket.

She lifted the little thing to her face. "He's panting and I couldn't get him to drink any water. I, uh ..." Then she shoved him at Rayen, who took the little critter before Gabby dropped him.

Gabby grabbed her head. Her entire body started shaking. More like vibrating.

Tony's anger slide away and his mouth fell open. "What's wrong with you?"

"I-I-I ... d-don't know." Gabby's teeth chattered. "I-I ... hear ... ev-ev-everyone."

Gabby was scaring Rayen. "What do you mean everyone?"

"In ... th-th-the ... *school! I can't block them.*" Gabby clenched her eyes shut and all at once the trembling stopped. She stumbled sideways and stuck her hand against the wall. Tony reached over to steady her, but Gabby said, "No! Don't touch me right now. It's quiet again and I'm afraid you'll set it off."

"What do you think is happening, Gabby?" Rayen asked.

"I have no idea, but I've been feeling strange, even before they gave me drugs. I'm not sure what's going on. Maybe the drugs are making it worse."

Rayen considered how Gabby had been the most sensitive to things yesterday. "Do you think it's a reaction to visiting the Sphere?"

Gabby shook her head. "I think it might be a reaction to me coming back here."

Tony made growling noises and hit his fist in the palm of his other hand. "This is why you shouldn't go back. It's making you sick."

Gabby didn't seem to have the energy to snap at Tony, but she sent him an evil, one-eyed look. "I'm not sick. I'm having some reaction, but I think it's from being *here*, not there. Either way, I need to get help and that means seeing Jaxxson again."

Rayen agreed. "She might be right, Tony. They said she's a powerful Hy'bridt." The MystiKs had designated Gabby as such based on her different-colored eyes–one green and one brown–plus her ability to communicate mentally and heal others. But she wasn't healing *herself* now.

"Give me a break. Hy'bridts are from *their* time, not ours."

"We are the ancestors of people in the future," Gabby tossed back at him with more force this time. "They got their genetics from someone. Even you scientific types should be able to understand how traits are passed through DNA. Think they just woke up one day with their supernatural gifts?"

Rayen heard voices of someone approaching and this conversation was going nowhere. Tucking the computer against her chest, she stepped away. "People are coming. We need to move or get caught. Come on, Gabby."

When they reached the corner, the voices she'd heard were two students walking into a room, leaving the hall empty. Tony turned the opposite way from them, heading in the direction of the office. He called out in a whisper, "I have to find out what Hannah wants. You two be careful."

They waved him off and turned toward the girls' sleeping quarters.

Tony was right about one thing. They hadn't tried traveling through the computer with just two of them, or even one alone. That *could* work, but it didn't stop the sinking feeling Rayen had about trying to time travel without Tony this time.

"What happened with the Browns last night, Rayen?" Gabby asked. "I'm assuming that you get to stay since you're still here."

Gabby had been on her way to the women's clinic by the time Rayen's meeting with the Browns had ended. "I'm here for right now. Mrs. Brown seems to like me. She suggested that I might be on some lists of local Indian tribes. She bought me more time by setting up a meeting with someone called Takoda. She said they'd let me know when he can see me."

"Normally, that would make good sense to check the Navajo council to see if they know who you are since it's the largest tribe in the area, but you're a C'raydonian."

Rayen hadn't forgotten. "I know."

Gabby continued, "If this Takoda says you're not an enrolled member of any of the tribes, the Browns can kick you out."

Maybe she wouldn't be here to be kicked out if she could figure out how to get back to the Sphere and stay there. A big maybe. "I'll deal with that when it happens."

By the time they'd raced back to Gabby's room, Rayen's clean shirt was damp with sweat from worry and exertion.

Gabby put her sickly pupple on a pillow on the floor and locked the door to her room. "This is PPA day, so no one should bother us, but I'm not taking a chance of someone coming in unannounced." She turned to me. "Do you think we can do this? Travel through the portal with just the two of us?"

No, but that wasn't the right answer with Gabby's emotions held together by threads. "We'll know as soon as you're ready, but we can't do this here."

"Why not?"

"Your room is the first place they'll look for you."

"Shoot. You're right."

"Tony said he sent the clinic staff on a cyber goose chase, whatever that is, to buy you time. Hurry up and we might get out of here before someone comes for you."

Her odd eyes shimmered with hope. "Be right back."

The pupple made a whimpering noise.

Rayen walked over to look at the odd ball of fluff with legs. When she'd first seen them, they were cute in a bizarre way with spiked rainbow-colored hair at the end of their tails and around their paws. This one's spiky hair drooped and was bland as if the color had been washed out. No telling what time travel had done to the poor baby.

The door opened and Gabby emerged looking much like a healthy human pupple. Ponytails woven into braids stuck out all over her head, each tied with a mix of red, yellow, and purple ribbons. Instead of the dress from yesterday, she wore baggy purple pants that had pockets all along the legs. She'd pulled on a long-sleeved pink shirt of soft material, plus another sleeveless shirt over that but it had no buttons.

A vest?

Remembering a word was like receiving a shot of energy, but it didn't last long. Every time Rayen thought her memory was coming back, she got excited. Then nothing ... just that same black hole that had swallowed her life.

Freshly showered, Gabby had a smile in place, but it lacked heart. "I'm ready."

Then Rayen heard Gabby's voice chattering in her mind. *Oh, God, I can't believe I turned the water green ... and I reshaped the faucet ... and my head feels like it's expanding. What if my hair stands up again and Rayen notices?*

Her hair *was* floating up. "Are you having problems, Gabby?"

"No. Let's go."

"Not until you tell me what happened in the bathroom."

Gabby's face lost color, looking like her sick pupple. "Did you hear my thoughts?"

"Yes."

"You aren't supposed to listen to someone else's thoughts!" she yelled at me.

Rayen held up her hands in defense. "I can't help it. And if I hadn't heard you earlier this morning you wouldn't be here now."

Gabby put a hand to her forehead. "You're right. I'm sorry, Rayen. I just don't know what's going on." She was panting and sounding terrified again.

Gabby's ponytails now stood straight out.

That couldn't be good.

Not wanting to panic her anymore, Rayen kept her voice calm. "You can tell me everything. I'm not Tony. I know you have unusual gifts. Are you just having a reaction or is there more?"

Gabby was wringing her hands and let out a long breath. "There's more. I touch things and they change shape, but I'm not trying to make that happen. And I can't control my thoughts. Jaxxson taught me how to block someone else's voice in my mind. I was doing it until I got back here. I heard the nurses' thoughts, but I was too groggy to put up my mental shields."

"Can you make your hair lay down?"

"What?" Gabby rolled her eyes up as if she could see her hair then swatted a hand around, feeling her individual braids. She groaned. "I can't walk around this way."

"Can we tie them down somehow?"

Reaching with her hands to gather all the ponytails, Gabby twisted them into one big knot of some sort. "That might work for now, but whatever is happening to me is intensifying. If I can't make it back to get Jaxxson's help, I'm not sure what I'm going to do because I can't stop this and it's getting worse by the minute."

Rayen had a new worry. "What if traveling through the portal causes another type of reaction?"

Gabby clutched her hands together. "I just know that Jaxxson can fix this. You must take me back, Rayen. Please. If I stay here, they'll take one look at me and decide I'm possessed. You don't know what it's like to be treated like you're insane. It's awful. Don't make me stay here to face that or to be sterilized in their clinic. I'd call my father, but he'd just pull me out of the school. Then where would I be, or you for that matter?"

Rayen could feel her terror spread out and fill the room. Gabby was right to worry about the clinic. Rayen nodded at the critter. "Get your pupple."

Relief broke across Gabby's face. She hurried over and grabbed her little pet, voice anxious. "Where are we going to set up the computer?"

"The one place no one will look for us." Rayen just hoped she wouldn't end up killing both of them, and the pupple.

CHAPTER 5

TONY STRODE QUICKLY DOWN THE halls, nodding at three girls who paused from huddling in a girl circle to smile at him. Normally, he'd stop long enough to flirt with the trio he knew from two classes, but he didn't have it in him right now.

Xena and Psycho Babe were going back to a world full of dangerous crap that they'd all been lucky to survive yesterday.

What was wrong with those two?

Besides one being a C'raydonian–whatever that was–from the future and the other one possessed with twitches? He knew the answer. Boys. Gabby wanted to get back to Jaxxson who might or might not know how to fix her problems or could be behind all her problems.

And Rayen had Callan on the brain.

No one had missed that serious liplock Callan had put on Rayen before she dove inside the transender.

Hormones were going to get both of those girls killed.

So why do I feel guilty that I'm not going back?

Tony had responsibilities. His grandmother barely got along on her own now that he wasn't there to help her out. Tony had jumped at the opportunity to test for enrollment in the Byzantine Institute even though it meant leaving New Jersey. He'd walked away from everyone he'd known for the chance to offer his little brother a better life and to have the money to care for his grandmother.

If it were only about his dreams and future, he'd have gone with Xena and Psycho Babe just to keep them safe. But Vinny had no one watching out for him except Tony.

On the other hand, Nick Brown had screwed Tony out of his best chance at MIT when he got Suarez to stick Tony with Nick on the Top Ten Project, so maybe Tony was letting everyone down by staying here.

"Tony."

He glanced up, realizing he'd reached the front office where Hannah waited out in the hall for him. She always looked put together, today being no different in that baby-blue straight skirt and matching jacket. Uber business like and uptight. That ruffled white blouse did soften her strait-laced look and even he had to admit it turned her downright sexy. She *was* cute with her chin-length auburn hair and diamond-blue eyes, but he'd never caught her attention except when she sent him a wary look.

Only an ice queen would be impervious to Scolerio charm.

What'd she want with him on a teacher's day off?

Clamp down on the bad mood already. Hannah was only doing her job as an intern for the office and didn't deserve attitude. He gave his best try at a warm smile when his heart wasn't in it and said, "What's up, Hannah?"

She had a stack of papers and handed one to Tony. "Mr. Suarez wanted to let everyone know he'd be missing a day."

"Think I could figure that one out all on my own since it's PPA day."

"Not talking about today. Tomorrow. Mr. Suarez had something personal come up and has to leave later today. He said he'd try to be back by tomorrow afternoon, but he wasn't sure. I'm passing out his instructions for all his classes and extra notes for the Top Ten Project in case he isn't able to return for a few days."

Tony glanced at the paper. None of it sank in after he heard the words *Top Ten Project.* He had too much on his mind, starting with Nick and ending with two crazy girls time traveling right now.

What if it did require all three of them to open the portal and something happened to Gabby and Rayen trying to travel with only two? Tony wouldn't know what happened if they never returned. That thought turned his stomach.

Hannah chided, "Earth to Tony."

He folded the paper and shoved it in his pocket. "Got it. What else?"

Her pleasant face lost all softness and looked hurt.

Why? Because he was being an A-hole? "Sorry, Hannah. I've had a tough morning."

That brought the twinkle back into her eyes. She glanced around when a group of students passed then her gaze whipped back at Tony. "I want to talk to you about something."

She had the direct line to the office and knew everything that went on in there. Had she heard something about Xena and that tribal person? Or was she going to ask if he knew where Gabby was?

He said, "Sure thing."

Waving Tony to the side of the hall traffic, Hannah stepped into a corner.

He followed. It felt intimate to stand here with a pretty girl. Any other time, he'd be thinking about getting a kiss from a babe that had cornered him, but not the ice queen.

Make a pass at her and you'd get your butt hauled into the office.

Hannah chewed on her lip, nervous. "You're not happy being partnered with Nick, right?"

He went on defense immediately. Admitting to that and letting it out in public could get Tony canned from this school since Nick's parents pulled the strings around here. "I never said that."

"Are you happy about it or not?"

Where was she going with this? "It's okay."

Her entire attitude shifted to annoyed, from her fingers clenching the stack of papers to those pretty lips scrunched up. "I thought you wanted MIT and to go a year early, but if you'd rather suck up to Nick then never mind."

"Whoa, babe, I never said that either." He huffed out a breath and scratched his neck, debating. Hannah hadn't cozied up to any guy here, definitely not Nick. She'd just made a dig about sucking up to Nick so what would be the harm in telling her the truth?

Tony dropped his arm and leveled with her. "I do want MIT and I'm not happy about having Nick as my partner."

That transformed her face quick as a snap from irritated to hopeful. "I've got an offer for you. Trade Nick for me as your partner."

"What?" Oops. He might have said that with a little too much disbelief.

"Before you insult me any further–"

"I didn't insult you," Tony argued. Not intentionally.

"Yes, you did. You're in shock that I'd even suggest it, because seriously? Who could be as competent as you or Nick?" She crossed her arms, not the least concerned that she was crumpling her papers. "For your information, I rock in computer science. I'm just as good, if not better, than you *or* Nick."

That comparison might be going too far, but this was the first year he'd had a class with her. He'd never seen what she could do so he was still listening.

"I may not wave my accomplishments in front of everyone, but I do know what I'm doing."

"Hey, I'm not doubtin' you, babe, but you have to admit that Nick has major mojo bein' a Brown and all. I dump him, I'm tickin' off the Browns."

"True, but it won't matter if you win the contest. Anything worth having is worth fighting for." She glanced around with a slyness that Tony had missed about her until now. Hannah might not be the quiet little innocent everyone had made her out to be.

When she looked back at him, she kept her voice low. "In fact, Nick didn't test as high as you or me on Mr. Suarez's last evaluation."

That surprised Tony. "No kidding?"

"No kidding. Mr. Suarez put you two together because Nick asked him to do it. Nick wants to win bad."

That sucked. Tony got stuck with someone who talked a big game but couldn't pull his weight and expected Tony to carry him? On top of that, Nick would use the power of his last name to muscle Tony into accepting second position on their team, which meant if they won that Nick would receive first place of going to MIT.

That came with early entry and a full-ride scholarship for someone with Tony's IQ, but only if he won this Top Ten competition.

Hannah watched him as he processed what she'd offered. "You need me," she added.

That was going too far. "I don't *need* anybody, babe."

She wasn't even put off by his snarky attitude. The girl was smiling, and man was she hot when she smiled. "Yes, you do, Tony, because I can help you win the Top Ten Project, and I don't want the number one position. I have the most flexible schedule of any student because of being an office intern and I can sway Mr. Suarez to swap me with Nick."

She had a convincing argument. "How can you be so sure about Suarez?"

"Because I know that Mr. Suarez doesn't like the way Nick slides along doing the minimum to get by. Mr. Suarez comes from a wealthy family. He doesn't need this job. The institute needs *him*."

"Really?"

"Yes. Mr. Suarez rewards those who work hard. He only put you and Nick together because Nick said he suspected the person he'd been partnered with was cheating on his tests and he didn't want to be accused of aiding a cheat."

"And Suarez bought that?"

"Not really, but when Nick suggested you, Mr. Suarez thought it might keep you two out of trouble if you were competing for first place on the team."

Tony cut in. "Whoa. What kind of trouble?"

"Mr. Suarez thinks you two spend more time chasing girls than showing your potential."

"What?" Tony sputtered? He aced every test.

"*–buuut*," Hannah said, her tone letting him know he should let her finish. "Since you and Nick don't run together, Mr. Suarez thought the pairing might keep you both on your toes."

Tony tried not to look guilty about being accused of chasing girls. Catching them was the trick.

"Now me?" Hannah bumped her chest with her armful of papers. "I'm the conservative geek who gets her work done and excels in class. If I told Mr. Suarez that I'd like to work with you to improve my computer science skills–which would be a complete falsehood you understand–he wouldn't think twice about putting us together. Mr. Suarez would see this as a chance to tell Nick that he made the change to match weak and strong skills for a fairer competition."

"You sure about this?" Was he really considering this? Absofreakinlutely, if it meant a real shot at winning the competition when he'd thought all was lost.

She put a hand on her hip. "Why? Because I don't seem like a risk taker?"

"Well, to be honest, yeah."

"You can be so dense," she muttered.

"What?" Now she sounded ticked off at him. How had that happened? "Why would you be willing to take the second position?"

She didn't answer and that bothered him enough to back away from this offer. He didn't need to find out she'd had an ulterior motive all along that tripped him up later. "Come on, Hannah. I'm being straight with you. What's your goal in all this?"

"I need this."

Tony eyed her up and down, taking in the snobbish lines of her clothes. "With your family's money?"

Her cheeks turned pink. "I made a deal with the Browns. I trade tutoring hours with the younger students for nice clothes I plan to wear to college even if they will be a little out of date by then. I ended up in this institute as a ward of the state and I intend to leave with a full ride to Stanford, so first place and MIT doesn't matter to me. I believe I can win this with you ... or Nick. But I think you and I can beat Nick."

He'd thought prissy Hannah had come from money because of the way she carried herself and kept a distance from others. Had he missed looking deeper? If getting into Stanford was her ultimate motive, he could work with it no problem.

Hannah must have thought he was hesitating. She added, "I've got something to sweeten the deal."

"Oh?"

She reached into her shoulder bag and pulled out a colorful, but aged, booklet in a clear wrapper, placing it on top of her paper stack. "What about a 1968 Captain America?"

Tony couldn't believe his eyes. His voice dropped to a whisper. "Where'd you get this?"

"Won it a year ago on the Gamer Trading Post."

Tony jerked his head up at that. "You play?"

"Yes."

She was blowing his mind. "I can't take that, Hannah. Those are tough to come by on the trading post."

"I know and you would have won this one if you hadn't jumped off at the last second." Her eyes shone with pride that could only mean one thing.

"Are you the–"

"Dragon Goddess. Yes." She was nodding and looking embarrassed again, but in a sweet way.

Tony took a small step closer to her.

She backed up, bumping into the wall. Her eyes rounded. She clutched her comic and stack of papers to her chest.

She really did have gorgeous eyes. *Always watch out for the quiet ones. You'll never see them coming. By the time you do, they'll slip in and steal your heart.*

After being dumped on his granny by his parents, Tony's heart was safe from everyone except his tiny family, but that muscle was using his chest for a punching bag right now.

He put a hand up on the wall beside her head and leaned close, smiling at her. "You're one hot babe, you know that? I've been tryin' to beat the Dragon Goddess for months."

"I, uh, know," she whispered then looked horrified. "That's not what I mean."

"What *did* you mean ... Hannah?" Now he was teasing her, but she was so adorable flustered. Seeing this side of her made her more approachable.

"Uhm. I meant, well, I didn't mean I thought I was hot or a babe–"

"But you are."

She rolled her eyes at that and finished explaining, "I was *trying* to say that I, uh, knew it was you trying to beat me."

"How'd you know it was me?"

"Your handle–South Jersey Scorpion–and I knew your schedule, so it didn't take long to figure out when you'd be online."

"I see." He wanted to kiss her, but she might call out the PC police on him. He needed her too much for their computer project to screw this up but tell that to the crazy urge determined to convince him it would be worth all the fallout.

But he wasn't feeling the need to play games with Hannah like he did with the other girls. They were good for a laugh or a quick flirt. Hannah was ... different. Now he knew she was also special. He'd never had special and wanted to impress her, not make her uncomfortable. Plus, she might change her mind about teaming up with him, then where would he be?

He had to do his part so they both won.

The last thing he'd do was let her down after the opportunity she'd offered him. He felt the burden on his shoulders grow heavier. Just what he didn't need was one more person depending on him, but this was his one chance at winning the Top Ten Competition and he would not squander it.

For either of them.

She got that serious look in her eye like he'd seen in the past when someone teased her. It finally dawned on him that she turned stiff and serious when she was nervous.

When that happened, she shifted into her abrupt office voice like now. "Do we have a deal or not, Tony?"

"Yes, ma'am, we have a deal."

Her shoulders relaxed with the breath she let out. "Then I should get back to work." She paused, eyes darting around then back to him. "We should probably start working on the project."

"Sure. When?"

"I'm free this, uh, afternoon at four for an early dinner, but if you–"

"Four works for me." He wouldn't be a minute late or she'd think he'd stood her up. She needed to know he wouldn't flake on her. He stepped back far enough to allow her room to stand away from the wall. When she started to leave, he stopped her with a word. "Wait."

She leveled him with her ice queen expression. "What?"

"Thank you. I'll do everything in my power to make sure you get what you want out of this competition, too."

The blush flooded her cheeks again. Her tongue swept out over that pair of kissable lips, driving him crazy with wondering just what she'd taste like.

She looked down at her stack of papers then picked up the comic and handed it to him.

He put his hand on hers and felt a buzz of energy. "No, I didn't win that, and you don't have to give me anything to partner with you."

Her smile was back in full force. If she kept that up his heart just might be in danger. She handed the comic to him. "Send it to your brother."

Talk about blindsiding him. "How'd you know about him?"

"You use your only postage credits to send things to your grandmother and your little brother. I've noticed the comics you won at the trading post, then a few days later you'd receive a package the size of a comic and following that there'd usually be a padded envelope the same size addressed to your brother. Go ahead and take it. I'd give it to a little brother if I had one, but ..." Her voice trailed off, then she shrugged and quipped, "Keep it and you can owe me. Maybe a dance at the prom this year."

She'd shocked him again with that hesitant suggestion. Hannah was interested in him like *that*? Hot day-um! He might get that kiss after all.

While he was congratulating himself on scoring Hannah's attention, her shoulders turned rigid.

She shoved the comic at him, muttering, "Or not. Just take it. I'm not dancing with you."

He caught her chin, and she froze.

She was some fireball when she got her feathers ruffled. He turned her chin gently until she faced him then he spoke for her ears only. "Oh, but I want to dance with you, Hannah. All night and then some. There's a lot of things I'd like to do with you, but we'll start with a dance."

Then he kissed her cheek. "Tell Suarez that Tony Scolerio is your new partner."

"'Kay." She walked away and Tony could swear he'd heard her sigh.

Things had taken one heck of a turn in the right direction. He just needed a computer that would smoke anything Nick could build with his limitless resources, because the minute Nick found out he'd lost Tony, the kid would turn to his dad who would open his wallet.

Tony knew just the computer he needed, too. All he had to do was talk Rayen and Gabby out of going back to that hellhole Sphere so he could use the crazy time-travel computer.

He pulled out his phone and texted Gabby.

Three minutes later, still no answer.

Were they gone?

CHAPTER 6

"WHAT'S WRONG, RAYEN?"

She turned to Gabby who stood next to her in front of the desk in Tony's room. Rayen started to tell her that she had no idea why their special computer wouldn't work but Gabby's hair stopped her. The ponytails had snaked loose from the wad Gabby had tied them into and the wild hair now danced around her face.

The ribbons were changing colors.

Changing. Colors. All by themselves.

Telling Gabby would only increase her stress, so Rayen pulled the palm of her hand off the computer monitor to address her question. "I don't know what's wrong with this thing. The monitor just sucked my hand in yesterday, but I can't make it work now."

Two of Gabby's eight ponytails were poking at each other, and her hair had turned a bluish color. She'd been shaking hard again a few minutes ago, but that had ceased. Rayen couldn't get her to Jaxxson or help her with whatever was causing that crazy reaction.

For someone who had killed a monster much taller than this two-story building with nothing more than a spear and her own internal power bomb, Rayen felt helpless.

The lock on the door clicked.

Gabby and she stared at each other. Rayen looked toward the bathroom, but that would only delay the inevitable.

The door swung open. Tony walked in and stopped short. "What the 'ell are you two doin' here?"

Gabby opened her mouth then jammed it shut when she started shaking again.

Rayen answered, "It was the only place we figured no one would look for either one of us."

He looked at the computer, Rayen, then noticed Gabby's hair standing out on end. "What the–"

"*Tony!*" Rayen warned. Gabby didn't need more reason to be stressed. "Her reactions are getting worse."

"Understatement, Xena. We can't take Gabby to anyone here with her hair doin' *that*."

Gabby's shaking slowed. She unleashed her frustration on Tony. "Well, duh. Did you fall out of the stupid tree and hit every branch on the way down?"

"Very funny. At least I don't look like Medusa."

Rayen growled, "*Tony!*"

"What?"

"Did you see Hannah?"

"Yes."

"Is anyone looking for me or Gabby?"

"Hannah didn't mention either of you. I didn't see security runnin' the halls, but they will as soon as they figure out Psycho Babe escaped her padded room. How'd you two get in here?"

Nodding at Gabby, Rayen said, "She did what you told me about with the two metal sticks."

That surprised him. "You picked my lock?"

Gabby gave Tony a sour look. "You think you're the only one with nimble fingers? What are you doing back here when you should be working on your computer project? That's the only thing you care about, right?"

"I came back here because this is *my* room and I care about a lot of things, but I have to win the Top Ten Competition. Even more so now."

"Why? World domination isn't enough for you?" Gabby snickered.

Rayen had to stop the fighting between these two and convince Tony to help them, because she wasn't going to make that computer work without him. She had no idea why they needed him, but that didn't change the fact that the computer screen failed to morph into a portal with just two of their group.

Tony sent a hurt look at Gabby–really?–then swung his gaze to Rayen. "It's not just about me winning now. Hannah offered to be my Top Ten partner and I accepted."

A whimper squeaked.

Gabby turned her back on Tony and dropped down to where she'd left her pupple. It was barely moving now. "No, baby, please keep breathing."

The dugurats in the future bred constantly but losing that one pupple might push Gabby's reaction further in the wrong direction. Rayen really didn't care about that stupid Top Ten Project right now, but she wanted to show Tony she was interested in his goal in hopes he'd be interested in helping with hers and Gabby's.

She congratulated him. "Good for you, but I thought Hannah was my partner and Nick was yours."

"She was, but even you have to admit you're not the best computer partner," Tony said with a wry twist of his mouth. "Hannah has a way to switch her and Nick so that she's on my team." He paused, his forehead scrunching with a thought. "Ah, man, that means you'll be stuck with Nick, Rayen. I didn't think about that."

She waved off his concern. "I'm glad you got it changed. I don't plan to stay here. The minute that Takoda guy I'm supposed to meet figures out there are no records on me, tribal or otherwise, I'll be shipped somewhere else. I'm not risking anything that will prevent me from getting back to the Sphere."

Gabby stood, clutching the pupple to her and trembling with her shakes. "W-Why'd you agree to t-take Hannah if she's inferior ... t-to you and Nick."

Tony's frowned turned to fury. "She's *not* inferior."

The shaking stopped as quickly as it had come on. Gabby said, "Excuse the heck out of me."

"You just don't know her," Tony said sheepishly, sounding a little embarrassed by his outburst.

Gabby shrugged off his irritation. "You think you and Hannah can win?"

Tony's anger lost steam. "Yes, if I can get the right computer." His gaze tracked back to our time-travel computer.

"You want that one?" Rayen asked.

"I'm thinkin' you two couldn't make it back to the Sphere, which is probably a good thing. If you're not using the computer, I'd like to borrow it and build our supercomputer with an AI function."

Gabby stopped petting her pupple. "No."

"Why not?"

"Rayen and I need it so we can travel through the portal."

"You two are safer here."

Rayen butted in. "That's our choice to make."

"But it's not working." Tony sounded desperate.

"It would if you'd help us," Gabby said, and they all stopped talking.

Tony grabbed his head with both hands and walked in a circle. "I can't believe you're blackmailing me."

"We are not," Gabby argued. "But that computer belongs to all three of us. Help us out and we'll help you. That's a fair offer." She looked over at

Rayen and winked then her body started shaking again.

Rayen grabbed the pupple from her, because Gabby wouldn't want to risk harming it.

The room started moving, shaking like they were in the middle of an earthquake. Gabby began bouncing an inch off the floor. Rayen grabbed the chair to stay upright.

Tony stumbled right and left then his feet slipped out from under him.

Gabby stopped shaking and everything went still at the same moment.

She slapped her hands over her ears. "Make it stop! They're all shouting in my head." Tears trickled down her face.

Watching her in misery and not being able to do something for her was killing Rayen.

"That's screwed up," Tony grumbled from the floor.

Rayen gave him a hand up. "We've got to get Gabby back to Jaxxson. I have no idea how to help her and she says they'll lock her away here."

Tony clutched his forehead. "She's right. They'll put her in a freakin' straitjacket."

Rayen didn't ask what that was because it sounded suffocating enough just by the descriptive name.

She waited with Tony for Gabby to calm down.

When Gabby started taking deep breaths and lowered her hands, Rayen asked, "Do you think you can handle the trip through that portal, Gabby? It's not going to be easy for you."

"I have to." She raised tortured eyes to them. "If I stay here, I might destroy this whole building next time. I don't want to hurt anyone."

Rayen didn't want to ask Tony to travel with them again, but every outbreak of Gabby's shakes was increasing in intensity. She offered Tony what she hoped he'd see as a fair deal. "If Gabby agrees, you can have this computer as soon as we're through traveling with it. Help me return to the Sphere and I'll ask V'ru how to travel by myself through the portal so that when we come back there will be no reason to ask you to go again."

"If anyone knows how to do that, it'd be the boy wonder," Gabby agreed, her voice full of respect for the eleven-year-old historian of the MystiK Records House. "I'm onboard to do whatever it takes to make it back there like right now. Staying here with these reactions might get someone killed."

Including Gabby, but Rayen had come to realize that Gabby always thought of others first.

Tony cracked his knuckles in an unconscious manner, talking quietly to himself. "I can do this and V'ru could help me. I have to make this project work."

Gabby arched an eyebrow in question at Tony. "You may be the first to end up in a straitjacket if you keep mumbling to yourself."

Tony's brown eyes sharpened with a serious glint. "Here's the deal. I doubt I can make that laptop function for the two of you, but I'll go back–"

"Yes!" Gabby gasped.

He silenced her with a hard look and finished. "But I'm only going for an in-and-out trip. One-hour tops. And I want information from V'ru on turning this computer into something Nick can't beat."

Rayen glanced at Gabby who nodded. "I'll do whatever I can to help you with V'ru," Rayen offered.

Born with the knowledge of all history through his time, V'ru could be stubborn about sharing technical information if he deemed the other person unworthy of it, but Tony didn't need anything from a hundred and fifty years in the future. He should be able to complete his project with knowledge from just a few years forward in time.

That sounded doable.

Tony stepped over and turned the lock on his door then reached in his pocket to withdraw his phone. He tapped on it with his thumbs and a light in the corner of the room near the ceiling blinked on and off. An alarm.

She and Gabby had been lucky he'd only locked the door when he'd gone to the office, or they'd have set the thing off.

Tony walked over to the desk where Rayen had placed the time-travel computer. He opened a drawer, digging around until he pulled out a small square object he stuffed in the pocket of his hooded jacket.

Gabby got to her feet and wobbled her way to one side of the computer. Just like last time, Rayen stepped up between the two of them. She handed Gabby the pupple, which ended up in a baggy pocket covered by a flap.

"What's not working on this, Xena?" Tony grumbled. "You didn't need me the first time you stuck your hand through the monitor."

She hadn't mentioned that earlier when she and Gabby tried on their own because she didn't want to see the disappointment now invading her friend's eyes. Rayen had serious doubts about this working even with all three of them here, but Gabby needed reassurance and that's what she gave her when she answered Tony.

"Yes, but you were standing close by and that had to be important."

He gave Rayen a you-can't-be-serious look. Gabby smiled with hope and that was enough for her. "Everyone ready?"

"Should Tony keep that backpack on?"

"I'm wearin' it. Takin' notes this time–"

His phone buzzed. He lifted it from where the phone was clipped on his belt and Gabby lunged for it, fingers grabbing air. "We need to go now!"

"Wait a minute. It's a text from Hannah." He scrolled it one handed, read the display, and said, "They're lookin' for you, sweet cakes."

Rayen stared ahead as if the wall would give her the strength to keep from strangling him since Tony called all females that at some point. "Which one of us are you talking about this time, Jersey?"

"Ah, crap." He kept reading. "Both of you actually. Hannah said the office thinks you figured out how to get your ankle cuff off, *Xena*, and escaped the school property. They think Gabby might have left with you." He lifted his head. "She wants to know if I have any idea where either of you are, because the office is alerting security."

Those uniformed people who brought Rayen here had threatened to take her away if she caused any problem at the school.

"I'm not leaving here with anyone at any time," Rayen stated with no room for argument.

"Me neither," Gabby added. "Not even if my dad shows up, but that's not really a possibility since he'd have to actually remember he had a daughter first."

"Sit tight for a second." Tony tapped fast on his phone. Rayen had the urge to snatch it away to find out what he was telling Hannah. When he finished, he glanced up and took in their faces. "What?"

"You didn't squeal on us, did you?" Gabby accused him.

"No, but I should have after that dig. I told Hannah that I didn't think either one of you would try to run off. Last I heard Gabby was in the clinic and Rayen said something about going somewhere quiet to study."

Gabby's eyes shifted away. "Sorry, I'm just not myself right now."

Rayen should apologize, too, since she had expected the worst, but then Tony went and ruined her generous mood when he added, "Of course, if you two don't come back in an hour like we agreed, I may change my story, plus I told Hannah you two would probably show up in a few hours."

For a happy girl, Gabby could give lessons to a nightmare when she wanted to alter her face to scare someone. Tony was ignoring the deadly stare she put on him.

Gabby placed her hand on Rayen's arm. "Can we do this today?"

She could feel Gabby fighting to contain a chaotic energy. Was that the voices?

Gabby ordered Tony, "Grab her other arm."

He reached over and hesitated until Gabby reminded him, “What’s riskier? Traveling through this computer again or staying here and letting Nick win the Top Ten Competition?”

His fingers clamped Rayen’s forearm.

Rayen placed her palm over the three swirling circles on the monitor and, once again, there was no resistance.

Her body was sucked forward. She gritted her teeth, knowing what to expect this time and not looking forward to having her torso stretched like a rubber band.

Gabby’s fingers dug into her arm and started trembling again.

Tony cursed.

Gabby shuddered harder.

Rayen’s teeth banged together.

Everything erupted into a vibrating kaleidoscope of disjointed shapes and colors.

This was not the same.

Rayen had made a huge mistake.

CHAPTER 7

Byzantine Institute, Albuquerque, New Mexico

PHEN T-112 HID BEHIND A corner where he'd watched the boy called Tony walk into his room in the Byzantine Institute. Phen smiled at how things were falling into place. In a moment of luck, he'd peeked out of his dorm room just in time to catch the backs of two girls sneaking through this area. That Rayen girl and her friend.

And now Tony shows up.

Phen stroked the black bird on his forearm, his only companion in this miserable place.

How could SEOH send him back here when Phen's entire world existed over a hundred and sixty years in the future?

Because Phen was nothing but a number to SEOH.

Disposable.

Not anymore. Phen had a way of upping his credit value.

SEOH wanted a specific computer. This antiquated place had many of the outdated electronics from back when computing required hardware.

Living through every minute here was like an unfolding nightmare.

SEOH had laid the blame at Phen's feet for the problems which had been caused by three intruders entering the Komaen Sphere. Like Phen had any control over what happened there or anywhere? Only the top reigning TecKnati had power to make choices and live the lives they wanted.

The rest of the TecKnati were just various levels of servants no matter how they tried to justify their sad existence. Phen had given his all, been one hundred percent loyal, and where had that gotten him?

Stuck in the dark ages where transportation required wheels that touched the ground and people still used paper for documents.

The black bird dropped its head to be stroked.

These sentient beasts had been works of art at one time, then cursed as a demonic invention. SEOH hadn't said anything about a sentient beast being in the past, but the minute Phen arrived he'd recognized it from having seen one on display in a controlled zootech where Phen had worked his first job.

He'd become friends with that one, too.

Now, while Phen waited and observed Tony's room, he had the beast for company. Tony was still in there with those two girls. Phen had fought the tall girl with black hair in the Sphere. She had the attitude of a warrior. He'd found out something special about that one. That other girl with her hair sticking out everywhere might be an AI with a corrupt motherboard.

Three boys walked out of another room further down the hall and turned in Phen's direction.

He pulled back and held his hand up, palm out to the bird who immediately focused on his palm. Then Phen gave the order to shift and, in the next instant, the bird changed to a blue and purple lizard no longer than his index finger.

He dropped the lizard in his pocket and waited until he heard footsteps close to his corner before he walked toward them.

The boys cast a glance his way and he ignored them. When they rounded the corner out of sight, Phen slowed next to Tony's door and placed his ear against it.

Not a sound in there.

He tried the handle–or was it called a knob? How was he supposed to know the names of antiques?

The knob didn't give. Locked.

He smiled.

When Phen had been captured in the Sphere by the MystiKs and locked up with Tony, he'd thought the guy was a joke or crazy for acting like he could travel in and out of the Sphere without SEOH's permission.

But the MystiK traitor had told Phen the three intruders claimed they traveled from the past through a computer.

SEOH wanted the Genera-Y computer that could time travel in both directions.

Phen wanted to go home.

That computer was his ticket to get there.

CHAPTER 8

RAYEN KEPT HER JAWS CLAMPED against the jarring that tried to rip her bones apart. Colors flashed and blurred at a blinding speed as they traveled in a whirl through the portal.

They!

Where were Gabby and Tony?

Had Gabby's reaction exploded in the portal and cut them loose from Rayen?

She felt her body coming back together and remembered the last time they'd traveled that she landed hard on the metal floor of the transender. She tucked at the last minute and hit, then rolled forward, slapping into a wall.

She didn't think a body was meant to take the abuse hers kept getting.

A loud thump followed then Tony's deep groan of pain.

That was one of them.

She opened her eyes as Gabby appeared out of thin air falling on top of Tony who grunted. "Killin' me, Psycho Babe."

"Sorry. My bad," slurred from Gabby.

Rayen righted herself and leaned back, getting her breath. She studied Gabby to see if the trip had caused any new reactions. "Are you okay?"

Gabby crawled off Tony who made more grunting sounds like an angry animal. At least he'd had a backpack on to break his fall. Gabby sat to the side of him, leaning against the silver wall that hummed with energy. Red lights flashed and streaked around the top, outlining the cylindrical shape.

Gabby brushed hair off her face. "I'm fine."

She didn't sound fine. She sounded squeezed dry of all her life force.

Tony shoved up on his knees. "She lands on me like a bag of cement, and you want to know if *she's* okay? Nice, Xena."

Rayen stretched her legs as they tingled with the return of feeling. "I'm just as concerned over you, Tony. I was only asking if the portal trip had affected Gabby's issues. Can we get back to where we were working together so it's a more pleasant visit than last time?"

"Whatever." He pushed up to his feet. "Let's do this and get it over with."

Gabby stood and began the rewinding of her ponytails, which had turned even bluer. "I don't think I'm any worse, but I admit this stupid reaction is making me crabby." She eyed Tony. "What's your excuse?"

This was going to be the longest day of Rayen's life if these two kept at it. "Gabby, please? Tony didn't want to come here, but he did. How about a truce, you two?"

Gabby finished tying down her hair. "Sorry. Truce."

Tony ignored us both. "Let's just get moving."

Getting to her feet, Rayen said, "Keep in mind that we can't lower our guard and assume we know what we're doing in this place even though we've done this before."

Tony frowned at me. "What should be different?"

"If the TecKnati control the transenders, then *anything* and *everything* could be different this time."

Taking heed of her own words, she wondered at the silence inside the transender.

On the last trip when they'd landed in this thing, she and Gabby had realized they needed to get out of the transender quickly, but Tony had argued staying put was their best chance at going home.

Then a loud siren had started and ...

"There's the alarm again," Gabby shouted. "We have to go."

Tony walked over to the end where an arch created by a purple glow looked just like the spot where they'd exited through on their first trip. He grouched, "Wasn't that what I was tellin' you two?"

Rayen stepped up beside him then Gabby appeared next to her. The pupple lump in her pants pocket wasn't moving even with the screeching noise that should wake the dead. Rayen kept that observation to herself. If the pupple hadn't survived the trip, Gabby would know soon enough. Rayen was just glad that her friends had come through alive.

"Hurry up, Xena, before my ears start bleedin'."

A sulfuric smell bloomed. Another sign to leave.

She lifted her hands. Gabby and Tony touched her forearms again. When she placed her hands on the humming surface, she thought *Out. Let us out.*

The opening formed and they tumbled forward through a purple haze that blinded her for a moment. She lost her footing and smacked face first on the ground where a low-hanging mist surrounded her head.

There had to be a better way to travel here without landing on her face and butt all the time, but she hadn't figured it out. She spit out what should be dirt or sand, but it was spongy and tasted bitter.

Lifting her head slowly, she took in the pinkish-orange mist hovering ankle-high above the ground. It had a soft fragrance that drew her back down to it.

As she leaned down to inhale the sweet scent, Tony said, "Holy crap. This can't be."

Gabby's gasp raised chill bumps on Rayen's arms.

She was afraid to look up and see what they'd found, but when she lifted up to her knees, everything was just like she expected. A wide-open field covered with rubbery grass that extended to the jungle, or what they'd called a jungle. She could see the same strange-colored plants and trees bordering this landing area that were here the first time.

The transender started spinning and made the high-pitched sound she now recognized as its departure signal. They all jumped out of the way as it disappeared in a whirlwind of red haze.

Rayen dusted off her pants and smiled. Just thinking about seeing Callan soon had her excited. Her world had been in turmoil since waking up in that desert back in Albuquerque, but Callan anchored her in a way she couldn't explain.

He gave her a sense of safety she felt nowhere else.

She wanted to see his smile and feel his lips on hers again. Her skin felt too tight just standing here, knowing he was close.

"What are you so happy about, Xena?" Tony asked in a cautious voice that warned she'd missed something.

She looked over at Gabby who stared at her with just as much question in her gaze. Rayen asked, "What do you mean? We landed in the right spot. All we have to do is head toward the village and we'll probably meet up with Callan's group. They watch the sky for green slashes when a transender shows up." She raised her eyes to where the green stripes signifying their arrival were fading against the purplish-red sky.

There was the same fat red moon hanging in what would be a mid-morning position back at the school.

"You don't see the destruction, Rayen?"

Her heart stuttered at that question because Tony had called her by name. He wasn't joking around.

She turned, taking in the landscape, and not seeing what he was talking about. "No, I don't."

He frowned at Gabby. "Tell her."

"Tell me what, Tony?"

Gabby's eyes were bright and damp. "It looks like a bomb hit. The jungle is part destroyed and part burned to the ground. Something bad happened after we left."

"You're wrong." Rayen shook her head, refusing to believe their words. She turned around all the way until she faced them again. "I'm looking at a lush jungle."

"Somebody's hallucinatin' and it ain't me," Tony declared.

Gabby walked over to her. "What do you see over there?"

Rayen swung around, expecting more wide-open field and saw a croggle sleeping. A baby croggle ... but those creatures were massive and dangerous as adolescents. They lived underground and burst through the dirt to attack unsuspecting prey.

Seeing a potential threat, she went on offense with her arms out, stepping in front of Gabby and Tony to protect them. "You two head toward the jungle and I'll keep an eye on the croggle. If it wakes up before we get out of here, I'll deal with it."

"It's not a croggle," Gabby whispered, sounding frightened.

"Yes, it is."

Tony walked over. "No, it's not, Xena. It's a pile of dead trees."

No. She could see the scales as large as her hand and the horn that stuck out the top of its head. Its body was lifting and dropping with each breath, but she did wonder why the creature hadn't attacked when the arrival of a transender acted like a croggle call for dinner.

Gabby said, "I'm going to try something to see if it will help you."

She touched Rayen's arm, and the world shifted, blurry at the edges, but she saw the pile of trees she'd thought was a croggle.

Then flashes of devastation bombarded her.

Gabby cried out and jerked her hand back. "Oh, fudge, that burned my brain."

The minute she broke contact, the landscape returned to pretty and lush again with a baby croggle sleeping nearby.

Rayen's eyes were lying to her for some reason. "Why can't I see what everything really looks like?" she asked no one in particular.

"I don't know." Gabby's voice dropped to a level of despair. "What happened to the heat from last time? Yesterday this place felt as humid as Georgia in July."

That's when Rayen noticed the dry wind had a brittle chill. She rubbed her arms. It wasn't so cold she couldn't handle it, just unexpected after this place had been hot and thick with humidity last time.

Gabby and Tony had to be just as confused, because neither one spoke.

"You will see what you need, when you need," a gruff voice behind Rayen said.

She turned to find the old guy she'd first encountered in the desert yesterday. His hair hung in two long gray braids to his waist. His face was still carved with many years of life. He still wore tanned animal skins on his body and feet.

And he was still a translucent ghost sitting with his legs crossed, floating above the ground.

She hit her limit of patience right then. "What do *you* want?"

"Who's she talkin' to, Gab?" Tony asked from behind her.

Gabby sighed. "I don't know."

The ghost stared at Rayen and through her. "The future is in the past."

He had yet to tell her anything helpful except that her name was Rayen, she was seventeen, and she was allergic to peanuts, whatever those were. "I don't have time to talk right now so either tell me what happened here or go away."

"Oh, crap," Tony whispered, but she heard him. "She's hallucinatin' *and* talkin' to invisible people, just like when we were in the prisoner hut here. This means I'm the only stable one."

That was a frightening thought.

Her ghost said, "One will seek, and all will forfeit."

More useless words of wisdom.

"Rayen?" Gabby asked tentatively.

Sighing, she turned to Gabby. "Yes?"

"Who are you talking to?"

When she looked back, the ghost was gone. Explaining wouldn't help their situation since it was obvious that neither Tony nor Gabby could hear or see the ghost. Besides, Rayen only cared about one thing right now. Finding the MystiK village. "It's not important, Gabby. We need to locate Callan and the children."

Tony said, "He may not have sur–"

She shoved her pent-up frustration at Tony. "He *is* alive."

Tony backed up. "Take it easy, Xena. I'm just sayin' you don't know what we'll find."

"I *will* find him." She had to. Callan couldn't be dead. She had no family and no world to go back to since hers had been destroyed and Albuquerque was not her home.

If she only had the time here with Callan, it was more than she had anywhere else. She refused to accept anything but that he had survived.

A sickening thought hit her. Had Callan turned eighteen while she was gone? If he had, then the black wraiths had come for him like they had for Mathias.

No. That can't be.

He was alive in her heart.

That was all she needed for right now.

Tony pinned her and Gabby with a steely gaze and announced, "I'm going to the village with you two, but don't forget this is an in-and-out trip."

"What about the flower?" Gabby asked. "How are we going to get back if we can't find it?"

On their first trip, a huge pink flower attached to a carnivorous vine had attacked Tony. Later, they found out the TecKnati had created a lifelike image of the pink flower to hide their control unit for calling back a transender.

Gabby brought up a valid concern.

Tony looked around. The fake flower had been installed at the edge of the jungle where nothing had survived based on what she'd seen in the moment Gabby touched her.

Tony's gaze turned desperate the longer he stared at the tree line. He had one word that covered a lot of things. "Unfreakinbelievable. We can't get out of here without that control panel."

CHAPTER 9

RAYEN'S HEART DROPPED. SHE HAD not wanted Tony to be stuck here.

He scrubbed a hand over his face, cursing under his breath. "We find V'ru, we'll find answers. Someone will tell us how to locate the control panel."

She noticed Tony hadn't suggested that V'ru hadn't survived the destruction, and that was too horrible for her to consider as well. With no way to call up their ride home, they had limited options. The one thing they'd learned last time was that if they tried to use any other transender than the one they'd arrived in, they would all die upon return.

Tony had discovered that their molecules were suspended during the ride through space and time. Land in the wrong place and those molecules rearranged out of sequence.

Their bodies would explode.

A cheerful thought.

For now, Tony's logic of asking V'ru beat her despair over their situation and waiting any longer to find out what had happened to the MystiKs.

Gabby wrapped her arms around herself.

Rayen opened her mouth to ask why, but Gabby's shaking started. Her fingers dug into her sides. Was she trying to force her body to be still?

She sat down hard. The ground beneath them immediately bounced and buckled. Rocks that sparked green, orange and blue pushed up to the surface, plopped on the ground and started crawling around. Some were as small as her thumb and others were too large to put her hand around.

Or at least, that's what she saw.

When Gabby's flurry of shaking finally subsided, Rayen asked, "Are those rocks?"

"No, they're beetle things." Gabby picked up a bright orange one and studied it on her palm. The round shape started growing until it was double in size.

Tony's eyes bugged out at that. "Day-um, sweet cheeks. I wonder if that works on anything *else*?" he asked with a lot of innuendo in his voice.

Gabby dropped the bug, rock, whatever on the ground and informed Tony, "Don't even *think* about it. They make little blue pills for that."

Little blue pills?

Tony huffed, "I'm Italian, babe. We never need that."

Rayen was used to their picking at each other, but she was feeling edgy and couldn't stand here another second. "Are you two done?"

They both looked at her like she'd been the one wasting time arguing over whatever a blue pill did.

Adding to the tension wouldn't get them to the village any faster, so she took a calming breath and explained, "With the shape the jungle is in, it shouldn't grow back behind us like last time. If that's so, then I'll lead since my power is the only weapon we have at this point. I should be able to retrace our path to the village."

Tony chuckled. "You're liable to walk into a tree if you lead, Xena."

"Then you better warn me before I do, *Jersey*, unless *you* want to lead."

"Chill, Xena. You want to lead, no problem. First man in, first man hit."

Where did Tony come up with the things he said?

She had to get a grip on her emotions, but her heart ached at what they'd found here. She'd been so ready to come back and even told the other two, things might be different, but she hadn't been prepared for this devastation. She was scared for Callan and the children he protected.

What or who had attacked the Sphere?

SEOH had to be at the root of this.

She waited for Gabby to give her a nod then she started forward, stumbling over ruts until she reached the jungle, which had a similar damp and decaying smell as before, but mixed in was a charred odor.

And death. Animals had died.

She had no idea how she knew what that should smell like, but she did. At least, she hoped it wasn't human death she smelled.

In the next minute, that sweet scent from the mist rose up to greet her.

Gabby coughed. "This stench is awful. Stinks like burned rubber and some weird chemical."

Rayen would take the mist scent over any of that. She banged her knee and hissed. "How about some help, Tony?"

He started calling out, "Go right." Then a minute later, he yelled, "Got a pile to climb over in two steps."

Once she got the hang of it, they moved along pretty good. They stopped twice for Gabby when she had episodes. She put her hand on a tree at one point and the roots burst from out of the ground, sending them all off their feet.

Returning to the Sphere was doing nothing to help Gabby.

With Tony calling out signals, Rayen realized the terrain undulated the same way for both of them, but things looked and felt different. She walked through what appeared to be pearl-white velvety plants only to have a thorny vine rake across her jeans, snagging the material and cutting through to skin.

She ignored the burning sting.

That pain was nothing compared to what she felt in her chest the longer they went without Callan finding them. He had to have seen the streaks in the sky by now.

What if he hadn't survived? What if none of them had?

That meant she'd come back here for no reason and had no way to call up the transender to go home. She'd gotten Tony trapped and had no way to help Gabby.

She asked, "Gabby, how're you doing?"

"No worse."

"Depends on your point of view," Tony interjected. "Her hair is–"

Gabby hissed, "Stuff it, Tony."

Rayen stopped and turned to face both of them. Gabby's hair was still blue, not her natural color, but not that bad. "What about your hair?"

"You can't see it, can you?" Gabby said more to herself than Rayen. "My hair has turned into flat ribbons. No hair strands."

Really? Rayen walked back to her and touched her hair. It felt normal, but she didn't pick up any sensation from Gabby so the locks of her hair must be ribbons. How could Rayen see some things about Tony and Gabby that were correct, but other things escaped her?

She took Tony in from head to toe and asked, "Is anything different about him?"

Gabby was quick to answer. "Nope. Still an A-hole."

"You're stompin' on my last good nerve, Psycho Babe."

The chuckle that followed had a decidedly nasty sound. Gabby liked to poke at Tony, but she'd never been unkind about it. Whatever affected her was altering her personality, too.

Rayen couldn't talk. Her reality was so far gone she looked at her hands wondering if she had changed. "Is anything different about me?"

Gabby and Tony exchanged a look then Gabby said, "Your eyes are still aqua but they're ... glowing."

"Like a blue-eyed demon," Tony confirmed.

Spearing Tony with a deadly glare that did not belong on her face, Gabby asked, "Ever hear the saying a closed mouth gathers no foot?"

Tony rolled his eyes at her and waved at Rayen to get moving again.

She might as well since there wasn't anything she could do about glowing eyes. She turned around, plodding her way forward again. The MystiKs believed she was C'raydonian. A group of people who had turned rabid after a virus invaded their world.

Would Callan and the MystiKs think she was infected with something now?

"Whoa, Xena, take a step to the right," Tony called out.

She did as he said, but her left shoe still sucked down into something that reminded her of mud. When she dropped her gaze to the ground, she saw bright orange sand and tiny purple flowers covering the ground.

No mud.

Disgusted, she yanked her foot up and kept going.

They'd been walking for a while and should have found the village by now. The closer they came to where it should be and wasn't, the more Rayen's muscles tensed. She pulled at the neck of her T-shirt. The jungle was closing in on her. She couldn't breathe.

Where was the stupid village?

Had the TecKnati burned it to the ground? They *must* have done it. What other explanation was there for all the destruction? Those murdering TecKnati hated the MystiKs, and the MystiKs hated them. There were grave problems in the future, but why do this to children?

Callan was seventeen and a few of the others were between that age and fifteen, but many were much younger.

She smacked a leaf out of her way, stomping faster. She would make the TecKnati pay if they had injured any of Callan's group. Especially if they'd harmed *him*. She would draw on her power and burn them from the inside out, just like a croggle.

Her chest heaved as each breath got harder and harder to pull inside.

Where were the MystiKs?

Their village had been no small place and a protective fog had enclosed it.

Blood thundered through her veins. She could feel the surge, hear it rushing in her ears. Her body pushed her to do something. Strike back at the enemy.

How? She needed a target.

She opened and closed her fingers, wishing for a spear to slam into the enemy. They would bleed out as she laughed at them, right before she used her power to blow their heads off. Her fingers curled into tight fists. She felt each heartbeat pulse in her throat. Was that the power inside her swelling?

Or was it a warning that the enemy was close?

Where was that village? They should have seen it by now.

"We're here, Rayen," Gabby called out.

She jerked her head up.

Her heart started beating fast at the sight before her. There was the building the MystiKs had created by using pinkish and lavender bird feathers as tall as her for walls. Bowls of fruit sat on slabs of wood that floated waist-high above the ground. Pango orbs made of the brightly colored feathers from little pik-pik birds still hung on vines strung between trees just like last time continued to glow. Three sweet young girls had created those for Mathias' BIRG Day celebration.

The day of his birth eighteen years ago.

The day of his death in this place.

But she couldn't speak about his death.

Only Callan and she knew the truth, and she'd been sworn to secrecy. She couldn't tell the MystiK children, and she couldn't tell Tony or Gabby either. The TecKnati had found an evil way to circumvent a penalty built into a treaty and sealed with powerful magic. The treaty decreed that a TecKnati child's life would instantly be forfeited for any MystiK child killed intentionally by a TecKnati.

And vice versa.

SEOH had figured out a nasty way to kill teens, the future MystiK leaders, in this Sphere when they reached eighteen, and with no repercussion.

Bile raced up her throat at remembering how Mathias had died.

Ignited by her emotions, power began rising inside her, expanding and threatening to erupt. Her clenched fists burned hot as two chunks of smoldering coals.

Her hands smoked. That was new.

She heard Gabby sobbing. Tony cursed quietly.

Something wasn't right. She looked at the village again.

There were no children in sight. This place would be a hive of activity. Her mind forced her heart to accept what it was trying to deny. This was not real. "Gabby?"

"Yes?"

"Is the village still standing?"

"No." Sniffle.

"Is anything left?"

"Shreds of buildings. That peach-colored mist is carpeting the ground. No sign of ... life." Her voice was raw.

No. Rayen's heart ached. Callan couldn't be dead.

"Let's go, Rayen," Tony said in a voice thick with emotion and disappointment. "We gotta try to find the controller for our transender."

She couldn't leave. Not yet. "I want to keep looking."

Tony's deep sigh said it all. He hesitated to push her to let go of Callan but staying was foolish. She knew this.

Her mind knew it. Her heart had lost the ability to care about anything beyond this moment. She had to help Tony and Gabby get back, but she couldn't make her feet walk away.

She couldn't make her heart stop crying out for Callan.

Had he died the same way Mathias had?

No, please tell me he didn't suffer that agony.

Her chest burned with power that begged to be released. The warrior inside her cried out for vengeance.

A noise to her left snapped her head around.

Someone came busting out of the jungle two hundred feet away, heading straight for them.

Silver-gray uniform. Short black hair. A TecKnati scout running hard.

Finally, someone worthy of her rage.

"You will die, TecKnati!" she promised and raced toward her enemy.

Gabby screamed, "*No, Rayen!*"

Tony shouted something, but the pounding of her heart was beating in her ears too loudly for her to hear their words.

The TecKnati coming at her shifted and blurred from one shape to another. He was a jumble of arms, legs, faces and colors. She was sick of being fooled by the TecKnati. Whatever was making her confused in this place had to be their doing.

Had they tricked the MystiKs, too?

If that was so, why could Gabby see the truth?

She had no time to think about that, only to react and prepare for battle.

Where was the TecKnati's weapon?

He slowed to a jog and smiled. Laughing at her was a deadly mistake. She would teach him one last lesson in life. He would pay for what he'd taken from her.

She kept running, but he stopped and stared hard. Confusion crawled across his face.

She launched herself at him, drawing back to slam a fist into his confusion. He ducked, barely in time to miss her strike. But the power of her leap took them down hard with him landing beneath her. She let go of all her hurt and anger, yelling and pummeling him with her fists, but his strength surprised her.

He grabbed her arms. They rolled over and over, down an incline. He kept shouting at her.

She refused to listen. She hated him.

He'd killed Callan.

He'd ripped her heart into pieces.

They stopped tumbling and she struggled to break his fierce hold even though she was on top and should have the advantage. She didn't, though. Where was her power when she needed it?

"Rayen. *Stop*."

The sound of his voice rushed through her. He sounded ... like Callan. Another trick. One she would not fall for. She stopped fighting and waited for him to relax his grip. The minute he did, she snatched her hands away and clutched his throat, strangling him.

Rage roared through her veins.

Heat banked inside her. She called to it, begging for that flicker to burst into a flame. When it spread through her center and seeped into her arms, she was the one smiling. "You *will* die, TecKnati."

CHAPTER 10

"RAYEN, PLEASE LISTEN," CALLAN BEGGED her, trying to wrap his mind around her being here again. He stared up at her, pulling on her arms to break her chokehold on his neck.

The deadly mist had invaded her mind. It wasn't her fault that she couldn't recognize him, but if he didn't find a way to stop her soon, she'd kill him.

Her hands began heating around his throat.

He clamped his fingers tighter on her forearms, but he couldn't bring himself to break the bones. He couldn't harm her, not even to save himself. Instead, he had to do the one thing he'd never done without permission.

Force himself inside her mind.

Callan only hoped he could get through to her quickly then pull back without going too far. But what if he had to break the veil in her mind to reach her?

That was forbidden until ...

Stars danced in his vision. He couldn't draw a breath. Her strength was superhuman when she tapped her power.

There was no time left for what ifs.

He pulled inside himself and searched for a connection to her. The pressure in his head kept building, threatening to explode. Entering the mind of another was wrong and dangerous, but it was the only way he could save both of them.

If she killed him, she'd never forgive herself. He had to protect her from that as much as the damage the mist was doing to her mind.

He nudged at her mental walls and got slapped back.

Blinking, he shook off the strike and fought through the darkness trying to swallow him. He was seconds from losing consciousness.

Shoving with more force this time, Callan lunged into Rayen's mind and was swept into a firestorm of chaos that jerked him back and forth, battering him.

Anger, disappointment, and fear warped her thoughts.

But above all that, her enraged mind kept screaming, *You killed Callan! Why did you kill him?*

Her pain was raw and living. Now, would she even listen to him?

It's me, Rayen. It's Callan, he tried to tell her.

No, you're not tricking me anymore.

I'm not the TecKnati. You can't see my face, but I am Callan. I healed you after the croggle ripped you open. Remember?

She froze but held tight to his throat.

He struggled to stay lucid and kept trying to reach her mentally. *A TecKnati would not know that you and I were the only two to witness Mathias' death.*

Her grip loosened a tiny bit.

A hesitation that encouraged him, but darkness kept clawing at him. He blinked past the sharp points of light in his vision and sent words softly into her mind, hoping to calm the pandemonium going on. *You helped me heal a little boy. A TecKnati would not know that either.*

She was still breathing erratically and the muscles in her arms were pumped up tight, but her voice finally whispered in his mind. *Callan?*

His chest squeezed at hearing the hope fueling that one word. In his world, nothing was more intimate than a bonding of minds, not even the physical act of mating. He reminded himself to be careful with how deep inside he went.

He could not touch the veil in her mind and, by all that was holy, he could not pierce it and start the bonding.

Some lines couldn't be crossed, no matter what. He answered her, *Yes, it's me, Callan. The mist is influencing you, Rayen, but I can help you.* He hoped.

No, she cried in his mind. *I can't just accept what you say. Tell me something else. About someone else.*

He wanted to tell her how much he'd missed her and how he wanted to feel her close, but not like this with her emotions shredded by the effect of the mist. This was why he hadn't wanted her to come back, not to this danger. *Remember that V'ru told you that you're a C'raydonian and that he tested Tony's blood and determined Tony was from the past. V'ru's eleven and skinny, too serious by far. He–*

She gasped and released his throat to grab his shoulders. When she spoke out loud, her voice squeezed with a tortured sound. "I'm so sorry, Callan. You look like one of their scouts. I thought you were dead."

"Close your eyes and I'll fix it." He could clear up her confusion, but it would only be temporary if she remained exposed to the mist surrounding them.

Footsteps came pounding up.

Callan lifted a hand at Tony and Gabby. "Go back. I need a minute, or I won't be able to pull her from the grasp of the mist."

They looked at each other, silently debating his order.

He put power beneath his words. "Back away now before the mist overtakes her mind completely!"

Throwing their feet into reverse, Tony and Gabby didn't stop until they were far enough away to allow Callan a measure of privacy that he needed to prevent anyone distracting Rayen.

She angled her head and studied him as if she could use her will to make him look like the right person, but the mist prevented that. "It's really you?" she whispered.

"Yes, and I will prove it to you if you close your eyes." Callan brushed his hand over her hair, smoothing it gently to calm her. He'd rather not have to force his way into her mind again.

What he'd seen there the first time had tortured him. It had taken all he could do to reach her. Her agony over thinking the TecKnati had killed everyone in the village had spun her thoughts toward a black void.

She'd been prepared to kill the ones responsible.

To see her so exposed and hurting was painful.

Callan had sworn that if he ever got his hands on SEOH, the TecKnati leader would not draw another breath for killing Callan's twin brother. But he would now have to think up something more deserving for SEOH than mere death for what he'd put the village of innocent children–and Rayen–through.

Rayen's body tensed and shook with shock.

He could not clear her mind unless she released her anger and fear. Wrapping his arms around her, he pulled her toward him.

She wouldn't budge.

Callan said, "Please."

Her arms bent and she slowly lowered her chest down to his. He reveled in the feel of her close again, but as usual he had no time to allow himself the simple pleasure of a stolen moment. He had to work quickly, or the mist would seep into her mind again and they'd be battling once more.

Rubbing his hand up and down her back, he whispered soothing words of healing. Those words worked on others, but Callan had no idea if they'd heal a C'raydonian. The TecKnati and MystiKs before his time had joined forces against the C'raydonians who'd killed so many because they'd become rabid from the incurable K-Virus while the world had struggled to recover from the viral devastation.

All C'raydonians had been infected.

But Rayen must not have been. Why? Had she found a portal to escape the virus and the genocide only to lose her memory?

He didn't know. He was just glad she seemed infection-free.

Rayen's breathing became shallow and breathy. Her muscles went limp. She felt warm and so soft in his arms.

Many MystiKs hated all C'raydonians based only on what their parents and grandparents had told them about that secluded race. It was an inherited bias against a race of people who had died out many years before Callan was born.

He'd always thought of C'raydonians as a deadly threat, one he should hate after all the stories of MystiKs lost to rabid attacks.

How could he hate Rayen?

Not possible.

He told her one more time, "Close your eyes."

She did and he felt her resistance fall completely. She'd attacked him, thinking she faced a TecKnati who'd killed him. No one *ever* waded into battle for him, but she'd done so more than once. It was his job to protect all the others, but this girl had tossed all care for herself aside to face a deadly enemy. For him.

Before Callan thought better of it, he snuck a kiss against her hair. She murmured something but remained still with her heartbeat gradually slowing.

In a few more seconds, he'd be able to enter her mind with surgical precision this time. Breathing deeply, he inhaled the scent that he'd longed for since she left in the transender.

When he felt her heartbeat fall into pace with his, he swept forward cautiously to enter her mind.

She flinched a little and pushed back, but he blocked her from entering his mind. She was not skilled in this, at least he didn't think so, but she was aware enough to protect herself–to prevent him from sliding in easily.

Rayen would never drop her mental shields without mutual trust. The only way she'd give that trust would be if he showed her that same respect first.

He lowered his mental shields and whispered, "Try now."

She murmured something that he didn't understand then he felt her sneak inside. Curiosity swirled and heat followed. She touched his mind gently, her tentative probing an intimate and sensual stroke. So much that heat stirred uncomfortably in his body. He had to hurry up or this would get out of hand.

Callan forced his thoughts back to dealing with the mist invading her mind. *Can you hear me, Rayen?*

Yes. How is this possible?

Answering that would take explaining that he'd shoved his way in the first time. He didn't think he'd caused any permanent change, but better to avoid that conversation. *Telepathy is possible because you trust me, but first we have to clear away the influence of the mist.*

Then he'd have to make sure she told no one about speaking mind-to-mind with him. He had enough to handle without taking grief over doing this with anyone but a MystiK.

He told her, *Now that you know how to move your thoughts, return to your own mind.*

She frowned again but her swirl of heat withdrew from him like smoke evaporating.

He released a sigh of relief. There was only so much a man could take and having her inside his mind threatened to cut the leash on his control.

When he tried to enter her mind this time, he hit no resistance, but he could feel the mist still working to confuse her. Infusing his order with steel, he told her, *Follow me around your mind, and when I show you the mist, you force it out.*

I can do that.

She didn't sound convinced though and he couldn't do this part for her, or he would. He pointed out a boiling mass of mist and warned her that was the enemy trying to harm her. She did nothing. The mist gained confidence at her reluctance and began to spread.

Callan changed his tactic and told her, *That mist is coming after me and wants to kill me.*

Her thoughts warred for only a second before she turned on the mist, slamming it over and over into her mental walls until the pocket of trouble disintegrated.

Callan rushed from spot to spot, showing Rayen everywhere the mist hid. When he was done, he had to withdraw without leaving her vulnerable to anything slipping in behind him.

Her mind was strong, but he'd been correct in thinking she was unskilled. A novice when it came to mental engagement.

But he was not and recognized the desire to linger as unacceptable behavior on his part. He'd never spent time deep inside a mind and had no business wanting to feel more of Rayen's.

What little time he'd spent in there was putting him on edge, so his words came out a little abrupt. *When I pull out, drop your mental shields.*

I don't know how.

Yes, you do, Rayen. You knocked my mind back with a natural defense move when I tried to enter the first time. Ready?

I guess.

He wasn't and paused, which was stupid because that was testosterone influencing *his* thoughts. He wanted to stay right where he was, but an entire village depended on him. His life had never been his own and never would be. A selfish part of him considered kissing her mind, just to be the first to do it. But that was wrong.

No man should ever do that to a woman unless he'd bound himself to her forever.

Callan? Are you glad to see me?

Her mental voice swept across his senses, curling heat into places it had no business being. Was he glad to see her? So much he'd thought his chest would burst when he first spotted her standing near their empty village.

But was he glad to see her *here* again?

Not even.

She shouldn't have come back. He'd told her to not return. He wasn't so selfish that he'd encourage her to return again or stay. If she did, she'd eventually die here. Just the thought of anything happening to her fouled his thinking. He could barely keep small children alive.

If SEOH caught Rayen in here, there was no way Callan could protect her.

Callan?

Anger at the idea of her being harmed turned his tone abrupt. *Prepare to drop your mental shields. I'm backing out now.*

He withdrew rapidly and clenched his teeth at the ache that drove through his head, but it shouldn't have caused her any distress. He quickly tried to poke again, but she'd done as he said and blocked him. His last words were too harsh. Before he could say a word to soften his reply, Rayen slid her hands to his chest.

He let out a lusty sigh over the pleasure of her hands on his skin until she shoved down hard enough to force a grunt from him. She leaped to her feet.

He gazed up at her and a glow from the red moon kissed her skin. She was pretty.

No, she was beautiful. Her blue-green eyes were–

Giving him a look that would fry a croggle. What was wrong?

"Guess that answered my question," Rayen snapped.

"What question?" He'd lost the ability to think straight when her hands had crawled over his chest.

"It doesn't matter."

He raced back through their silent conversation. She'd asked if he was glad to see her. He hadn't said anything, but if he'd told her the truth, that he'd missed her every waking moment, he'd have an even harder time convincing her to go back to the past and stay there.

Stay somewhere safe. Not in this deadly place.

She'd argue that she'd given her word to Mathias who had asked her to remain here and help protect the children in the village.

Callan would not hold her to that.

He lifted his knees, and with a quick arched leap, he landed on his feet in front of her. Determined to get her out of here as soon as he could, he leaned down and said, "Here's your answer. I told you not to come back."

She yanked her head back as if she'd taken a hit.

His stomach twisted at that. He'd never been cruel to anyone, especially a female, and definitely not to one he cared for. He'd cut his arm off before hurting Rayen, but she wore her feelings like a cloak for all to see. Right now, he could tell how much she wanted to hear something different from him.

If she only knew all the things he wanted to say differently and to pull her into his arms. But he would not risk her life for anything. He couldn't control what SEOH did to create more death traps in the Sphere or how many MystiKs were constantly dumped here, but Callan *could* keep Rayen out of this place.

And he would.

With no memory, she didn't even know what day she'd turn eighteen. If that happened here, the death wraiths that had taken Mathias might come for her.

Callan couldn't breathe for a moment just thinking of her dying.

He would do anything to protect her. Even let her think he didn't care for her, because the truth was that he felt more than he should for this girl.

"Can we come back?" Gabby called.

Callan started to wave them forward, but Rayen did it first, her eyes daring him to override her command. She propped a hand on one hip and leveled him with a glare that could bludgeon. "You may not be pleased that

I'm here, but I'm sure *others* in your village will be. Where are they?"

"A short hike from here."

Tony strolled up. "You two finished booty wrestling?"

Rayen's gaze stayed on Callan when she said, "Callan was only wiping away the mist influence. Nothing more. He's made it clear that I'm not welcome, but I didn't come back for him. I'm here for the children."

That struck deep, cutting him, but he deserved it after pushing her away. He couldn't shove her back and expect anything other than an honest response. It didn't change the fact that his insides were getting chewed to pieces by her chilly stare.

Gabby came up next, her worry over Rayen evident. "*Sooo*, you can finally see what we see?"

Rayen nodded. "Everything looks as grim as you described." Then she tossed a scathing look at Callan. "A lot has changed since we left."

Gabby's eyes flicked back and forth between Callan and Rayen, pausing on Callan. Gabby crossed her arms and glared at him.

Had Gabby and Rayen spoken mind-to-mind?

Callan didn't think so. No, this was the same silent dialogue that happened between girls at home all the time. Rayen hadn't said a word, but Gabby picked up on Rayen's hurt and was letting Callan know he was not high on her list either.

Women.

"What happened here?" Tony asked, taking in the destruction from this point.

"The TecKnati deposited a ground-covering plant that attached to the surface then went underground. It spread quickly and literally emerged during the night, growing fast enough to bloom and emit a mist within hours. We noticed it the first day you were gone but didn't realize the mist was a gas that affects the mind."

"First day?" Gabby asked. "We've only been gone overnight."

Tony chimed in. "Best I can figure, four hours here passes for one hour back home, so that means we've been gone over two and a half days in Sphere time."

Callan continued. "Right. We lost two children when the ground cover initially appeared. One child shoved his face into what he thought was a stream but was really an army of blood ants that can strip the skin away in seconds."

Gabby covered her mouth. "No."

"Yes," Callan said.

"What about Jaxxson?"

"It hit the children fastest, but the minute Jaxxson noticed something invading his mind, he attacked the gas and cleansed it then taught all of us how to prevent the mist's influence. That's why we moved the village and warded the ground against the mist-producing plant before relocating the children."

Gabby started trembling. Was she cold?

She shook so hard she fell to the ground.

Callan reached toward her.

Rayen shouted, "Don't touch her. She's having reactions of some kind. That's one reason we came back, but it seems to be getting worse here."

Nearby, dead trees swayed back and forth, tossing broken limbs to the ground, then it all ended just as quickly.

Gabby sat up, holding her head.

Callan asked, "Is she sick?"

"No." Gabby shifted around and gained her feet again. "She also speaks for herself. I don't feel ill, but I can't control these reactions."

He started to ask what other reactions she was referring to but noticed that her hair was missing. Maybe replaced would be more accurate. She had red, gold, and purple ribbons like he'd expect, but in place of actual hair she had blue ribbons. "What happened to your hair?"

Gabby huffed out a breath. "What part of reactions are you confused about? How many times do I have to explain this?"

Callan sent a what's-going-on look at Rayen.

She shook her head. "This is hard on Gabby so the fewer questions the better until she can talk to Jaxxson."

"Who's that?" Gabby asked with obvious female admiration as she strained to look past Callan.

He swung around to find a grinning Kaz strolling toward his group. Callan was glad to have another skilled MystiK Warrior his own age, but sorry that his friend had been trapped in the Sphere with him.

When Kaz reached them, Callan said, "This is Kaz of the Warrior House of City Two. He arrived here a few hours after you three went home. Kaz, these are the three from the past we told you about." Nodding at Gabby, Callan said, "This is Gabby. That's Tony and–"

When Callan turned to introduce Rayen, he realized Kaz had been paying attention to only her. That rubbed a raw spot, so he made a quick introduction. "And this one is Rayen."

"*This one*?" Rayen snapped. "Guess I really have fallen out of favor if I'm *this one* again."

What had he said wrong? He gave up and ordered everyone, "Follow me."

"Only if I have to," Rayen muttered.

"I know the way there, too," Kaz suggested, but it hadn't been for Callan's ears.

Tony asked, "I just realized we didn't run into a croggle back at our transender site. What happened to them? Not that I wanted to be a snack for one, but did they just disappear?"

Kaz answered, "There aren't any croggles left at this transender site. They probably left to find a better food source, but they're still around the other landing locations."

Callan had taken ten steps when he glanced around to find Gabby right behind him, then Tony.

Rayen brought up the rear with Kaz walking beside her.

Not just walking next to her but smiling and talking the whole time. Kaz had a reputation with girls back home that had made it around the entire Warrior House. He was standing entirely too close to Rayen.

White hot anger burst through Callan.

Gabby paused, her gaze running over him from head to toe. "I didn't know your skin changed. It was always the same pattern of color last time I saw you."

Callan locked down his emotions.

Those born of the Warrior House had natural camouflage pigmentation in their skin that shifted and changed with strong emotional reactions. But he'd learned how to control his before he reached ten years of age.

Or he thought he had.

The last time his control slipped had been around Rayen.

Did he need any more signs that having her here was a bad idea?

When everyone's forward progress stopped because Callan hadn't moved, Kaz and Rayen finally looked up. Kaz worked to hide a smirk, but not very hard.

Rayen's face had been soft and open while she was staring down, but the minute she raised her head and met Callan's gaze, hers changed into a fierce expression, closed off to him.

Kaz took in Rayen then Callan, causing his stupid smirk to grow into a full grin.

Callan couldn't allow Kaz to remain with Rayen while she was here. Not that he had a sound reason for thinking that way, but he was the leader, which should be reason enough for ordering anyone to separate.

Yes, that sounded ridiculous, even in his head.

At a loss for what to do to get out of this predicament with any pride left, Callan asked Kaz, "What happened on the hunt?"

"I was successful. We have meat for this week. Had I killed any more, it would have gone to waste before we could consume it all."

"You should be at the village cleaning the game."

"I finished that and would have stayed but I saw the green stripes and thought more children were coming. You were the one who said no less than two were to run the transender lines. They told me you had gone alone. So here I am."

Callan couldn't argue with his own rule.

When Mathias lived, the minimum number had been four to run the transender lines due to the constant threat of attack by croggles, but Callan wouldn't risk any of the younger ones on these runs.

What if Rayen had met a MystiK child when she'd first arrived today and thought it was a TecKnati?

Even as he thought it, he knew that wasn't a real concern. Knowing Rayen, she'd protect a TecKnati child as quickly as a MystiK child.

"Did you forget the way?" Kaz asked, his grin growing.

Rayen's lips twitched at that.

Kaz brought a smile out of her? Callan clenched his jaw to keep from snarling at someone he called friend. The guy enjoyed life too much, even in this place. "Just keep up."

Callan turned back to leading and set a fast pace he hoped would limit any talking. Gabby grumbled as she stumbled over uneven ground and Tony cursed, but not a peep of complaint from Rayen. The last time he checked on her, she was laughing at something Kaz said as they ran side by side.

There was nothing Callan could do about that, not until they returned to the village where Kaz would find his duties were about to increase significantly.

And Rayen ... would have to leave as soon as Jaxxson did something about Gabby's reactions.

CHAPTER 11

RAYEN COULDN'T GET OVER HOW much the landscape had changed since leaving the Sphere.

Just over two and a half days—in Sphere time—for the jungle to be burned away as if slashed by a giant hand of fire. Callan led them into an area with lots of trees that were gnarled and stunted. And the colors became more intense, acid greens and shocking oranges. Gabby should like them, but the colors made Rayen uncomfortable, as did the soft pink soil that puffed with every footfall.

She cleared a downed log with little effort, glad to finally be able to see what everyone else did even if the sight of the damaged landscape sickened her. Kaz jogged beside her, leaping just as smoothly over the log without missing a step.

He moved with a fluid grace, as effortless as a wild cat on the hunt. Tony and Gabby were doing their best to stay up with Callan who pushed everyone harder than seemed necessary.

What had gotten into him?

Even though the exercise was creating body heat to ward off the chilly air, she considered yelling for him to slow down for Tony and Gabby's benefit.

He tossed a look back her way. Eyes she'd seen go from blue to hazel now flashed the color of a striking sunset before he turned his back to her again. A beautiful back with muscles that bunched and flexed with every move, his skin a mix of muted blue and brown colors that shifted at will to camouflage his body.

Just as ruthlessly as he camouflaged his emotions.

Callan backed off the swift pace.

Had he heard her thoughts? She doubted it, because if he had, he'd take any request to slow down as a sign of weakness on her part. She would not give him the satisfaction of asking him for anything. He'd cleared the mist out of her mind, but she could take care of herself in this place, and she'd help with the children even if he didn't want her here.

Still, why hadn't he missed her?

The ache that had started when he told her that she shouldn't have come back kicked her in the heart again.

Stupid.

"That's all you know about yourself?" Kaz asked. "Only that you're a C'raydonian?"

"Pretty much." She ducked under a branch and noticed the terrain was now becoming bluish-green and brown with yellow spots, less intense in color. "I hope to find out more this time, something that might break loose some memory cells."

"How are you adjusting to living in the past?"

"I haven't been there long, but since I have no memories of anything else, I suppose it's fine. I don't want to go back."

"Why?"

"Because they keep trying to identify who I am. If they don't come up with something soon, which they won't, they'll send me away from the school where Gabby, Tony and I live." Then she'd really be in trouble and have no way to return to the Sphere.

Not that Callan cared. He should be the one asking about her life back in that world, but no. He just wanted her to get out of his. She'd leave when she was good and ready. When she'd fulfilled her promise to Mathias.

Kaz fell silent for a moment as they ran, then asked, "What's going on between you and Callan?"

"Nothing." She'd said that too quickly, but it was the truth. Whatever she'd thought was happening between them had been an illusion. Something else that her confused mind had generated. A fantasy. Nothing more. She'd convinced herself that she belonged here, even though she knew it was only for a short time.

With no home to long for, she'd been willing to come back here to be with the MystiKs and protect them against the TecKnati.

Now, she wasn't welcome here either.

"There's some good news," Kaz murmured.

"What?" She looked over at him and his smile lit up the air.

He chuckled and shook his head at some silent thought. He was just as tall as Callan and had nice muscles, but not as carved up as Callan's.

Kaz was toned, where Callan was all power.

Thick, cinnamon brown hair fell in shaggy waves that managed to look attractive on Kaz, maybe because he had gorgeous green eyes and a mouth that had no doubt been born grinning. Kaz wore a vest made of woven light gray material over his strong chest. He was built to be fluid and quick. His skin had the same type of mottled colors as Callan's, in similar shades of blue, but Callan seemed to be able to control his shifting colors better.

Why was she comparing Kaz to Callan?

Kaz wanted to be friendly, which was more than she'd gotten from Callan. She *should* pay more attention to someone engaging and nice, right?

A part of her argued that no matter how much she denied it, she wanted to be alongside Callan.

That part could go hang out with her lost memories, because no matter what she'd thought, she was not here for Callan. She was here for the children.

Nothing else.

Certainly not for an annoying, full of himself, grouchy leader.

Stop thinking about him! she silently ordered herself.

I'm trying.

She'd talk to Kaz. At least he was interested in what she had to say. "Tell me about your world, Kaz."

He lunged ahead of her and lifted a branch out of her way then caught up quickly again. She tried not to notice how much that small consideration meant right now.

He scratched his chin. "My world, hmm. Let me think where to start." Two more strides and he said, "We have ten cities."

"I did hear about that," she admitted. "I'm not familiar with anything in the past to know where those cities are now geographically, but to be honest I know just as little about the land in the past where my friends live."

He explained, "The general area where civilization congregated after a terrible virus wiped out most of my world is in what was originally called North America."

"I think where Tony and Gabby come from in the past is also known as North America. Callan said your House is in City Two. What's that like?"

Kaz's voice took on a longing. "MystiKs of all Houses live in all the cities, but the ruling force of the Warrior House is in City Two. It is also called SAN, which I've heard was once known as San Diego. It's a beautiful place on the edge of an ocean and the weather tends to be sunny more than overcast, and it has everything I could ask for with mountains, ocean, and city."

"Sounds nice."

"It is, or it would be if we didn't live in constant struggle with the TecKnati leader. He continues to send MystiKs here. I'm not the only new one in the last few days."

Would SEOH forever make the lives of MystiKs miserable? She wished he'd show up in this Sphere. "That situation doesn't sound as if it's getting any better with MystiK children still being captured and hidden away here."

"No, it's not." Kaz lost his smile.

She wished she hadn't asked about his home. She had probably made him homesick, something she could identify with even if she didn't have a home. That was a whole different kind of sick feeling.

"I hear you have mad powers," Kaz quipped, his mood light again.

She laughed. "I don't know what exactly my powers are, or if they are mad. They just show up sometimes with no warning then other times I can't beg them to work." As soon as the words were out of her mouth, she wanted to bite her tongue. Why had she told Kaz that? *Never give anyone something to use against you*, rumbled through her mind. She'd learned that somewhere.

Until now, she hadn't admitted that she had no control over her powers. What if–

"What's bothering you, Rayen?"

She glanced over, expecting him to be laughing at her, but he was serious. Talking wasn't wise if she couldn't keep her secrets to herself.

He turned to the left when the path angled down and away, the fine powder becoming more copper colored here. When she caught up to him again, Kaz said, "I'm not your enemy. I won't use anything you tell me against you."

She pretended to be confused. "What are you talking about?"

"You just told me your powers are intermittent and uncontrolled. It bothers you that you told me."

"How did you know that?"

"It's a gift." He chuckled and his eyes twinkled when he looked over at her, which he'd been doing pretty much the whole time. How did he manage not to fall on his face?

She chanced another quick glance at him and almost tripped.

Kaz caught her arm when she stumbled then released her once she was steady again.

Some warrior she was. She couldn't stay upright on her own. If the splash of heat in her cheeks was any indication, he could see her humiliation.

But when she tossed another glance at him, he wasn't the least affected by her misstep.

Splotches of color on Kaz's face rearranged to make a wild pattern over his skin. He crossed his eyes then burst out laughing at my reaction of horror. The guy was too full of life to ignore.

She said, "Thanks."

"Why?"

"I needed a reason to smile today." She enjoyed a comfortable silence for the next few minutes. When she pushed her gaze his way again, all joking had vanished.

He stared at her with heavy eyes that hid his thoughts. "You're unusual."

"I know, but I can't decide if that is good or not."

"Oh, it's definitely good, Rayen. There are too many girls stamped out from the same mold. I've always been interested in custom creations."

She wanted *someone* to look at her the way he did and say her name in that gruff tone. Kaz was extremely attractive, but ...

She was thinking about *him* again, their stupid leader, and refused to even think his name.

He hadn't looked at her the way Kaz was doing right now, even after she had traveled through the portal again, ready to take on all the TecKnati here if they had harmed he-who-shall-not-be-named.

He'd ignored her from the minute Kaz had shown up.

If that's the way he wanted things between them, then she would lick her wounds in private. But out here?

Out here, she would not allow *that one* to know how much he'd hurt her.

Yeah, he was now *that one*, like he'd called her.

Giving a smile back to Kaz, she swallowed the lump in her throat and continued her interest in his world. "Tell me more about growing up in these cities in the future."

Kaz finished their last ten minutes of jogging by recalling his life as the youngest boy in a family of warriors. That he'd been doted on was obvious because he did not lack confidence.

"We're close to the village," Kaz said as they left the cover of trees and started up a rocky hill, but he paused and squinted at the sky.

"What's wrong?" She searched ahead of them for some sign of a village. If it was near, it was hidden by the hill they were climbing.

Callan looked up at that same moment, seemed to freeze then exploded into a run.

That's when she saw smoke rising above the crest.

Kaz raced up the incline with her right behind him. Tony and Gabby were just reaching the pinnacle, too.

Callan shouted, "The village is under attack," and disappeared over the top.

She slowed next to Tony and Gabby, yelling, "Stay here. I'll come back for you."

Not waiting for an answer, she pumped her arms and spun her feet toward an unknown danger. It didn't matter. She would fight alongside Callan and Kaz.

Now would be a great time for her powers to show up and be of use. She could plead with them all she wanted, but the strange energy had let her down in the past. Whether her powers manifested or not, she would protect the village children with her last breath.

CHAPTER 12

WHATEVER PREPARATION RAYEN THOUGHT SHE'D done mentally was of no use for what she encountered. At first, she hadn't seen the village, but as they approached, Kaz yelled at her to follow Callan through an opening in a protective ward they'd placed around the village to hide it from view.

What had happened to allow the TecKnati to break through a ward like that?

Once inside, she could see the village and the damage.

This scattered grouping of huts was a pitiful replica of where the MystiKs had lived in their last village.

Smoke tendrils curled toward the sky, rising from what appeared to have been two hut-like structures large enough to sleep ten to fifteen children. A burning stench filled her nostrils and choked her.

Children cried and wandered around looking lost.

Broken gourds were scattered across the ground, a water-like substance spilled into the soil, turning the copper color blood red.

Callan picked up a tiny little boy and carried him to a young girl who was ushering small ones into one group. Tears streaked her face, but she took the boy from Callan and added the child to her bunch.

Kaz looked nothing like the easy-going guy who had teased and joked with Rayen on the way here. His face took on the edge of a warrior ready to trounce an enemy that had dared to touch his home.

But if Kaz looked threatening, Callan looked deadly. He had his usual unemotional mask on, but she'd been around him enough to see past the façade he wore for the benefit of the children. Everything about him had lethal sharpness. The aggression flooding his bones was there but leashed behind the rigid control he maintained.

Still, she felt his pain over what had happened and wanted to put her arms around him. Tell him she was here to help, to stand by him, fight by him, care for him.

But he didn't want her, or her feelings, so she kept them locked safely out of view.

Kaz stepped up to Callan. "There are impressions of many boot heels. The TeK invaded our village."

Callan nodded his agreement then lifted his head and roared, "*Zilya!*"

The entire place quieted, all gazes fixed on their leader. And it was no question that they accepted Callan for that role. Frightened eyes on every child wanted to believe that someone could, and would, protect them. That someone was Callan. He'd said something once that made her think he didn't want the role of leader. He wanted to be a warrior.

He'd lead a team of warriors into a bloody battle any day, but he had never yearned to govern anyone. Here he had to do both.

A tall girl with white-blond hair and a sprinkle of jewels embedded on one cheek came rushing out of a structure enclosed in rough striped bark. Zilya. She craved power and hated TecKnati.

C'raydonians? They didn't count enough to be hated as far as she was concerned.

"Where have you been?" Zilya yelled at Callan, clearly not noticing how close he was to ripping someone apart for what had happened here. She was too striking to just call beautiful. Her tunic-style gown still had the strange half-moon designs sewn in a deeper burnished gold down the front, but it looked battered and worn. Her arrogant attitude made her appear as tall as Rayen was while her white-blond hair was so pale it reflected the vivid purple sky.

"You knew I was running the transender line." Callan's voice dared her to contest him.

Smearing a dirty streak across her forehead when she wiped at sweat, Zilya caught sight of Rayen and sneered, "What's *she* doing here? I thought we were rid of her kind."

Muscles corded on Callan's arms when he crossed them. "She's not important. What happened here is."

Callan's gaze had skipped to Rayen and bounced away just as she flinched at his words. She knew what he meant, that the village was important, but she couldn't stop the involuntary reaction.

For a mere second, he looked like he was going to apologize, maybe tell her he was glad to see her. But that had been her imagination because he turned on Zilya again. "How did the TecKnati scouts break through our protective wall?"

Zilya forgot about Rayen at the unspoken accusation that she'd failed to protect the village while he was out. Based on what Rayen had learned the first time here, Zilya came from the Governing House and should be ruling this village, but Mathias had been in charge and was from the Governing House as well. Before he left the village for the last time, he'd dictated Callan as his successor.

At the time, everyone had thought the TecKnati were removing Mathias from the Sphere and imprisoning him back home until the MystiKs and TecKnati worked out their differences.

Mathias had known his terrifying fate even as he'd smiled at the children and pretended that he enjoyed his eighteenth BIRG Day.

The day that MystiKs became fair game for the blood thirsty SEOH.

Zilya hadn't been happy about Mathias' choice of Callan as leader and let Callan know it, just as she seemed determined to remind him again. She jutted her chin up. "How did those TeK get in? You tell me. You were supposed to check the perimeter before you left."

Callan glanced around then back at her. "I did. Everything was secure."

"Then explain to me how a scout found a way inside and brought ten more with him?" She shifted her anger at Kaz next. "You should not have gone out again."

Kaz kept his voice even, almost bored when he replied, "I followed protocol established before I arrived here that dictates two on the transender run if two capable warriors are available. From what I understand, you ratified that, plus if you had precognitive information of an impending attack, it was your duty to inform me before I left."

Rayen admired the way Kaz had turned the argument back on Zilya and took the power from her verbal attack on Callan.

Callan lifted a hand, silencing Kaz and Zilya. "Where is Jaxxson?"

Zilya shook her head. "He's gone."

What? Rayen clamped her mouth shut to keep from shouting. Gabby needed Jaxxson. How could he just leave?

"Where?" Callan demanded.

"To search ... for the children."

Callan moved quickly, shoving a finger into Zilya's face. "One warning. That's all you get. Tell me everything and do it quickly before I lose what little patience I have and forget your position."

Her flat gray eyes flashed with a caution signal, but she replied, "The TeK kidnapped three of our children. Jaxxson followed to find out where the scouts might be taking them."

Callan's skin color moved a tiny bit, but that was huge because he held his control in a ruthless grip. "You stand here speaking of insignificant issues when the first words should have been about three of our children ending up in the hands of the enemy? What is wrong with you?"

She backed up a step and glared her hatred at Rayen. "The attack is her fault."

Mine?

Tony called out from behind, "How do you figure that, sweet cheeks?"

Rayen turned to find that it really was Tony who gave voice to the words she'd thought. He and Gabby were jogging toward them. She was glad to see them and that they'd found the opening Kaz had made, but they hadn't known what they were walking into.

Rayen softened her rebuke. "You should have waited for me to come back."

Gabby laughed with an evil sound. "And miss Robo Barbie's drama queen interpretation? Not a chance."

Tony stepped up next to Rayen. Gabby flanked her other side.

It was a blatant show of support that Rayen felt deep in her bones. She might not have family, a future or a past, but she did have two friends who would stand by her against a threat.

Just as she would for them.

Etoi chose that moment to show her face and stepped up next to Zilya, making her allegiance obvious then shoving her attitude at Rayen. She still wore a muted tunic with a braided gold edge that mimicked Zilya's but not quite as ornate. Her hair was much darker than Zilya's, falling in ringlets woven of blond and black.

One other thing that hadn't changed.

Etoi's beady eyes slapped Rayen with icy hatred when she stated, "It is true. The destruction, the mist, this attack–it all happened because you turned our enemy loose and he reported to SEOH."

"Oh, look, Mini-me is here." Gabby had her hair woven into one big ball again that gave her a more mature look when she addressed Zilya. "Explain how this–" She opened her arms wide. "–is all Rayen's fault when we just got here."

Zilya had been wary of Gabby last time, especially after Jaxxson declared Gabby a Hy'bridt, someone rare, powerful, and highly valued in Zilya's world.

But that didn't prevent the acid burning through Zilya's words. "The TecKnati did not bother our village until you came and she–" Zilya pointed a long finger at Rayen. "–showed herself to them."

Rayen didn't need anyone to speak for her and started toward Zilya, a challenge seeping into her voice. "I had no choice last time when the TeKs were harming one of your new arrivals. Did you want me to leave that child to face a croggle?"

Everyone sitting around observing the conversation sucked in a breath.

Callan shouted, "*Enough!* Kaz and I will go after the children."

"I will, too," Rayen added and thought Callan would argue, but he nodded quickly in her direction.

Zilya didn't like that idea at all. "She and Kaz can go. Your place is here, Callan."

Another round of air was sucked in.

Callan became very still then in a quiet voice that packed a lethal warning, he said, "Do not ever think to tell me what I am or am not to do. You constantly claim this is your village to rule. Now is the time to stop talking and start showing that you are more than a voice box. The guards inside our perimeter should have caught anyone breaching the wall and alerted everyone telepathically. When I return, you and every guard will explain why that did not happen. We can't survive unless we *all* do our jobs, starting with you."

Rayen didn't think Zilya was capable of embarrassment, but her cheeks turned ruddy. Her narrowed eyes held a venomous look for Callan then slashed over at Rayen with a promise of who would pay for her humiliation.

Rayen cocked her head at Zilya in a silent response of, *By all means, give me a reason to wipe that arrogance from your face.*

A skinny little boy in a robe walked cautiously into their midst. V'ru, the boy wonder who had been born with the knowledge of all history from the beginning of time. His eyes were red and swollen with lingering fear.

Callan visually calmed and spoke gently to V'ru. "Are you harmed?"

"No." The tiny word barely made a sound. "We lost three."

Walking over to V'ru, Callan shook his head. "I'm going after them."

"What about ..." V'ru looked at the clumps of children huddled together and finished with, "Them?"

Anyone could tell the boy needed reassurance that the TecKnati would not return to take the other children and *him* once Callan left. Where Zilya's screeching hadn't chipped at his resolve to go hunt TecKnati, seeing V'ru so frightened had Callan hesitating to walk away.

Tony surprised everyone by speaking up. "No worries. I'll stay but fix whatever perimeter defense you have before you go, show me how it works, and I'll watch over this place."

"You?" Zilya made that single word sound like an insult.

Tony sighed. "I'm not a superpower X-man, but I'm from South Jersey, part of the Black Scorpions, and we don't let no one mess with our territory." He winked at her. "I'll keep you safe, babe."

Etoi started toward Tony with a spear in her hand.

Callan stopped her with, "Etoi. You will listen to him while I am gone. If you do not do as he says, you will answer to me."

In two steps, Etoi went from furious to horrified and froze. "You would put me *below* a TecKnati?"

Rayen had forgotten that V'ru had declared Tony not a TecKnati of the future, but that he carried the genetic marker for one. A possible TecKnati ancestor.

"Did you not understand my words?" Callan asked and the silence that followed made it clear all discussion on the topic had ended at that point. He turned to Kaz. "Find the breach in the reflective wall. Take Tony with you and explain how the wall acts as an external repellant. Show him how I expect the internal guard stations to be staffed."

Kaz nodded and glanced at Tony, giving a silent command to follow.

Before Tony could walk away, Rayen said, "Kaz, I need a minute with Tony and Gabby."

He waited without a word.

Callan stepped further into the center of his battered village and started giving everyone instructions of what he wanted done while he was gone. He didn't even acknowledge that she had spoken, but neither did he deny her request.

Rayen turned to Tony and Gabby.

"What, Xena?"

"First of all, thank you, Tony."

"No problem, but don't forget our agreement about in and out," he reminded her. "I'll get with V'ru to find out what he knows about the computer and the transender control. You just make sure you get back here as soon as you can."

"I will, but I also need to find out how to travel here without either of you, so ask V'ru about that, too."

Gabby said, "Wait a minute. You really want to come back without us?"

"That's her choice," Tony argued quietly. "Just like it's mine to not make another trip here. I have to take care of my family first."

Rayen hated the hurt she heard in Gabby's voice and didn't want to give up either one of these two, but she didn't belong in their world. "It's not that I don't want to stay with you two, but I have no home in the past. I'll never be able to explain my existence and at some point, my powers or lack of knowledge about your world is going to give me away. That might end with me being locked up because they don't know what to do with me, or me possibly hurting someone because I can't control this energy. I can't go forward to the world these children come from or I'll die, because I no longer exist in that world either."

Gabby got more distressed by the moment. Her hair was moving around, trying to free itself. "What's your plan?"

"I'm going to stay here and do what I can to help Callan and the MystiKs return home."

"So, what? You're just going to stay here?"

Rayen shrugged, trying to show a calm acceptance she hadn't quite reached yet. "This might be the only place left for me. I'll figure that out once the MystiKs go home." Now that these two knew what she was thinking, she needed their cooperation to say nothing. "Promise me you won't tell anyone here what I just shared with you."

Rayen had expected Tony to pipe up with a quick agreement, but he and Gabby were exchanging glances then Tony told Gabby, "She's got a point."

"I don't care," Gabby grouched. "She'll be alone here."

Callan finished what he was doing and turned to them.

Rayen had to get this done before he heard anything. "Look, we'll talk more later, but I need your promise to hold my confidence."

Gabby grumbled, but in the end they both agreed.

When Tony strode off with Kaz and Callan went in another direction, Rayen whispered to Gabby, "Will you be okay while I'm out hunting for those kids?"

"I'll handle it. Just get Jaxxson back here as soon as you can. He'll know what to do."

"I will." She noticed Gabby dragging her nails down her arms, leaving red marks, and asked, "Why are you doing that? You're digging into your skin."

"I can't help it. My hands won't stay still."

"What else is bothering you?"

"You mean other than Jaxxson possibly captured or killed by the TeKs? Nothing."

Rayen felt for her. Gabby had thought of herself as a freak of nature until she met Jaxxson. The healer taught her to appreciate her gift of mental communication and how to block out so many thoughts invading her mind around large groups of people. But more than that, Gabby's eyes had been bright with excitement after her time with Jaxxson. She'd gotten close to the healer and clearly missed him as much as Rayen had missed Callan.

But Jaxxson would probably be happy to see Gabby.

At least, Rayen hoped he would.

Gabby stopped clawing at her arms. "It's passed again. I'm going to do what I can to help the little ones." The pocket on her pants started moving. She glanced down to find the pupple's head sticking out. Gabby let out a long "ooh" and pulled the little thing up to smile at it.

The fringe of hair around its paws and poof of its tail were vibrant colors again. She hugged it to her cheek and its tiny pink tongue came out to swipe a wet spot on her skin.

One of the girls Rayen recalled had worked on the decorations for Mathias' party, walked up. She hoped she remembered her name correctly. "Hello, Phoebe."

"It is good to see you again, Rayen."

Not everyone blamed her for the apocalypse that happened here.

Phoebe looked at Gabby's hands and exclaimed, "You have a pupple?"

Gabby smiled. "Yes, it traveled back with us and almost died."

"We have none for the children. The fires killed many animals."

Rayen asked, "What caused the fires?"

"It rained from the skies. SEOH sent it."

How could one man hate a group of people that much?

Gabby told Phoebe, "As soon as we can clean up an area for treating the children, we'll pass this one around to the ones who you think need it the most."

Phoebe acknowledged the compliment by smiling. "I will be happy to help you."

Gabby stood very still. Rayen worried about a new bout of shaking, but she started smiling. "What is it?"

Angling her head, Gabby called out, "I'm over here." Then she told Rayen, "Be'tallia, the little girl that Jaxxson and I healed, just called to me telepathically."

That had been the little girl Rayen saved from a croggle attack. Looking to be around five years old, Be'tallia came hurrying through the groups of children. Her intricate braids had fallen loose, her silver dress had lost its shine, and her dirty shoes no longer sparkled, but her smile glowed at seeing Gabby.

Be'tallia paused, eyes bright. "I am glad you came back. We were attacked."

Moisture gathered at the corner of Gabby's eyes.

Rayen had come to know how very important protecting any child was to Gabby, but this one was special to her. Be'tallia had played a part in teaching Gabby how to embrace her telepathic ability.

"I am even more glad to see you," Gabby said as she squatted down and opened her arms. Be'tallia ran to her and hugged Gabby's neck.

Rayen's heart swelled at seeing Gabby not just touch someone but share a hug. The relief in her friend's voice was tangible. It wasn't until that moment that she realized Gabby must have been worried all the way here that Be'tallia had been one of the children Callan had mentioned losing to the mist.

Callan, Kaz, and Tony returned.

Rayen noticed that Zilya and her assistant Etoi had disappeared, but she seriously doubted that Zilya would let anything go wrong while Callan was gone this time.

No one would want to face his wrath.

That included Rayen, so she'd keep her thoughts to herself around him and focus on finding the missing children.

Once everyone was set, Callan handed Kaz two spears like the one he carried. When Kaz walked over to hand Rayen one of his weapons, she realized Callan had intentionally raised an invisible wall between them with that one act.

She was not hurt. She wasn't.

When they headed out on their hunt, she looked back at the village, which literally disappeared from view. The protective shield Callan and his people had created absorbed its surroundings and showed nothing of what it hid.

Much like Callan could be with his emotional shield.

He didn't want her inside his personal walls, but would he allow her to remain inside the village walls?

Kaz slowed and glanced over his shoulder at her. "Coming?"

Callan had moved way ahead. Leaving her. She needed a friend on her side here in this place and Kaz was the only one present willing to giving her a chance. She smiled at him. "Yes, sorry I slowed down. I'm fine."

He grinned. "Yes, you are."

His unexpected attention warmed her. Not the way Callan's had, but she had to forget about that. Callan kept putting as much distance as he could between them.

She didn't know if she'd ever spent any time with boys like Callan and

Kaz, but she didn't need experience to know that Kaz was being nice and trying to make her feel better. She should acknowledge and appreciate it.

Picking up her pace, she fell into step with him.

Callan took a sharp left at the same moment, tossing a look her way.

Their eyes met. She kept her face neutral, though it hurt to ignore him.

She couldn't tell what he was thinking from here, or even up close because he hid his thoughts so well, but for a moment her heart skipped a beat at what she wanted to call longing in his expression.

Then he turned away and moved faster.

Why did she keep trying to convince herself that he cared? Maybe she would stay in the past with Tony and Gabby after all.

CHAPTER 13

2179 ACE, in ORD/City One

SEOH FINISHED REVIEWING A BULLETIN and sat back, waving his hand past the holographic document that disappeared from above his desk.

Vice Rustaad, his second in command, entered SEOH's private office where he ruled the TecKnati empire from the hundred-and-seventieth floor of the ANASKO building. Others had tried to emulate SEOH, but none had built anything this spectacular and nothing of significance stood near the prime location of this building that overlooked Lake Michigan.

Rustaad strode up to SEOH's desk and lifted his hand, palm facing the twenty-foot-tall ceiling. A small hologram shot up from his hand and Rustaad began his report. "No additional MystiK families have disappeared in their entirety since the first two earlier this week. This gives us reason to believe Phen T-112 has made successful contact and informed our staff in the past of step two in the sterilization program at the Byzantine Institute."

"If it wasn't so close to the furkken BIRG Con, I'd let our people at the Byzantine Institute continue destroying eggs they're removing from female MystiK ancestors. I'm still chuckling over how those MystiK descendants disappeared this week in three of our cities. Entire families. That's damned encouraging, Rustaad, but now that we know it works, we don't want to continue destroying eggs and draw undue attention too early."

SEOH paused and chuckled. "I do look forward to seeing the faces of holier-than-thou MystiK leaders when they gather and realize how many MystiK families have just vanished. It'll show that they aren't the only ones with magical powers."

Rustaad angled his head in what sufficed as a nod sometimes. "Then we proceed as planned. Our team in the past will continue sterilizing anyone they DNA screen as MystiK ancestry, which is nothing more than extra insurance at this point."

SEOH enjoyed a moment of early satisfaction. Leaders of the seven

Houses believed they were coming to the BIRG Con to sign a new five-year treaty.

They were coming to witness the end of their time on this planet.

The fools really believed they held the upper hand because of their next generation of G'ortian rulers coming of age. SEOH had been forced recently to finally admit that MystiKs were a real threat to technology. Rustaad had delivered solid evidence that two MystiK leaders had used their power to sabotage the HERMES shuttle program.

Plus, SEOH had experienced the MystiK power infused in the treaty firsthand. His eldest son, who had been seventeen and the next SEOH in line, dropped dead at the very second that Rustaad's people killed the G'ortian known as Jornn of the Warrior House. SEOH had considered it a necessary risk to prevent the MystiK prodigy from uniting the seven Houses at this BIRG Con.

But a child of SEOH's blood was worth far more than any MystiK child.

Speaking of the furkken prophecy, SEOH asked, "Have we located the other five G'ortians?"

Rustaad never reacted with enthusiasm or concern, just the stone-cold ability to impart information. "No. We are on the trail of one we should capture shortly. I have teams searching for the others, but I don't expect to find them with the BIRG Con only days away."

"And our decoders working on the prophecy still believe one G'ortian in particular will unite the MystiKs?"

"As best as they can tell, yes. The Damian Prophecy is still in play."

SEOH hated loose ends, and not capturing the rest of the G'ortians represented just that. "You say it's still in play, but who's to say we haven't created a corruption in the prophecy by killing Jornn and locking his twin brother in the Sphere? With Callan gone, the Warrior House has no G'ortian to stake its future on. The prophecy doesn't specifically say the G'ortians will rule, does it?"

A sound escaped Rustaad that might have been a sigh. "This is not something you can throw logic at, SEOH. The Damian Prophecy is an intangible provocation, but one we must respect, as was shown by the proven threat of losing one of our children if we killed one of theirs."

Few things had meant as much to SEOH as his first born. Losing that son cut deep, a wound that would never heal until the MystiKs were made to pay. Rustaad had argued that the spell woven into the treaty by MystiK elders was viable, but as one who accepted only science and hard evidence, SEOH hadn't been capable of believing words on lambskin could touch his child.

He'd learned the truth the hard way and was now after retribution as a bonus to getting the MystiKs out of his world.

If that meant accepting the validity of the unnatural, he'd do it to win.

SEOH waved his hand for Rustaad to continue. "Explain where we are on the prophecy."

Rustaad reached for the hologram that floated above his palm and flicked a finger at one corner. The hologram turned into a four-foot-wide display that hung in midair at Rustaad's left. He moved his hand over the panel, sliding up text until he stopped at one point and expanded the text for both of them to read easily.

"Our code breakers are working around the clock on this, but they believe they understand one part that is in the second half of the prophecy."

The words on the screen read, *A friend enters as an enemy and an enemy departs as a friend.*

Rustaad pursed his lips. "They believe this is our traitor who came to us as an enemy and left as an ally."

SEOH grunted an acknowledgement and Rustaad continued to the next words, reading out loud. "Day of birth as Red Moon rises. Night of end when last Moon sets."

"The fact that we created the Sphere that red moon now orbits should point to our superiority in this whole prophecy business," SEOH pointed out.

"Possibly," Rustaad allowed. "Our decoders have determined that this part of the prophecy aligns with the timing for the start of the BIRG Con meeting. In fact, the Red Moon circling the Sphere will set at the exact moment of sunset on our planet as the MystiK leaders enter the BIRG Con meeting. At that point, they will realize all the MystiK Houses are missing children, specifically their G'ortian heirs."

"The only reason those MystiK fools haven't figured it out yet is because they either aren't talking to each other, as usual, or they suspect other Houses are kidnapping the kids and probably plan to finger them at the BIRG Con in a power play." SEOH smirked. "Of course, I've created a campaign to drive rumors of those suspicions through their world."

"That was a masterful plan to feed covert information into their rumor mill and turn paranoid MystiKs on each other. The Warrior House has not come looking for blood, so they don't know who to hold responsible for the death of Jornn."

Cupping his chin in thought, SEOH suggested, "We may be going to a lot of trouble for naught. The MystiK distrust runs so deep among the Houses that they might attack each other at this BIRG Con and solve our problems by decimating most of their population."

"One could only hope, but–"

"I will not risk a maybe over an absolute," SEOH finished.

"Correct." Returning his gaze to the hologram screen, Rustaad said, "We cannot let the red moon set in the Sphere without a successful execution of the laser grid first, or the combined MystiK power can be turned on us." He looked over at SEOH. "You, specifically."

That might frighten a weaker man, but SEOH had not reached the pinnacle of his success by letting an intangible threat put him on defense. He was pure aggression and offense if he was anything. "Is that all?"

"No, I do have something to report that I just learned on the way here. The three intruders have returned to the Sphere, which means they successfully traveled from the past, returned home and traveled forward again."

Few things stunned SEOH but the magnitude of Rustaad's words hit him. He stood. "They really are from the past?"

"Yes. The MystiK traitor said the three claimed to be students from the Byzantine Institute, which pinpoints specifically where they are in the past. Brilliant on your part to have assigned specific names to each year the Institutes were created in the past."

SEOH was still digesting the significance of this. "Then we could not have sent Phen T-112 back at a better time." He grinned at his own joke. "Literally. We dropped him exactly where those intruders live."

"That's true, which means Phen T-112 should be able to locate the computer these three are using to travel."

"That has to be the Genera-Y computer." SEOH started laughing. "The furkken myth was true. There really was a sentient computer in the past." His brow furrowed tight. "Phen T-112 will find it, just as he was ordered."

"I certainly hope so." Rustaad lifted his left hand and the hologram disappeared. "If he doesn't, those three could cause us problems. From all accounts, they are allies of Callan and his people."

"Phen T-112 will do as told and locate the Genera-Y computer. He was chosen for his ability to follow orders without question. And based on what he told us about being captured by the MystiKs and tossed in a hut with an intruder, it only stands to reason that one of the intruders is the one who built that computer. The one who the MystiKs believe to be a TecKnati."

Rustaad offered, "That intruder could very well be a TecKnati ancestor."

"Exactly what I was thinking," SEOH said, nodding. "I want that one captured."

"We won't be able to transport him here without killing him since he did not originally travel to the Sphere in a transender from this planet."

"We don't need to keep him alive indefinitely, only until he tells us everything he knows. Once that happens, we'll deal with him."

Rustaad was clearly confused by that. "Even if he is a TeK ancestor?"

"No, I don't mean to kill him, just have a medic inject him with Zy-M serum to wipe his memory."

"Ah. Of course."

"Continue to send scouts to the Sphere but allow none to come home until this intruder is captured."

"What of the younger ones sent to train as future Scouts?"

"Everyone stays until this job is done. They'll be motivated to work together." SEOH ignored the disparaging intent of Rustaad's question. The TecKnati Scouts had a mission to execute in the Sphere and sometimes having enough warm bodies made the difference. Sure a few of the Scouts were seven and eight, but this was career development. They knew what risks they were taking.

"Your middle son is scheduled to leave on the next transender shipment there, which will trap him as well."

Where SEOH's first born had been his greatest treasure, his middle son was his greatest disappointment. "Thylan claims he wants to impress me. We'll see if he does."

"I understand. I was only thinking that there will be more risk if these intruders are in fact aligning with Callan."

SEOH grinned. "Then it's a good thing you captured Callan's nemesis within the MystiK Uberon Warrior House and sent that entire unit to the Sphere. Fight fire with fire by putting one powerful MystiK Warrior group up against another who has something they want. Trying to survive that should keep Callan busy."

CHAPTER 14

CALLAN CONSIDERED DROPPING HIS PACE to give Rayen a chance to catch her breath, but when he looked back, she was striding alongside Kaz with no problem. Nodding and answering Kaz as well. No one could stay around Kaz long and not talk. Even though he was from a Warrior House, Kaz talked as much as the newsmongers on the vid screens back home.

Or old women spinning rumors.

What could he be saying that was so interesting to Rayen? It had been a mistake to bring her.

Rayen should have stayed at the village. She was constantly putting herself in danger for others.

But she wouldn't have remained behind if Callan had refused her offer. The girl was as willful as they came.

That was really the only reason Callan agreed to bring her along. *It had nothing to do with you missing her and wanting to keep her close?* his conscience asked.

When had his conscience turned into a meddling voice?

If Rayen had been left on her own, a TeK scouting party might have caught her. V'ru had warned Callan that SEOH would consider her a prize to use like a lab experiment or to put through a public killing to show how the TeKs were the protectors of all ten cities.

What was it going to take to convince her that being here was a death wish?

Callan! Jaxxson's voice called telepathically, breaking into his thoughts. Jaxxson was the only person besides Zilya who could project his voice outside the power structure of the village. As far as Callan knew. Maybe Kaz could.

Where are you? Callan answered. Unlike when he entered Rayen's mind, this was a surface touch on the mind for communication only.

You must be close if you can hear me. I've been calling out for a while.

I'm not sure how to tell you where to find me, but I'll keep talking so you can track my thoughts.

Have you found the kidnapped children?

One, Jaxxson acknowledged. He sounded beaten down. *And she is injured. That is the only reason the scouts let her go.*

Callan turned off the trail, hoping Kaz and Rayen kept watch because he had to hold his telepathic focus to locate Jaxxson. Since they had to continue communicating, Callan asked, *How was there no alert from the internal guard points in the village?*

The breach was in Etoi's quadrant. Etoi claimed she had to help Zilya by feeding the children and that doing such a task was beneath one of Zilya's level.

Callan's jaw dropped. Both girls had failed to tell him that, and he could see why. Walking away from a guard station for anything short of a crisis was unacceptable and punishable in painful ways for a warrior. He'd have to think on how to discipline Etoi.

Did Zilya condone this action? Callan asked.

I don't know. In fact, Zilya may have instigated it, but those two are cut from the same cloth so the truth is a juggling act carried on between them.

All at once, Callan knew exactly where Jaxxson waited. Callan made a sharp left and in two long steps he spotted Jaxxson not far away holding a girl of four years who cried into the healer's shoulder. Her red hair flared all around her head and the ragged gilded dress she wore had originally been handmade for a child of a ruling family.

She was terrified, in threadbare clothes and had almost been taken hostage by a TecKnati.

Callan was failing as a leader.

Mathias would be disappointed in him. The children had been kept fed and clean while Mathias lived, but chaos had erupted moments after Callan returned from witnessing Mathias' death and then Rayen's departure. Overnight, the mist had grown, confusing the highly susceptible MystiK children into hallucinating. One fifteen-year-old girl who had been exceptional at finding herbs for Jaxxson had strayed from her group when she thought she'd seen her mother. She followed a turgo lizard over the side of a rocky drop-off and fell to her death.

Callan's throat thickened at the memory of every child he'd had to bury since coming here. He was the worst leader ever. He would never measure anywhere close to the leader Jornn, his twin brother, would have been, and *should* have been.

The sound of Kaz and Rayen catching up to him pulled Callan from his morose thoughts as he jogged up to Jaxxson.

The healer wore his usual cloth wrap that tied at his waist and fell to mid-calf. His bare chest was cut and bleeding from a punishing run through the woods. He wouldn't use any of his power to heal himself in case the children needed it.

Callan had warned Jaxxson more than once to take care not to overextend himself in healing or Jaxxson would be susceptible to something in this Sphere. If that happened, it would be a brutal blow all the way around from Jaxxson's suffering to losing an elite healer they were fortunate to have.

Jaxxson raised his head at their approach. "It's good to see you. I was torn between taking her back and staying in case they released another child." He angled his head looking over at Rayen with a look of disgust that bumped Callan off center.

What would cause that reaction in Jaxxson when there had been no conflict between him and Rayen the last time they'd met?

Jaxxson stood with the child in his arms. He asked Rayen, "Did Gabby come back with you?"

"Yes, and–"

"Do you care for *no one* but yourself?"

"Of course, I do." Rayen bristled at Jaxxson's veiled accusation that she'd intentionally put her friends in danger.

Callan was angry that Rayen put herself in jeopardy again, but she would not have returned with Tony and Gabby unless they'd both wanted to come.

Before Callan could interject to find out what was going on, Jaxxson went back on the attack. "How could you bring Gabby back here? Is it not enough that you have caused us more misery than we had before?"

"What are you talking about?" Rayen shouted at him. "Gabby is having a bad reaction and we can't fix it in her world. She begged me to bring her back because she thinks you can help her. But it doesn't sound like *you* care about anything but throwing blame where it doesn't belong."

"Gabby is not well?" Jaxxson's hostility deflated with that news.

"She claims she feels fine physically, but she shakes a lot, and her hair is flying up in the air and things change shape in her hand."

"That is all? She can fix that," Jaxxson groused and was right back to being angry with Rayen. "A weak excuse to come back and create more problems."

"Why is everyone blaming *me* for your problems?" Rayen exclaimed.

Callan wanted to know why as well. "What's causing your anger,

Jaxxson?"

Jaxxson shifted the child in his arms. "While I've been healing this one, I was able to learn something about the TeKs–something she gleaned while they were holding her. The TeKs have watched us since the three intruders first came here. As soon as the green stripes streaked across the sky, the TeK scouts attacked because they knew there was no MystiK delivery expected. They took our children as hostages. If this one had not thrown up on them and claimed her bile was poisonous, they would not have left her."

At least one lesson with the children had gotten through. Callan had told them if they were ever grabbed and thought they could be sick on their attacker to use their powers to make the contents of their stomach "sting" then claim it was deadly.

He could feel the air turn practically icy with the chill coming off Rayen. She wouldn't even look at him, as if Jaxxson's attitude was Callan's fault? Determined to get to the bottom of Jaxxson's caustic tone, Callan asked, "But that doesn't explain why you blame Rayen."

Jaxxson swung a gaze heavy with disappointment at Callan that slashed at his confidence even more.

"The TecKnati want the intruders," Jaxxson explained. "When the scouts put this one down, they waited until I was in sight and said they would exchange our children for the intruders. They were absolutely certain the transender arrival brought the intruders back. Did that Tony not say it took Rayen's touch to open the portal between our worlds? Had *she* not returned, the TeK would have no reason to take our children." His troubled gaze went to Callan. "It is your job to protect our village from *all* threats."

Rayen's skin lost a shade of color. She stuttered, "I-I'm sorry. I didn't know..."

Jaxxson tucked the child close and cut off Rayen with the speed of a sharp knife. "I must return. This child is in shock and the others need me at the village."

Rayen asked, "Please look at Gabby once the children are taken care of."

Jaxxson's normally pale features arranged into a dark look for her only, then he left without another word.

Callan had heard enough. Jaxxson and the others blamed Callan for Rayen's return. He was as much at fault for the TeK attack because he was sure Rayen had come back for him.

She'd promised. Right after he'd kissed her.

His heart would be holding a celebration at her return if not for how her presence impacted everyone else and her own safety. He was responsible for his entire village. Any encouragement from him toward her at this point would be a betrayal to his people.

Yes, Rayen had returned to protect the children, just as she'd promised, but that kiss had sealed her commitment to Callan as much as anyone else.

She would stay if he asked. He was sure of it.

That meant it was up to him to make her leave and not return.

Rayen started to say something, but he needed time to process all this and decide how to choose the right words for sending her back. "No more talking. We hunt."

Rayen's face fell. Her shoulders drooped with hurt.

Why did he always say and do the wrong thing? Callan wanted to pull the words back where they wouldn't harm her or to find a way to explain what he was thinking.

Then again, that would make *him* feel better, but he'd only dig a deeper hole if he said anything right now that gave her the impression that he wanted her with him.

Because he did. He wanted her in his arms.

But he had a duty to his people first.

He would work twice as hard to be a better leader. And a strong leader would put his people before his own needs and feelings. He looked into Rayen's eyes, wishing he had the luxury of choosing what he wanted over what he had to do, because he would choose her.

CHAPTER 15

RAYEN THOUGHT SHE WAS GOING to be sick.

Did Callan *also* blame her?

He wouldn't even look at her now. Just ordered her to start tracking the TeK scouts, then walked off in a new direction.

Kaz gave her a consoling glance, which she ignored as they both followed.

She was too busy trying to breathe past the pain in her chest. What had caused everything to be so different since the last time she'd seen Callan? They hadn't spent a lot of time together before, but it had been intense. They'd killed two croggles, fought the TeKs, and healed as a team.

Callan had used his gifts to repair the huge gash across her chest and stomach that a croggle had laid open.

She'd felt him close to her then and later when they'd joined hands and powers to save a child at the village. Then he'd kissed her with so much hunger she wouldn't have left if Tony and Gabby hadn't needed her to activate the transender.

She and Callan had shared something special.

Hadn't they?

At this point, she didn't know. Maybe she remembered their time together as more than it had been. Maybe she was the only one who thought the universe had trembled during that kiss. She believed he'd given her a message during that embrace, one that promised he felt the same deep yearning for her that she'd felt for him.

Replaying the scene in her mind again, she honestly still believed he *had* felt something strong at that moment.

So, what had happened once she left, and what was the reason for his distance now?

Jaxxson blamed her for the TeK attack. Callan hadn't argued, so did that mean he blamed her, too?

Could she fault any of them for that after what Jaxxson had shared?

She *was* the reason those children had been captured. Guilt swelled until she thought it would strangle her. Jaxxson had been right to insinuate that her reasons for coming back were suspect.

Even though she came back to fulfill her vow to help protect the children, all she'd thought about since leaving this place was Callan.

She was starting to see why everyone pointed at her for their world turning upside down. It had been *her* touch that pulled the three of them into the computer time-travel portal. Just like it had taken her touch on the transender control to call it back.

She didn't belong in the past or the future. She was the only one who shouldn't be here. Maybe her presence truly was a catalyst for all the bad things happening.

"Stop thinking so loud," Kaz whispered over his shoulder. "Or he'll hear you."

She hurried up to Kaz just as he slowed before reaching a cluster of trees where Callan knelt. "Can he hear my thoughts?" she asked just as softly.

"Not if you don't want him to." Kaz's eyes danced with mirth.

She frowned at him. "Then why did you say that?"

"Because I can feel your distress and it bothers me."

"Are you telling me the truth?"

"Yes. I'm empathic. The perfect male who is both attractive and sensitive, don't you agree?"

"You forgot humble."

"No, I didn't." He grinned. "I would never claim so simple a trait."

She stopped short of reaching Callan, unwilling to see the rejection in his eyes.

Kaz kept going until he could see what Callan observed.

When Callan stood up, Kaz said something under his breath that caused Callan's posture to turn rigid then he pushed a look her way just long enough for her to feel guilty again.

She hated this place. What had made her think she'd want to return and stay here?

Because she couldn't live free in the past with Tony and Gabby when she had no identity there? She didn't like that Byzantine Institute very much either. Scrubbing a hand over her face, she tried to clear away the confusion.

Didn't work.

She still had no idea what to do.

What had she done in her life to end up with no memory, no family, and no hope for a life anywhere? Had she been sent to the past as punishment?

When Kaz lifted his chin in a "come here" motion, she walked over to them. She assumed if Callan didn't want her to hear their conversation, he could order her to back off. It wasn't as though he had any problem pushing her away.

Gathering her confidence back, she asked, "What'd you find?"

"Boot tracks."

Two whole words from Callan. Next thing she knew they'd be sharing complete sentences. "Can you tell the direction the TecKnati went from here?"

"No."

Kaz made an exasperated sound in Callan's direction then explained to her, "They stomped all over the place then left by other means than hiking. We haven't seen transports, but that doesn't mean their machines are not here."

"Thank you, Kaz." She said that with as much sweetness as she could dig up, because she was grabbing at any straw to feel welcome. Pathetic, but true. Just to let Callan know that she didn't need him either, she kept her attention on Kaz only. "What's our next move?"

Kaz's eyes could smile with the slightest crease. "I'm thinking–"

Callan growled something then said, "*I* want us to search the area."

She ignored him and kept addressing Kaz. "In that case, which direction are we going?"

"Allow me to show you." Kaz reached for her arm and got his hand knocked away.

The fingers of Callan's right hand wrapped gently around her arm.

She was torn between yanking her arm back and curling into him. Energy sizzled across her skin at the contact. Was his body trying to send her a message to overlook Callan shoving her away? At moments like this, she wondered what part of him made his decisions–his head or his heart?

Her body was more than ready to agree with his, but she wasn't. Not as long as she was treated as nothing more than a major inconvenience.

Taking a breath, she warned Callan, "Remove your hand unless you are content to throw spears and eat your meals left-handed for the rest of your life."

"Rayen."

His deep voice dove inside her and wrapped itself around her heart with a squeeze, but he was the one who didn't want her here. She couldn't continue to leave the door open to her soul only to have him walk out every time he changed his mind.

"Callan," she said with far less warmth than he'd spoken her name. She looked up at him and had to move her gaze past the emotionless mask on his face to hide her own emotions. Narrowing her eyes at him, she said, "Heed my warning. Do you want to hunt for those children or not?"

He dropped his hand. "The terrain has changed since the last time we were here. I don't want you to get lost."

"Really? Because it sure sounds like you wish I'd fall off the edge of this world."

Kaz snorted at that.

Callan's anger rumbled when he pointed to his right and ordered, "Kaz, head out a hundred yards that way."

She started to follow Kaz, but Callan said, "Wait, Rayen. You and I need to talk."

Her heart thundered in her chest, but she stayed. The minute Kaz was out of earshot, she unloaded on Callan. "What could we possibly have to talk about? The fact that I foolishly pushed my friends to come back here because I couldn't make the portal work without them or that I was stupid enough to think you'd appreciate my help?"

"You don't understand–"

"Yes, I do. I heard your message just fine. You didn't want me to come back and now you blame me for what the TeK scouts did."

"I do not," he said, shaking his head. "That was unfair of Jaxxson."

In a fit of honesty, she admitted, "No, it wasn't. I didn't intentionally cause all this, but my presence clearly is an issue. As soon as we get those children back to the village, I will leave."

Callan started to protest again, but she stopped him with, "Just tell me one thing. Do you or do you not want me here? The truth."

Silence built between them, filling the vacuum that anger had created until Callan finally looked away and admitted, "No, I don't want you here."

What had she been thinking?

That Callan would change his mind? That he'd sent Kaz ahead and asked her to stay back so he could tell her he'd missed her and didn't want her to leave?

He wasn't stupid.

She was. And that ended right now.

Swallowing the ball of hurt in her throat, she shrugged. "In that case, there's nothing else to talk about, is there?"

He shook his head and wouldn't look at her. "I guess not."

"I'll stick with Kaz. He doesn't seem to mind my company."

Callan swung a vicious gaze in the direction Kaz had gone and gripped his spear hard enough his knuckles turned white. He drew a long, labored breath and called out, "*Kaz!*"

Kaz turned and waited.

"You two will hunt as a team." Callan's next words were for her, but he kept his gaze averted. "Go and don't wander."

"Where will you be?"

"Close enough for Kaz to find me."

For Kaz to find him, but not her, because she was nothing more than a tagalong at this point. She turned and walked quickly to Kaz. When she reached him, he took in her face and sighed. "Is there something between you two or not?"

At one time there might have been, but not now. "No."

"You're sure."

"Yes."

"Good. Let's take this path."

She stomped her way behind him and once she could no longer see Callan behind her, she asked, "Why did you say, 'good'?"

He turned around and searched over her shoulder before meeting her confusion with a wolf's smile. "Because I would rather not have to bloody myself with Callan, but I will do it to win a prize such as you."

Kaz dipped his head and kissed her so quickly she didn't have time to react. His lips were firm and sure, teasing and nipping just enough to take her breath, then he lifted his head.

He didn't kiss half bad. The universe hadn't shifted, but all men couldn't kiss like Callan.

Stop, she ordered her mind. She had to cease comparing everyone to Callan.

She would. Right away, but first she had to find out what was going on. "Why did you kiss me?"

Kaz cocked his head as he studied her. "Has Callan taken you inside his kamara?"

"What is that?"

"A large, white dome shape that we create as personal quarters."

Oh, yes. The white bubble they used for healing, too. She snickered at the ridiculous suggestion. "Callan can barely tolerate having me around right now."

"I'm not entirely sure about that."

"Trust me, it's so. The minute I first saw him today, he told me I shouldn't have come back. I just asked him point blank if he wanted me here and he said no. I don't think it needs to be any clearer than that. You still didn't answer my question, Kaz. Why did you kiss me?"

Happiness glimmered in his face. "Because I've wanted to do that since the moment I first saw you, but I would never touch any girl who belonged to another."

That was sweet and his interest soothed her wounded ego. He wasn't Callan, but she'd just promised herself that she wouldn't keep sizing everyone up against stone face. "Are you saying you don't have a problem being my friend?"

Kaz lowered his head again and she thought he might kiss her again. She didn't know if she wanted him to or not, because no matter how much she told herself she was nothing to Callan, she still felt wrong kissing another boy.

That feeling should be added to the definition of stupid.

But Kaz didn't kiss her. He only said, "I am your friend, and I would be so much more if you would allow me."

He waited for her to say something.

She was out of her depths here. She had no memory to fall back on that would instruct her how to act around either boy, so she had to go with her instincts and right now they were telling her to take cautious steps. "You're sure you want to be friends, because the other MystiKs are blaming me for the TeK attack."

Kaz took a step back, putting some distance between them.

Distance she needed.

He'd clearly been expecting her to say something else and address his offer for "so much more," but he didn't press that issue.

Instead, he said, "Angry people speak when they should hold their tongues until they are calm enough to think intelligently. I heard the story of your first visit and that you promised to come back to help protect the village. That doesn't sound like a person bent on causing destruction and the only person responsible for all of this is SEOH, thus you are acquitted of all charges in my eyes."

That was perfectly reasonable. Why couldn't Callan have said something that nice?

"Everyone speaks of your unusual power," Kaz continued, changing the subject, for which she was thankful. "You'll have to show it to me some time."

She hoped she could and, with equal enthusiasm, also hoped that she wouldn't have to. "I can only draw on it when the power is needed. Or when my power thinks it's needed. It's really unpredictable."

"Interesting. We'll move in a zigzag pattern for a while then touch base with Callan."

"Lead on."

This area gradually became dense with a growth of plants she'd originally seen in the jungle area near their transender landing spot. On her initial visit, they'd traveled through a jungle on one side of the original MystiK village, then a forest on the other side. The land Kaz and she traversed now was a blend of forest and jungle, but the colors still jarred her as did many of the shapes as if even the vegetation hated being in this place.

"Something cut through this area," Kaz told her without turning around. He squatted down.

She did, too, and could see a snaking path with freshly broken branches bleeding in colors of black and purples. Torn leaves had started growing back. It reminded her of when Tony was attacked by that deadly flower. The thing had been after blood.

Had a pink flower captured someone?

Concurring with her silent thought, Kaz suggested, "This looks like a frazzle vine flower has raced back to the host plant."

"You know about those, huh?"

Kaz's voice was somber when he said, "Warriors must learn the terrain quickly or die even faster."

That struck her as something she'd once been told but chasing the memory was a fruitless action, so she looked around the area. There were quite a few of the huge pink flowers with green dots that opened wide enough to stick her head inside. Not that she would since the flower was attached by long vines to a meat-eating host plant. "From what I remember of those flowers, the path seems too narrow for dragging a body, even a small child."

"True. It could have captured a dugurat or another animal, but the animals have been scarce in this area since the fires. Let's follow the trail before it disappears and see what prey it captured ... just in case."

Using his spear, Kaz whacked vines and plants that had entwined themselves together.

The trail had grown completely over in another ten minutes, just like the jungle had on her last trip to this artificial star.

"Now what?" she muttered to herself.

"I'll call to Callan and–"

A child's high-pitched cry yanked Rayen to look in the same direction as Kaz. Her heart thumped fast. She felt the pull to battle, to protect. "Can you find that child?"

"Yes, but I can't call Callan until I find the child." Kaz was already pushing through branches, breaking a path for them.

They heard the pitiful sound again and Kaz adjusted, angling slightly to the right.

Rayen looked up through an opening in the branches ahead to see a tree with a massive trunk that grew six feet in diameter and grew tall, breaking through the lower canopy of trees. At different places along the trunk, the bark reshaped to look like tiny human faces staring out with empty eyes.

"Kaz. There's the host plant."

He paused only for a second, nodded and took off. When he reached the area around the base of the tree, the ground was clear in every direction for about twenty feet.

The only one of those trees she'd seen before had a smaller two-foot-thick trunk and a huge host flower with petals the width of her shoulders.

Three of them had almost died fighting *that* plant.

She could use *one* of the petals on this flower as a blanket to wrap her entire body. The thing breathed in and out, an opening in the center fanning like a mouth with long black spikes as teeth.

This plant could be the mother of the first one she'd fought.

A post made from a smaller tree as big around as her arm had been sank into the ground two strides in front of the host plant.

Tied to that post was a boy who might be seven or eight years old. His feet and hands had been tethered with ropes woven of brown vines. A palm leaf wrapped around his head and partially covered his mouth.

The plant wouldn't have done that.

But a thick, dark-blue vine that had probably been the one that raced back to the host plant had wrapped around and around the boy's body. It was pulling tight, hard enough to make the post lean.

She started forward.

Kaz stuck his arm out, blocking her.

"What?" She sounded ready to take his head off and would if he didn't hurry up so they could save this child.

"You do know that's not one of our children, right? That plant will attack anyone. Trying to free a prey this close to the host is suicidal."

She stared at the child, finally seeing his short haircut and a piece of the metallic gray-green uniform.

He was a TecKnati and the MystiKs held all TecKnati responsible for the deaths of their children.

Her heart thudded harder with every tug that vine made on the child. She was going to lose what might be her only MystiK friend, because she couldn't let that child die.

CHAPTER 16

RAYEN LOOKED AT KAZ. "THAT'S a child. I don't care whose side he's on so get out of my way." Her voice sounded calm when she was anything but right then. Her insides thundered at the thought of that deadly plant eating a child.

Of course, the idea of attacking a plant twice the size of the one she'd barely escaped could be playing into the adrenaline coursing through her, too.

Kaz raked fingers through his wild reddish-brown waves. "I don't like it either, but Callan would take me apart for allowing you be injured or risking my life to save a TeK when our children need protection more than ever. I'm willing to die to protect a child, but they have killed many of ours without regret. I would be putting the lives of ours at risk if I died saving this one."

If that hadn't come out swimming in guilt, she might still be angry with him, but she understood the conflict warring inside him right now. She wanted to rail at him over his hesitation, but she couldn't. She battled her own issues about the MystiK and TecKnati conflict.

One minute, all TecKnati deserved to die.

The next minute, she ran in to rescue one of their people.

Why had children and teens been put in a life-or-death situation? All because SEOH was afraid of the power the next generation of MystiKs presented to technology in his world? From what she'd heard, these two groups needed things from each other. Why couldn't the MystiKs and TecKnati find common ground for a peaceful existence?

She didn't know and all she cared about was saving this child, because while she might understand Kaz's position it didn't mean she agreed.

Kaz was deep in thought, staring at the child.

She interrupted, telling him, "I don't want to stand here and watch him die."

"I don't want to do so either."

Did that mean he'd help her? "What are we going to do about it, because that post is not going to hold?"

"You wait here and–"

Was he serious? "No. I've killed one of those vines before. Have you?"

He studied her with new respect. "No, but this is not your war either, Rayen." He hesitated, then said, "If I don't survive, please don't tell the others what I did and stay to help the village regardless of what Callan thinks."

That sounded too much like the words Mathias had spoken just before he died. She was tired of people she barely knew dying and handing her another secret to carry that would eat her up inside like Mathias' death had.

She took another tactic. "I don't know how to get out of here on my own."

Her comment did as she'd hoped and distracted Kaz. When he turned away from her to search their location, she raced forward.

The vine dragging at the boy must have felt a threat coming close because it unraveled quickly, coiled like a snake with the flower at the end lifting to attack.

Heat roared through her center.

Finally, the energy flooded her body.

Kaz yelled, "*Move before it strikes!*"

She dove at the little boy and grabbed a handhold on his tethered body, wrenching him and the post up out of the ground. Using the momentum she already had going, she flung the boy back at Kaz and hoped she didn't kill one or both of them.

With a glance back, she was relieved to see Kaz snag the child from mid-air and slice the tethers holding him, freeing the boy.

Yes! But the energy pulsing through her dissipated with her relief.

Shoving hard on her heels, she pivoted to spin away so they could escape, but she got knocked sideways by the flower and vine. The hit rattled her brain. That plant had a stronger punch than she would have expected from something so delicate in appearance.

Landing on her side, she rolled twice and bounced against the base of the host tree. Of course, the thing had driven her towards the mouth.

She jumped up and lunged away. She made it ten feet when a vine wrapped around her leg multiple times, yanking her off her feet. It started dragging her to the host plant whose massive base flower opened to expose sharp, clicking, stick-like teeth.

Kaz used the spear he clenched to slice another vine that had sprung up. As she came close, he dropped the spear to catch her arms and dig his heels in, pulling as he backed up. He was inching her away, which meant he was far stronger than she'd originally thought.

He started to say, "I called–" Another vine flashed into view and wrapped around his neck. Kaz tried to hold her with one hand and fight the vine strangling him with his other.

That wouldn't work. They both slipped toward the plant with him still holding onto her.

She let go of his hand and dug her fingers into the ground, trying to anchor herself.

Had Kaz been saying he'd called to Callan? Or that he tried and didn't hear?

Could she reach Callan telepathically after he'd spoken in her mind today? *Callan, can you hear me?*

Nothing.

Sharp points stabbed her captured leg. Her calf and thigh muscles burned. She chanced a look and saw black needles coming out of the vine that wrapped her leg from thigh to calf. Blood trickled from each stab. The vine and host plant that had attacked Tony hadn't done *that*, but it hadn't been as gigantic and mature as this one.

On the plus side, these vines were no stronger, but that was a small benefit when her power had abandoned her.

The burning sensation changed to the feel of a thousand stinging bees shoved into each cut. She couldn't stop the cry of pain that ripped from her lips. This thing could be poisoning her for all she knew.

Trying to break free wasn't working.

Kaz was on the ground, wrestling his vine and making horrid gasping sounds. He was using some kinetic force to keep from being dragged to the plant, but his heels were digging a slow trough. He wouldn't last long.

He freed one hand and lifted it. His spear flew up from the ground to him, but just before he could catch the weapon the vine attacking him whipped several loops around his forearm and pinned it to his side.

She gave up clawing the ground and lifted her body in a fast move, twisting around to bend as far as she could to reach past her ankle. Tears burned down her cheeks from the searing pain. She grasped where the vine extended back to the host.

It started dragging her again.

She called on her power, begged it to come forth.

Not a hint of heat.

Kill, she demanded in her thoughts. Nothing.

She was losing strength.

Kaz managed to rip a section loose from his neck. The host made a snarling sound.

Another vine flew out of the forest and circled Kaz's waist, yanking him off his feet.

Was this thing sentient? Did it call in reinforcements?

They were going to die. Neither of them would be here to protect the children and, once again, it was all her fault, but she couldn't regret saving a life even if it belonged to a TeK.

A roar of fury shook the woods and Callan burst in from a different direction than they had come.

No, Callan couldn't save her. The MystiKs had to have him. She let go of the vine and lurched for a handhold. She only needed long enough to make him go back.

He ran toward her.

She yelled, "*Nooo!* Save Kaz. I can't be saved."

The savage look on Callan's face should have frightened this plant to death, but it must not have because the minute he reached her a vine flew at him.

He swung around and slashed his arm at the plant. The vine went flying sideways.

What kind of kinetics did Callan have to do that?

He raised both hands and shoved forward hard.

The invisible blow knocked the host flower back with a snap and it lost several petals.

The tension against her leg relaxed. She was no longer being dragged. The vine on Kaz went limp for a second.

Kaz yanked his pinned arm free and went back to fighting the vine around his neck.

Callan reached down to hook his hands under her arms to lift her. He looked into her eyes, telling her with one look that they would get out of this.

She wanted to live more than anything in that moment. She nodded, unable to talk because her throat muscles were numb. Everything in her body was going numb from whatever the plant had stung her with.

What a simple way to kill.

Render the prey incapable of fighting.

As Callan lifted her, she looked past his shoulder and saw a huge pink flower descending.

Look behind you, she screamed in her mind because her tongue wouldn't work.

His eyes flickered with surprise then he swung an arm out, twisting around to strike at the vine. He cut through it with a crushing blow.

Her leg yanked backward so hard right then, Callan lost his one-handed grip on her.

Kaz was making headway at freeing himself. It seemed the host plant would abandon Kaz to be sure it captured her for dinner.

Callan lunged and grabbed both of her wrists. "Call up your power."

She tried to speak, but she couldn't so she just shook her head and used her eyes to beg him to understand. In her mind, she said, *Let me go and save Kaz. Your people need you both.*

Callan's voice shook. "You will not die."

His muscles were bunched and tight. His body vibrated with the effort to hold her from the host.

In another two feet, she would be in the grasp of its mouth.

Callan couldn't let go long enough to throw another invisible hit at the plant. For the first time, she saw true terror in his eyes and realized it was for her.

He worked his hands up her forearms, gripping with the strength of steel. His eyes were tormented. When he spoke, he said the last thing she expected. "If it eats you, then it eats me, too."

No, no, no screamed over and over in her mind. Callan's beautiful face would never be in the bark of this tree.

Let me go! she yelled in her thoughts. Tears spilled down her face.

He shook his head and entered her mind. *I will not lose you.*

The vine dragging her gained another foot. She was inches from going inside the clacking teeth. Kaz still struggled with the last thick vine wound around his neck.

Kaz looked at her and she saw their deaths in his gaze.

His eyes were wild. His hands jerked at the vines tearing them from his body, but he'd never get free in time.

I will not lose you either! she yelled at Callan in her mind, not sure if he heard her. She would kill anything that tried to harm him. Energy started in her center, coiling, and growing, then wicking up her arms.

The plant drew her closer. Her body was being pulled apart. Pain dug past the numbness. She latched onto it to stay lucid.

The host's teeth snapped and cut through her shoe to slice her foot.

You can do this, Callan whispered mind to mind. *We can do this.*

She nodded. Thinking the word "kill" hadn't worked before. This was carnivorous so she thought, *Bleed and die.*

Her energy surged, but the plant wasn't dying.

She silently told Callan, *It isn't working.*

He glanced up at the monster plant and back at her. Then his words flooded her mind. *Will your power to surge through your blood and kill it.*

I don't know how. Tell me how and I'll do it.

There was a microsecond of hesitation then his voice rushed into her head. *Come all the way into my mind and do as I say.*

She didn't think twice. She shoved at his mind, shocking herself when she got in. Her body was seconds from being destroyed, but right now she felt safe inside Callan. She never wanted to leave, but this was no time to get comfortable.

What now, Callan?

Pull your power inside.

She closed her eyes and drew hard on her power. She couldn't call it up at will, but once her power showed up, she was starting to learn how to control the surge inside her. She just didn't know how to do what Callan wanted. Energy flooded the area where Callan had her cocooned in his mind. She started to tell him to use it if he could, but she felt him take control and wield it immediately.

He sent a fiery path back through her to her leg, driving it into the plant.

She screamed with the pain.

The plant screamed louder and snapped its jaws faster.

They were still going to die.

The next seconds were a blur. Petals exploded away from the host and the vine on her leg started crumbling.

Kaz was there, yanking everything off her leg, pulling the spikes out with it. When he had her free, he yelled at Callan, "The host isn't dead. Vines are starting to regenerate."

Callan was up and scooping her over his shoulder, then he turned and ran hard.

She blacked out only to hear him shouting at her. She opened her eyes to find he'd pulled her into his arms. She looked up at him. The muscles in his neck were rigid with the strain of crushing her to his chest and running all out.

She caught a glimpse of Kaz's reddish-brown hair blown back by the force of him running.

Callan and Kaz had lived. The village would be safe.

Her eyes drooped.

Callan came into her mind. *Don't sleep. Fight whatever it injected into you. Please don't sleep.*

But she wanted to sleep. She was so tired. A sudden peace was drawing her to a place that felt pleasant and welcoming. She had no family, no place to call home. No one cared what happened to her so why should she stay here and face the pain?

To face being alone.

Just let me go, she pleaded.

No! Callan shouted in her mind, and she flinched. Then she felt him gently kiss her mind. *You're not alone. I care. Live for me.*

Her heart thumped slowly, but she felt him inside her, pushing her to wake up.

When she did open her eyes, he had slowed to a walk and was drawing heavy breaths. She blinked to clear her blurry vision. Trees and the purple sky came into view.

Dead skeletons of trees. They'd gone quite a distance.

The red moon peeked through gnarled and twisted branches.

"We're far enough away here," Kaz said from nearby. "I'll keep watch while she heals."

Callan sat down with her in his lap. He held her tight, still chugging hard breaths. "You have to heal yourself. Remember what you did last time?"

Her mind raced for an answer. Yes. No. Sort of. Remembering took effort that she didn't have the energy for.

He eased his grip on her, holding her so that she could look up into his face. She searched for Kaz. He stood twenty feet away with his back to them, searching in the direction where the forest turned lush again.

He was likely watching for new vines from the host plant.

"Rayen?"

She swung her gaze back to Callan. Hearing her name spoken softly on his lips sent a thrill through her. She would face another deadly plant to finally be back in his arms. She tried to speak, but her throat and tongue still wouldn't function.

She tried reaching his mind again. *What?*

You can't speak yet?

Everything is still numb.

Callan looked over at her legs.

She lifted one up and made a gasping sound at the sight of her attacked leg turning black.

His voice came into her mind in a soothing sound. *Use your power to search for the damage. See if it's poison.*

With a quick nod, she closed her eyes, remembering how she'd been able to do this last time. But that had been with Callan's help. She tried for a moment then shook her head and told him, *I can't see it.*

He put his hand on her chest where her heart was thumping at a slow beat. He told her, *Cover my hand.*

Looking up at him, she placed her hand over his. When she did, it was like having someone open up her body. She could see through his eyes again, but this time she was inside his mind looking through his thoughts.

That was different than last time. Much more clear and vivid.

His mouth tightened into a grim line. Then he told her, *Follow me through your body with your power.*

My power has a mind of its own, she reminded him.

You can do this.

But I don't feel my power.

He watched her for a moment, hesitation shifting through his eyes until he made some decision. *I feel your power.*

You do? How is that possible?

That's not important right now. Just follow me through your body and do as I say.

Okay. She stayed close to his presence as he moved through her. This was very different than the last time they did this. His presence filled her body as they searched their way through, but not going straight to her damaged leg. He found a streak of black in an organ and told her to grasp the tendril and destroy it.

She reached for the inky stream and crushed it with all her strength until it shattered and dissipated into nothing.

They kept that up, clearing out pocket after pocket of whatever the plant had injected into her until they reached her leg. Much like they had done this morning with the mist in her mind.

There was still a lot of black in her system.

Callan whispered near her ear, "Don't stop now. You're more powerful than you realize."

Now that Callan had shown her how to locate her power even if she couldn't call it up at will, she grabbed a fist of it and shoved hard into her leg.

Bad move.

She arched at the pain that exploded from thigh to calf, but she didn't stop because she was blasting the black away.

Callan's arms held her tight. He whispered soothing words, but she couldn't understand them. She could only focus on finishing what she started. She hissed at the burning sensation, ready to do anything to make it stop. When the last of the poison was gone, she fell limp against him, panting.

His lips were on her forehead and cheek, kissing her.

She reached for him. His lips found hers, kissing her with a desperation she could appreciate. His tongue swept into her mouth, taking possession in the most primal way.

Here was the kiss that she had dreamed about and longed for. His lips moved in sync with hers in an instinctual dance. She felt him in a way she hadn't before. It was as though their bodies had locked together as one. His fingers grazed her face then brushed gently along her cheek and down her neck.

This felt real and dragged her heart back into the fray again.

When they took a breath, they stared into each other's eyes with questions on both sides. Why had he pushed her away earlier if he did care for her? She felt the honesty in his touch.

She brushed her fingers along his face. A muscle in his cheek jumped.

He covered her hand and angled it to kiss her palm, but when he turned back to her his eyes were haunted and distant. "I need to tell you–"

Kaz shouted, "Someone's coming!"

Callan immediately lifted her up to her feet as he stood.

The bottom of her foot was still cut, but she was too spent to heal another part. There was no poison left in her and that was enough for now.

Kaz held two spears and tossed one that Callan caught.

Rayen listened for any sound but heard nothing. Keeping her voice low, she asked, "How does Kaz know someone is coming?"

"He's a powerful empath, but he wouldn't be able to feel the emotions unless someone failed to keep theirs shielded. Sometimes he can pick up enough pieces from many to realize a group approaches."

Kaz backed up, taking a position on one side of her and Callan on the other. She needed a weapon, but hers was back where they'd fought the plant. She had her doubts about calling up her power again.

Everything was deathly calm, then the woods came to life, moving in on them. It took a moment to realize those were children moving toward them, because the markings on their skin blended with any nearby vegetation.

They had skin pigments like Callan and Kaz.

MystiK children.

She smiled, glad to see allies coming forward, then noticed Kaz and Callan's faces. They weren't happy. In fact, they looked like they were preparing to fight an enemy.

Twenty children of both genders that appeared to range in age from eight to fifteen emerged from every direction, all carrying deadly looking spears, some with two blades.

They stopped in a circle thirty feet in diameter.

She, Callan, and Kaz were at the center.

Then a female stepped into view. She had to be at least six feet tall, with defined muscle and Rayen guessed her age at seventeen. If she was eighteen, she'd already be dead in this place. Her hair was a striking mix of dark red and black. The mottled shapes on her skin went from polished bronze to an iridescent purple that didn't seem real, but she'd blended in with dead wood and dried leaves only a moment ago.

Her eyes swirled grayish green in color. Swirled.

She wore an animal skin top, but it wasn't any kind of skin Rayen recognized. Iridescent and smooth as if the covering was taking its colors from her. Leggings covered her lower body, showing the strong muscles in her thighs. Her feet were not covered by hard shoes like Rayen's, but soft material that made it easy for her to travel silently.

And she was as terrifying to face as that plant they'd fought.

If the silence lasted any longer, it would reach a detonation point.

Callan and Kaz remained mute, spears at the ready.

When the female warrior spoke, her voice held enviable confidence. She took in all three of them. "You released our TecKnati bait. The punishment for treason during war is death."

CHAPTER 17

GABBY WIPED SWEAT OFF HER brow and surveyed the area that she'd helped clear of wrecked tables and chairs, primitive furniture the MystiKs had made by hand. The TecKnati had stormed through here with destruction in mind as much as kidnapping.

But soon she'd have a place to treat the children.

Jaxxson had taught her that unless a child was in critical condition, to first create a safe environment and half the battle was won.

Her muscles ached from suffering two more bouts of the shakes. They'd worn her out as much as dragging debris out of the way. The last episode had tumbled everything down that she'd straightened, but at least a child hadn't witnessed it.

Now that she'd felt calm for a fairly long stretch, she was ready to offer help to children withdrawn from shock.

The older ones around thirteen to sixteen were recovering more quickly, but the younger kids had both physical and mental damage.

Who wouldn't have emotional trauma just from being captured and tossed into a dangerous world where home was on another planet?

Gabby's pupple had bounced back quickly in the Sphere and followed at her heels. She looked down at the happy animal that poked its nose at a plant that had two tiny yellow flowers. "I should name you."

"They don't talk."

Gabby turned to the child who had said that with total sincerity. A little girl with curly golden ringlets falling to her waist stood there wearing a pitiful, faded-red robe that matched her sad expression.

Gabby offered her a smile. "I know the pupple can't talk, but I like to talk to animals."

"Why?"

"They're always nice to me. How old are you?"

"Five point seven."

That was a strange way to say her age. Did it mean five years and seven months or five years and seventy percent of a year? Something else different in the future. "What's your name?"

"Ahji. We lost our pupples when the firestorm came."

The tear sliding down Ahji's face threatened to break Gabby in half. "I heard about that, but this one belongs to everyone now. And I need a name for him, her, it."

"It is female."

"Really?" Gabby wanted to ask how Ahji knew, but she wasn't sure she wanted to get in a conversation on the physical difference between male and female pupples.

Ahji nodded solemnly, intent on instructing Gabby. "The girl pupples have an orange tongue and the boys have a green one."

Yay for color-coding baby animals. "I get it. Like girl babies come in pink blankets and boy babies come in blue blankets."

Ahji frowned, concentrating on that. Maybe pink and blue didn't designate gender in the future.

Ahji stared up at Gabby's head. "You changed your hair."

How to explain hair changing into ribbons? Gabby couldn't wait until Jaxxson showed up to explain it to her, so she just went with it. She touched one of her ponytails and said, "Yes I did. Like it?"

Ahji nodded, her eyes too serious for one so young.

What would it take to make this little girl smile? Gabby pulled one of the little yellow flowers off the plant and placed it in the palm of her hand.

Would her trick work twice?

The flower started changing and growing until it covered her hand and the yellow petals had purple speckles. That was strange, but harmless. She handed the flower to Ahji whose eyes lit up. The child murmured, "You are one of those."

"One of what?"

Etoi interrupted, striding up in her usual rude way and shouting, "You should be cleaning up, Ahji."

The little girl tensed.

Gabby stepped between the two and informed Etoi, "Ahji is helping me, and do you have any volume other than loud and obnoxious?"

"Watching you play games with making something grow is not helping her people."

"You know, that sounds like jealousy to me, *E-toi*, but I'm willing to shake hands and see if I can grow that seed pit you call a heart into the real thing."

Etoi would need a facial muscle makeover to smile. "Joke all you want, outsider. Your days here are numbered."

"And how is that bad news?"

Etoi stepped up close, set to spew something else snotty, but before she could do it Gabby got up in Etoi's face and warned, "Callan said you had to obey Tony. Do not bother Ahji or any of the other children waiting to come over here or I'll ask Tony to give you a task to keep you busy. I might even come up with a suggestion for Tony because I can be very creative when it comes to making someone regret being unkind to a child. Do I make myself clear?"

A storm brewed in Etoi's eyes that Gabby would probably have to ride out at some point, but the twit backed up and left.

Ahji looked up at Gabby like she was her fairy godmother and made her feel … invincible. That was worth any fallout from Evil Etoi.

Gabby started to reach for Ahji's hand to lead her over to a cleared area, but the shakes started again.

This time they went straight to violent.

"B-b-back up, Ahhh-ji," Gabby warned. She'd been radiating more power with every episode and that radiation had affected the ground, plants, trees, anything near her. The last thing she wanted to do was injure Ahji or frighten her any more than being attacked by TecKnati had done.

"You should not do that," Ahji said, taking tentative steps back.

Tell me about it. Gabby was shaking so hard her head nodded up and down. She let that stand as her answer.

The debris piled over on one side of the clearing started bouncing and moving in a circle until it was spinning in a tornadic motion.

Not good.

Gabby wrapped her arms around herself and tried to will her body to calm down. Chunks of damaged furniture, broken bowls and water gourds were spinning faster and moving with the power of a giant horizontal buzz saw as wide as a picnic table. It ran into a newly created structure built with those huge feathers and disintegrated it upon contact.

Ahji went running away, yelling, "*Jaxxson, Jaxxson!*"

Gabby would do the same if she could talk, but her jaws were vibrating from being shaken so hard. Plus, there'd been no sign of Jaxxson since Rayen, Callan and that new guy left.

The ground started cracking and Gabby's foot fell into a wide opening, forcing her down on one knee. She shoved her hands to the ground, pushing to raise her caught foot, but it was pinned tight, and she couldn't keep her hands still long enough to gain any leverage.

Etoi stepped into view and said nothing. Just watched with mild curiosity.

Fighting to keep her balance, Gabby turned her head at the whirring sound and found the tornadic yard sale spinning toward her. She glanced over at Etoi who smiled and turned her back, walking away.

Wood chips flying from the spiraling wind struck Gabby's skin. She yanked harder at her leg, but the ground was not giving it up. The tornado was going to batter her body and peel her skin off.

"*Make that stop!*" Jaxxson shouted.

Relief gushed through her at hearing his voice until Gabby looked up and realized he was shouting at *her*.

She shouted right back, "I. Can't." And wanted to add, *You idiot*, but feared she'd bite her tongue.

The edge of the rotating debris touched her arm, slashing across her exposed skin. She gritted her teeth to keep from screaming.

Jaxxson boomed a word Gabby had never heard that sounded something like "ole-itchy-kader-ish" and the world froze.

Her body had frozen, too, but at least she wasn't getting beaten to pieces by a demonic funnel cloud.

She felt a bump on her mind she recognized as Jaxxson wanting to speak to her telepathically, which meant he couldn't speak out loud either. When she opened up, he said, *That will only hold for a minute. Call your power back inside you.*

Really? You say that like you think I know how to do it.

Focus on your center, Gabby. See the origin of the power and contain it. You must never, ever let that kind of power run free.

Did he just chastise her?

After hours of suffering through the shakes and now facing death by garbage pile, she snapped back at his mind, *I didn't let anything happen, Mr. Know It All.*

Stop arguing and do as I say before the spell gives out.

Gabby closed her eyes and searched inside herself, for what she had no idea. The wind started to move slowly.

A bowl bumped her arm.

She was running out of time. Concentrating harder, she saw green lightning strikes inside her that shot in different directions and exploded into white bursts of light. Searching deeper, the center of the green energy spikes came into view.

That was crazy looking.

Wind started picking up speed slowly around her and sticks slapped her cheek.

Jaxxson called into her mind, *Hurry up.*

She shouted back, *Shut. Up.* Then she locked down her mental walls the way Jaxxson had taught her.

That's when she realized the green lightning bolts seemed to notice *her* and got excited again.

Her body trembled with oncoming shakes.

Oh, no. Not now.

Wind whipped across her back with the leading edge of sharp bits and pieces jabbing her. She arched away. The spell or whatever Jaxxson had done was wearing off, but she couldn't move her legs yet.

Reaching mentally, she grabbed at the neon-green sparks and wrapped her mind around them, drawing the frenetic energy into one cluster.

That worked?

That really worked.

She pushed the vibrating energy back down inside her until it all turned into a pulsing green glow that was now icy where the white sparks had been hot.

That's when she noticed the silence and opened her eyes slowly. No tornado.

Putting her hand down firmly against the ground, she pushed and freed her leg easily this time, then got to her feet. Dusting her hands, she was so happy to have control of her body she started laughing like an idiot who'd won the lottery.

Or someone on the verge of hysteria.

"That was not funny!" Jaxxson snapped.

She turned on him, ready to give him a piece of her mind. She'd forgotten just how nice the smooth muscular cut of his chest and abdomen was and shouldn't be sidetracked noticing that, but some things were out of a girl's control. He had the lean build of a runner or a gymnast, strong in a fluid way. Jaxxson also had dark shadows beneath his eyes she hadn't seen last time, and he'd lost some weight, but she wasn't feeling sympathy at the moment with him glaring at her.

She clamped her jaw shut and warned, "Oh, no you didn't."

"Didn't what?"

"Dare to yell at me after all I've been through." She started toward him with fists clenched. She'd never struck another person, but she was seriously reconsidering her aversion to violence right now.

Jaxxson's face went through an overhaul from furious to surprised to wary. "What is wrong with you, Gabby?"

"Me? Nothing other than dealing with idiots who have the bedside manner of a hedgehog."

"What is this hedgehog?"

"Don't change the subject," she ordered, marching up to him.

"How did I change the subject?" he muttered.

"Is that how you're healing these days, Jaxxson? By ordering your patients to figure out their own diagnosis and just get over it? Not even my cold-hearted father is that insensitive with his patients."

"Gabby, I didn't–"

"No, you *didn't* consider that I was in distress, and you *didn't* consider that yelling at me wasn't helping, and you *didn't*–"

"I miss–"

"Yes, you mistook me for a girl who puts up with that kind of crap."

"You're impossible to talk to."

She wished just this once that he wore a shirt so she could grab the collar and shake him. "I'm done talking to you."

"Finally, we agree." He dropped his mouth to hers and kissed her, smothering her words.

Did he really think a kiss would ... uhm, he was so wrong if he thought ... good grief, what a great kisser. She put her hands on the body she'd spent last night dreaming about. She'd never been so close to a guy, much less touched one, before Jaxxson. And she hadn't actually touched him last time, not like now. He still wore the sarong. Nice. She let her fingers glide over his oh-so-warm chest and wrapped her arms around his neck.

His arms went around her waist.

So, this was what it felt like to be kissed? She hadn't been hugged or touched since she was a little girl, always afraid of hearing another person's thoughts through any contact.

She'd missed out on so much and craved this connection.

Craved the feel of Jaxxson's body all around hers.

His fingers threaded through her hair then clutched a handful, holding her mouth close to his. She opened for his tongue and found a whole new playground she'd never known about. His arm hooked around her waist, tugging her up against him and all that hot body.

When Jaxxson broke the kiss, Gabby started to say something, but he kissed her quickly again. He stopped her from getting a word out three more times the same way until she gave up trying to speak.

His eyes held amusement she should wipe off his face, but she was too happy to see him and be in his arms to take him any further to task. He whispered, “I was trying to tell you I missed you.”

Well, crap, now he was going to make her cry.

He kissed her cheek. “You didn’t miss me?”

“I might have ... up until you started yelling at me.”

He let a sigh escape that was heavy with frustration. “I’m sorry. When I heard about your shaking and growing things in your hands, I dismissed it as you just adjusting.”

“Adjusting to what?” This time, Gabby softened her question, because it was becoming obvious that he’d been under a lot of strain recently.

“Your Hy’bridt powers.”

“*That’s* what’s happening?”

“Yes.” He was smiling, no doubt at the shock on Gabby’s face. “I have heard of such things with the Hy’bridt, but I have never witnessed this transformation. The blue was pretty on you, but I’m glad to see your hair is back.”

She reached up and, yes, she had real hair again. Not all ribbons. She couldn’t think of what to say for a moment, just digested that Jaxxson really believed she was gaining powers. “But I’m not a Hy’bridt, Jaxxson. That’s someone from your world in the future.”

“We do not just exist only in the future. Our genetics did not just show up one day.”

Hadn’t she told Tony the same thing? Duh.

Jaxxson explained, “You are an ancestor of Hy’bridts in my time. But in fairness to you, they did not emerge until after the K-Virus if my knowledge of history is correct. V’ru would know for sure.”

She lifted an eyebrow at him in reprimand. “That would explain why I had no clue what was going on.”

He had the good sense to look chagrined when he nodded. “I have had a lot to deal with lately and did not consider you would need healing.”

“I’m not sick, but I am dangerous if I don’t keep this under control.”

“True. Do you think you can manage the power now that you’ve contained it?”

Could she? Gabby wouldn’t risk saying yes since she had no idea how the power had gotten out of her the first time. “I don’t know. Is there a manual on being a Hy’bridt? Anyone I can talk to about it?”

What happened? Why had her question made him sad? “Jaxxson? What is it?”

“I believe Mathias may have had a Hy’bridt gene.”

“But he didn’t have mixed eyes like mine.” Gabby had been treated as a freak most of her life for having eyes in two different colors. That was reason enough to hide her ability to hear what other people were thinking.

“No, he didn’t, but when I first arrived Mathias and I healed together. That’s when I felt that same type of hot-and-cold power as yours, just not as pure. He had one eye that would sometimes look more red-brown than purple. A recessive gene perhaps.”

“You’re right. What I feel is like that and looks green when it’s cold then it turns white hot.”

“Exactly.”

Gabby stared into Jaxxson’s suddenly shuttered gaze. “Have you seen Mathias again after he left?”

“No.”

“You don’t think he’s coming back, do you?”

Jaxxson’s eyes strayed from hers. “No. He would have been back already.”

“But you don’t think he’s safe either,” she guessed.

He quietly admitted, “No.”

She wanted to ask more, but Jaxxson lifted his head the way he did when someone was calling to his mind. When his gaze returned to her it shielded a burden he didn’t share.

It didn’t take a mind reader to see that Jaxxson was carrying a heavy load with healing everyone and saving nothing in reserve for himself. She brushed her fingers across his cheek. “I’m here. You don’t have to do this alone.”

“You have no idea how much that means.”

Gabby smiled to offer encouragement Jaxxson clearly needed. “Let’s get this village in order.”

She hoped her power was truly buckled down but had her doubts. It felt stable for the moment in a way that reminded her of a tired wolf that stops to rest before resuming the hunt. If that ball of green energy exploded again and gained more strength the next time, she presented a greater danger than the TecKnati to everyone here.

But she couldn’t take this home to the past before she had it under control either.

CHAPTER 18

RAYEN CLENCHED HER JAW. HAVING this warrior girl threaten her was one thing, but she must not have heard that girl correctly when she threatened to kill Callan and Kaz, too. Plus, she admitted that she'd staked a child like a sacrificial lamb.

Rayen asked, "Aren't you a MystiK?"

Warrior girl angled her head, looking at her with the same interest someone would study a pupple upon first inspection. Curious about what type of animal had appeared but quick to dismiss it as of no importance.

Callan answered Rayen. "Kenja is MystiK by birth, not necessarily by definition."

He knew warrior girl, huh?

Kenja's eyes narrowed, which only added to her exotic beauty in a sinister way. Her surly tone issued a snub directed at Callan and Kaz when she clarified for Rayen's benefit, "We are not merely MystiK. We are Uberon warriors."

Call her paranoid, but Rayen had a feeling that was not encouraging news. She just didn't know why. Wouldn't all MystiKs work together in this place? She wasn't going to ask that in front of this girl, so she tried to push the question at Callan's mind.

It was like walking straight into a steel wall. Rayen mentally bounced back and stifled the urge to rub her head.

She shouldn't feel rejected that he'd blocked her out, but evidently, she had no control over her reactions around him because that wounded her, especially after what had felt so intimate earlier.

"When did you arrive in the Sphere, Kenja?" Callan asked, not addressing her threat to kill them.

"I have been here two moons."

"You can't tell me you've been here that long and didn't know there were other MystiKs here. Not with the Uberon ability to track a scent."

"I knew you were here."

Callan was less flustered than Rayen would have been over her admission. Why would she and her warriors not join up with other MystiKs in this place?

Callan remained calm, but his words were clipped. "Why haven't you made contact?"

"I was on my way to your village when I captured one of the stragglers of the TecKnati scouts who delivered us to this pit. Once the TecKnati came for their boy, I would have dealt with them first and gotten answers on how to return home, then I would have visited you next. Which brings me back to your treason."

Placing the blunt end of his spear on the ground, Callan crossed his arms. His spear stood by itself next to him. Was he doing that as a show of power?

He told Kenja, "We captured a TecKnati three moons back who escaped. We would not free one voluntarily."

Uh oh. Rayen tried to reach Callan's mind again and hit that same barrier.

Kenja arched a wicked eyebrow. "I should not have to remind you that my people are incapable of lying ... to me. We staked a TecKnati bait one hour ago at the flower plant that eats human flesh and she–" Kenja pointed a long fingernail at Rayen. "Released him."

Callan turned to Rayen with disbelief on his face. "You risked your life, *and* Kaz's, for a TecKnati?"

Kaz started to speak, but Callan silenced him with a look then speared her with his anger, waiting on her reply.

"Yes, but he was a small child, as defenseless as V'ru. Would you leave V'ru to face that fate?" Then she turned on Kenja. "What kind of warrior kills a child, even if he is the enemy?"

"We would not have killed him," Kenja said, sounding confused by her assumption. "The TecKnati had been alerted that one of theirs was in danger. Had you not released our bait, we would have captured the scouts, maybe even their leader here. As it is, you destroyed our best chance at gaining information."

"Don't expect me to be sorry that I saved that boy's life," Rayen tossed back.

"We'll discuss this later," Callan said in her direction with bite in his voice.

Well, that hadn't sounded good. She cut her eyes at Kaz. A silent apology wrapped his face that said he'd tell Callan all later. She shook her head and whispered, "It was my decision. Don't make this worse."

"Silence." Callan barely spoke, but the command was clear.

She started to tell him he had no say over her, who she chose to save, or when she spoke, but she was distracted by Kenja walking over to them. Warrior girl had a strange look on her face.

Callan's order was louder this time when Kenja got within ten feet of them. "That's close enough."

"What *is* she?" Kenja demanded, indicating Rayen.

"Not your concern."

Kenja found that amusing. "I will not war unnecessarily with another MystiK, but there is a price to be paid for her actions."

When Callan said nothing, Kenja's next words came out with the edge of a blade. "I demand her life for releasing the TeK."

"No." Callan stated that with just as much menace.

Just great. Rayen wanted to scream at what went on in this screwed up place. How could she fix this? Kenja really intended to kill her for saving that child from being eaten by a plant. Rayen would consider this conflict too bizarre to believe if not for everything *else* that had happened to this point.

Kenja warned, "If we war, it will be bloody, and I will win."

A growl came out of Callan that was half disgust and half warning as well. "We should be working together to survive this place and find a way to get *all* of our people home so we can stop whatever SEOH is trying to do."

"I will capture TecKnati and interrogate them. Once they give me what I need, I will take *my* people home."

"What about the other MystiKs," Callan argued. "We're searching for two of our children captured in a TeK raid. You could help us track them to wherever the TecKnati are staying."

"I know where the TeK camp is."

"Then show us."

Kenja said nothing.

Shaking his head, Callan sighed. "Many of the problems we have back home are for this very reason. No one House trusts the other six. Our elders keep their distance and refuse to share gifts or information. If not for the BIRG Con meetings every five years, they would never speak, and even then, they do nothing to build unity among the MystiKs. And if they were communicating now, they would know that all Houses are losing their next generation. We have joined ranks in our village in this Sphere and, when we go home, I assure you the next generation will make changes."

Kenja lifted her chin, looking down her nose when she said, "Regardless, I do not risk my people for just any MystiK in this place. Only for an Uberon warrior."

Kaz snarled, "You should be careful with your words and actions, Kenja. Think about once we're out of here. Callan is the G'ortian in line to rule the Warrior House. He *will* unite all seven Houses. We all face the Damian Prophecy outcome."

She snorted at that. "No. The *first* born was meant to bring the Damian Prophecy to fruition." She faced Callan, not an ounce of compassion in her voice when she declared, "You are not your brother. Only a poor copy."

Callan didn't visibly flinch at the reference to the twin he'd lost, but Rayen caught a tiny shift in his skin colors that gave credit to her vicious strike. She wanted to shove Kenja's hateful words back down her throat.

Sounding unbothered, Callan said, "Your point?"

"You are Warrior House, but you could not protect your own brother from being murdered. How can you bring the prophecy to light?"

"I'll worry about the prophecy after our people are out of here. *All* of us, including you and your group. That is our duty as MystiK Warriors," Callan said, every word chiseled.

What was this prophecy everyone kept referencing?

"My people have scented more Uberons here. I will come for what is mine."

Callan shook his head once. "Any Uberon warriors in my village are staying there."

Kenja was undeterred in her single-minded drive to get what she wanted. "I had intended to come in peace to discuss my Uberons, but this treason changes everything. However, I will offer a compromise to show my willingness to work together. Either give me this female or the Uberon warriors in your village."

"The answer is still no."

Kenja looked at Rayen more closely and flared her nostrils, taking a deep breath. Her face contorted with disbelief. "What *is* she?" Kenja asked again, but with more than mere curiosity.

Rayen was tired of being discussed. "I'm a C–"

"Be quiet!" Callan ordered.

She glared at him. They were definitely having a talk as soon as this was over. If he raised his voice to her again, he would regret it.

Kenja watched them with deep interest. "Tell me I don't smell the beginning of a–"

"You don't," Callan said, cutting her off just as quickly. "You cannot have *anyone* under my protection, including Uberon warriors in my village. If you don't want to join us, then do not make the mistake of crossing me."

"The mistake will be yours if you do not hand over my people, Callan. I will give you until moonrise on the morrow. If you hand them over, I will tell you where the TeK camp is and allow that one–" She cocked her head at me. "–to live. If not, I will fight and I will win. When I do, my warriors will leave with me, and she will die."

"What about duty?" Kaz bit out.

"I know my duty, but you two have forgotten yours." With that, Kenja backed up until she was with her warriors, then she spun in place, and they literally vanished into the background.

Rayen turned to Callan. "Do you believe her?"

"Yes." He wouldn't look at her.

"What do you think she'll do?"

"Exactly what she says, and we don't have warriors capable of fighting Uberons. The few we have are young and they will not battle their own nor would I ask them to."

"This is ridiculous," Rayen snapped. "Why is this happening?"

She heard her condemnation in Callan's silence.

It was simple. She showed up and the village was attacked. She freed a TecKnati and almost got Kaz killed. Now Callan was going to war to keep her alive instead of handing her off to appease Kenja.

He had to be thinking twice about saving her from that plant. Whatever bridge they'd rebuilt between them just came crashing down.

CHAPTER 19

TONY HAD INFINITE PATIENCE WHEN it came to unraveling the secrets of a computer, charming a girl, or reaching a goal he'd personally set.

But trying to get through to an eleven-year-old boy who took everything literally was testing even Tony's limits. He had no choice. V'ru had the answers Tony needed locked in that little head, hidden underneath all that shaggy black hair the boy kept shoving up out of his eyes.

"Come on, V'ru Man, give me something to take back," Tony coached from where he sat cross-legged opposite V'ru. "I get that you're the keeper of all knowledge since the beginning of time–"

"Incorrect," V'ru said, swatting at a lock of hair that had fallen forward. Again. "I am limited in that I only have access to any history recorded in various means during relevant time periods, which includes verbal history confirmed by..."

Tony sighed.

Everyone cut V'ru off when he went into one of these monotone recitations, but Tony wasn't going to do that. Adults had done that to Tony as a kid, ignoring what he had to say and talking over him because they thought he didn't know what he was talking about.

He did.

Unlike adults, he listened when it mattered. Like talking to Vinny. Tony paid attention to his little brother to make sure Vinny knew that he counted. He would always make sure Vinny knew that he mattered even if their parents had dumped them on their grandma, throwing them away like yesterday's garbage.

Now Vinny lived with strangers, foster parents who collected a check for giving kids food and shelter. Decent foster parents existed, he supposed, but Tony had talked to Vinny twice by phone before the foster parents had changed their number.

Vinny had been more withdrawn each time.

Food and shelter didn't equate to love. Tony had to get his little brother back before Vinny shut down completely, which was why Tony sat here listening to V'ru explaining how he only knew more than all the computers stored in Tony's world.

V'ru had been born with this knowledge, and it included how Cyberprocessors work in the future—Tony's future.

Tony salivated to get a look at how those functioned, but he would be content with just enough information to beat Nick at the Top Ten Competition. What would that take? Information on computers created a year or two beyond the present-day world he lived in?

When V'ru paused to take a breath, Tony said, "You'd be a national treasure in my time, V'ru."

The boy cocked his head one way then the other, thinking. "The term national treasure comes from the pre-K-Virus time of the eighteenth and nineteenth century. It was considered a cultural asset shared by an entire nation. I am not that."

"Oh, but you are, V'ru Man. Your knowledge is something to be treasured and appreciated. I'm not asking for all that and, even if I was, I couldn't possibly hold that much in my head."

"True."

"Hey, don't be so quick to discount me."

"I only confirmed what you stated."

He had Tony there. So much for trying to schmooze this genius squirt. Tony noticed for the third time that V'ru's gaze strayed to the backpack that had thankfully stayed with Tony when he traveled through the time portal.

Maybe a change of topic away from what V'ru knew to what Tony knew would help.

Tony lifted his backpack and opened it up, pulling out his calculator that fit in the palm of his hand. He offered it to V'ru, explaining, "I thought this would work here since it's got batteries, but it won't turn on."

V'ru took the unit in his skinny little fingers, holding it carefully and turning it from side to side, examining every inch. "I know of this, but to hold one is ..."

The awe in his voice touched Tony. He'd been like V'ru as a child, mesmerized by every electronic he could get his hands on no matter how insignificant it might seem to everyone else. But V'ru wasn't impressed by anything as antiquated as that calculator.

He studied it the way a gemologist would look at a rare diamond that had been lost and just rediscovered.

V'ru held his hand open, and the calculator floated above it.

Tony would never get used to these MystiKs.

Moving his little fingers in the air above the calculator, numbers began to appear in a holographic image that replicated the way they'd look in the calculator screen.

Tony had never envied anyone for their knowledge but sitting so close to all that information and knowing he couldn't tap it was physically painful.

V'ru seemed to catch himself and stopped playing with the calculator. He handed it back to Tony. "Thank you."

"For what, buddy?"

"Allowing me to touch history."

Didn't this kid just have fun sometimes? "It's not like something powerful."

"But it is," V'ru argued. "Just as *Nezarr the Calculator* was powerful." His lips snapped shut.

This kid was a closet comic aficionado?

Tony kept his excitement in check and asked, "You wouldn't know anything about *Captain America*, would you?"

V'ru's eyes opened wide. He started rattling off dates and details that would make him the main attraction at a comic convention. "*Marvel Superhero* first appeared circa March 1941 in *Timely Comics*, the predecessor of *Marvel Comics* that ..."

Tony eased back, smiling at the excitement in V'ru's face. This was a kid he understood, because V'ru reminded Tony of his little brother. Vinny could get just as excited over a comic book and had gotten his love of comics from Tony.

When V'ru took a breath and paused, he clammed up, immediately self-conscious over something. Worry jammed his face.

Tony prodded him with, "That's impressive, V'ru."

The boy hung his head. "I would be chastised for expending energy on something that has no value in our world."

No value? What about the sheer pleasure of reading for hours? Didn't V'ru's people want their kids to read? These MystiKs needed to be jacked up for the pressures they put on their youth.

Tony reached into his backpack and pulled out the comic he'd gotten from Hannah. Normally, he wouldn't let anyone touch this since it was so old and fragile, but V'ru would know the value and delicacy.

"V'ru Man, take a look at this."

V'ru lifted his head and sucked in a breath. "That's-that's ... real," he said with an awe reserved for something too rare to exist. "It's a *paper* comic."

"Not just any paper comic, this is a 1968 Captain America, issue number one-o-seven. Have a look at it." Tony offered it and V'ru stared at him. The boy's hesitance dug at Tony's heart. "It's okay, V'ru. Belongs to me, and you can hold it if I say so."

Reaching out with trembling hands, V'ru took the comic that was in a plastic wrapper. He lifted the clear flap and started to reach in then raised eyes to Tony that begged permission.

The kid was killing him. "Sure, take it out."

V'ru did and held the comic in both hands, staring at it with the wonder a young child should have. He slowly turned the pages as if each one might disintegrate if he moved too quickly.

His eyes raced over the colorful characters and artwork, then he did something that almost hurt to observe.

V'ru smiled. A real smile.

When was the last time this kid read something for fun?

Once V'ru had finished the comic, he carefully replaced it into the clear sleeve, but he did not return it. Instead, he looked at Tony and those intelligent eyes were calculating something.

V'ru squared his narrow shoulders and swallowed, then asked, "What would you trade for this?"

Way to kick me in the gut, kid. Here was Tony's chance to get the answers he needed to build a supercomputer when he returned to the school. People were depending on him. Hannah put her faith in Tony to beat Nick at the Top Ten Project. Vinny was stuck with foster parents until Tony could provide for him, and their grandmother's health was starting to go down.

He'd give one of his comics away in a heartbeat. He'd give all of his comics in trade for what V'ru could tell him, but Tony had promised Vinny a surprise for his birthday that was coming up quickly. Vinny had always wanted one of the classic Captain Marvel comics but would never ask for it.

This particular comic could be the difference in cheering up a boy who Tony feared was falling into deep depression.

V'ru waited with barely contained anticipation.

Tony fought against the sick grind in his stomach, but he had to be honest. His voice was low and sincere when he said, "I'd give it to you if I could, V'ru Man, but this is for someone special."

The words were out before Tony realized how they sounded to V'ru. The kid's lips trembled, then V'ru pulled himself together in the blink of an eye and handed the comic back. "I understand."

Could Tony feel any lower than he did right now? Probably not. "That's not how it sounds, V'ru, because–"

"No more words. We are done here. I can share no knowledge with those of the past." V'ru stood quickly and walked away with disappointment heavy in each step.

Tony dropped his head in his hands. How could he fix this? He couldn't. Family came first, always.

But what about V'ru? He had no family here, just like Vinny had no one back home. Who watched out for V'ru?

That wasn't Tony's problem, but he was going to make it his for whatever time he was in this place even if it was only for today.

Tony jerked his head up. The transender. He'd forgotten to ask V'ru how to find the controller, because if that knowledge existed V'ru was the only one who would have it besides the TecKnati.

Would V'ru now ask for the comic in trade for the key to leaving this Sphere? No, it was much worse than that.

V'ru's parting words rang through Tony's mind.

I can share no knowledge with those of the past.

CHAPTER 20

"THIS IS USELESS," KAZ MUTTERED.

Rayen hated to agree, but he was right.

The three of them had been traipsing around the woods, going from areas that had been blasted by fire to lush stretches filled with healthy plants and birds. Even lizards with yellow skins.

But every trail Kaz or Callan found that might lead to the TecKnati camp would just vanish at some point.

Had the TecKnati created all these false trails in hopes Callan would give up? If so, they didn't know the level of determination he possessed for protecting his people.

"We have to head back," Callan announced, surprising her.

"Why? We still have light left," she argued even though the red moon would drop out of sight soon. Tony was not going to be happy with her when she returned late. This fell way short of their agreement to get in and out, but they had to find the TecKnati camp and get those two children back.

"We return because I have said so."

Callan was clearly still angry with her. He'd walked ahead of her and Kaz for hours, no longer willing to split up from them again. Anything he had to share, he told Kaz. She found out only because she was present, but she wouldn't be put off so easily this time.

Speaking to Callan's back, she announced, "Well, I'm not willing to give up."

He stopped six strides ahead of her and turned, his face rigid with some emotion he kept locked behind that blank gaze. "Do as I say."

Where had he gotten the idea that she would just defer to his orders? "And what if I don't?"

Kaz coughed and covered his mouth, doing a poor job of hiding his grin.

Callan's dark eyes shifted to Kaz who lost all amusement, nodded, and walked forward. Before he passed Callan, Kaz slowed to say something that Callan acknowledged with a stiff chin nod.

Kaz disappeared around the next curve in the path before Callan spoke. "The woods are dangerous once the moon sets. I've ordered everyone inside the village before darkness each night."

That made sense. "Thank you for explaining."

"Kaz asked me to, but it shouldn't be necessary."

Great way to ruin her happy moment thinking they were communicating again. She put her hands on her hips, giving him a sign that she was ready to have this out. "Well, it is necessary, just like it's necessary for us to talk about what happened with Kenja."

"I'll deal with Kenja."

She stormed up to him, her jaws tight with wanting to yell, but she didn't. "You aren't the only one who can do things here, Callan. I'm here, too."

"I'm all too aware of that."

If he'd said that in a different tone, one filled with teasing, it would have healed her heart some.

But there was no joy in Callan. She understood why.

At home, he'd lost his twin brother, his best friend who everyone had hailed as the prodigy expected to govern the Warrior House and bring all seven Houses together in a way that would strengthen the splintered MystiK population. The old guard had ruled too long and harbored prejudices to the point of paranoia against other MystiK Houses.

They silently fought the wrong enemy.

SEOH was their enemy. Not each other.

With his twin dead, everyone expected Callan to accept his duty by stepping into his brother's vacated shoes, but Callan didn't want to govern at home any more than he did here. As the highest ruling member of the Governing House who was captured, Mathias had ruled here until he appointed Callan to succeed him here right before Mathias died.

She might not have believed what happened to Mathias if she hadn't seen it with her own eyes. Black wraiths had swarmed and killed him, and the death had been painful. The TecKnati scouts had told each captured MystiK that they would only stay here until the day they turned eighteen. The MystiK children believed they'd go home at that point. It was a deadly trap, and SEOH sent MystiK children here knowing they'd never leave.

SEOH clearly planned to destroy these children emotionally by offering hope then having it yanked away in the most hideous manner imaginable. But Mathias had circumvented that by holding her and Callan to secrecy.

She understood Callan's burdens.

For that reason, she *would* be patient and find a way to reach past his cold exterior to make him realize she could stand with him to protect the village.

The one he'd put at risk over her safety. "I came back to help you, Callan, not to cause you more misery."

He'd been staring at nothing, but his eyes dropped to hers at that.

She ignored the harsh gaze trying to look through her and continued. "I promised Tony that I'd take him and Gabby back as soon as I figured out how to travel here without both of them. If V'ru can tell us how to do that, I'll take my friends home and come back. That is, if Jaxxson is able to help Gabby, because she can't remain in her time with the problems she's having."

"No. Return with them and stay."

She didn't recoil at Callan's blunt words, determined not to lose her temper. "Are we back to that?"

"My stand on your not being here has never changed. This is not your battle."

"Even if I'm *willing* to return and help you?" she asked gently to keep this from escalating into an argument.

Yearning slid into his gaze and stayed only long enough to tug on her heart before he shook his head. Why wouldn't he let her support his efforts to protect his people? If she figured out how to travel through the portal again on her own, she didn't need his permission to come back, but she wanted him to be glad to see her.

Using the words that had reached him when the plant was trying to kill her, she said, "I have nothing in the past and nothing in the future. But here with you and the village, I feel like I have something. That I *am* someone."

His lips flattened into a line of determination. He shoved a hand over his face and dropped it, frustration pouring off him. "SEOH will not allow you to live. Kenja wants to kill you and that's without knowing that you're C'raydonian."

A small thrill rolled through her at hearing his concern was more about her safety and not about wanting her out of his sight. "I get that C'raydonians were not liked–"

"Not liked?" Callan's voice was hoarse. "They were hunted because the K-Virus had turned them rabid. The TecKnati put a bounty out on them and MystiKs brought in heads to claim their credits. Kenja's Uberon Warrior House led the hunts and took pride in slaughtering the greatest number of C'raydonians. She would consider it a moral duty to end your life. Hate is too simple an emotion to describe how those in the future feel about C'raydonians."

That was sobering, but she had no illusions about returning to Callan's world with him. She only wanted to have this time in the Sphere if he'd let her. Returning to Tony and Gabby's world was filled with uncertainty. This seemed to be the only place she belonged, even if it was for a short time.

But she wouldn't force her presence on Callan if he didn't want a reminder of the rabid people who had killed MystiKs. "Do *you* hate C'raydonians, Callan?"

"They were before my time."

"But I'm here now." Her voice was whisper soft.

She waited while the silence between them built until it threatened to crush her.

"You know I don't hate you," he admitted in a voice so low it drifted like smoke through her senses.

She held her breath, because the colors on his skin moved around slowly, showing her that his emotions simmered just beneath the surface where he tried to contain them.

He could stand there all day and declare that he wanted her to leave, but the fact that he wasn't keeping his skin color fixed told her more than anything else that he wasn't the cold leader he tried to convince her he was until he spoke again.

"Go back to the past, Rayen." His words were rough and sad but loaded with sincerity. "You can't survive here now that SEOH knows about the three of you and you can't go to the future, but you *can* stay alive in the past."

He was giving her permission to abandon him like everyone else had, but she had never walked away from those she cared about.

She blinked at that realization. A tiny memory of her standing alongside others to defend their homes and lives fought its way to the surface of her mind. C'raydonians?

She shook off the déjà vu moment and sidestepped agreeing or disagreeing with Callan. She didn't want to spend the rest of her time here fighting with him, so she just said, "If that's what you want."

Noncommittal, but still an answer.

His neck moved with a thick swallow. "Yes."

"I can't return until we find a control panel for the transender. When we arrived, we couldn't find anything like the fake pink flower that held the switch for calling up the control panel the last time."

"There has to be one." But Callan hadn't sounded as convinced as she'd hoped since she did want to find a way to take Gabby and Tony home.

Waving his hand to the side to get them moving, he said, "We'll talk of this back at the village. We have to move quickly."

"What's so dangerous out here at night?" she asked, following when he led her down the path Kaz had taken.

"The mist plants spread underground and emerge in places you don't expect at night."

She thought out loud. "But it didn't affect you?"

"No. Jaxxson instructed all the older ones first since the mist would have the most difficult time with us. The orange haze attacked the imagination of vulnerable MystiKs before we realized what was happening." He made a sharp angle when the path turned to the left, going silent again.

"What, Callan? Between having no memory and traveling between two worlds where everything is unfamiliar, I'm constantly guessing. Please at least tell me what you're thinking."

He glanced over at her, considering her words. "The mist obviously infected you, too. I have no way to shield you from that."

As always, Callan was determined to protect her. "If that's the reason you're calling off the search early, I'll go back to the village alone."

"The mist is only one of the threats. Most of the dugurats disappeared overnight. Something is eating them. A few survived, but so many disappeared that first night after the firestorm we realized something hungry roamed after dark that would be looking for a new food source. I think the mist drives the beasts wild. We sometimes hear screams at night."

"Croggle attacks?"

"No. It walks on four legs like the prantheer, but twice the size. We found an eaten prantheer and those can take down a full-grown human."

That raised chill bumps on her skin. She didn't ask another question as they changed their gait to a faster pace and caught up with Kaz.

As they approached the village, Kaz lifted his head, pursed his lips, and released a high-pitched sound.

She couldn't see the village. Callan had explained how they created a reflective ward that repelled anyone who was not MystiK, which left her out.

At Kaz's whistled signal, an opening appeared that they were able to pass through. That was clearly for her benefit.

A TecKnati raiding party had slipped inside the MystiK defenses the same way.

Much of the area had been cleaned up during their absence and the children were sitting on mats woven of dried plants and vines she recognized from the jungle and woods. They were eating from plates made of thick palm leaves and drinking from a gourd passed around.

They sat in a general circle around piles of multi-colored rocks that glowed with an internal light. The exterior of the stones had a cracked translucent finish.

Etoi sulked over at the far side of the clearing.

Rayen called it sulking, because Etoi eyed them with resentment with the bulk of her anger for Callan. He'd embarrassed her by forcing her to answer to Tony. But if Callan hadn't done that, they would probably have come back to find Tony being roasted over the fire pit instead of the tangy smelling meat now cooking. Jaxxson sliced off pieces and placed them on palm plates to be served.

Gabby very close to him. When she noticed Rayen entering, she came walking over with a smile.

Rayen hoped that meant positive news about her reactions. She needed someone in their trio to be doing better here than she was. "How are you feeling?"

Gabby expelled a deep breath. "I might have my shakes under control."

"Did Jaxxson fix it?"

"Not exactly unless you consider tough love an acceptable treatment procedure."

Rayen had no idea what tough love was, but if it made Gabby smile, she was all for it. "Where's Tony?"

"Right here," Tony said, walking up from their left.

Callan joined the group. "Any problems?"

"Depends on how you define problems," Tony quipped, being as clear as Gabby had been.

She started to warn Tony that this was not the time to be cryptic with Callan, but Zilya interrupted when she called over, "Callan, I want to see you."

Callan said nothing to her.

"If you want this public, so be it." Zilya came forward, each step a warning that she was one unhappy person. "Where are the other two children the TecKnati took?"

"We didn't find them. Yet. We will tomorrow."

Rayen noticed that Callan failed to share that they might be fighting Kenja by daylight.

"Tomorrow will be too late," Zilya charged. "They could be dead."

Callan's grim expression turned hard as stone. He lowered his voice. "Do not say such things within hearing of these children."

Kaz interjected, "Besides, the TeKs will not harm the children, because of the treaty and they want to trade them for the three from the past."

"Then you should trade them, Callan," Zilya hissed at him. "Or must you be reminded of your responsibility to this village first?"

"No, but perhaps you need to be reminded. The TeK should not have gotten inside our walls to begin with. Care to explain why Etoi left her position, Zilya?" Callan crossed his arms. His words were sharp with censure.

"I do not answer to you or anyone else. Our wall had a defect. That is all. Speaking of Etoi, how dare you undermine my authority by telling Etoi that she had to do as this one says?" Zilya jabbed a finger toward Tony who gave her an amused eyebrow arch.

Callan must have hit his limit for dealing with everything, because he unfolded his arms and took a step forward.

Gabby murmured, "Shouldn't have poked the bear."

Zilya finally realized she'd opened a door that had been better left shut. She backed up a step, mumbling, "We'll speak in my office."

When Callan replied, he didn't try to shield his words from anyone. "You don't *have* an office. This is not the Governing House, the Warrior House, or any of the other five Houses. This is not some vid game. This is more than war. This is about survival and my orders are to be followed without question. Put your ego aside and grow up. Now is the time to *act* like a future leader of a House if you really expect to be one, because what happens here will be reviewed in detail when we go home."

Color washed out of Zilya's already pale skin. The splatter of black and silver jewels on her cheek dimmed into a dull finish.

Zilya spun around and stalked away.

Callan ran both hands through his hair and whipped back to Rayen, Tony, Gabby and Kaz, but his orders were for Kaz. "Let the children finish eating and get settled then call me and we'll meet to discuss tomorrow."

When Callan turned away, Gabby asked him, "Do you want something to eat? There's plenty and we're almost through feeding the kids."

He just shook his head and kept going.

Rayen started after him and Kaz caught her arm. "What?"

"Don't make this more difficult than it is for him."

That stung, coming from Kaz. She'd begun to think of him as a friend. "What do you think I'm going to do?"

Kaz released her arm, waiting as Gabby and Tony moved back over to where Jaxxson continued to feed the village. The warmth in Kaz's eyes softened the blow of his words. "Callan carries a responsibility that is beyond all of ours. He is not just the next leader of the Warrior House, but he has to take his brother's place."

"I know this." Her protective instincts rose to the surface. "I seem to be the only one who notices how hard he's working to be what everyone wants. No one seems to care what Callan wants."

"You're missing my point."

"What is it, Kaz?"

"That Callan doesn't get to choose some things about his life, like taking his place in society or ... who he will rule over the Warrior House with as his wife."

"He doesn't get to choose who he ends up with forever?" she asked, thinking the future was not a place that offered much for a young person.

Kaz scratched his neck. "No, that's not what I'm saying. I'm trying to avoid being unkind so I'm not explaining this the best way."

"Then just say it. The truth is what it is."

"Callan can choose a girl from among his people, but he would never, could never, consider being with a C'raydonian. If others see what I've seen between the two of you, Callan will be decried a betrayer of the MystiKs. He forces the village to accept you and your friends, but to ask more of him would be wrong and unkind."

His words hollowed out her chest and left a cold desolate emptiness in place. No wonder Callan was trying so hard to send her away. First, because he was concerned over her safety, but even if this was not his home these were his people and he had to maintain a proper existence even in the Sphere.

The more she pushed to make him admit he wanted her here, the more pressure she added to his already overloaded shoulders.

It took a moment before she could speak without her emotions giving her away. She would not make Kaz feel bad for delivering the truth. Wasn't that what she kept asking for?

Rayen swallowed the ache of accepting that she didn't belong here any more than she did in the past or future. She told Kaz, "Thank you for being honest."

"All is not lost," Kaz said, a smile building in his voice.

She couldn't agree and reached for a word that wouldn't make a bigger fool of herself than she already had. "Oh?"

"No. Unlike Callan's parents, one of mine had a roving eye and other parts that led to me being only a half-blooded Warrior, which means I don't have the limitations he does." Kaz winked. "I am free to choose any girl who catches my eye."

That was sweet and flattering, but as much as she wished she could just let go of what she felt for Callan, she couldn't. But neither would she continue to create conflict for him. She said, "That's good to know."

Kaz sighed. "I can see that you are not so easily swayed, and I told you I would never touch anyone who belonged to another."

"I don't belong to Callan."

Kaz stepped close and whispered, "There is evidence that a bonding ritual has begun between the two of you but know that Callan must not complete it. You must let him go and allow him to sever what has been started."

She stood with her mouth open as Kaz sauntered over to pull a piece of meat off the roasting carcass and chew on it while Gabby loaded a palm frond for him. She loaded one for Rayen that she took without a word. Gabby gave her a frown but returned to help the children, leaving her to face her thoughts.

What was Kaz talking about? Callan and she had done no bonding. Had they? When?

Kaz thought she could end something when she had no idea what had been started?

Wasn't it enough that she would back away from Callan? What else was she to do besides leave?

And how was she going to leave without a controller for the transender?

Her stomach growled. She ate a bite of the meat that had a sweet taste to match the aroma. That silenced her stomach. If only all problems were solved so easily.

Why would she want to stay here when her presence caused constant conflict and others thought so little of her? But neither was she thrilled at going back to a place where she didn't exist.

Why was she even alive at this moment when no one else from her time was left?

Or were they? Callan had shared only the parts he wanted her to know from what V'ru had told him of her lineage as a C'raydonian.

V'ru would know all.

Callan was nowhere in sight, having vanished into the wooded area inside the village. She had a chance at getting answers from the one person who held all the knowledge.

V'ru.

If she could get him to talk to her without asking Callan's permission first.

And V'ru was the one person who might be able to tell her how to travel through the portal alone.

CHAPTER 21

RAYEN FINISHED HER MEAL AND found the young boy all alone sitting under a shimmering silver tree that she hadn't seen before. He was far from where the rest of the village shared food. Why wasn't he eating with the others?

"Hi V'ru. Can we talk?"

"Why?" He lifted his chin.

She expected to see the same eleven-year-old she'd met last time who had been surprisingly confident when uttering obscure details about history. This child looked lost. His skinny arms wrapped around bony knees tucked up to his chest. He wore the same toga-like cloth wrapped around him that had held up fairly well only because he was shielded from everything, including the other MystiK kids.

Callan once told her that V'ru had to be protected at all costs.

She made a swift change in plans and decided to put her need for answers aside for now and sat down in front of V'ru, crossing her legs as she did. "How are you?"

"I am well."

That was a statement of his physical being, but nothing that addressed the sad inward curve of his shoulders. What had made him so unhappy? Could it be a physiological change? "You seem bothered by something. Were you influenced by the orange mist?"

"No. My kamara prevents anything from touching me. I stayed inside until it was safe to come out."

"Do you stay inside a lot?"

"Yes. It is important that I not be exposed to the others any more than necessary. I am a natural resource for our people."

He lived most of his time in a dome, secluded from others. He didn't see himself as a child or a person, but a resource. Oddly, that attitude was parallel to Callan's view of his own life, which was not about what he wanted but what everyone expected of him.

She smiled at V'ru who cocked his head to the side, studying her. He asked, "Why are you smiling?"

If she were honest with him she'd say she had no idea since everything in her world was in turmoil, but sharing her problems would not solve his. He needed encouragement. "I'm just happy to visit with you."

"Interesting."

Strange answer, but she let it go. "Did you get something to eat? Whatever Jaxxson is cooking was good."

"Yes. It was acceptable."

Could this boy be any more depressed? She had no recollection of any experience with sad children to draw on that she could use to help him. She decided being direct was her only option. "Who has upset you, V'ru?"

"No one. I am not upset. I am ... contemplative."

"That's not true."

His eyes bulged. "Do you accuse *me* of lying?"

"Maybe." She held a serious face to hide the fact that she was teasing him.

"I ... I ... you can't say that."

"Sure, I can. I just did. Now, why don't you tell me what's going on?"

He looked away. "Nothing."

And that meant something had definitely happened. She mentally ran through all the people who might have caused V'ru distress and hit on the obvious one. "Has Etoi yelled at you?"

If she had, Rayen would find her and make Etoi think twice about ever being mean to this child again.

"No." Was there any hope for reaching the heart of this issue before Rayen grew old and gray? "Who have you spoken to today?"

He lifted a shoulder, dismissing her question.

Ah, that meant she was getting close. This boy was considered the fount of all knowledge and was proud of his ability to call forth any information needed. He would not take being challenged on this ability lightly, so she switched tactics and said, "I'd love to stay and visit, but I have to find someone who can answer my questions about the C'raydonians."

She got to her feet.

V'ru frowned up at her. "There is no one else to ask besides me."

"I'm sure there is. Someone like Jaxxson."

"Poor choice."

"Zilya." She fought to keep a straight face on that one, because she'd ask a TecKnati a question before Zilya.

V'ru sounded exasperated. "Zilya will not answer you. Even if she would, she lacks sufficient information."

This kid sounded like a book with legs instead of a person. Rayen waved her hand dismissively. "There are others with plenty of information to share."

"No there are *not*, especially that stingy Tony," V'ru muttered so low she almost didn't hear his last four words.

Tony was the one who had upset V'ru?

Rayen was torn between not wanting to believe it and irritated if Tony *had* left V'ru in this state. She'd give Tony a chance to explain himself, but one thing was clear in V'ru's long face. Someone had hurt his feelings.

Still pushing the child to break free and act like any other boy, Rayen shrugged. "I'll just have to piece together what I can from the rest of them. I'm sure they'll know enough."

"Hardly," V'ru scoffed, shoving a mop of hair out of his eyes. He sighed heavily and said, "Sit and ask."

This was the confident V'ru who she'd met on her first trip to the Sphere. The one who held his knowledge in the highest regard.

She hid a smile and sat down again with her legs once more crossed.

"You sit as a C'raydonian," V'ru noted.

"Who are ... *were* they? I know nothing of my people and if I never regain my memory, I won't even know where I came from, because no one in the past has any knowledge of C'raydonians."

That must have finally reached V'ru. He nodded and lifted his hands. A holographic screen she'd seen him conjure during her last visit appeared between them. With a slash of his hand, he moved it to the side where she could read it as well.

She smiled at him for that consideration. "Thank you for helping me. I know you're the only one with the answers I need, but I wasn't going to bother you. I appreciate you sharing your amazing grasp of history."

He blushed under the compliment and cleared his throat, his voice finding strength with him now in his comfort zone. "C'raydonians have always lived apart from the MystiKs and TecKnati. They descended from people once known as Navajo who were original inhabitants of North America."

"I've heard Navajo mentioned around the school Tony, Gabby, and I attend in Albuquerque."

"Correct." Scratching his nose, V'ru continued, "Long before the K-Virus came to be, it is believed–though not physically documented–" V'ru qualified, before going on. "That one group of Navajos living in an area called New Mexico seceded from the entire Navajo Nation. They were driven by the charismatic leadership of a young medicine man known only as C'ray who had powers that amazed even the formidable elders of the Navajo council."

Her ancestors had been rebels. Maybe that explained why she fought to do things her way? She remained silent, afraid to interrupt V'ru.

"This C'ray taught his people to turn their backs on what was considered the modern world at that time."

"Why?"

"There are conflicting records on when North America was actually discovered." V'ru's grave tone criticized those who failed to keep adequate records. "Navajos and other true natives of this North America fought the invaders who came to claim their lands, but eventually the natives were outnumbered and overpowered by advanced weapons. More than that, the invaders brought disease that destroyed many. The natives of this land ended up on tracts of property allotted them, which were called reservations."

Her heart hurt at the atrocity. "That was cruel."

V'ru nodded. "This C'ray wanted to effect change, but he faced a battle of mixed attitudes among the Navajo population, which was the largest Native American group. Some were willing to hold fast to traditional beliefs, but others, tired of poverty and dismal living conditions, embraced the modern ways and commerce offered by the invaders, or Americans, as they were known."

"What did C'ray have against his people finding ways to earn money?"

"Because many casinos were built on the reservations. These businesses provided gambling or games of chance to buy their way out of poverty. A fool's dream at best. This industry did bring wealth to many, but not all, and especially not to those not in power. C'ray felt their next generation was deteriorating morally and abandoning their roots. He believed the future of the Navajos was inside the hearts of their youth if he could reach them."

"What did C'ray do?"

"He traveled by foot through the Navajo nation for three years, searching for those who would be worthy of their Athabascan ancestry."

"I haven't heard about Athabascan."

"Athabascans were considered by some to be the ancestors of Navajo and Apache who could be found in the Pueblo population. The Athabascans originated in a country later known as Canada, but tribes migrated south for hunting and food. Some remained in southwestern lands like New Mexico. C'ray hand-selected a core group of Navajos during those three years."

"Why Navajos?"

"Of the Native Americans he believed had descended from Athabascans, Navajos had held out the longest against allowing their lands to fall to commerce. C'ray felt this showed a strong faith among their people. Once he had his tribe, he settled in an area where his family had lived for many generations known as the Sandia Mountain range. He began to show his followers how to once again not just live, but to thrive."

She wanted to ask if V'ru had an image of this C'ray, but the boy had calmed as he embraced the topic, so she let him continue.

"Eventually details of the C'raydonians seeped out from time to time and that is what we have of their history."

She hated to interrupt, but she was confused. "Were they hiding?"

"In a way, yes. C'ray spent his lifetime showing his people how to live without depending on the rest of the world. After a while, they were forgotten ... until the K-Virus was introduced to our world, then they came out of the mountains to strike a deal with the TecKnati."

Rayen raised an eyebrow at that. "Why?"

V'ru appeared perplexed. "Oddly, there is no written record of this meeting, so I am unable to claim this as confirmed history, but it was said that SEOH's grandfather refused to allow your people inside any of the cities. He didn't trust the C'raydonians not to open the city gates to their families infected by the K-Virus."

Her people had been forced into extinction. "You said this C'ray had powers. Was he a MystiK?"

"No, the MystiKs evolved after the K-Virus. Based upon verbal history passed down since his death, we know that C'ray was sent by spirit guardians to save his people and prepare them for the Damian Prophecy."

There was that prophecy again. "What is that?"

"The prophecy?" V'ru's little frame stiffened. "I am not at liberty to share those details with you."

"But my people knew it," she argued.

"And if you had prior knowledge, I would discuss it with you, but you do not."

He could be so irritating when he got all righteous over protecting his precious history, but it sounded as though the Damian Prophecy belonged to her as much as it did him. She'd have to ask Callan about that later. For now, she wanted to keep V'ru talking so she went back to where he'd left off. "What happened to the C'raydonians after the K-Virus?"

"Native Americans still living on reservations around North America fell to the virus as quickly as the rest of the population, but C'ray's tribe survived ... at first."

"What protected them?"

"Isolation, the same thing that protected the future TecKnati and MystiKs. Scientists and others in technology who worked in secluded environments learned of the virus first and were safe from it as long as they did not have contact with infected individuals. That was one hundred and six years ago. Those who survived joined forces later and eventually became known as the TecKnati."

She could see how that transformation happened, but not how the MystiKs came to be. "What about the MystiKs?"

His eyes moved back and forth as if he searched through a thousand pieces of history, which he very likely might be doing. V'ru said, "MystiKs were individuals and small groups who had withdrawn from society long before the K-Virus to study their beliefs and become better acquainted with the natural order of their world. Some were monks, some were spiritualists, some were just isolationists who wanted to do what was called 'living off the grid.'"

"That sounds similar to the C'raydonian tribes," she pointed out and admitted only to herself that she was grasping at threads to find a connection with the MystiKs. V'ru's people held Gabby in the highest regard as a Hy'bridt. They at least respected Tony's technological ability, but her?

Rayen was the lowest vermin in their world.

"No, there is a difference between your people and MystiKs," V'ru replied, smashing any hope she had. "The C'raydonians were strictly of one belief that went back to the beginning of time for their people. They would not consider joining forces with any others. That was why they remained in the mountainous area close to ABQ/7, known as Albuquerque in the past."

She'd been stepping all around what she really wanted to know and finally asked, "Do you know who my family is … or was?"

"No." His whisper doused the hope she'd been clinging to. "When I tested your blood, I could only determine that it was C'raydonian and that you had been born after the K-Virus first arrived in our world. There is little information on the C'raydonians, because they preferred to keep to themselves, which did not allow for much recorded history once the virus began infecting them."

"You must have had something recorded in history for comparing my blood. Otherwise, how would you know the era I was born?"

His eyes strayed away from her for a moment. "Samples were stored from C'raydonians the TecKnati captured during the first few years of the virus outbreak. They sent sentient beasts to hunt C'raydonians and tasked them with bringing back blood samples that were used for genetic dating. With any other population where there is annual blood testing, I am able to determine a year of birth or a decade of birth as a minimum, but all we had were a few C'raydonian samples from pre-viral outbreak then the ones the beasts returned that were post outbreak. All I can determine is that yours is post K-Virus."

She would never find out who she was or who her people had been. She just had to accept that truth, even though her mind was having a hard time explaining it to her heart.

V'ru watched her with solemn eyes. "I am sorry."

"It's not your fault, V'ru."

"I know. I'm sorry that I have nothing more for you."

"Are you sure all the C'raydonians are gone?"

"SEOH's predecessor released a report detailing how the sentient beasts released to hunt the C'raydonians were infallible in search and destroy. The MystiK leaders at the time realized these same sentient beasts could be turned on MystiKs. That prompted the first treaty to be signed that same year, which included a provision going forward that outlawed any sentient hunters capable of wiping out an entire population."

One sentient hunter still existed, but I wasn't bringing that up right now. "Why did the MystiKs come to live in the cities if they disliked TecKnati so much?"

Her question must have hit a nerve, because V'ru squirmed and stopped talking.

"V'ru, I won't judge anything you say. And I won't bring this up around the others if it causes you discomfort. I just want to understand why my people no longer exist."

Maybe it was the raw honesty of her words, but V'ru sat quietly for a moment then continued. "The MystiKs were mixed bands of people who began to realize they had both similar and individually different powers. For example, many have different degrees of telepathic ability, while a limited number of others develop exceptional healing abilities like Jaxxson and yet others are born with elite warrior skills like Callan."

Admiration flowed when V'ru mentioned Callan. She could appreciate his respect for Callan's skills. "Go on," she encouraged.

"It is believed that MystiK power rose with the fall of technology, because life turned primitive for a period of twelve years after the K-Virus hit. During that time, the Houses divided up according to how each group developed powers. The TecKnati bred for intellectual ability more than anything else. I suppose it is only fair to point out that MystiKs have benefitted by TecKnati creations, *but* we have also suffered," V'ru was quick to add. "If not for the TecKnati, there would have been no K-Virus."

She held up her hand. "Wait. Explain that. How did the TecKnati release a virus if they weren't even in existence when it spread?"

"Pardon me. That was a technically inaccurate statement on my part," V'ru explained. "It is believed that the TecKnati *ancestors* were at fault for bringing the virus back to our world from outer space."

"No wonder your two groups don't trust each other."

V'ru nodded in earnest, his voice picking up speed with his passion for this topic. "Right. *They* created the problem and now they want to do it again. Our MystiK leaders are trying to make them see that the TecKnati desire to explore other planets is putting our world at risk. Look at this Sphere. It's proof of how dangerous other worlds can be."

She pondered this and admitted, "True, and SEOH clearly chose the deadliest elements to put in this place, but why go to so much trouble?"

"That is obvious."

Did he know what Callan and Mathias had discovered? SEOH's plan hadn't been clear to Callan until they accompanied Mathias outside the village where Mathias was killed. Then it all made sense. SEOH couldn't kill a MystiK under the age of eighteen without sacrificing a TecKnati child due to the spell infused in the treaty. But once a MystiK turned eighteen here, the Sphere had a killing machine in place.

When she didn't comment fast enough, V'ru must have taken it as confusion on her part. He sighed, letting her know it was tedious trying to educate someone so far beneath his intelligence level. "The treaty between the MystiKs and TecKnati is renewed every five years and the spell remains in it to protect our next generation of leaders. Many are rare G'ortians."

"Like you and Callan."

The kid beamed at her including him in the same company as Callan.

"Correct," V'ru said. "We G'ortians were foretold by the Hy'bridts who also warned that the TecKnati would betray the treaty, but our leaders refused to believe that was possible. They had added a clause that stated if any of our adolescents were killed intentionally by a TecKnati, that a child of equal status would die immediately."

"This is so cruel to children on both sides."

V'ru's hands cupping his legs clenched with anger. "Why would the penalty be any less than the crime?"

"I'm not arguing that point, just saying adults should not use children in a war of blood."

V'ru lifted eyes that said he would not return home the same child who had left.

She just wanted him to make it home again. She waited for him to say he'd figured out what had happened to Mathias. If he had, what could she say?

Shoving a handful of dark hair off his forehead that flipped right back, V'ru asked, "Do you think Mathias made it home or ..."

Hesitating would kill any chance she had of convincing V'ru that Mathias was still alive. "Yes, I do think he made it back. He's probably in a secure TeK facility while the MystiK elders work out a new treaty."

V'ru's narrow shoulders eased with that confirmation until he realized something. "But the TecKnati would not be able to prevent Mathias from communicating with his House telepathically."

"Are you sure?" That wasn't much of an argument, but it was all she had.

V'ru stared off at nothing, his eyes twitching with tiny movements as that Cyberprocessor-level mind sorted through every potential outcome. When he finally had a bazillion possibilities worked out in less than a minute, he looked at her for the first time like she had a smidgen of intelligence. "That is possible. We made the mistake of underestimating the TecKnati once and should not again."

No truer words had been spoken. She had something else bothering her that V'ru might be able to answer. "Tell me how bonding works between MystiKs."

His eyes widened and his narrow cheeks blushed. "Why?"

"I'm curious."

"Why?"

"You want to know why I'm curious?" she asked. "Maybe because I have no memories, which means very little past knowledge. I have no idea if someone has bonded with me."

"Of course, you'd know." He clearly didn't believe her.

"No, I wouldn't. Not if I don't know what happens. Is it painful or nice or what?"

"It's not painful." Now he was exasperated as if he had to explain breathing to a novice. "But you would definitely know if someone pierced the veil in your mind."

Oh, so this bonding thing did have to do with Callan coming into her mind. Had he broken through her mental veil? When? Then it hit her. Had to be when they fought the plant.

She struggled with spiraling emotions from wanting to celebrate that they had a connection to disappointment that there was no future in this bonding.

Trying to sound casual, she told V'ru, "I understand now. Thank you for explaining."

"Is that all?" V'ru was clearly ready to end their meeting.

"One more thing. If that veil is pierced, can it be fixed?"

"That's a complicated question, but one you'll never face since you are not MystiK." V'ru's eyes strayed from her, embarrassed again, but in a different way. "I mean no harm in this, but if someone bonded with you, they would face being an outcast."

CHAPTER 22

2179 ACE, in ORD/City One

SEOH GLANCED UP AND DID a double take when his middle son walked into his office wearing the metallic green uniform of TecKnati scouts. "Thylan?"

"SEOH. I wanted to see you before I departed for the Sphere."

Waving his hand to close the holographic monitor on his desk, SEOH sat back. He should take more interest in this one now that his oldest son was gone, but Thylan had never shown the gift with technology that his other two sons had.

Still, family was important to him. He had a dynasty to build after all. His youngest would be the next shining star in SEOH's universal domination, but this son might become useful at some point.

"Have a seat, Thylan."

"I'd rather stand if it's the same to you. I don't plan to stay long. You have a busy schedule."

Why did SEOH have the feeling there was an undercurrent to this conversation he was missing? He stood and stepped around the desk, because he allowed no one to talk down to him. "What's on your mind?"

"I want to prove to you I can play a significant role in ANASKO."

"Of course, you will. We need someone with your skill to manage the scouts and find that computer." SEOH had told Rustaad to share only what was necessary when he briefed Thylan on his responsibilities.

His son had been given one task. Bring the computer back, or the schematics to build the Genera-Y computer.

Thylan put his hands behind his back and stood with his feet apart, just as the scouts had been taught since the moment they turned eight. But Thylan had never been through any such training. He'd preferred vid games and girls over studying and work.

Was this pose supposed to impress SEOH when they both knew how much money SEOH had spent to keep him out of juvenile and adult detention centers? His son had aggression issues on top of not testing at the genius level of his other two, but no son of SEOH's was getting locked away just because some little whore at school accused Thylan of rape.

"I'm aware of your plans for the BIRG Con," Thylan started. "The real reason I stopped by was to tell you I know how to ensure that your laser grid will function correctly and at the appropriate moment to neutralize the MystiK power."

SEOH hadn't expected *that* to come out of Thylan's mouth since this boy wasn't supposed to know about the laser grid. "Who have you been talking to, son?"

Thylan's lips lifted in a faint smile. "I listen to you even though you think I don't. I know I'm not your favorite, but I believe I can prove myself to be your best."

This was a dilemma.

Should SEOH ask what Thylan knew or turn him over to Rustaad's extraction specialists to get the answers? That seemed cruel to do to a son, but SEOH had never cared for anyone to know his business unless he shared it himself.

On the other hand, maybe he'd overlooked potential. SEOH put a question to his son that would decide how this ended. "Have you allowed someone to leak ANASKO secrets?"

"Never. I spent sixteen months getting to know an engineer on your design team. On my way here, I sent word to Vice Rustaad about this leak once I determined the engineer had spoken to only me. I would suggest replacing that one at this point. I doubt he'll be able to function once Vice Rustaad is through with him."

Ruthless. SEOH admired that quality, but he suspected anyone who worked behind his back. "What was your goal in all this?"

"To show you that I have a skill for finding the weak link in your organization and containing the problem. Plus, while I was flushing him out, I learned quite a bit about the laser grid. I had time to think on the issues we're facing in the immediate future. You're concerned about being sure the grid will function properly and at the correct time it's needed. I have determined a way to insure one of those two."

Hard to imagine anyone surprising SEOH, but if Thylan's bold claim held up he'd be the first. "And what can you insure about the grid?"

"I'll tell you as soon as I return from the Sphere."

Thylan was negotiating to return soon, but he was not coming back until he had the computer. SEOH doubted that Thylan had any earth-shattering idea, but he extended his hand and shook with his son, saying, "Looking forward to having you on board."

"I'll be leaving shortly. I have a list of supplies and equipment I'd like sent with me today."

"Oh?"

"I think you'll be pleased with something I have in mind for your MystiKs there."

If this boy survived that Sphere, he might just be of value in SEOH's organization. "Give your list to Rustaad."

CHAPTER 23

"HERE'S YOUR FOOD."

Callan eyed the palm plate that Kaz carried. "I don't need anyone to wait on me."

"You're welcome." Kaz put the plate on the stump of a tree at his left then stepped back and crossed his arms. "What are you doing with Rayen?"

Not what Callan would like to be doing, but that wasn't where Kaz was headed with his question. "I'm doing nothing with her."

"Then why did Kenja smell a bonding in process?"

"She didn't say that." Callan was dodging and would quickly run out of directions to sidestep.

"Only because you cut her off, because an Uberon would be the only one able to detect a bonding this early."

"I am not growing a bond with Rayen. I would never do that with someone not approved by my elders and certainly not a C'raydonian." That should have shut down any further conversation on the topic, but Callan could see he'd failed to convince Kaz it was true.

Probably because it wasn't.

Callan had broken through the veil of Rayen's mind when he thought he was going to lose her to the blood-eating plant. Rayen believed her life was of no value. What was he supposed to do when he saw her slipping from him? He'd done the only thing he could and roared at her to fight, then dove inside her mind to make a connection.

He'd broken the veil that shielded contact with her power.

That had been the moment the bonding started.

But he would keep it from continuing. He would not bind Rayen to him when she could never bond with another as a result.

Kaz waited with stern patience.

Callan could order him to go away, but that would be no different than a slap to the face. Kaz had been a tremendous asset from the minute he showed up, plus they'd become close friends over the past three years while training back home.

Sighing, Kaz scratched his chin and studied the dark sky then lowered a suspicious gaze to Callan. "Why do I think you are saying what you must say as opposed to the truth?"

"Because we all have responsibilities and mine is to this village. I don't deny that I find Rayen interesting–"

"Understatement," Kaz murmured.

"–but," Callan said, sending Kaz a warning look. "Any attraction is only because we've been thrown together here. Circumstances that have been beyond anyone's control. She'll leave with the other two at moonrise and not return again."

"That's what you want?"

No, Callan wanted to spend every minute he could with her but keeping her here was putting her life in constant jeopardy and tempting him beyond the limits of his restraint.

She had to leave, and he had to do his duty.

He would figure out how to stop what he'd started. He didn't want to ask V'ru how to sever a bonding that had been activated, accidentally or otherwise. V'ru would be appalled to think Callan had acted without thought for his position in the Warrior House. But the little historian was the only one Callan knew of who was capable of answering his questions.

It seemed logical that he only needed to know how to shut down the bonding on his end, which should be much simpler once Rayen was gone.

Kaz watched him with keen intelligence that would not be easily swayed, but Callan was determined. "Yes, that's what I want, Kaz, for her to leave. That's what's best for Rayen and this village."

"And you know what's best for her?"

"You're starting to annoy me."

"Only just now? And here I'd been putting my best effort into it," Kaz quipped, always the joker. "There is one way to stop a bonding immediately."

Pushing away from the tree, Callan ordered, "How?"

When Kaz's eyebrows lifted, Callan considered biting his tongue for answering so quickly.

Kaz scowled at him. "Don't give me that threatening glare. I'm on your side here. First, I want to know how you happened to start this bonding if it was not intentional?"

Kaz would not let up once he had a meaty bone to chew, which had Callan admitting, "It happened when the plant tried to eat her. She couldn't talk. The venom in her blood had turned her muscles numb. I ... wasn't thinking about anything except helping her get away, so I shoved into her mind and it ... just happened."

It being the one thing he should never have done.

That was the lamest explanation ever, but Kaz for once didn't challenge him. Instead, his friend started pacing and tapping his jaw with his forefinger. "Hmm. Then nothing particularly deep happened between you two, right?"

"No." At least, Callan didn't think so. Unlike his brother Jornn who had been groomed as a leader and expected to bond with a chosen gild-level female soon after his BIRG Con, Callan had shunned being coached in bonding. He'd planned to remain single so long as he possibly could.

If … no, *when* he returned home, that would all change and he'd have to face his duty. Maybe that was why he'd allowed his desire to overrule his head here.

This place gave the illusion of freedom to make choices he couldn't at home.

Kaz stopped and snapped his fingers at Callan. "Are you listening?"

"What did you say?"

"I was explaining how to sever the forming bond."

Callan shoved the crazy attraction he had for Rayen out of his mind along with the odd reluctance he felt at breaking this connection with her. If he paid attention to Kaz, he wouldn't have to bring V'ru into this. "What do I do?"

"Nothing. That's the beauty of this."

"I could have a more enlightening conversation with a rock, Kaz."

"You remind me of a black thundercloud whose only purpose is to pass over sunny areas and rain on someone's pleasure."

"I'm considering doing far more damage than raining on your pleasure if you don't start making sense," Callan warned then muttered to himself, "What made me think you really knew what you were talking about?"

"Because I've seen this done." Kaz was the epitome of smug.

"When? Who?"

"My mother and my natural father," Kaz admitted in a flat voice, all humor gone. "We both know I'm not of pure lineage. I overheard my mother speaking to my warrior father who has always accepted me despite my not being his blood child. He realized she had begun bonding with another and ordered her to end it immediately or face being turned out."

Callan's mother and father had been manipulated into marrying to join influential warrior families, but his parents had fallen in love along the way.

He knew he was fortunate and offered his friend understanding. "It's never easy to live with the decisions adults make that affect our lives."

"There is the benefit of my not being expected to choose a mate by my BIRG Day as you have to do. I can enjoy my bachelorhood for many more years." Kaz lifted both shoulders as if his mother's betrayal to his warrior father really didn't matter to Kaz, but Callan knew better. He'd seen the ever-happy Kaz in low moments that were brutal. That's why he pushed his friend back on topic.

"You were telling me what you figured out, Kaz."

Taking a deep breath and exhaling whatever gnawed at him over his parental issues, Kaz grinned. "It's actually very simple. If you break the bonding, there will be a residue from her left inside you that will always be there for another female to see since you're the one that opened the path between your minds. You don't want that, right?"

"Right."

"That's why it's imperative that Rayen disconnect from you."

"Will it cause Rayen any problems?"

"Not if she is the one to do the severing. If she releases you, there will be no residue in her mind because she did not break the veil."

Callan felt the loss already just by talking about it, but if that's what it took to free her from him then he would let her go no matter the cost to him. And he was sure that even if ending the bond was painless, losing her would not be.

But there was one more obstacle to overcome.

Rayen.

Callan suggested, "This all depends on whether Rayen will agree to end the bond."

"You think she'll want to keep it?"

Would she? Callan shut down that direction of thinking because it was not productive. "Uh, no, I don't think so."

"And you do want to sever it, right?" Kaz asked, suspicion floating through the air.

Callan growled, "Of course I do."

"In that case, there is nothing for you to say or do, because it works best if she lets go without being coerced or guilted into it," Kaz explained, but a hint of mischief in his voice alerted Callan that he was missing something.

"What exactly are you saying, Kaz?"

"That it's really very simple. You just make sure she knows you aren't interested in her and all she has to do is shift her heart to another male for the bonding to begin disintegrating."

Callan envisioned Rayen with another boy when she went home with Tony and Gabby. It took a moment for him to realize his skin colors were shifting. He fisted his hands and stopped the reaction. When he had control of his voice, he flipped his reply at Kaz with an indifference he didn't feel.

"I suppose I'll just have to wait until she finds someone when she returns to the past."

"Not really. I forgot to mention something."

"What?"

"It doesn't work unless the female becomes attached to another MystiK male."

Callan almost chuckled in relief and replied too quickly, "That's not going to happen."

"Don't be so sure."

"It's illogical," Callan argued. "She's going back to the past where there are no ..." His words trailed off at the knowing gleam in Kaz's eyes. He wouldn't dare. "What are you really trying to say, Kaz?"

"It depends on if you're truly sincere about ending the bonding connection with Rayen and keeping knowledge of it from everyone else. You know I'll always hold your confidence, but I'm only going to ask once more. Are you *sure* you want to break this connection with her?"

Kaz had never addressed Callan in a tone this serious.

If Callan said no, he was turning his back on his people and his duty to the Warrior House. If he said yes, he was handing Rayen to Kaz. His gut was tied into a hundred knots and the word had to be dragged from his throat. "Yes."

"Then you won't care who she turns to now, will you? Because if you do, you'll prevent the bond from severing. Do you care to whom she moves her affections?"

"No."

Kaz gave a brief bow meant to acknowledge his position beneath Callan's rule. When Kaz stood upright, he said, "Then by your consent, I will do my best to break this bond before daylight."

He walked away and Callan forced his feet to stay rooted in place. He didn't want to bloody his best friend.

Callan finally released the pent-up breath he'd been holding when he realized his lungs were threatening to explode. Wait. He was getting stressed for no reason.

Daylight would be in a matter of hours. Not even Kaz could win Rayen's affections that quickly.

Could he?

CHAPTER 24

RAYEN LEFT V'RU AND WANTED nothing more than to find a hole to climb in and wallow in her misery. The harder she searched, the less she found out about herself and the more she hurt for C'raydonians.

When she stepped back into the central area of the village, most of the children were gone. The few who remained were being walked to a communal structure where she'd seen several bedding down.

She spotted Tony who was helping Jaxxson carry what was left of the meat into that same building. When Tony came out licking his fingers, he walked over to her. "We have until mid-morning here to get back home in time."

"For what?" Not that she wanted to keep him here any longer than necessary, but she wasn't as concerned over this Takoda as she probably should be.

"Gabby said you got some tribal guy coming by to see you and I told Hannah I'd meet her at four. I can't be late."

"We're doing okay on time, though, right?"

He scratched his neck. "I'm keeping an eye on time the best I can, but with four hours here equaling one hour back home it's only an educated guess without a functioning watch. Smart money says to err on the side of returning early and we still don't have a control panel for tomorrow, Xena."

He could be annoying at the worst times but calling her Xena was becoming something she recognized as his way of being friends. "Did you talk to V'ru?"

"Yes, but I forgot to ask about the control panel. He got cranky so I didn't push it."

"Cranky?" she asked, confused over that term.

"Irritated with me."

That reminded her. "Did you two have a disagreement over something?"

Tony was studying his hands and scrunched his mouth into a frown. "Sort of. He has the information I need to build a winning Top Ten computer and won't give it up."

"Did you yell at him?"

Tony lifted his appalled gaze. "No. Did he say that?"

Now Tony sounded wounded. What was with those two? "No, but he seemed ... sad and I know he likes you."

"Not anymore."

"He's just a little boy."

"I know that, Xena. I wouldn't do anything to hurt his feelings and I'd like to go a round with that SEOH who put V'ru here, but SEOH's a pansy. He'd never show up here and get his hands dirty."

What was a pansy? Never mind. She didn't want to know. "Will you try to fix things with V'ru before we leave?"

"Sure, but we ain't goin' nowhere without a control panel. You didn't happen to ask Warrior Guy while you were out huntin' the kids, did ya?"

"No, but I will ask Callan."

Kaz stepped up beside her. "Ask him what? I might be able to help."

Tony didn't wait for her to answer. "Do you have any idea what happened to the transender control panels in the burned-out area where we landed?"

"No, but I doubt Callan would either. I can go search for it in the morning," Kaz offered.

"Sounds good to me, buddy," Tony said.

Kaz added, "We can't go to transender sites with less than two though and I would rather not pull another warrior from the village." He turned a smile made of solid charm on Rayen.

Tony cocked an eyebrow at her. "Well, Xena?"

"Sure. I'll go." What else could she say?

All at once, she felt eyes on her back, which couldn't be Zilya and Etoi because they were approaching from behind Tony, who faced her. Gabby and Jaxxson walked out of the communal building glancing back and forth at each other with a secret smoldering between them.

That left only one set of eyes that would be drilling a hole through her. She turned and so did Kaz at the same time. His arm bumped hers. She cut her eyes at him in time to see him staring down at her with heat stirring in his.

What was going on with Kaz?

She searched for Callan who was emerging from the heavily wooded area he'd disappeared into earlier.

His gaze took in Kaz, then landed on her.

Their eyes locked for a moment, which was over too quickly when Callan snatched his attention away from her faster than a thrown spear. She felt his rejection deep in her stomach. Kaz had made Callan's position about her clear and Callan was keeping his distance. She had to do her part, so she leaned over toward Kaz who dropped his head close to hear her when she turned to speak to him.

"Remember what you were telling me about Callan and that connection thing?" She didn't want to say bond with the risk of someone hearing her.

"Yes."

"How do I disconnect? I want to do it so it's easy for him."

Kaz let go of a breath that rushed out like a sigh. "By making him believe that you are not interested in him. The minute he sees that you no longer care for him, it will begin to sever naturally."

There was nothing natural about the ache clawing through her at the thought of convincing Callan she didn't care about him. But she had no right to interfere in his life. Unlike her, he *would* have a life once he got out of here and his family *would* expect Callan to bond with his future wife. She had to accept that he'd forget about her when a new girl came along.

She couldn't leave this connection thing dangling between them.

Breaking it was going to leave a gash in her heart that not even her power could heal.

But for her to allow this start of a bond to continue would be dishonorable.

She nodded to let Kaz know she understood.

When Callan called everyone over to where he stood, Kaz walked at her side. Callan didn't look right at her, but she knew he missed nothing in his peripheral vision.

Zilya and Etoi stood on one side. Kaz and Rayen were opposite them with Callan on their right, leaving Gabby and Jaxxson on their left.

Kaz took her hand.

She almost snatched it back, but his grip was tight, and she didn't want to cause a scene.

Callan started to speak but glanced at their hands and paused. The silence that ensued had her squirming inside.

She swore she saw a flash of anger in his eyes, then hurt, but he cleared his throat and spoke with authority, ignoring her, so maybe she imagined it. "We have to make plans for tomorrow's defense."

Etoi jumped in. "Give these three over to the TeK and we will need no defense." She glared at Rayen. "Two children sleep in an enemy holding tonight because of you."

Rayen would not miss Etoi once she left here. She told her, “I’d trade myself for those children in a heartbeat. We couldn’t find the TecKnati camp, or I would have.”

“Didn’t try hard enough,” Etoi countered.

“Enough!” Callan shouted at Etoi. “I will not tolerate constant dissent in this village.”

“You are not our leader. Zilya is.”

Callan moved so fast Rayen wondered if he did it with magic, but one moment he was standing next to Kaz and the next he had a hand around Etoi’s throat.

Her eyes flared with fear, but she didn’t say a word. Callan’s grasp didn’t appear to be harming her, only silencing her snarling words.

Zilya said, “Showing your brute force isn’t–”

“Shut up, Zilya, or you’re next.”

Zilya’s lips parted for a second in shock, then she closed her mouth and kept her thoughts to herself.

Rayen glanced at Kaz who was watching Callan with a strange look of confusion that she shared. Callan prided himself on not losing his temper, but if she had to guess he was a hair from everyone finding out just how dangerous that temper could be.

He spoke whisper soft, a threatening sound with a core of steel. “Who am I? I’m the person who will make you regret the day you were born if you do not start pulling your weight and showing respect. The lives of these children depend on us working together. I don’t care what your opinion is of me, but you will keep it to yourself, and do as I order or your presence is of no use to any of us. Am I getting through this time? If so, blink once. If not, blink twice, because I have a place to hang you upside down until we come to an understanding.”

Etoi blinked once very carefully.

He released her and she stumbled back a step, eyes filled with reluctant respect that hadn’t been there before.

Callan returned to his original position. Once there, he continued with what he’d been saying. “We must ensure that our defenses are secure, because there’s a tribe of Uberon warriors who have threatened to come for the Uberons within our village after I refused to hand them over.”

“We’re being attacked again?”

They all turned at the sound of V’ru’s voice. She heard Callan’s sigh end on a growl. He muttered, “I should have been more careful.”

She started to go to V’ru, but Tony stepped away from their group and walked over then squatted down. "There's nothin' to worry about, V'ru Man. Callan's just makin' sure everything's buttoned up." Tony turned to Callan. "I'm goin' to check out V'ru's area like you wanted."

V'ru's wide eyes moved from Tony to Callan who seemed relieved.

Callan hadn't said a word about Tony checking out anything, but he said, "Thanks."

Tony gave a nod of understanding and stood up, talking low to V'ru. "Show me your crib, V'ru Man."

"I am too old for a crib and the only furniture of that type is now in museums."

"Your cultural references need some updating." Tony's voice trailed off as they walked around the corner of the communal building.

Then the rest of them turned back to Callan who started issuing orders. "Etoi will take first watch and rotate through all four security points every twenty minutes."

She said nothing, but there was no doubt that she would do as ordered as long as Callan was in the village.

He turned to Zilya next. "Since you pulled Etoi from her guard duty last night, you can take the second watch."

Zilya's eyes held a threat that promised blood would spill at some point. She might have been slapped down, but that didn't stop her from having her say. "The intruders can*not* bed down in the central area. This poses too much of a risk to the children unless you intend to stand guard over them tonight, *Callan*."

Jaxxson interjected, "Gabby will stay in the healer's hut where I can have use of her gifts for healing the children." He took Gabby's hand and led her away, not waiting for anyone's approval.

Gabby tossed a quick look over her shoulder at Rayen and winked or she'd have gone after her friend to make sure Gabby wasn't being dragged off involuntarily.

No, she'd gone very willingly.

Rayen seriously doubted Gabby was going to be doing any healing tonight, but maybe that was Jaxxson's way of saying he intended to help her figure out more about her reactions. If he'd said anything about that, Zilya would have started shouting about how Gabby was a threat to the village.

"You didn't answer me, Callan. Where will this one sleep?"

"Worry about your duties, Zilya," Callan said, dismissing her question.

Zilya and Etoi left in a huff, whispering to each other.

Rayen stood there with Kaz, feeling all kinds of uncomfortable. Where would she stay?

Kaz took her hand in his and she turned into a statue, unsure of what to do when Callan's eyes zeroed in on them. He didn't move. Didn't say a word, but his jaw muscles flexed.

She guessed that pretty much confirmed what Kaz had been trying to get across to her. Callan might feel something for her just as she did for him, but he would put his people first.

Kaz tugged her to the left, telling her, "I can find a place for you."

They made two steps when Callan ordered, "Rayen!"

Her heart jumped in her chest. Every brain cell was screaming at her that she was being a fool to consider turning around.

Was he calling her back because he couldn't let her walk away? Or would she turn around to find out she was creating possibilities in her mind that had no chance to be reality?

She wasn't sure what Callan wanted, but her name had been issued as an order. She tried to turn back.

Kaz wouldn't let go. What to do?

Callan spoke again and with just as much power, but she wanted to believe she heard a yearning, too, when he said, "Come here, Rayen."

She whispered, "Let go, Kaz."

Kaz lifted her hand and kissed her fingers. "If you turn around, it will be a mistake."

He was right, but that evidently had no influence on her wayward heart. "It's my mistake to make."

He gave her a grim look of acceptance and released her.

She swung around. "Yes?"

"Follow me."

She didn't have a chance to ask where because Callan had turned and was striding off. Did he think she'd just follow like a lost pupple?

Evidently, because Callan never even glanced back.

She was losing count of how many times he'd been high-handed today, so she turned back to Kaz who had observed the whole thing. "Where's he going?"

"My guess would be to create a kamara for you to stay in tonight so that nothing can get to you, and so you won't be moving around on your own."

"He thinks he's going to lock me in some bubble room and expects me to go willingly?"

Kaz said nothing, just watched her with those gorgeous deep green eyes.

"I have no idea what life was like where I grew up, but I *do* know I am not someone who bows to anyone. What did *you* have in mind?"

His skin colors shifted, but the emotion was easy to read when his lips spread with a smile that probably had hearts doing backflips where he came from.

Kaz extended his hand. "Would you like to come with me?"

Should she? Why not?

Callan hadn't asked her anything. If what Kaz said was true, which she had no reason to doubt, Callan thought to lock her away. She took a step toward Kaz.

He reached for her hand.

She pulled away from him. "Don't, Kaz. I've already made the mistake of letting my heart get twisted up over one MystiK. I can't do that again. You're both returning to a world I can't go to, plus I'm leaving here tomorrow."

His fingers caught hers. He leaned close enough for her to feel the heat from his body. "I am not bound to a future like Callan. I am my own man and I want to spend whatever time we can together."

His lips moved slightly. She knew he wanted to kiss her.

She put a hand on his chest that was covered with smooth muscle and gave him a small push.

He backed off an inch, then cocked his head and declared. "You will fall to my charms. I will not be denied."

"How have you managed for so long on so little self-esteem?"

He laughed from deep in his chest. "I like you. Let's go." Then he grabbed her hand again, undeterred by her sigh.

How could she not like this guy? He made her smile when it was the last thing she thought possible. She followed Kaz past the communal building and through the wooded area. They walked beyond where she'd stopped to see V'ru earlier but stayed inside the secured area.

She would not wallow in hurt over Callan's abrupt attitude.

Should she have gone with him?

No.

Tagging along after he'd ordered her like one of his MystiK underlings would have made her look weak. She hated giving up what little time they had left, but evidently it didn't bother him, because he hadn't come after her.

How did things get so confusing?

When Kaz let go of her hand, she looked up to see a strange netting stretched horizontally between two trees. It was made of woven vines and had a carved limb on each end that kept it open wide.

"This is where I'll spend the night," Kaz announced, watching her for some reaction.

She studied his hanging bed. "What is that?"

"An old design my uncle taught me. It's called a hammock. They had them in the past. They were once made from weaving ropes and were beds on ships that crossed the oceans."

"Are you a historian, Kaz?"

He winked at her again. "Sometimes."

Grabbing one edge of his hammock, he flipped his body onto the odd-looking bed that swung gently with the movement once he landed and stretched out. "Want to try it?"

Some niggling feeling told her the correct answer was no, but her other choice was sleeping on the ground or locked in a giant white bubble.

CHAPTER 25

CALLAN STORMED AHEAD, GRINDING HIS back teeth. He couldn't allow the bonding between him and Rayen to gain any strength, but how was he going to do his part to help sever it when his blood still boiled at seeing Kaz touch her?

Killing his best friend would be frowned upon but knocking the grinning fool off his feet was acceptable.

Callan would find a quiet place to talk to Rayen and explain about what had happened. Then he'd tell her that he'd figure out how to fix what he'd started once he had a chance to speak with V'ru.

V'ru would know what could be done and he'd have no ulterior motive. Callan would trust Kaz to protect his back in any fight but not with a girl like Rayen. Kaz enjoyed a challenge and Rayen was every bit of one.

Once Callan explained everything to Rayen ...

All of a sudden, the silence caught up to him.

He turned and found ... no one. What happened to Rayen? She'd been right behind him.

Hadn't she?

Was she lost?

Not Rayen. She was just as at home in the woods as he was, and this entire area was secure so she wouldn't be in danger. Had she wandered off?

He stared, trying to see her among the weave of trees, but she wasn't there. Did she not understand to follow him? Or did she think he was going to chase after her? That day would never come. He had never chased a girl.

The ones back home had always come to him.

Pretty females, who were easy on the eyes and did not cause constant trouble. They smiled and agreed with whatever he asked them to do, like following him.

They were easy, period.

Rayen was the complete opposite.

Nothing was easy or simple about her. She didn't listen to him and, if she did, she ignored what he told her to do. Then she put herself in danger for everyone, even the TecKnati.

But that's what makes her special.

He slapped his forehead at that thought. She was not someone to think of as special. She was someone he had to break the bonding with and send back to a place where she'd stay safe.

So where was she now?

Callan took several steps back the way he'd come, not because he was going after the hardheaded girl. She was simply his responsibility for as long as she remained in this village, and he wouldn't leave her to bed down on the ground when everyone else had a place to sleep.

Even Kaz slept in his swinging bed.

Callan paused on his next step.

Kaz wouldn't dare take her to sleep there.

His common sense said, *Of course he would.*

Hot rage rushed over Callan's skin at the image of Rayen in Kaz's swinging bed.

Kaz would need that bed to heal in if he touched her. Callan reminded himself that he needed Kaz healthy to face the Uberons tomorrow.

He took a step and halted. What was he thinking? To go after Rayen? What if he did find her with Kaz?

Callan would look like a jealous idiot.

No girl was worth acting a fool over.

Especially one that turned his insides into a battleground every time she came near him.

He gave another long look at the path, struggling against indecision, the Achilles heel of a warrior.

CHAPTER 26

"DO YOU MISS YOUR TREE house?" Gabby asked Jaxxson.

Jaxxson had been stacking feathers into two piles on the floor of the hut if you could call a space with no roof a hut.

He replied without looking up, sounding distracted as he corrected her. "It was not a tree house. It was a Healing Hut."

She smiled at his need to be specific. "You were *inside* a ginormous tree. That qualifies. But you are correct. An actual tree house is built really high *up* on the limbs sticking out from the tree."

"What?" He looked over at her, his face scrambled with trying to figure out what she was talking about.

Gabby laughed, enjoying his company again. She'd never spent time with boys her age. They didn't want to be around the weird girl, and she wouldn't risk touching anyone and opening the door to their thoughts. When Jaxxson taught her how to shield her mind, he'd given her the freedom to enjoy a simple hug.

He'd also wound himself around her heart and raised her blood pressure every time he smiled at her, which he wasn't doing right now. She stopped chuckling and explained, "Where I come from, a tree house is built for kids around V'ru's age."

"I didn't think children in your time exhibited powers. Can they levitate?"

"No, they can't."

"Then why would you put children in trees?"

Gabby made a mental note to be careful what she teased Jaxxson about. "It's a playhouse with a ladder to the ground. The kids climb up there."

"Why? Are they unwelcome at home?" He was concentrating hard now.

For Pete's sake, this was getting complicated. "No, I mean yes." She had to hold her patience. "Kids think of a tree house as their personal space, a place to hide out–" She held up her hand. "Before you ask me, nothing is hunting them. It's a private place to play. See?"

"Not really, but I will ask V'ru to show me this from the past."

Gabby had a feeling V'ru would be just as confused about children his age climbing trees and hiding out to play games, but a picture had to be worth twenty words if not a thousand. She gave up. "Anyhow, do you miss your Healing Hut or do you like being in this open space better?"

"I do miss it." He didn't complain, just stated a truth.

"Why haven't you done the same thing here? I saw a big tree inside the protected area that should work."

"We actually chose this setting because of that tree, but I'm closer to the children out here and more available for defense if need be. Besides, I haven't had time to set up a proper hut yet."

Gabby looked around the fifteen-by-twelve room formed by walls of huge feathers that were strapped together and attached to a frame of rough-hewn posts. She stroked her hand down the closest feather. Her fingers sank into thick blue plumes that started as a blue fit for royalty and ended with gold and red tips. The thing had to be six feet tall. "What kind of bird has feathers this big?" she mused out loud.

"Not a bird. A tortalone."

"What the heck is that?"

"It would be easier to show you than explain it. We find the feathers left behind after they shed them but have not spotted the group."

"Then how do you know what it is?"

"V'ru."

Of course, the miniature technological and supernatural prodigy who could spout any detail of history, call up a holographic computer monitor from thin air and determine what era you were born in by simply rubbing a drop of blood between his small fingers.

But Gabby would bet he'd never dressed up like a pirate or gotten his hands dirty playing in the dirt.

Jaxxson finished piling feathers into a makeshift bed and checked drying plants that were strung on a length of vine, just like he'd kept in his tree hut. Her gaze tracked to the stack of bowls he used to mix herbs, but they were sitting on the floor in one corner. He didn't have the counter space he had in the tree hut or the floating bed he'd levitate to a height for dealing with his patients.

Everything reminded her of just how hard this life had been on all the children, but especially on the older teens who struggled to provide food, clothing and lodging for the village while trying to keep them safe and healthy.

What would happen to all of them? Would Jaxxson and the others really get to go home? Gabby would never see him again, but nothing was worth his staying here.

Even when never seeing him again already hurt just to think about.

The trembles hit her out of the blue. She thought it was the ground shaking with an earthquake until Jaxxson snatched his hands back from the plants and swung around to face her.

"What's happening, Gabby?"

"I don't know ... I thought I was fine ..." She saw a face waver into view on the far side of the room. "Who is ..."

Jaxxson blocked her view when he lunged forward and grabbed her shoulders. "Look for your power."

Everything was out of focus, like a picture shaking. "Do what?"

"Pay attention, Gabby!"

She yanked her mind together enough to shout, "Don't yell at me."

"Take possession of your power. Now. You're going to wreck the village and hurt the children."

That got through when nothing else could. "Okay." She closed her eyes and searched for what she'd found earlier today when her body had tried to nuke the place.

She found the glowing green mass of energy inside that was throbbing and shooting tiny lightning bolts she knew from experience would grow more powerful, and quickly. Using what she learned earlier today, she tried wrapping her mind around the energy.

But that didn't work.

Heh. What now?

She trembled harder.

Jaxxson was whispering words of encouragement or at least that's what she hoped he was doing because she couldn't understand him. His hands were clamped on her shoulders, an anchor in a wild storm. Her teeth started chattering with volcanic eruption going on in her muscles.

She opened her eyes. "I can't do it. I tried what I did today, but it's not working."

Concern deepened in Jaxxson's gaze, but his voice was the kind of calm that came from functioning under pressure all the time. "Tell me what it looks like."

"You don't know?"

"I'm not a Hy'bridt." He was urgent but gentle when he said, "You must hurry. I have wrapped you in a spell, but nothing can contain a Hy'bridt for very long."

"Can you see it if you come into my mind?"

Jaxxson hesitated when he'd been pushing hard for her to fix this. "If I do, I'll have to pierce the veil in your mind to witness your power."

"Will it hurt?"

"No, but to do that is to open the path for bonding. That is something only done between two who wish to begin the ritual of an eternal bond."

She was not in the best place to make life and after-death decisions, but her entire body started vibrating. That energy started seeping into the ground at her feet, buckling jagged slashes of dirt.

"Do it, Jaxxson."

When he still hesitated, she said, "It only starts a bond, right? No harm to you?"

"Correct."

"Then. Do. It."

He pushed inside her mind and in the midst of all the crazy shaking she had a moment of bliss that she'd never be able to describe to a normal human.

Jaxxson's rich voice spoke inside her head. *Show me the core of your power.*

Gabby shoved everything away except getting Jaxxson to plug the well of power threatening to explode inside her. She felt his mind partner with hers as she turned and headed straight for her base of energy, which was now sprouting brilliant green lightning bolts in all directions. Shouldn't that hurt? But it didn't. Being inside her body was like going underwater and feeling wrapped in a safe cocoon. But no one else would be safe if she didn't get her power under control.

Jaxxson spoke softly. *Join with your power. The problem is that you somehow trigger the energy into reacting and it has no direction.*

How do I join something like that?

By diving into it.

No way.

Do it, Gabby, he ordered, echoing her words back at her. *The energy won't harm you. It serves you and right now it's looking for you.*

Only *she* would have pet energy that could get lonely and blow up a small city. She mentally squared her shoulders and forced her way into the center of all that fiery green. It was like diving through heat, then into a cooling bath. Not icy as she'd thought, at least not to her. No telling what it might do to someone else.

Green wrapped around her in a lazy fog, swirling and soothing. She could make millions off a spa made of this stuff. No stress. No doubts. No weirdness. Just a healing balm that she never wanted to leave.

Gab...by, a faint voice called from far away.

Hmm?

Come back...

Too far.

We need you. Come back. Please, come back.

She stirred at that. No one had ever said they needed her. Not unless there was more attached like "I need you to go away and leave me alone" or "I need you to get your homework done on your own." She listened for the voice.

Then she leaned toward the last place she'd heard the voice and pushed her way out of the cocoon, searching for the person who needed her. It was a dream. An illusion. Just like the rest of her life.

Nobody would ever need a freak.

You are not a freak! Jaxxson roared in her mind.

That snapped her back to life. She shoved him out and opened her eyes, telling him, "Stop yelling at me."

But the look on his face silenced her. She'd seen icy indifference, anger, and a sweet calm cross that handsome face, but never the terror riding his eyes right now.

He wrenched her to him in a crushing hug. "You disappeared."

Really? "You told me to join with the energy," she mumbled, since her face was pressed against him. His chest moved in and out with deep gulps of air.

And what a nice chest. Solid and warm. She'd missed so much in her life, afraid to have any physical contact. She wanted to stay right here in this moment with Jaxxson's arms wrapped around her. This was what she'd longed for, to be held as if she were cared about.

"I almost lost you."

She barely heard that, but the words sounded wrenched from him. Her heart wobbled. "I was right here."

"No, you weren't. You can't do that again. I'm the wrong one to help you. I thought you only needed to take control, that your powers might be evolving, but I didn't think they'd do that until–"

Sliding a hand up between them she pushed back a little. "Whoa, take it easy. I'm fine. No harm, no foul. I didn't wreck the village. All's good."

He eased his hold, looking down at her. "You don't understand. I heard rumors about a Hy'bridt who disappeared while being trained. She just vanished one day. I didn't believe it because there is so much misinformation sometimes, but I saw you starting to vanish. I could feel you slipping from me."

"What did I do wrong?"

He lifted his hands to cup her face. "I don't know. I'm the one who was wrong. I've been ordering you to gain control but–" He swallowed, his eyes for once hiding nothing. A jumble of emotions raced across his face, but one was very clear, and he gave it words. "I thought I'd lost you. Losing both hands would be easier."

She'd never heard anything so wonderful.

He leaned down and she went up on her toes, meeting him halfway on the kiss. This one started slow and sweet, his lips moving over hers with teasing gentleness, then heat rushed through her when he deepened the kiss. She hooked her arms around his neck, and he lifted her closer, answering the urgency of her kiss with a hungry desire of his own.

Jaxxson's mouth was almost too perfect, but in a very male way. Firm lips. He kissed with experience, where she was a novice. If she thought about it, she could get good and jealous over someone else in her shoes.

What if he did have someone back home?

What if she was better at this?

No one kisses better than you, Jaxxson whispered in her mind.

She paused the kiss and asked, "Did you enter my mind without an invitation, mister?" But she was only teasing.

"Never. It's the start of the bonding. If you're distressed, I can feel it and as soon as that happens, your thoughts come flying into my mind unless you stop them."

"So, you heard my stupid thoughts."

"Gabby, I don't–"

She pushed away and crossed her arms. "As long as you heard them, then tell me. Is there someone at home?"

"No."

"But you've been with other girls, and I've been with no one."

His eyes darkened and, for a healer, he had a surprisingly intense air about him at times. "I'm the first to kiss you?"

A simple question, but the words were so loaded with testosterone that Gabby fought off a shudder at the intimate sound.

He hadn't asked for confirmation and shouldn't need it, since he was the one who'd taught her how to shield her mind when someone touched her skin.

Evidently, she needed remedial training since he'd heard her thoughts a moment ago. She scowled at the male gleam in his eyes. "Of course, you're the first to kiss me. That doesn't mean I'm happy about ranting mentally like a jealous twelve-year-old."

He grinned.

She might dig out a wad of that green energy and blast him with it. "Not helping your case right now."

"You forgot what I told you."

"You say a lot of things. I try to ignore most of it." Liar. But she wasn't admitting she hung on his every word at this point.

Taking a step forward, he was so close she could see tiny flecks of gold in his brown eyes. If she were like any other sixteen-year-old girl, she'd know what it was to be kissed by a guy. One very hot guy.

But for all that she'd tested Mensa level, she was a loser when it came to relationships. Had never had one. Didn't know how to act.

Jaxxson watched her with patience that was starting to get on her nerves. She growled at him. "What do you want now?"

"I'm just giving you time to work it all out in your mind."

What should she say to that? "I'm done."

"Good, because I want you to hear me this time."

"Hear what?"

"That kissing you is like nothing else I've ever felt."

How did he do that? Tick her off one minute and fix it with a handful of words the next?

She felt a thump on her mind. Let him in or not? She did and he swept inside, telling her, *Close your eyes.*

Why?

I want to kiss you in a way that I've never kissed anyone else.

Oh. She closed her eyes. Then she felt his warmth fill her mind at the same moment his lips touched hers. It was as if their mouths joined into one, the emotion filling up every space inside her with a rush. Colors swirled in a kaleidoscope river, churning, and rolling, until she was in that river and part of it.

Jaxxson's deep voice rumbled inside her. *Never doubt that you are amazing. Unequaled.*

She kissed him back but could no longer tell where she ended and he began.

The flush of bliss she'd experienced when he'd first pierced that veil in her mind was nothing compared to the rush of incredible sensations that barreled through her now.

The kiss ended and she couldn't get her breath. Her fingers gripped his upper arms, but his hands cupped her waist. Always holding onto her.

Raising her eyes to his, she whispered, "Never."

"Never what?"

"You'll never lose me, Jaxxson."

He stared into her eyes for so long she thought he was going to speak to her in her mind, but he voiced his words. "Never is a long time. I can heal anything physical, but I don't know how to repair the veil."

"Why would you?"

His fingers slid into her hair, gently removing one ponytail at a time as he explained. "A bond is a union of two souls that can never be broken. It lasts forever."

"Like marriage?" She sounded breathless, but Jaxxson either didn't notice or liked what he heard and left it alone.

"Much more than uniting as a couple. In my world, men and women join as one in marriage and love deeply, but some bond their souls so they will always find each other every time they are reborn."

Gabby had never been able to imagine finding one man to spend the rest of her life with much less one to go through eternity with. Having Jaxxson fingerbrush her hair loose was so relaxing she should be falling asleep but hearing him out on this bonding was imperative. "What else happens?"

Once he had her hair falling to her shoulders and below, he seemed content to return his full focus to her. He put the palm of his hand on her face and brushed his thumb over her lips. "Once bonded, the souls will feel each other's emotions and know where the other one is when they are apart."

That sounded like the ultimate commitment of love. "Why wouldn't everyone who got married bond?"

"Because not everyone is willing to risk their future. Every time their soul returned to live in a body, it would not love until it found its eternal mate."

"What if that didn't happen?"

"Two bonded souls always find each other."

She wanted that. To know she had a connection forever with someone. No, not with someone, but with Jaxxson. But she wouldn't ask that of him because it would mean him never bonding with someone at home. Was there another girl who would ever feel what she did for Jaxxson?

A light glowed behind Jaxxson, drawing Gabby's attention.

There was that figure again—the face she'd glimpsed earlier, right before she'd almost disappeared into her own power. The shape wavered in and out of view, trying to form. Dark shadows moved around the light, poking at it, but the figure was turning into a boy.

She asked, "Do you have ghosts here?"

Jaxxson looked down at her then twisted around to look where she was staring.

The boy's form shimmered again as if the dark shadows were trying to prevent his body from filling in, but his image kept developing from the legs up.

"What are you looking at, Gabby?" Jaxxson turned back, frowning with confusion.

She lifted her head to face him. "You didn't see something like a spirit?"

"No. What or who does it look like?"

"I don't know–" The words died in her throat when she looked back. "That can't be right."

"Why?"

She studied the translucent face of an attractive teenager who had skin the color of cocoa and the regal bearing of one born to rule, because this one had come from the MystiK Governing House. She was staring at Mathias, but that couldn't be him if he'd gone home.

Were MystiKs capable of projecting an image?

"What is it, Gabby? You're worrying me."

She felt a cold tap on her mind and opened it without even thinking. The voice that came inside was not Jaxxson's, but a chilling version of Mathias' that said, *Do not tell Jaxxson you can see me if you wish to live. I can help you with your powers or I can turn your energy against you, Hy'bridt, and you will die.*

The image vanished and the cold sucked out of her head just as quickly.

"Gabby, talk to me."

And tell Jaxxson what? That she'd just talked to a ghost of Mathias that everyone thought had gone home? Clearly, Mathias did not want it known that he hadn't survived.

She took the threat to heart.

She was careful this time and shut her mental shields, but she couldn't look Jaxxson in the eyes when she said, "I, uh, I was confused. I'm tired and the lights are playing tricks on my eyes."

CHAPTER 27

THE RED MOON HAD VANISHED, leaving a chill in its wake that seeped through the air and left Rayen feeling even more alone.

She stared up at Kaz who stretched across his floating bed of woven vines. He offered her a hand to help her get up there, since his bed was strung at shoulder-height for her.

It wasn't that she couldn't hoist her body that high, but that she couldn't make herself climb in with him.

He bent an elbow and propped his head, letting his free hand dangle over the edge. "What are you afraid of, Rayen?"

"Nothing."

"Really? Nothing scares you?" he teased.

She hadn't been entirely honest. She was terrified at the possibility that she'd never regain her memories and feared spending her life in a place where she had no one except Gabby and Tony. Even if she could go home to her time, it would be a suicidal wish since all C'raydonians had been wiped out by the K-Virus infection and being hunted.

Oh, yes, she had plenty of fears, but Kaz wasn't one of them.

He rocked his bed with a touch of his foot. "You are worrying, and I want to make it better. You'll be safe with me, and warm. I won't try anything. I give my word."

Was that what was holding her back, a concern that he'd expect something physically from me?

No, she believed Kaz.

She knew what was stopping her from reaching up. She had the ridiculous feeling that if she climbed into that bed, she would be betraying Callan.

How did that make any sense when she wasn't supposed to still be caring about him? She shivered with the falling temperatures and rubbed her arms. "Why aren't you cold, Kaz?"

"I possess a high metabolism. Makes me a natural furnace." He took a deep breath and his chest stretched, which she had a feeling was for her benefit. She had to admit that he had a beautiful body.

Not as nice as Callan's, but ... argh.

She had to quit comparing everything to him.

And she had to admit she was still waiting for something with him. Where was her backbone? Where was her determination to snip this bonding thing?

Callan was the one who'd walked off and hadn't even come back to see what had happened to her.

Forget about him.

There. She was done with stubborn, irritating males.

If she could only get the image of his face out of her mind.

Wind slithered around her, and the chill settled into her bones. She murmured to herself, "I guess this is my only option."

Kaz rolled his eyes. "Try to contain your enthusiasm."

She looked away, not wanting to hurt Kaz's feelings, but unable to show him the same interest he had in her. She should be flattered, and on some feminine level she was, but she was only interested in Kaz as a friend.

Kaz's voice dropped conspiratorially low, barely above a whisper. "Callan has not told you everything, has he?"

She lifted her chin slowly in his direction, using the time to figure out what she wanted to say. But she had little choice other than to admit, "I don't know what you mean."

After a long thoughtful moment, he said, "With Callan's twin brother dead, Callan is the one expected to take his place to unite all the MystiK Houses."

"What if he doesn't want to lead?"

"Whether he does or does not, Callan will do what is expected of him."

She'd seen the lonely place inside Callan that he kept hidden, the part of him that longed for a life he was being denied. She'd heard the echo of that in his voice when he talked about duty and returning home. "It sounds unfair to expect so much from him before he's had a chance to live his life."

"Our world is a turbulent place where we must constantly plan for how best to protect MystiKs in the future. Callan is a born leader, whether he ever recognizes that within himself or not. Right now, he only sees it as a duty, but the truth is that we need him. And for him to lead all seven Houses, he must bond with a MystiK mate equal to him in power and respect. A G'ortian. One has been chosen for him."

"Another warrior G'ortian?"

"No. She is of the Creativity House."

G'ortian, and was there any doubt that she'd be beautiful as well? No.

"Who is she?"

Kaz's eyes softened with sympathy. "Talking about her will only make it hurt more. The point is that he can't take a broken bond to his marriage. He can't allow this to continue with you. Have you ever heard the phrase, any port in a storm?"

"No. What does it mean?"

"My uncle who taught me about ships and hammocks said it meant that a captain turned to any port in a storm. And it also meant that sometimes a man found comfort with a woman at hand even when he might have another at home. Have you considered that this attraction grew only because Callan was stuck here?"

No. She didn't say it, but her face must have answered for her, because Kaz said, "I don't mean to hurt you, only to help you face the truth of your situation and Callan's obligations back home."

Every word from his mouth stabbed her heart, but she would not fault him for being honest. She was not so selfish she would interfere with the life Callan had ahead of him.

But neither would she ever truly be free of him.

"I, however, am quite the available man as I've mentioned," Kaz said, raising his voice and infusing it with levity.

When she pinned him with a don't-go-there look, he merely laughed and extended his hand again. "My word that your virtue is safe ... until you change your mind." He winked.

The word *rogue* slipped into her mind, and it fit him. Unable to scowl in the face of his grin, she gave in and chuckled. She hoped Kaz knew he couldn't take Callan's place in her heart, and he wouldn't risk Callan's wrath by being inappropriate.

She gave in and reached up.

Just as his fingertips touched her, a wash of energy rushed up from behind her. She was scooped off the ground and slung over a shoulder.

She drew back to swing a hard fist at the head attached to that shoulder until a hand came up, catching her fist.

Callan said, "I've got this, Kaz."

He turned and walked off without a word to her.

Was she going to let him get away with this arrogant act again?

She raised her head to see Kaz staring after her with a forlorn look. Had there been more to his offer than only a place to rest? In a matter of seconds, she lost sight of him and turned a day of frustration on her closest target.

"Put me down, Callan."

"No. You don't follow when I tell you."

"Maybe because I don't take orders well."

"That is not news to me."

She couldn't kick her legs, not with them locked in his iron grip. To be honest, she *could* if she was willing to hurt him, but that was the problem. There was no way she would lift a finger to harm Callan.

The next high step he made over a fallen tree shoved his shoulder up into her stomach. She sucked in hard to draw a breath and warned, "I'm going to lose my meal."

With a move made easy by his formidable strength, he pulled her down until he cradled her in his arms. His muscles bulged and flexed with the movement. Kaz had a beautiful body, but he didn't have Callan's powerful build. He was sleek as a deadly predator in the night.

He smelled of the woods and distinctly male, a scent that raised a primal reaction she could deny all she wanted, but her body recognized his and missed him.

He would put her down if she demanded it, but she was beyond tired of fighting and tired of being alone. She didn't want to think about what she faced tomorrow, so she gave up and leaned her head against his shoulder, taking what she could tonight.

This moment.

His body relaxed as soon as she did. He curled her to him. Heat wafted off his skin and she inched closer to soak up his warmth.

Neither of them spoke as he moved through the darkness with the ease of one born to the night. Kaz's words about Callan's future haunted her. Why couldn't she have been born in his time? Why did her people have to end up rabid? Why was she thrown into the past?

Why, why, why? Her head hurt from constant questions.

Callan finally stopped in a small clearing, one just wide enough to take three long strides across the middle. She thought he'd put her down. When he didn't, she looked up to find him staring at her.

He asked, "Why were you with Kaz?"

She was so relaxed from being tucked up next to his heat she said the first thing that came to mind. "To sleep in his floating bed."

Callan's face turned into a stone mask. "Kaz clearly doesn't value life as much as I'd thought."

She snapped out of her lethargic state. "What? No, wait. What are you saying?"

"I said nothing. You're the one who said you intended to bed down with him." Callan dropped her feet to the ground.

She stepped away and crossed her arms. "It wasn't like that. He was just offering me a safe place to rest."

Callan strode over to the center of the clearing, not turning around when he said, "I'm sure."

She'd thought it meant something that Callan had come for her. Why? She knew he would go home to find someone else, so why keep twisting her insides up over him? She wished she had a logical answer for that. He had her emotions flying all over the place. She hated feeling so out of control over a reaction she *should* be able to command.

The temperatures continued to plummet with each passing minute and without Callan's heat she was soaking up the cold.

Her teeth chattered. She was tired and she'd willing left a perfectly warm place to be all but accused of climbing naked into bed with Kaz.

She didn't know which way they'd gone, but she was sure she could find Kaz and he would give her another chance. She was not speaking to this, this ... jerk, to use Gabby's word, again.

Callan just stood in the middle of the clearing, staring away from her.

What was he doing? Conjuring up a bubble room?

Did he really think she'd let him lock her away in a place that she couldn't get out of when she wanted to? She hugged her arms around herself, trying to ward off the chill, but it wasn't working. That reminded her of another new term she'd heard Tony say back at the school.

Screw this. She was leaving.

She made it ten steps and two arms came around her body.

How did he move without her hearing him? "You get one warning, Callan. Get your hands off me or I *will* hurt you."

"Where are you going?"

She wanted to say back to Kaz, but the words caught in her throat. "Leaving. Let. Go. Now."

"No." He drew her back against his chest. "You're freezing."

That was because he'd dragged her away from the only offer of a warm bed she'd had tonight. "Whose fault is that?"

"Mine."

She hadn't expected that answer. "I'm not staying here."

"You haven't seen what I made for you."

"I know. That kamara thing." Why couldn't he just hold her like this all night? She didn't want to sleep locked away by herself.

She felt the briefest touch of his lips on her hair. What was that all about?

"Please come back and see what I made for you." His voice turned rough. For the first time, she noticed how tired he sounded.

Just like that, he melted her resolve. She was clearly demented when it came to him. "I'll come back, but it doesn't mean I'm staying."

He turned her in his arms.

She snuggled up to all that rugged male and lifted her face to his. "You're confusing me."

"I know, but I don't mean to."

"Then don't. Just tell me what's going on."

His hand came up and brushed across her hair, smoothing it down to her shoulders. "There are so many things I wish I could say, but I can't."

"Can't or won't?"

He smiled, a very sad smile. "Sometimes those two are one and the same."

"I don't want to cause you problems."

"You don't," he assured her. "I'm the one who's causing problems."

"Not for me," she whispered.

His eyes met her and the hunger in them stirred an equal one inside her. She understood all the reasons that she shouldn't care for him and that he shouldn't care for her, but what she felt refused to be reasoned away.

She lifted her hand to his face and ran her finger over his lips. He turned, kissing her finger and drawing it into his mouth, teasing the tip with his tongue.

A shiver ran through her that had nothing to do with the temperature outside and everything to do with being this close to him.

She moved her hand up into his hair. He hesitated, then dropped his head, covering her mouth with his. The kiss was everything she remembered from the first two times. Better. She wrapped her arms around his neck. He lifted her with strong arms and a gentleness that left her weak in the knees. He knew she wouldn't easily break but held her as if he wouldn't risk it.

She loved feeling that gentleness inside him that no one else saw. She'd seen shades of him the first time they'd joined their powers to heal a child. He hid pain inside over the brother he'd lost and now more with Mathias gone, but Callan shielded a tenderness she reveled in and had a feeling only she knew about.

His lips demanded and teased. She couldn't get enough of him. Wanting more, she parted her lips for his tongue to sweep in and touch hers. Grabbing his hair, she held on for the kind of kiss she knew she'd never feel with anyone again.

How was she going to leave tomorrow?

She didn't want to be another dark spot on his soul, but neither would she give up even one minute with him.

Maybe she was selfish after all. She could live with that fault for the few hours they had left together.

Callan lifted his head and drew one deep breath after another. She was just as breathless. She slid a hand over his chest until she felt his heart pounding. He covered her hand with his and released a long exhale. "Tomorrow will be here too soon and we'll face another threat. You should go to bed."

Was he going to put her inside then leave?

She hid the turmoil churning through her. He didn't need more grief from her on top of what everyone else dumped on him, so she filled her voice with false enthusiasm. "Show me what you created."

He held her another minute, just long enough for her to die a little more inside at the thought of never feeling his arms around her again. Then he took her hand in his large one and drew her around to face the clearing again.

A shimmering kamara floated just above the ground. She'd been in one of those before. It was shaped like a luminous white bubble about the size of a small bedroom. Jaxxson had made one for healing children who had reactions to the Sphere. He'd infused it with a calming spell of some kind, but she didn't think Callan had that power.

This would just be a place to sleep.

Walking her over to it, he placed her hand up on the wall of the dome and covered it with his. "Lean in and you'll pass through."

She did and the next thing she knew she was inside a space that felt much larger than it appeared from the outside. In the middle was a fluffy cloud bed. That was the only way she could describe it. The temperature inside was as comfortable as being in the sunshine on a mild day in the desert.

Callan stood next to the bed. "Try it out. I know it doesn't look solid, but it is."

She went over and lowered herself to the bed that surprisingly held her. Then she stretched out and it hugged her. The bed really did hug her, and not in a confining way.

When she looked up at Callan, she wanted to ask him to stay with her. To help keep away the empty feeling of being alone that she'd struggled through last night at the school.

But he stepped toward the wall and, without looking back, said, "All you have to do is say when you're ready to leave. I'll hear you."

Then he leaned forward and vanished.

The walls had been glowing, but now they dimmed slowly until it was only a soft glimmer given off by tiny lights. The dome turned into a night sky with twinkling stars. Just enough that she wasn't left in pitch-dark.

She curled onto her side and should have been warm, but she felt cold and hollow. Where had Callan gone that he could hear her if she said she wanted to leave?

He didn't say she had to speak out loud.

Would he hear her thoughts?

Probably not. The only time he'd heard them had been under duress when he had to come inside her mind. But what if he could?

What would she tell him?

She closed her eyes and composed the letter she would write him if she had the materials to do so.

I already miss you, Callan. I know we can't be together, but I wish we had tonight. Am I wrong to want the time we have left? I wish you wanted me to stay. I would. I know you're going home, and I hope you go home soon, but I still want to be with you while you're here.

I understand that you can't allow yourself to care about me, and even if you could, I'm an undesirable C'raydonian.

Energy flooded the dome. All the lights went out.

"*Never* think that I don't desire you," whispered next to her ear as Callan wrapped his arms around me from behind.

Her heart tried to race out of her chest. In that moment, she was cloaked in happiness. Snuggling back against his warmth, she made an *mmm* sound then realized what had happened. "You heard my thoughts?"

"Yes."

"How?"

"I'll explain tomorrow." His lips touched her neck and she shivered. "Sleep now or I'll have to leave."

"Why?"

His sigh was so strong it ruffled her hair. "Because I'm a warrior, not a saint. If you move around much more, I'll have to leave for any hope of showing my face with honor tomorrow."

She smiled at the grumble in his voice. That was as much of a declaration of caring for her as she'd get from him, but it was enough to hold her. For now, and once she left.

But what about the bonding?

She tried to decide if she should bring it up now or wait, but his heat must have been all her body needed to relax and give in to sleep.

The last thing she heard was his whispered words.

"Some things can't be broken."

CHAPTER 28

TONY FORCED HIS EYES TO stay open and hoped this was the last game even if he'd give up a family jewel to see the software design for this thing.

V'ru moved his stick fingers with practically inhuman speed as he played a multi-level game of Capistine Universe on the holographic display. V'ru's private quarters was a giant bubble where they sat on the floor. The skin, or whatever made the dome shape, was a strangely soothing aqua color with clouds. It contrasted with the orange glow of captured planets on the holographic game board shining over V'ru's face.

The game was a futuristic mix of chess and interspace Monopoly played on three planes at one time throughout the holographic board. Gamers back home would be salivating over this thing.

And Tony had no doubt this half-pint genius would destroy the best of them.

V'ru was a closet gamer.

If Tony hadn't offered to play tic-tac-toe with the kid, he'd never have found out about this. V'ru's response had been to give Tony a look normally reserved for someone incapable of tying their shoes.

Once Tony got past the insult, he'd come up with an idea to find out if there was a real kid inside that grim shell. He'd told V'ru, "If I had my electronic games, I could show you some crazy stuff you could take home and use to beat your buddies. See, I don't have any problem sharing, especially a game. I could make you look good."

V'ru had raised that sharp chin and said, "I am certain electronic competitions from my time are far beyond your comprehension."

Nice comeback from a tweener.

Instead of letting his hackles rise, Tony shrugged. "I'm sure you kick butt with little guys your age, but I only play those at elite level. Never met anyone with *those* skills below the age of fourteen. No disrespect, dude, but it takes experience to reach my level."

V'ru Man had gotten that tough guy look in his eye that he had anytime someone dared to question his ability. "I am sure you could not defeat me."

"Guess we'll never know, will we?"

That's when V'ru lifted his hand and made a slashing motion to the side that brought up a hologram of a three-dimensional game with the sickest graphics Tony had ever seen. That had been worth sacrificing a smidgeon of his ego to the munchkin.

At least that was what Tony had thought two hours ago before the kid turned into a four-foot-six, eighty-pound intergalactic conqueror.

V'ru had been generous enough to play the game three times for practice.

The minute Tony cracked his knuckles and declared "game on," V'ru's entire demeanor switched to life-and-death intensity. The mark of a true gamer.

V'ru made a soft growling sound when he concentrated hard, like now as he made two moves and finished the fourth game.

He'd won all four.

Never had Tony accepted defeat with a smile, but he respected ability and more than that he'd finally met the real kid, not a historical data machine walking around in a toga.

V'ru leaned back against his weird cloud bed and released a breath of exhaustion, but the healthy kind that came from doing something that filled your soul. V'ru glanced over at Tony, trying to contain a grin and in a respectful voice offered, "You played well."

"No, I didn't." Tony chuckled. "I got my ass kicked by a half-pint, world-class gamer." He immediately felt guilty for using the word ass in front of V'ru, but the little guy busted up laughing until he fell back on his bed.

Anything that brought this kid out of his funk was worth a little guilt.

"How many others do you game with back home?"

V'ru's laughter died a swift death. "One."

"One? Are you kidding me? You should be playing hundreds, thousands, and showing them who's king of the game."

"Frivolous use of time is frowned upon. If I were at home, I would not be playing games."

What kind of place did these kids live in? "I don't see it as frivolous. Keeps your mind sharp. It's good for hand-eye coordination." Tony could see V'ru listening, but not accepting so he added, "And it's good for your health."

V'ru sat very still, staring ahead, something he did when he searched the vast sea of files in his mind. He angled his head in that confused puppy look. "How does it improve health? Exercising finger muscles?"

"No. Your heart muscle."

"That has never been documented."

Tony knew better than to argue with the ultimate Wikipedia, but he wanted V'ru to realize he was right to enjoy playtime. "But you're wrong. It *has* been documented that all work and no play is unhealthy emotionally, which affects you physically. Health is about balance. You're special and I don't want to take anything away from you about that, V'ru Man, but being a human receptacle for all the known history of man is not who you are entirely. You're a master-of-games and that's no small feat. You deserve to enjoy your life, too. Just remember that and speak up for yourself."

V'ru had stared at Tony, mesmerized by his every word. His mouth opened in a small O and his hands were clasped in his lap. He shut his mouth and shoved a handful of hair off his forehead. "My opinion is never requested, only my information."

"Then give your opinion. It matters. I don't care if anyone wants to hear it or not, you have a right to say if you're not happy with something. You're capable of making your own choices and decisions about things that affect you or your people. Don't ever doubt that."

Every time he got around V'ru, he thought of his little brother. Tony had taught Vinny to stand up for himself and couldn't tolerate anyone walking over V'ru.

Tony stood. "You need to get some sleep. Get me outta here and I'll see you in the morning."

Shoving up to his feet, V'ru stepped over to Tony who took his hand. The next thing Tony knew, he was standing outside in the icy darkness. He let go of V'ru to hurry the kid back inside his toasty hovel.

V'ru turned to his white balloon palace and paused. His head dropped and his shoulders hung low.

"What's the matter, V'ru Man?"

The kid mumbled something.

"Turn around so I can hear you." Tony squatted down to face him.

"I hate sleeping in there." V'ru studied Tony's face, clearly watching for a negative reaction. His teeth started chattering.

Tony stood back up and pulled his hoodie off. "Hold your arms up."

Two matchstick arms shot straight up. Tony slipped the jacket over V'ru's head and arms, tugging it down until it stopped mid-shin. As he lifted the hood up to protect V'ru's head, Tony asked, "Where would you like to sleep?"

"With the others."

The kid was crushing his heart. Of course, he'd want to be with the other kids. "That's where we're taking you."

"But–"

"No buts. Anybody has an issue with that, send them to me." Tony put his hand at V'ru's back to gently get him to start walking to the communal building where kids had bedded down all over the place. The floor had been layered with palm-like branches then covered with something this group had woven from that weird pik-pik bird thread.

Gabby had tried to explain it to Tony, but he didn't need to know about jungle yarn.

When Tony found an open spot among the sleeping children, he motioned for V'ru to take it then Tony looked around for another feather like the ones these kids were using for a blanket. He found a stack in one corner and brought a big feather back to cover V'ru.

"Thank you."

The peace in V'ru's face would be worth any argument Tony faced tomorrow. "You're welcome, V'ru Man."

As soon as Tony started to step away, V'ru whispered, "... tomorrow."

Tony turned back and leaned down, keeping his voice just as soft. "What, V'ru Man?"

"Ask me about the computer tomorrow."

"What do you mean?"

V'ru smiled. "I will tell you what is coming soon to your time. It will not harm the universal order of things to know this."

That was the last thing Tony had expected. He didn't want the kid to feel that he owed anyone for being nice to him. As much as Tony needed that information, it wasn't worth giving this kid the wrong message, but V'ru's eyelids were drooping.

Poor kid probably hadn't had a decent night's sleep since coming here. "Okay, buddy," Tony said. "We'll talk tomorrow."

But there was no way Tony would be leaving with the information he needed now.

CHAPTER 29

RAYEN STIRRED IN THAT HALF world of not awake but not asleep, somewhere she'd been before in her life.

A crackling sound filled her mind just as a small campfire came into view. Yellow and red flames licked at the darkness cloaking the image in her mind. Three figures stood around the fire, chanting a familiar sound, but she couldn't figure out what the words meant.

Two men and a woman, all with a pair of long gray braids that fell to their waists. They wore thick, woven robes that had beautiful geometric designs in subtle, soft browns and muted reds down the sides. The robes were slit and tied together with a complicated weave of thicker threads.

These elders raised their hands up, then dropped them in a pleading motion as they chanted and performed individual roles in some ceremony.

The chanting lost strength until it faded away like mist under a strong sun.

That's when she noticed that none of them stood on the ground. They all hovered inches above the sand and rocks.

Drifting around, they came together as a group to face her.

I knew their faces. Blue-green eyes stared back at her. Was this a memory?

The man on the left had taught her to craft a narrow strip of wood into an *atlatl* that was used to throw a streamlined spear at higher velocity. He'd tied a red-and-black feather to one end as he'd told her that the weapon had originated with their ancestors.

And he'd called the spear a lance.

She tried to dredge up more, but the memory slipped away.

The woman standing in the middle was just as familiar. Rayen stared into an older version of her own face but with wrinkles. A lifetime of experience slept behind eyes just like her aqua blue ones.

Her irritable ghost was the third one in the trio and stood, or floated, on the woman's right.

Did that mean they were all ghosts?

As one, the group drifted forward until they paused two arm lengths away from her. The man on the left spoke first. "You must not turn away from your destiny. Your people have only you to save them."

Her heart was breaking because she *couldn't* save them. They were already dead. What did these ancestors think? That she could do anything to help her family when she was living a hundred years in the past where she didn't belong? They had confused her with someone else.

She told him, "I'm not who you think I am."

The woman said, "We know all about you, *Ashkii Dighin*."

Her heart thundered at the name. She recognized it, but she had to be wrong. If she was right, it meant *sacred child*. Someone who would have been watched over and cared for. If that was the case, why had she ended up here?

Why wasn't the grumpy old ghost who'd informed her that her name was Rayen arguing with this woman?

So confused, she asked, "Who are you?"

"We are your ancestors. I am Yanaba." She lifted a hand toward the man on the left. "He is Gaagii."

Rayen knew those names, too. Her breathing kicked up to keep pace with her racing heart. Gaagii was a name that translated to *raven* and Yanaba meant *brave*.

Yanaba waved at the old ghost on her other side, the one who appeared whenever he wanted, said just enough to confuse her, then disappeared. Why hadn't she noticed that his eyes were like hers during other meetings? Now that she thought about it, his image had never been this sharp or his face so lifelike the other times he'd shown himself to her.

Yanaba said, "This is Bisahalani. You may call him Acheii. He is your great-great-grandfather who watches over you now."

Rayen nodded to acknowledge what she told her. She'd heard the name Bisahalani before. It meant *one who speaks for others* and Acheii was the same as grandfather. She finally recognized something. These people were family. She could at least find out who she was and where she had lived.

This had to be her memory coming back.

Or was it nothing more than a dream driven by the hunger of a girl desperate to have something to cling to? "I have so many questions. Who are my–"

Acheii ordered, "Silence. We did not come to play a child's game of questions."

What? He wasn't going to allow her to ask any questions? That stunned her as much as getting slapped, but she shook it off. She deserved answers. "But I don't know–"

"You know what you must know," Acheii said in his gravelly voice. "We have come to remind you of your duty and your destiny."

"Destiny? What destiny?" she snapped. "How can you expect me to do something when I don't even know who I am?"

Yanaba's voice was calm and soothing. "You are ... Rayen. The blood of C'ray ... through your veins. You were chosen as the one who will save ... and the Damian Prophecy has ... power ... to destroy ..."

Yanaba's words faded with her image, wavering and translucent.

"Wait!" she yelled. "What about the prophecy? I don't understand."

Gaagii said, "A power ... to kill or ..." He flickered in and out. "You must not ... fail." His body lost shape and blinked out. Gone.

"Don't go. Not yet," she cried out. "Help me. Tell me what is going on."

Acheii drifted back as if pushed by a wind. His form shrank, smaller and smaller, and his voice boomed in her head. "The gateway will open. A path will close." He vanished.

"No, please don't leave me!" she screamed, reaching for them. Tears spilled down her face. "Please ... don't leave me."

"Rayen, wake up, sweetheart."

She opened her eyes. Callan leaned on his arm, staring down at her. He was shaking her gently. His eyebrows were drawn tight. "You were reaching out for something. What were you dreaming?"

How could she explain something she wasn't even sure was real? "I don't know, just a ... I don't know."

Using his thumb, he brushed away a tear from her damp cheeks. "You were begging someone not to leave you. Did you mean me?"

She could see in his eyes that he wanted it to be about him, but he also didn't want it to be. She shook her head and gave Callan as much truth as she could. "I think my memory was trying to come back to me. I recognized some people in my dream and when they started disappearing, I guess I panicked."

He leaned down and kissed her forehead then he rubbed his cheek along hers. "I would keep you with me if I could do so without putting you at risk, but nothing is worth that."

Her heart thumped at the deep longing in his words.

But he couldn't keep her, and she couldn't keep him.

He had to go back to his home where a G'ortian beauty waited for him. Someone his House would not just approve of, but a girl who would grow to be the woman other Houses would adore who would stand at Callan's side as he led his people.

Rayen had only one option and that was to return to the past where she'd have to run and hide.

Or face having no control over what they did with her. The Browns would eventually stop trying to find records that didn't exist.

She touched Callan's cheek and kept her hand there when he raised his head. Before he could say something else that would make departing today that much harder, she told him, "I believe you, but we both have people depending on us. Your people need you at home, your village needs you here, and I have to take Tony and Gabby back to their world."

She'd returned to the Sphere expecting to find a way to travel here alone and stay, but that had been a fool's quest. She knew in her heart it would take all three of them to travel through the portal. Maybe she'd forgotten to ask V'ru yesterday, but she probably hadn't wanted to hear the truth. She and Gabby hadn't been able to activate the computer without Tony this time.

They'd all have to be together to return.

She owed Tony for coming this time and had to get him home soon. With the way the time moved here compared to back at the school, they had until the red moon reached what would be mid-morning in the Sphere as their deadline to call up a transender and leave.

Maybe two hours after daylight. And they still had to find a controller first.

It hurt too much to think about leaving so she changed the subject. "When is daylight?"

"Soon. In a little over an hour."

"Kenja said she'd be here this morning. What are you going to do about her?"

Callan's hazel eyes changed, glowing with sparks of red like flickering embers in a fire. "She can't take any of my children, but I don't want to fight her either."

"Your best chance at survival is for her to join your village and you two to work together."

"Agreed. She won't be here until after daylight since the deadly mist prevents traveling while it's still dark. She may be annoying and single-minded, but she's an exceptional warrior who will know the mist rises at night. When she shows up, I'll try to reason with her again. If that doesn't work, I'm not giving up children when I know she will make them fight. The ones I have are young and have not been trained for the threats in this

Sphere."

Callan spoke with the conviction of a leader who would face anything to protect his people, just as Kaz had said.

Rayen wanted Callan to know he wasn't alone. "I can't leave until we find a controller. I'll fight beside you."

"Then I'll be worried about you, too."

All she did was arch an eyebrow at him in response. "Did you just insult me?"

He ran a finger along her cheek. "You're as deadly as any warrior I've ever met, Rayen, but that doesn't stop me from feeling protective of you."

"Just as long as you realize that you can't stop me from standing with you."

"Understood. I'm hoping it won't come to an actual battle. I've been thinking on this, and I have a plan. If Kenja's warriors were older this wouldn't work, but over half of the ones we saw with her are V'ru's age. I'm going to send Zilya, Etoi, Kaz, and Jaxxson out as soon as it's safe and put them in strategic positions. Jaxxson will shield their presence with an herbal concoction that stinks so the Uberons will not smell them."

"We should have had that with us yesterday."

"True. From now on, no one leaves without some in hand. Once my four are in place, I'll wait outside the protective barrier for Kenja to arrive. She'll position her people close enough to cover her back. As soon as Kenja and I start talking, Jaxxson will send a calming spell over her warriors. Kaz, Etoi and Zilya will then create a ward to surround the warriors once Jaxxson has them held in place."

Rayen felt the need to point out, "I like your plan, but Kenja might react badly to that."

"Once I tell her what's at stake, she'll either work with me, or walk away with nothing."

"What's at stake?"

"One of the two children the TecKnati took is Uberon, a second cousin of hers. If you think Kenja is possessive of her warriors, she's ten times more reactive if someone touches her family. I didn't want to tell her yesterday about the boy, because she might have attacked us out of anger at that point. She knows I won't harm any of her warriors, but what she doesn't realize is that once we have control of her force, I will take her children into my village and lock her out."

"Can she survive on her own?"

"Better than with caring for others. At the age of nine, Uberons are dropped in the wilderness during winter without even a knife and left to find their way home—at least a five-day walk."

"What do you think she'll do when she gets here?"

Callan thought on it and said, "She might decide to fight me, but that would be a mistake. She's assuming her skills are superior and they aren't. If we were both MystiK only, we would be well matched. But I'm G'ortian and my powers have been developing faster here than at home. I would never touch a woman in anger, and I have no intention of battling Kenja, but we are taught from day one that to face an Uberon is to face death."

Rayen shivered at the threat in Callan's voice. "How will you keep her out if the protective wall around this village allows MystiKs to enter? She could enter now, couldn't she?"

"I took the time to infuse a warning I would sense if she entered last night. Had any MystiK inside or out touched the protective ward, I would have known immediately and alerted the best fighters. When I take my four outside at daylight, we'll close the ward to all MystiKs. Even us."

"Like I said, I'm fighting with you, and just so you know–I have no qualms about going up against a female warrior."

Callan ran his fingers into her hair and that one touch turned her skin to fire. She felt him everywhere and wanted to feel him closer. She focused on the energy inside her and reached out to bump his mind.

He jerked back and smiled, but she felt the access give way to telepathy.

She sent a question. *Did I hurt you?*

No, but tap a little lighter on anyone else.

The minute his voice filled her mind she was happy.

What are you smiling about? he asked.

You.

He gave her an odd look at that.

She explained, *I like looking at you. I love the colors on your skin, the way your eyes darken and change. I think you're ...* She stopped before embarrassing herself.

I'm what? he prodded.

Might as well tell him or he'd figure it out if her thoughts wandered. *Sweet. I think you're sweet.*

He burst out laughing.

She huffed at his irritating reaction. *Never mind.*

Kissing her on the nose, he said next to her ear, "A warrior isn't sweet, unless it's a female with raven hair and eyes the color of an island lagoon."

He pushed up off the bed and offered her his hand. Swatting his offer away, she slid past him and gained her feet at the foot of the bed, muttering, "I wouldn't want to accuse you of something that might undermine your manhood."

A deep chuckle answered her.

She pulled her hair out of the lopsided ponytail, trying not to think about just how messy she looked first thing in the morning.

"Trust me, sweetheart, you're beautiful in the morning," he said.

She spun around. "Did you hear my thoughts?"

His expression slid from amused to embarrassed. He ran a hand over his own mussed hair. "I guess I caught that thought without thinking. Close your mind and think something. I don't want anyone else picking up your thoughts."

She did as he asked and thought, *I wish you'd kiss me again.*

When his face showed no reaction, she asked, "Well? Did you hear me?"

"No. Be careful to keep your shields up."

"I will." She turned to the domed wall, preparing to leave when she felt him behind her.

He turned her around and kissed her. When he ended the kiss, she said, "You said you didn't hear my thoughts."

"I didn't need to hear the words when I could see it in your eyes."

That might be a bigger problem than someone picking up her thoughts if Zilya or Etoi saw the same thing on her face. She had to pull it together before they got around others.

Starting now, which was why she claimed, "The kiss was nice, but you guessed wrong."

"Why would you lie about that?"

Because she had to start backing away at some point or she'd never take a step toward leaving. "You want the truth? I'm trying to get my face to where it doesn't reveal what I feel when I look at you."

He took her hand, placing it between his and the wall. Nothing happened and she realized he was hesitating. He didn't look at her when he spoke. "We're agreed that you will leave today ..."

"Yes." She knew this was it for them, but that hadn't been the last thing she wanted to hear before they stepped out of here.

Kaz's *any port in a storm* comment chipped away at the happiness she'd allowed herself to feel. She wanted to ask Callan about the G'ortian girl Kaz had mentioned. Had she only been a diversion until Callan returned home or because he expected to never see her again?

She said she would accept last night with no regrets.

She stood behind her word when she gave it to others. It had to count with herself, too.

"All I'm saying is–"

She finished the sentence for Callan. "We deal with Kenja then find the controller for our transender and we get out of everyone's hair."

He frowned, but said, "Basically, yes."

His sigh came out so heavy that she felt the need to make this easier for him. "We both knew we would only have last night, Callan."

Looking away from her, his chest heaved with a deep sigh. "I wish I could send the rest of this village with you. Even if it meant sending them to the past. They would be safer with you than me."

She hated the lack of confidence she heard in his voice. He wasn't being fair to himself. "You are the leader your people need, the one they respect and the one who will get them out of this."

He started to shake his head, but she wouldn't let him deny it. "I didn't meet your brother, Callan, but I know that you're every bit as capable. This village believes in you. I believe in you. You just have to believe in you."

Pulling her hand from the wall, he kissed her fingers. "Thank you. Ready?"

The truth wouldn't change anything, so she lied. "Yes."

He placed her hand on the dome again and in the next moment they stood in the early morning light that filtered through the trees.

Now that she was outside her safe little bubble, she started wondering what would happen if things didn't work out as Callan hoped with Kenja. Just how powerful was that female warrior? How could Rayen leave if Kenja injured, or killed, any of the older teens? If she harmed Callan ... "I might be able to convince Tony to stay a little longer–"

"No."

She pulled her hand away. "You didn't even hear me out."

"It's been decided. You agreed."

"Well, I might unagree."

Callan crossed his arms and put on his don't-argue-with-me face. "What changed from a moment ago?"

If she admitted she had concerns about Kenja, he would dismiss them. "I need to be convinced that Gabby is better for one thing."

"She looked fine last night."

What was it about someone this stubborn that drew her? Did all the women in her bloodline have a genetic defect of idiocy? Maybe it was a good thing that she was the last one. "I might stay here just to prove to you that I make my own decisions."

"You. Are. Leaving!" Veins in his neck were rigid.

"Stop. Giving. Me. Orders!"

Callan uttered a harsh word in a language she didn't know, but it sounded like a curse. Then his head snapped up to stare past her.

She followed the direction of his gaze to find Kaz running toward them.

Kaz skidded to a stop ten feet away, staring from her to Callan then back to her.

She was prepared for him to criticize both of them when it was obvious they'd just left the bubble together, but that was not what came out of his mouth.

"Kenja approaches with her warriors."

They were too late to set up Callan's trap.

CHAPTER 30

CALLAN IGNORED THE CONDEMNATION IN Kaz's eyes and asked, "How do you know Kenja approaches?"

Kaz said, "When we met up with her yesterday, I searched each of her warriors empathically. She is like touching the emotions of a stone, but a girl around thirteen was sending out waves of irritation at Kenja. I focused on her until I could pick up her emotions again."

Rayen said, "I don't understand what you're saying."

Disappointment and censure raked across Rayen with one sweep of Kaz's gaze.

Callan had to fight the urge to warn him not to give voice to his turbulent thoughts. He was having enough trouble calming anger at himself for letting his last private words with Rayen turn harsh. But he'd just come to terms with her leaving when she changed her mind.

Kaz told Rayen, "Female warriors between the ages of twelve and sixteen are excused from training to allow them time to become accustomed to the changes in their bodies. They're too emotional to risk putting in combat, but Kenja clearly disregarded this rule. Once I had a lock on the girl's emotions yesterday, I was able to sense her again this morning."

Callan heaved a deep breath. "From what direction are they approaching?"

Pointing to his right, Kaz said, "South by southwest."

"How close?"

"A half-mile."

A half of a mile would not allow enough time for Callan to get his people in place. He ordered Kaz, "Wake everyone. Tell Zilya and Etoi to meet me at the bent tree near the southwest wall of our defense."

Kaz asked, "Have you changed your mind about sending Rayen and the other two back to the past?"

Callan gritted his teeth at Kaz digging into a raw wound, especially when Rayen stiffened next to him. "They'll return after we deal with Kenja."

Sending a loaded look Rayen's way, Kaz told her, "I'll still go with you when you're ready to find the controller."

Rayen shrugged. "Sure, as soon as–"

"I'll go with her when it's time," Callan snapped, drawing a heated glare from Rayen, but she didn't argue for once.

"Do you think that's wise?" Kaz asked, which would have sounded like concern if not for the incensed sweep of his words.

Intending to end this conversation, Callan said, "You should be more concerned about Kenja not annihilating this village."

When Kaz didn't move fast enough for him, Callan shoved power into his next order. "Do as I say, Kaz. Now."

Kaz looked properly disciplined and Callan felt lower than a croggle's butt for talking to his friend that way, but Kenja was coming and Rayen was shooting feral looks at him.

As soon as Kaz took off, Rayen rounded on Callan with a frown marring her pretty face. "What is wrong with you? Kaz was only trying to help you."

No, he wasn't. Kaz was angry that he hadn't ended up with Rayen in his bed. Callan said, "I don't need his interference. If he wants to help, he can do his duty. Let's go."

She grumbled something but caught up to his long stride, talking the whole time. "He was only sharing his thoughts and yesterday he offered to hunt for the controller with me."

"I expect him to hold his tongue unless he's asked for his opinion, and I said I would go with you to hunt the controller. That discussion is over."

"Really? Just because you say so? I don't think so. You may not want my opinion but you're going to get it. Sending Kaz to hunt for the controller makes more sense than you going, because they need you here to run this place. It's been attacked and your village is facing another one from Kenja."

Everything Rayen said did make sense, but logic wasn't Callan's problem right now. Knowing Rayen would not be here for long was causing chaos in his head. The idea of Kaz being the last person she saw before she left turned that chaos into a mental apocalypse.

How could he explain that? He couldn't.

Unwilling to let it go, Rayen kept her voice down as they headed for the meet spot. "Yesterday you didn't care if Kaz spoke his mind."

"Yesterday we weren't facing an enemy."

"Yes, we were," she argued. "We were chasing TecKnati, fighting a plant and facing off with Kenja. I'm just trying to get you to realize that you can't afford any division of loyalty here. Kaz is on your side, but you just shoved him away."

Guilt dug into Callan's stomach and wallowed around with a load of worry over the threat headed this way.

He had an Uberon force coming with the intention of attacking. The only elite warrior among them was Kenja, but the rest of her group was by far better trained than any of the younger ones Callan had in the village.

He pushed a branch out of Rayen's way, irritated at her incessant logic that he couldn't debate, so he fell back on what worked best.

Giving orders.

"Don't argue with me and don't interfere when I'm dealing with my people. Nothing is more dangerous than a break down in command when facing an enemy. Kaz is not a child who needs defending. He's a warrior who knows better than to voice his opinion when it's not requested."

That silenced her and Callan knew immediately that quiet was not a positive sign with Rayen.

He considered what he could say to put things right between them, but time had slipped through his fingers. They'd circumvented the communal building and were closing in on the bent tree.

Zilya and Etoi stood together, talking. Both turned at Callan's approach.

He spoke softly to Rayen. "We'll discuss finding the controller later. For now, just do as I say." He took another breath and added, "Please."

She gave it a moment then answered just as quietly. "I will do as you *ask* unless I have no choice. And as soon as Kenja is handled, I'll leave and no longer be a problem for you. Satisfied?"

Callan grunted a noncommittal answer. No, he wasn't satisfied. He wanted to pull her aside and strike down the hurt in her words, but he had an audience. Never a moment to himself. Except for last night. He'd hold that in his memories and protect it like a secret treasure.

Then it hit him that the beginning of the bond was still in place.

He reached out mentally and tapped on Rayen's mind to speak to her telepathically and ran up against a wall of silence.

"Kaz tells us the Uberons are on the way," Zilya spat at Callan with enough acid in her voice to burn skin. "If he had not heard them coming, we could have been attacked with only Etoi and myself to sound the alarm. Two of us could not defend this village against Kenja while waiting on you. You're the one who criticized everyone for the last attack. How is this any different?"

He was not in the mood for Zilya's grandstanding but taking her down a notch in front of everyone would serve no purpose. She had become so undependable she might decide to retaliate in the middle of trying to defend the village. "We don't have time for that debate right now, Zilya. We need to step through the warding and seal it against MystiKs to prevent Kenja from coming in."

"You want us to go out and fight Uberons?" She looked stricken. "That's suicidal."

"What I want is for you and–"

"I'm here," Kaz announced, running up with spears in hand. He handed one to everyone, but he presented the first one to Rayen.

Callan noticed and gave himself credit for not allowing his irritation to show. Before he could continue, Jaxxson came jogging up. Callan shook his head. "You're not going with us, Jaxxson."

"You'll have a better chance at containing Kenja's young ones if I'm there."

"We can't risk it." Callan would give him an order to stay if he had to, but he'd rather not. If he kept yelling at his best MystiKs, they'd eventually ignore him.

Tony and Gabby must have followed Jaxxson because the two of them walked up at that moment.

In his usual way, Tony butted in. "Callan's right. If anyone gets injured, you're the doc."

"You have no opinion, TecKnati," Etoi snarled.

"Button it, magpie," Gabby sniped right back.

Jaxxson argued, "I am not pleased about the idea of agreeing with Etoi, but she is right. Tony has no say in this."

Gabby rounded on Jaxxson. "So, you're going out to risk your neck when all these kids depend on you, and you have the best healing skills?"

"They need me, Gabby."

"Everyone does. Tony makes a valid point, regardless of him being a TecKnati *ancestor* or not."

Tony made the same point that Callan had before this turned into an argument. Callan lifted a hand, and everyone quieted. "There will be no more discussion on this. Jaxxson stays here to defend the village and keep the children calm."

Jaxxson understood the order Callan infused in that statement and nodded.

Tony said to Jaxxson, "Thanks, man. V'ru's a little stressed over a potential attack. I think he may need your woo-woo stuff to calm him down."

"It's not woo-woo, you moron," Gabby grumbled.

Callan looked over at Kaz and asked, "Why does V'ru know about the attack at all?"

Kaz shook his head. "He was in the communal area when I announced it. I don't know why he was there before someone escorted him over for the morning meal."

Tony scowled. "He slept with the other kids last night. That's why he's there."

"Was that your doing?" Zilya asked, venom dripping from her words. "How dare you put our historian at risk."

"Yeah, it was my doin', babe, and if you don't like it, tough, because that kid's having a hard time with being alone so much."

An enemy was bearing down on the village and Callan's patience frayed more with every word uttered. He boomed, "E-*nough!* I will deal with this later. Right now, the five of us have to move outside the warding and seal it against any MystiKs or the confrontation will end up inside here."

"Make that six," Tony said.

Callan shoved his irritation at Tony. "Are *you* volunteering?"

"Yep. You got anything besides those oversized grill skewers?"

Callan asked Rayen, "What is he saying?"

She shrugged, looking just as confused by her friend's words. "He can handle himself in a fight."

Gabby slapped her forehead with her hand. "Tony means the spears."

Kaz stepped up and handed a spear to Tony, leaving himself empty handed.

Accepting the weapon, Tony asked, "What are you going to use?"

"My powers, which are far more dangerous than a mere skew-er," Kaz bragged.

Tony eyed the sharp blade on the spear. "You plan to use this on kids?"

"Yes," Zilya and Etoi answered just as Callan, Rayen, Kaz, Jaxxson, and Gabby shouted, *"No!"*

"Day-um. Glad I'm not runnin' this side show," Tony muttered.

"Listen up," Callan ordered. "No children are to be harmed unless you're in danger of being killed and your first goal is to injure only as minimally as possible." With that said, he finished the instructions he'd been trying to get out. "I will attempt to reason with Kenja. While I do that, Kaz, Etoi, and Zilya will spread out slowly. As soon as her warriors show themselves, the three of you will form a circle with your power and prepare to enclose them with a containment spell."

Zilya grouched, "I seriously doubt that Kenja will allow us to flank her and, if she catches us, she'll retaliate."

Rayen spoke up. "I understand how Jaxxson feels now because after having met Kenja, I am actually going to agree with Zilya." Rayen angled her chin up at Callan. "And you expect Kenja to retaliate, don't you, which means you intend to cause a diversion if your talk doesn't go well."

She had guessed correctly, but Callan wasn't ready to share the idea he'd been formulating on the way here. He wasn't sure if he could depend on his G'ortian powers. If he told this group that his goal was to take control of Kenja's mind long enough to circle her warriors, they'd all think he was insane.

And he might be. If he stabbed at her mind and missed, she'd unleash everything she had on him, but while that was happening, Kaz would drive the children and Callan's warriors inside the village warding.

In answer to Rayen's observation, Callan said, "I do have an idea on how to give our three time to circle the children with the containment spell. If I *am* forced to engage Kenja, it will allow Kaz, Zilya, and Etoi an opening to move the children inside the warding."

"But *I* can create a diversion," Rayen argued, knuckles turning white where she clenched her spear. "Kenja doesn't know what she's facing with me. No matter how skilled she is, no warrior is going to attack an enemy without knowing her strength and weakness."

Tony's head moved up and down. "Xena's got a point."

"Who is Xena?" Kaz asked.

Rayen raised her hand to stall that question. "Is that all you have to tell us, Callan?"

Zilya's frown deepened. "How can we trust this one–"

"My *name* is *Rayen*. Not *this one*."

"–not to provoke Kenja into killing you," Zilya finished, ignoring Rayen's death glare. "If Kenja kills you then she'll turn on us while we're powering the spell."

Rayen slammed the end of her spear down into the ground. "Do you *ever* try to make something work? All you worry about is your own hide. What about all these children on both sides?"

"Don't speak to me in that tone or I'll–"

"What, Zilya? Attack me? Hasn't Etoi told you how I used my power to burn a croggle from the inside out?"

Zilya's face paled. She slashed her bad temper at Callan. "You trust a TecKnati to fight with us and now you stand there and allow a C'raydonian to threaten me? What is wrong with you?"

Rayen took a step toward Zilya.

Callan put his arm out, blocking Rayen, then pulled his temper back in line. Taking down a croggle would be easier. He told Zilya, "If you wish to live in this village, you will defend it the way I tell you to." Then he turned on Rayen. "Do not threaten the life of any MystiK."

She looked as if he'd slapped her then stepped away from his arm. "I wasn't threatening anything. I was simply reminding her of the danger she would face by attacking me."

Callan was starting to hope Kenja did attack him. He wanted an opponent of equal power to fight.

Rayen raised both eyebrows at him in a challenge he'd find adorable under different circumstances. At this moment, he wanted to shake some sense into her, because the only constant with her power was that it was unpredictable.

If it failed to show at the right moment, even someone like Zilya was capable of meting out serious injury to Rayen.

But Kenja would kill her and not even blink while doing it.

Kaz said, "Kenja will be here in two minutes at the speed they are moving."

Callan nodded and gave his last instructions. "Zilya and Etoi, follow Kaz's lead. Pay attention to his hand signals for position and when to begin the containment spell."

Picking up that point, Kaz added, "I will cross my arms as a sign to start the spell. Zilya will begin, Etoi will join her, then me."

"Where will that one be?" Etoi asked in her surly way, indicating Rayen.

"Remember my warning from yesterday?" Callan asked in a voice filled with serious warning. "It still stands. Do not question me."

Etoi said nothing.

Everyone looked at Callan, waiting for his answer. "Rayen and Tony will stay with me. If Kenja attacks and I can't stop her, Rayen and Tony will be our last line of defense."

Kenja would toast Tony with one swipe of her hand, but he'd volunteered and Rayen's power tended to rise up as soon as someone she cared about was in danger.

Power or not, Callan couldn't stop her from walking out with them, but he didn't want Rayen in this fight.

The Uberons back home were secretive and refused to cross train, so others in the Warrior House rarely had a chance to go up against one. Callan had told Rayen his G'ortian powers would defeat Kenja, indicating his physical powers, but in truth he had no idea what he was facing.

But he should be able to keep her busy long enough for the other three to contain her warriors.

Once he stepped outside the wall protecting the village, he'd send a telepathic message to Kaz and Zilya that the minute they had control of Kenja's warriors, to drag the children inside the walls while he fought Kenja.

And Callan would send a private message to order Kaz to use his kinetics to push Rayen back inside as well.

If Callan's plan to negotiate failed and Kenja forced him to use his full power against her, Kenja might defeat Callan, but he would give his last breath to ensure that she was in no shape to battle anyone else once she was done with him.

He walked over to the wall and lifted his hands, opening a path for all of them, allowing Rayen and Tony to pass through first.

CHAPTER 31

RAYEN STEPPED INTO THE OPENING Callan created in the warding around the village. Cool air turned charged, raising the hairs on her arms as she passed through.

Callan had something in mind for this confrontation that he wouldn't tell her. She could see it on his face. He would sacrifice himself before he'd allow any of them to be harmed.

She just hoped she could find her power if Kenja struck at him.

There was no point in wasting her breath to argue with him over strategy.

She'd already wasted what little time they had this morning in a useless debate. If she'd been honest, she'd have admitted that she was frustrated at their situation. Instead, she'd turned all that pain into anger. She needed time when this was done to repair the damage she'd done.

Or maybe Callan would be better off if she just let everything end that way and left.

The sky had brightened to its usual purple but was smeared with deep crimson reds and slashed with shades of bright violet. Outside the protective wall, shin-high dark blue grass and black and white striped flowers covered a patch of land maybe a hundred feet between the village and a tree line of the forest.

Tony popped out of the ward opening right behind her, then Zilya, Etoi, Kaz and finally Callan. The four MystiKs turned back to the ward that she could no longer see because the whole point was for the village to disappear into the landscape.

Raising their hands, the MystiKs chanted in a low vibration.

Tony took a look around then tilted his head up at the red moon that was just rising. He turned a solemn face to Rayen. "We gotta find that controller soon, Xena."

"I know. I wish you'd stay inside and make sure you and Gabby can get out of here."

"We can't make that transender work without all three of us. I'm keeping an eye on your back since you've got as many enemies on this side as you have on the other."

No matter what reason he gave, it didn't change the fact that Tony had walked out here with nothing more than a spear against a small army powered with magic.

Admiration built into a lump in her throat.

Rayen leaving in the transender would benefit everyone from Tony to Callan, but what if she died fighting Kenja? Would the sentient ability of the transender still require her presence then?

She started to tell Tony to make sure to try no matter what, but Callan walked up at that moment, so she just lifted a finger, hoping Tony read her signal that they'd talk later.

And hoped there would be a later.

Callan positioned her two steps away on his right and spaced Tony the same distance on Callan's left. They had their backs to the warded wall, facing the open field and the forest.

Kaz moved way left then motioned Etoi and Zilya to spread out to the right of where Rayen stood, with all three of them working their way ten feet closer to the tree line.

Kaz had just stopped when he cocked his head and sent a nod at Callan. His eyes stared off for a moment and Rayen realized he was listening to someone. Then his face registered concern over something, sending his glance at her then back to Callan with a second nod.

They'd just spoken telepathically and wore matching fierce masks of determination.

What had they discussed? Rayen bumped Callan's mind. No response. She did it again, but harder.

He didn't even blink.

He'd shut her out.

She stared at him, trying to will him to look at her, but he wouldn't. Hiding disappointment over being ignored, she faced forward.

The forest shimmered with shadowed movements.

Kenja stepped out and never slowed her stride. Her gaze swept over each person, clearly assessing her opponents.

When she reached the point of being in line with Kaz, Zilya, and Etoi, Kenja stopped. She wasn't going to allow those three behind her. A wise decision, but one that would inhibit Callan's people from working the spell.

Callan crossed his arms. "We have no reason to battle, Kenja. We're on the same side."

"You are wrong. There are MystiKs then there are Uberons. I want mine."

"The children are safe in this village. If we joined forces, they would be even better protected."

Kenja found something amusing about what he'd suggested. She asked, "You would invite me to stay in your village?"

"I would invite you in if you gave your word to follow my orders." He spoke with absolute authority.

"The day will never come for an Uberon to willingly follow a mere Warrior House spawn. Second best spawn at that."

Callan appeared unaffected by her scorn, but her snub of discounting him as a poor copy of his twin raised Rayen's temper to the boiling point. She still didn't see Kenja's warriors. Where were they? Had she left them at her camp?

Did she have enough to even mount an attack?

Kenja roared, *"Give me my Uberons!"*

"No."

"Then I will take them."

Callan warned, "You won't get inside. We've warded the village against any MystiK entry. You can try to break the ward, and you might, but you won't be capable of fighting a pupple off when you're done."

Kenja moved her hand so fast Rayen barely saw the action. When she flicked her fingers, dirt burst from the ground in an explosion at Callan's feet.

He didn't flinch and maintained a calm tone. "I will offer you one chance to recall your challenge."

She angled her head, first one way then the other, studying Callan. "I will offer you the only words you will get from me. Prepare to die."

Rayen searched inside herself for the power that could fry a croggle from the inside out. Nothing flickered. Why was finding her power impossible when *she* believed she needed it?

Callan shook his head. "Power does not equal strength."

"It does with my people," Kenja assured him.

"Then you and I will fight. Leave the children out of this."

"If you surrender now, I will not have to damage your pretty face, Callan."

"The Warrior House surrenders to no one. Only a fool attacks a G'ortian warrior, and I have never heard of Uberon warriors being fools."

Callan was giving his best at trying to talk her out of this, but Kenja would not be swayed. She lifted both shoulders in a shrug and continued conversing as if they discussed where to share a meal and not the possibility of doing serious bodily harm to each other.

"Have it your way, Callan. I have been as fair as an Uberon can be when my people are being held against their will."

"They are *not* being held against their will," Callan scowled at her.

She turned her head from side to side, searching. "Then why are they not here to greet me? The way I see it they are not free to leave your village. I am through talking. We will fight and the winner will decide the fate of the Uberons."

That sounded logical, which meant it had to be anything but if it was coming out of Kenja's mouth. She fully expected to walk away from this fight the victor.

Callan muttered something Rayen couldn't hear then told Kenja, "If you're determined to do this, I give you my word that once you lose, I will take the rest of your warriors inside the village to protect them."

She smiled the way someone would at a child who had said something silly. "I only need your word that your people will not interfere." She paused then added, "Or must I dispose of them first?"

Rayen narrowed her eyes at Kenja, trying to send a message that she was ready to serve her words back to the warrior girl for a meal.

Callan sighed. "I give my word that my people will not interfere if you call out your warriors and order them to not attack while we settle this between us. Mine are in sight."

Kenja did nothing.

Callan lifted a shoulder. "I did not think Uberons hid behind their leaders. My people are in front of me, but then I don't doubt their ability to defend themselves."

Kenja lifted a hand but kept her back to the forest. Ten, no, twelve children ranging in age from around seven to thirteen emerged from where they had melded with the trees. Today, Kenja's warriors had the same copper-and-gold swatches of color as her skin.

She raised her voice, her back still to her people. "By my word, my warriors will stand down as long as no one tries to harm them."

She was so sure that Callan and his MystiKs were just as bloodthirsty as Uberons that she'd left Callan an opening. His people would not harm the children, but they did intend to capture them in an invisible net.

Callan shouted, "By my word, no Uberon warriors are to be harmed and no one is to interfere when Kenja and I battle. You will give your word."

Once Kaz, Zilya and Etoi all consented verbally, Kenja indicated Rayen with a tilt of her head. "What about her and the other one?"

Rayen was normally *that one*, so she meant Tony by the other one.

Callan said, "They will speak for themselves."

Tony snorted. "You got it, babe. I won't hurt any of your little soldiers."

She stared at him. "What *are* you?"

"Your worst nightmare if you touch any of our kids." Tony cracked his knuckles.

Kenja gave it a second then dismissed him to focus on Rayen who said, "I will not harm a child, but I have no qualms about making *you* bleed."

"You and I will speak before I kill you," she told Rayen with the confidence that her death was a foregone conclusion. "You will tell me where you come from and why you are here."

Rayen must have been channeling Gabby, because she said, "Have you always had these fantasies or is it a recent problem?"

Tony snorted.

Callan made a noise that sounded like he wanted to strangle her.

He could get in line.

Based on the look Zilya slid her way at that comment and the hunger for blood in Kenja's eyes, there might not be anything left to strangle if Rayen's power let her down.

Kenja began backing up and waving Callan forward as she did, calling out, "This will give us room."

Rayen spoke to Callan under her breath. "I can distract her now."

He turned to me. "If you make any attempt at fighting her, I will hold you back with my kinetics. If you divide my attention to do that, you give her an advantage."

He couldn't be serious. "I can do this, Callan."

"Do you really think I would stand by and let you get anywhere near Kenja? She's as deadly as ten of those killer plants you faced. Do. Not. Move."

He didn't give Rayen a chance to say another word before his expression lost all concern and he turned toward Kenja, heading to where she waited in the center of the field.

Rayen stared at him in disbelief. Did he really think she would stand by and allow him to sacrifice himself? That's exactly what would happen if he pulled his punches to keep from harming Kenja.

Callan would defend himself, but Rayen didn't see him unleashing the full brunt of his power to fight one of his own people, much less a female.

She searched inside herself again, forcing her mind to focus on nothing but finding the core of her power. Sweat broke out on her forehead despite the chilly morning.

Her arms shook.

Then she saw it. There was her energy pulsing. She called it up.

Nothing.

She should have asked the ghosts about her power this morning.

Acheii would probably tell her again that she asked useless questions.

There were a lot of things she needed to know, but the opportunity to find out more about herself had passed. She was standing here with no idea of whether she could bring on her powers or not.

It didn't matter.

Kenja bled therefore she was vulnerable.

Callan paused, leaving twenty feet between him and his opponent. He shifted his feet apart and lifted his arms slowly.

Kenja, on the other hand, jerked both of hers up quickly, crossing her chest then slashing her hands straight out in front of her.

Toward Callan.

But he could move fast as a thought when he wanted. His hands whipped up at the last second and kinetic power blocked whatever she had thrown at him.

Then he side-armed a whip of power back at Kenja.

She swatted it away.

The diverted power ripped a groove two feet deep and fifteen feet long in the ground. Kenja's smile said it all. She had plenty of untapped energy she would use when she was ready, at the best possible moment to do the most damage.

What about Callan?

Rayen was sure he had more. But he'd once told her his G'ortian powers were not stable. Or had he said they were evolving? She couldn't recall. Whether he had all his abilities or not, Callan could never live with himself if he used lethal power against a MystiK, or a girl.

Not even Kenja. Not unless she tried to harm one of his people.

This battle went against all Callan believed in. Rayen might not know who she was, but she knew who he was.

He rolled his shoulders then his hands came together, palms facing out, to shove forward sharply. Just as quickly, Kenja put up one hand to block whatever he'd sent.

She wanted everyone to see that she was the stronger of the two.

But she didn't seem to realize it was a case of *would* not harm her instead of *could* not.

While Kenja and Callan tested each other, her warriors moved up, closing the space behind her in a half-circle.

Rayen glanced at Kaz. When was he going to give the signal to start the spell?

Kenja pointed two fingers out to the side and moved her arm in a horizontal swipe in front of her.

A slash ripped across Callan's rib cage and blood trickled. He growled, but Rayen also heard a sharp intake of breath.

He might not kill her, but Rayen would. Slowly and painfully.

Callan took a two-fisted swing at Kenja.

She bent backwards at the waist to avoid the invisible shot, never losing her balance.

The hit missed her completely. He'd aimed high.

Her warriors ducked at the same moment she did, but the shot would have flown over their heads even if they'd stayed upright.

Callan's hit of energy landed against a tree as thick as Rayen's waist on the far side of the field. The tall tree snapped in half and crashed to the ground.

Kenja started laughing. "I can do this all day long. Tell me, have you had a real taste of battle yet?" She prattled on, all her attention finally on Callan.

Kaz crossed his arms, giving Zilya and Etoi the signal to start the spell.

But Kenja moved her head, distracted.

She wasn't thoroughly engaged.

Rayen took a step toward her.

Just as she expected, Kenja's gaze shot to her while she still harangued Callan. The scary truth was that she was just as powerful as he'd said and she was playing with him, which had Rayen thinking that once Kenja had humiliated Callan enough she would kill him.

Until this moment, Rayen hadn't believed it was possible.

But Kenja didn't have the same code of honor that Callan held himself to. She would inflict whatever damage she felt was justified to get to the children she believed were hers.

Rayen felt equally justified in using her power to stop Kenja. With Rayen's next step, she sensed heat building inside her.

Please let that be her power coming to the forefront.

Kenja's face had been relaxed as she'd fought Callan, but her eyes sharpened, and her jaw hardened when Rayen stole a slice of her attention.

Callan tossed a quick glance at Rayen and shouted, "No." He raised his hand to use his kinetics against her.

And just as he'd warned, Rayen had divided his attention, giving Kenja an advantage over him.

He was batted backwards fifty feet in the air and slammed up against the village ward ten feet off the ground. His back hit with a sickening thud and he stayed pinned up high, held there by a force Kenja wielded mentally because her arms fell to her sides.

Callan wouldn't forgive Rayen for stepping in, but she'd cost him that break in concentration. At least, he'd be alive to be angry.

If she didn't make another mistake.

Rayen took one more step toward Kenja who stood there, waiting calmly for her.

Tony called over, "Xena, we're gonna need a fifty caliber for that one."

She couldn't waste a microsecond to figure out what a fifty caliber was, but maybe she should have. Tony started toward her, clearly planning to help her.

Was he crazy? "Stay out of this, Tony."

Kenja flicked a mere glance his way and Tony skidded backwards forty feet until he was pinned against the ward wall, too, but with his feet still on the ground. He swatted at whatever held him, yelling curses, and threatening to maim the Amazon witch.

At least, Rayen thought he had said witch.

Kenja made a move that televised she was going to look over her right shoulder.

If she turned far enough around, she'd catch Kaz and his group who were busy with the spell.

Rayen yelled at Kenja, "Is that all you can do? Shove people around? I'm not impressed."

That brought her back to Rayen. "You will be when I hold your heart in my hand while it still throbs with life. But I must know what you are first. I may keep you alive, like a pet to amuse me for a while."

Rayen would show her a pet with fangs.

Out of the corner of her eye, Rayen saw Kaz turn a worried look her way. She sent him a warning glare that he'd better interpret as not interfering. He had to hold that spell. She didn't know if it was even working but getting bloodied by Kenja would be all for naught if they didn't contain the children.

Kenja had said the winner would decide the fate of the Uberons.

That could not end up being Kenja.

When Rayen didn't feel anything coming from Kaz, she took that as a sign he realized he'd only put her at a disadvantage if he tried to help. Her conscience pointed out how she'd committed the same crime by distracting Callan, but Callan had no intention of fighting Kenja with all his resources.

Rayen would.

Kenja focused far more intensely on Rayen than she had on Callan, taking her time at making a move.

That's right, I'm the unknown, warrior girl. Kenja had no idea just how much about Rayen was unknown, but she was going to get a chance to find out.

Hopefully. If Rayen's power didn't go into hibernation.

She must not have been covering the forty feet left between them fast enough for her, because Kenja raised one hand and cupped her fingers toward her twice, like she was waving Rayen forward. Rayen started to snicker and ask her what her rush was until she heard Callan groan.

When she spun around, she found what Kenja was really doing.

Not waving, but kinetically raking her nails up Callan's arms, leaving four jagged gashes on each forearm. Blood ran down his arms. Pressure hit him again, harder. He balled his fist and roared, fighting to break her hold.

Fire seared Rayen's back.

She arched away from the pain.

Kenja had done the same to her. Rayen wheeled around fast and charged forward, ready to draw some blood of her own.

Kaz had moved around the rear of Kenja's warriors. Their collective gazes were fixed on their leader Kenja.

Zilya and Etoi had altered their positions to encircle the children. Both girls held their arms out to the side like Kaz did. Rayen hoped that meant they'd locked their power and the spell was under control.

Kenja reached out a hand, fingers curling as if grasping for something.

Rayen kept heading for her.

Kenja jerked her arm to the side.

The spear flew out of Rayen's hands in the same direction. She didn't stop or slow down. If she hesitated, she might think about just how outmatched she was.

But Callan was bleeding and Kenja was crushing him.

Rayen picked up speed and called up her power. It answered her this time, rushing through her body in a raging river of energy. Finally. Her hair felt like it stood on end.

Maybe it did.

Kenja raised a hand, murmuring something into her palm then she heaved whatever it was at Rayen.

Still running, Rayen lifted her arms in an X across her face and turned her hands out.

Power hit her hard, jarring her teeth, and throwing her out of step.

Her arms burned hot as a fire, but it was her own fire. Rayen shoved back and Kenja's power burst away from her in a blast of blue sparks.

Kenja had yet to show any fear, but surprise rolled over her eyes for an instant. Then her gaze lit up glowing yellow. She dropped into a fighting crouch.

Twenty feet. Rayen fisted her hands.

Kenja was chanting words louder this time. They came out with bite.

Fifteen feet. Rayen lowered her head for a straight on hit.

The ground trembled.

Five feet away an explosion struck behind Rayen, blowing her off her feet. She hit the ground, rolling head over butt. The world spun. Sound disappeared.

Instinct screamed at her to get up.

She pushed to her feet and sidestepped when the world tilted. Her ears were ringing.

Kenja was rolling to her feet as well.

Callan had dropped to the ground and stumbled forward. So did Tony.

Kaz shouted. "*We're under attack. TecKnati!*"

CHAPTER 32

RAYEN SHOOK OFF THE DIZZINESS as another blast hit, tossing Tony off his feet.

Callan fell to his knees and got up. He turned to Kaz whose shoulders bunched with strain and arms extended out from his body shook. The effort of holding the invisible field of magic showed on Zilya's face and sweat poured down Etoi's arms even in the brisk morning temperature still chilly.

Kaz was yelling something at Callan who took off running toward the children.

Rayen couldn't hear what was said over the screams of Kenja's little warriors. They were racing around inside the containment spell, running into the sides in a panic.

Kaz, Zilya, and Etoi were being jerked back and forth as they struggled to hold the spell.

Rayen started toward the children, too. Her hearing was coming back. She caught a high-pitched whining noise that pulled her gaze to the sky.

A stream of light shot up from deep in the forest. The light glowed blue as it developed into a tubular line as thick as her head. It went straight up then arced high in the air and angled back down ... heading for Kenja.

Rayen took off running and called on her power. A blaze of energy seared her legs. Her feet spun with inhuman speed.

Kenja came to her feet facing Kaz who clutched at the containment spell. She roared, "Free my warr–"

Rayen hit Kenja with all she had, knocking her off her feet, tangling with her as they went airborne.

Kenja's hand moved fast as a rattlesnake striking at heat and grabbed Rayen by the throat, yanking her with Kenja as she fell. She got a good lick in on the way down, jarring Rayen's head, but Rayen hammered right back, hitting Kenja's jaw with a fist that snapped her head back.

They smacked down hard and slid over rough ground, chattering Rayen's teeth and taking another layer of skin off her arms. She wasn't sure she hadn't broken something.

Her punch must not have been as well placed as she thought, because Kenja yanked Rayen's face to hers, still choking her with one hand. "You–"

The blue streak hit right where Kenja had been standing and blew a hole in the ground, shaking the earth hard enough to rattle Rayen's bones.

Clumps of dirt rained down on them.

Rayen clamped her hands on Kenja's forearm, which was solid as an ancient tree limb. Heat rushed up her arms to her hands that started smoking.

Kenya's eyes bulged. She yanked her arms out of Rayen's grasp and had burn marks where Rayen had touched her.

Rayen snarled, "Stop being stupid and get your people to safety."

Then she was on her feet and heading for the kids caught in the spell.

When she got to the wobbling mass of little bodies, Callan was shouting orders. "Drop the spell and move them into the village.

Kenja appeared next to Rayen, not even winded where she was chugging air as hard as she could. Unbelievable. Kenja told Callan, "They will not follow you."

He turned on her. "The TecKnati aren't *supposed* to kill the children, because of the treaty, but that doesn't mean we won't lose a child who runs into one of those laser beams. I'll block the next beam they release. If you stand here arguing, your warriors will die."

Rayen thought Callan was wrong about the TecKnati not targeting bodies since they'd almost killed Kenja, but maybe they hadn't seen her standing in that spot. She had no idea what kind of weapons they possessed.

Lasers sounded familiar, though.

"They will follow my orders," Kenja clarified about her children. "Open the ward and they will go inside."

Callan gave the word to Kaz, and the spell disintegrated.

Children raced toward Kenja who merely turned and pointed in the direction of the village. "Take formation."

Tony yelled, "Incoming!"

Rayen had forgotten about him. He was running toward them and pointing up. Blood ran down the side of his face.

Tony was only human with not the least bit of supernatural power. He would be the easiest to kill of everyone. And he wasn't a MystiK, which made him fair game for the TecKnati.

A glowing streak shot from deep in the forest, but this one was radiating yellow and pink. A laser beam shouldn't curve.

But this one would. She was sure.

Rayen had seen one like it before and knew that the pink-yellow beam was far worse than the blue.

Why? And how did she know this?

What did it matter?

There was no time to explore another piece of memory.

Callan and his people circled around behind the pack of kids, herding them. The children had fallen into line upon Kenja's order. They were running toward the village with her at their side.

Callan shouted, "Kaz, take Zilya and Etoi. Open a passage in the ward."

The three ran all out, passing the children whose legs were short, but spinning as fast as they could.

Rayen told Tony, "Go with them."

He shook his head and waved a dismissive hand in Kenja's direction. "They got that. Soon as you two do whatever you got in mind to stop that laser, we all run for it. I'll watch the woods and give you a heads up if anyone shows up."

What did he think he could do that wouldn't get him killed?

Callan said, "That beam is taking too long to get here. Why?"

Rayen looked up, gauging where the soaring twist of pink-and-yellow would hit.

Tony jogged a few steps toward the trees and stopped, doing his own evaluation of the laser. He waved us back toward the village. "You're too close. Gotta back up."

Callan started toward the village with his gaze locked on the threat. "The TeKs can't break through our ward with a laser."

The whistle of the approaching attack turned into a high-pitched scream.

Tony covered his ears.

Rayen fell into step with Callan, backing up as he did. He ordered, "Go to the wall."

She slowed to stand next to Callan when he paused. "No."

"Just once I wish you'd do what I say."

"Do a better job of keeping yourself alive and that might just happen."

Bracing his feet shoulder width apart, he grumbled, "I'm locking you up after this."

Looking back toward the village then up at the laser that was coming slower than the last two, her palms started to sweat. There was something bad about that pink and yellow mix.

What was it?

Callan lifted his arms. His hands glowed with power.

Rayen knew he hadn't been using all he had against Kenja.

Raising her hands, she called upon her power. The heat built in her chest and rolled through her with a buzzing pulse. It swam through the muscles in her arms. Her head was so hot it felt like her brain would explode.

The twisted pink-yellow glow was getting bigger the closer it came. She chanced a look at the wall.

Nobody had gone inside.

Why not?

Callan looked around and cursed. He roared, "Open the ward!"

Kaz yelled, "We can't. Don't have enough energy after the spell."

Rayen had kept track of the glow that was definitely turning toward the village. If it couldn't break the ward then what could it ... oh, no. "Callan, I know what that glow does. It's heading for the village. We have to stop it."

"I told you it can't break the ward." He started toward the village.

Rayen grabbed his arm and jerked him back to her.

He shoved his face down to hers and ground out his words. "Let go so I can help them."

"You won't get the ward open in time and if you do the damage will be worse. Pick me up and throw me."

"What? *No!*"

"Do it or your entire village will die. That glow doesn't blast anything. It's sentient, searching out life. It will coat the ward and anything near it. No one will get out, so they'll starve to death. I can stop it with my power."

The glow was generating a louder screech.

Callan looked at the wall then back at her, torn between how to save everyone.

"Please, Callan, I promise to do what you want next time, but I can't throw you up there. One of us must stop it in midair. Trust me that I can do it. My power is coursing through me."

He made a vicious noise that could have come from an enraged animal then his hands gripped her hips.

She stared into his eyes and bent her knees to get a strong push off. "Thank you."

He promised, "If you die, I'm following you to the other side just to chew you out."

Then he whipped her straight up at the glow that shot forward.

But the beam altered, trying to avoid her.

Callan must have thrown his kinetics because he forced it from diverting.

She lunged and caught her arms around the beam of undulating energy.

She gripped it to her, yelling, "*Tenadori!*"

Spinning energy ground into her body, driving a wild shock through her from head to toe. Then the beam whipped back and forth, energy building and gyrating around her, engulfing her body. It rolled and jerked.

Clutching the beam to her, she drew on her power that meshed with the beam, confusing her as to what was hers and what was not. The screech turned into a hellish howl.

She felt her insides being twisted and wrenched.

The world passed by in a blur of vivid yellow then radiant pink, sliding in slow motion until everything exploded into a million brilliant sparks.

White light blinded her.

CHAPTER 33

"RAYEN!"

She moved her hands from her eyes and looked toward Callan's voice. He was down below, racing toward her, but she didn't think he could see her yet. She could hardly see him through a mash of light purple, mint green, and gold colors.

Whatever she sat on moved.

She blinked to clear her vision and looked to find she sat high in a tree, lying on top of two long branches with a garble of leaves.

One tree limb had broken and drooped down onto a second one. They both supported her. The air was thick with a eucalyptus smell.

Had she landed all the way over in the forest?

That must be why it felt like someone had beaten her with a stick.

"Is anything broken?" Callan yelled as he ran up to the tree and pushed off with his feet, leaping fifteen feet to grab a thick limb.

"I don't think I broke anything," she called down then tried to swallow against her sore throat.

Callan grabbed one limb after another, climbing up to her. She had to be sixty feet off the ground. When he got close, she warned him, "One of these limbs has snapped. I'm not sure if it'll support my weight if moved, so don't come out here. I'll have to find a way to climb down."

He told her, "I don't want you to climb anywhere. Just sit very still."

"What are you going to do?"

"You promised you'd do as I said if I threw you."

True. "Okay. I'm sitting still."

He stood on a branch as thick as his waist and leaned back against the trunk of the tree. Blood no longer trickled from his chest and arm wounds. He was regenerating. She might let Kenja live after all.

Callan extended one hand in her direction.

She felt herself being lifted. He cupped his other hand and curled his fingers into his palm.

She floated on a cushion of air toward him.

It seemed forever until she reached him, but the second she was close, Callan caught her around her waist and pulled her to him. She lunged at the same moment and almost sent them tumbling.

He steadied her up against his chest and murmured, "Whoa, sweetheart."

There was that word again. He had no idea how much she loved his saying it. Just hearing his voice made her heart sing, but sweetheart turned it into mush. She clutched him tight and hugged her face against the warm skin of his chest. He had a scent all his own that she'd know with her eyes closed.

"I don't know what's worse," he murmured. "Knowing you're going to leave or having you here where you could die."

She smiled. She wasn't the only one struggling with her leaving. But her smile was a sad one, because their time had come to an end. After this, Kenja had to realize the MystiKs were stronger together than as enemies.

With Kenja here, Rayen couldn't even justify trying to stay or come back for the protection of the children.

It was quiet. "What about the ward, Callan?"

"I tossed you up in the air and ran to the wall. Took like six seconds. They all got inside while you fought that beam."

With the MystiKs safe inside the village and three powerful warriors between Callan, Kaz, and Kenja to protect them, the MystiKs had a real chance to survive.

"Maybe that's why the TecKnati stopped attacking, because everyone is safe."

"You probably broke their weapon. The explosion ricocheted back along the laser beam's arc to its origin then a flame burst into the air." Callan's hands rubbed up and down her back. "We have to go."

He sounded as reluctant as she felt.

"I can climb down," she told him, although with a glance down, she had her doubts. She was having a hard time breathing, but she wasn't in a panic. Really, she wasn't.

Callan caught her chin and lifted it until she faced him. "You destroy croggles, go up against an Uberon warrior who could crush an army on her own, and attack a laser beam, but you're afraid of heights?"

Evidently. But she wasn't admitting a weakness, not even to him. "I'm just a little winded."

His eyes twinkled, calling her on the lie.

She let it go. Probably because he was so attractive. Must be her defective gene at work again.

The twinkle disappeared and his eyes darkened. He lowered his head, kissing her along her cheek and throat. He was driving her crazy. His lips touched hers and sparks burst inside her. This might be their last kiss since he wouldn't want to engage her around his people.

Her arms found their way around his neck. He held her secure. Safe. Cared for. They stayed like that, caught in the moment. Her energy swirled, moving through her as if seeking something. It pushed at the walls of her chest.

That was odd.

She tapped on Callan's mind, and he opened to her, pulling her in and surrounding her in a cloak of emotions. Her energy surged through the opening and followed her inside.

Callan stopped kissing her and propped his forehead against hers. In a gentle telepathic voice he said, *Take your power back inside yourself, sweetheart.*

She was so lost in the moment, he had to tell her again before she withdrew from his mind and pulled her power back.

Leaning away, she met his stormy gaze. "What did I do wrong?"

"Nothing." That word had been stuffed with guilt and worry.

Kaz had said they couldn't bond for Callan's sake. Did this telepathy have something to do with that? "Are we able to talk mind to mind because we're bonding or is it the other way around."

Instead of answering her, he wrapped one arm around her waist and said, "Hold on."

She didn't have time to wonder why.

He stepped off the branch and her stomach tried to crawl up her throat as they plummeted past limbs.

She yelled, "Are you trying to kill us?"

Right before the ground, they slowed until touching down softly. He explained, "I slowed our descent with my kinetics."

"What if they hadn't worked?"

"That particular gift finished evolving yesterday."

Had he used it to fight back against Kenja?

No. He'd only blocked her hits when he could.

They were walking back to the wall when Callan stopped and looked around.

She did, too, but she didn't know why. "What are you looking for?"

"Tony."

Her skin chilled. "He isn't back inside the ward?"

"No. He was watching you and took off when the laser shot you back toward the forest. I passed him and got to you first. I thought he was still here."

She yelled Tony's name over and over.

Two boys walked out of the forest. They wore the silvery green uniforms she recognized as TecKnati scouts.

Callan stepped in front of me. She thought about cuffing him upside his head, then dealing with the scouts, but she moved up beside him instead and warned, "Do not treat me like one of your children."

"I was treating you like a young woman. One I keep trying to protect no matter how difficult you make it."

One scout carried a weapon that she guessed might send a projectile the size of her fist. It must be made of light material, because it was huge and the small scout managed it alone, holding the weapon propped on his shoulder.

She wasn't sure if Callan's kinetics could stop what came out of it or not.

The other scout raised a hand to his mouth. When he spoke, his words boomed with a mechanical sound. "We have one intruder. Bring us the computer. He is not a MystiK. His death will cause no repercussion. You have until tomorrow at moonset."

They backed up and vanished into the woods.

CHAPTER 34

INSIDE THE VILLAGE WAS CHAOS.

Rayen had turned into a numb blob, putting one foot in front of the other.

The TecKnati wanted a computer, or they would kill Tony. *What computer?* The only one she could think of that mattered was the one they used to travel through time.

How were they supposed to bring that here?

First, she had to find V'ru to determine if he knew any way Gabby and she could travel back without Tony. She'd find a computer and bring it to them now.

But Tony's electronics didn't work here. How was she going to make a computer function in this place if he hadn't been able to?

She and Callan walked apart, but he kept stealing glances at her. "We'll get him back, Rayen."

She knew he meant every word, but without a computer they had nothing to bargain with. "I have to talk to V'ru about traveling back without Tony."

Shock drew Callan's eyebrows together before she rushed to explain, "I'm not leaving Tony here. I'm going to get a computer, so we'll have something to trade."

"They might be lying."

"Doesn't matter. I want to do this without putting anyone else at risk if I can."

Gabby came walking up, ponytails flying and her two different colored eyes dark with threat. "Where did you find that crazy chick, Kenja? She's demanding all kinds of things and telling everyone she's in charge. We can't get the place under control until she shuts up."

Kenja had no idea just how dangerous Rayen could be if she caused any delay in getting Tony back.

Callan said, "I'll deal with Kenja. You two talk to V'ru."

Gabby watched him walk off and asked, "Why do we have to talk to

V'ru?"

Rayen gathered her thoughts and gave it to Gabby straight. "Tony's gone."

"What? He wouldn't leave us."

"The TecKnati caught him."

Gabby paled. "Are you sure?"

Rayen told her about the scouts coming out to make a demand and provide their terms. "The only thing I can think of is for the two of us to go back and get a computer if V'ru can tell us how."

Worry washed away her anger. "He's in his kamara." She led Rayen there and called to V'ru who appeared outside a second later.

Gabby spoke to V'ru in her don't-frighten-anyone voice. "Can you tell us how to travel back to the past with just two of us?"

"Why?"

"Rayen and I may have to make a quick trip back."

"Why?"

Rayen took over, hoping to get past the one-word obstacle. "Because we need to get something for Tony."

V'ru searched their faces. "Why?"

Gabby said, "Just tell him."

"The TecKnati have Tony."

The boy's eyes doubled in size. "They'll hurt him."

They would do far more than hurt Tony, but she didn't want V'ru terrorized. "No, the TecKnati want a computer, so Gabby and I are going back to get one if we can figure out how to do it."

"I don't think that's possible."

"Why?" Now Rayen sounded like him. Just kill her now.

V'ru was wearing Tony's pullover with the hood. The bottom edge fell below his knees. V'ru said, "Because Tony told me how the portal didn't open until Rayen put her hands on the screen and that it wouldn't open without him this time. Your power is needed, Rayen, but so is Gabby's and Tony's."

Gabby scoffed. "Tony doesn't have power."

"Yes, he does," V'ru said in sharp defense. "Everyone does, but MystiKs have developed theirs where TecKnati power has gone dormant."

Well, that was interesting. But this information wasn't helping Rayen return to the past where she could find a computer. "Back to our travel problem."

V'ru sighed with the heaviness of a genius trying to solve a problem two idiots couldn't comprehend. "A portal is an unknown science, or it would have been duplicated many times by now. MystiKs have never discovered how to open one on demand and the TecKnati keep trying to create one scientifically. It appears that a two-way time travel portal requires both science and supernatural power. The one you opened is unique to itself. That means you must replicate the power and electronics the same way each time to expect the same results."

Gabby wore discouragement on her face and in her shoulders. "Then what are we going to do, Rayen?"

V'ru looked to her, too. "How are you going to get Tony back?"

"She will ask me nicely and I will show her how."

They all turned to find Kenja and Callan standing behind them.

Rayen asked, "What are you talking about, Kenja?"

"Callan tells me one of mine is inside the TecKnati camp. I will show you where the enemy beds down at night and take mine back. It will be up to you and Callan to extract the other MystiK boy and that loud one who is not worth the risk, but that is your choice."

Gabby asked, "Do you trust her to do what she says, Rayen?"

Rayen looked squarely at Callan when she answered Gabby. "No, but I trust Callan to have gained an agreement I can depend upon."

He gave one short nod and that was enough for her.

They spent the next ten minutes sorting out who went to the TecKnati camp and who stayed at the village. In the end,

Rayen walked out of the village with Callan, Kaz and Kenja.

Zilya had not been pleased to be left in charge of feeding another twelve mouths and was reminded that if she failed to offer her help, she'd face Callan's wrath. Etoi was just as unhappy to be instructed that she would be personally responsible for any breach in the wall regardless of who was at fault.

The moon had passed its zenith and was slowly dropping.

Rayen couldn't figure out how close they were on time to know if they could still return Tony to the school by four, but she did know they had to activate that transender before moonset or they'd face another night here.

Once they reached the woods, Kenja picked up the pace. Kaz was right behind her, then Rayen with Callan bringing up the rear. Kenja stepped off the path. She broke through thick brush and emerged on a new path that had been hidden. This one hadn't been beaten down for long and was probably something she'd created that the TecKnati hadn't known about.

The ground crunched beneath Rayen's shoes and buzzed. Had Kenja figured out how to create a path through the forest that was protected from the mist?

That would explain how she'd arrived at the village before daylight.

Kaz ran up an incline ahead of Rayen.

She spent the majority of the run staring at his back in silence. He'd said little to her since this morning and kept his distance from her now. The one time he'd looked at her while he slowed to hold a drooping branch out of the way, she wished she hadn't noticed.

There'd been no hiding from the disappointment staring back at her. Kaz had figured out that Callan hadn't just come to get her this morning, but that he'd been with her all night.

She suffered a moment of guilt. She hadn't encouraged Kaz's attention even though he'd made it clear that he was interested. But his brittle attitude hadn't changed since seeing her return to the village with Callan after the battle.

His silence was so loud she couldn't get away from it.

She mentally added him to the list of people ready to send her back to the past.

Rayen had said she'd leave, and would, but she couldn't do that until they rescued Tony.

Kaz stopped and she was so lost in thought after an hour of keeping her head down that she almost ran into him.

She stumbled and felt her shirt yank her back before she collided with Kaz. Looking over her shoulder, she caught the wry twist of Callan's lips that said he'd caught her daydreaming.

He was correct. But she'd admit to that right after she conceded to being afraid of heights. Never.

Kenja gave a hand signal with one finger pointing to the right. Kaz slipped through the foliage and stopped on that side of her.

She sent a two-finger signal to her left.

When Rayen moved to the left, Callan stepped up between them. She peered through slits formed by a crisscross of palm fronds.

The TecKnati camp was a series of tents painted in colors that matched the woods, camouflaging them from the sky, plus one single-story metal building which stood in the middle. The tents were half-round shapes set in rows around the structure.

Trees had been taken down and land cleared in a broad sweep around their camp, but the widest section of open space was on this end.

A thin mesh fence enclosed a square patch of land that was seventy feet across and nothing but fine-powdered orange dirt. It was a small part of the open area.

Tony and two young boys Rayen guessed to be around eight years old sat on the ground in the middle. They had their backs to a post, facing in three different directions.

One boy was a pale version of Kenja's colors. Rayen remembered the other child from when she'd entered the old MystiK village on her first trip here.

He'd been levitating.

Could he levitate over the fence? It was only chest high on her.

Two TecKnati scouts guarded the area. One on each side. They faced out toward any approaching threat.

Kenja had laid out the plan with Callan before they left the village. She'd described the tents, saying she hadn't seen the MystiKs there on her first visit or she'd have gotten her Uberon kid the first time.

Callan pointed out that the child hadn't been there at that point.

Callan whispered, "What's with the fenced area?"

Kenja shook her head. "Wasn't here the last time."

What did the TecKnati plan to do? Just leave Tony and the boys outside at night? What about the mist?

The TecKnati were heartless enough to make that fence be deadly, then let the mist attack the MystiK children and watch them race wildly into it. TecKnati would not put up a simple barrier. Rayen figured this one would burn someone to a crisp.

Callan said, "We need to take out the guards silently or we'll have to face the entire TecKnati force."

Kenja said, "I will deal with the guards. Do not fail to bring my Uberon out alive."

Callan didn't answer at first then told her. "No child will be left or harmed as long as there is a breath in my body."

That must have been enough for Kenja because she said, "I must wrap myself in a cloaking spell before I leave."

With that said, Kenja let her arms fall to her sides and closed her eyes. Her lips moved with silent words.

Energy pricked at Rayen's skin.

Callan motioned for Kaz who drew close to hear Callan's orders. "When the guards are neutralized, I'll go inside and pitch each prisoner out to you."

Rayen leaned in. "I'm going in with you to watch your back."

"No. We need you to take the boys as soon as Kaz hands them off. The boys have been traumatized. After having been in fear for their lives, they might panic the minute they're free and start running. Kaz will need you to hold them and keep them quiet."

She couldn't argue with that, she mused, but she didn't like not going in with him. "Would this be better at night?"

Callan shook his head. "Kenja created a temporary path through the jungle. We don't have any way to do that so we can travel at night without you and the boys being affected by the mist. I can help you, but Jaxxson is better with the children and he's running himself into the ground healing."

Once again, she felt like a burden, but Callan was right. They couldn't risk the children or putting Jaxxson under more strain.

But there was too much land between where she stood and the fenced area with no way to shield any of them from sight as they approached. At the far end of camp, a thin stream of smoke rose from an area where scouts were clustered.

Someone was cooking. That meant the scouts were occupied.

Waiting until dark might also mean more scouts to contend with once they finished eating.

Kenja lifted her head. Silver swirled in her eyes and her skin turned translucent. She murmured, "Be ready. I'm leaving."

Rayen said, "Are you just going to walk out there?"

She bared her teeth at Rayen in the semblance of a smile. "You will witness the gift of Uberon as I blend with the wind."

Rayen cut her eyes at Callan who didn't scoff. O-kay.

Lifting her hands above her, Kenja lowered them slowly until her body shimmered in place.

Rayen blinked, sure her eyes were playing tricks.

Kenja stepped out into the open and kept moving. She really did blend with the wind. Rayen could hardly see her once she was ten feet away.

Holding her breath, Rayen expected one of the scout guards to turn on Kenja any minute now and fire the weapons in their hands.

But two minutes later, each guard began to droop. Their heads fell forward. That was the only obvious change. From a distance, nothing would appear amiss, but up close?

They looked sound asleep.

Callan pulled a knife from its scabbard at his hip and handed it to Rayen. "You'll need this to free their bindings."

When he moved forward, she and Kaz followed.

They hurried across the open space. Her skin crawled at the feeling of being so vulnerable. She didn't like anything about this. Instincts that had kept her alive to this point were warning her to pull back.

How could she leave Tony and those children sitting there?

She couldn't.

Seeing him safe and not being tortured lifted her spirits. When they got closer, she saw that all three prisoners had their hands and feet tied and a clear wrap around their mouths.

Uncomfortable, but the upside was that the children wouldn't give away their approach by making any sounds.

Callan shoved up and rolled forward in the air, using his kinetics to vault over the fence. She heard energy sizzling along the mesh, but he'd cleared it with an easy two feet to spare and landed lightly on his feet.

So far so good.

The small boys started jerking their heads back and forth as soon as they saw Callan. Tony was turned to the side of them but wrenched around at their movement.

Callan put his finger to his lips and the boys quieted.

Kaz stopped several strides from the fence and Rayen stepped up next to him.

In the next second, Callan lifted a boy and tossed him to Kaz who handed the first one to her. She put the child on the ground. He jerked his arm, trying to free it from her grasp and made grunting noises. She shushed him. "I'll take the cover off your mouth as soon as we leave."

Kaz handed her the next boy who acted the same way.

Callan lifted Tony kinetically and sent him floating toward the fence.

Tony's eyes searched both sides of him, clearly worried about being dropped.

Kenja appeared next to Rayen practically out of thin air. She immediately started taking the covering off her Uberon child's mouth. Rayen thought it was a bad idea until they were far enough away to not be heard, but she wasn't going to argue.

The minute the boy's mouth was uncovered, he shouted, "*It's a trap!*"

Tony's body had just cleared the fence with Callan still holding both arms out, controlling his kinetics, when brilliant yellow and blue lights shot up in a cross pattern from under the orange dirt.

Callan wrenched his arms in and yelled in pain.

Tony hit the ground and yelped.

The closest tent belched out a wad of scouts from the other side of the fenced area. At least twenty came running and carrying weapons.

Rayen started forward and Kenja grabbed her. "*No!*"

"Let go or I will break your arm," Rayen told her in a cold voice that warned of much worse if anyone stopped her from getting to Callan.

"That grid has shut down his powers. If you go in there, your powers will not work either. Do you think he wants that?"

The scouts fired hard pellets at them. One popped Rayen in the arm. She stepped in front of one child and Kaz protected the other.

But Kenja threw up a wall of kinetic protection and ordered the boys to run to the woods. They ran like wolves were after them.

Rayen watched Callan fall to his knees, twisting and fighting against whatever those lights were doing. She tried to reach him telepathically, banging on his head, but he didn't open his mind to her. Maybe he couldn't.

One of the scouts yelled, "*Cease fire!*"

The silence hit with the power of a steel fist and the same scout ordered, "Dim the grid."

The grid lights dropped. Callan struggled to his feet. He took a step and almost went down again. His gaze searched until it landed on Rayen.

She moved forward.

He shouted, "Go back."

She shook her head. She would not leave him here.

Scouts were spreading out and taking in their sleeping guards. She hoped they were sleeping and not dead. With Kenja, it was hard to gauge.

One of the TecKnati lifted his hand to his mouth and his words came out in a clear metallic sound. "Bring us the computer. We can't kill him, but we can make him beg for death."

Rayen yelled, "What computer?"

"The one you used to travel here."

That one? How were they supposed to bring the one they traveled through? "Who wants this computer?"

"SEOH."

That was the man who had put the MystiKs here. She demanded, "What does he want with it?"

"I don't know and don't care."

"If you turn the MystiK loose, we could get it to you faster." That suggestion had little chance, but she had to try.

The scout called back, "Speed is not going to be a problem. We can't go home until we have the Genera-Y computer, so he doesn't walk away until you show up with it. There is an old saying that time is of the essence. If you want Callan of the Warrior House back undamaged, or at least with minimal damage, then bring the computer by the third moon set from now.

That should give you plenty of time."

They knew who Callan was.

And this TecKnati spoke like he knew the difference between the passage of time here versus back at the school. That information had to have come from the traitor in Callan's village. But what was a Genera-Y computer? Her feet were moving before she realized it.

Kenja caught her upper arm and held her back behind the protective field.

Rayen said, "Let go. I'm only getting Tony." She watched the scouts for any aggressive move as she walked over to Tony and squatted down. Pulling out the knife Callan had given her, she sliced the bindings on Tony's hands and feet, then handed him the knife.

While he cut the covering off his mouth, she stood up and called to the scouts. "If you harm Callan, you will pay ten times over, because I *will* return with your stupid computer."

Callan said, "No, Rayen. Don't come back."

The yellow and blue lights glowed bright again and Callan arched backwards.

"Stop it," she ordered, "Or I promise you'll never see that computer."

The lights dimmed and that tall scout in charge called out through his mechanical device, "Oh, you'll bring it back. And if you try to rescue Callan without the computer, we'll start cutting off parts. Nothing that will kill him. We'll sear the skin with a torch to make sure he doesn't die. And since he's male, we have plenty of choices. Allow three moons to pass and you may have to carry him out."

She was shaking with the need to attack the scout who threatened to touch Callan's body. "What's your name?"

"Me? I'm Thylan." He laughed.

Tony pulled on her arm and urged me, "Come on, Xena. We'll get him back. The longer you're here, the longer it'll take to free him."

"They want a computer, and it will have to function *here* to convince them it's the right one."

"Piece of cake. Let's get moving."

Was that supposed to reassure her? Cake was food. Had Tony been influenced by the hallucination mist?

Tony tugged her again, his expression as serious as she'd ever seen. She took a step, keeping her eyes on Callan's.

Every inch of distance that grew between them clawed a chunk out of her heart. Callan's eyes begged her not to come back.

She shook her head. She would crawl through fire to get to him, and he would do no less for her.

Their group made it to the trees without being attacked again, but the scouts had no reason to come after them.

SEOH wanted a computer.

The scouts wanted to go home.

She wanted Callan safe.

Everyone was going to get what they wanted because nothing would stop her.

The minute they reached the cover of the forest, Tony said, "We got one big problem, Xena."

Bigger than saving Callan? She doubted it. "What?"

"We still don't have any idea where the controller is for the transender. We're stuck here until we find that."

She would not be defeated before she got started.

Straightening her back, she was ready to take on anything that got in her way. She snapped out instructions. "Kaz and Kenja, carry the boys so we can make good time. Tony, you follow them, and I'll cover our rear."

Kenja bristled. "You do *not* give me orders, outsider."

"Fine." Rayen got up in her face. "Then you *Uberons* can stay here and fight on your own if the TeKs come after you, because we're leaving and not slowing down for anyone." Nodding at Kaz, she said, "Lead the way."

Kenja snarled something under her breath and snatched up her warrior boy then ordered, "Everyone will follow me." She took off at a pace that would test all of them.

Tony grunted something, but he fell in behind Kaz who followed their self-proclaimed leader.

Rayen took one last look at Callan who was still in the middle of the fenced area with the scouts jeering at him. He stood tall, proud, and silent. A warrior willing to face whatever the enemy threw at him. His gaze swung to where she hid in the forest. That grid had harmed his gifts. They couldn't talk telepathically, but she didn't need words to know he'd rather face being dismembered than have her come back to this place.

As Gabby would say, *tough.*

Watching him stand there so alone thrashed Rayen's insides and was doing nothing to shorten his imprisonment. She hurried to catch up to the group.

Solve one problem at a time.

Find the transender controller.

Travel back through time to the past.

Get a computer the scouts would believe was the Genera-Y.

Piece of cake.

Now she was losing her mind.

CHAPTER 35

WHEN RAYEN ENTERED THE VILLAGE, the sound of young voices shouting told her they had new problems.

Tony was flagging physically by the time they reached the central area where a group of thirty-plus children stood on one side of an imaginary line and twelve Uberons faced them from the other side.

Angry shouts flew back and forth.

The Uberons were bellowing, "We are superior," and "We will not tolerate insolence," and "You will serve us."

Callan's MystiKs snarled and yelled, "I'm Governing House," and "We are gild level. You are nothing." One called out, "I'll serve you my foot." Zilya and Etoi stood back, watching with weary faces.

Gabby came running up from the other side. "What is going on?"

The shouting went up a level.

Rayen had no time for this. She roared, "*Shut. Up!*" But she believed it was the punch from her churning power that forced the entire place to go silent.

Rubbing her forehead where she was sure someone banged a rock against the inside, she took a breath and tried for calm. "This is not the time to be fighting. Callan has been captured by the TecKnati." A massive gasp whipped across the silence. She continued, "We will get him back, but not if we fight. We *must* all work together."

Kenja lowered her child to the ground and stepped forward. "This is not my problem. My people will not stay here."

That was it. Rayen snapped and wheeled on her.

Kenja shoved a wall between them that Rayen slammed into.

The Uberon leader smiled. That was the wrong move.

Rayen called up her power. A flood of it roared into her hands that glowed green. That was new, but she wasted no time considering it.

She shoved her hands against the kinetic wall.

The invisible barrier didn't just break. It shattered and knocked Kenja twenty feet back. She slammed against a tree, shaking limbs that sent crystal-clear, thin leaves falling like rain.

If Rayen hadn't been so worried about Callan, she'd have taken a minute to enjoy the full-blown shock on Kenja's face. As it was, she didn't want to let on that she was just as surprised. This gave her the edge she needed.

Crossing her arms, Rayen told her, "I have to go back and find this computer. If you do not stay here and help protect this village, I will hunt you down when I return and make you regret your selfish decision. Callan put himself at risk for your warrior as well as the other two captives. A true warrior would not leave that debt unpaid."

Kenja got up and knocked leaves out of her hair and strode forward. "Do you even know that you can bring a computer back?"

Without taking her eyes off Kenja, Rayen said, "Tony?"

"Not a problem, sweet cakes," he answered, directing his sweet cakes address at Kenja. "I can handle the computer, but can you handle the security here with Jaxxson and Kaz being the only older males left?"

Kenja's eyes swirled icy silver when she turned her gaze on Tony. "Do you dare to suggest that I require a male for protection, when so few are worthy of breathing my air?"

Tony lifted his hands. "No insult meant, babe. Just checking to make sure you got this."

She mimicked him. "I got this, *babe*."

Rayen almost smiled at realizing Tony had soothed Kenja's dented ego by giving her a chance to posture in front of the MystiKs *and* he'd managed to gain her agreement to stay. Now that everyone had calmed down, Rayen took advantage of what Tony had maneuvered by making it clear that challenging Kenja was not a wise idea.

She turned on Zilya. "With Kenja here to oversee security, you and Etoi will be free to govern the village, but you have no say over Kenja. Understood?"

Zilya's eyebrows drew tight, and her mouth sharpened in response, but Gabby stepped in before Zilya destroyed the fragile peace Rayen was trying to weave.

Gabby smiled at Zilya. "I can call Jaxxson to have him weigh in on this, but I warn you he will not be happy about being pulled away from treating the child in his hut right now. Plus, you and Etoi will have to deal with security if you give Kenja reason to leave." Gabby shrugged. "It's your choice."

Callan had left Zilya and Jaxxson jointly in charge. Zilya respected

Jaxxson's power too much to challenge him, but she had a chance to make decisions right now without his input, which would up Zilya's value in the eyes of the village. Callan would have no quarrel with that.

Zilya stood straighter. "As the Governing House elder of our village, I accept the offer of protection from Kenja of the Uberon Warrior House. It should not be taken as insult that I cannot offer shelter for sleeping until more is constructed, but we will share our food with you."

Rayen was prepared to tell Zilya that she and Etoi could give up their sleeping areas for these children, but Kenja answered with pride.

"Uberon warriors are not coddled. We sleep outside."

Rayen asked, "Even in this cold?"

The smirk on Kenja's face taunted her, suggesting *she* had been coddled. "We are adept at living on the land and know how to maintain heat on a cold night. As for meals, we will feed ourselves if I do not find the food here acceptable."

Tony laughed. "They need to film a *Survivors* segment here."

Kenja and Rayen both turned a confused look at him then Kenja spoke some odd word in the direction of her warriors. They were silent after having been in a shouting match earlier.

Every one of them, including the new one Kenja had brought back from the TeK camp, snapped to attention, and raced to fall into two lines, side by side. Rayen considered suggesting that Jaxxson check the health of Kenja's warrior they'd rescued, but that wouldn't go well.

And to be honest, the Uberon child appeared strong and well.

Pointing a long finger toward the wooded area inside the secured warding, Kenja said, "Wait for me twenty yards from here."

Once her warriors marched away, she spoke to Rayen, but swept a cutting look at the others. "I will stay for now. If you have not delivered this computer by the third moonset, my obligation to Callan will be repaid and I will leave the next morning."

"Callan is gone?" V'ru asked in a squeaky voice.

Rayen groaned inwardly. Callan would have wanted her to break the news of his imprisonment gently to V'ru before she left, but some things couldn't be avoided.

Tony said, "We'll get him back, V'ru Man."

"That's what Callan told me about you," V'ru replied.

"And I'm back."

Rayen waved V'ru over to her. He stepped forward looking even smaller in Tony's gray hooded pullover. His toga robe hung to the ground, tattered along the bottom edges.

Zilya called out, "What are you wearing, V'ru?"

The boy froze.

Rayen sent Zilya a frown edged with threat if she said another word. She wisely quieted.

Softening her expression, Rayen told V'ru, "Callan is a strong warrior. He'll be fine until I return." She wished she could convince herself as easily as everyone else who nodded their heads in agreement. She took V'ru's little hand in hers. "I promise to come back, and Tony knows what the TeKs want. It's a simple trade then Callan will be free."

V'ru shook his head and used his free hand to swipe black hair out of his eyes. "What about the prophecy?"

There it was again. "What prophecy?"

"The Damian Prophecy," Kaz said. "If you do have the computer that SEOH wants and you give it to him, he'll use it to destroy the MystiKs."

Could just one thing be easy?

She started to say that she'd bring another computer back—one that would fool them long enough to get Callan set free, but Callan thought there was a traitor in the village. She wouldn't risk sharing anything in front of the group in case the traitor was passing information to the TeKs.

Why would a MystiK do that? For a chance to leave.

She didn't know for sure, but she couldn't risk the truth spoken in the open, so she whispered, "This is just between us. Understand?"

V'ru nodded, intent on what she was saying.

"From what the TeK scout said, it's the computer we need for traveling from the past to here and back. Maybe Tony can figure out how to replicate that to give SEOH a similar one without fulfilling the prophecy."

Tony turned a face on her that questioned her ability to walk upright and speak a known language. She narrowed her eyes at him, and he just huffed quietly.

Letting go of V'ru's hand, she stood up. "What else should we know about this prophecy?"

V'ru answered in the voice of a child who was losing faith. "Callan is necessary for the prophecy. But he's stuck here. If he does not unite all the Houses, our entire world may fall anyhow."

Kenja made a nasty scoffing sound. "If you truly believe in the prophecy then you'd realize it's falling apart. Jornn is dead and Callan is not the equivalent of his twin. We do not have the computer and, if we did, we would destroy it, not hand *any* version of it over to the TeKs."

She quirked an eyebrow in Rayen's direction to let her know she'd heard what Rayen had told V'ru. But Kenja didn't like these MystiKs so she might not share that with the others.

Rayen started to warn her not to speak so harshly to V'ru, but the little guy jutted his chin up and got that righteous look in his eyes. The look she'd witnessed coming over him just before he'd proceeded to clear up incorrect facts.

V'ru sounded a foot taller when he spoke with authority. "The prophecy does not just vanish because something changes and who is to say that Jornn was definitely the one to unite the Houses? Callan could very well be the one."

Several intakes of breath echoed through the air.

V'ru crossed his skinny arms, sinking his teeth into his opinion. "The prophecy states that '*the last will lead when others cede*,' which exemplifies Callan. He has led us when we've had no other here. Mathias left us and never came back."

Gabby flinched at the same time Rayen did, but Gabby was probably just reacting to the anger in V'ru's voice.

Rayen's was due to guilt since she and Callan were the only two who knew the truth about Mathias. She felt bad keeping the truth from the others, but she'd given her word and Mathias had demanded it so that these children would not lose faith by learning what had happened to him.

V'ru didn't sound like an eleven-year-old when he got riled up, but she had no idea how eleven-year-old prodigies spoke. He was clearly not intimidated by Kenja, who listened with a surprising calmness.

Kaz said, "He has a point."

Zilya had been silent longer than expected. "You can twist the words to mean anything. I heard one part of the prophecy is "*the future is in the past ... one will seek and all will forfeit*." She turned her wrath on Rayen. "We've been under attack and on the run since you showed up asking questions. How do we know that *you* aren't the one the prophecy is talking about who will seek and cause all to forfeit?"

This whole conversation was wasting time. Zilya would think I was dodging her question, but I honestly didn't care. "I can't do anything about a prophecy, but I can get Callan back. Until then, I'm done with talking."

"Then go," Zilya said. "Come back without that computer and you will be left outside the ward to fend for yourselves."

There was no if in Rayen's mind. She was bringing back a computer.

Dismissing Zilya's worthless threat, Rayen asked, "Does anyone know how to locate the controller to our transender site?"

Jaxxson came walking around the corner of the communal building in time to hear her question. He looked around. "Where's Callan?"

She asked Gabby, "Would you fill him in?"

Gabby waved a hand in acknowledgement and walked over to him where they spoke off to the side.

"I think I can find the controller," Etoi volunteered.

Had she heard that correctly? Etoi was going to help them? Call her suspicious, but she had to ask, "Why do you think *you* can?"

That's all it took to bring out Etoi's surly side. "Do you want my help or not?"

Tony said, "Let it go, Xena. Beggars can't be choosy."

"I did not beg her," she let him know, adding an angry cut of her eyes.

Gabby called over, "It's just a saying, Rayen. It means getting something is better than nothing."

Rayen would never understand how everyone talked in the future or the past. "We have to leave now."

Kaz stepped up. "I'll go with you."

Etoi exchanged a guarded look with Zilya and told Kaz, "I do not need your help."

"I didn't offer my help to you. I'm going along to guard these three as per Callan's orders, then I intend to hunt. We need more food for tonight.

Kaz had to be lying. Callan couldn't be reached telepathically while he was standing on that grid and, before now, Callan had no reason to order Kaz to protect them at this point. But she wouldn't refuse his offer in case Etoi had some other agenda in mind.

Like leading the three of them into a croggle nest.

Gabby and Jaxxson hugged then she walked over to Rayen and Tony. She looked at them. "What?"

Tony scrunched up his face. "You're not getting sweet on the doc, are ya?"

Instead of her usual come back, Gabby grinned and asked, "Maybe. You're not getting sweet on Zilya, are ya?"

"Be serious." Tony glanced at Zilya who thankfully was too far away to hear his soft words. "Got my eye on someone back at school, but she's gonna light me up when I show up late."

"I'm sorry, Tony," Rayen offered. "This wasn't what you agreed to."

Jaxxson walked up to them with Tony's brown backpack slung over one shoulder. He slipped the strap off and handed the pack to Tony.

After thanking Jaxxson, Tony hooked the bag with one hand and told Rayen, "None of this is your fault, Xena, but I'm ready to roll."

She noticed V'ru had gone stony quiet. The child seemed to be pulling in all his defenses, prepared to be left alone.

Tony must have noticed, too. He stepped over and squatted down in front of the child. "I don't want you to worry, V'ru Man."

V'ru moved his head up and down. His eyes were shiny with unshed tears.

Sighing, Tony scrubbed a hand over his face and tried again. "This place sucks, but I *am* comin' back. I need you to do your best to stay healthy and safe, okay?"

Another nod.

"Play your games," Tony whispered.

V'ru shrugged.

Tony stared at V'ru for a few seconds then seemed to come to some decision. He dropped his backpack on the ground and reached inside to pull out a colorful booklet that he handed to V'ru.

The child's entire face lit up with disbelief and awe. He whispered, "For me?"

"It's yours, V'ru Man."

The boy ran his hand over it with the care you'd give a precious possession. "But ... but you said it was for someone special."

"It is. You're special. I'll be very sad if I come back, and you aren't okay."

A tear slid down V'ru's face. He sniffled. "I will be okay."

Gabby's eyes were damp. Rayen had to swallow at the tender way Tony handled this child.

V'ru glanced around then back at Tony and spoke low. "The computer you bring back must convince the TeKs that it is not just any electronic from the past."

Tony said, "I know, and I'll do my best. I promise."

The child leaned close to Tony and started whispering a rapid string of words. Now Tony had a look of disbelief mixed with awe.

Zilya came marching up. "V'ru, do you forget yourself?"

V'ru stood up and backed away from Tony with fear in his face.

Tony shoved up with his hands fisted. He shouted, "Do *not* yell at that child again."

"He can share nothing of what he knows with your kind. He is a G'ortian of the Records House, a rare descendant, one that must never share this knowledge with outsiders and most definitely not one of TecKnati blood.

You should show more care for this child and not put him in a position of shaming himself."

So that's what V'ru had been doing. Telling Tony something about computers. Rayen was with Tony about Zilya yelling at V'ru, but she didn't want to put the boy under more strain. Rayen told Tony, "I'm sure you can do this with what you know."

He was shaking with unleashed anger, but to his credit, Tony pulled himself under control when he told Zilya, "Then treat him like he deserves and be nice to him."

There was no question about the threat within those words.

Kaz strode over with Etoi at his heels. "We can leave when you say the word."

Rayen wasn't happy leaving V'ru with Zilya, but the boy looked up at Tony and winked as he slid the booklet under Tony's pullover.

Out of the blue, a word struck Rayen. Pluck. The kid had pluck.

She told Kaz, "Now," which everyone took as the word, and they left.

Almost an hour later, they stood watching Etoi hunt through burned and broken jungle debris.

Tony eyed the sky. "That moon's gonna set in another fifteen minutes. If it does, we lose our window of time to travel until it rises again tomorrow."

"And they have to get back before the mist hits," Rayen said in Kaz's direction.

He stabbed his spear hard into the ground. "If she finds it soon, we can return to the village much faster with our power." He asked Tony, "How soon can you return?"

Scratching his chin while he mentally calculated something, Tony said, "We have to get back inside the school and explain where we've been then get our hands on a computer. I need time to figure out how to do what V'ru told me. If the crazy girl hadn't gone off on V'ru, I could have asked questions."

"I don't support Zilya's actions," Kaz said. "But she is technically correct. V'ru broke rules to share that knowledge with you."

"Sometimes you gotta break a few rules to do the right thing," Tony pointed out.

"I'm not criticizing. I'm only telling you the situation he's in."

"Fair enough, but you should keep her off his back."

"I'll do as much as I can, but I'm the one who feeds our children. I can't depend on Kenja to do it. She'd expect them to live off of tree bark." Kaz ran his hand through his hair, leaving wild sprigs of cinnamon locks behind.

"You were going to tell me when you plan to return."

Rayen asked, "Why does it matter as long as we come back in time to get him out before sunset?"

"Because the prophecy does circle around Callan, and he must–"

"Found it!" Etoi shouted, waving from thirty feet away where she stood next to a pile of branches and dried vines. She'd pushed it aside and there was a slightly scorched pink flower that looked like the fake one that held the controller.

"Hot *day-um*!" Tony exclaimed and rushed over to shove his hand down inside.

Rayen reached him just as the holographic panel appeared and the smooth feminine voice from last time announced, *"Twelve minutes left to request transender return from Sphere."*

"It's ready for ya, Xena."

She stuck her hand on the holographic panel and a red light immediately traced the outline of her hand, then started blinking and turned solid green.

So far, so good.

Out in the open space next to the destroyed jungle, a whirring sound started. When the spinning ended, the transender appeared as a metallic cylinder. If everything stayed constant, they had three minutes for all three of them to put their hands on the side of the transender. That would open a panel to allow them to climb in.

Tony said, "Let's not make it a photo finish this time, okay, Xena?"

"I'm ready." But she wanted Kaz to finish what he was telling her. "You said Callan is at the center of the prophecy and he must do something. What were you going to say?"

Grim concern entered Kaz's eyes. "It may not seem important to others, but we must continue with our tradition just as we would at home for any hope that the prophecy will not destroy us. I was only saying that Callan must fulfill his role in three moons."

Tony and Gabby had already started toward the transender. Rayen took a step that way, but asked, "What's so important about three moons from now?"

"Callan's BIRG Day. He'll be eighteen and must perform a ritual for the prophecy."

The blood froze in her veins. If she didn't get Callan out of that TecKnati camp, not only would they torture him, but he'd also have no defense against the wraiths.

Etoi made a pfft sound. "Callan will leave us just like Mathias did."

For once, the mouthy MystiK was right. In three moonsets, Callan would be swept away by the black wraiths that took Mathias away screaming.

Callan had to get out of this Sphere.

"Rayen, you gotta hurry," Tony yelled. He and Gabby already had their hands in place.

No truer words had ever been spoken.

She tore across the rutted field and slapped her hands on the cold metal.

A panel opened and they dove inside just as a screeching alarm pealed and the panel shut.

CHAPTER 36

RAYEN'S BODY TWISTED AND JERKED in different directions as they flew through the multi-colored ether again. She might be another inch taller after all the stretching she was going through.

The computer spit her out on the floor of Tony's room.

Muscle memory sent her rolling to the side to keep from being slammed by Tony. He must have had the same muscle memory.

He jumped out of the way before Gabby hit with a thud.

All Rayen heard for a moment was a chorus of their groans. Then she struggled to her feet and took in her appearance. Torn to pieces. The last time they arrived, she had to go straight to a meeting in Dr. Maxwell's office. He hadn't been pleased with the way she'd treated her clothes, but she'd had no defense.

Not unless she had wanted to tell him that a three-story monster called a croggle had attacked her.

Tony rubbed his neck and dragged himself to his computer chair. He leaned against the backpack he still wore.

Gabby stood, arching her back. "That sucks."

Rayen asked, "Any idea of what time it is?"

Reaching over to the desk where the portal computer sat, Tony lifted his phone that had been sitting face down. "Five-o-eight. PM. I'm in so much trouble. I promised Hannah that I'd meet her at four."

"You're only an hour late."

"Yeah, but ... never mind." Tony shook off whatever he was going to tell her.

"Well, they're probably still looking for me from the infirmary," Gabby said and started repairing her loose ponytails. "I'll have to find a good hiding place until you two are ready to go."

"Can't stay here," Tony said. "You get caught in the boy's dorm they'll boot you in the next second. Me, too."

"We can't lose either one of you," Rayen warned. "I'll help Gabby hide.

Tony, you find us a computer and fix it up."

"About that–"

Rayen held up a hand. "We'll talk later. What time do we need to leave here to be back in the Sphere no later than an hour before moon set? Two hours would be better to avoid the risk of traveling at night to get back to the village."

Tony stared off at nothing, but he was clearly calculating. "Best I can tell, the third moonset will be forty-eight relative hours in their time. That equals twelve hours in our time, which would be five in the morning. If we want to have a two-hour window, we need to leave here no later than 4:30 AM."

"I understand." Rayen thought on it and wanted plenty of time. "No matter what, Gabby and I will be in the storage room where we first found this computer by 4:00 AM at the latest. That way, if you can get there sooner, Tony, we'll be waiting on you, but you have to arrive by four-thirty."

Tony stared at the computer with a grim expression.

Understandable, because they were all mentally, physically, and emotionally drained.

She looked around the room and caught sight of herself in a mirror on his bathroom door. "I have to clean up and find out if the front office has been looking for me for that Takoda guy. I can't go like this to Dr. Maxwell's office. Have you got a shirt I can borrow?"

Tony walked over to a dresser and pulled out a long-sleeved blue shirt with the words "AND YET DESPITE THE LOOK ON MY FACE, YOU'RE STILL TALKING" in white. He tossed it to her and claimed, "Hannah will know what's going on."

She pulled the shirt over her ragged one. At least the sleeves covered her scraped arms. "You think she'll tell you?"

Tony's voice lowered a notch. "If she's still speaking to me, she will."

"I'm sorry, Tony. You did your part and I got you back late."

He waved her off. Charm and confidence blended in his next words. "Give me a couple minutes and I'll smooth this over. I know her soft spot."

Gabby missed nothing. She eyed Tony. "Is *that* who you've got your eye on?"

"Maybe," he said, grinning.

"But she's a bitc–"

Tony warned, "Gabby, stop right there before you stick your foot in it. You just don't know her."

"If you say so."

"I do. I'll text her and see what's been going on ..." He punched a button on his phone and whistled. "Everybody's been blowing up my phone."

His phone looked to be in one piece to Rayen, but asking him to explain would take time, the one thing none of them had.

While Tony punched more buttons, Gabby spoke to Rayen in a voice too soft for him to hear. "I need to talk to you about Mathias."

Rayen did not want to discuss that and used the only excuse she could for avoiding it. "Let's talk later when it's just the two of us."

"Okay."

Tony chortled under his breath then grinned to himself before sharing what was funny. "Hannah's texting me back. That's a good sign. She said she figured something important came up."

"Are you sure it's the same Hannah we know?"

Shooting a dark look at Gabby, Tony said, "Give the girl a break already." When Gabby rolled her eyes, Tony went back to reading messages on his phone to them. "Hannah says Suarez was looking for me. Probably wanted to confirm the change to Hannah as my partner. The front office is looking for me. That's probably for Suarez. Security is looking for me. That would be because they came to my door, and I didn't answer." He rubbed his hand over his stubby hair.

Gabby started floating up.

Tony lowered his phone. "What the ..."

Gabby flailed the air with her hands like she was trying to push herself down.

Rayen reached over and tugged on her shirt. Gabby floated down.

"That's not good, babe."

Tony, master of the obvious. Rayen didn't say it though.

"I can't help it." Gabby grabbed the footboard of his bed, fingers clutching tight. "It just happened."

They had to get her hidden soon. Rayen asked, "Anything on your phone about me or Gabby?"

"No." He thumbed buttons quickly and waited. "Hannah said she'd meet me outside the boy's dorm and fill me in." He closed the time-travel laptop and slipped it into his backpack then went to his door, unlocked it, and looked both ways. "Everyone should be at dinner. Let's make a run for it."

Gabby followed Tony. Rayen was right behind her to keep an eye out that she didn't float up again. Pulling the door shut softly, Rayen padded down the hall that seemed impossibly long. The double doors loomed ahead like a gate to freedom. Her heart was thumping faster with every step, because she and Gabby couldn't afford to be caught here.

Thankfully, when they reached the doors no one was on the other side.

Rayen took a deep breath as soon as she stepped out.

Based on the timeline Tony had provided, she felt confident that between her and Gabby, they could find a place to hide until they met up and opened the portal again. The only questionable part of this plan was if Tony could make the second computer work, but he was a genius and V'ru had shared some secrets with him.

She had to put faith in her friends.

They had been there for her and still were.

Hannah came walking up with a fast clip clop of her short heels. She was perfection as much as Rayen was the opposite. She wrinkled her nose in Rayen's direction.

Tony turned into Mr. Charm. "Hey, Hannah. You're lookin' good as always."

The girl who had been so abrupt with Rayen when she'd escorted her around the first day turned into a ball of sunshine for Tony. "Thanks, but where have you been?"

Hannah sounded concerned.

Gabby gave Rayen a look of disbelief and she just lifted her shoulders. Guess Hannah *could* be nice if she tried.

"It's a long story, hon," Tony crooned. "I just need to know who's lookin' for these two and what I gotta do to appease Suarez." He paused and added, "But the good news is that I have what we need to win that competition."

She smiled, but not with any enthusiasm to match Tony's excitement over his news on the competition. Hannah said, "The Clinic is looking for Gabby. The Browns have sent me everywhere looking for Rayen. Takoda wants to see her. He was here a half hour ago. I don't know if he's still here or gone."

Rayen told Gabby, "We should get moving." Hannah might think they meant to go to the clinic and front office, but Gabby nodded her understanding that they had to hide quickly.

"You won't make it far if you stray," Hannah warned Rayen.

"Why?"

"Security is monitoring cameras to catch you three."

Tony frowned. "Three? Why me?"

Embarrassment flushed Hannah's cheeks. "No one will tell me, but security wants to talk to you about something."

Rayen took in the worry in Tony's face and asked, "Is this serious?"

"No, they must think I went AWOL or something's happened to me physically."

"AWOL?" she asked.

"We need to update your vocabulary, Xena. It means absent without leave. Military term." Tony asked Hannah, "Would you do me a favor?"

"Sure, what?"

"Would you hide Gabby?"

"Why?" Hannah and Gabby said together.

He arched an exasperated look at Gabby then became Mr. Charm again for Hannah. "They had Gabby scheduled for an invasive procedure in the hospital. Until her dad can get here to straighten it out, she's afraid to go back to the clinic. Right, Gabby?"

"Uh, yes, that's right."

Tony continued. "No one would look for you in Hannah's room and it's only for tonight."

Gabby caught on. "Good point." She asked Hannah, "Do you mind?"

"No, I guess not. I'll do it for *Tony*."

"Thanks, Hannah." Tony turned to Rayen. "That Takoda guy is probably gone by now. Tell the Browns that I was tutoring you on computers and I didn't realize my phone died."

"For eight hours?" Hannah asked.

Tony threw his hands up in the air. "She can tell them she fell asleep and thinks she's narcoleptic. I don't care, but we need our stories straight."

Before Rayen could ask, Tony told her, "Narcoleptic means you fall asleep practically walking around."

"Why are you helping her?" Hannah had her arms crossed and she looked suspiciously at Rayen. "What's *this one* to you, Tony?"

This one? Even here? "I am Rayen!"

Hannah bumped a shoulder up in her direction. "What. Ever."

Tony stepped up to Hannah and pushed a lock of hair behind her ear, melting the scowl on her face. Then he leaned in and kissed her cheek. "Not what you think, hon. She's a friend, nothin' more. You on the other hand are *very* special."

The girl sighed.

Gabby coughed into her hand and said something derogatory. He glared at her then swung his backpack around and handed it to Gabby. "Keep this until I come for it."

"Why?"

"Because I don't know what security wants but the first thing they'll do is search my backpack, and I hate anyone touching my stuff." He spelled it out slowly.

Gabby's gaze brightened with understanding. "Got it." She pushed her arms through the straps and grunted as if it was heavy.

Rayen hoped the weight of the backpack would keep Gabby's feet on the ground. Hannah was going along with them and helping because she clearly liked Tony. But she might not be so calm and agreeable if Gabby started levitating.

Hannah waved a hand at Gabby. "Let's go this way."

"Through the boy's dorm?"

"There's a cut across to the girl's dorm with a narrow passage that's blocked from cameras."

"What if we get caught in there?"

Grinning slyly, Hannah lifted a plastic covered piece of paper that would fit in Rayen's palm. It had her photo and a bunch of impressive writing. She said, "I have the master badge. They send me to deliver messages everywhere. If anyone stops me, I'll tell them I've just located you and was heading back to the clinic, which is in the same direction."

Tony said, "I don't want you to get in trouble, Hannah."

"I won't. If I do run into anyone, once I put her in my room, I'll just tell them she got away from me."

"That's my girl," Tony crooned.

Rayen thought Gabby would gag.

She smiled at Gabby then asked Hannah for her room number and made a mental note that it was on the second floor. "I'll come get Gabby as soon as I finish with the Browns." Then it hit her that Takoda might be there. "What does this Takoda want when he comes to the school?"

Hannah shrugged. "He'll talk to you and try to determine what tribe you're from. He'll take what you tell him back to the council then it takes a while to find your family unless they've already contacted someone about you disappearing."

That eased the tight muscles in Rayen's chest. It might even be a benefit if Takoda was here so she could get the meeting with him out of the way then no one would be looking for her.

When the double doors to the boys' dorm closed behind Hannah and Gabby leaving, Tony said, "Let's go face the music."

Rayen walked along beside him. "What music?"

"If you stay in the past, you're gonna need a crash course in current pop culture and old sayings. It means we have to go find out how much trouble we're in and face the possible consequences."

They'd just turned down the last hall heading to the office when two men in uniforms approached them. She recognized the men as the ones who were security officers for the school.

The intense look in their eyes raised hairs along her neck.

Tony murmured, "Wonder what got their panties in a wad?"

She was not going to ask about their panties.

Students passed them as they stopped and waited.

As soon as the pair of security officers reached them, the taller one said to Rayen, "You're to report in at the front office immediately."

Tony waved her on.

She walked past the two men, but ducked into the doorway of a broom closet, close enough to hear the conversation. It wasn't difficult. Those men could have taken Tony somewhere private, but they seemed determined to make a show of this conversation.

The man who sounded in charge said, "Tony Scolerio."

It was not a question, but Tony answered, "You found me. What's up?"

"You've been charged with stealing a laptop computer. Where is it?"

Oh, no. Did they want the portal computer?

Tony bristled. "I haven't stolen a computer. I'm in Mr. Suarez's class. He'll tell you that I'm working on the Competition project."

Thank goodness Tony handed off the portal computer to Gabby.

"Mr. Suarez is the one who reported the theft."

"What? No!" Tony was shaking his head. "I have an old beat-up computer from the storage room just like everyone else. I got the crap stuff, in fact."

"It was Mr. Suarez's personal computer that went missing. It will go better for you if you return it now."

This couldn't be happening.

Tony said, "I don't have it. Why point the finger at me? I wasn't anywhere near his class today and he's supposed to be gone."

"There was an eyewitness who saw you sneak out of his classroom early this morning with a laptop matching the description of Mr. Suarez's. The timing fits for when Mr. Suarez was out of his room before he left the Institute at noon on a personal matter."

"Impossible," Tony argued, his body starting to vibrate with aggression. "Who is this eyewitness? I want to meet the twerp that dares to accuse me of theft."

"Nicholas Brown."

Tony's face refelected Rayen's horror at hearing the name of the Brown's only child uttered.

The security guy ordered, "Okay, that was your one chance. You're going to detention where you'll remain until the police arrive."

Panic entered Tony's voice. "When will they be here?"

"The Browns will want to be present when law enforcement questions you. My best guess is sometime tomorrow afternoon since the Browns have left and won't be back until morning at the soonest."

Rayen stuck her head out. Tony caught sight of her just before he turned. She mouthed the words, *I'll find you.*

He gave a tiny move of his head to let her know he understood, but he still looked like he was on the way to face a killer frazzle vine with his hands tied.

The Browns were gone until tomorrow. All she had to do was check in at the front office so they would stop looking for her then promise to be back whenever the Browns wanted to meet her if Takoda wasn't here.

Then she would free Tony somehow.

Turning back down the hall, she passed a group of girls talking and two boys punching each other's arms. They were arguing about something called football.

The bodies parted and she almost ran into Phen.

This just got better and better.

He had something in his hand. When she reached him, he opened his fingers and a frog stared up at her with huge black eyes. The frog yawned, showing off a mouth full of fangs.

And it stank.

Phen was holding the sentient beast that had been a three-legged animal the size of a buffalo when it chased her in the desert.

She might as well find out what this TeK was up to. "Hello, Phen."

"Rayen. Where have you been all day? Everyone was looking for you."

Of course, she didn't answer him even if he had guessed that they'd returned to the Sphere. Maybe he would give up some information by accident if she annoyed him and kept him talking. She wanted to find out who their enemies here were and doubted Phen would tell her if she asked.

She tried another idea. "Who are these people looking for me? Are they the TecKnati you got sent here to serve? How many do you answer to in this place?"

He snapped his hand shut. His eyes darkened with menace. "Listen up. I'm willing to make a deal."

That wasn't what she'd hoped to hear.

"Are you without a lick of survival instinct?" she asked, leaning toward him. "You tried to kill my friends. I do not make deals with the enemy."

"I heard about you. You're not from this time either, Rayen. You need me to go home, too." He grinned. "Yes, I know you're C'raydonian, but I haven't told anyone. Yet."

The traitor had told him. That was the only way a TecKnati could know where she'd come from. "I'm listening."

"I'm willing to work together if you'll help me get back to my world. You must have it figured out to be traveling back and forth to the Sphere."

She ignored the shuffle of footsteps passing them, accompanied by the hum of conversation. She had no idea how to make the portal work or she'd send every MystiK home. Even Callan. Why would Phen think she could do more than travel to that artificial star? She'd been told that if anyone could perfect time travel in two directions it would be SEOH and the TecKnati.

TeKs had already tricked them once today. She would not play into another trap. Phen was here in the past where mentioning that she was a C'raydonian would mean nothing, even if they believed him. "Stay away from me and my friends, Phen. If you harm even one of them, I'll make you very sorry."

If hate could be molded into a mask, it would look like Phen's face right now. "I *will* find how you're traveling. I'm not staying in this decrepit excuse for a world."

Maybe he really did just want to go home. She started to reconsider her words, because if that was the case, he might actually help them.

"Rayen!"

She looked past Phen's shoulder to where Dr. Maxwell stood at the door to the front office. Waving to let him know she'd heard him, she stepped past Phen and whispered, "Let me think on it."

If nothing else, that might keep Phen out of their way until they could leave again. With Gabby hiding and Tony locked up somewhere, they didn't need any more people creating obstacles.

She hurried into the main office, ready to be humble and tell Dr. Maxwell anything he wanted to hear.

As soon as she walked into his private office, he said, "Here she is. I told you we'd find her."

Standing in Mr. Brown's usual position next to the bookcase behind Dr. Maxwell's desk was a man a few inches taller than her with skin the color of the dark liquid people called colas in this time. His face was carved with sharp edges and his nose had a distinct curve. Black hair hung past his shoulders. He wore a faded checked shirt that might have been green once, tan pants and soft shoes. Around his neck was a necklace with a rock-sized turquoise stone shaped as an oval and mounted in silver metal.

This had to be Takoda.

His deep-set brown eyes studied her face ... no, her eyes, for a long moment, but he kept his reaction hidden. Had the odd pale, blue-green color of her eyes caused him to dismiss her outright? Would that work in her favor?

Takoda spoke in a deep, weathered voice. "Hello, Rayen."

"Hello." She was still staring at him but couldn't help it. He had a familiar look about his face and body that she couldn't place. Had she seen him the first day she was captured by the Albuquerque Police? Had Takoda been one of the native-looking men around the police station?

So many people had been there. It had turned into a confusing blur.

Takoda ordered, "Remove her cuff."

Dr. Maxwell started to argue. "The Browns–"

"Have no say over a Navajo."

Disgruntled, Dr. Maxwell pulled a key from his drawer and walked over to drop down on one knee. He pushed the edge of her pants up with the back of his hand, then unlocked the the metal cuff. Then he went back to his desk.

Her leg felt so much better with that weight off that she said, "Thank you."

Takoda gave an abrupt nod. "I have questions."

How long would this Takoda want to talk to her? She told herself to be patient. She'd rather answer his questions than face the Browns. If Phen could be here from the future, others could too. Were the Browns TecKnati? What about this Dr. Maxwell?

The silence pulled tight with tension. Rayen said, "I'll answer anything I can."

"Good." Takoda looked over at the doctor. "Are the papers ready?"

Dr. Maxwell gave a sharp nod. "Yes."

Rayen looked at each of them. "What papers?"

Takoda answered, "Releasing you into my custody. I will take you to my reservation and send out an alert that I've found a missing daughter. Your people will come for you, or we will find a home."

The walls started caving in on her. She backed up. "No, I like it here." She looked at the doctor. "I want to talk to Mrs. Brown first."

"She waited to meet with you and signed off on the papers before she left."

Rayen took another step back and the door opened behind her. A pair of security officers entered. One had a strange object in her hand that she held like a weapon.

Takoda ordered, "Do not try to run, Rayen. You will only hurt yourself."

Rayen called to her power, but she couldn't feel it. She tried to think, but her mind froze with panic. She was breathing fast and sucking air like she had high up in the tree.

The male officer held up a plastic strip and said, "Put your hands out."

They were going to bind her. "No. I'm not going." Her heart hammered fast as the hooves of a spooked horse racing across hard ground. She begged her power to help her.

The security man said, "Put. Your. Hands. Out."

Takoda said, "Do as they say, Rayen."

She had to get back to Callan. "Noooo!" She lunged forward to escape.

The female officer fingered her metal unit, and something shot out of it, stabbing Rayen. Pain exploded in her chest. Her body vibrated with a charge of energy that shook her like a rag. She screamed, falling to the floor, begging for the buzzing energy to stop.

It did.

She fell into a black hole of pain and horror.

TIMELOCK

RED MOON TRILOGY
SCIENCE FICTION TIME TRAVEL BOOK 3

DIANNA LOVE & MARY BUCKHAM
WRITING AS
MICAH CAIDA

CHAPTER 1

RAYEN WAS DOWN TO HOURS to save Callan's life. He'd never see eighteen.

At this rate, she might not either.

Callan was trapped in a place far into the future known as the Sphere, an artificial planet, and she was trapped in a small, cramped room somewhere out in the desert an hour away from a place called Albuquerque. The time-travel computer portal for returning to the Sphere was in an Albuquerque boarding school in Tony's backpack, which Gabby had. Tony had been locked up by security. Gabby hid in another student's room.

She needed both of her friends to open the portal.

Minutes raced past.

Her heart beat a frantic speed.

"Come on," she begged her power and gripped the doorknob. That stupid power had yet to show up since she'd been taken from the school and locked in this room. She'd drawn on it to kill a huge croggle monster in the Sphere, but she couldn't open a locked door right now. *Why?*

Nothing she tried worked. She was hitting a new level of panic. Holding onto the doorknob, she slumped to her knees on the wood floor.

There had to be a way out of here. But how? The last time she'd used her power it was to save someone else.

She sat upright. That was it! Someone had been in immediate danger each time she'd drawn on her energy.

The danger to Callan wasn't happening right this second, but it was real and deadly. Could she use that to wake up her power?

Clenching her fingers tighter around the doorknob, she dredged up an awful image of Callan's enemy—the TecKnati—swinging a sword and lopping off his beautiful hands. Nausea crowded her throat and she flinched at the gruesome image.

A spark of energy warmed her chest, swirling, then the heat spread to her arms and hands. Yes!

The doorknob heated beneath her fingers. She closed her eyes to see if she could picture the lock parts the way she had when she and Tony had opened a door. A vision of metal parts blurred in her mind. The parts tumbled and clicked, banging into each other, faster and faster until she couldn't tell what they were doing.

Metal jangled together in a loud crash.

She snatched her hand away and fell backward, expecting Takoda to burst inside any minute with another stun gun in hand.

She'd learned about that weapon the hard way.

What she'd learned since coming awake in the desert a couple days ago was terrifying.

She still had no memory, except for a few bits that had emerged to form a strange puzzle still missing too many parts to make sense. Takoda was a Navajo on some council who'd found her at the school. When he came to take her away last night, she'd tried to run. The guards had used that stun gun on her.

Silence outside her room taunted her.

No Takoda.

The door should open.

What if he had someone guarding this building?

Takoda had said he'd be back in the morning, which might be hours away if midnight was as close as she estimated. But it could already be past. Her guess could be way off. Blood pounded in her ears, thudding with each heavy beat. If they caught her escaping, would they shackle her and lock her away somewhere her power would not work?

This was not the time for fear.

She had no idea how long it would take her to walk back to the school. To *run* back. Everything hinged on her returning before four in the morning.

She had to hurry and hope that Tony was still there, and no one had found Gabby's hideout. So many things had to happen for her, Gabby, and Tony to return to the Sphere.

Callan and the other MystiK children who'd been captured were stuck there waiting for them to come back.

Returning too late meant Callan would first suffer torture at the hands of the TecKnati, then he'd die a horrible death.

The minute the red moon above the Sphere set and Callan turned eighteen, black wraiths would swarm him. He'd vanish into the ether just like Mathias had, but the other MystiKs in the Sphere didn't know that.

Rayen stood up. She was the only one besides Callan aware of his horrible fate—the same fate of any MystiK who turned eighteen in the Sphere.

She couldn't stop the moon from setting on the day he turned eighteen, but she might be able to do something to prevent his death.

I will not lose you, she vowed silently, repeating the words he'd said when he'd fought to protect her from a deadly plant in the Sphere.

But she couldn't change anything if she didn't get out of this room.

Caution from the awful memory of being shocked by the weapon had her hesitating to see if anyone had heard the internal lock parts clanging, but she couldn't stay here any longer.

She put her ear against the door and listened.

No footsteps were coming this way. Takoda had driven through miles of desert on the way here last night. He said only a few locals lived in this small town, but he hadn't told her if he was one of them.

She tested the doorknob again and ... it opened. Her power must have worked. This time.

Outside, the air was dry and cool where it had been hot as an oven during the day. The glow from a giant, not-quite-full moon washed over the stacked pueblo rooms built high into the night sky. Takoda had used the term pueblo, but it was unfamiliar to her. To be honest, with few memories returning so far, most of the things she'd encountered were unfamiliar to her.

Once she regained consciousness last night, Takoda had talked continually during the drive. He acted friendly and asked if she knew about Acoma Pueblo.

No, she didn't, and they weren't friends. Her friends had never electrocuted her with a weapon.

He'd explained what a stun gun was, then apologized.

Apology not accepted. She was still a captive.

Moving quietly, she kept picking her way through the quiet town, looking all around. The place had been built on a high plateau. In the distance, mountaintops dusted by moonlight rose against the dark skies. She had to get down from this sandstone mesa to the desert floor.

Had this place still been standing in the future when her people—C'raydonians—lived in the Sandia Mountains somewhere around Albuquerque? V'ru would know. She'd gained the only information she had on C'raydonians from V'ru, an all-knowing, eleven-year-old MystiK in the Sphere. Based on his records, it was believed that she had been born over eight decades into the future.

Her people would eventually live here.

And they would all die here, leaving no one.

Longing hit her with the swift strike of a sharp arrow for a family she couldn't remember and a life beyond the reach of her mind.

She had nothing. No one.

In the brief, grueling days she'd been in this time, she'd formed a connection with Gabby and Tony back at the school, plus Callan and the MystiKs trapped in the Sphere.

And now someone wanted to take even *that* from her.

She continued sneaking through the town. No life stirred.

When she finally found the main road leading away from here, her feet picked up speed with each step toward the desert. Freedom was within her reach.

The road dropped off at a steep angle.

She embraced the adrenaline pushing her to go and started running faster through the moonlit night, using the broken white lines on the center of the road to navigate.

How long could she maintain this pace?

She didn't know, but at least she had a trail to follow. Also, at this hour of night, no one would hear her sneakers slapping the hard surface.

Would this route lead her all the way to the school? She had been unconscious during the first part of the drive.

Breathing hard, she'd been on the desert level only a few minutes when she heard thunder.

She looked up. Not a cloud disturbed the vast sky.

The noise grew louder.

Not a storm, but the thunder of hooves pounding the ground.

Panicked, she looked over her shoulder. Four men on horses raced toward her.

"No!" She pushed her legs harder and spun her feet, searching all around. Where was a place to hide or a way to lose them? Nowhere. She stared at nothing beyond a vast ocean of sand interrupted by an occasional juniper tree.

Racing ahead with all the speed she could beg of her legs and feet. Pain gripped her side. She clutched it and kept running.

"Rayen, stop!" Takoda shouted as he closed in on her.

She was gasping for air. There was no way she'd outrun horses. Slowing down, she stumbled to a stop and spun to face him.

Raising her hands, she begged her power to come forth.

Energy buzzed beneath her skin and hummed in her chest, but nothing reached her hands.

The horses pulled up hard, sending a cloud of dust billowing around her. When it cleared, Takoda climbed down and walked up to her. "You can't leave."

Tears would do her no good. She blinked them away and pleaded, "Please let me go back. Cal … a person's life depends on me returning."

"Your people need you." His voice gentled. "You are special, Rayen."

How could she tell him that *her* people lived eighty years in the future and all of them were doomed to die because of a virus? She'd found out the C'raydonian race *had* descended from the Navajo and other tribes that had intermarried with the Navajo.

But the people Takoda had talked about were not *hers*.

When the K'ryan Virus, or K-Virus as it was also called, came along over a hundred years in the future from now, it turned C'raydonians into rabid animals who were hunted to extinction.

Her throat was dry from running and the dust didn't help.

She coughed and croaked, "I can't ... save anyone here."

Takoda said something to one of the riders, who tossed him a bottle of water. He handed it to her. "Drink."

She grabbed it and guzzled down the cool liquid. When she wiped her mouth, she asked, "Why won't you let me go back? I don't have any family on your reservation. I'm not from here."

He studied her for a long moment. "Where *are* you from?"

If she told him, he'd think she was insane. "You wouldn't know the place."

"You were sent by the spirits."

Just when she thought she had exclusivity on being strange, he one-upped her. "I, uh, don't know what you mean."

But she had a bad feeling that she just *might* know since she'd met a few spirits yesterday while she slept. Callan had held her during the night, consoling her after the spirits had told her they were her ancestors, that she had a destiny, then disappeared before she could get answers.

That seemed so far away now.

Takoda spoke in a calm voice as if he were trying to cajole her into doing as he wished. "Come with me, Rayen. I have someone you must meet."

She considered the situation she was in and wondered if she could draw on her energy again if she envisioned Callan being hurt. But she knew in her heart that she would not harm this man and his friends. Not if he didn't threaten her first.

What was she going to do?

She felt a new presence join them and glanced to her left, then closed her eyes for a moment, searching for patience.

The glowing image of an old man, in a seated position with his legs crossed, floated above the ground. Her annoying ghost was back.

He was also Acheii, her great-great-grandfather.

Acheii said, "You must listen before you can be heard."

Rayen curbed the urge to give him a biting retort about how he always showed up at the worst times, with unwanted advice, and never helped her out. Such as during the dream when she met the other spirits. Acheii was the one who'd kept her from asking questions.

She wanted to convince Takoda to return her to the school. That might be hard to do if she started talking to the wind since no one else could see the old guy but her, so she ignored Acheii.

She looked at Takoda. "What time is it?"

The ghost answered, "Time for you to learn more of your destiny."

Rayen refused to even glance in his direction.

Takoda looked at his watch. "The new day began four minutes ago."

Just past midnight.

Licking her dry lips, she asked, "How far away is this person you want me to meet?"

Takoda pointed to his left where a tiny campfire burned bright as a candle in the sea of darkness. "Not far."

"If I go with you, will you take me back to the school?"

"I will do what our shaman decides."

They wanted her to see a shaman and that person had final say. She couldn't get away from four men on horses. If she convinced this shaman to let her return to the school, horses or a vehicle would be faster than on foot.

She asked, "How far is the drive to the school? I wasn't awake for the whole trip."

"Sixty-five minutes."

That meant she had to be out of here by two-thirty to have enough time to return to the school and still have about thirty minutes to find Tony and Gabby before their four o'clock deadline to leave. Heading to the school sooner would be better.

"You waste precious time," Acheii said with brusque impatience.

"Don't you think I realize that?" she snapped at the space where Acheii had floated. The space was now empty.

And Takoda had witnessed the whole thing.

As had the three silent men on horses.

She didn't want to see the wariness in his eyes, but she rarely got what she wanted these days, so she turned to Takoda.

No wariness. No questions about talking to herself. He waved his hand toward his horse. "We should go."

Once she was seated behind Takoda, he made a clicking sound and his horse flew across the desert.

Wind blew hair loose from her ponytail. A memory swirled in her mind of riding at night through a desert with her hair whipping in the wind. She reached for the memory, dragging it to her with anxious fingers, begging her mind to give her something from her past.

The memory unfolded slowly. She and her father were on separate horses.

He'd ridden with her to someone he said would protect her.

She could see it all so clearly now.

A beast was after them. Red demonic eyes glowed. The same type of sentient beast that had chased her two days ago when she'd awakened in the desert.

That deadly thing had come from the future, too. It had followed her here, to this time.

The vision wavered like a reflected image disturbed by ripples in a pond. She focused all her attention again, desperate to mine more of this one memory. Her father yelled at her to keep going and to do as the elder told her. She would never disobey her father, but when he'd turned off to lead the beast away from her, she'd panicked momentarily.

She pulled around hard to change direction and go help her father fight the sentient killer.

But a second beast appeared, charging toward her.

Whipping back around, she drove her horse hard toward the opening between two sheer rock walls where her father had told her the elder waited in a narrow canyon. When she passed through the rock gap, the beast was close behind, but it crashed against an invisible force. She looked behind her. The beast backed up, changing its form to a giant bird with a six-foot wingspan, long talons, and a vicious beak, watching her with the glowing eyes of a predator.

She reined in her horse, stopping before she ran down the elder on the other side of a small fire.

He wore faded colors of the sunset woven in geometric patterns on a robe that brushed the ground. For a frail man, his voice was strong. "You are Ashkii Dighin, and you have a duty."

That was the same name the spirits in her dream had called her. It translated to sacred child.

His eyes were two milky orbs incapable of seeing her.

Smoke-filled air teased her nose.

The bird-beast charged, once again slamming up against some invisible field that prevented it from passing through the gap in the stone. The elder's wrinkled brow furrowed at the bird's screech. In one hand, the elder lifted a scuffed and battered gourd covered with faint black-and-red images of warriors fighting. He told her, "You must hurry. My magic will not hold the protective wall long. Come closer."

Every detail of that next minute roared to life.

She slid off her horse and walked toward the fire. The elder began chanting and allowed sparkling granules of sand to sift through his fingers into the fire. He shook the gourd, and it rattled like the tail of a deadly snake. The fire rose into a cyclone of swirling blue and green flames that moved away from the elder and toward Rayen, engulfing her.

A scream rose in her throat, but the flames didn't touch her skin. She was mesmerized by the strange sensations flooding her. Energy surrounded her then her body stretched and pulled.

The elder shouted a warning.

She couldn't grasp what he was saying. She was lifted off the ground inside the cyclone as it picked up speed. She could feel the power pulsing through the whirling funnel, spinning faster and faster.

The elder's voice boomed, but she still couldn't understand his words.

She pivoted in slow motion, suspended as the world warped around her. The sound of a thousand voices chanted a melody that blended into a kaleidoscope of colors. As she came around to face the narrow opening for the canyon, she realized what the elder was shouting.

The sentient bird slammed the invisible barrier once more, bursting through this time. It flew at her, beak open to rip her to shreds. Then it dove into the cyclone and—

"*Rayen! Rayen!*"

Takoda stood above her with worry etching his face.

She was lying on the ground, staring up at him and the moon that hung over his left shoulder. "What happened?"

"You passed out the second we stopped. I couldn't catch you before you fell to the ground. Does anything feel broken?"

She sat up, gave the dizziness a moment to diminish, then shook it off.

Bending her knees, she rocked forward and pushed up from the sandy ground to stand, dusting herself. "Nothing broken. I don't know what happened."

That was a lie.

Fear at being attacked in that fire cyclone had been too much. She'd blacked out. But now she knew how she'd ended up here in the past with that sentient beast chasing her. It had gotten sucked into the same cyclone firestorm.

"Are you all right?" Takoda asked.

She would never be all right.

Her life and family lived almost a hundred years in the future. She'd grown attached to Callan, who'd been born fifty years after her entire race had disappeared from this planet. Plus, she was running out of time to save him.

But if she could convince Takoda's shaman to allow her to return to the school, she still might save Callan.

When Takoda sighed patiently and nodded at someone past her, she turned to find his shaman standing on the opposite side of a small fire.

They were in a narrow canyon, like the one in her memory.

That wouldn't have been so disturbing if the shaman had not been the spitting image of the elder in her dream, right down to the painted gourd in his hand, the milky eyes, and his next words.

"You are Ashkii Dighin, and you have a duty."

She started backing away.

No, this couldn't happen again. Not now.

CHAPTER 2

RAYEN TRIED TO MOVE BUT Takoda anchored her in place with his hand on her shoulder. He said, "The shaman won't harm you."

She couldn't decide if his hand was to comfort her or keep her from running. No one could reassure her right now, and with her level of adrenaline reaching a new high, she doubted anyone could prevent her from running, either.

Looking around, she saw the other three horsemen still mounted and waiting a hundred feet back.

Were they positioned in case she took off again?

Sweat ran down the side of her face and pooled at her neck. Her fingers fisted and she was alert to every sound as she turned back to the shaman.

"Do not fear me, Ashkii Dighin," the shaman said in a voice gruff with age. "I only wish to speak with you."

She found her voice. "How do you know who I am?"

"I have seen you in a hundred dreams. The last one was yesterday. That is why Takoda came for you."

Could this man really have answers? *Finally.*

Could she trust any of this?

The spirits in her dream had also called her by that name, but this shaman couldn't even see her.

The shaman must have taken her silence as disbelief. He asked, "Do you have the blue-green eyes of the sea?"

Hard to deny that with Takoda standing here. "Yes."

"Do you have magic that comes from within?"

Takoda didn't know about her powers, so he couldn't have told anyone. Her palms dampened. Hope coursed through her at just how much this shaman did know, so she said, "Yes."

"Do you come from another time?"

That caused the skin on her arms to prickle with warning. How should she answer that question? Instead, she asked, "Why would you think that?"

A smile formed on the elder's lips. "This is the one, Takoda."

"Wait a minute," she complained. "I didn't say I was from another time."

Takoda said, "But neither did you deny it."

This was getting stranger than being dropped at the Byzantine Institute and finding a laptop that opened a time portal to another world. The one her hand had gone into the monitor on.

Into. The. Monitor.

She'd survived that, plus time travel to the future and back. This shaman couldn't be any scarier than facing monsters in the Sphere, so she admitted, "Yes, I'm not from this ... place." She chickened out at the last minute when she was going to say not from this time in life.

No one reacted, so she added, "If you know so much about me, maybe you can tell me who exactly my family is, because I have no memory other than pieces that fall together sometimes."

The elder nodded. He started chanting and opened his hand.

"*No!*" she shouted and raised her hands even though he couldn't see her. Or could he? "Stop that."

He paused his chanting and angled his head as if he *could* see her. "What is wrong, child?"

What wasn't wrong?

She ran her palms over her wind-blown hair and dropped her hands. "I will tell you the truth and answer your questions if you promise to return me to the school by three-thirty this morning." In the ensuing silence, she added, "And don't use your magic to send me to another place."

"I can not send you home, Rayen."

She hadn't really considered the possibility of going home until he said that, but the reminder that she had no way back to her family ripped a piece of her heart open.

Everyone belonged somewhere. Except her.

The only place she'd felt as though she belonged at all had been in the Sphere with the MystiKs.

And with Callan.

But that was temporary. Hoping for more was a fool's dream.

"You do not have much time, Rayen," the shaman warned.

"For what?" Everyone kept telling her what she could and could not do, and that time was running out, but none of that made sense to her.

"You have a destiny to fulfill."

She kept hearing that, too. "To do what?"

"To save your people."

Her eyes stung and her voice shook with emotion. "I can't."

Takoda had observed silently with his arms crossed. He asked, "Why do you say that when you have yet to hear what the shaman has to tell you?"

She was too weary to keep pretending that she was anything except what she was—a seventeen-year-old girl sent back in time and stripped of her family and her memories.

Lifting her hands to ask for a moment, she said, "This might be hard for you to believe, but I'm going to tell you the entire truth and hope that you will let me save the people that I can. I came awake in the desert just a few days ago with a beast chasing me that was capable of changing forms. It wasn't a real living animal. It was a creation built for one purpose—to kill. I escaped it, but then I was arrested with other young people. The law enforcement called us runaways. They couldn't find any identity for me here, because I haven't been born yet in this time. I *am* from the future."

The shaman had lowered his gourd and kept his cloudy-eyed attention on her, so she continued.

"They dropped me at that private school where I met two students. The three of us accidentally found a portal to the future. We landed in a place called the Sphere where other young people known as MystiKs are imprisoned by SEOH, a man who is the leader of all the TecKnati in their world. I found out that I am a C'raydonian, that—"

Rattling erupted from the gourd, and the shaman stabbed it toward the sky. He stared up and chanted softly.

Words froze in her throat.

Did he see someone up there like she sometimes saw her old ghost man, Acheii?

She was terrified that she'd say the wrong thing and he'd flash her out of here to another place in time. He'd said he couldn't send her home, but that didn't mean he couldn't send her further back in time.

After several long seconds of the elder shaking his gourd and singing a chant to the heavens, he calmed down and lowered the gourd to his side, where it quieted.

He said, "You *are* the one."

Clearly, what she'd just shared had not influenced his thinking one bit.

Trying again, she said, "I really think you have the wrong person. My people are C'raydonians and while they *are* descendants of the Navajo, their group broke off to live in solitude. They were killed almost a hundred years from now, wiped out completely by a virus. I'm the only one left."

The MystiKs believed the TecKnati had brought the deadly K-Virus back from space explorations. After the virus killed much of the world, pockets of reclusive people from spiritualists to dedicated scientists and researchers who hadn't been infected came together in ten cities in this place called North America. From what she'd learned, the C'raydonians hadn't been so fortunate, and the virus ran rampant through their population.

Any who didn't die outright had been hunted to extinction.

Both the MystiKs and TecKnati had killed C'raydonians to protect their fragile populations—the ones who had not been infected—but it seemed the TecKnati leader had taken a special interest in wiping out C'raydonians.

"You have a destiny that you cannot avoid," the shaman repeated. The man was still stuck on one track.

"If I listen to what you have to tell me, will you answer some questions *then* let me go?" she asked, just as determined to gain what she needed.

The elder's reply was to raise that blasted gourd again and begin chanting. They were getting nowhere.

She decided to let him move ahead with his ceremony in hopes that once he finished, she could leave. But if a cyclone blew up out of that fire, she wasn't sticking around.

The shaman sprinkled crystalized grains over the fire that poofed and shot a flame high in the air, then died down. She wasn't sure he was still with them when he began talking in a strange tongue to no one in particular.

Then he spoke words she understood.

"The future is in the past ... One will seek and all will forfeit."

Her blood turned to ice. She'd heard those phrases in the Sphere.

The shaman continued, "When three become one ... the end has begun. The gateway will open ... a path will close."

Her ghost grandfather, Acheii, had said that to her.

As if she'd called him, Acheii appeared next to the shaman, who smiled and angled his head toward the ghost. Was he acknowledging the specter? The shaman continued speaking. "A friend enters as enemy ... an enemy departs as friend."

These were words from the Damian Prophecy the MystiKs spoke of during her last trip to the Sphere.

She'd heard only bits and pieces of the prophecy. This man's version might differ from the one she'd heard before. She repeated the shaman's ramblings in her mind, determined to remember every word to share with the MystiKs.

If she ever saw them again.

She started to speak.

Acheii raised his hand, palm out, and shook his head at her.

The shaman chanted another few seconds, then lifted his blind gaze to the sky again as he spoke. "Day of birth as Red Moon rises ... Night of end when last moon sets. Three must unite ... for the scales to right. The last will lead when others cede."

He dropped his chin and those empty eyes stared at her. Through her. She couldn't breathe, waiting for his next words.

"All turn to the outcast. The past speaks to alter the present ... a bond of two will set us free."

All turn to the outcast echoed in her mind.

She trembled at the push of power that rushed around her.

Was she the outcast?

Acheii gave the shaman a nod of approval and vanished.

The night was deathly silent, and the flame flickered gently.

Takoda didn't speak or move an inch. They waited on the shaman's next words. He frowned and angled his head as if listening to some voice she couldn't hear. He nodded and seemed to listen again, then his hands trembled, and his mouth opened in shock.

When the shaman's frightened face turned to her, he said, "Go now, Rayen, or you will miss the window you must pass through. If Callan dies, all is lost."

"How do you know about—" She stopped in mid sentence when what he'd said hit her. He was allowing her to leave.

No, the shaman had *ordered* her to go and whatever he'd been listening to had frightened him.

Her skin chilled at realizing the prophecy was more than a bunch of words in the future. She was tied to it.

And so was Callan ... if he lived.

CHAPTER 3

RAYEN CLUTCHED A HANDHOLD ABOVE the passenger seat in Takoda's truck as it raced over the road.

He slowed only when they approached a turn that she recognized from the first time she'd been delivered to the Byzantine Institute.

She'd ridden in silence, afraid to ask what Takoda believed, but she couldn't risk that he'd change his mind and come back for her or tell the people at the school what she'd said. "Do you believe what I told the shaman?"

"I believe in our people and the elders who guide us."

No answer there. She pressed her point. "So do you believe that I'm from the future?"

Seconds passed on slow feet as Takoda weighed his answer. "I have witnessed some unusual things in my life, but I have never met someone who time traveled." His dark gaze swept over to her. "That does not give it less credibility."

All the way back to the school, her body had vibrated with worry over Callan, fear that the Browns, who ran the Institute, had sent Tony away or found Gabby, who should still be hiding.

Gabby's powers had begun evolving when she'd entered the Sphere, but she was having a tough time gaining control of them. The last time Rayen saw her, she was having issues such as uncontrollable levitation.

Rayen didn't know which one to worry about more—Tony or Gabby. Tony had been locked up yesterday for a crime he hadn't committed after another seventeen-year-old lied. Gabby was hiding from hospital staff in the Institute who wanted to sterilize her.

Gabby was only sixteen.

On top of all Rayen's concerns, she wondered if Takoda would hand her back to the Browns and declare her mentally unfit, or if he really accepted what the shaman had said.

In the distance, the school shimmered beneath security lights, growing brighter as they approached.

Takoda pulled to the side of the road before reaching the gates. He parked and turned to her. "When you don't know what to believe, believe in yourself and be true to your heart. You can never go wrong if you do both."

"Are you leaving me here?"

"Yes. The Browns sent me a message last night informing me they were reporting you as part of the theft ring that your friend Tony is leading."

"What? Tony didn't steal anything. Nicholas, the Browns' boy, lied about Tony."

Takoda nodded with understanding. "If I enter with you, they will be alerted that you are returning."

What he was trying to say dawned on her. "I have to find my own way in."

"That would be safest for you. My shaman said that you would either find the passage back to the place where you will fulfill your destiny or that you would return to us."

She was not returning to Takoda's people. Because that would mean she had failed to reach Callan in time to free him. She put her hand on the door handle.

Takoda touched her arm, stopping her. "You will always be welcome among your people, no matter the year. If you come back to us, I promise that we will protect you."

The words were heartfelt and sincere. She reached over and squeezed his arm. "Thank you. But you cannot protect me from what I must do. What time is it?"

"Two-twenty."

Smiling her thanks again, she slipped out of his vehicle and headed for the school, searching past the lights for any sign of someone on patrol.

One glance over her shoulder confirmed that Takoda was gone. His taillights were quickly turning into tiny red spots.

When she reached the school, she found it strangely amusing that she had fought so hard to escape this place the first day, and here she was planning to break in.

No one guarded the gate, but a current ran through the metal bars. She could feel the energy of it as she drew near. It felt like the same kind of power that had struck her body that first day here when she'd tried to leave with an ankle cuff strapped on. The electric charge had been even stronger than the stun gun.

Her cuff was gone—Takoda had made the school remove it—but she was fairly certain the current in the gates would burn her.

The gates were attached to a high wall the same adobe color as the pueblos. It had intermittent square columns of layered sandstone. Going over the top was the only way in that she could figure, but there were only shallow handholds and the columns soared twenty-feet high.

Her palms started sweating.

She hadn't known she feared heights until she'd ended up in the top of a tree after a battle in the Sphere. Callan had been there to help her down. No one could help her now.

She had to get inside, and every second counted.

Heart pounding at a crazy beat, she studied each column and chose a spot that would land her in the shadow of the two-story school. That area would put her near the access to the dorm side of the building.

If she could make it all the way up there, then back down again.

What was worse? Facing her fear of heights or showing up too late to prevent Callan's death? Pretty equal when it came to her level of terror, but saving Callan won hands down.

She could do this. Had to.

Drawing a couple of deep breaths, she reached above her head and sank her fingers into a recess in the column's structure. She started climbing, proud of herself when she'd reached six feet off the ground in the face of her trembling.

All was going well until Gabby's voice shouted in her mind. *Rayen, where are you?*

Shocked, she let go and fell, landing on her back with a grunt of pain.

She'd heard Gabby telepathically once before here at the school, but she had yet to figure out how to answer her.

Standing up, Rayen calmed her startled heart, rubbed her behind that had taken the brunt of the fall and faced climbing one more time. Now she had even more reason to be afraid.

What if she let go at the top and fell?

What if Callan faces the wraiths alone and with no way to use his power? Quit whining and just do it.

She lunged to grip the stone structure again. From handhold to handhold, she made it to the top where the column had a flat surface two feet square. The small surface would be tough enough, but it was slanted toward the outside of the wall. Struggling to balance, she was in a half crouch, trying to catch her breath when Gabby called out again.

We're running out of time, Rayen!

She jerked at the sharp sound of Gabby's voice in her head and lost her grip, sliding sideways and grabbing at anything to stop her fall. She ended up draped half on and half off the top of the column.

We need to go, Rayen, Gabby's voice boomed in her head once more.

"I know it. Shut up," she snarled quietly, trying to keep her mind on not looking down or letting go. Gabby couldn't hear her words, but it made her feel better to answer.

A bird flew past her. It stank like the sentient beast.

Hugging the column, she twisted to look around, trying to determine where the bird was or which way it was flying. Wings fluttering, it dropped to the ledge of a window on the second floor. The window slid up just high enough for the bird to enter.

That was one of the forms the sentient beast had taken since she'd arrived here two days ago. It had also turned into a three-legged creature with the size and speed of a buffalo as well as a whippet-shaped animal, among others.

Why had it not attacked her this time?

Now that she thought about it, the beast hadn't attacked her since she'd seen it with Phen yesterday when she, Gabby, and Tony returned from the Sphere. Phen must have trained the beast to perform on his command, but Phen was a TecKnati from the future and liked Rayen no more than that creature did.

Especially after she'd refused to help Phen find a way to return home. SEOH had sent him here from the future, but those TecKnati knew how to time travel in only one direction—the past. That was why they wanted the computer that she, Tony, and Gabby had used to travel forward in time to the Sphere.

She couldn't stay in this spot much longer. The muscles in her arms were screaming in protest.

Now would be a great time to have Callan's kinetic ability to slow her descent. But she'd also need his lack of fear about jumping to the ground. She wasn't entirely sure what her powers were capable of, but since they weren't reliable, she was stuck with figuring out how to get down the normal way and without breaking both her legs.

Forcing herself to release the death grip she had on the edge of the column, she kept her gaze on her hands. Anything to stave off the panic that kept painting pictures of her on the ground with a snapped neck. She moved her feet until she caught a toehold and carefully slid her fingers down to find a handhold, then to the next. One foot and one hand at a time. Even if the fall didn't kill her, even a damaged ankle would destroy her chance of finding

Gabby or Tony without being caught. *Don't look down or think about how far it is*, she kept telling herself. She continued moving lower and lower tediously until she was close enough to drop to the ground.

She landed on trembling legs.

Give her a croggle monster to fight anytime rather than face another climb like that one. Wiping her damp palms on her pants, she gave herself a minute to allow her breathing to calm down while she listened for the sound of guards running toward her. She heard nothing. Even the wind moved too gently to make a sound.

She rushed to an exterior door that led to the boys' dorm, the quickest way to get inside. The door had two sets of locks.

More locks, really?

Where was Tony with his lock-pick skills when she needed them? He was the one who'd taught her how to unlock a door. Combining her powers and his knowledge had made it work.

The door she faced swung open slowly.

She shifted her feet into a fighting stance.

Phen appeared, same wide forehead, dull eyes, and twenty-something attitude. He held the door open. His cruel gaze swept over her with contempt. The black bird was perched on his shoulder. "What do you want, Rayen?"

"I need to get back inside the building."

"We all need something."

If Phen raised an alarm right now it would destroy any hope of finding Gabby and Tony. "I told you I'd think about helping you find a way home."

His eyes lit with interest, but he refused to admit how much he wanted that. "I don't trust you."

"I don't trust you either," she countered. "But we need each other. Let me in and I'll try to help you."

"Try? That's not good enough." He gave a casual look over his shoulder then glanced back at her with a sly smile. "Wonder what the Browns would say if they knew you were on Byzantine property."

She didn't like making an offer for something that she had no certainty she could deliver, but every second they burned here would cost Callan on the other end. "Fine. Let me in and I'll share our time travel secret with you, but you have to help me get to my friends for that to happen."

For the span of two seconds, hope and longing bloomed in Phen's face. He pulled the momentary weakness back under control and stepped aside for her to enter. "We have a deal."

She rushed past him and tried not to worry about how she could possibly make good on her offer when the portal only worked between here and the Sphere. She reached the end of the short hallway from the outside access and pushed through the door, then took a fast right.

Phen was close behind and hissed, “Hey. Where’re you going?”

She paused to tell him, “To the girls’ dorm.”

“Is that where the computer is?”

The laptop with the portal should be in the backpack that Tony had left with Gabby but telling Phen would cause him to follow her when she needed to lose him. Instead of outright lying, she said, “The laptop is in Tony’s backpack.”

“You’re screwed. He’s still in detention.”

That was encouraging news, but she didn’t want to admit it to Phen. She nodded and gave him a concerned look. “I have to go find Gabby and see if she knows what’s been happening while I was gone. I’ll talk to you later.”

She turned and raced away before he could stop her.

He wasn’t supposed to enter the girls’ dorm, but who knew what Phen would or would not do?

Phen watched the miserable MystiK-loving twit run into the girls’ dorm. He’d gotten caught there once last night while trying to track down Gabby. It wouldn’t have been a problem if the Browns had been here, but they weren’t on site right now. When the Byzantine security found him in the wrong place, Phen had barely gotten away by acting totally confused over what area he was in.

They’d cut him a break since he was so new.

He lifted the bird off his shoulder and stroked its head. At one of his jobs back home in the future, he’d been responsible for tending sentient beasts at a zootech. They’d turned out to be simple to manage if you understood the hard coding in their systems. He gave this one an order and the bird rolled into a black-feathered ball in his hand. Bones poked out at odd angles and the feathers morphed into the smooth skin of a chameleon.

Phen squatted down and placed the sentient critter on the floor then ordered it, “Follow Rayen until she’s with Tony and Gabby, then return to me.”

He’d programmed images of Rayen, Tony, and Gabby into the beast’s memory.

The chameleon took off, flattened itself to crawl beneath the door, and scurry down the girls' dorm hallway.

CHAPTER 4

RAYEN REACHED THE SECOND FLOOR, hunting the room number that Hannah had given her before all of them separated. Hannah had agreed to hide Gabby as a favor for Tony, who'd poured on the charm for her help.

But that had been prior to Tony being accused of theft and locked up in detention.

Hannah was a perfect student, all about the rules, and worked part time with the office staff. If she'd heard about Tony's detention, she might have given up Gabby.

That nauseating thought jammed Rayen in place. Where would Gabby be if Hannah had turned her over to the staff?

Rayen, hurry up and get back here, Gabby called in her mind again. Louder this time.

Rayen's pulse jacked up. She searched the numbers on the doors and found the one for Hannah. She'd tapped twice on the door and it whipped open.

"There you are!" Gabby launched herself at Rayen, hugging her.

They'd never hugged before. Rayen's throat tightened with emotion. She'd found one of the two real friends she had in this world.

Gabby pushed away and backed into the room. She wore her yellow and purple hair in multiple ponytails that jutted out all over her head in a signature Gabby style. On the last trip to the Sphere, she'd started having issues like dancing hair and her feet leaving the ground involuntarily.

Still wearing the heavy backpack Tony had given her, Gabby ushered Rayen into the room. "I'm so freakin' glad to see you. Where'd you go?"

"Takoda took me to a place out in the desert, one of the reservations, and I just now got back." Rayen looked around. "Where's Hannah?"

"I told her I couldn't explain, but that I needed to get to Tony. It's two-thirty already. We're running out of time."

"You still haven't told me where Hannah is."

Gabby lifted her shoulders. "She took Tony's hoodie and went to see him."

"We have less than an hour to open that portal." Of course, that would do Callan little good if they didn't have a computer to hand over to the TecKnati. "What about computer parts?"

"I don't know what parts Tony needs."

Rayen clutched her head where a stabbing pain had camped out. "Do you have a way to reach Hannah?"

"She gave me her phone number, but she said she might not answer if she didn't feel it buzzing when she put it on silent. She didn't want to risk having the ringer on while she was sneaking into detention."

"Let's go find computer parts then we'll break Tony out of there and get back to the Sphere."

"I have doubts about breaking him out," Gabby admitted.

Rayen was herding her out the door and toward the computer lab. "Why?"

"They put an ankle cuff on him."

"Like the one I had?" Rayen was *so* glad hers was gone.

"Yes, but yours was programmed to stop you if you tried to step off the property."

"Yes, I remember." Hard to forget after she'd gotten a nasty load of electricity when she tried to walk out the front gate. "What's the deal with Tony's ankle cuff?" she asked in a whisper, closing the door.

"His is programmed to set off alarms if he steps out of his detention room."

How were they going to get him out of there?

CHAPTER 5

TONY IGNORED THE FOOD THEY'D brought him in the windowless basement room the Byzantine Institute designated as their detention facility.

How had he screwed up so badly?

He'd left everything he'd ever known in Jersey to come to a freaking desert school for a chance to get into MIT.

Right now, it looked like he was headed to juvie. Or worse.

Callan was in a bigger jam in the Sphere. Rayen was probably going postal by now. Those two had something going on that had no chance of working out, but that was between them. Tony had no desire to play the fatal messenger role. He'd do what he could to help save Callan *if* he got out of here in time. Right now, that wasn't looking promising at all.

Everyone would lose.

All because of Nicholas Brown, that lying sack of—

"Tony," a voice whispered on the other side of the door.

He walked over and leaned against it. "Who's there?"

"Hannah."

He heard a card swiping through a reader, then a key jangled, because security didn't trust Tony not to figure his way past just an electronic lock.

When the door opened, Hannah stepped in and quickly closed it behind her. She usually wore prim skirt-and-jacket suits that carried an air of authority. In truth, that perception was more about *her* than the clothes. He'd thought she was an ice queen but changed his evaluation when he'd gotten to know her.

She was sweet and smart, and looked adorable right now wearing pink flannel workout pants and a gray hoodie like the one he owned. The girl could rock anything from business suits to cutoffs.

Her hand trembled, causing the ring of keys to tinkle.

Dark auburn hair hung straight to her chin and swayed with her slight head movement. She speared him with an icy look he couldn't read.

Had she come in friendship, or to ream him out for screwing up their chance to win the Top Ten Competition? She'd convinced him to partner up with her yesterday and he wouldn't blame her if she sorely regretted that move.

"Tony." She said his name with a breathlessness that had his brain short-circuiting, but she might just be nervous about seeing someone in the school equivalent of death row.

"Hey, Hannah. Why ya here?"

Her face fell.

What had he said wrong?

She stared away from him. "See if I come to visit you in detention again."

"Whoa, babe. I'm glad to see you. I just ... figured you're pissed at me."

"No. I'm worried about you."

"Really?" He scrubbed a hand over his face and stepped over to her. "How'd I get lucky enough to find someone like you?"

Her eyes twinkled and he knew all was forgiven.

He didn't deserve it because he'd let her down. Through no fault of his own, but he'd still let her down. He ran his knuckles up along Hannah's smooth cheek. "You're the sweetest thing I've ever met."

Surprise glowed in her. She licked her full lips in a way that Tony would bet his comic book collection was an unconscious move. Her surprise shifted to a coy gleam. "Did you miss me, Tony?"

He couldn't resist the invitation when he might not ever see her again.

He pushed his hand into her hair and cupped her head, leaning down to kiss her. Man, she had amazing lips. He'd only planned to give her a quick peck, but he couldn't stop himself from indulging another few seconds. Hey, death row inmates got a last meal, right? He'd gladly take a taste of Hannah as his.

How had he spent so much time around her and not realized until recently what a babe hid beneath that uptight exterior?

That's what happened when you assumed you knew someone.

Her fingers touched his shoulder then tentatively moved around his neck and the room got hot.

Lifting his mouth from hers, he smiled at her. In the middle of his entire life falling apart, just looking at her could make him happy.

This one was a keeper. He sighed.

If only he could figure a way out of being in trouble.

The glaze over Hannah's eyes cleared and she blinked, snapping back into Miss On The Ball. "I came to tell you what's going on. When I found out who had fingered you for the theft, I did some checking. Nick must have heard about you changing to have me as your Top Ten partner, because I put the paperwork in before Mr. Suarez left yesterday. I heard Nick went to talk Mr. Suarez out of allowing you to drop him as your partner, but Mr. Suarez told him a little adversity would build character."

Tony was touched that Hannah had enough faith in him to not jump to a conclusion that he was some lowlife thief, but Nick had done a number on him.

Stepping away from her, Tony cracked his knuckles then pounded his fist into the palm of his hand. "Suarez is wasting his time on Nick. His character is pretty much ingrained at this point. He's got me in a corner. They're gonna expel me and throw me in jail. I can't even defend myself against his lies."

"I'm sorry, Tony."

"Not your fault, babe." Tony relaxed his hands and gave her a smile. "Thanks for finding out what you can."

Hannah pulled a hand from behind her and stuck a folded-up sweatshirt toward him. "Here's one of your hoodies. I used my passkey to get into your room."

Good thing Tony had forgotten to set his room alarm after he returned from the Sphere. He took the hoodie and pulled it over his head. "Thanks. I was getting cold down here ... until you showed up." He winked at her.

She blushed and looked away. Cute.

He stepped close again and took her hand. "How's Gabby?"

That got him an eye roll. "Strange as usual. She won't take the backpack off that you gave her."

Jealousy lurked behind Hannah's frown.

"Hannah, baby, that backpack is keeping Gabby balanced. She's having ... vertigo issues." Not really. Not unless vertigo included floating in the air. That backpack was probably the only way Gabby could keep her feet on the ground right now.

"Okay."

Girl-trouble bullet dodged. "Have you seen Rayen?"

Hannah stepped back, crossed her arms, and scowled. "I'm the one who comes to see you and you want to know about other girls?"

For the love of St. Christopher. "I only asked because I promised to do something with Rayen and Gabby. We're just friends. Why would I be interested in them when I already have a girlfriend?"

"You do?" Hannah's pretty lips softened.

Tony would have laughed if not for fear of really ticking off Hannah. He touched his finger and thumb to her chin. "I hope so. I don't kiss just any girl. Only the *one* that matters to me."

Hannah was emotional, but she wasn't slow on the uptake. Happiness glittered in her eyes. She whispered, "I'm your girlfriend?"

"Of course, you are, but I'm not sure you want to have someone who's headed to juvie."

"We have to get you out of here."

Tony held his breath a second. "Are you sayin' you're gonna help me break out?"

She looked defeated by the idea. "I can't. I accessed the security system. The alarms will squeal the minute you cross the threshold to leave this room."

"Crap. I thought this cuff was just programmed for if I tried to leave the property."

"Nick warned them that they couldn't be too careful with a genius like you."

Tony snorted. "The guy finally admits he's intimidated by me?"

She grinned. "Not exactly, but we both know he is." Her pocket hummed. She patted it and fished out her cell phone. "Who would be texting me at this time in the morning? More like ten minutes ago. Stupid cell service sucks here." Her eyes flicked back and forth. She clutched the phone in her shaking hand. "Oh, no."

"What, Hannah?"

Looking up, her gaze was full of concern. "You asked about Rayen. Security shocked her with a stun gun and —"

"What?"

Hannah let him know with a look to not interrupt her. "Not now. Last night. I heard that guy from the Navajo council, Takoda, was in the office waiting for Rayen right after you were put in detention. She tried to run so they zapped her. The last I heard, Takoda was driving her to some reservation." Hannah looked at her phone as if it had lied to her. "I thought she was gone, but Gabby just texted me that Rayen's back and they're headed to the computer lab. What's Rayen doing here and what are they doing at the lab this time in the morning?"

He didn't want to lie to Hannah, but it wasn't like he could tell her he'd time traveled to a place way in the future either. "I promised to do something for them, and I'd tell you more, but if it goes bad, I don't want you involved."

She didn't give him any indication of what was going on in her mind at first then finally said, "I'm going to trust that you're telling the truth."

"I am."

"Is what you need to do illegal?"

Insane maybe but building a laptop to save Callan was not technically illegal since Tony had permission from Mr. Suarez to use parts to build a computer for their project.

Tony shook his head. "But it's hard to explain right now."

"Gabby and Rayen won't get into the science lab."

Tony recalled how Rayen had used her weird powers to unlock a door when they'd busted Gabby out of the clinic. "They'll get in. Rayen has a gift at getting past locked doors."

Hannah's lofty attitude surfaced. "But can Rayen get past a security system?"

"That area is not alarmed."

"It wasn't until Mr. Suarez reported a theft."

Tony sucked in a breath as if he'd taken a punch to his solar plexus. He grabbed his head. "Text Gabby. Tell her to stop. Please, Hannah."

Her attitude vanished and she tapped furiously on her phone screen. She stared at it a second then looked up. "It's not going through."

"They're gonna get caught."

CHAPTER 6

"WHY CAN'T YOU GET THE lock open?" Gabby whispered so close Rayen jumped. Her shoulder bumped the computer science lab door.

"I don't know." Rayen put her hand back on the knob and tried to concentrate again, but her stupid power wasn't coming through. "I can't make the power appear the way you can just talk in other people's heads."

Gabby shifted the backpack that she had to be tired of carrying. "I do not talk in other people's heads without permission."

"You did in mine." The metal knob still hadn't changed temperature.

"I never know when you hear me," she argued.

Rayen started to tell her that it didn't change the fact that she heard Gabby's voice in her head sometimes, but she caught sight of the clock above the door for this hallway. Two-forty-one.

She warned Gabby, "Stand back. I have an idea. I'm going to try something different to call up my power."

Gabby shuffled away.

The lock at the pueblo had sounded as if Rayen had broken it. She had to be careful not to destroy the door, but she closed her eyes and blocked out everything. Next, she started imagining Callan being attacked. Blood running down his face and—

Her chest warmed.

Good enough. The knot in her stomach loosened.

She opened her eyes and took a moment to let the energy swirl then she focused on her fingers cupping the lock. Nice and slow, she felt the energy pushing out through her fingers and warming the metal.

Slowly this time. Don't push too hard.

An image of the tumblers appeared in her mind. Click, click ... the next one stuck. Maybe she had to put more power behind it. Her hand trembled. She drew again on the power, and it flooded her arm then her hand.

Click, click, *bang* then *pop!*

Rayen released the knob and looked up at Gabby with a smile. "I think I got it."

Gabby grinned, ready to move forward and enter with her. Rayen had just touched the knob again when she heard, "*Stop!*"

Hannah came running up to them.

What was she going to tell Hannah? *This doesn't look like what you think?* Any idiot would realize exactly what she was doing.

Rayen didn't get a chance to say anything, because Hannah said in a rush, "If you open that door, you'll set off alarms."

Gabby groaned. "What are we going to do, Rayen?"

"I don't know."

Hannah said, "Lucky for you two, I have access to the code. Stand back."

Rayen looked over at Gabby who gave her an I-don't-have-a-clue-why-she's-helping-us look. They both gave Hannah room, and she slid a keycard into a slot next to the door that Rayen had ignored because all the doors had those.

When a tiny light beamed green on the card slot, Hannah said, "Now you can open it, but you have five minutes."

Gabby asked, "Why?"

"Because I just saw Tony and he said you had to come see him before three AM. It will take me ten minutes to get you into his detention cell."

Hope surged so fast and hard through Rayen it should have exploded her heart. "We'll hurry."

But the minute she stepped inside the room, the sheer volume of technical supplies against the wall overwhelmed her. She had no idea what they had to collect in computer parts. She was not the techno geek that Tony and Hannah were.

Asking Hannah for any more help at this point would open the door to questions she didn't want to answer.

Rayen nudged Gabby in her side. "How do we know what parts to take for Tony?"

"Select them the same way you chose the laptop that can—" Gabby looked over at the door and said, "—you know what."

She meant the laptop computer Rayen had accidentally found that had opened a time travel portal. She hadn't really chosen it. The computer had chosen her by pulling her hand to it as if the laptop had been a magnet and she'd been made of steel.

Had the laptop recognized the power inside her?

She followed Gabby to a wall of cabinets that were six feet tall and a foot thick. Plastic drawers started at four inches square at the top and grew larger with much wider ones across the bottom.

This was where she'd seen Tony grab computer parts the day they'd first met and he'd gotten stuck with her as a project partner.

But Tony was a technological genius who knew exactly what he'd needed that day.

Catching Rayen's attention, Gabby held her hands up, palms facing the bins. She whispered, "Hold your hands like this."

Rayen did as she asked. Nothing happened. "We only have four minutes. Maybe we should just start grabbing—"

Fifteen drawers opened out toward them.

Gabby laughed and started pulling out odd little parts, which she handed to Rayen. "Put them in the backpack."

"That was bizarre," Rayen muttered, carefully filling Tony's backpack.

Still speaking softly, Gabby quipped, "Is it any more bizarre than traveling to the future, meeting kids with all kinds of gifts, and fighting everything from croggles to attack vines?"

She had a point.

She handed Rayen a part the size of her fingernail and said, "That's the last one."

"Maybe we should grab some more."

But Gabby was distracted by something on the other side of the room. She said, "Pick out some more parts and I'll be right back."

Rayen had her hands full when she returned, holding a shiny silver laptop. "What are you doing?" Rayen hissed, watching for Hannah.

"You need a computer to save Callan, right?"

"Yes."

"This is it."

"We can't steal someone's computer." But even as she said the words, she knew she wasn't leaving without something to bargain with to keep Callan alive.

"This computer is donated. Stick it in the backpack before we run out of time."

Rayen was loading the laptop and parts into the backpack while trying to make sense of Gabby's explanation when Hannah stuck her head in and said, "Let's go if you want to see Tony."

Speaking of Tony, he'd have a meltdown if he saw how they'd selected parts.

They hurried out the door. Hannah locked it behind them, then she swiped her card back through the slot. When the light turned red, Rayen assumed the alarm was set again.

Hannah took off and they had to jog to stay with her.

Gabby's shoulders were sagging from the weight of the backpack. Rayen offered, "Want me to carry that?"

She sent back a pained look and shook her head. "I'd love for you to take this thing, but I'm afraid of going airborne without the weight."

Nodding, Rayen grabbed a strap to lift the backpack and lighten the weight some.

They had been lagging, but now she and Gabby were really moving. She glanced over at her friend and did a double take.

Gabby's feet were moving, but not touching the floor.

When Hannah finally stopped at an elevator and turned to check on them, Rayen let go of the backpack faster than she'd intended.

Gabby stumbled under the sudden weight and glared at her.

She murmured, "Sorry."

Hannah might be pleasant to Tony, but with them she was abrupt. "I don't have all day. Hurry up."

While the elevator carried them down to the basement level, Rayen asked Hannah, "Why are you helping us?"

Her mouth twisted up as if she'd eaten something sour. "I'm not doing anything for *you*."

This had clearly been for Tony, but that didn't explain why she'd take this much risk.

Gabby must have picked up on Rayen's thinking. She warned Hannah, "You better find a way to wipe your electronic trail out of security or they'll be questioning you about what you were doing in the computer lab this morning."

The elevator doors opened, and Hannah's haughty smile came out. "I didn't use *my* keycard."

As they followed her down the hall, Rayen asked, "Whose did you use?"

"Nicholas Brown's."

Gabby grinned and covered her mouth to smother her laugh.

Rayen found that funny, too, but was too worried about what little time they had left to open the portal to actually enjoy the moment.

Hannah paused at a door and pulled out the same keycard to slide into a slot, but it wouldn't open the door. "What the heck?"

She tried it two more times.

"Is that you, Hannah babe?" Tony called from the other side of the door.

Gabby made a silly face at the endearment.

Hannah said, "Yes, but I can't get Nick's keycard to work."

Sirens whined upstairs. An alarm had been set off on another floor.

Hannah's face drained of color. Her words rushed out in a flurry. "We must have tripped something by opening the computer lab door this early in the morning. If security contacted Nick, they know it wasn't him and that's why Nick's card has stopped working. We have to get out of here now. Security will be here in five minutes."

No. If they couldn't free Tony, then Callan would die. Rayen would not panic, but those sirens were sending her pulse into overdrive. Heat built in her chest and wicked out through every limb.

She pushed Hannah aside and called to Tony, "Back away from the door and protect yourself, Jersey." Gripping the knob, she called up her power and forced it into the lock.

The handle exploded and the door flew inward.

Tony stared at her then shook his head. "Daa-yum, Xena."

He rushed out and looked first at Hannah. She stared at Rayen with her mouth hanging open. Tony grabbed Hannah's arm, distracting her. "Can you get out of here safely?"

"Yes."

Then Tony kissed her in a way that should have set off the fire alarms. He broke apart from her, worry chomping in his gaze. "Go, Hannah. Get out of here first so if we get caught you won't be with us."

She nodded and started for the elevator.

Tony turned to Gabby and Rayen. "If someone chases us, we separate, then once we're clear, go to the computer storage room where we found the portal computer."

Sirens whined all around them on this floor and a mechanical voice shouted, "*A. Scolerio, return to your unit. A. Scolerio—*"

What if that storage room was alarmed?

They didn't have Hannah with a key card. They couldn't make it back upstairs and they couldn't access the portal computer if they had to leave it anywhere that people would find it while they were gone.

CHAPTER 7

"WE'LL NEVER REACH THE STORAGE room," Rayen told Tony and Gabby. "We've got to get out of here another way."

She thought Hannah was gone, but the girl turned around and ran back a few steps to shout at them over the intercom voice. "Take the stairs at the end to the next floor. Go to the door that says 111-B. The whole floor is for supplies and storage. Security will be looking for you on the street level above that floor."

Tony shouted, "Got it, now go."

Hannah ran to the elevator, and they took off in the opposite direction.

They made it up the stairs and raced down a hall that was silent other than the muffled sound of sirens from above, plus Tony's name being shouted below us.

At 111-B, Tony opened the door.

Rayen was glad it hadn't been locked. Glad she didn't have to depend on her power this time. With all the adrenaline shooting through her right now, she might blow up the whole room. Once the three of them were inside, Tony closed the door and locked it by pushing a button on the knob.

The room was deep and had rows of wide shelves built of steel to support the big cans and boxes of food stacked on them. She looked at the top of the closest shelf, which stopped two feet down from the twelve-foot ceiling.

Gabby was red-faced and panting from the run.

Rayen pulled the backpack off Gabby's shoulders and slipped her arms through the straps. "This thing feels heavy enough to be a dead body."

"It has everything we need. At least I hope it does," Gabby said as her body rose a foot off the floor and stayed there. It was a sign of how much he'd been through in a few days that Tony didn't spare Gabby's levitation a second glance.

He was too busy looking around. "We need a place to set up the laptop."

Rayen pointed above her head at the top of the shelves. They were four feet deep. "We can go up there."

Tony gazed up at where she indicated. "Looks strong enough and wide enough for us to fit, but we'll have to lay down."

When Gabby stretched her neck to see what they were talking about, the movement caused her to float a little higher. "That's a great place to hide the laptop, but unless you two can levitate, I'm the only one who might reach it if I keep floating up."

Rayen started searching around her. "Let's find something we can stack up for climbing." She ran through the room, hunting between shelves, and found exactly what they needed. A folding ladder. Lifting it, she hurried back to them.

"Attagirl, Xena." Tony took the ladder and set it up next to the shelves. "I'll hold this while you two climb up there."

She told Gabby, "Just grab my shirt."

When Rayen had a grip, she climbed until she could move close enough for Gabby to crawl onto the surface. Then she had to stand on the very top of the ladder to hoist herself up to their hiding spot.

Tony took down two one-gallon cans of tomato sauce from the middle shelf and placed them next to the foot of the ladder as if someone had been interrupted while retrieving supplies.

Smart guy. Rayen had the feeling this wasn't the first time Tony had been forced to evade someone.

He pushed himself up onto the top of the shelf and stretched out along one side of her. Gabby hovered on her other side. They were positioned the same way they'd always been when traveling through the portal.

That didn't stop Rayen from having a moment of anxiety that it might not work this time. Gabby pulled out their portal laptop and that lightened the backpack Rayen carried only a little. Tony took it from her and opened the lid against the wall they faced.

Rayen glanced over her shoulder to check the door, but she couldn't see it from this location. Someone would have to climb all the way up there to find the laptop.

Tony powered it up.

Three circles of gold, silver, and bronze formed on the screen, moving in and out of each other. It was time to go.

Tony slapped his hand down. "Oh, man."

"What?" Gabby and I shouted together.

"We don't have the extra laptop to take with us and give the TecKnati in trade for Callan." Tony sounded sick.

Gabby said, “We have that computer.”

“Where’d you get it?” Tony asked.

“Hey,” Rayen said. “We have a computer. We have parts. We have to go. Now.”

Tony eyed them with suspicion. “How did you two know which parts to get?”

Gabby wiggled her fingers. “Rayen and I used touch.”

“For the love of St. Christopher. We are so screwed.”

“Listen, Jersey Jerk,” Gabby growled.

The door jangled like someone was trying to open it.

They froze. Rayen pushed her palm at the monitor and her hand passed right through. Gabby grabbed that arm and Tony latched onto her other one.

The doorknob rattled again, a key scraped in a lock, then the door squealed open as her arm was sucked into the screen and her body stretched thin as a rubber band.

CHAPTER 8

RAYEN WAS JERKED AND BOUNCED at warp speed.

Wait a minute. Did she know what warp speed was? That thought flashed by as she spun in a twisting blur.

Just as she had revolved when she was in that fire cyclone.

She hated time travel. All of it.

Everything slowed at once. She had a whole second to prepare herself before hitting the floor of the transender. She bounced and forced herself to move because ...

Bam! Tony hit hard in the spot she'd left vacant, but he must have recalled last time, too. He groaned but quickly rolled away before Gabby landed on his chest again.

Rayen waited. No thump. "Gabby?"

Tony pushed up onto his knees. "*Gabby!*"

A ball of color rolled from the air and landed gently on the floor. Gabby sat there a moment then broke into a fit of giggles.

"Are you kiddin' me?" Tony grumbled. "How'd you do that?"

For once, Rayen was with Tony. "Why didn't you land like a bag of rocks?"

Gabby caught her breath and stretched, pushing hair off her face. "I didn't actually do that on purpose. I panicked and curled into a fetal position, thinking that I didn't want to hit the floor or land on Tony again. The next thing I knew, I'd stopped. Then I was worried I wouldn't get here. I started moving and here I am."

Tony shook his head. "Only you would have auto-pilot woo-woo powers."

Rayen struggled to her feet, wishing she had *her* powers. Her body had taken a beating over the past few days.

Red lights flashed around the top of the round transender, and a siren cranked up.

She stretched out the kinks in her body. "We know what that means."

Gabby said, "Time to get out of Dodge."

Had she heard that right? "What is Dodge?"

Tony let out a painful sigh. "If we get out of this mess, we're puttin' you through Pop Culture 101, Xena." He turned to the end of the transender where they'd exited the last two times.

A purple glow shaped as an arch brightened then dimmed then brightened again.

Tony muttered, "And there's our blue light special." He lifted a hand. "Before you ask, I do know that glow is purple."

She tossed back one of his usual replies. "Whatever."

When they reached the end of the transender, she lifted her hands to rest on the humming wall. Tony and Gabby each grabbed one of her arms again just as the familiar sulfur stench began flooding the air.

Rayen thought, *Please let us out.*

Then she held her breath because the last time they'd entered the Sphere it looked as if an apocalypse had hit.

And a ground fog had infected her which caused hallucinations. She almost killed Callan because she thought he was a TecKnati who'd harmed the MystiK children.

The hatch that formed where she touched the transender wall disappeared, and they landed on rock-hard ground on their hands and knees.

Why couldn't one place have something soft to land on?

When she realized she and Tony were the only two on the ground, she looked around to find Gabby hovering upright again.

Gabby tried not to smile and failed. "I'm getting used to this."

A whirring sound that turned into a high-pitched squeal announced the transender was about to spin then leave in a cloud of red dust.

Rayen and Tony jumped up. They started to run but Gabby shouted, "Don't leave me!"

Gabby was moving her arms like she was trying to swim but was going nowhere. Rayen ran back and grabbed her shirt, dragging her along and getting away from the transender right before it spun furiously, then disappeared.

All Rayen could think was *please don't let anyone find that laptop in the supply room.* It was their only way back.

She watched where she stepped. The ground was still torn up from the prior destruction. Overhead, the red moon offered a weak light, but the vegetation glowed pink, orange, and blue. Not just glowed, but the colors pulsed, and the air was steamy. Add that to the sweet-sour smell and she was ready to get moving.

Tony stopped and muttered, "Give me a break."

Gabby sucked in a breath.

She raised her head to see what was going on.

An oversized reptile had stepped from the woods.

Just once, she'd like to have an easy trip to this place.

When the creature turned its head toward them, it emerged from the broad orange palm fronds, where darker-blue branches behind it had regrown since the last time. The thing was shaped like a huge turtle. It stood eye-to-eye with Rayen when it lifted its body on chubby legs and wobbled out into the field.

Then it fell and fumbled around until it was up again. The head stuck out on a skinny neck that had a thick tuft of blue and white hair resembling a chopped-off horse's mane.

It made a chittering noise.

Gabby floated next to Rayen. "I think it's a baby something."

Tony wasn't as willing to downgrade the creature and reminded Gabby, "I remember Rayen fighting a *baby* croggle in this very spot, Sweet Cakes, that tried to eat us." He turned to Rayen. "Think you can call up that crazy power of yours, Xena?"

She had no idea. Tony had a point, but she couldn't harm something that posed no immediate threat. "Not all baby reptiles are killers, Tony."

"Snapping turtles are dangerous back home."

Gabby whispered, "It looks pretty harmless."

At that moment, the critter angled its head to one side then the other, studying them. It yawned, exposing two rows of sharp, pointed teeth.

Tony said, "If it's got teeth, it's got potential."

The baby turtle thing took two more tentative steps their way.

It wasn't often that Rayen agreed with Tony, but she did this time. "Maybe we can scare it off," she suggested and raised her hands to wave back and forth.

That was the wrong move.

The turtle thing let out a blood-curdling scream, and dropped to the ground, sucking in its legs and head.

Something huge crashed around in the woods, making a loud grunting sound.

A head Rayen wouldn't be able to wrap her arms around shoved out from the trees. Way up. Another ten feet in the air. The eyes in that head zeroed in on the clammed-up baby and let out a screech of fury that forced them all to cover their ears.

Then it plowed out of the woods, heading straight for them.

CHAPTER 9

POWER EXPANDED AND BURNED RAYEN'S insides, then rushed up her arms and down her legs.

She jumped in front of Tony and Gabby, raising her hands again, ready to throw a blast of energy to stop that mama-turtle-thing from charging over to where they stood in the transender landing spot.

"*Ah-jeet!*" a deep human voice roared from the forest.

The mama-turtle-thing halted and squatted next to her baby.

"Do not harm them," another shout boomed. The guy making all that noise was coming closer to them.

Did he mean for Rayen to not harm the creatures or for the mama to not eat them?

And who was he that she should care?

This might be nothing more than a TecKnati trick to steal the computer.

There was a sound of branches breaking as someone rushed through the woods, then a tall young man with skin mottled a mishmash of blue and brown splashes burst into the opening.

Kaz.

Her heart leaped with happiness. Only seeing Callan would have made her happier.

Kaz rushed forward but halted next to the mama creature where he spoke soft words.

The mama dipped her huge head down and Kaz stroked her iridescent skin. A full, blue-and-silver-striped mane growing along her neck gave her a regal flare. Her body had a similar shape to a turtle's except that her shell was flatter on top, more streamlined, and appeared furry. Dark-blue layers rimmed in a shimmering gold ran along the edges of the fluffy surface covering her shell.

The animal made soft grunting noises and lifted a paw instead of a foot to nudge Kaz gently. Silver hair flowed down over her paws and dragged the ground. Large round eyes with a blue center and gold iris looked down at Kaz with what Rayen could only describe as affection.

But those curling horns with sharp tips that stuck out the sides of her head could do some major damage if she changed her mind about attacking.

Once he had her settled down, Kaz waved them over.

Tony didn't move and Gabby was stuck hovering above the ground unless someone pulled her along. Gabby had come a long way since Rayen had first met her. Two days ago, she wouldn't allow anyone to touch her for fear of hearing another person's thoughts, but a MystiK healer named Jaxxson had taught her how to shield her mind.

"Come on, let's go," Rayen urged and snagged the hem of Gabby's pink shirt to tow her along.

Following several steps behind them, Tony lifted the pendant hanging on a chain around his neck. He kissed it then let the round disk fall back inside his shirt as he mumbled something about St. Christopher.

When Rayen reached Kaz, she let go of Gabby who remained floating a foot off the ground.

Kaz lifted an eyebrow at her, but anxiety rode his face in the place of his usual easy-going expression. "Why did you wait so long to come back, Rayen?"

After all she'd been through to even get back to the Sphere, she hadn't expected Kaz, of all people, to criticize her. "We got here as soon as we could."

"Callan is down to three hours."

Gabby had no trouble sharing her opinion. "Rayen was zapped with a stun gun and taken away from the school last night. Tony was accused of a crime he didn't commit and locked up. I had to hunt down a computer and parts while hiding this levitation problem, then we ended up breaking Tony out and had to make a run for it before they caught all of us." She put her hands on her hips and leaned forward, her mismatched eyes—one green and one brown—staring Kaz down. "Whatever's eating you must be suffering horribly."

Kaz took a step back and scratched his head. "Sorry, but I've been here for four hours waiting when I should be back at the village."

It didn't take much to appease Gabby. "Apology accepted."

Rayen didn't care if Kaz was being short with them because she was in the same mood, and they needed to get going. "Tony needs time to build the computer."

Kaz raked Tony with an angry burst. "How long will that take?"

Tony moved forward, shoulders bunched, and disgust peppering every word. "I haven't even seen the laptop we brought back. Since Sweet Cheeks here picked out parts using your woo woo system, I have no idea how long."

Rayen put a hand up between Tony and Kaz before they took any more steps toward each other. "We don't have time to argue."

Something bumped her in the back, knocking her off her feet.

Kaz grabbed her before she face-planted on the ground.

He swung her up by her arm and caught her to his chest. It's good to be an extra-strong MystiK warrior, she mused. His skin had an interesting woodsy smell she hadn't noticed before, but then she hadn't been this close to him before now either.

He didn't need to clutch her so tightly against him.

She'd explained more than once that she wasn't interested in anyone but Callan. Kaz contended that she and Callan wouldn't work out. She knew all the reasons, but it didn't stop her heart from calling out to Callan, and only Callan.

She pushed away and stepped back, dusting herself off. If anyone asked her, she'd say that turtle creature had intentionally shoved her. Giving the animal her threatening look didn't faze her one bit. She asked Kaz, "What's with that ... thing?"

"She's a tortalone, not a *thing*."

Was he insulted on the creature's behalf?

Gabby leaned forward. "So that's what a tortalone is. Jaxxson said it would be easier to show me one than to explain it. I thought they were wild."

"They are." Kaz put his thumb and first finger in his mouth, took a deep breath and let out a shrill whistle.

Three more tortalones crashed their way out of the woods, moving slowly but on large paws that could push down small saplings. A MystiK warrior rode each one. The warriors appeared to be thirteen or fourteen and had splotches of color like Kaz's. Tony called it camouflage skin.

As they made their way over to them, Kaz explained, "We found a small herd yesterday and have come to an agreement."

Gabby quipped, "So you're a turtle whisperer?"

Kaz frowned at her then at Rayen, waiting on an explanation.

Rayen eyed him and the tortalone. "I think Gabby was asking if you can talk to them."

"I told you my gifts were different than Callan's."

"Right." They were both warriors, but Callan possessed powerful kinetics where Kaz's were not as strong, but he had empathic ability. Kaz sensed emotions, which was another reason she had to be careful to keep hers locked down when she was around him.

He motioned with his hand and the mama tortalone dropped to the ground, spreadin out her her front legs. Kaz explained, "I don't actually speak the tortalone language, but this female leads the herd. She and I understand each other."

The animal made a gritty sound in her throat and the other tortalones dropped to the ground, too.

A MystiK warrior climbed off one animal and climbed onto another one, doubling up. Kaz pointed at the tortalone left without a rider and told Tony, "You and Gabby will take that one, because you only need to hold on. He will follow mine."

Tony sized up their situation. "You're telling me we're gonna ride something I can outwalk and they're safe as long as you don't tick her off and she decides to have us for lunch?"

Kaz's easy-going nature had come and gone. "If you were not needed for the computer, I would allow you to walk and learn for yourself who is quicker."

Tony raised his hands to ward off Kaz. "Chill, bro. I'll ride. How tough can it be to sit on a turtle hump?" Tony held his hand out. "Give me the backpack, Xena, and just worry about holding on."

She gladly passed off the heavy pack.

Kaz had already climbed up on the mama creature and sat on his knees. He leaned over and offered Rayen a hand up. She had to step on the mama's two-foot-thick leg to reach Kaz's hand.

She pushed up and stretched at the same time, extending her hand to Kaz.

Their tortalone scooped her head under Rayen's butt and pushed up, tossing her high. Kaz caught Rayen around the waist and swung her around in front of him.

Had he somehow told the tortalone to do that?

Kaz made a strange chattering sound in his throat. The tortalone raised her head until Kaz leaned around Rayen on one side to grip her mane.

He held her mane lightly. She curved her neck forward and rose all the way up on all four legs then made a sharp bark.

The little baby next to them came out of its shell and jumped up on springy legs, bouncing back and forth, squeaking happy sounds.

Mama tortalone took the lead, plodding across the long open field. Checking over her shoulder, Rayen saw Tony holding the mane on his ride and Gabby sitting at his back, clutching his shoulders. The other two tortalones moved in sync with Tony's, all of them maintaining the same slow pace as the leader.

She agreed with Tony.

They could walk faster. How could Kaz snap at her for taking so long to come back, then bring turtles to ride?

This was going to make her nuts. "We have to get to Callan before his BIRG Day, Kaz."

"I know I said it was important to continue embracing our customs, but Callan turning eighteen is not the issue at the moment."

Yes, it was, but she couldn't tell Kaz about the wraiths that would come for Callan. Not unless she had no other choice. It didn't matter. They still weren't going to reach Callan in time to rescue him from the TecKnati. She tried to sound patient about their transportation. "Kaz, it has to be faster to—"

"Shh. Don't say a thing," he whispered close to her ear and wrapped his free arm around her waist.

She tried to push his arm away. "I think I can manage to stay on a turtle."

He just tightened his hold.

Their tortalone started moving faster.

She smiled. Kaz hadn't said this creature could run.

The shimmering gold-and-blue fur covering her shell swept away from each side and started flapping.

Feathers? Wings?

This thing could ... fly?

Kaz chuckled as they took to the air. If he hadn't held her, she'd have fallen off out of shock.

Wind slapped her ponytail all around. It must have been beating up against him, because Kaz tucked his head next to hers, pinning her hair, and spoke words that were as disconcerting as the intimate feel of him behind her. "You must not go with us to free Callan."

"Why?"

"It is not my place to explain."

"Then I'm going with you."

"If you do, you will put his future back home in jeopardy."

How could that be? "What changed after I left?"

Kaz sighed. "I learned of another MystiK imprisoned at the TecKnati camp who is royalty from one of the Houses."

Rayen recalled that the MystiKs had seven Houses based on different gifts or powers, but she was still confused. "I don't understand, Kaz. If the TecKnati have another MystiK, I'd think you'd want my help."

He was slow to respond. “Normally, yes, but not this time. You are not able to hide your feelings for Callan from others, especially another empath. And when you are near him, neither can he.”

It was probably the wrong reaction but hearing that about Callan made her happy.

Kaz ground out a noise.

Guess he caught her reaction.

He wasn’t through warning her. “As Callan’s best friend, it is my duty to protect him. Even from you.”

That deflated her moment of pleasure. “Who’s this other MystiK at the TecKnati camp?”

“I’m not sure how much Callan wants to tell you about her and it is his place to explain.”

Her?

CHAPTER 10

WATER HIT CALLAN IN THE face. He jerked his head, slinging droplets from hair that clung to his neck.

He sat with his knees on the hard ground in an enclosed room. His arms stretched above his head, hanging from metal wrist cuffs attached to cables. Not just any metal, but one infused with an electronic component to interact with the grid outside that the TecKnati had used to capture him. After all these years, the TecKnati had finally designed something that would neutralize MystiK gifts like Callan's kinetic and healing abilities.

But the laser grid had to be powered up high to completely shut down his kinetics and telepathy.

The thing had short-circuited once.

He'd either dreamed about a woman's voice or the cuffs were running so low on power they weren't preventing his telepathy. But when he opened his mind, the female voice he'd heard had been all wrong.

It hadn't been Rayen's.

When Rayen spoke, Callan felt her rich voice all the way to his heart.

He might just be hallucinating at times. Sleep had been impossible and Thylan, the TecKnati in charge, had taken great pleasure in driving up the grid power when the urge hit him. That was only when Thylan was too tired to use his electric whip on Callan, striking the minute Callan's head lolled from exhaustion.

Who knew if it was telepathy he heard or if he was slowly losing his mind? He hadn't been able to send or receive telepathy when he'd stood in the middle of the grid and the TeK in charge had turned up the power to the point of frying Callan from the inside out.

He had burn marks on his skin that ached intermittently.

The grid was buried just deep enough in the ground to hide it, so when Callan had entered an enclosure to rescue a pair of MystiK children and Tony, he hadn't known it was there until the TecKnati activated the lasers in the grid.

How long ago?

He was losing track of time.

Icy water crashed into his head again.

He coughed and sputtered, slinging his hair like a soaked dog trying to shake off the excess. Water ran down his naked chest and pooled at the ragged skins he wore for pants.

When he stopped choking, he raised his head and looked through wet hair stringing over his eyes. His body hurt no matter how he tried to find a comfortable position and he couldn't heal the cuts on his chest while bound by these cuffs.

"You awake?" Thylan chided. "No sleeping on my time."

Callan said nothing, maintaining his silence just as he had since his capture. This was the leader of the TecKnati in the Sphere. Big man on a small pedestal. He was not SEOH, who ruled all the TeKs back home, but this one had SEOH's arrogance.

Thylan stood just inside the door of Callan's prison cell. He was decent size, but his soft middle bulged over the black belt strapped around the waist of his gray green TecKnati uniform. Not a warrior. His blended alloy belt buckle had a holographic element that showed the ANASKO triangle emblem one moment and the name SEOH II the next.

Ah. Now Callan understood. This was SEOH's son. The II meant he was second born. This would be the middle son, the one often brought up on charges for abusive acts. A soulless predator.

SEOH's genes ran true.

Thylan smoothed a hand over black hair cut close enough to expose his pale scalp, then he twisted his thin lips in a cruel smile. "I haven't heard a word from your friends, or your girl."

Callan could only hope that Rayen had made it back to the past and stayed there. She was too headstrong for her own good. She would battle anyone and anything to protect an innocent or someone she cared for ... and she cared for Callan.

He'd tried to convince her that he didn't reciprocate her feelings, but he'd failed at that. More than failed. He'd climbed inside the kamara he'd made for her and spent the night with her. He was honest enough with himself to admit that he wanted to share *his* kamara with her, a major step toward bonding.

Regardless, he would be glad if she didn't return.

Never seeing her again would hurt, and that pain would cut deep, but he would be content with her being safe.

She'd given him memories he'd treasure for a lifetime if he survived this.

Thylan snapped his fingers. "Pay attention, warrior boy."

Callan lifted his chin. "Uncuff me and I'll show you who is the boy in this room."

A grin broke out on Thylan's flat face. "He speaks. And here I thought you were silent because I intimidated you."

"I would have to notice you first," Callan pointed out.

Thylan's thick black eyebrows drew together into one angry caterpillar. "You won't be so arrogant once we get that computer."

"She isn't coming back." Callan hoped. His chest felt empty without her nearby, but he didn't have much longer to live. He could endure until then.

"Oh, yes, she's coming back. I saw the look on her face. She'll return and she won't be empty handed."

It pained Callan to realize there could be truth in Thylan's words and, wrong as it was, a part of Callan admitted he would trade all his tomorrows for one minute to see Rayen again. But even if she came back, she wouldn't hand over the actual Genera-Y computer. She knew the danger of the TecKnati using that computer to destroy the entire MystiK population on and off the Sphere.

No one really knew what this Genera-Y computer could do, but it was supposedly a computer built two millennia ago that could allow travel both ways through time. Was that the computer Rayen, Gabby, and Tony used to travel here or just the product of some mythological tale? Callan didn't know and didn't care so long as Rayen stayed safely in the past.

If she did return, Callan trusted Kaz to stop her from coming to this camp. But that was the extent of trust he would allow when it came to Kaz being around her.

Kaz had better keep his hands off Rayen.

The sole time Kaz had tried to gain her affections, Callan had considered skewering his best friend over a fire. But Kaz was still the friend that Callan could depend on, the one person who would do his duty.

Callan huffed a tired sigh he hoped sounded bored to Thylan. "Even if you get the computer, you won't be able to operate it without a MystiK."

Thylan leaned back on the closed door, overconfident at facing someone shackled. "You MystiKs have a high opinion of yourselves. We don't need you. By now, you should have realized that SEOH is far superior to your MystiK leaders. Your people don't even know how many of you are missing. They'd have to talk to each other to have an inkling of what's going on."

Shame flushed over Callan. He couldn't deny that claim. The leaders of their seven MystiK Houses had once been close while rebuilding their world. A world devastated by a virus they were pretty sure had originated in outer space.

The K-Virus had been introduced to Earth because of an aggressive space program the TecKnati were still pushing.

But somewhere along the way, the MystiKs created as many problems for themselves as the TeKs presented.

Thylan was on a roll, chuckling. "SEOH kidnaps the majority of future MystiK leaders, G'ortians no less, and your people won't realize how widespread it is until all your leaders meet to sign another treaty with us." He grinned and studied Callan with condescension. "You're one of those rare G'ortians with special powers, right? Look at you now."

This TecKnati needed to have a dose of reality.

Callan slung his hair back so that Thylan had to stare into eyes promising his death. Even in these cuffs, Callan managed to summon enough power to shift his eyes from brown to a searing, glowing green. The ability to make that change had developed only in the past few days, along with many of his other G'ortian powers. Even the powers he'd had for a while had grown stronger as he approached his BIRG Day.

When Thylan paled, Callan nodded. "You would be wise to consider who you taunt. I *am* one of those. We are powerful, and when we join forces, we will destroy your dangerous space program and protect our world."

Thylan puffed up at that. "You think so? You people kill me." He thumped his chest as he spoke. "Our technology has created laser curtains to protect the ten cities where both TecKnati and MystiKs live. Our technology has created hospitals that are state-of-the-art facilities for all citizens. *Our* technology continues to develop programs that better our world for *everyone*, even for you miserable, unappreciative MystiKs."

"I don't disagree, TecKnati. I can acknowledge that there are benefits to both MystiK and TecKnati skills, but you are too ambitious and risk bringing another virus back to our planet. What if you do that again?"

Thylan hunched his shoulders, acting unconcerned. "There's no proof we did that the first time."

"There could be, but your people refuse to work with ours to screen what you bring back. And from what SEOH has done here, there will be no treaties in the future. Only war. And we will win."

"You are so full of crap." Thylan was getting louder, the way a person did when he was frightened or trying to prove an indefensible point, or both. "You don't understand that you've already lost. You think the BIRG Con means a new treaty and the ascension of future MystiK leaders coming into power, but it doesn't. Instead of your symbolic end-of-childhood ritual, this year's BIRG Con will mark the death of all MystiKs. Why do you think we tested the grid on you?"

Callan hadn't felt real fear until now.

"That's right, warrior boy. We didn't test it here just to see what it would do. That baby holding your power in check is just a taste of the big one that has been installed back home for the BIRG Con." He snorted. "Basking In Reflective Glory Convention? Sounds like a summit for tarot readers."

Callan ignored Thylan's snide remarks. SEOH's spawn had shared important information, but there was no way for Callan to get word to the MystiKs back home.

The TeKs intended to use that grid on MystiK leaders? Callan had experienced the grid eating his power during the times he'd been exposed to the activated lasers. If Thylan hadn't backed off the power when he did, Callan was certain he would have eventually died as the grid continued attacking his gifts.

"Now you're getting a clear picture," Thylan chortled. "You people aren't very smart, you know that? You haven't even figured out that we have a hotline straight from your camp."

A traitor in our village. Just as Callan had thought.

Someone shouted outside the door.

Thylan called back, "On my way." Then he bent over with his hands on his knees, putting his face eye level with Callan's. "You're just a bunch of fanatics with a little power."

Callan lunged at Thylan, who panicked and stumbled back, landing in the water that covered the floor. He scrambled to get to the door. When he made it back to his feet, he snarled, "I was going to kill you after we got the computer, but I'm going to hold off. Killing would be too easy for you."

Callan vibrated with the need to get his hands on Thylan. He didn't think he could harbor any more rage until Thylan explained, "I don't want you to miss the show. Once your girl arrives and I capture her, I'm going to lay her out right here in front of you. Close enough for you to watch me take her."

Callan lunged again, straining, and sounding like a furious animal. This time, the cables groaned. He spoke through teeth clenched hard enough to break a rock. "You touch her, and I will kill you with my bare hands."

Thylan wisely rushed out and locked the door.

Callan fell back against the metal wall, breathing hard. His wrists bled where he'd punished them against the cuffs. His body shook, drowning in adrenaline and gut-wrenching worry over Rayen.

He prayed that she had not been able to find a computer or return.

CHAPTER 11

THE TORTALONE RAYEN AND KAZ rode swooped low over the carpet of fluorescent trees, a sea of peach, aqua, and purple vegetation below them that gave way to dark blue and white. They landed in a large clearing and the tortalone trotted slowly across dark blue grass that would be shin-high on her. Black-and-white striped flowers that looked feather-soft darkened to coppers and reds in the shade. When they stopped, it seemed as if they were in the middle of nowhere, but she knew better. Callan and a handful of the MystiKs around his age had used their combined power to create a ward that mimicked the surrounding woods to hide their village.

The cool air that had wafted over them while flying disappeared, and the sticky heat returned with a vengeance. But once that red moon vanished beneath the horizon, the air near the ground would chill.

She climbed off the tortalone and ran over to help with Gabby. Tony passed her down to Rayen, then Gabby once more floated at her normal space above the ground. Rayen snagged the hem of her shirt then the three of them followed Kaz. He could have passed through the ward easily since he was a MystiK, but they couldn't. He paused and lifted his hands, then spoke an incantation for ten seconds before turning to them.

"You may pass through."

They did, and the other three warrior boys followed them.

While Kaz closed the ward, they continued in the direction she recalled as being toward the village, but they were quickly surrounded by a new group of warriors.

This bunch looked threatening even at six and seven years old. That was because they were Uberons, part of an elite MystiK Warrior division.

A young woman Rayen's age, known as Kenja, led the Uberons.

Rayen had been through her share of run-ins with that one.

Kenja appeared in their path, so fast and close they almost plowed into her.

Gabby shrieked and paddled her hands in the air, trying to back up.

When Kenja smirked at Gabby, Rayen wanted to strangle her, but Gabby wielded words the way Kenja handled a spear.

Tony gave Gabby's shirt a tug and she floated forward. Gabby used her lofty advantage to rake Kenja with an imperial look. "Did you give up fighting your inner demons and just join them, Kenja?"

"Your sarcasm is wasted."

"It generally *is* on the ignorant."

In a blink, Kenja's expression switched from calm to the promise of retribution.

Rayen didn't want a repeat of her last altercation with Kenja. There was no time for it. "Either help or get out of the way, Kenja."

With a tiny move of her head, she redirected all her aggression at Rayen. "You have less than three hours until my agreement to stay at this village has been fulfilled."

Then Kenja disappeared as quickly as she'd arrived.

Gabby muttered, "I've got levitation-itis, I just climbed off a flying turtle, and we still don't know if that computer is going to work. She does *not* want to mess with me."

Kaz stepped up beside her. "Problems?"

Rayen shook her head. "Nothing new."

He led them into the center of the camp where more sleeping quarters had been created from tortalone feathers hanging from poles and vines to form walls. Some of them had red tips as well as gold. Now she understood where someone would find a six-foot-long feather.

She caught the approach of another female. Headache number two. Zilya of the Governing House and senior pain in Rayen's backside.

Short, white-blond hair flared across Zilya's head, and a smattering of black and diamond jewels were embedded in her perfect cheek. She had that mix of haughty and exotic that would always cause easily distracted males to drool. Her tunic-style gown was an odd yellowish, almost golden, material, not shiny, but elegant in its simplicity. Strange half-moon designs were sewn in a deeper burnished gold down the front. Callan had mentioned they indicated her status, but having her clothes speak for her seemed unnecessary. Her arrogance announced her status all on its own.

She stepped into their path.

Rayen ground her teeth. *What was with everyone wanting to get in my way right now?*

Zilya spoke with the single purpose of commanding attention. "Do you have the computer?"

Tony sounded impatient. "We have *a* computer, but I don't know that we have *the* computer, and until I get a chance to work on the device we do have, I won't know if we can use it to scam them."

She brought out her tone of superiority. "You were supposed to—"

"Hey, sister," Tony snapped. "We've had our own troubles. I need time and a workspace. If you can't provide that, then you're in the way."

Everyone was on edge.

Tony, Gabby, and Rayen had barely found each other and left before someone caught them. Kaz had taken lead on the warrior duties, which included keeping this group safe and alive. Zilya was a pain of the highest order, but she looked worn around the edges, too.

Rayen raised her hands. "Can we all call a truce for a couple of hours until we free Callan?"

Kaz crossed his arms and addressed Zilya. "I will see to what they need." When she started to interrupt him, Kaz was quick to cut her off. "Where is Jaxxson?"

"In his healing hut."

"Take Gabby to him."

"I am not a servant." Zilya stomped off.

Kaz smiled at Rayen. "Problem solved for now."

Jaxxson shouted, "*Gabby!*"

They turned as one toward the path that led to his hut. Jaxxson stepped forward, his naked chest showing above the skirt-like covering that reached just above his ankles. He was muscled in an athletic way, not like Callan's powerful build. His blond hair was a dark honey shade, and his rich brown eyes were for Gabby only.

He rushed up and stopped short. "Gabby?"

She sighed. "At least I'm not sick this time and my power isn't trying to kill everyone, but I can't fix this—" She pointed her finger at her boots. "Or figure out how to move around when I'm up here."

Jaxxson smothered a chuckle, walked over, and pulled her into his arms.

Red flagged Gabby's cheeks when she looked at Rayen, then at Tony, who smirked. She asked Jaxxson, "Can't you just pull me through the air? That's what Rayen does."

Jaxxson walked off, explaining, "I would never risk you bumping into a tree."

Rayen doubted there was any real issue with drawing Gabby along by her hand, but those two had something special going on that had changed over the past two visits.

She was happy for Gabby but hoped her friend didn't end up with a broken heart.

Who was she to talk? Rayen was in just as deep when it came to caring about Callan.

She wasn't backing away, but where Gabby had a life to go back to, Rayen had nothing. She would take what little time she had with Callan and be thankful for it.

Kaz pointed across the clearing to a small structure. "That hut has a table and chairs. Callan and I have used it for planning sessions."

Tony was looking all around. Half listening, he said, "Sweet. Okay, I need V'ru."

Despair graveled in Kaz's voice. "V'ru has been in deep depression since learning of Callan's capture ... and since you left. He speaks to no one."

Nothing was deterring Tony. "Take me to him."

Rayen followed Kaz and Tony toward the isolated area V'ru had chosen for his kamara, the bubble thing that some MystiKs could create to use as personal quarters.

She didn't recall V'ru's kamara being this deep in the wooded area. Maybe he'd moved it.

V'ru and Callan were G'ortians, a type of rare MystiK that was more powerful than normal. Even though V'ru was only eleven, he was a prodigy who'd been born with his brain holding all the known history of mankind up to the current year in his world.

Tony salivated to have the knowledge that V'ru held in one tiny finger, but he'd also grown close to V'ru, who reminded Tony of his own little brother, Vinny.

On the way to the kamara, Tony shook his head at Kaz. "You can't leave a little kid alone like this."

Kaz turned defensive. "We respect the privacy of others, particularly a G'ortian."

Tony turned on Kaz, fury rumbling in his biting words. "He's a freakin' kid. Little freakin' boy, not a G'ortian, not a future MystiK ruler, just a kid who's frightened and who just lost the one person he believes will take him home."

The look in Kaz's eyes hurt Rayen.

All the MystiK children captured and sent to this place had suffered. Kaz had been one of their most fierce protectors. Rayen touched Tony's arm. "No one meant to mistreat V'ru."

It took Tony a minute to pull himself back under control. He exhaled hard and spoke with compassion this time. "I'm not yelling at you, Kaz. I'm yelling at the way your leaders have treated him. V'ru has no identity. No sense of who he is beyond being a resource. All I'm saying is that it's up to us to take care of him. He's only a kid."

Rayen's throat swelled at the way Tony cared for V'ru. Tony had put everything at risk to help her, Callan, and everyone else here. His little brother was in a foster home. Tony was determined to get into a school called MIT as soon as he could so that he'd eventually be in a position, which would allow him to bring his little brother home.

After what had happened back at the Byzantine Institute, Tony might not be able to do that for a long time, if ever.

Kaz reached over and gripped Tony's shoulder, looking him straight in the eyes. "You are right. We will do a better job of caring for V'ru."

"Thank you."

Another fifty feet into the woods, they found V'ru's kamara. Rayen recalled the one Callan had made for her to sleep in on their last visit to the sphere. It had been more luminous than this one.

She frowned at V'ru's. It was as though the energy fueling his kamara had dimmed.

Tony put his hand on the kamara and called out in a cheerful voice he must have pulled out of his pocket, because he was anything but cheerful right now. "V'ru Man, it's me, Tony."

No reply.

"Need you to come out and talk to me."

Silence still.

Shoulders down, looking defeated, Tony lowered his voice and said with genuine worry, "I'm concerned about you and Callan both, V'ru. I can't do anything to help either one of you unless you help me. Callan's depending on you, and I am, too."

The kamara's glow brightened, and in the next instant V'ru stood beside Tony. V'ru's skin looked pale. "What can I do? I'm just an information vessel."

Tony sent a sharp look at Kaz who, to his benefit, merely gave a quiet nod of understanding.

Dropping into a squat that put Tony closer to eye level with V'ru, he smiled at the boy. "Still got the hoodie on, huh?"

V'ru nodded. Tony's dark gray hoodie swallowed the kid and hit him past the knees.

Putting his hand on V'ru's shoulder, Tony said, "You're the most important person on our team. I can't even get the computer I brought to boot up without you."

V'ru's eyes lit up. "You brought a *real* computer?"

"Yes, sir. And I'm pressed for time. So, if you—"

V'ru waved his hands around. "Where is it? Show me."

Tony stood and led the way back to the hut Kaz had pointed out. He spoke in a low tone the whole way, talking computer terms, with V'ru nodding enthusiastically.

Kaz walked beside Rayen and leaned down to say, "He's right. None of us realized that V'ru is kept on a virtual pedestal and not allowed to be a part of this village. His knowledge is revered, but he is more than that and we should have noticed the hardship his position puts on him."

Finally, things were smoothing out. "Thank you for recognizing that Tony has V'ru's best interest at heart."

Shrugging, Kaz quipped, "Even a TeK has useful information on occasion."

She turned to remind him that Tony was not the enemy here just because V'ru had determined Tony carried TeK blood markers, making him an ancestor of the people in Kaz's world.

But Kaz's lips twitched with a smile, so she gave him a shove and he surprised her with a chuckle.

Tony and V'ru had almost reached the hut when Zilya's voice rang out. "You cannot share knowledge with him, V'ru of the Records House."

V'ru froze. Poor thing was terrified of Zilya.

All the good Tony had accomplished by getting V'ru out of his bubble was about to disintegrate.

Tony wheeled on Zilya. "I thought we had this straight about not messing with him."

"We have nothing *straight*, TecKnati. You will not access V'ru's database."

"Then Houston, we have a problem, because that's exactly what I'm going to do."

CHAPTER 12

RAYEN SHOVED HER HANDS IN her hair and growled to keep from throwing a blast of energy at Zilya. Pulling her hands down, she continued to where Tony and Zilya were facing off.

Zilya snarled at Tony, "I will not warn you again, TecKnati."

"You're always fightin' the wrong people, blondie. I'm trying to help Callan and your village. So is V'ru. So back the heck off and stay out of my way. And if I catch you trying to bully V'ru one more time, you'll regret it."

Zilya lifted her hands.

Rayen warned, "Make a wrong move and I *will* fry you."

Shoving a shocked look her way, Zilya said, "You would not dare touch me."

"Yes, I would, and you won't like it."

"You are not more powerful than I," Zilya argued without conviction.

Tony chuckled, a dry nasty sound. "Bad move, blondie. You've never been present when Xena unleashed her power and cooked a croggle just by stabbing it with a spear. But you know what? Go ahead and keep pushing Xena. I'd like to see you toasted."

Rayen sent an arched look at Tony.

He opened his arms. "What?"

She squeezed out a sigh. "I'm trying to help so you can get moving on the computer."

"She started this crap." Tony put his hand on V'ru's shoulder. "Let's get busy, little man."

Zilya started, "V'ru, if you—"

Tony swung around and raised a hand so fast Rayen was worried that he had kinetic powers, but he only pointed at Zilya. "I've told you before and I'm only saying this one more time. V'ru is under my protection. Don't mess with him." Then Tony and V'ru entered the hut.

Kaz finally said something. "Zilya, this is the time to work together, not to fight. You should trust that V'ru will reveal nothing more than is needed to prepare that computer to trade for Callan."

She didn't acknowledge his words, merely replying, "When we return home, this will all have consequences."

Etoi, Zilya's assistant and closest friend, came into the clearing then. She wore ankle-high boots made of something like leather and a muted burgundy tunic with a braided gold edge that stopped short of her knees. Swinging her blond-and-black ringlets at Rayen, along with a full load of bad attitude, she warned, "If you threaten our Governing House leader again, you will not be allowed to remain inside the village."

"Says who?" Kaz asked.

Tagging him with her furious gaze, Etoi answered, "Says me, if you are not willing to do your duty as a warrior."

Rayen just rolled her eyes. "I'm tired of the threats. Do you or do you not want Callan to be freed?"

She'd said that just to break up the friction, but Etoi shrugged. "He's only a warrior, not a leader."

Now she wanted to strangle her for real. "Mathias left Callan in charge of this village."

Zilya lifted her nose. "*Then* Callan left me in charge."

Kaz interjected, "He left you and Jaxxson in charge. You have *joint* authority. We are done here. Return to whatever it is you do to fill your days and we'll deal with bringing Callan back."

Zilya's cheeks flamed, then she returned to her natural annoying self. "You have enjoyed too much autonomy here, Kaz. It will not go well for you when we are home again."

With that, Zilya and Etoi marched off.

Muttering to himself, Kaz said, "I'll worry about that if I ever see home again."

Rayen wanted to comfort him and reassure him that he would go home again, but she was in no position to be making false promises.

Tony stuck his head out of the hut. "Need you in here, Xena."

She couldn't imagine why he'd need her with the computer, but she followed Tony as he ducked back inside. He had the keyboard off and V'ru stared at the electronics with a fascination she couldn't appreciate.

"What do you need?" Rayen asked. "Didn't Gabby pick a good computer?"

"She did better than good," Tony said. "She got Nick's laptop, and he has state-of-the-art everything. This baby is loaded with every option available."

Had Gabby known that was Nick's computer when she grabbed it?

Knowing Gabby, the answer was yes. "I don't see what the problem is then."

V'ru looked up and his straight black hair fell over his huge brown eyes. He shoved a lock off his face, a futile effort when it fell again. "We made several alterations that emulate what Tony tells me your portal computer does, but this is not the same configuration."

The sound that came out of Kaz could only be called relief. "You are saying we won't be giving the TeKs a computer they can time travel with, correct?"

"Correct," V'ru confirmed. "That's not the problem. This has to at least power up long enough to pull a fast one."

Kaz frowned. "What do you mean by fast one, V'ru?"

V'ru shrugged. "I don't know. That's what Tony said."

Tony chuckled and explained, "We're going to have to convince the TeKs to trade Callan for a computer that isn't going to do what they think. That's going to require some slick talking and sleight of hand to get him out of there, thus pulling a fast one."

V'ru nodded as if Tony had imparted a wisdom to be archived, then he said, "I was able to power this unit for only ten seconds with my residual power, but I'm not strong enough to keep it running very long. My power is focused on retaining information, not driving something physical. We need a superpower."

Everyone looked at her.

"What?" She protested, "I couldn't turn the last computer on by myself. What do you expect me to do with this one?"

Tony pointed at one spot. "See what happens if you touch that. And don't blow it up."

Good advice if she had any control over her power. Half the time it wouldn't even show up without someone facing death or torture. She hovered her hand over the spot and felt no tingle of energy, so she dropped her finger down to touch the part Tony had indicated.

Nothing happened. She looked at him. "I told you."

Running a hand over his short hair, Tony stared at the laptop. "Kaz, you try it."

He did. Nothing again.

Tony put the keyboard back in place and once the laptop was whole again, he handed it to Rayen. "Try it again."

She felt like an idiot standing there holding the laptop with nothing happening. "What do you want me to do this time? I can't just call up my power."

"Well, I can't do it," Tony snapped back at her. "Your power is what runs the other computer we used for traveling here. Way I got it figured, we need this one to function for about a minute. That's all."

She gripped the laptop tight. "I have no control over the other one and this one is clearly not the same."

"Just try harder, Xena."

She had to make this work for Callan. She closed her eyes and pleaded with her power. Not so much as a flicker. Opening her eyes, she placed the computer back on the slab of wood they were using for a table and asked V'ru, "Can't you wave your hands and make a computer work?"

V'ru held her gaze with a tolerant one and flipped one skinny hand without looking up. A holographic screen popped into view. "You mean like that?"

"Yes. If you can do that, why can't you make this computer work?"

He sighed, sounding like someone a hundred years old instead of a stick-thin eleven-year-old. "That is like saying why can't you use your power to fly or teleport. Those are two unique energy sources just as your power and mine function differently."

Kaz looked out the doorway. "The moon will be setting in a little over an hour. We must leave soon."

When would this day get any easier?

Tony crossed his arms. "Call up your power like you did to unlock the doors. That's all we need. Not croggle-killing level."

Frustration boiling inside her burst out. "Don't you think I would if I could?"

"I don't know," Tony argued. "How important is it to get Callan back? Or don't you care enough."

She took a step toward him. "How can you say that?" Heat coiled and spun inside her like a whip of fire.

"'Cause you ain't makin' much of an effort." Tony lifted his shoulders. "Hey, if you don't care about him being tortured, that's fine by me."

She yelled at Tony, "Make that stupid thing work!"

"Not my problem."

"I'm going to make it your problem if you—"

"Look, it's working!" V'ru shouted.

She jerked her gaze to the table where the computer had three circles whirling on the screen. She started laughing out of relief. "It *is* working."

Tony scrubbed a hand over his face. "Getting you upset enough to power up is killing me, Xena."

"Oh, no," V'ru whispered.

The computer died again.

Kaz said, "That's okay. She'll make it work again. We have to go."

Rayen caught the resignation in Kaz's face when he acknowledged that she had to return to the TeK camp with him. She'd do her best to hide her feelings about Callan once they were around the female captive. A royal.

Tony wrapped up the computer and started to put it in his backpack, then changed his mind. "I'm leaving my pack with V'ru. We'll just take the computer."

Tony, V'ru, and Kaz were ready to walk out when Kaz turned to Tony. "I would rather you stay here and keep an eye on ..." He glanced down at the top of V'ru's head and said, "The village."

Tony looked to Rayen, and she nodded. There was nothing he could do once they got to the TecKnati camp if powering this thing was up to her.

"Sure thing," Tony agreed, though not looking all that happy. She didn't blame him as they were sticking him with Zilya, Etoi, and Kenja.

She held Tony back when V'ru and Kaz walked out. "Tony, you said we needed the computer to operate for a minute. It only powered up for fifteen seconds."

"You weren't even focusing on the unit and the overflow of your power got it running. All you need to do is concentrate when you get there and you'll do fine, Xena. Plus, you don't have a choice." Tony glanced outside and back at her. "Kaz said you have to leave now, or you'll miss your window of time."

If her power showed up, she'd either make the computer work or take down the entire TecKnati camp until she found Callan.

If her power failed to show up ...

No. She couldn't accept the possibility.

With no other choice, she headed out with Kaz to the tortalones.

CHAPTER 13

GABBY HAD TRAVELED THE WORLD with her surgeon father, and they'd stayed in five-star hotels where the staffs had catered to her every whim. Not one of those places had been memorable, not like Jaxxson's hut.

She'd missed the simplicity of his space with its dried herbs and tree stumps for chairs. Being back in his personal space filled her with a joy she'd never found in her own world.

Okay, to be honest, having Jaxxson carry her into said hut had a lot of influence on her frame of mind.

He still had the pile of blue-and-gold tortalone feathers on the floor where he'd placed them during her last visit.

Another reason to smile for no real reason.

She was officially an idiot. Over him.

But being with Jaxxson felt like coming home.

All semblance of home had vanished for Gabby after her mother had died in a car wreck. That death had been Gabby's fault. She'd been a small child, but even then, she could hear a person's thoughts if she touched their skin. She'd blurted out something she'd heard in her mother's mind, a secret love affair that had been playing through her mother's thoughts. Gabby had terrified her mother to the point she'd raced away from her demon child and lost control of her convertible, rolling it.

In all the years since then, Gabby had isolated herself, refusing to touch or allow human contact. She'd gone from one location to the next with no urge to return or stay anywhere.

Jaxxson's hut had changed little since she was last here. Gabby had spent fourteen hours back in Albuquerque, but in that same time, two days had passed here in the Sphere.

Stopping in the middle of the room, Jaxxson lowered her feet to the ground.

But her feet refused to stay down, as if she wore anti-gravity boots instead of her scuffed black ones. Floating a foot above the ground was strange, but not a bad strange except for when she had to move around.

She lifted her hands. "What now?"

"You have to take control of your power, Gabby."

She would not bite Jaxxson's head off again about telling her to do something as if she could just snap her fingers and make her power perform. "Okay, let's take this one step at a time, Jaxxson. First, I don't feel that bright green power like I saw inside myself last time when you showed me how to find it."

He smiled. "You are annoyed with me."

"I was trying to not let it show."

"Your thoughts are hard to hide from a healer."

She cocked an eyebrow at him. "Then why don't you get busy healing and fix this?"

"Because if you recall, last time I made a mistake by tampering with your power and almost lost you. I will not suffer that moment again. You are the only one who should be controlling your power at this point."

She grumbled, "Then get ready for me to turn the village into a category-three weather event."

His smile slipped. "No, do not do that."

"It was a joke."

"You have a twisted sense of humor at times for such a pretty girl." If he hadn't smiled when he said that—and added the compliment—she might have been insulted, but Jaxxson would never say anything unkind to her. "Back to your power."

"What am I supposed to do to make this stop when I don't want to float? Why can't I see that green power inside me?"

"That's because the power is becoming one with you. When you're unfamiliar with it at first, the power feels like something added on or stuck inside you."

"I remember that feeling."

"Since then, your body has joined with the power, so you do not have to go search for it, but you do have to *feel* it."

Gabby crossed her arms and stared almost eye level with him. She could get used to this floating thing if she could reverse it when she needed to walk. "Well, I don't know how to *feeel* it."

Jaxxson crossed his arms now, which she read as impatient. Not a good sign. "Sit down on that stack of feathers, Gabby."

She gave him the stink eye, which turned out to be a wasted effort when he ignored it. Unfolding her arms, she flapped, trying to push herself down the way she would if she were in water. "Clearly, ordering me to sit doesn't work. Not that you'd miss that in your diagnosis, being a skilled healer and all. Just ignore me while I do what I've been doing since I left here. It's worked so well up until now. I only had to wear a thirty-pound backpack to keep my feet on the floor."

"There must be something wrong with me, because I have missed your caustic tongue." Jaxxson sighed. "You are not even trying to use your powers."

Gabby stopped flapping. She was not going to say another word until he figured out that telling her to just *do it* was not working.

His eyebrows jumped up. "Well?"

Nope. Not answering him.

"Let's try this. Close your eyes, Gabby."

She hoped this meant he was finally going to tell her something useful, so she closed her eyes and waited on his next instructions.

"Now tell your body to breathe."

Her eyes flew open. "What? That's ridiculous."

"Exactly. You do not tell your body to breathe, just as you should not have to tell your feet to stay on the ground. Your body knows what it must do to keep you alive, and your power will know what to do when you direct it. Close your eyes again and envision standing on the ground."

Here we go again.

She pictured her feet moving down and taking her weight again. She pictured weights dragging her feet down. She tried a couple of mental commands. *Down, girl. Feet on the ground, now!*

When Jaxxson said, "Try picturing yourself sitting on the feathers behind you," she instead pictured grabbing Jaxxson by the neck and shaking some sense into him.

Her skin chilled, then a voice whispered in her ear. *I told you I would help you if you kept my secret. Let go of your anger and I will move you to the feathers.*

Her neck muscles tensed.

She recognized that voice. It was Mathias, the former MystiK leader for this village. She'd seen him in ghost form last time she was here. Jaxxson hadn't seen the ghost and Gabby didn't tell him that she had.

Mathias had warned her not to, for one thing.

"Very good, Gabby!"

She opened her eyes and looked up from where she sat cross-legged on the feathers.

She whispered, "How'd you do that?"

"I didn't do that. You did." Jaxxson grinned at her, and she felt like a star student, when she was anything but. "See how it works now?"

No, she didn't see. Mathias had moved her, but she couldn't tell Jaxxson about her invisible consultant. Like the rest of the village, Jaxxson believed that Mathias had left the Sphere and was being held in a TecKnati facility back in Jaxxson's home world.

She rubbed her eyes with the heels of her hands. When she dropped her hands and looked up at Jaxxson, he was still smiling at her.

But standing next to him was the translucent image of Mathias frowning at her.

Reacting to either expression was not going to go well since Mathias might take offense to her returning Jaxxson's smile and Jaxxson would question her glaring at Mathias.

Jaxxson's gaze strayed away from her, staring at nothing. She'd seen him like that before when someone called him telepathically.

He swung his attention back to her. "Zilya is calling for me, because Kenja is arguing with her. Those two are making me crazy. Stay here and practice using your powers. I'll be back as soon as I can. Sound good?"

She gave him a plain smile and nodded.

The minute Jaxxson stepped outside, and the sound of his footsteps faded, she arched an eyebrow at Mathias. "Okay, time to start talking and tell me what is going on. What happened to you? Everyone thinks you're back home."

"I cannot stay long so listen closely."

"Do you really think you don't have my full attention by now, Math—"

"Silence!"

She scowled and crossed her arms. "Yelling at me is not a good way to gain my help."

His form wavered in and out. "I don't have much time."

Now she felt bad for snapping at him. "Sorry. Tell me what you came to say."

"The prophecy must be fulfilled."

"What's with this Damian Prophecy anyhow? All I hear is that it has to be fulfilled and time is running out and the world is coming to an end."

"You made that last part up. I heard nothing of the world coming to an end."

She crossed her arms and rolled her eyes. "Okay, so no world is coming to an end part, but everyone acts like there will be dire consequences."

"That part is true. I did not understand the significance of the prophecy until I died. I have moments that things come to me, but I have not been able to relay what I learn to Callan."

Gabby perked up at that. "Does Callan know about ... you?"

"Yes. So does Rayen."

"Are you serious? And she didn't tell me?" Gabby was so giving Rayen a tongue lashing over holding out on her.

"She gave me her word. You should know by now that Rayen will not break her word no matter what."

True, but Gabby still intended to bust her on it. Friends told each other things. Like when someone freaking *died.* "Why can I see and hear you, but no one else can?"

"Because you are a Hy'bridt. Your powers are ancient and formidable. The Hy'bridts who live in our time are revered for their abilities to move between worlds."

Gabby shook her head. "I don't want to move between worlds if you're referencing the world that you're in right now. I have no control over my powers. I'd never make it back here and I might destroy your world at the same time."

"That is not necessary." Mathias waved her comment off with his ethereal hand. He moved across the hut, pacing back and forth, if you could call it pacing when his feet didn't move.

Maybe she should give him the "just put your feet on the ground" talk.

He paused and focused on her. "You must ensure that the prophecy is fulfilled."

"How am I going to do that?"

"By following your heart when it comes to caring for people. You hide your feelings behind a sharp tongue, but you will not stand by and allow these children to remain trapped here."

"Are you saying I have the power to do that?" She shoved up to her feet, stomping over to Mathias. "Are you saying I could have gotten them out of here by now? If that's the case, you should have come to me sooner."

"It's not that easy."

"Why not?"

"I don't have time to explain things that you will not understand."

"So now I'm a moron?" she groused, hands on her hips, not backing an inch away from him.

His image shook with anger and the room vibrated around her. "How does Jaxxson deal with you when no one else can?"

"By not talking to me like I'm an idiot." Could he choke her as a ghost?

"I don't think you are a moron or an idiot, Gabby, but you are unfamiliar with all that goes on in this Sphere and in our world."

"Like I said, maybe if you'd have come to me sooner, I would be more up to speed by now."

"I couldn't come to you before or I would have."

She grabbed a handful of her ponytails and growled. "Why not?"

"Because it is difficult to shield myself from the wraiths for long."

"What wraiths, Mathias?"

"No! Never say my name!" The terror that filled his eyes bled through his body, shaking his form to the point it was hard to identify the wobbling mass as any version of Mathias.

Howling started inside the hut, but it sounded as if it was coming from somewhere beyond the Sphere. Mathias looked right and left, shouting at Gabby, "You must send the children home."

"How?"

"The prophecy. Fulfill it and ..."

Dark shapes flew into the hut, coming out of nothingness to form and fly around the room. Wind battered everything, slapping her ponytails against her face.

Gabby backed up, waving her arms. "What can I do? How do I stop them?"

"Nothing. They won't ... touch you," Mathias choked out before his head jerked back. The muscles in his face and throat stood out in thick cords. He clenched his jaw and groaned, struggling against an invisible force that yanked him right and left.

Her ears should be bleeding from the noise those things were making.

Mathias forced out his next words. "V'ru ... has ... prophecy. Help him ... decode it. Bonding ... *must* happen—"

Black shapes flooded the room, swarming Mathias. He cried out, swinging his arms, and fighting them until his arms were snatched behind him and he was dragged up toward the open roof of the hut, where the sky arched overhead.

The black swarm spun into a tight knot, then ... poof. They were gone and so was Mathias.

Gabby's knees gave out. She hit the feather bed hard and looked up to see nothing but a sky losing light with every second that ticked toward moonset.

Ten minutes later, Jaxxson came walking back in. He glanced around at the hut, noticing herbs blown into a corner and gourds on the floor. "Did you have a weather event?"

I'm going to take one for the team, Mathias. Gabby nodded.

"Come on, Gabby. I thought you were going to practice. You shouldn't be intimidated by your power. It is yours to control."

She moved her mouth like a guppy struggling for air. Breathing wasn't a problem. She was trying to figure out what to say. "Did you hear anything while you were gone?"

"Like what?"

"Wind noise. Howling wind noise?"

Jaxxson's forehead creased in thought. "No, I heard nothing." He looked more closely at her. "Are you okay?"

No, she wasn't okay, but neither was she ready to talk about what she'd just witnessed. Poor Mathias had died a horrible death if those wraiths are what killed him.

And she was the only one who could hear or see him, so it was her job to do what he couldn't and make sure these children returned home.

She recalled what he'd said.

Fulfill the prophecy and the MystiKs would go home.

Plus, something about a bonding that had to happen.

The only problem with what he'd told her was that she didn't have any idea how to unravel the prophecy. That meant she had to talk to Mathias again, but this time she wouldn't waste time arguing with him and she sure as heck wasn't saying his name again.

Finding a smile for Jaxxson, she asked, "Would V'ru have information on Hy'bridts?"

"Some, but he will not be able to tell you how to manage your power."

"That's not what I'm after. I want to know the history of the Hy'bridt abilities."

Jaxxson pondered that. "What exactly are you looking for?"

"You know, things like if they all have telepathy and if they all levitate." She let her words trail off, because what she couldn't tell Jaxxson was that she wanted to find out if she could cross over to another world and come back.

If Hy'bridts were so powerful and could walk between worlds, then why couldn't she go into the place where Mathias was caught and free him? It was the least he deserved after sparing Rayen, Tony and her on their first visit to the Sphere.

CHAPTER 14

CALLAN SHIFTED HIS BODY, BUT there was no comfortable position. His raw skin bled where the metal cut into his wrists and the room stank of rotted food he'd ignored.

Or maybe he was to blame for that obnoxious odor after all the time he'd been stuck here.

TecKnati scouts laughed and carried on outside. Someone shouted, "Red moon setting soon, warrior."

They'd been doing that for the past two hours.

Closing his eyes, Callan leaned his head back, determined to keep his wits about him no matter what they did. The minute it was dark, Thylan would be back with an army to hold Callan down.

Will Thylan cut off my fingers first? Or my hands?

He fisted his hands, shaking with the urge to break these chains.

Music pushed inside his mind. Someone was singing.

A girl.

Callan focused on the words that he'd heard sung at home. That voice was as sweet as any songbird's. Within seconds, his heartbeat slowed, and he relaxed his hands. The lyrical sound curled inside him, soothing the fury that had raged for days. Exhaustion and pain left him. His body welcomed the relief.

His breathing dropped to a calm rhythm. The pain wracking him subsided for the first time in so long he just wanted to stay in this state of disconnect.

Something tapped on his mind.

"Hmm?" He drew a deep breath and let it out slowly, unwilling to disturb the tranquility wrapping him.

The second tap on his consciousness brought him back to alertness. He stilled and opened his mind a tiny bit, just enough to determine if this was friend or foe, but a TecKnati would not know how to execute telepathy.

He sent out a silent question. *What?*

I'm so glad you answered. I have tried to reach someone, anyone, since I was captured two days ago. What House are you from?

I am with the Warrior House. And yours?

Creativity House.

Callan's mother was fond of the Creativity House and mentioned it often, hoping to pique Callan's interest in the females there. Now he was interested in only one young woman, and she didn't live in his time. If he survived this Sphere, he'd be expected to choose a future mate when he returned home.

The Houses were big on long engagements. They still struggled to rebuild the population of MystiKs, and encouraged proliferation, but only after two people had made a true commitment.

He wished the Houses were big on allowing teens to have a life first. Some did, but not the MystiK teens expected to assume roles of leadership at some point.

To be honest, right now he'd take being home and facing the decision about a mate over sitting here worrying that his little village in the Sphere was vulnerable.

When he didn't hear from the girl again, Callan reached out to her telepathically again. *Were you singing?*

Yes. Her answer held a shyness that would be a rosy blush if sound had color.

His mother thought he would be content with a shy, accommodating woman. That just proved how little his mother knew about him.

Callan was attracted to a stubborn, argumentative female with eyes the color of a turquoise jewel and hair dark as midnight.

The songbird's voice poked at his mind again. *Are you alone?*

You mean here in the TeK camp or in the Sphere?

I guess the Sphere if that's what this world is called.

That's what we call it, Callan explained. *There's a whole group of MystiKs living in a village we've warded.*

How can that be? She sounded shocked. *I didn't know anyone was gone until they captured me.*

That's the problem with our Houses. They rarely talk. Even when they do, it's not about anything significant or there would be an outcry by now.

The quiet stretched so long that he wondered if she was okay. He started to ask when her words flowed into his mind.

Do you have any idea of how we can return home?

He hated the longing in her voice. It was no different from that of any other adolescent MystiK newly captured and delivered to the Sphere. By the time they were here a month, the longing changed to despair.

He had to give her an answer, but he stayed with the truth. *No, I don't have a way home yet, but that doesn't mean we won't find one.*

Her silence answered with more anguish than if she'd used words.

He'd like to give her encouragement, but he might not be here long himself. Now he knew how Mathias felt as his eighteenth BIRG Day neared. Callan had considered Mathias a close friend and respected him as the senior teen from the Governing House, which had given Mathias the authority to rule the MystiK village he'd created in the Sphere.

Governing had not gone to Mathias' head either.

He would have made an outstanding leader back home ... had he lived. The minute the red moon had set on the day Mathias turned eighteen, the deadly wraiths had dragged him away.

Callan clenched at the memory of his friend screaming.

He and Rayen had been the only two present to witness that hideous moment and had given their vows to keep Mathias' death a secret from the others in the village.

Mathias had good reason. He'd wanted the rest of the children in the village to maintain hope. He'd explained how it was best that they think SEOH had taken him back to their home world and locked him away until the treaty was signed again.

And now Callan faced that same fate. He could only hope that Kaz, Zilya, Jaxxson and the others would believe the TeKs had killed him.

Turning eighteen hadn't seemed like a big deal when Jornn, his twin, had been alive and slated to be the next Warrior House leader. But SEOH had murdered Jornn, leaving Callan as the next in line. Callan had never wanted to lead a House. Give him an army of warriors any day, but politics and stuffy events had turned reaching eighteen into a monumental pain in the butt back home.

Or so he'd thought until he'd been captured while tracking down a lead to prove SEOH had been behind Jornn's murder. Then he'd been transported to this Sphere.

Now reaching the age of eighteen equated death, because he doubted the MystiKs would find a way out of the Sphere before the red moon set on his BIRG Day.

He felt another bump on his mind and telepathically replied, *Yes?*

Are you feeling any better?

His chest didn't hurt as much as it had, and one of the gashes had closed. It was no longer bleeding. *I do. Did you do that?*

I could feel your pain, she answered, then added, *The TeKs don't know. I pretend I can't do anything, and I scared the leader into thinking I'm crazy. Who are you?*

Callan of the Warrior House.

She didn't answer at first then she said, *I thought it might be you. I'm Becka.*

He bounced his head back against the wall and locked down his mental shields before she heard him groan. Was the universe bored and had no one better to toy with today?

Her gentle thump was back.

To ignore her would be a major breach of protocol. Even in this place. He carefully dropped his shields just enough to talk, but not enough to allow her music to pass through again, or she'd get the wrong idea.

Becka?

Thank goodness, I thought the TecKnati had activated their laser grid again. I can ease more of your pain.

No. He shouldn't have replied so harshly.

Why not?

I'm fine.

I can feel that you are still hurting. Why won't you let me ... Her voice faded to silence then she came back. *Are you bonded with ... someone?*

The hurt in her voice radiated through their mental connection. Callan thunked his head back again and admitted, *No, I'm not bonded to anyone.*

Oh, good. You had me worried there.

And that would be because his mother and her mother had discussed a possible future alliance. Why couldn't parents stay out of things like that?

Becka's mother had three daughters and intended for every one of them to marry well. One was a year older than Callan and lived to be served by others. The second daughter was a year younger than him and had always looked down her nose at him when they ran into each other, as if he were unfit to be in the same room with her.

As the youngest and two years behind Callan, Becka was the quiet one. She was the only daughter he could tolerate spending time around, but that didn't mean they were well suited.

He wasn't bonded, but to act as if nothing had changed since he had been captured would be a betrayal to Rayen and dishonest to Becka. He might not be able to bond with Rayen, but his heart was his own to give away and Rayen held his in her hands. It mattered not that he'd never see her again. That was the way he felt.

Up until now, Callan had not actually admitted to himself that he never expected to go home, but he must have always doubted that he would. Otherwise, why would he have opened himself up to Rayen when he still had commitments at home?

Such as Becka.

She was the one his parents had encouraged him to consider. By the time she turned eighteen, he would be well on the way to taking his place in the MystiK hierarchy. His parents hadn't done anything archaic like demand he choose her as his future wife, but there were expectations that came along with responsibility.

They wouldn't understand if he told them he wanted to spend his life with someone unsuitable.

A C'raydonian no less.

Becka wouldn't understand either.

Callan could avoid telling Becka the truth since there was little chance that either of them would escape the TecKnati camp, but to allow her to think there was any hope between them would be dishonorable.

He took a breath and answered her telepathically. *Becka, I need to tell—*

Shouting erupted outside his door. He slammed his mental shields down and prepared for Thylan. The moon shouldn't have set yet.

What was going on?

Becka tapped again, but Callan needed to remove all distractions to face what Thylan had planned for him.

Thylan opened the door. Six beefed-up TecKnati stood behind him. He grinned. "Time's up."

Then Thylan told his men, "Bring him outside."

CHAPTER 15

RAYEN CLIMBED OFF THE TORTALONE in a clearing barely wide enough to contain the two creatures. The heat here was thicker, with a dirty yellow hue and a sulfuric smell like rotten eggs. Maybe it was because of the TecKnati presence, or maybe because the trees and shrubs in this area looked stilted, more bleached bones than soft foliage.

Kaz had maneuvered his mount to come in very slowly until it dropped vertically out of the air.

He'd shown her how to handle riding one by herself so that they could bring two for the trip back to the village. He said the creatures didn't mind several people, but they tended to become unstable with more than two riders of their size.

That was fine by her.

It meant she and Callan would be riding home together.

She was not leaving here without him. She could already feel his arms around her. He would hold her close when they rode back to the village and Kaz could fly on the second tortalone.

The TecKnati camp sat three hundred feet ahead.

Dropping down beside her with an easy move, Kaz pulled the laptop out of a shoulder sling. He'd carried it so that she could focus on handling her tortalone.

Once he handed the precious computer to her and tossed the sling on top of his tortalone, he whispered to the creatures. They immediately settled down and tucked inside their shells.

She asked, "Do you think any of the TeKs will come out here?"

Kaz shook his head. "They should keep all of their scouts in close to have as many as possible for when we return, but I do worry about the tortalones being here. They disappeared on me once yesterday."

If they had to return on foot, they'd just suck it up and do it. "Do you think the TeKs have hurt Callan?"

"Possibly, but they want this computer, or they want the one you traveled here through if that is indeed the Genera-Y. To harm Callan ahead of moonset would work against them."

She hoped he was right.

Speaking of moonset, she had made a decision on the way here so that Kaz would understand why they *had* to break Callan out before the red moon disappeared. "About Callan's BIRG Day—"

He scowled at her. "I wish I hadn't told you about that. It *is* important to MystiKs that we hold true to our ceremonies, but the celebration of his birth is trivial at this point. Stop obsessing."

She hoped Callan would forgive her, but she couldn't leave Kaz in the dark and expect him to be as committed as she was to getting Callan out *now*. "You don't understand, Kaz. Callan's birthday is *not* trivial. He'll die when the moon sets unless we can find a way to protect him from another threat in this Sphere besides the TeKs."

That clearly surprised Kaz. "What are you talking about?"

"I gave my word to Mathias, but I think he would understand why I have to break it, given this situation."

"Mathias? You think I care anything about a leader of the Governing House who left our people here to fend for themselves?"

She understood his feelings since Kaz didn't know the truth, but she was about to enlighten him. "We don't have much time, so I need to tell you this quickly and explain more later. The minute the moon sets on any MystiK celebrating an eighteenth BIRG Day while in this place, that person will die a horrible death from these awful wraiths. *That* is what happened to Mathias. I saw it."

Kaz's lips moved with his struggle to form words. "Why would—"

"I'll explain later, but Mathias was the second one to reach eighteen and die in this place. Callan will be the third if we don't get him out of the TeK camp and give him a fighting chance. I don't know what it will take to stop the wraiths, but I intend to unleash all my power on them." She swallowed and still that lump of worry wouldn't go away. "I don't care what we have to do to free him now, but we're not leaving without Callan. Understood?"

The dark gaze of a ferocious warrior slid into Kaz's eyes. "Agreed, but we have to rescue *two* captives."

"The girl who is here? Who is she?"

"Yes, her, but just as you said, we have no time. I will explain later. Let's get moving."

Something told Rayen she wasn't going to like that explanation, but nothing could be worse than Callan facing death with his hands tied and no way to fight.

They hurried through the woods. Her palms were damp. She clutched the computer tighter to prevent dropping it. When they reached the edge of the bone-colored trees, Kaz held up a hand and studied the terrain.

The fenced area where the TecKnati had captured Callan now stood empty, which explained why there were no guards around it. It was seventy feet wide and covered in fine-powdered orange dirt that had hidden a dangerous grid capable of stealing power. She had to assume the grid was still in place. Between where she stood and the single-story metal building at the far end of the camp, a series of tents had been erected in two rows that bordered the walkway to the metal building. The tents had been painted in colors that matched the woods, hiding them from the sky if she and Kaz hadn't already known the location.

The TecKnati had removed trees, leaving a broad sweep of cleared ground around the camp with the widest open area at this end.

She saw little activity and, even at that, it was all down near the metal building where a handful of scouts moved around.

Kaz said, "They must have Callan locked inside the building." He eyed the sky where the moon dipped closer to the horizon.

"We need to go, Kaz."

He grunted, his gaze sweeping the TeK camp once more.

She was done waiting and started to move.

He caught her arm. "You must do as I say when we meet with the TeKs. I know them better than you do."

Her first thought was to remind him that she was not receptive to being ordered around, but there was no give in Kaz and Callan when they were in protective mode. "I understand."

"No, you don't. I shouldn't even be bringing you here, Rayen. Callan will be furious with me, but after seeing how Tony brought V'ru out of his kamara, I had to leave Tony to watch over him."

"That TeK Thylan is expecting *me*, not Tony or you," she reminded him. "Callan can't be angry unless he's alive. I'll smooth everything over with him, but if you try to tell me to leave before we have him back, I'm not going. Are we clear?"

"Yes, but—"

She didn't want to hear any more. "Callan doesn't get to make that choice and neither do you. Besides, we both know what I can do."

"*If* your power comes when you call to it," he pointed out.

He would bring that up when she was already worried about making this computer work. She ended the conversation by telling him, "The longer we wait, the less time I have to make this thing work."

He waved his hand forward. "Go."

As soon as they emerged from the woods and started across the open space between them and the structures around the camp, TecKnati scouts came out of the tents. The scouts followed them on their way to the building that sat dead center. Ahead, more boys from age ten to older teens poured out of the camouflaged tents.

She and Kaz moved through a sea of metallic gray-green uniforms and clipped haircuts much like Tony's short hair, but that's where any resemblance ended.

Tony would never mistreat someone.

Several of the younger ones spun around and shouted for Thylan.

That was the arrogant TecKnati who had taunted her after he captured Callan. Thylan had enjoyed telling her how he was going to cut parts off Callan if she showed up after moonset today.

She hated watching that red moon. It drifted toward the horizon with no care for what was happening here. In another thirty minutes, it would be gone.

The scouts they approached jeered at them, and the ones following behind picked up the mantra, lifting the noise to an angry rumble. There had to be sixty or more. Kaz continued walking, not giving heed to anyone or anything.

Of course, the scouts all stood back from the menace emanating from her and Kaz.

The Teks wanted blood?

Harm Callan and she'd show them their own.

Fifty feet from the building, guards stepped into her path. "No further, MystiK."

Should she correct him and say she was a C'raydonian?

Kaz would kill her. She said nothing, waiting for the all-powerful Thylan to make his way to her.

The men parted for Thylan and filled in behind him as he moved toward her with a cocky gait. He stopped in front of her, grinning and sweeping a slow look over her in a way that made herskin crawl. "I can see why Callan would want you, but not why you'd want him."

She hadn't seen *that* comment coming.

An arm bulging with tense muscle went around her shoulder. She looked up at Kaz who didn't spare her a glance. What was he doing? It looked as if he was staking claim in front of Thylan.

Did Kaz think she cared what this creepy guy thought? Or that she couldn't take Thylan in a battle? The mouthy TeK was slow and, in a fight with her, slow would lose.

She tried to ease away from Kaz, but he squeezed her tighter against him.

Then Kaz pinned Thylan with a bold stare, making it clear who he was addressing. "She and Callan are friends. Just as Callan and I have been friends for many years. We're here to deliver your computer and take our *friend* back to the village." His voiced dropped with an edge of threat. "Just to be clear. She is mine. If you insult her again before our exchange is completed, you will regret your words."

Since waking up in that desert, she'd prided herself on assessing a threat situation quickly. She didn't understand what Kaz was up to, but he wouldn't be doing this unless he had a reason.

He must realize something about Thylan that she'd missed. Was Kaz doing all this to prevent Thylan from thinking she was of value to Callan? If that happened, she *would* become a liability in this negotiation. That had to be the reason behind this posturing. Kaz was diffusing the notion that her presence had any significant value to Callan, so the Teks would focus on the exchange, which meant Kaz was protecting his friend.

In that case, their goals were the same.

Thylan rubbed his chin, taking Kaz's measure with a long look. "Show me the computer."

"Not until we see that Callan is unharmed."

This commanding voice of Kaz's was one she hadn't heard before now.

Thylan laughed. "You do realize you're outnumbered, right?"

Kaz's gaze hardened. "You do realize that MystiKs sabotaged the last ANASKO space launch using only natural powers, right? Would you care for a demonstration?"

That wiped the attitude off Thylan's face.

She wasn't sure Kaz had chosen the right approach, considering they were at a disadvantage if they were standing above another grid.

"Show me how the computer works first," Thylan demanded.

"No." She and Kaz said that together.

She added, "You can't be trusted after what you did to capture Callan."

"Don't like getting outsmarted, do you?" Thylan laughed. "All I'd have to do is throw a switch to capture you two."

She wanted to use a blast of power to make Thylan think twice about that laser grid.

Kaz warned, "If you turn on that grid, you risk destroying the sentient component of this computer. Now, where is Callan?"

The Tek gave her a taunting smile. "He's been out here the whole time."

Thylan's eyes lit with mean happiness. He kept his attention on her while he called over his shoulder. "Callan? We've got your ... well, not *your* girl since she's with someone else, but she's back with the computer. You want to say hello?"

Forcing herself to remain planted in this spot was a battle when all she wanted to do was run to find Callan.

Someone thumped against her mind so hard it jarred her, and she sidestepped to keep her balance.

Kaz jerked his gaze down at her. "What?"

Everyone else was watching, too.

She couldn't let Thylan misread the stumble as her reaction to Callan being close by. She said, "Nothing," and shook it off, ready to negotiate.

Callan came blasting into her mind shouting, *What are you doing here? I told you—*

She slammed her mental walls down, shutting him out. There was no way she could handle these negotiations with Callan yelling at her at the same time.

He thumped again, hard, and she pushed back.

That silenced him.

Thylan's men cleared a path between where they stood and Callan.

When the crowd parted, she finally saw him. Her heart thudded.

He was alive, but he was far from unharmed with bleeding wrists and gashes along his chest and shoulders as if he'd been struck with a whip. One nasty cut had closed, but none had healed entirely.

What was stopping him from healing?

The laser grid.

She didn't sense any such power operating beneath her feet at this moment. Based on the last time she'd been here Callan wouldn't be able to contact her telepathically if the laser grid was activated.

Callan slung wet hair off his face and split his furious glare between her and Kaz.

It took a moment for her to realize how this picture looked to Callan.

She tried to step out of Kaz's hold, but he had an unyielding grip on her shoulder. She tugged again.

Kaz yanked her closer and told Thylan, "She'll show you the computer, then you will uncuff him."

Callan's fierce stare was all for Kaz and, after a moment, she had the feeling he was trying to communicate telepathically with Kaz, too, but Kaz must not be opening his mind either.

Growling like a trapped animal, Callan shouted, "Kaz, get her—"

Someone threw a bucket of liquid straight at Callan's face. Energy crackled at his wrists, and he jerked as if shocked.

She flinched, the urge to fight trembling through her.

Kaz slid one word at her through his gritted teeth. "Don't."

She hoped he knew what he was doing.

Thylan tucked a gadget in the pants pocket of his uniform before she could see what it was. He stepped closer to her and held his hands out, palms up.

She placed the laptop there and lifted the lid. Flexing her fingers, she hovered her hand over the keys.

Every TecKnati gaze was locked on her hand.

Callan yelled, "Do not—"

More water hit him. Just hearing him choke and the sizzle of energy shocking him hurt her. She'd thought about how she would do this on the way here. To make her power surge, all she had to do was envision them hurting Callan.

Holding the computer in one hand, Thylan yanked the gadget back out that was just big enough to fit in the palm of his hand. Silver and oblong shaped. He lifted it in Callan's direction and Callan went silent.

What had he done to Callan with that small device? Energy stirred inside her, and she snapped back to her task.

Callan thumped hard on her mind once more. It had to be him. Kaz wouldn't interrupt her right now.

Calling hard for her power, she envisioned the TeKs taking a knife to Callan—

He bumped her again mentally, over, and over.

She lost her train of thought. Poof. The energy settled down.

Thylan shifted his feet, getting antsy. "What's the holdup? Does this thing work or not?"

"Yes," she was quick to assure him.

Kaz stepped closer and questioned Thylan. "Why can't the TecKnati build a two-way time travel computer?"

Good. He was distracting Thylan. She dug into her memory for more nightmares, such as Callan being attacked by the croggle.

But they had defeated the beast together.

Thylan said, "Who's to say we haven't built a portal computer that will time travel in any direction?"

"*I'm* saying you haven't if you need this antique," Kaz pointed out. His foot nudged her, which she took to mean hurry up.

She changed her mind on searching for a vision of Callan and started thinking about Tony and Gabby attacked by the deadly vine.

Heat stirred inside her once more. Thank goodness.

Energy balled and twisted, churning.

Tony warned her not to feed too much power into the computer and blow it up. She pulled the power slowly toward her arms and into her hand.

The monitor flashed on.

More than anything, she wanted to let Callan know they were close, but she kept all her attention on the three circles moving in and out of each other across the screen. The blue, green, and red colors weren't the same as the image on the actual time travel computer, but no one here would know that. Tony and Gabby had been the only people other than her who had seen the real portal computer.

When scouts behind her saw the monitor come to life, they started murmuring.

Now was as good a time as any to turn it around and make their swap.

Kaz's gaze tracked the monitor screen, but he kept up his conversation with Thylan. "We informed you the computer requires a MystiK to operate it. What are you going to do when you take it back to SEOH?"

Thylan found Kaz's question amusing, but then he found everything about the MystiKs amusing. "You think my father doesn't have MystiKs on our payroll?"

What? This was SEOH's son? And they had MystiKs working for them?

She lost her focus in that one second.

Thylan had just looked down at the screen when it flashed twice and blinked off.

One of his guys shouted, "They're trying to trick us."

"No, I'm not," she lied. "It'll come back on in a minute."

For the first time, Thylan was not amused. He slapped the lid shut. "Lock these two up."

Kaz jerked her back to him and shoved past her. He lifted his hands in front of his chest, then behind him, shoving a fast kinetic blast in a circular arc to stop scouts in front and those who surged toward their backs.

They slammed into the invisible wall and bounced off.

Thylan yelled, "Blast them."

Callan roared and lunged. Metal screamed as the chain mounts started ripping away from the wall.

She screamed inside her head, begging her power to come back. Nothing. What good was the stupid power if it couldn't show up when she needed it most?

The noise of Callan struggling snatched Thylan's attention and offered her the perfect opening.

She shot past Kaz, snatched the computer from Thylan's hands, and spun around to stand in front of Kaz, holding up the computer. "Shoot us and you'll lose the Genera-Y computer. Then who's going home?"

Everyone stilled.

Kaz whispered, "Smart, but give it to me and get behind me."

"Not going to happen," she murmured. Keeping her gaze on Callan, she spoke to Thylan. "The computer works. I can prove it, but I'm not even going to try again unless you release Callan."

"Then he dies."

That was a greater threat than Thylan knew, because that blood red moon was sinking faster every second. "If you harm him, I will destroy this computer."

"Do that and SEOH will destroy this Sphere."

Kaz shouted, "Have you forgotten the counter measure bespelled in the Amity treaty? SEOH wouldn't risk killing a MystiK child and lose a TecKnati youth of equal standing. The majority of MystiKs in this Sphere are future leaders, the highest ranked in our Houses."

"That's the thing, MystiK. There has been no loss of TecKnati children from all the deaths here, so SEOH *would* destroy this Sphere."

Kaz answered, but confidence was absent from his statement. "Yes, but none of those deaths met the requirements of the treaty."

"Or so you think," Thylan said, not the least bit concerned.

Callan had shared the details of the current treaty with Rayen. It was signed every five years between the TecKnati and the MystiKs. Due to a spell infused by the MystiK leaders who signed the original treaty that continued through each resigning, if a TecKnati intentionally killed a MystiK child younger than eighteen then a TecKnati child of equal political stature would die immediately, and vice versa. Callan said SEOH's oldest son had died the minute Callan's twin had been murdered, proving the treaty had teeth.

Thylan said, "I'll make you a deal."

She'd trust that as much as making a pact with a wraith. "What's the deal?"

"I'll trade Callan now for the computer ... and you."

Kaz and Callan shouted, "No!" Callan lunged against the chains again.

Bolts holding Callan's chains squealed.

Another bucket of water hit Callan. She was going to hurt whoever held that bucket as soon as she had the opportunity. There had to be an evil reason for keeping him wet.

Thylan held up his hands. "I'm trying to be reasonable."

If Kaz got Callan away from here, Kaz knew about the wraiths and would help Callan fight. That would only happen if Callan was free to use his power.

She stepped forward. "I accept the deal."

Kaz's hands landed on her shoulders, pulling her back. "I said no."

Callan drove his body hard against the chain mounts. Metal twisting against metal screamed. "Get her out of here, Kaz!"

Driving forward hard again, Callan forced the supports to give another inch.

Looking panicked, Thylan fished his gadget out quickly and pointed it at Callan's wrist cuffs that glowed blue.

Callan arched up and back, shuddering against power being activated by Thylan's remote controller.

She yelled, "Stop or I won't trade."

Thylan held the button down an extra second then clicked the device off.

Callan fell to his knees and hung forward. His arms pulled back against the chains that were stretched tight.

He was hardly breathing. Unconscious.

Thylan erupted into laughter, a nervous one, but his scouts joined in.

The noise covered her words to Kaz. "Let me make this trade. Keep Callan alive, then come back and get me out. I trust you to help him fight off the wraiths and for you both to come back for me. You trust me to deal with Thylan."

"No."

"It's my choice, Kaz. I'm doing it with or without your help. If you don't help me, we're going to all end up captives. Or dead."

She yelled at Thylan, "Make up your mind. Deal or not?"

The laughing died down. Thylan ordered Callan unchained and carried to just short of the tree line.

She stepped out of Kaz's grasp. When she turned to look at him, sick disappointment stared back at her. He was worried for her. She wished she could return Kaz's feelings, but her heart belonged to Callan. She mouthed the word *please.*

Kaz inhaled deeply and followed the men carrying Callan.

She hoped she would see them both again.

"Bring the girl and the computer," Thylan ordered.

Rayen swung around and jerked her arm away from the first scout who reached for her. When Thylan snickered at her reaction, it occurred to her now that Kaz's protective attitude might have been entirely for her benefit.

If that was the case, she would need her power for more than lighting up this computer.

CHAPTER 16

"WAKE UP!" SHOUTED SO CLOSE to Callan's face he jerked away.

Pain clawed up his arms, dragging him back to consciousness as much as the loud voice and someone shaking him. He opened his eyes and saw the sky peeking through branches.

"Get up!" Kaz stood and pulled on Callan's arm.

A burning pain raced up Callan's shoulder. He snatched his arm back. "Do you want to die?"

"No, but you must if you're not going to get up and fight. You have only minutes until moonset."

Callan shoved himself up to a sitting position and looked around. The woods surrounded him. Kaz was here. The TecKnati camp ...

He launched to his feet. "Where's Rayen?"

"She traded herself and that computer for you," Kaz snapped, eyes accusing Callan over the trouble Rayen was in.

Callan shoved up into Kaz's face, his voice threatening to maim. "I told you not to bring her back. How could you leave her in that place?"

"If you had told me the truth about Mathias, I might have had a chance of talking her out of it." Kaz shoved him back.

Callan didn't retaliate. Something was seriously off with this conversation. "What does Mathias have to do with anything?"

"Rayen told me what happened to Mathias and that you two were sworn to secrecy, but *you* should have told me that Mathias hadn't abandoned the village."

Callan shoved both hands over his face then back over his wet hair. Thylan liked to zap him with a charge of electricity when he was saturated. "There was no reason to tell you until the right moment."

"And when would that have been?"

Callan had never seen Kaz this angry. "Tomorrow. I was going to take you with me when the time came so you would see what happens just as

I had to watch Mathias. Then you would understand why I have held his confidence."

Kaz raised his fists, shaking them at the universe. "Tomorrow? Have you lost all track of time? We'll talk later. The wraiths will be showing up any minute now."

"No, they won't."

"Is this not your BIRG Day, moron?" Kaz shouted at him.

"Today? No. My BIRG Day is tomorrow." Callan put it together and fury ignited. "You told Rayen it was *today*? That's why she traded herself so I wouldn't be defenseless against the wraiths?"

Confusion wiped the anger off Kaz's face. "It's not today?"

Murdering your best friend was generally frowned upon, but Callan had never cared about what society thought before so why hold back now. "You get the date wrong every year. Jornn was born today just before midnight, and I was born six minutes later."

Kaz muttered, "I don't recall you correcting me."

"I did when we were little. Later I stopped because it didn't matter to me. Jornn and I celebrated together."

"Then it's your fault I told Rayen the wrong date," Kaz spat back. "If anything happens to her, the wraiths will have to stand in line behind me."

Rage blinded Callan so fast he just reacted and lashed out a kinetic hit that slammed Kaz back twenty feet into a tree. "I want her out of there now! You, I'll deal with later."

Kaz banged into the tree and groaned. Then he dropped to his feet, rolled his shoulders and came walking back over. "I'm not done with this."

"Neither am I," Callan made clear.

"How do we get to her?"

"That's not going to be easy."

"Why?"

"Because the TecKnati have run a narrow grid around the perimeter of that metal building. Thylan doesn't trust putting the grid beneath the floors of the building."

Kaz snorted. "Doesn't trust their technology? I'd say he was intelligent if Thylan wasn't SEOH's son. What do you think they're going to do with the computer?"

Callan stared off at the camp in the distance. "SEOH wants the computer sent back to ANASKO so he can destroy it, but Thylan thinks he can make it work for time travel in both directions. He's determined to outsmart his father on this."

"Rayen says it's just a computer with no special ability."

"That will keep Thylan from harming her for a while, but not for long." Callan's hands trembled with just thinking about her inside there, subject to that animal, Thylan. Getting Rayen out of that camp and to safety came before all else.

Callan forced his emotions into the hole where they would stay out of his way and not distract him. "We've got to find a way to enter the camp without them knowing so Thylan doesn't turn on the laser grid."

CHAPTER 17

2179 ACE, in ORD/City One

SEOH'S OFFICE FACED THE EAST. From the one-hundred-and-seventieth- floor of the ANASKO building that towered above Lake Michigan, he could see reflections created by the last glimmer of sunlight dissolving into the calm water. Very soon, the MystiKs would no longer be a problem. He leaned back, smiling.

One more day until the BIRG Con.

The moment of reckoning for those furkken MystiKs was finally approaching. Furk, that worthless old board member who had died *after* he'd made the tiebreaking vote *for* the treaty, deserved to have his name live on in posterity as a favorite curse.

A light on the control panel built into SEOH's desk glowed, then a hologram of his female AI assistant appeared. Leesa announced, "Vice Rustaad will arrive in your office in eight seconds."

SEOH replied, "Acknowledged."

The holographic woman disappeared and Rustaad entered, silent as a killer in the night, a role he'd performed exceptionally well from time to time.

Before Rustaad began his report, SEOH asked, "How close are the leaders of the MystiK Houses to arriving in our city for the BIRG Con?"

Holding himself with the posture of one born to money, Rustaad considered the question, never rushing to answer until he had the exact words required. "Based upon tracking the vehicles we sent for the leaders, none should arrive prior to noon tomorrow, but all should be on site by an hour before sunset. However, two H'ybridts have arrived already, early and within thirty minutes of each other, which I find odd."

"Everything about those people is odd." SEOH waved a hand, dismissing the issue. "I detest them personally, but they're not an issue for us. Even their own people treat the Hy'bridts as reclusive wackos. It's the G'ortians we need to keep an eye on."

Rustaad inclined his head. "Agreed."

"Any news on the remaining five to capture?"

"Some," Rustaad admitted. "We had a small bit of fortune. A Hy'bridt went to the Creativity House and, from what I've gathered from our snitch in that House, the Hy'bridt raved that Callan was at the center of the prophecy and must bond to see it fulfilled."

"Callan?"

When Rustaad nodded, SEOH stood and leaned forward with his hands on his desk, speaking softly. "Are you saying we killed the wrong twin? Because if that's so, my son died for no reason."

Anyone other than Rustaad would be shaking in his boots, but Rustaad was cut of the same shark cloth as SEOH. The TecKnati leader might regret losing his first-born son, but he had a natural indifference to things like having possibly murdered the wrong MystiK teenager.

Rustaad said, "There is no way to know for sure until tomorrow and even then, it may all be a moot point. At the time that you ordered Jornn's death instead of Callan's, everyone was of the belief that Jornn represented the greatest threat to TecKnati if he managed to do what no one else had and unite the fragmented MystiK Houses."

"I know why I had him killed," SEOH snarled.

Rustaad remained silent for several seconds, the equivalent of a sigh from anyone else. "My point is, had Jornn not been killed he would still be a threat because so many were willing to follow him when he took over leadership. But even if Callan is central to the Damian Prophecy, he is no longer in a place where he can influence change."

"But he's a G'ortian," SEOH argued. "You're the one who finally convinced me to take the G'ortian power seriously. Now you're dismissing it."

"No, I'm not." Rustaad continued in a calm voice. "As long as the G'ortians we've captured stay in the Sphere, we shouldn't have an issue here. If their powers transcended that Sphere, they would have been able to contact someone via telepathy by now, especially a Hy'bridt, but they haven't. The Hy'bridt who spoke at the Creativity House managed only to further your plan."

Settling back into his chair, SEOH asked, "How's that?"

"Becka is the youngest of the Creativity House ruling family, but she has been singled out as Callan's future mate since she's also G'ortian." Rustaad's lips slanted up a tiny degree, just enough to televise his pleasure at what he was about to share. "She felt it her duty to inform Callan of the Hy'bridt's revelation, so she—"

SEOH started chuckling, seeing where this was going.

"—rushed to tell Callan," Rustaad finished.

"And we caught her, right?" SEOH added, enjoying the moment.

"Absolutely. We now have three G'ortians with Callan, V'ru, and Becka. Plus, Thylan is holding Becka captive and away from Callan to prevent their bonding."

"That's right. You said the Hy'bridt mentioned them bonding." SEOH studied on that. "I wonder if we can feed her to a croggle to keep her from Callan."

"That would be dangerous, SEOH. We've been fortunate to have no loss of TecKnati children when the MystiKs died on their own in the Sphere, but intentionally feeding Becka to a croggle would—"

"Constitute murder." SEOH waved him off. "I won't risk my youngest son." SEOH had Bernardo surrounded by guards and medical professionals twenty-four-seven, but his firstborn had died of asphyxiation in front of several people. He just couldn't trust that furkken treaty not to kill his progeny.

Rustaad picked up where he had paused. "There have been reports of Kenja and Callan battling, so sending in a group of Uberon warriors is turning out better than we'd hoped. If she kills Callan, we don't risk losing a TecKnati child."

SEOH hadn't believed in any of this mumbo jumbo until his son died, but he acknowledged the risk now. He asked Rustaad, "What about the other four G'ortians still at home?"

"They are all kept within their respective compounds and protected by heavy security, but my resources tell me none of those G'ortians have a desire to lead, nor are they being groomed for such. It appears that as long as we keep the powerful ones segregated in the Sphere until tomorrow night, we will eliminate the threat of MystiKs joining forces."

Propping his elbows on the chair arms, SEOH steepled his fingers. "Any news on deciphering the prophecy?"

"Nothing new from our technicians working on it, but the Hy'bridt who spoke to Becka's family confirmed the prophecy will be fulfilled when the red moon sets tomorrow."

SEOH pushed an eyebrow up. "You told me our sun will set at the same moment the red moon sets in the Sphere. Did the Hy'bridt specify the location of the red moon referenced?"

"No, and we aren't due to have a blood moon visible in this country for another four years. That's the closest we would come to a red moon here, which leads me to believe the Hy'bridt meant a red moon somewhere else. If we're to give credence to their powers, we must assume she meant the Sphere's moon even if she does not know the Sphere exists."

"She couldn't know about that," SEOH argued, then leveled Rustaad with a don't-go-there look to cut him off before he reminded SEOH, again, that the MystiKs supposedly had psychic perception or *visioning* powers as well. "Let's move on to things that we know we can control. The laser grid must be ready to activate city-wide tomorrow, but only after all MystiK leaders are inside the boundaries of our city. I don't want any MystiK leader to become suspicious and remain outside the power grid."

"They won't turn back," Rustaad said, planted as still as a statue in the middle of SEOH's office. He rarely sat. Everything about him was contained, as if Rustaad held his body in constant readiness for any situation. "As long as the MystiKs continue to be distrustful of each other and paranoid that every other House is a threat to their power bases, they'll be too busy watching each other to worry about us. I'm only concerned about the grid performing consistently across such a massive area. We haven't tested as much—"

SEOH slapped a hand down on his desk. "The grid was tested successfully in the Sphere, based on the report delivered by the last scout brought back."

Patient to the point of being annoying, Rustaad blinked slowly in the face of SEOH's anger, then said, "The scout said that Thylan had turned the grid sample up to eighty percent to neutralize Callan's power. The grid he created covers an area slightly larger than a basketball court. Our grid is over twenty miles square. We can't just run it up to eighty percent the first time it's powered across the city."

"If our engineers say it's safe, then it's safe. I have faith in technology."

"I do too, SEOH, but you've used a skeleton crew of engineers to do this secretly. Every project designed and built as a prototype requires more beta testing than we've executed."

SEOH rubbed his forehead and sat back, considering how much nicer life was going to be once he was the only ruler.

Rustaad made a valid point, but a miniature version of this laser grid had also been tested in City Three with a majority population of MystiKs over TeKs. SEOH's MystiK snitch in that city had helped carry out that test. Sure, there was always a chance of a misfire with any new project, but the element of surprise was far more important than worry over one section of the grid not functioning properly.

He crossed his arms and reminded Rustaad, "Based on what our engineers determined, we need only sixty percent of the grid functioning to contain the power of the MystiK leaders."

"True. As long as that sixty percent of the grid is in direct contact with the BIRG Con meeting hall." Rustaad paused and touched his lips with a finger while in thought. He pulled his finger away before adding, "There is still a certain amount of gamble to all of this. I don't like that we have no Plan B in place."

Grunting his acknowledgment, SEOH lifted a hand and a hologram appeared at his left shoulder displaying a map of the ten cities left in North America. "Oh, I have Plan B."

For the slightest moment, Rustaad's eyebrows flinched with surprise before his indifferent mask slid back into place. "Would you care to elaborate, SEOH?"

"If the grid doesn't work, we send word to the past immediately to destroy the eggs of all MystiK ancestors being stored in the female research center at the Byzantine Institutes across the world and order the K-Virus to be released."

Rustaad argued, "But you were going to wait until you were sure we had the MystiK power under control before unleashing the virus."

"Not anymore. No need to wait once the MystiK population is reduced to a fragment of what they have now."

"That would be almost a month ahead of schedule. How would we know our people in the past have located the genetic ancestries for *both* of us?" Rustaad asked, his voice tight. "Plus, based on the schedule we set and assuming they're on track in the past, we would still lose a third of our TecKnati population by releasing the K-Virus too soon."

"Stop worrying. They were told to find the DNA links for both of us first. Nothing has changed with the orders we gave our people sent to the past. Unless we send another person back with new orders, our people will continue on track. But you wanted a Plan B, so there it is."

SEOH waited for Rustaad to ask what SEOH had told Phen before sending the TecKnati scout to the past, but Rustaad's ruthless control exerted itself. His rigid posture relaxed only enough for SEOH to notice, and that was only because SEOH had spent years watching for those rare tells. Rustaad had been SEOH's right hand of justice for over ten years, the one person he trusted with many of his secrets.

Not all, but many.

Switching topics, SEOH asked, "Has Thylan gained the computer yet?"

"His last report indicated he would have it by tomorrow." Rustaad's unruffled demeanor had returned. "Thylan may surprise you yet, in a positive way."

"That'd be a welcome change after years of fixing his screwups. Why couldn't the MystiK treaty have targeted Thylan instead of my oldest?"

"One of life's mysteries," Rustaad muttered. "Speaking of Thylan, he did mention something odd about those three intruders in the Sphere."

"What's that?"

"The traitor said the girl called Rayen claims to have no memory and that she only recently arrived at the Byzantine Institute in the past."

Shrugging, SEOH said, "Why should that matter?"

"Because this Rayen also claims to have been hunted by a sentient beast." Rustaad's cool gaze studied SEOH. "There were no sentient beasts during that period of history. The technology wasn't developed until after the K-Virus infected our country. Except for a few that have been deprogrammed and reside in the zootech, no others should be roaming our land. Correct?"

"Yes. You're not one to be subtle, Rustaad. Make your point."

"If we have a sentient beast that has *not* been decommissioned, but is in fact active and traveling through time, the ANASKO board will turn on us."

"Of all people, I know that." SEOH held Rustaad's unwavering gaze. "If you're asking if I've got one on the loose, I'm insulted you think I'm reckless enough to risk my freedom, and life, by hiding or activating a sentient beast."

"I would never insinuate such, SEOH."

"Good, because that would put a crimp in our relationship."

SEOH's holographic assistant appeared, saying, "Vice Rustaad, you are wanted in R&D."

When Leesa disappeared, Rustaad gave a slight dip of his head as his way of saying goodbye, then left.

SEOH sat back and pulled up his online vault of private information that no one else could access.

Rustaad thought SEOH had a rogue sentient beast, huh?

The board turning on him would be the least of his worries. Possessing sentient beasts or shielding knowledge of their existence could earn someone convicted of the crime a lifetime in prison.

Transmissions from six security videos surfaced on a holographic screen. When he tapped keys on a holographic keyboard, one of the vid feeds doubled in size. Three sentient beasts growled and pawed the ground. A four-legged jungle cat prowled across one cage, then paused and morphed into a bird of prey that had a sickle-shaped beak.

Chuckling, SEOH pointed a finger and the screen disappeared.

Rustaad didn't think SEOH had a viable Plan B?

That was understandable since Rustaad had no idea that Plan B was to inject a body with the K-Virus and ship it into the past, day after tomorrow, regardless of whether they found Rustaad's genetic origin or not. SEOH knew *his* had been located, because the uncle he'd never liked simply disappeared eight months ago, along with his entire family.

SEOH had sent his first TecKnati team back to the past with orders to locate his specific ancestors, then separate the DNA for his mother's side that led to the uncle he hated, then destroy that line.

SEOH hadn't told Rustaad any of that for the simple reason that Rustaad would have focused too much on his own survival and not on doing his job.

Rustaad's only living relative, a cousin, had *conveniently* died in an explosion at one of their test facilities. That left no specific indicator to ensure the staff at the Institutes had located Rustaad's ancestry.

More important to SEOH had been insuring he did not lose a TecKnati engineer who had been a part of creating the ANASKO Empire to this point. Every leader of ANASKO since the onset of the K-Virus in their world had hand selected engineers from eight specific families.

SEOH had seen confirmation that his people in the past had located the ancestors of those families.

Plan B was most definitely in place.

SEOH even had one more play to make.

Once the laser grid was activated in this city and these furkken MystiK leaders were out of SEOH's hair, he was transporting three sentient beasts to the Sphere and programming them to attack anything that was not TecKnati.

CHAPTER 18

RAYEN SAT IN A TWELVE-FOOT-SQUARE metal room of the same building where the TecKnati had held Callan captive, but it didn't appear to be the actual space where they would have put Callan.

This room was too clean and sterile feeling.

Thylan had brought her here and he now stomped back and forth in front of the dull silver table. She sat on the opposite side of the table, studying the laptop that stared back at her in total silence.

"Why isn't it powering up?" Thylan asked as he crossed in front of her for the fiftieth time.

"It takes concentration to make something electronic come on with power derived from a human." That sounded pretty good for being totally made up by someone with zero electronic knowledge. She was no technical whiz like Tony and knew nothing about this computer, but the flat screen monitors at the Byzantine Institute had seemed familiar so she wasn't completely clueless. She hoped.

On the other hand, the only real memory that her mind had given up had involved horses in the desert, not buildings and equipment.

"I suggest you start concentrating a lot harder or I'll have to motivate you." Thylan's words slid and shifted, viscous as thick slime.

"*Threatening* me interferes with my concentration." She moved her hand over the keys, ignoring him as best she could.

"It wasn't necessarily a threat. You might enjoy yourself."

She paused her hand and took a closer look at Thylan.

He hadn't stopped moving since he walked her into this room. His eyes were bright, too bright. Everything about him said he was agitated and nervous, but in an intense way. His last words settled into her mind, warning her that Thylan might be mentally unstable.

Her skin prickled with the way he leered at her. Thylan had more on his mind than just what she could do to make this computer operate. Did he intend to force himself on her?

The room and Thylan blurred, then all her senses sharpened.

She could hear his watch ticking with loud clicks. He shifted his stance, scuffing his boot heel over the gritty floor. It sounded too loud to be natural. He smelled of hate and fear.

Her skin heated from the inside out. She warned him, "Don't underestimate me."

He turned rigid. A muscle jerked in his jaw. "You do *not* give me orders. The last girl who tried regretted it."

She didn't want to kill anyone here, but she would not allow him, or anyone else, to assault her. She warned softly, "If you touch me, *you* will be the one to regret it."

She heaved one breath after another. Her body fed off the tension, preparing to fight.

Thylan unbuckled his belt.

Images on the buckle flickered between a triangle design and letters, then he started pulling the belt through the loops on his uniform. "You're clearly not motivated, but I'm going to fix that."

Energy stabbed through her like a lightning bolt.

In her peripheral vision, the monitor flickered, but she kept her eyes on the predator in the room.

He whipped his belt out of the last loop with a snap.

She flinched.

Thylan smiled, pleased at her reaction.

Her heartbeat picked up speed, beating faster.

The monitor flashed bright, drawing her attention. She caught the flick of the belt being swung and put an arm up to protect her face. A sharp sting slashed across her arm.

Clearly, her power had no loyalty to her, or it would rise to the surface and protect her.

Acting like a rabid animal, Thylan raced around the table and grabbed for her.

She shoved him back, but he didn't fall. The belt rained blows over and over in a chaotic attack, biting her shoulder, then it popped her face.

Slamming a hand down on the keyboard, she used her other hand to grab for the belt on the next swing, catching it before the whip slapped her again.

Light exploded from the computer.

It screamed at a high pitch. Out of instinct, she clamped down her mental shields, which thankfully muted the sound.

Scouts started yelling outside the room. The door flew open, and two scouts ran in with hands over their ears.

Thylan released the belt. She yanked it away, tossing it to the ground. He doubled over, cupping his ears, and screaming, "*Shut it off*!" Blood trickled from his nose.

She grabbed the computer and slapped it shut. The thing kept screeching. That worked for her. It was incapacitating the TecKnati. She raced out of the room and entered a cramped hallway. Narrow strips of light from odd fixtures in the ceiling shone a green glow over scouts fighting each other at the end of the hall.

As she moved closer, she realized the scouts were actually jerking around, still holding their ears.

Not really fighting.

The screech from the computer she clutched was disabling them, but they still blocked the only way out she knew about. This sound could die any minute. She headed toward the scouts.

All at once, bodies flew backwards, hitting each other and the walls before falling into piles. It was as if a giant arm had swiped across them.

Two figures rushed forward through the cleared space.

Not a giant arm, but one with powerful kinetics.

Callan stormed toward her. When he reached her, he grabbed her to him in a fierce hug with the screaming computer sandwiched between them. He cupped her face in two hands and pulled her head back so he could look at her.

Warm liquid trickled from where the belt had cut her cheek.

Callan growled, "I'm going to kill Thylan."

She was both glad to see him and wanting him gone from here. "We don't have time, Callan. I don't know how long this computer will keep making noise and they'll probably turn the grid on as soon as it stops."

Callan kissed her forehead and stepped back. "Go with Kaz. I'll be right behind you."

She grabbed his arm. "No. I'm not leaving you here again."

"Just go outside and give me a minute."

"Why?"

"I have to free another MystiK."

That's right. She'd forgotten about the second one. "Hurry."

As Callan vanished down the hall, Kaz stepped into view and yelled over the sound blaring from the computer. "I was ordered to take you out of here even if I had to use my powers."

"I'm coming." She gave him a hand motion to get him moving. They ran past bodies of unconscious scouts. A few were groaning and shaking their heads against the torturous noise. She had a hard time feeling sympathy for them even if some might not have wanted to be here in the Sphere.

None had raised a hand to help the MystiKs.

Or to help Callan.

When they stepped outside, she searched the area and sky. Dark was choking off the last hint of twilight. Even outside, scouts had fallen to the ground, gripping their heads. Some rolled around as if that would stop the noise.

She looked up at the sky again and realized... "The moon is gone, Kaz." Her gaze snapped to his face. "What happened with the wraiths?"

"They didn't come."

She searched his eyes for the truth. "Are you joking?"

"No, I'm not." Kaz sounded grim enough to be serious.

How could he be so unhappy? She was thrilled that Callan had survived. She wanted to run around shouting and dancing.

Callan would not die.

And now he would be free from the TecKnati, too. Where was he?

Callan shouted, "Get moving. I'm coming out."

She turned with a huge smile breaking on her face until she saw who Callan had gone back for. A young woman held his hand and looked up at him like he was her world.

The same way Rayen looked at him.

Callan slowed only long enough to shout, "Why aren't you running? Let's go."

She suffered a rush of embarrassment she couldn't explain and took off in the direction of the tortalones. Kaz caught up and fell into stride next to her.

Tossing a glance over her shoulder, she noticed that Callan was falling behind them because that girl was slower. And he was still holding the girl's hand. Swinging her attention forward again, she asked, "Who is that, Kaz?"

"It's not my—"

"Stop telling me it's not your place."

Kaz lowered his voice as they reached the edge of the forest. "He can hear every word you say. So can she."

Heat blossomed in her cheeks, and it wasn't from her core energy. She was making a fool of herself. Callan had told her not to come back, but she'd thought that was for her safety.

Maybe she was just dense and missed the fact that he had been trying to tell her their time was over.

It didn't matter. She would have still come back for him.

Fool that she was, she still cared.

In the forest, Kaz turned his hands palm out and a glow pulsed on the ground ahead of them or she'd have fallen over roots and downed trees. The computer under her arm continued to pretend it was a siren.

They reached the tortalones first. Kaz walked over to the one he'd ridden here and put his hand on her shell. Nothing came out of the holes of either his tortalone or the male she'd ridden.

Kaz frowned in her direction. "Turn that squawking thing off."

She opened the laptop and colors flashed repeatedly. Holding her hand over it did nothing. She tapped keys. Still nothing.

Kaz stepped over to her, lifted his hand to shed light on the keyboard, then he pressed a button, and everything went silent.

She asked, "How did you do that?"

"I pushed the power button."

When he returned to his tortalone, a head slowly came out followed by a long, snaking neck. Kaz whispered something and the head nudged him in a sweet way.

The female tortalone then swung her head over and bumped Rayen's tortalone's shell. Another head emerged.

She could see the glow of Callan's hands coming through the woods. He was still a bit farther back. Rayen caught Kaz by the arm to gain his attention.

"What?"

"Don't snap at me."

He dragged his fingers through his hair. "I'm sorry. What?"

"Just tell me who she is. Please."

"Her name is Becka. She is the youngest of three daughters in the Creativity House."

"Thank you." That wasn't what Rayen had specifically been after, but the friction between them seemed to be dissipating so she pushed for a little more. "But who is she to Callan?"

"Not now."

At this point, Callan and Becka were approaching and Kaz was silent again. Rayen stood there, watching the pair illuminated by the glow Callan was generating. He held branches out of her way and guided her carefully as if she were fragile.

Kaz took the laptop from Rayen and slid it into the sling he once again strapped across his chest and back. Once he had the computer loaded, he pushed the thing around to his back. Then he shined light from his hands on the tortalone she'd ridden here, telling Callan, "That one is yours."

Rayen waited for Callan to hand Becka off to Kaz and ask her to ride with him.

But Callan lifted Becka up on his tortalone.

Shock rolled over her.

Callan was so busy getting Becka settled that Rayen was invisible to him. Or was he ignoring her on purpose?

She stood there like an idiot with no clue what to say or do.

Kaz's light disappeared then his hands hooked around her waist and lifted her up on his tortalone before she could protest. She was not fragile. She could climb up on her own.

He jumped up behind her and grasped the mane with one hand, hooking his other arm around her waist.

She started to tell him that was not necessary either but then she felt a bump on her mind.

Callan was paying attention after all.

Her heart raced at the contact she'd missed so much, but she did not want to do this mind to mind. If he wanted to talk to her, he could do it in person and to her face. Plus, she wasn't sure she could hold back all the hurt banging around in her head if she opened her mind.

Rayen told Kaz, "I'm ready."

He clicked with his tongue and the tortalone rose high on all four legs.

Callan said, "Be careful with—"

Kaz cut him off. "I've got Rayen. You worry about your passenger."

Their tortalone flapped its wings rapidly.

"What's your tortalone doing, Kaz? I thought she needed enough area to run and take off."

He kept an arm tucked securely around her middle. When he spoke, he was right next to her cheek. "It's more difficult to lift straight up, but she can do it. She knows it is important."

What had Gabby called Kaz? The turtle whisperer? That fit.

Why couldn't Rayen's heart yearn for Kaz? He'd made it clear that he liked her, and he had no obligations back home that mattered. They could enjoy the time they had left here.

But that wasn't how she was built. She had opened her heart to Callan and the stubborn organ didn't want to give him up.

Turning enough to look over to where Callan and Becka flew maybe fifty yards away, she could see them only because Callan continued to shine a soft glow from his hands.

He had his arms around each side of Becka, holding the mane of his tortalone.

The words came out before Rayen realized she was speaking. "Why are his hands still glowing?"

"I sensed that Becka was afraid of flying on the tortalones when she first saw them. Callan is talking her through it and keeping enough light available that she doesn't feel lost in the darkness."

What girl could feel lost with Callan's arms around her?

Maybe Becka was a friend, and he was just protecting her as he would any defenseless female. He knew that Rayen could handle herself in a fight, where Becka looked ... delicate.

And pretty. Rayen hadn't missed the fall of blond hair that hung like long strands of corn silk, or the smooth skin on her perfectly sculpted face.

She probably had fine hands that were soft, where Rayen's were rough from the gritty work of staying alive.

A wave of a dark emotion plowed through her. Jealousy. It dug deep and twisted her feelings into a warped animal that howled in pain. After a bit, the sound quieted and there was nothing left but her.

Alone. Just as she'd been when she woke up in that desert and just as she'd be when this last trip was over.

Kaz hugged her. "Stop feeling so sad. It's killing me."

She'd forgotten she was with an empath. "I'm not sad."

"And now you lie to me."

Kaz had been here for her when she needed his help to meet the TecKnati and he'd managed to get Callan out of the camp when she asked him. She would not weigh him down with her self-inflicted misery.

Rayen swallowed her sinking pride and admitted, "I'm being silly, sitting here feeling like I've been rejected when Becka is just another young woman captured and sent here. Right?"

They flew in silence for a moment, the chilly wind whistling past her ears. She couldn't say she was cold with Kaz's heat so close to her back.

His chest moved against her back with a deep breath. "When Callan's brother was killed, the Warrior House was in an uproar until Callan accepted that he had to take his brother's place. To do that, Callan will be expected to make an acceptable choice for a future mate. Based on how things were left back at home, many Houses will be watching for an indication of Callan's decision by the BIRG Con."

Blood rushed too loud in her ears. "When is the BIRG Con?"

"Tomorrow. Becka is the G'ortian Callan's parents expect him to choose and Callan will not shirk his responsibility. Nor will he humiliate Becka. I have tried to warn you off him so you would not be hurt, but I was unsuccessful."

In other words, that was the woman Callan would spend the rest of his life with and she would not have even one more moment with him.

Rayen blinked back tears. She would not cry, but it hurt worse than any physical wound she'd suffered.

This one would never heal.

CHAPTER 19

CALLAN CRUSHED HIS JAWS TOGETHER, watching a glow Kaz created for a moment, illuminating Kaz and Rayen while they flew too far away for Callan's peace of mind. Then the glow extinguished. Had Kaz done that to hide any actions from Callan's view?

Was his arm still around Rayen? Callan hoped not. She was clearly no wilting female like Becka.

He took a deep breath, trying to clear his head. He was not being fair to compare Becka that way.

She'd been raised in a sheltered environment, the baby of the family. He wasn't sure how Rayen had been raised, but she had fighting skills and he had no doubt she could live off the land. Two completely different women. For example, Rayen must have ridden one of the tortalones here for there to be a pair of them waiting.

If that was the case, then Kaz had no reason to be wrapped around her for the ride back. Callan glanced over and now ground his teeth at not being able to observe the pair.

Becka's grip tightened on his arm, drawing his attention back to her. She'd slipped from side to side when they first lifted off and she'd latched onto him in terror, so he'd been forced to wrap an arm around her and hold her against him.

But this wasn't the body he wanted to hold.

She had her long hair clamped in one hand, holding it to the side. Her hair was such a bright gold color it should glow. Any man would want her for his wife.

Any man but Callan.

If she had not been so terrified by the time that they reached the tortalones, he would have handed her off to Kaz. But Kaz and one of Becka's older sisters had a falling out last year. Becka had tensed the minute she noticed Kaz, and he hadn't been any more hospitable. He'd pointed out which tortalone belonged to Callan as Kaz's way of saying not to stick him with

Becka.

"How will we escape this Sphere, Callan?"

Her words flew past him in the whipping air. He could pretend not to hear her, but that would be wrong on his part. "I told you before that I don't know. We haven't found a way back yet."

"This is your time to lead. They need you at the BIRG Con tomorrow."

"There's always someone else to lead." Taking over his brother's position was the least of his concerns.

Becka twisted to look at him over her shoulder. "The Damian Prophecy must be fulfilled."

"Then it may have to happen without me," he said, only halfway listening.

"No, it can't."

He finally paid attention to her. "What are you talking about, Becka?"

"A Hy'bridt came to our House. She's precognitive and explained things about the prophecy she'd seen that included you."

"Did she see that I would be captured by the TeKs?"

"No," Becka admitted.

"Then she must not have gotten the entire picture in her visions."

Becka was shaking her head. "This Hy'bridt has never been wrong, and she did say that MystiK children were at more risk than normal."

Astronomical understatement. "Did the leaders of your House tell mine what she said?"

"You know our leaders do not talk."

Callan didn't shield his bitterness. "And that is something they will regret when they walk into the BIRG Con tomorrow evening only to realize they have no future leaders ready to move up in the ranks."

Becka turned back to face forward.

Had he somehow insulted her? She had to realize that the future they both had expected was not going to happen. No one even knew the timing of the prophecy. Oh, sure, many had speculated that it was intended to happen at this BIRG Con, but that could have come from someone's wishful thinking that turned into rumor and eventually became a concrete belief.

The only thing Callan believed in right now was that his days were no longer numbered. At this point, his hours were numbered. He would do all in his power to protect the village and ensure that Kaz and Jaxxson were ready to take over after the red moon set tomorrow.

Until then, Callan wanted only one thing for himself. Rayen. That shouldn't be too much to ask of the universe.

He looked at the back of Becka's head, feeling a twinge of guilt, but only for the sake of their families who were pushing them together. There was no chemistry between him and Becka, only responsibility. She was too subservient for her own good. Before tomorrow night, he would explain to her that if they both managed to get out of the Sphere, she deserved to choose the person who made her heart beat fast and someone she missed when he wasn't nearby.

For him, that person was Rayen. They had no future, but they had right now.

After what Becka had gone through, Callan could give her until tomorrow morning to adjust before he explained how she should accept nothing less than someone who truly loved her.

When Callan's tortalone began descending, he realized it was following Kaz's and allowed the animal to continue.

Becka leaned right with the slant of the downward shift. She turned to look at him again. "The Hy'bridt knew much about the prophecy, and she did say that I would have trouble finding you, but that I would find you."

Anyone could say that, but Callan kept his thought to himself.

Becka wasn't finished. "The Hy'bridt said it was imperative that you know the details she shared about the prophecy."

"How did she expect you to tell me when we weren't going to see each other again until the BIRG Con ceremonies?"

"She said that we all must make decisions and it was up to me to decide if I would tell you in time or not."

Callan realized how she'd been captured. "Did your father take you to my father's House?"

"No. He refused. That's why I snuck away and went to find you, and that's how they captured me."

She was here because of him. Callan closed his eyes, wishing the world would give him a break. He shook it off and opened his eyes, listening to the soft flap of large wings.

Becka turned her back to him again as the tortalone slowed to land with a walking trot across the open field leading up to their warded village.

Callan was glad to be back, but it was hard to rejoice when he was bringing Becka here and she'd been captured while trying to reach him.

As the tortalone stopped and dropped to the ground, Becka released her fall of hair. Her tense shoulders relaxed. She'd been terrified the whole ride, but she hadn't cried or carried on. He was thankful for that. It wasn't that he didn't like Becka. She was nice enough, but ... she wasn't a raven-haired beauty with eyes the color of a tropical sea.

He leaped off and reached up for Becka as she slid down. When he started her forward, she jerked around and said, "One more thing. You have a traitor among you. I heard the TecKnati talking about it."

"Did they mention a name or if the traitor was male or female?"

"No, but whoever it is believes they are leaving this place with the TecKnati. You must be very careful with what details you share about the prophecy."

"I will." But he was thinking more about finding the person who aided the enemy and making that person pay. Children had died and the traitor had opened the ward around the village to the TecKnati once already.

When Callan got Becka moving, they walked over to where Kaz and Rayen had dismounted from their tortalone. Kaz was shining a glow from his hands that illuminated a twenty-foot-wide circle.

If Callan could get Kaz to just escort Becka to the village, then Callan could have a moment alone with Rayen. He was still seething over her injuries and wanted to hold her, to know she was safe.

He tried once more to reach Kaz telepathically, thumping his mind.

Kaz finally answered, *What do you want, Callan?*

A little help with Becka for one thing.

Why? She is your intended. Not mine.

She's not my intended. I've made no formal claim and right now I want to see Rayen. Do me a favor and walk Becka to the village, okay? Callan had just pushed that thought back when he reached where Kaz and Rayen stood.

Kaz replied telepathically, *I'll try, but no promises.* Then Kaz spoke to Becka. "Let me show you where the village is."

She looked at him then at Callan, waiting on Callan to say something. When he didn't, she huffed a weary sigh. "Fine. Show me."

Rayen said nothing the whole time she observed the exchange. The minute Kaz and Becka started toward the village, she turned to follow them.

Callan sent a thump to her mind. She hadn't answered him the last several times, but there was no danger here that would prevent her from replying.

He felt the moment she lowered her shields, but she said nothing.

He spoke to Rayen telepathically. *I want to talk to you.*

She replied, *About what?*

Why are you not talking to me?

Rayen stopped walking and turned around, returning to him.

He opened one hand and allowed a soft light to glow.

This time Rayen spoke her words. "I understand that you didn't want me to come back, but I couldn't not come back and free you from the TecKnati.

That's done. Now that you're free and the village will be safe again, I'll be gone tomorrow."

Callan hadn't wanted her here where she was in danger, but neither did he want her gone right now either. That was so messed up, but he blamed it on two days with no sleep.

She was here for one more night.

He wanted to share this time with her.

She'd seemed thrilled to see him when he returned for her at the TecKnati camp. Where had this indifference come from that he was sensing now?

He lifted a hand to touch her cheek and she stepped back so quickly the air turned brittle between them. "What's wrong, Rayen?"

"Kaz told me who Becka is. I have no right to be spending time with you"

Now he understood. Callan would have a talk with Kaz about keeping his mouth shut, because although there was truth among those words, Kaz did not know the entire truth. He'd deal with Kaz once he sorted this out with Rayen. "Becka and I share no commitment."

Rayen's gaze drifted away from his. He feared she was drifting away from him as well.

When she finally looked back, her eyes hid emotions that churned and struggled to be released. "I'm not supposed to be here or in the past with Tony and Gabby. I don't belong anywhere, but you do. And Becka does and all the other MystiKs do, but not me. Everyone should just pretend that I'm not here, because soon I won't be. You have a responsibility, and it doesn't include me."

She turned and walked away, dragging chunks of his heart in her wake.

CHAPTER 20

RAYEN PASSED THROUGH THE OPENING Kaz made in the warding and ignored the way his eyes searched her face for answers. When she put her hand out, he handed her the laptop, then she continued on.

On her last visit here, he'd tried to tell her that she was stepping between Callan and his destiny, interfering with the natural order of the MystiK world.

It took a while to sink in, but she now accepted the truth.

Callan was not hers to feel jealousy over, or this deep, wrenching loss that she couldn't make stop. Yes, she accepted that, but it didn't mean she had to be happy about it.

When she reached the central area of the village, children were eating and arguing and running around.

Gabby and Jaxxson stood in the middle of the chaos, handing out food and keeping peace between Kenja's Uberon Warriors and the kids of Callan's village, some warriors and some from other Houses. Except for their leader, not one of the Uberons was over the age of thirteen, but they were a deadly lot that had to be kept under control.

Gabby stood on the ground. Huh. Evidently, she'd solved her levitation problem.

Kenja strode into the scene, at least six feet tall and strongly muscled. She surveyed her warriors as one would look over an army at rest, then her gray-green eyes swept over to Rayen.

They'd had their differences, one that had ended with her sending Kenja flying across fifty feet to slam against a tree. She hadn't tested Rayen since then. Rayen's power was hiding again, but the look on her face should warn anyone against crossing her now. She would do what was right and honorable, but she couldn't be held responsible for any reaction to someone's bad attitude.

While she'd kept track of the Uberon leader, Kenja crossed the village common area and stopped in front of Rayen. "So? Were you successful or not?"

Callan chose that moment to walk up. "I'm back, if that's your question, Kenja."

"Then I have fulfilled my duty and will take my Uberons away from here."

"The TecKnati are going to attack."

Kenja's tone dismissed Callan and his claim. "I am not worried about my people. They are skilled in ways the TecKnati will never understand or be able to combat."

Tension sheared off Callan. Rayen wasn't empathic like Kaz, at least she didn't think she was, but she could feel Callan's anger seeping out with every harsh breath.

He made a rough scoffing sound. "You know what? Fine. My duty is to my people, the ones who trust me to protect them. My people believe me when I tell them the TecKnati have created a laser grid that can neutralize our powers, and *you* witnessed it being used on me."

Kenja's eyes flared as if insulted, but even if she had wanted to speak up, Callan wasn't done.

"If you're so independent you can't see past your nose and realize that we're stronger as a unit, then take your Uberon children and lead them to their deaths. As they die, remind them what a powerful leader you are and how they should feel honored to die for you, because the TecKnati are coming for all of us. All. Of. Us. You step outside the ward around this village and you're on your own. I'm not risking *any* of my people to come after you, because *my* duty is to keep the MystiKs in this village safe."

Zilya and Etoi had just walked into the common area when Zilya noticed Callan and changed direction to join them.

Just great.

Rayen found a tree to lean against so that she could stand to the side and not fall on her face from lack of sleep. She was growing more tired as the adrenaline rush subsided, too tired to interfere in whatever was going to play out between Kenja and Callan.

Kenja hadn't liked what Callan said. From the fire in her glare, Rayen wondered if they were going to have a replay of their last battle. Unlike that time, when Callan pulled back to keep from harming Kenja, he might not be so considerate right now with her threatening to take children from this village.

He would do anything to protect these children, even fight Kenja for real.

Zilya stepped up between Kenja and Callan. "What's going on? As senior leader from the Governing House, I—"

"Shut up!" Kenja shouted as Callan snapped, "Stay out of this."

Zilya took a step back as if she'd been hit. Her mouth dropped open. Etoi gripped her spear in a tight fist, but wisely held her tongue for once.

Kenja turned to Callan and one side of her mouth curved up with a ... smile? Yes, Kenja found something humorous about all this tension. She told Callan, "I may have judged you too quickly. Your brother was groomed to be the next leader, but I would never have followed him into battle. I will stay and we will defend this pitiful village together, because that is what warriors do."

Callan let out a long breath and after a moment he extended his hand. Kenja gripped it, and they shook.

When she released him, she swung to face an audience of children and called out, "Silence."

Quiet fell over the rumble.

Kenja said, "Uberons, when you finish your meal, which will be in no more than six minutes, you will meet me at the west wall for our evening drills."

A resounding "Yes, *Doyen*!" shouted, then the kids returned to eating.

The term *doyen* bumped around in Rayen's mind until she brought up the meaning as one of respect.

Before Kenja walked away, she told Callan, "If the TecKnati bring the weapons they had the last time, your ward may not hold."

Rayen heard a noise of someone moving up to the group and Becka appeared. The royal girl said, "The TecKnati complained that equipment they used as weapons was taken out of the Sphere, but I heard Thylan speaking to his scouts about taking the grid components apart and turning it into a weapon to use against you ... if he didn't get the computer."

Everyone looked at Rayen right then.

She had the computer tucked under one arm. "They can't have this. Thylan believes this computer is something called the Genera-Y computer, but it's not. Until he figures that out, he isn't going to risk destroying it, but the minute he realizes he's been played he *will* attack this village and destroy everything. He's insane."

Zilya found her voice. "Who is Thylan?"

Callan answered, "SEOH's son."

Zilya shook her head and sounded appalled. "Attacking us would be the height of insanity. If the TeKs could kill us outright, SEOH would have done that already. If they wipe out this village, an equal number of TecKnati children die at the same moment back home."

Gabby and Jaxxson were heading over as Rayen told Zilya, "I understand the whole treaty thing and Thylan probably does, too, but I'm not sure he cares. I really don't think he's mentally sound."

Callan's gaze had strayed to her while she spoke. She could feel him staring at the cut on her cheek and wanted nothing more than for him to come over and hold her. No matter that she could defend herself, the memory of Thylan's attack was an ugly blotch that lingered in her thoughts.

But then she caught Becka looking over at Callan with big round eyes, begging him to notice her.

Or was she looking past Callan to where Kaz had quietly joined them? No, that was a bad case of wishful thinking on Rayen's part. She and Kaz apparently disliked each other because she'd obviously not wanted to ride his tortalone. He hadn't offered either.

Etoi shouted because that was her only volume, asking Becka, "Who are you?"

For all of Becka's delicateness, she whipped a haughty glare at Etoi. "I am Becka of the Creativity House, and you are not to speak with that tone to anyone at my level."

Etoi surged forward, but Zilya touched her arm and that produced the same result as giving an order to a well-trained animal. Etoi glowered at Becka, but she backed down in the face of Becka's arched eyebrow daring her to speak.

Lifting her chin with regal arrogance, Zilya said, "I'm sorry you were captured, but you are welcome in our village. You are G'ortian, correct?"

"Yes, I am."

"I am Zilya of the Governing House. We have food and will find you somewhere to rest tonight."

"Thank you. I would like a bath as well."

A bath? To be honest, Rayen would like a bath, too, but since she didn't recall anything resembling the bathroom back at the Institute, she was out of luck and so was Becka.

Kaz had refrained from speaking until now, but Callan must have spoken to Kaz telepathically because Kaz jerked around to Callan and shook his head.

Callan said nothing and moved no muscle. He just stared at Kaz until Kaz took a deep breath and called out, "Zilya." When Kaz had her attention, he said, "Once Becka bathes, let me know and I'll create a kamara for her."

Becka swung around and tossed a look from Kaz to Callan, then back to Kaz. "You? That's inappropriate."

Callan finally said, "Things are different here, Becka. We do whatever it takes to survive. I'm too drained to build one. Zilya's power is for the children first. We assume you'd like privacy. That being the case, it's either a kamara by Kaz or you sleep outdoors."

She looked as though Callan had suggested running naked through the village. "I must have a kamara."

Callan told Etoi, "Get with Kenja and fortify the perimeters." When she opened her mouth, he added, "Don't give me a reason to discipline you. I'm not in the mood. Push me, and you won't like the way it turns out."

Gabby came over to Rayen and touched the cut on her cheek. "Are you okay?"

No, she wanted to find a corner to curl up in and sleep, but that wasn't happening yet.

Callan started toward her.

Kaz sent Rayen a condemning look as if she was pulling Callan's strings.

She straightened from the tree and told Gabby, "I'm fine."

"No, you aren't," Callan said, contradicting her. "You have a cut on your face, and I saw another cut on your arm. Where else are you hurt?"

"Nowhere that you need to be concerned about."

"Rayen—"

"Don't." That was the only word she could get out between the painful thumpings of her heart. That single word managed to cut off whatever Callan was about to say.

If he comforted her right now, she'd forget about her resolve to do what was best for everyone.

Well, everyone but her.

Kaz stepped up, clearly trying to draw Callan's attention. "We need to talk about the warding."

Callan kept his eyes on Rayen. "What's the problem?"

"The ward isn't going to hold. We have to redo it, but we need more power."

That broke her and Callan's staring match. He asked Kaz, "How do you know it's weak?"

"We had a dugurat get inside last night."

Gabby exclaimed, "You found some more dugurats?"

Only Gabby would miss the point about the weakness in the perimeter and focus on something that reminded her of a pet back in her world, but these animals had peculiar hair and a brain that never grew beyond puppy stage.

Jaxxson put his hand on Gabby's shoulder, smiling at her. "*One* dugurat and I have her locked away for now because they can be aggressive when expecting."

"She's pregnant!" Gabby's smile took over her face. "We have more pupples coming."

"Yes."

Rayen had to laugh at the thrill in Gabby's voice. If only they could all be that happy in the darkest of times.

Gabby's ponytails bounced with her animation over the news. "When can I see her?"

Her question interrupted something going on between Kaz and Callan, who were exchanging murderous looks again.

Breaking away from Callan, Kaz replied, "I have to inspect the ward with Callan then ... take care of Becka, but Jaxxson will be able to take you to the dugurat once he's free. Don't go without one of us, because she's not friendly in her condition."

Gabby waved the issue off. "That's fine. I want to take care of Rayen's injuries first anyhow."

Callan whipped around at the reminder that Rayen had been hurt.

She was done with all this tension and told Gabby, "I'm not hurt that badly." At least not physically. "But I'll let you do your healing thing if you can find a place away from ... everyone." Before Rayen turned her back on Callan, she reminded him, "V'ru needs to see you and know you're safe. He was deeply depressed while you were gone and wouldn't leave his bubble. Tony got him to come out and help us. I think V'ru is better, but he's still a scared child."

"I'm on my way to see him next." Callan held himself still, but she could tell he wanted to say more. If she had given him any encouragement, he would've, but she didn't. She turned to follow Gabby.

"Follow me." Gabby walked away, tossing a look at Jaxxson, whose eyes were only for her. Gabby returned the look with a flirty one.

She waved at Jaxxson and nodded, another silent conversation. Two happy people in this place, but for how long? Gabby had to go home and so did Jaxxson.

Rayen wanted everyone to be able to go home.

In fact, she wanted to go home. She wanted to be somewhere that it mattered whether she lived or died.

The vision of riding across the desert at night with her father had replayed through her mind all day. Had he sent her to the shaman knowing she would be spun away to another time?

"Here we are," Gabby announced.

With being so lost in her thoughts, Rayen hadn't realized where she was going. Six-foot-tall blue tortalone feathers strapped together formed the walls. They were attached to some rough posts, something the MystiKs had created by hand.

She dropped her head back to look up. There was no roof. "Whose place is this?"

"Jaxxson's healing hut."

"Does he care if we're in here?"

"No." To prove her words, Gabby went about picking up bowls and a woven piece the size of two hands. Pointing at a slab of blue-gray wood supported by two tree stumps, she said, "Have a seat."

Rayen obeyed and watched her friend carry a container over that she set in front of her. It was a scooped-out piece of wood, the size of three hand widths, with a carved exterior, and full of water, or whatever they had here that passed as water. "First," Gabby suggested, "why don't you clean up?"

She handed Rayen a rag and a chunk of something that smelled floral.

Rayen used it to scrub the dirt from her arms and face, feeling better with being clean. Gabby kept herself busy while Rayen washed under her shirt and anywhere she could get to without stripping off all her clothes since Jaxxson might walk in at any moment.

When she was done, Gabby came over carrying a stump. She placed it on the ground in front of Rayne and plopped down. Gabby opened her hand and waited until Rayen held her arm out. She carefully turned it, studying the gash on Rayen's arm. "It's not bleeding any more. What'd you get hit with?"

"Thylan thought he was going to force himself on me. When I told him it was a bad idea, he pulled off a wide belt and started hitting me with it."

Her lips scrunched up with a bitter twist. "What a coward." Then she placed her fingers over Rayen's cut and whispered a jumble of words.

Whatever she was doing soothed the aches everywhere Rayen had been hit. When Gabby let go of her, Rayen could still feel where the cut had been, but now it was a scar on her arm and when she touched her cheek.

Gabby said, "That will be better tomorrow. I focused my attention on the ones that I sensed were more painful. You should be able to heal yourself."

"I can, or at least I've done it before, but I needed Callan to show me how to direct my power. You've figured it out though. Thanks."

"You're welcome. I only wish you'd have made that slimeball pay."

"I did when my power finally showed up. It has a mind of its own sometimes. But when it did come through, I had my hand on the computer. My power turned the computer into a screeching animal. Thylan's ears and nose bled. I got him back."

The computer! Rayen slapped a hand on her forehead at forgetting about the stupid thing. "Where are Tony and V'ru?"

"Tony said he was going to help V'ru with the prophecy and do some geek therapy. I heard V'ru laughing a little while later. Jaxxson called it a miracle. He said no one had been able to get through to V'ru after Callan was gone."

"I'm sure Callan stopped by to see him."

"Let's forget about them and the computer for now," Gabby suggested. "Let's talk about Mathias."

Rayen stilled. What could she share with her friend without breaking her word again? "What about Mathias?"

"To begin with, he's dead."

Holding her breath from shock, Rayen struggled to figure out what to say. Who had told her? Callan wouldn't have, but he and Rayen, plus Kaz, were the only three who knew. Had Gabby told anyone, like Jaxxson? "Uhm..."

"Hold it, Rayen. I know you gave him your vow that you wouldn't tell and although I think we're close enough friends by now that you should have told me, I'm not holding you to the friend rule."

Rayen let out her breath. "How did you find out?"

"Mathias told me."

That was not what she thought Gabby was going to say. Rayen opened and closed her mouth, at a loss for words that would be right in this situation. She gave up and said, "You're going to have to explain this to me."

Gabby sat with her hands clasped between her knees and gave her the most serious look Rayen had ever seen on her face. "Mathias came to me. I can see him, but Jaxxson can't. He's telling me things." She waited for Rayen to say something. When that didn't happen, she said, "You must see a ghost sometimes, too. You've talked to someone at times that Tony and I couldn't see or hear."

True. Rayen's grumpy ghost. "Yes, I have an ancestor who shows up from time to time, but I have no control over when he appears. What about Mathias?"

"He appeared briefly before we left the Sphere the last time."

"Why didn't you tell me?"

"I tried, but we were a little busy if you recall."

Yes, they'd been rushing to make the transender so they could find a computer to bring back. "You're right. We haven't had time to talk about anything. So, uhm, do you know how Mathias died?"

Gabby's eyes were shiny with unshed tears and her voice came out raw. "It was awful. The wraiths that took him came and found him when he was talking to me. I screwed up the first time I saw him on this trip and said his name." She swallowed. "I won't make that mistake again."

"Again? How many times have you seen him?"

"Three. The first time was on our last trip and twice today. He's trying to tell me about the prophecy, but he gets dragged away. His spirit is weakening all the time. We have to save him. If he doesn't cross over soon, he'll be stuck forever with the wraiths and his spirit will remain a shadow of itself for eternity."

Rayen grabbed Gabby's hands. "Tell me what we have to do, and I'll do it."

"Mathias says we have to fulfill the prophecy."

Dropping her hands, Rayen sat up and ran a hand over her face. Why couldn't the answers ever be easy? When she lowered her hand, she asked, "How are we going to fulfill the prophecy with Callan and the other MystiKs stuck in this place? I don't see any chance of them going home before that BIRG Con ceremony tomorrow and it sounds like all the parts of the prophecy must happen there. I have no idea what to do. It's taking all everyone can manage to keep the MystiKs alive while they're here."

"Mathias said he's watched V'ru search archives when V'ru thought translating the prophecy might save Callan from the TecKnati. Mathias said there was a legend about an ancient analog computer that was created by the first TecKnati sent back in time, which didn't make sense at first."

"Why?"

"Because as far as we know, the first machines that we consider real computers back home were built in the mid 1940s."

Rayen did a quick calculation. "That means the ancient analog one would have been created long before your time."

"Right. A TecKnati was sent back in time as the first test for time travel, but he ended up further in the past than expected. He landed in ancient Greece."

"How did he build a computer back then?"

"It wasn't one with components like the computers we have today or, uhm …" Gabby waved her hands around. "You know, not *today* as here in the Sphere, but current day in the past where I live." She took a breath and muttered, "That sounds so screwed up, but whatever."

Then she continued. "The story Mathias told me was that this TecKnati sent back in time picked a name from the era he landed in. He called himself Antonis because that was the day he arrived in Greece."

"You mean like the day of the week?"

"No, the Greeks actually named *every* day of the year back then. Based on that name, Antonis arrived on January 17. Weird, but whatever. Antonis was not thrilled to be sent back to primitive life in Greece, but it wasn't so bad once he fell in love with a woman called Lysandra who had unusual powers."

"Was she something like a MystiK?"

Gabby shrugged. "Maybe. That's how it sounded to me. Anyhow, when Lysandra showed her powers to Antonis, he told her about how the world was headed toward destruction in the future. She convinced him it was their duty to fix things so that technology and natural gifts could coexist in a balanced world, and she showed him how he could live in peace with someone who had natural gifts. This Antonis decided he would create a computer that would send him and her far into the future. He figured out what had gone wrong during the first time he traveled back in time and believed he could travel forward in time until just before the K-Virus showed up, then keep it from killing so much of the population in the future."

Rayen wasn't the person to argue computers or technology, but even she knew that didn't make sense. "How was Antonis going to make this computer work two-thousand years ago with no power source?"

"That's what I asked. Mathias said the computer had to be a sentient machine, which meant that Lysandra would have to power it using her gifts."

Call Rayen impatient, but she was exhausted from no sleep last night and dealing with Thylan. She was having a hard time following Gabby. "How does all that have anything to do with figuring out the prophecy?"

"I'm getting there and jumping ahead is only going to confuse you."

Nope, she was already confused. "Please continue."

"One of the fetial came to Antonis and his wife to warn them about—"

"A fee *what*?"

"I knew you were going to ask that." Gabby scratched her head in a spot between the multi-ponytails. "From what I gathered, a fetial was a group of twenty Roman officials, sort of a cross between priests and peacemakers. They worshipped the god Jupiter. Anyhow, one of them was not quite like the others. His skin was darker than most Romans and he had the sharp cheekbones found on those from Eastern Asia. He had shamanic-like powers that the others didn't, so they tiptoed around this guy."

Rayen held up her hand and counted as she pointed out what she knew. "Antonis was a TeK sent back to ancient Greece. He met a MystiK woman name Lysandra and built a sentient computer. What did the fetial-shaman-priest warn Antonis about?"

Gabby gave her a look she usually saved for Tony. "I know your day probably sucked more than mine but have a little patience Rayen. I'm trying to explain this."

Rayen hadn't meant to sound so irritable. "Sorry. I'm just ready to fall over and I have a bad feeling this story isn't going to end well."

That would have been a great time for Gabby to smile and tell her to have a little faith, too, but she didn't. Rayen's sense of impending doom expanded, threatening to suck the air from the room.

She nodded at Gabby. "Go on."

"It took Antonis almost two years to build his device out of cyprium, their name for copper. The shaman guy shows up one day and tells Antonis that rumors were flying about Antonis building a war device. Antonis denied it and this shaman guy believed him, but that didn't change the fact that Antonis stood to have his head cut off or die some other horrible way. He finished the device, but he and his wife had not been able to get it to work, so when the shaman came to tell them they had to flee, Antonis packed up his wife and the device. They joined the shaman, who smuggled all of them onboard a ship leaving port that day."

As if a switch had been thrown, Gabby stopped talking, sat up straight and stared at nothing.

Rayen whispered, "What's wrong?"

Gabby held her index finger up for her to wait then nodded to herself and returned to Rayen. "There's a problem with the ward. I have to go help Jaxxson and the others, but I want to tell you this first."

"Did you just talk to Jaxxson telepathically?"

She smiled and her cheeks pinked with embarrassment. "Yes."

"That's amazing." Rayen smiled back at her, glad to have Gabby and Tony with her. She hated for them to be subjected to all this, but she couldn't ask for better friends right now.

Gabby got serious. "Listen up. This is pieced together from spoken history, mythology, and MystiK visions so I'm just going to tell you what Mathias told me. As the ship Antonis was on left the dock, his wife had a vision that they wouldn't survive the trip, so while Antonis and his wife hid below deck, he tried once again to make the device work. Nothing happened until the shaman came down and told Antonis that he would change the course of the world, but not the way Antonis thought."

That sounded like the shaman Rayen had spoken to in the past who made no sense. Why couldn't people just say what they meant? But she kept her thoughts to herself, letting Gabby get out what she had to say.

"Antonis ignored the Shaman, but his wife suggested combining their power for the device. The details get a little vague at that point, but someone on the Greek island of Antikythera saw the water spinning up around the ship, then an explosion of light and the ship sank. That sunken ship was discovered in the early 1900s along with an engineered mechanism made of copper gears. That mechanism has since been called the Antikythera computer."

Rayen's lips parted in shock. "How is that any help?"

"I had the same reaction, Rayen, but Mathias said the point is that it's believed they overloaded the power, and the device blew a hole in the ship instead of activating the time travel."

Gabby stood up, floated a moment. The muscles in her face showed the strain as she came back down to the ground.

"You figured out the levitating?"

"Jaxxson thinks I did, but Mathias actually showed me how to get control of my power."

"You didn't tell Jaxxson about seeing Mathias?"

Gabby hit her with a sharp stare. "No, just as you didn't tell me about Mathias. I gave my word."

Point taken. "Is that all you have to tell me about the prophecy, because I'm still confused."

"No, but I have to hurry. I can tell Jaxxson is getting anxious waiting on me." Before Rayen could ask how she knew that Gabby finished explaining. "The prophecy supposedly originated with that shaman named Damianus who received the words in a vision and told the prophecy to Jupiter before leaving on the ship. Jupiter has since passed it on to others through visions. Mathias is convinced we need a sentient computer with MystiK power sources to fulfill the prophecy and once that happens the MystiKs will be sent home."

Rayen jumped to her feet. "Gabby, there's no way to bring the real computer we travel through here and this one—" She lifted the laptop. "—wouldn't work today. It *isn't* sentient and all I managed to do was shove so much power into it that I almost destroyed it."

Gabby swatted a lock of hair out of her eyes, a motion more about frustration than her hair being a problem. Her voice was thick with emotion. "If we don't figure this out, Mathias will never cross over. But that's not why he's coming to tell me all this. Mathias continues to guide this village even from death. He said if the prophecy is not fulfilled by the time the red moon sets tomorrow, everyone still in the Sphere will die."

CHAPTER 21

"I ONLY ASKED YOU TO HELP with Becka," Callan said, hacking at the vines that had grown in the two days he'd been gone. They needed to keep a path inside the ward cleared for the warriors to move quickly between security points.

And for the children as well in case they had to run for their lives.

Kaz retorted, "I did help. I walked her through the ward. That should be enough."

Why did he sound so surly? "I'm not asking that much."

"Yes, you are, Callan. You want me to handle Becka completely while she's here."

"What's your problem with her? You told me you and her sister had an issue, not that you and Becka did. Can't you two let whatever happened back home go while we're here?"

Kaz grumbled, "That doesn't matter. Becka is not *my* responsibility. I know my duty and she isn't part of it."

Meaning Callan was shirking his duty? When had he not given his all for everyone here and back home? What else did they want from him?

"She's not—" Callan stopped before the whole village heard them and lowered his voice. "She's not *my* duty either."

"What of the betrothal?"

"There isn't going to be one."

"Because once you're betrothed, you have to—" Kaz caught himself. "What did you say?"

Callan raked his hand through his still-damp hair. He'd visited V'ru then swung by to wash off in a trough of water fed from a spring they'd magically tapped when they created this village. "I knew my mother was planning with Becka's, but my mother has been so depressed since Jornn's death that I didn't have the heart to say anything. Right before I was captured, I told my father I didn't see this as a wise union. I told him I didn't want it."

"Why not?"

"Becka gets on my nerves."

"What's wrong with her?"

Callan cut his eyes at Kaz's sharp tone, but he tried to explain. "She's too ..."

"Too what, Callan?"

"Give me a minute. I'm trying to tell you."

"Fine." Kaz cursed under his breath.

"She's too neat and tidy and looking for someone to be the perfect husband. I'm never going to be that. She's too proper."

"More like she's too perfect," Kaz murmured.

"What'd you say?"

"I said you're being overly picky. She's a nice girl. You should be glad to end up with one that is pleasant and pretty."

"She's boring."

Kaz turned on him. "She is not."

Callan finally grasped something that was going on with Kaz and poked at him. "She's not even that pretty."

"Are you blind?"

"She talks too much."

"Because she has something to say," Kaz argued, shoulders up, and defensive.

Callan crossed his arms and leaned back. "If that's so, why don't *you* date her?"

Kaz snapped his lips shut and stalked off.

Oh, no, he was not getting off that easily after busting constantly on Callan. After catching up to Kaz and jumping ahead to block his path, Callan said, "I thought you didn't like her either."

"I never said that."

"Then what *is* the deal between you two?"

Kaz inhaled long and slow then let out the breath. "I wanted to date the middle sister in her family. She had a reputation of being wild, probably because she wasn't expected to marry the head of a House. All I'd heard about Becka was that she was the baby. Their father doted on her and treated her like a princess. I took that to mean she was a brat. When my mother visited friends in their city, I met Becka's sister at a party and asked her out. That was a mistake." Kaz grabbed a dangling limb and yanked it out of the way with more force than was necessary.

"What went wrong?"

"Her sister told me she would never date a half-bred warrior, but if I wanted to mess around, she'd meet me in secret as long as I promised to never tell anyone." A sound of disgust came from deep in his throat. "She acted as if she was being magnanimous to make me her dirty little secret."

Now Callan felt bad for pawning Becka off on Kaz. "That was cold."

"Unfortunately, I was not as mature a year ago and told her if I was looking for someone to breed with it wouldn't be the useless middle daughter of the Creativity House."

Cringing, Callan asked, "How'd that go over?"

"About as good as you'd expect. I was banned from the Creativity House permanently."

"Sorry about pushing Becka off on you. I didn't know you despised them so much."

Kaz was silent a moment then he lifted sad eyes. "I don't despise Becka. I saw her for the first time as I was being thrown out of their House. She tried to stop her father's men from tossing me down twelve stone steps. When they ignored her and did it anyhow, she came down to see if I was okay. I was seeing stars. By the time I could speak and my eyes focused, her father's men were escorting her back inside."

"Then I don't understand why you're avoiding her."

"Becka didn't know what I'd done to provoke her sister and end up thrown out, but I'm sure she's been informed since then that I'm the closest thing to a demon that she will ever meet."

Callan had found little to smile over, but he grinned now.

Kaz lifted an eyebrow. "I will have to reconsider my basis for choosing friends if you find my misery amusing."

That brought a chuckle from Callan, and it felt good to laugh. "I do find this humorous, but not for the reason you think. None of Becka's family is here."

"For that I'm grateful, but what's your point?"

"I'm not interested in her. When we finish with the ward, go spend time with her. If you have to, tell her I ordered you to watch over her."

Kaz's eyes lightened at the notion. "She may still shove me away anyhow."

"If that happens, then you aren't as good as your reputation, Kaz."

"I'm better than that." Kaz got a wicked gleam in his eyes, then frowned. "What about Rayen?"

"You mean what about how badly you messed it up for me with Rayen?"

"She can't go home with you, Callan."

"I know all the reasons she's wrong for me." He studied the ground.

"Don't misunderstand me. I don't care that Rayen is C'raydonian, but if we ever figure a way out of here, you two can't travel to our world or to the past together. I just ... don't want to watch your heart get ripped to pieces over something you can't change."

It was too late for that.

Callan tried to explain what he'd figured out while he was in the TecKnati camp. "I've always accepted my responsibilities, never backing away. I stepped in when Jornn was killed even though I've never wanted to lead all the Houses, and still don't. I tried to make Rayen stay in the past, but she came back, and I'd be lying if I said I wasn't thrilled to see her." Callan searched Kaz's face for judgment, but there was none. "I've done everything I had to do and by this time tomorrow I'll probably be dead unless by some miracle we find a way home."

Kaz stopped walking and his eyes filled with disappointment. "I'm not much of a friend. With all that's happened, I'd forgotten you still face turning eighteen in this place. Rayen asked me about the wraiths when you were freeing Becka from the TeK camp. I didn't have time to explain. She thinks they never came for you. You have to tell her the truth, that your BIRG Day is tomorrow."

"I'll think about it." Callan didn't want her to come back to him out of pity, but because she wanted to be with him.

It had been a long time since he'd felt wanted instead of needed and he longed for that from Rayen.

He had no future to look forward to, but there was still hope for the rest of this village and his duty would always come first.

Thylan and his TecKnati scouts were no doubt planning an attack, if not already heading this way.

Rather than address new questions cropping up in Kaz's face, Callan said, "Show me the weak spot in the ward. We need to figure out how to reinforce it by ourselves."

"You, Jaxxson, and I don't have the power required to strengthen it."

"Jaxxson is bringing Gabby to meet us. We can't risk anyone else helping until we find out who the traitor is, because he or she will leave a spot in the ward that we won't know about until it's too late."

Kaz stopped close to the invisible wall protecting the village and lifted his hand until the ward hummed softly. "Any idea who is contacting the TecKnati?"

"No." Callan lifted his hands to feel the energy from the ward. The humming grew stronger as he neared it, energy swirling in preparation for parting to allow him to pass through. When he stepped back, Callan looked around, considering the entire compound. The ward had been created so that it was a hundred yards from the closest structure.

He took in the area around him. “I have an idea, but it requires restructuring the ward.”

Kaz’s mouth dropped open. “Rebuild the ward? You have to be joking. We’ll be lucky to just strengthen the one we have.”

“That’s not what I’m thinking about doing.”

Dropping his chin to meet Callan’s gaze, Kaz’s eyebrows cinched together with curiosity. “I don’t understand.”

“You will when I show you how we can catch the traitor.”

CHAPTER 22

RAYEN DIDN'T WANT TO SIT around Jaxxson's hut being miserable alone, so she went searching for Tony and V'ru. Those two were their best hope at figuring out what to do with this computer and the prophecy.

At V'ru's kamara, she lifted her hand and stalled it in midair when she heard V'ru shout, "Yes! I win."

Tony's deep voice chuckled. "You would be a legendary gamer in my time."

What had happened to the mouthy Jersey boy she'd met only days ago? It felt like eons since she'd first walked into the Byzantine Institute.

"Would you like to enter, Rayen?" V'ru called out.

Lifting an eyebrow at him that V'ru couldn't see— or could he? —she answered, "Yes."

"Put your hand on the exterior."

She did and the next thing she knew she was standing inside his bubble. From the outside, it appeared the size of the room she had in the girls' dorm back at school, but inside made a liar of the exterior. "How is it that your kamara is so much larger on the inside than it is on the outside?"

V'ru and Tony sat cross-legged three strides from her with a holographic screen hovering between them displaying some game. V'ru tilted his skinny chin up. "Can you comprehend multivariable calculus?"

"No. Never heard of it."

"Then explaining the interior of this kamara would be impossible with your limited intellect."

Just when she thought she was going to like this kid he spits out an insult that she can't even counter.

Tony's failed attempt at hiding his snort only annoyed her more. Pinning a gaze in his direction, she said, "When you finish enjoying yourselves at my expense, let me know because you two can use all that intellect you're so proud of to solve our problem."

Coughing and clearing his throat to wipe away his humor, Tony said, "Sit down and tell us what you need."

She squatted down and debated on sitting. That was only one step from stretching out on this cushy floor that looked like the surface of a cloud.

Her body cried to sink into it, but she persevered and ended up cross-legged, too. "We have to figure out the prophecy and make that computer work."

"What have you been smokin', Xena?" Tony clearly thought she was out of her mind.

V'ru scratched between his eyebrows for a moment then explained, "I have spent many hours researching the prophecy. I know more than anyone here and *I* am not able to decipher all the meanings behind the words."

That didn't mean someone else couldn't even if V'ru might find that unimaginable. "We have to search until we find answers," she countered.

Tony watched her with a little more concern. "What's the computer have to do with anything?"

"The prophecy came from a shaman named Damianus in Greece two thousand years ago. Isn't that correct, V'ru?"

"That was the belief. Damianus was a fetial."

"But he was possibly a shaman, too, right?"

V'ru eyed her suspiciously and explained, "Damianus appeared physically different from other Greeks. He is thought to have come from what was later known as Siberia on the Asian continent."

She'd meant to ask Gabby about Greece, but they ran out of time. "Is any of that near Albuquerque, Tony?"

"Uh, no. Asia and North America are separated by an ocean."

V'ru waited patiently then interjected, "During the twenty-first century, a discovery about North American Indians was made based on the oldest human genome possessed at that time, which supports a theory that a major number of North American Indians originated in the same area as Damianus, so that does support the idea that Damianus could have been a shaman."

She took that information and turned it around in her mind. "I met some men in Albuquerque this morning before we left. I was told they are Native Americans. I think at least one is Navajo. Are you saying they came from another continent, V'ru?"

V'ru sighed and she knew it had to be in direct relation to the confusion that was inhabiting her face. "I cannot share what came to light years later after the discoveries made in Tony's time, but to put all of this in simple terms, the genetic makeup of North American Indians originated in the Siberian region, and they were believed to have crossed the Bering Sea over a land bridge that later disappeared."

She wondered if Takoda knew about this.

"Regarding Damianus," V'ru said, getting them back to the root problem. "There is no way to absolutely confirm the history tied to the prophecy as it was supplied by verbal and written word plus visions, but Damianus supposedly shared the prophecy only with Jupiter who then passed it to worthy record keepers through visions and dreams."

Tony's eyebrows crawled up his forehead at that. "As in the mythological god Jupiter?"

V'ru nodded solemnly.

"How'd we end up with it called the Damian Prophecy, V'ru Man?"

"Over time, names and terms shorten or morph." V'ru lifted his shoulders. "As centuries passed, the Damianus name in society shortened to Damian. Someone interpreting a vision or dream was susceptible to altering the name to one that was current or familiar."

When V'ru spoke with such authority and knowledge, it was easy to forget that he was only eleven, but the return of his confidence was a good sign that he was feeling better.

Rayen hoped.

He lashed a suspicious look in her direction. "How do you know so much about those details?"

How could she reply without giving away where Gabby got her information? She was an unknown to V'ru so she should be able to manufacture her own truths. Especially if she didn't have to outright lie. "I speak to those who have crossed to the other side."

For the first time since meeting the kid, V'ru's eyes widened, and he appeared impressed.

Tony's widened, too, but she thought it might have been apprehension. "Is that what happens when it looks like you're talking to yourself, Xena?"

The old ghost hadn't been the one to tell her the information she'd gotten from Gabby, but he *had* shared parts of the prophecy, so she wasn't lying when she answered, "Yes."

"What can you tell us?" V'ru asked, completely convinced that she had a direct line to information since she knew about Damianus.

That was the problem.

She had all kinds of information from Gabby and even from her ghost, plus references to the prophecy mentioned by the shaman back in Albuquerque, but none of it made sense. "I'll tell you what I know then we all have to figure this out. One person can't do this alone. If they could, you'd have come up with the answers by now, V'ru."

The kid squared his little shoulders, pride coloring his face.

But it was true. If anyone could have sorted out this puzzle by now, he would have. The fact that he hadn't was evidence of just how much trouble they were all in.

But she was not going to tell this child that the lives of everyone in this Sphere depended on solving the prophecy. He carried enough weight on those slender shoulders as it was. Tony had been right to bark at everyone over how they'd forgotten to treat V'ru as an eleven-year-old child.

V'ru was brilliant and certainly special, but at the core he was still a little boy who had been through enough.

She explained everything she'd learned from Gabby without saying they would all die tomorrow if no one figured out the prophecy. When she finished, she asked, "Do you have a way of displaying the prophecy so we can see what we've figured out and what's still missing?"

"Of course."

While Rayen rolled her eyes at the superiority in his tone, V'ru moved his hands in the air and the hologram that he and Tony had been playing a game on disappeared. In its place was something more like the white board that Mr. Suarez had written on back at school.

Guilt pinched her hard at the reminder that every minute here was putting Tony in more trouble back home. And Gabby.

Her, too, but nothing in the past mattered to her since that wasn't her world. If she ended up there when this was all done, she faced a life where she might be sent to a place where she'd never see her only two friends or Takoda in that world again.

When V'ru sat back, the prophecy appeared on the holographic screen.

The future is in the past
One will seek and all will forfeit

When three become one
The End has begun

The gateway will open
A path will close

A friend enters as enemy
An enemy departs as friend

Day of birth as Red Moon rises
Night of end when last Moon sets

Three must unite
For the scales to right

The last will lead when others cede
All turn to the outcast

The past speaks to alter the present
A bond of two will set us free

Tony ran a hand over the stubby hair on his head. "I don't understand how someone thousands of years ago wrote that and knew something would happen now."

His lack of belief was an obstacle they didn't need. If Tony wasn't totally committed to this, he wouldn't be much help.

Rayen suggested, "You didn't understand how we could travel through a computer to land here either, Tony. Or how I could use only a power inside me to burn a croggle from the inside out. Or how V'ru makes a holographic screen appear in thin air."

Pushing his bottom lip up hard against the top one, Tony studied the board then said, "You're right, Xena. Let's get busy figuring this out."

V'ru pointed a finger at the prophecy and Rayen's name appeared in brackets at the end of the line *One will seek and all will forfeit*."

"Wait a minute," she complained. She hated that part about *all would forfeit*.

Tony defended V'ru. "He's right. You're the only one looking for answers, because you don't have your memory."

Blowing out a puff of air, she said, "Okay. What else?"

V'ru lifted his finger again. "Prophecy" appeared at the end of *The future is in the past.*

That made sense in a strange way. The prophecy was telling them that they had to understand the past to figure out the future.

She ran down the list and told V'ru, "Put Callan's name next to *The last will lead when others cede.*"

Nodding and smiling, V'ru made that addition.

Tony suggested, "Put Rayen's ghost next to *The past speaks to alter the present.*"

Technically, that wasn't correct, but she couldn't tell them words from the past should be attributed to Mathias. On the other hand, her ghost *had* mentioned parts of the prophecy. When she'd met with the shaman this morning, she'd thought the outcast was her, but she didn't want this to be about her since the prophecy belonged to the MystiKs, so she didn't suggest adding her name again.

But that brought up a question that had been nagging her.

Why would her ancestors know anything about this prophecy?

No ghost appeared with an answer, so it would just have to continue nagging her.

Beside *A friend enters as an enemy*, V'ru added *traitor* and it stopped her cold. She glanced at Tony before asking, "V'ru, why'd you put that there?"

V'ru looked at her, then at Tony, then back at her, as though he were weighing how much to say. "Earlier, Callan asked me to review the histories of everyone in our village." V'ru spoke quietly, as though saying the words felt wrong to him. There was an edge of hopelessness in his gaze. "I had to know why before I could give him that information. He said he was afraid one of the MystiKs was helping the TeKs. He told me it wasn't either of you or Gabby, and that I could trust you three and Kaz."

Tony blew out a breath. "You can trust us, V'ru Man. But don't let anybody else see this diagram unless Callan or one of us says so, okay?"

V'ru nodded, then turned back to his hologram, but to her eyes, his shoulders had drooped a little. She wanted to make it better, but she had nothing to say that would help. Being a genius didn't mean a little boy could really understand that kind of betrayal.

When V'ru added *Tony* and *three powers,* she reviewed the list.

The future is in the past [Prophecy]
One will seek and all will forfeit [Rayen]

When three become one
The End has begun

The gateway will open
A path will close

A friend enters as enemy [traitor]
An enemy departs as friend [Tony]

Day of birth as Red Moon rises
Night of end when last Moon sets

Three must unite [three powers]
For the scales to right

The last will lead when others cede [Callan]
All turn to the outcast

The past speaks to alter the present [Rayen's ghost]
A bond of two will set us free

"I still don't get why this has to be figured out by tomorrow," Tony mused, studying the hologram.

"Oh!" V'ru lifted his finger and Callan's name appeared at the end of both "Day of Birth when Red Moon rises" and "Night of end when last Moon sets."

She gave V'ru an understanding smile, happy that Callan had been spared from the wraiths, but V'ru was wrong. "If it's tomorrow, then that can't be Callan because his birthday is today."

V'ru angled his head, a small line forming across his forehead with the frown. "No. He turns eighteen tomorrow."

"But Kaz said it was today."

V'ru laughed. "It's a joke in Callan's House that Kaz has gotten Callan's birthday wrong for the past six years."

Air backed up in her lungs as she mentally rewound the conversation with Kaz outside the TecKnati camp when they were escaping.

She'd asked, "What happened with the wraiths?"

Kaz had answered, "They didn't come."

That was because they would come tomorrow for Callan.

She forced her anxiety behind a calm front and told V'ru, "There is nothing Callan wants more than to take all of you home. If that part of the prophecy does relate to Callan's birthday, then let's surprise him by figuring this out by tomorrow."

V'ru came alive with hope. "We could ... we could go home?"

Mathias had told Gabby that. If that wasn't correct, this child didn't need to know the only other possibility. "That's right."

Tony's expression darkened, which she understood. He thought she was giving V'ru false hope, but she wouldn't be able to explain what was going on until she had Tony away from V'ru.

And right now, she needed those two working on this.

She pointed at the computer. "That is key to all of this, Tony."

He reached for the laptop and pulled it over to him. "I can't make any promises, because I'm not going to paint fake rainbows." He paused to slam her with a judgmental gaze. "But I'll see what we can do."

"Thank you and I'll explain more later." She emphasized later, hoping Tony would stop condemning her with every glance her way and allow her a chance to explain.

He dipped his head in a short nod.

She'd been given a reprieve for now.

Standing up, she asked V'ru, "Would you please put me outside?"

"Are you coming back?"

The apprehension in his voice twisted her heart. "Yes, but not right away. I need to talk to someone else first. Send for me if you need me, okay?"

V'ru nodded and waved a hand.

She was standing outside in the cold again. How did this place go from suffocating heat to bone-chilling cold so quickly?

Probably an extra torture treat devised by SEOH.

She wanted to find that man and make him pay for what he'd done to these MystiKs, but that wasn't her main concern right this minute.

Of all the people she worried about right now, Callan topped that list, which was saying something since she would put her life on the line for Gabby or Tony.

She had to return them to the school before the red moon set in this Sphere tomorrow, but Callan and all the MystiKs also had to be safe before she left.

Less than a day from now everything would change forever.

She had one last day with Callan and she couldn't stand the crushing pain of spending it away from him. Every second they'd been apart was killing her.

But Becka was here and Kaz claimed she was part of Callan's future. When Callan had tried to talk to Rayen once they'd arrived at the village, she'd thought he was going to tell her that he didn't care for Becka. That he'd sent her with Kaz so he could be with Rayen.

Then she'd chastised herself for imagining what she wanted to hear. She'd been too angry and hurt to listen. *Had* he been trying to tell her goodbye or that he still wanted to be with her?

She should have given him a chance to speak his mind.

There would never be another person who meant as much to her as he did. She knew that with every fiber of her being even without knowing any more than she did about her past. She couldn't get back to her home and she couldn't control her future.

All she had was right now.

Pointing her feet toward the glowing common area, she took a step toward what she wanted.

Callan.

CHAPTER 23

"IT DOESN'T WORK THAT WAY here, Becka," Callan said for the third time while he stood in the village common area. Or was it the thirtieth time? Darkness had fallen long ago, and he did not want to spend his last night dealing with Becka.

What did Kaz see in this girl?

She was high maintenance. Too contained. Every move seemed thought out in advance.

Kaz had called her too perfect. Maybe *he* appreciated that trait.

Callan called her a pain in the—

"Regardless of where I am, I can not allow a male to create my kamara unless he is my *intended*," she argued on and tossed her hair over her shoulder. Again.

Did she have some affliction that caused her to constantly sling that mane around?

He held his patience by a thread that threatened to snap any second. Hadn't he instructed Kaz to build her kamara? Where was he? "You've got it wrong, Becka. It is not acceptable for you to *share* a male's kamara unless you're committed to each other."

"My point exactly. I should be sharing yours."

Callan bit down to keep from shouting that he didn't want her within a solar system of his kamara. He lowered his voice. "We have no commitment and we have not bonded. Sharing a kamara requires one of those."

"Not necessarily, because we could share a kamara *then* bond."

She would argue with an empty room. Bonding was the last thing on his mind.

He took a breath, admitting to himself that wasn't entirely true. He'd been thinking about bonding since returning from the TecKnati camp, but it had nothing to do with Becka.

Zilya and Etoi drew his attention to where they huddled on the far side of the common area, whispering as they watched. Were those two joined at the hip? At least the children were all bedded down. Neelah, her strawberry-colored cornrows bouncing with each step she took, carried a bowl of fruit as she crossed the clearing. She paused to glare at Etoi. "If you have no more to do than gossip then you could help the rest of us who actually accomplish work every day."

Etoi slashed a threatening look at Neelah, and Callan started counting in his head to keep from yanking them apart before those two got into it one more time. Etoi snarled, "Do your work and I will do mine. Never think you are high enough to speak down to me."

Before Callan could intervene, Neelah gave Etoi a smug look and whispered, "When we leave here, you will no longer have this high position you've assumed."

"Hold on to your fantasies."

"We will see who is fantasizing." Then Neelah moved on.

Callan had to get Becka settled and out of his hair pronto. "Where's Kaz?"

Becka waved her hand in the direction of Zilya and Etoi. "Last I saw of him he was a little bit that way."

A little bit that way? Becka would be of no use outside the village or searching for anyone. She might end up lost *inside* the village.

Sighing, Callan said, "Let's go see what he's done."

Becka let out an undignified noise.

He took her gently by the arm to get her moving. When he reached the other side, he slowed long enough to ask Zilya, "What time does Kenja have you and Etoi on guard duty tonight?"

Fury rolled through Zilya's eyes. "You will not bully me into that again. We have been on our feet all day. Must I remind you that I am of the Governing House and abusing one of my position is punishable by MystiK law? Continue to harass me and you will be brought before our leaders when we return. You have others to place on guard duty."

Was that last shot directed at Becka?

Or maybe Rayen.

Callan was not going to ask Rayen to do anything else for him or this village. If he asked her for anything, it would be to take down the walls she'd thrown up the minute she'd encountered Becka. Callan would have explained their convoluted situation, but Rayen hadn't given him the chance once Kaz had shared his misinformation. She'd just taken what she'd heard and shown no consideration for Callan's side of all this.

Was it so easy for her to cut ties and walk away?

For the first time, he questioned whether the partial bond that had started between them before she left was still in place. Or had her change of heart severed it?

"I take it your silence means you agree, Callan," Zilya proclaimed.

Kenja came striding into the common area just as Zilya made that announcement.

Callan's jaw couldn't clamp any tighter. "If ignorance is bliss, the Governing House must be in a constant state of euphoria with leaders like you."

Zilya's faced warped with rage.

Speaking in a clear and calm voice, Kenja interjected, "Fear not, Governing House, because the Uberons protect this village tonight."

It took a moment for Zilya to regain her composure even as her attack dog Etoi made threatening noises that Callan shut down with one look of warning. He'd lost all desire to deal with either of these two who set themselves above everyone else.

Gaining height by pulling her chin up, Zilya gave Callan a snide look. "See? *Some* MystiK warriors understand how the hierarchy functions."

What a fool. Callan had caught the flicker of threat in Kenja's voice that had obviously flown right over Zilya's head. Becka watched the entire scene with a curious slant of her eyebrows but kept her opinions to herself.

One blessing.

But allowing Zilya and Etoi to get away with shirking their duties was not fair to the rest of the village. He told Zilya, "We are fortunate to join forces with Kenja and her Uberons, but they are not expected to bear the entire burden for protecting this village. Find your rest but be prepared to take your place on the security schedule when I call for you or you'll find yourself sleeping *outside* this village."

The dual gasp of Zilya and Etoi confirmed that he'd finally gotten through to the petulant pair.

When Zilya spun to leave, Kenja added, "And you should prepare as well to face reprisal from the report I shall make upon our return."

Zilya turned back. Her eyes would have burned a hole in Kenja if Zilya had possessed that gift. She pointed a finger at Kenja. "You dare to threaten me?"

Kenja shrugged. "Threaten? Telling the truth has never been deemed a threat unless you see it as such." Then she put steel in her voice. "On the other hand, I find your tone and attitude offensive, but I will allow the insolence to pass this time. Cross me again and I will not be as understanding, and you do not possess Rayen's powers. Any battle between you and me would be over swiftly."

Becka was tapping her foot and making impatient noises that were barely audible, but Callan heard them. *Grant me the patience to survive the women in my life.*

Zilya surprised him by silently turning and walking away.

Until now, he wasn't sure she'd possessed enough survival instinct to recognize a more powerful adversary. Kenja was just as deadly as she projected.

Having witnessed the whole exchange, Becka shook her head. "Zilya should be removed from office. I'm a G'ortian, which puts me above her if she wants to be technical. It's fortunate for her that I'm not interested in governing, but neither do I want to be ruled by someone who annoys me. I think we need a committee created to discuss how to run this village."

Callan wanted to pound his head into the nearest tree.

Kenja sent him a sympathetic glance that he appreciated. She was the sole female not giving him grief at this moment.

"Let's get you settled," he said, towing Becka by her arm again. He shined light from his hand to guide the way or he'd end up carrying her. Not happening. "Have any of your G'ortian powers manifested yet, Becka?"

"Some, but nothing consistent yet."

"What about shining light energy from your hands?"

"Oh, no, that's discouraged by the head of our House. It's far too ... pedestrian. There are plenty of servants capable of accommodating us."

Callan mentally added needy to the list of Becka's unattractive qualities. He was drawn to strong women not little girls.

The image of Rayen attacking a croggle single-handed filled his mind. That was the woman for him.

When he reached the cleared spot in the woods that was much closer to the common area than he'd prefer a sleeping unit, Callan could see why Kaz had chosen this for Becka. She was within shouting distance to call out for service since she viewed everyone around here as her servants.

He released her arm and she kept walking then stumbled, flailing for her balance.

"Callan, where are you?"

Was she serious?

He shined the light at his body. "Right here."

She extended her hand. "Please. I don't want to fall since this is my only outfit until more can be produced."

He didn't even want to ask her what she expected for production of clothes.

A remnant of energy hovered over the spot where Kaz had started her kamara and Callan intended for him to finish it.

Standing only six feet away, she still held her hand out.

He caught her by the wrist just to shut her up and moved her over to where she could stand on a perfectly smooth section of ground.

It was identical to the spot she'd just vacated.

She grabbed his shoulder with a desperation that should be reserved for clinging to the edge of a cliff, then she maneuvered herself up against his chest.

It took all his control to keep from flinging her away.

Callan called out to Kaz telepathically. *Where are you?*

Near enough to watch Becka paw you.

Then come and get her off me.

I'm just making sure you haven't changed your mind.

Not. In. This. Lifetime.

Becka dug her sharp little nails into his shoulder, clutching tighter. "Thank you for making my kamara, Callan. Our parents would want this for us."

There is never going to be an us.

Callan couldn't put off explaining that there was no future for them together. He opened his mouth to tell Becka when a stick snapped behind him. Thank goodness, Kaz was going to peel Becka off Callan's body. Relief rushed through him until he turned and realized it was not Kaz walking up.

Just beyond the glow from his hands, Callan could make out every detail of anger rising in Rayen's face. She swung her gaze from Becka to him. "Please. Don't let me interrupt you love birds."

Becka replied in a sugary tone, "Thank you. We do require privacy."

Callan started, "Rayen, it's not—"

Her voice sliced through his words faster than if she'd used the edge of a broken glass. "Save it."

Then she was gone.

Callan roared, "*Kaz!*"

CHAPTER 24

WILL I EVER STOP BEING stupid! Rayen shook her head in disgust.

Maybe that's why her family sent her into a time traveling tornado. They didn't want to risk her reproducing.

Who could blame them?

Fallen branches crackled beneath the slam of her pounding footsteps. She had no idea where she was going, just away from Callan.

She didn't want to go back to the village to face someone like Zilya who would see emotions she couldn't hide right now. She hated this yearning for Callan. It made her miserable. Worrying about him dying tomorrow was hard enough but watching him and Becka so close together was almost as bad.

She should be the better person and support his future with Becka. A part of her wanted to because it showed she was honorable, but her heart cared nothing for honor. It screamed and stomped around in her chest, refusing to give up Callan to anyone regardless of how absurd it was to want him.

Kaz had explained how Callan was committed to Becka.

No matter how hard Rayen tried, she couldn't make herself think about the future when what she wanted was so far from her grasp.

"*We do require privacy,*" she mimicked in Becka's irritating voice. "*Thank you for making my kamara, Callan. Our parents would want this for us.*"

The word princess came to mind.

Had her memory just tossed her another nugget, or had she known of a princess while growing up? She didn't know, but that haughty image that raised fit Becka.

The prim girl had stood there with her ivory skin and shining blonde hair falling to her waist. Those pretty hands had never been abused.

Rayen lifted her hands, thankfully it was too dark to see them. But rubbing her fingers together, she could feel the rough skin and callouses that hadn't happened only in the last few days. Whoever she'd once been, wherever she'd grown up, she'd spent time with weapons and tending the earth.

Her hair hung limp around her shoulders. Certainly not the vision of perfection that had clung to Callan. What was wrong with her? That was Callan's world, and it didn't include her, never would. *Get over him and let this go.*

Swallowing was difficult and her eyes burned, but she refused to let a tear fall.

Not for someone who didn't want her.

As she stepped forward, a branch hit her in the face. She attacked it, beating the thing away from her until the limb was shredded.

Someone grabbed her from behind and she tensed, ready to fight. But then he wrapped his arms around her to trap her body against his. He lifted her away from the branch she'd defeated.

Callan.

She knew the feel of his arms and the musk that floated from his warm skin. He hugged her to him, laughing.

He dared to laugh at her?

"You must have a death wish," she muttered. "Put me down before I grant it."

"We won't have a tree left if I turn you loose."

Her heart was pounding viciously from anger. That was all.

And now she was lying to herself?

The emotions she suffered were not just anger. Her heart was holding a party because Callan was here and wrapped around her. She stopped fighting to see if he'd put her down.

No, and he showed no sign of tiring.

He nudged his face into her hair, inhaling. "You smell good."

She could swear her heart grinned at that.

Stupid organ had no sense whatsoever. It would follow Callan around just to hear his voice, but she had pride. She'd gone looking for him to hear him out but found Becka hanging all over his beautiful body.

Now was not the time to think about Callan's muscular chest and arms. He'd chosen someone other than her and she didn't want to hear anything else from him. "Are you through sniffing me?"

"No." His arms tightened. Not uncomfortably, but to send a message that she was good and caught.

Of all the reactions to choose from, contentment over being so close to him was clearly the wrong one.

"Put me down, Callan. Did you build a kamara that quickly?"

"No."

"So Becka is waiting on you to get back." An ugly feeling clawed through Rayen at the thought of those two together tonight.

"No."

She growled. "Is that all you can say?"

He chuckled and started walking, still holding her in front of him. "Why are you angry with me?"

"Because you're still holding me when I said to put me down."

"You were angry with me back when you found me with Becka. Why?"

Her muddled mind floundered for an answer.

Why was she upset with him? Because he was going to create a kamara for Becka. That sounded ridiculous in her head. She needed somewhere to sleep. He'd made her one when she'd had no sleeping quarters, but then he'd stayed inside it with her that night.

And that was the reason she was angry.

She did not want him sleeping in a kamara with anyone else and she did not want to admit that, because it sounded ... jealous.

She had no right to be jealous. Callan wasn't hers. Never could be.

"Rayen?"

"Yes."

"Are you going to tell me why you're angry?"

"I don't think so."

"Why not?"

"Because talking about it will change nothing."

He stopped walking and lowered her to the ground, then turned her in the circle of his arms. He held her lightly and let a soft glow emit from his hands. "You don't know that."

"Yes, I do."

"Talk to me."

"No. I don't like this feeling."

A tender thought softened his gaze. "You don't like how you feel about me?"

"No, I mean yes. I mean I don't like it."

"Explain what you don't like."

She snapped, "You won't let this go, will you? Fine. I don't like seeing you with Becka. Now I feel even more stupid for admitting it out loud."

He smiled at her.

Maybe if she called up her power and sent him flying into a tree it would knock some sense into him. "Laughing at me is dangerous."

"I'm smiling. Not laughing."

She pushed a handful of hair off her face in a frustrated move. "I don't see the difference."

Lowering his face to her, he said, "Laughing at you would mean that I find something you did funny. Smiling at you means ... you make me happy."

"Nice that one of us is happy," she grumbled.

His hands came up from her shoulders and cupped her face. "I want to make you happy, too."

"That's not possible." Could she sound any more morose?

"You haven't given me a chance."

She took in a deep breath and let it out slowly, trying to find the right words. "You can't fix how I feel. It's my own problem. Go back to Becka and let me work this out by myself."

"I can't do that."

"Why not?"

"Because that's not what I want."

There were a lot of things she wanted, starting with him, but she wasn't getting what she wanted so why should he? "Then it's nice to know I won't be suffering alone."

"Why are you suffering?"

His thumbs swept over her cheeks, soothing her, and breaking her heart. She wanted to have this forever, but that was not to be. Her patience was long gone. She was tired of playing twenty questions. "What *do* you want Callan?"

"You. And you want me."

Arrogant warrior. "Don't be so sure."

"I wasn't until now." He pinned her with that relentless gaze of his. "Admit the truth, Rayen. You care for me."

Admitting that would only make walking away from him that much more difficult tomorrow. Why was he doing this to her? Callan had never struck her as insensitive but making her admit her feelings when they'd never see each other again after tomorrow was inconsiderate. He'd have someone and she'd be alone again.

She circled back to the real issue at hand. "What about Becka?"

He dropped his forehead to hers. "Kaz was wrong to share so much."

"But it was right for you to keep the truth from me?"

"No. That's what I wanted to tell you when we got back here today. Kaz knew nothing more than speculation that had been going on between my and Becka's Houses. The truth is that no formal agreement has happened. Before I was captured, I told my father I would do whatever was required of me to take Jornn's place, but I could not commit to a woman I had no feelings for, and I have none for Becka. If I had, I would have to find a way to break the start of my bond with you."

Her crazy heart started beating out of control and she couldn't chastise the fickle thing because she was just as excited. The bonding had started when they were fighting for their lives. Callan had broken through the veil in her mind as a last-ditch effort to save her from a bloodthirsty plant.

They'd had a connection since then, but they hadn't actually fully bonded, based on what he'd explained.

She didn't realize until that very moment how much she wanted to bond with him, but to do so would be beyond wrong on her part. How could she bind him to her, which would prevent him from having a life when he returned home? He should have a full life with a family of his own some day even if she had no future waiting on her.

But he was right.

She did care about him. So much it hurt. Was caring for someone supposed to be this painful? Her stomach churned. Seeing Becka's hands on him had stoked a rage she was surprised to find within herself.

But she still didn't understand something. "If you feel that way, why were you building Becka a kamara?"

Lifting his head, he said, "That bothered you, didn't it?"

His smug tone got under her skin. "No. I'm only curious."

"Liar."

"Just forget I asked."

"But I like that you asked." He was grinning again.

"You find the most irritating things funny. Are you laughing, or have I made you happy again? I just want to know before I call up my power and blast that smile off your face."

He gave up a booming laugh that rumbled deep in his chest.

She'd had enough of being made fun of and pushed to back out of his grasp.

He let go of her face, but grabbed an arm, pulling her back to him in a fast move that ended with his arms locked behind her back. "You are prickly as a cactus sometimes. I'm smiling because you're adorable when you're jealous."

"I am not jealous," she lied. Just because he was right didn't mean she had to admit it and feed his ego.

He kissed her hair then her forehead. "It's okay, because I was jealous, too."

That was news. "When?"

"On the ride back from the TecKnati camp. I spent part of the time trying to contact Kaz telepathically. When he wouldn't communicate, I spent the rest of the time considering how many bones I could break without killing him."

"Callan!" She was appalled that he would consider harming his best friend. "Kaz did nothing wrong."

"He was touching you," Callan argued in a dark voice that held no humor. "No one touches you ... but me."

His heated voice claimed her as surely as what he'd declared. She had no defense against the way her heart jumped around at his words, even when she knew there was no hope for anything more than being here with him.

Maybe it was weariness from the past two days that allowed him to knock down her barriers, but she knew it was more. She would never care for another the way she did for Callan, and she was selfish enough to want what little time they had left.

The warmth from his body slowly drained the fight from her. She yawned and dropped her face against his chest to cover it. He smelled warm and male.

"You're exhausted, sweetheart, and I haven't slept since you left to return to the past the last time. Let's get some rest," he suggested in a voice that was gruff with gentleness.

"Where will we sleep?"

"In my kamara."

"But Kaz said—"

"I don't care what anyone says. Time is short in this place. I spent two long days without you, thinking about how I've done everything I had to do and gave it my best." His lips grazed her hair. "But with what little time I have left, I'm doing what I want to do and that's to be with you."

Time.

All the worry and fear over him dying exploded in her chest. She pushed them apart enough to face him. "Kaz let me believe your birthday was today and that you had survived the wraiths, but you're turning eighteen tomorrow. What are we going to do? We have to get you out of here."

Callan hid his emotions better than anyone here, but in that one moment she saw how much being here and knowing what was coming soon had beaten him down. He was seventeen, a mere day from eighteen. Adulthood in his world. He'd fought and bled for this village, and still had to bury children. He'd watched his friend Mathias be dragged away by wraiths with no way to help him and Callan knew that was his fate at this point.

When he spoke, his words were gentle like the wind. "I don't want to spend tonight thinking about tomorrow. I want to forget about everything else and just be with you."

She reached up and cupped his face, kissing him with all the feeling in her heart. When she stepped back, he stood perfectly still, clearly waiting on her decision.

Was there any doubt? "Take me to your kamara."

CHAPTER 25

GABBY COLLAPSED ON THE HERB-SCENTED bed of feathers in Jaxxson's hut and sprawled. She'd once been forced to run track with a bunch of physical overachievers.

It had taken her three days to recuperate.

That had been nothing compared to how beat up she felt now. "Do you think the ward will hold?"

Jaxxson stood at the entrance of his hut with his back to her as he sealed the passage. The opening disappeared, filled in with more indigo-blue feathers to match the rest of the walls, then Jaxxson turned to her.

Fatigue left dark shadows under his eyes. "I'm not sure, but Callan believes we're secure, so I will accept that."

Pushing up on her elbows, Gabby swallowed a yawn. "How are the children?"

On the way back to his hut from powering the ward earlier, Jaxxson had split off from her to check on two children who had shown signs of their magic reacting to the Sphere. "They had mild rashes. I was able to clear that up and ease them to sleep. What about V'ru and Tony? Any progress on the prophecy?"

"Some. They're working late. If anyone can figure out how to make that computer work, it's Tony."

"I don't understand how they determined that we need the computer," Jaxxson commented as he walked over to where he kept a gourd of water on a bench Gabby had used earlier for a chair. "I know the words of the prophecy, and nothing was said of a computer."

She chose her words carefully, trying her best not to outright lie to Jaxxson. "The way I understand it, a TecKnati got sent back two thousand years in time and he built an analog computer that sank a ship near a Greek island. The prophecy started back then. It's some parallel to that ancient computer."

"I've read some on that, but who made the connection to *us* needing a computer now?"

Gabby shook her head thoughtfully. "I would ask more questions, but everyone is working so hard to solve the prophecy and find a way out that I don't want to make it any more difficult than it is for them."

"Me either," Jaxxson assured her as he brought the gourd to her so she could drink first.

While she took a drink that soothed her parched throat, Jaxxson knelt on the bed.

He turned with a groan and sat hard. "Someone must have beaten me when I was asleep to make me this sore."

Gabby took the opening he gave her to shift the subject away from the prophecy. "I hear you. I feel rode hard and put up wet."

Jaxxson smiled at her. "You say the most unusual things. You are both beautiful and entertaining."

And he made her feel like an amazing woman just for bringing a smile to his face.

Why hadn't they been born in the same era?

She wouldn't dwell on that and turned the subject back to what had drained them physically so much tonight. "Once I understood how to push our power into the ward and got the hang of it, I started *feeling* the energy in the ward."

"You're getting much stronger and gaining more control. I'm so proud of you."

She smiled her appreciation, but she hadn't been fishing for a compliment. "What I mean is, I could tell the ward was struggling to stay intact. We need more power than we're generating. Do you think Rayen could help?"

Jaxxson's face paled. "She might be able to power the entire ward, but she also might blow all of us up. She has no control of her power."

He had a point even if he had made Rayen sound like the antichrist.

Gabby hadn't told Jaxxson that it appeared Rayen was important to fulfilling the prophecy. The minute she did, he would ask questions Gabby doubted she could dance around as easily as she had a moment ago. Keeping her encounters with Mathias from Jaxxson was chewing her up inside, but Mathias had been adamant that she would put the MystiKs at risk if they knew what had happened to him. Mathias worried that Jaxxson and the others would try to reach out to him and open a door for the wraiths to attack them before they turned eighteen.

Jaxxson drank his fill of the gourd and lay back, pulling her down to his side. A week ago, she would have panicked at merely touching anyone, especially a guy, because she had feared hearing thoughts. And she had no experience with boys, but Jaxxson was in a league of his own.

He made her feel safe and comfortable, and loved.

Not that he'd said the L word. That was *her* mind playing the love game, but she'd never had the opportunity for a relationship with a guy, and after years of not even being hugged she craved this closeness.

Jaxxson waved his hand and the glowing rocks dimmed, leaving the room almost completely dark. His voice swept through her with a calming quality that came from his healing powers. "You will eventually leave and not come back."

Those words yanked her right out of Calm City. "I don't want to think about that."

"I do."

"Why?"

"I've been thinking about ... us."

In the silence that followed, she considered what he was saying. At some point, the MystiKs had to go home. Gabby did, too. She had no idea what awaited her, Tony or Rayen in the past, but the longer they remained in the Sphere, the more dire the consequences when they returned. The idea of Tony going to jail turned her stomach and the thought of losing Rayen if they took her away permanently left Gabby with just as sick a feeling.

But the real killer would be waking up the day that she'd never see Jaxxson again.

That was reality, whether she wanted to avoid it or not.

"You are thinking about us, too," Jaxxson whispered.

"Yes." There was no point in trying to lie. He would know. "It's just that I know it's going to be hard to live without ever seeing you again, so I don't want to think about it right now."

He hugged her to him and kissed her hair. "There is a way to stay connected."

Gabby turned, pushing herself up to look him in the face. "We can be together?"

His grim expression was answer enough, but he lifted a hand to her cheek, brushing his fingers across her skin. "You are not of age for what I have in mind—"

He had an idea? "Don't even start with me that I'm too young for something at sixteen. In your world, they expect a lot more of someone my age than they do in mine, but I'm an old soul in a young body. It's not the age, but the miles, and I've had my share because of my gifts. I've lived alone for so long even among others my age that I'm tired of being alone. What are you suggesting?"

"I will tell you, but this is not something that can be changed once it has been done."

"I'm listening." She leaned down with her arm crossed over his chest and propped herself up inches from his face. Jaxxson wasn't built like Callan and Kaz, but more like a toned athlete. An Adonis athlete.

Both of his hands moved to her hair where he began to methodically undo each of her eight ponytails as he spoke. "There is a way to stay connected throughout time. It is called bonding, but it is only for a couple who believes they were meant to be together forever. We are halfway to bonding."

What? Wait a minute.

Hadn't Jaxxson executed the equivalent of jailbreaking her mind to help when her power was out of control during her last visit? He'd hesitated, saying if he pierced her mental veil, it would start a bonding.

Hadn't Mathias said something about the bonding *must* happen?

Now that she thought on it, Tony and V'ru had mentioned that even if they figured out how to fulfill the rest of the prophecy the last line would stop them.

A bond of two will set us free.

Was that why Jaxxson was bringing this up?

She stayed away from the prophecy discussion, wanting to hear what he had in mind. "Are you saying you have divorce issues in the future, too?"

His lips tugged up in a half grin. "There will always be those who treat a relationship as temporary or disposable, but some believe their soul is meant to unite with only one forever."

Her heartbeat tumbled along at a fast rhythm that was picking up speed as she realized what he was talking about. Was she really considering this? "Are you saying you want to finish forming the bond with me?"

Jaxxson's gaze moved over her as his hands kept unwinding the ponytail bands. "I have a hard time admitting the truth, but yes."

Call her idealistic, but she loved hearing that. "Why is it hard to admit?"

His gaze slid back to hers. "Because it would mean that you would never bond with another, only when you found my soul."

The light bulb flashed in her head, and it had nothing to do with solving the prophecy problem. "Wait, are you saying I could find you in the past?"

"Yes, but—"

"*Oh my God, oh my God ...*" She shoved up, ready to dance around the hut to celebrate this news. "Yes, a thousand times yes. Of course, I'll do this. I want only you!"

Jaxxson wasn't jumping around celebrating with her. What was wrong? He swallowed and studied on his thoughts for a moment before replying. "You won't find *me* in the past."

"What do you mean?"

"If we are bonded, your soul will search for mine and you will find it if my soul is there."

"Are you saying your soul travels through time?"

He did smile at that. "Not exactly. My soul—and yours—remain in the human body until that body expires then the soul moves to a new body. I researched this with V'ru while you were gone. The way I understand it, once souls are connected, they will continue to reunite with each other as soon as both reach maturity. One will always wait for the other one to return. The maturity part is a gray area, but the best I can tell, it means whatever adulthood is in each of our lives."

She eased back down to his chest, considering what he'd explained. "Then if we bond, I would be able to find you in my time as soon as I hit adulthood?"

"Give or take a year or two, plus the fact that it will not be me physically as you see me right now, but yes, your soul would recognize mine."

She massaged that thought, looking at the possible downside as well as the benefit. Would she be open to caring for someone who was not *this* Jaxxson? "What actually happens during a bonding?"

"We each cross the veil in the other's mind, which allows our powers to blend."

"Is it painful?"

"It is ... intense. Not painful, but life altering. I'm told you experience a level of understanding for everything around you that feels like the world is amplified at first. Once you become comfortable with the connection, then everything will recede, still more sharply in focus, but not as overwhelming."

She latched on to the part about their powers blending and couldn't ignore the question hanging in the back of her mind. Was this about solving the prophecy riddle? She just could not believe that Jaxxson would ask her to do this solely for the prophecy. Every ounce of her being wanted him in a way that she doubted she'd ever feel again, but she still had to know. Instead of asking about the prophecy, she chose a parallel that would answer her question.

"If we bond, will you and I be able to offer more power for shoring up the ward, Jaxxson?"

"We could, if I allowed anyone to know, but I won't because I refuse to have you used like a charging source." Jaxxson's calm voice boomed with protectiveness. "Your power is greater than mine. Combined, it would expand and grow, but it takes time to become accustomed to the change. You've seen what happened as your Hy'bridt powers developed. No, this village will have to survive without putting you under that kind of stress."

This really was only about the two of them.

For the next few minutes, she chewed on her lip, thinking how it would be better to take a part of Jaxxson rather than lose all of him.

Finally, Jaxxson groaned. "Please do not do that."

"What?"

"Biting your lip."

"Why?" She had a feeling she knew why but the vixen inside her had to tease him. It was Jaxxson's fault after all that she'd come out of her shell of cold indifference to live like a real person.

"Because I want to kiss you and will forget about this discussion."

Her hair now fell around her shoulders in a way that hadn't felt normal in a long time. She'd planned to live her life alone rather than face any more heartache over the gift that had been the catalyst for her mother's death. That was the reason she'd pretended to appear as strange as possible, to avoid connections.

But now?

Gabby considered her options now that she knew how to block the thoughts of others and had developed powers attributed to being a Hy'bridt ancestor.

Even if she could now be with another person and protect her mind, she would still be living in the shadows, hiding her gifts. She asked, "If our souls meet in the past, would yours be open to my powers?"

"If we bond, your soul *will* find mine and, yes, mine will have powers as well so it will feel protective of you and your power. However, since that will happen so many years in the past, my soul would very likely need you to help it understand those powers."

So, somebody in the past would need her, but the same question kept niggling. Could she bring herself to care for someone who was not physically Jaxxson? "What if I meet this person and I don't ... connect to him?"

Jaxxson's smile was full of warmth. "That is the beauty of bonding. You will care for him, but you will not be forced to stay even though it will be difficult to walk away."

"Why?"

"Because he will fall madly in love with you the moment he sees you and be ready to lay the world at your feet."

She laughed, a light sound that filled the hut. "Like that would ever happen."

"It already has."

Her heart clutched at the sincerity in his words.

Jaxxson lifted his head and kissed her. His firm lips moved over hers in a dance that was familiar now and had her forgetting everything around her. The next thing she knew, she was on her back, and he was still kissing her. His fingers wove into her hair and touched her so lightly it was if they had moved to another dimension.

When he stopped, he lifted his head, drinking her in with his eyes.

She drank her own fill of him at the same time. "If we do this, will you want to, uh, ..."

He cocked a look at her but didn't force her to say it. "To truly share my bed and have sex?"

Her face felt so hot she had to be tomato red. "Yes."

"No. That is a physical bonding that should never happen until you have reached the point when you are prepared for that step. In your time, it would be when someone was prepared to make a commitment. But in my time, it is a vow of commitment to marry and a union of Houses."

She probably shouldn't feel such relief, but she wasn't ready to take that step, even knowing she would never get the chance with Jaxxson. "Is it strange that the idea of bonding feels more important to me right now?"

He shook his head. "It *is* more important than a physical act. To unite two souls is eternal. If we had time to spend together, I would wait to discuss bonding, but I can't live thinking about you alone in the past." His chest moved up and down with a deep breath. "I would be dishonorable if I didn't admit that I have a selfish motive. I want you in my future as much as I want you to have someone in your world. I love you, Gabby, and my soul will never want another."

Her vision swam with tears. No one had ever wanted her, not like this. She trusted Jaxxson enough to believe that she could care for him—even if he looked like someone else in a few years—and that she'd recognize his soul when she met him.

And now she could do something for him and this village as well.

If they bonded, that would ensure a real chance at fulfilling the prophecy and sending Jaxxson home.

CHAPTER 26

Byzantine Institute, Albuquerque, NM

PHEN-T112 WATCHED HIS LIZARD RUN back and forth across the hall, clearly confused. This was the floor where Rayen, Tony and Gabby were last seen before they disappeared.

Giving a command Phen had programmed into the sentient beast, it began morphing from a lizard to the image of a hunting dog called a bloodhound that Phen had seen in a book.

These people still had books with paper pages.

Talk about primitive.

When the dog finished forming, he started sniffing just like the one Phen had read about. Now, would he have a nose for finding Rayen and her two friends?

The Browns might give Phen grief over a dog, but he could always order it to morph back into a lizard when they weren't looking. They thought they were so clever running this school under the noses of the government in this world. How difficult could it be to develop a school and be accepted as a superior operation when the people running it had been sent back 175 years in time?

Not Mrs. Brown, of course. Or her son, Nicholas. Mr. Brown must have adopted the kid since Brown hadn't been in the past long enough to have a seventeen-year-old child.

SEOH didn't place women in any vital position. He had less use for women than he did for MystiKs.

Or scouts.

Phen had never enjoyed being a TecKnati scout, but he'd been moving up the ranks until that stupid Rayen showed up in the Sphere. SEOH held Phen responsible for the intruders.

Twenty-three years as a TecKnati, fifteen of which had been spent either training or working as a scout, and he got sent back to a time when paper and physical computers were still in use.

No more.

TecKnati had served the civilization back home by providing solar energy to heat and cool homes, laser curtains to prevent rabid C'raydonians from entering the cities, and a space program that offered a defense system unlike anything ever seen before.

That was all fine, but Phen had been treated as a number for too long. SEOH thought he'd never see Phen again, but he was wrong. Phen would find that time travel computer and wait for Rayen to return then make her show him how to get out of this place.

He wanted to go home. Something this place would never be.

The sound of voices echoing from the adjacent hallway snapped Phen out of his musings. He needed to hide. He hurried forward to where the dog had stopped, sniffing at a door. Phen opened it and rushed inside the dark room with the dog at his side, closing the door softly.

"I don't like waiting." Phen recognized the voice as Dr. Maxwell's, because it was rough and sounded as if the man gargled with broken glass. "SEOH leaves us exposed by sitting on all these MystiK eggs we've harvested in the women's center. We've been here four years. It's time to move to the next location and get started."

"Based on the message Phen brought from SEOH, we may not have to continue *any* operation much longer."

And that would be Mr. Brown, the central cog in all this. He'd tried to get Phen to take classes, to fit in with the other students in the school. Phen had given him the thousand-yard stare he saved for idiots.

Take antiquated classes? He'd probably have to use a pencil and paper, too.

Did they still have pencils in this era?

Phen should find some of the USB memory sticks and take them with him to sell when he returned home. There was always someone who wanted to collect old crap.

SEOH's minions really thought Phen was going to just accept being ripped from everything he knew and thrown back in time?

"Speaking of Phen," Dr. Maxwell said as the voices came closer to the room where Phen hid. "What are we going to do about him?"

"Let him be. The minute SEOH sends the K-Virus back in time, we'll release it into the atmosphere. The virus will begin attacking anyone not inoculated. SEOH specified that we should inoculate ancestors of *only* the top twenty percent of TecKnati DNA based on intellect, plus the eight families protecting future engineers. Do you really think Phen came from that level of breeding stock?"

Dr. Maxwell chuckled and Phen considered turning his sentient beast into something with claws and serrated teeth to unleash on the obnoxious doctor.

So SEOH was even going to wipe out his own people?

"I hope his plan works," Dr. Maxwell said.

"We'll know in another day when the virus shows up. Once we see the first cases being reported on the news, it will be time to move to the next phase of this operation. We'll use—" Mr. Brown's voice trailed off as they turned down another hall.

Phen swung around and leaned back against the door. He had to find that computer now and he'd take it to a spot where he could hold Rayen prisoner as soon as she came back through the portal.

She would either help him or watch her friends die.

When his eyes adjusted to the semi-dark room, he stared at where the dog sat beside a ladder, with two commercial-size cans of tomatoes sitting on the floor at its base. Then he looked up at the top of the shelf.

CHAPTER 27

CALLAN LIT THE WAY THROUGH the woods with his palms and wished he hadn't had to move his kamara closer to the village, but he couldn't very well ignore his own security orders.

Still, this location was far from anyone else, and he'd built a personal ward fifty feet out around the kamara that blocked entrance and sound from both sides.

Kaz could reach Callan telepathically if any threat arose.

Rayen said, "I'm not sure I even know which direction the village is from here."

He held her hand, keeping a light shining from his other hand as he drew her along. "The good news is that you aren't going anywhere without me, and I can find it."

"You sound pretty sure about this. I might change my mind."

He smiled at the teasing in her voice. When was the last time he'd laughed or smiled before Rayen came along? He couldn't remember and he doubted he'd laugh or smile as much again once this night was over.

Don't think that way tonight.

When they reached his kamara, he stopped before entering and pulled Rayen around in front of him and kissed her. She wrapped her arms around him without hesitation. This was the woman he envisioned being with forever. Someone who was his equal in every way, and maybe even more powerful than he was. That didn't matter. If anyone or anything threatened her, he would bring the full force of his power to destroy that threat.

Her lips on his brought his world into focus and gave him a reason to hope beyond tomorrow and this miserable Sphere. Callan ran his hands into her hair, letting the wild strands flow over his skin. She had her hands in his hair, too, holding his head as if she feared he'd vanish if she let go.

Nothing could drag her from him right now.

She angled her head, and he took advantage, kissing her more deeply, tangling her tongue with his.

He would trade all his tomorrows for this.

When they broke for air, she stared up at him, studying his face for answers he was sure he didn't have. "What?"

"I'm just trying to memorize everything for when ..." She looked away, her jaw moving with unspoken words, then she came back to him. "For when I have to depend on memories alone. I have none and I'm filling up every available spot in my mind with you."

If he were honest with himself, he'd admit he was doing the same thing, but he didn't want to admit that. He didn't want to give up the one thing worth fighting for, if only someone would point out who or what he had to fight.

She tried to stifle another yawn.

He kissed her nose. "Let's go inside where it's warm."

"Mm. Chilly out here, but I'm so tired I could probably sleep on the cold ground."

Once he had her inside, she glanced around at the gray zero-gravity chair that emulated the one from his home and the floating, cloud-like bed, silently taking it all in.

Then she froze, turning as she studied the images of her embedded in the walls of his kamara. That was another reason he wanted no one else inside here.

This was the only place he found solace.

He went to sleep and woke up thinking of her, and those images now covered the circular walls.

She finished pivoting around until she was back to facing him. "How did you do this?"

"I could show you more easily than explain it, but generally a kamara is created from the most tranquil part of your mind and enhanced with everything that fills you with peace."

"You always pull images out of your mind and stick them on the walls?" she asked.

"No. I've never had pictures of anything, or anyone, show up on the walls of my kamaras in the past, not even of my family. But after sending you back to Tony and Gabby's time at moonset on your first visit to the Sphere, I woke up the next morning to find that image of your face in here." He pointed at the picture of her lying back while he'd treated her wounds after a croggle attack. Her guard had been down, and they hadn't been adversaries in that fleeting moment.

Clearing his throat, he added, "When you came back and we spent the night in the kamara I built you, I stopped by here for a weapon on the way to rescue Tony and the two boys from the TecKnati. All the other images you see showed up then."

She reached out to touch a vision of herself sleeping that floated past her hand. "Is it because we spent that night together?"

He couldn't waste even a second being apart, so he moved behind her and wrapped his arms around her waist, dropping a kiss on her neck. "No, I think it's because we started the bonding even on our first meeting."

Her hands covered his that were folded over her stomach. "Oh. I forgot about that."

While locked away in the TecKnati camp, he'd given two long days of thought to the bond and what it would mean if he left it in limbo the way they were right now. Kaz claimed what was started when Callan pierced the veil in Rayen's mind could not be left that way and Kaz had shared his ideas on how to sever it completely.

Rayen dropped her head back on his shoulder and he could see thick eyelashes brush her soft cheeks.

Callan pulled her back with him and sat beside her on the bed. Her eyes flew open, and she looked up at him. He bent down, kissing her with as much control as he could manage.

Did he want more? Well, yes, but he'd never dishonor her that way.

That wasn't to say he would be satisfied with leaving things the way they were right now, with them half-bonded. Hoisting her up, he tossed her to the side. She landed and bounced on the bed, laughing with a deep, throaty sound he felt deep in his bones.

He stretched out next to her and propped his elbow to support his head. Here was the picture to replace all others.

Her black hair spilled around her face like a dark fire. Blue-green eyes twinkled even more when her lips curved into a soft smile. Her skin was the color of perfectly steeped tea. When he brushed a lock of hair off her shoulder, he grimaced.

Her fingers touched his lips. "Why are you frowning?"

"Your skin is so beautiful. I never realized how unattractive the mixed colors of mine are next to you."

"I love the way you look, Callan."

She caught his hand that was still toying with her hair and pulled it to her lips, kissing his hand then his wrist. When her aqua gaze reached out to his again, she said, "Something is bothering you that you're hesitating to tell me."

Had she delved inside and lifted his thoughts? No, she wouldn't do that. He asked, "Why do you say that?"

"I don't know. I just ... sense it, I guess."

"It's the bond trying to form." He said the words as soon as he thought them.

Her gaze moved everywhere but to his face.

As much as he wanted to push to know what she was thinking, he had to let her work through her emotions on her own and see if she'd come to the same conclusion he had.

Finally, she kissed his hand then tucked it against her chest and addressed him. "We have to do something about this bond that was started."

"Agreed."

"Is it something we can do tonight?"

"Yes."

Her eyes shone, glossy with tears. He never wanted to hurt her and watching her struggle with this was more than he could take. "We can finish the bond now."

"What?" Her eyes rounded. "Finish it? That would mean we're bonded forever."

He drew back at her reaction. "Yes, it would."

"No, we can't ... you can't ... what are you thinking?"

That wasn't the reaction he'd expected. "I was thinking that you wanted to be with me as much as I want to be with you."

"I do."

"Doesn't sound like it."

"But you're talking about bonding our souls forever. I'm already dead by the time you return home."

"First of all, I probably won't make it back."

She shoved up in his face. "Don't say that! You *are* going home."

This was not going anything like he expected. "Then if I do, that's even more reason to be bonded."

"What if my soul ends up in a TecKnati body in your time? You can't be with a TecKnati." She started nodding. "See? You haven't even considered that, plus if you're bonded to me, you'll never bond with someone you have to ... marry."

"I don't care. I don't want to lose you. I know if we bond, we'll be together somewhere during our many lives. If I find your soul in a TecKnati, I'll deal with it."

"You hate the TeKs. They killed your brother. They sent you here. SEOH is trying to destroy the MystiKs." She paused and took a trembling breath. "Don't you see? I don't have a life to go back to or any type of future worth thinking about, but *you* would be losing any chance at happiness by bonding with me."

For the first time since his brother died, the vengeance Callan lusted after had been moved aside in his heart and something more important filled the largest spot. He caught Rayen's face between his hands and told her, "I'll lose any chance at happiness if I never find you again. I've chosen you as my soul mate. I want you to choose me. Just answer this. Do you want to bond our souls?"

She squeezed her eyes shut, holding the tears back, then opened them. "Of course, I do, but I don't have any way back to my home. If we do this and my soul is trapped in the wrong world it may leave yours in limbo."

Drawing her close until their heads touched, he said, "I don't care."

She reached up to fold her fingers around his neck. "That's just it, I do care, too much to allow you to be bound to someone who will prevent you from having a life. I care too much to do that to you. I will miss you forever once we're apart, but I can't bond with you. I couldn't face myself for doing that when I have no idea what it would do to you for eternity."

Could it be any worse than the pain crushing his heart at losing her forever?

CHAPTER 28

THE WIND BLEW THROUGH MY hair as I raced across the desert beneath a full moon on my trusty Yo-zon. I'd given him a name my grandfather had told me meant swift, because this brindle-colored horse had been fast even as a yearling.

We rode as one through the dark.

Always at night.

That was the only time a C'raydonian was safe from attack. The sentient beasts were not as adept in the dark for some reason. My parents had warned me to always travel with an escort, but I needed to ride and burn off the fear that had clawed at me for three nights straight.

I couldn't face sleep again.

Each night I saw a young man, tall and fit, a warrior as fierce as my father, who led our tribe. This warrior called to me in my dreams. He sounded as though he missed me.

How could that be?

I'd never seen anyone like him.

Soft blue-and-brown-colored shapes covered his wide chest and arms, all layered with muscle cut by hours of training. His body was a living sculpture of a fierce fighter. The tanned skins he wore for pants hugged muscled thighs and stopped at his boots. Wild locks of hair blew in the wind, brushing his shoulders and changing from dark brown to golden to a cinnamon color.

He stood in front of a small, waist-high table and told me, "When I do this and I'm gone, my soul will search for you. If I had the choice to lose only my *life in trade for just one more minute with you, I would do it." His throat moved with a hard swallow. "If others did not depend upon me, I would stay here with you."*

"What are you talking about? Where are you going?" And why did his words tear me apart?

Lifting his hand, he reached out to me.

I reached out to touch his hand and the world exploded.

Rayen lunged up, gasping for air, no idea where she was until Callan jumped off the cloud bed to stand in front of her, searching the kamara. He whispered, "What's wrong? Where's the threat?"

"Just ... a dream." One that felt as if she'd had it while living at home, but how could that be when Callan had not even been born by the time she died?

She sat on the bed, still breathing hard. He turned to her with tufts of hair sticking out everywhere from sleeping. Running both hands through the golden-brown locks, he shoved the wild locks down and wiped a hand over his face before squatting down in front of her. "Are you okay?"

Staring at him, she tried to come up with an answer that was the truth. "Just rattled with so much going on. Think it's daylight yet?"

"In a little less than an hour."

"How do you know this when there are no windows in the kamara?"

"My body is in sync with the red moon. I can feel its pull as the moon nears the time to rise."

She reached out and touched his cheek, wishing he was anywhere but this miserable Sphere. Before she could form a thought into words, he cupped her hand and kissed the palm.

Then that look entered his eyes. The same one that she'd seen the last time he tried to make her leave. She warned him, "Don't start on me to go back."

"Thylan will attack. If we can't hold this ward against him, he'll come for you. I don't want to run the risk that I can't protect you."

"I'm powerful enough to deal with Thylan."

"*When* your powers show up," Callan pointed out, reminding her of her hit-and-miss defense system. He added, "If we were bonded, I could direct your power."

Ah, his new tactic. "No. I will not condemn you to a lifetime without the chance to bond with someone else. Don't think it's easy for me to say that. There's a crazy woman inside me who wants to kill any female who touches you, but the warrior in me was taught to make honorable decisions. I can't tell you how I know that since I've regained so few memories I can count them on two fingers, but I can't take that choice away from you."

"You're taking away the choice I'm trying to make."

She kissed his cheek. "Nice try. Not doing it."

Callan sighed and was leaning forward to kiss her when he stilled, and his gaze lost focus. He jumped to his feet. "TecKnati have broken through the ward."

CHAPTER 29

RAYEN RUSHED ALONG BEHIND CALLAN who lit the way for her with his hands, but she could see other lights coming from the right and the left. "How do you know where to go?"

Callan leaped over a log. She followed him as he explained, "Kenja contacted Kaz, and he called out to me."

"How many TecKnati have broken through the barrier?"

"We're about to find out." Callan slid to a stop and held an arm out to block her from passing him.

"What are you doing?"

He leaned over and whispered, "I knew the ward would be breached once the traitor got word out, so I intentionally left several spots vulnerable. Then Kaz and I created a trap inside our ward in those areas and I told Kenja to keep her people clear of them."

"Kenja was in on it?"

"Yes. She wasn't in the Sphere when the traitor released the TecKnati we captured the first day we had you, Tony, and Gabby in our prison hut."

She muttered, "I remember that."

Callan kissed her. "That was before we realized you weren't the enemy. Anyhow, Kenja isn't the traitor."

"That leaves Kaz out, too."

"Right."

"Then who is it?"

"If we've captured a TecKnati or two, we'll find out."

Kenja came running up to them, but she was quiet as a whisper covering the same ground Rayen had just crashed through. If she spent much more time around Kenja, Rayen was going to get a complex about her warrior skills even though she'd used a dose of her power to blast Kenja across the common area one time.

Callan lifted his chin at Kenja. "How many?"

"None on the far side. Kaz and my warriors are watching the second weak spot we created to make sure this is not a distraction so that they can send an army through that area."

"Good. Ready?"

Insult narrowed Kenja's gaze. "I will not honor that with an answer."

Callan muttered something that sounded like a curse and led the way.

As soon as they neared the trap, Rayen could feel energy swirling in a tight weave of ward and spell that had the pull of a strong magnet. When she focused on the ward trap area, the light Callan shined on it blurred around the edges, allowing her to determine the perimeter of the trap.

Two bodies were stuck against an invisible wall much like oversized insects pinned against a huge sticky surface.

Their arms were stretched out. They struggled, then one of them cursed and they both looked up at Callan.

Or Kenja.

Either sight should put the fear in a TecKnati captured inside this village.

Callan said to Kenja, "I'll release them one at a time. You contain them then I'll transport."

"Fine by me."

Walking through an open area between the trap and the ward perimeter wall, Callan stepped behind the first TeK and placed a hand on his shoulder.

The guy screamed and fell to the ground, then curled up as if he expected to be kicked.

"What did you do?" Rayen called to Callan.

"Nothing. I only touched him, and he cries like a baby."

Callan sounded bewildered.

Kenja passed through the ward and ordered the guy, "Sit up, coward."

The TeK remained curled in a ball.

"Very well." She held her hands over him and spun one hand as if wrapping something in the air.

A fine blue film circled the TeK on the ground until he was completely covered.

Rayen asked, "Can he breathe? If not, he won't be of much use to question."

Kenja nodded. "Air flows through the entire wrap."

They repeated the process with the second TeK, but without all the drama. This scout stood as Kenja wrapped him from knees to head and announced, "You will walk."

When he didn't move, Kenja pointed at him and he started jumping around shouting, "*Stop it! Stop it!*"

She snapped her fingers and he wobbled to the side. "Are you ready to walk now?"

He nodded.

Callan used kinetics to lift the whimpering TeK from the ground and float him to a prison hut Rayne hadn't noticed, but there were still parts of this place she had yet to see.

The hut they tossed the prisoners into was four long strides across, much larger than the one she, Tony, and Gabby had been locked in that first time, plus it wasn't made of the same vibrating green material. This one looked woven of vines so thick she couldn't see through the seams.

Kenja did her finger trick and the wrap disappeared from the heads of both captives. The wimpy TeK had no choice except to remain balled up and hadn't shown any interest in unrolling himself anyway.

Callan ignored him and speared the standing TeK with an icy glare. "Who opened the ward for you?"

"I don't know."

Kenja didn't hesitate or warn the scout before she pointed her finger at him.

The TecKnati started begging, "No, please don't, I swear I don't know. Please, please …" Tears rolled down his face and he twisted one way then the other trying to stop whatever was upsetting him.

"What's he feeling?" Rayen asked.

Kenja calmly said, "It is much like having a thousand black ants attack your most sensitive and private areas."

The scout cried out, "I swear I'd tell you. I don't know. Please make it stop," he pleaded.

Callan gave Kenja a look. She shrugged then snapped her fingers.

The guy fell to the ground, shaking and jerking. His voice was much higher now, and raspy.

Callan squatted next to him. "Are you willing to tell me what you know now?"

"Yes, anything, please don't do that."

"How did you know the ward would be open in that spot?"

"Thylan told us it was marked on the outside."

"Marked how?"

"With a glowing section of grass."

"Is it still there?"

"We were told it would vanish as soon as a TecKnati touched it."

Callan pinched the bridge of his nose between his thumb and forefinger.

Rayen could feel his frustration. He'd set a trap to uncover the traitor. If this guy knew, he'd have screamed the name by now. He might have a level of tolerance for pain, but not the kind Kenja inflicted.

Kenja asked, "Why were you sent here?"

"To find the computer and take it to Thylan."

Standing, Callan stepped out of the hut. Once Kenja and Rayen were out, he sealed it shut and set a ward of power that buzzed with the three of them this close to it.

He clearly didn't want to risk the traitor letting these two go.

She directed a question at both Callan and Kenja. "How many MystiKs can make the grass glow?"

Kenja glanced at Callan who answered her. "All of them. It's a simple exercise learned as a child and when anyone other than a MystiK touches it the glow disappears."

"What are we going to do now?" Kenja asked and Rayen was glad she had decided to stay.

Callan moved them far enough away from the prison hut to talk without being overheard. "We can't set traps all along this ward. It's too much area to protect and we don't have enough people to cover what we do have. It's not going to take long for Thylan to realize his scouts failed to get the computer. Once he does, he may be crazy enough to attack. He must be getting desperate to send two of his people inside this village."

Rayen suggested, "What if we reduce the ward's protection area so that there's a smaller perimeter to protect?"

"We can't," Kenja said. "Remember the ground cover that emits a hallucinogenic mist?"

"Oh, yes." Rayen had encountered that on the last trip and shuddered at how close she'd come to killing Callan, because of hallucinating he was a Tek.

"It's mutating and poisoning the plants we've been using to sustain us. That in turn will affect the animals. This village is barely surviving on what we can forage inside this ward."

"Then we have to strengthen the ward."

Callan said, "We've tried. Gabby and Jaxxson exhausted all they had to get it to the point it is right now, and I only allowed that because I knew everyone was inside. We can't risk losing our strongest healers, but the ward is slowly failing."

"What about my power?" Rayen asked, thinking that was the obvious next move.

Neither Kenja nor Callan said a word.

CHAPTER 30

WHILE RAYEN STEWED OVER BEING told she couldn't help with the ward, Callan had called in every available power source. He didn't see the point in trying to trick the TecKnati again since they needed to capture Thylan to find out the identity of the traitor.

She believed she could power up the ward and not kill anyone, but from the looks on the faces surrounding her, no one else held that opinion. It was worth another shot at trying to convince them. "This is a ward," she began, "and I'm a power source. How difficult can it be?"

Kenja explained, "Your power is not MystiK so it may not merge with the current ward, or you could force too much power into it and blow up the village."

"She might blow up the ward, but not the village," Kaz offered, and Rayen wasn't sure if that was in her defense or not.

"It's too much risk to her," Callan said with the power of his authority that would normally end all debate and prevent anyone else from arguing.

Anyone but her. "I think I'll know if it's too much for me."

Callan, Kenja, and Kaz were grouped on one side of her. Gabby and Jaxxson stood on the other side. Zilya sort of stood with Callan, but in truth she hung back, staring a hole in Callan's back.

Unwilling to bend, Callan shook his head. "We try it again without you."

Zilya argued, "We're draining our power when we'll need it later."

Rayen was in shock. Had Zilya spoken up to support something she wanted to do? That surprise lasted only long enough to note the sneer she sent Rayen's way. No, Zilya just wanted to conserve her power for herself and would willingly sacrifice Rayen.

They stood twenty feet inside the ward. Rayen could tell there were weak spots when they'd passed through an opening the last time. The energy usually buzzed across her skin, but now it felt more like the brush of friction.

Before she could mount a new argument, Gabby said to Jaxxson, "We have to tell them."

Jaxxson nodded.

Rayen had noticed something odd about the two of them when they walked up but couldn't put her finger on it. Gabby always had a glow about her when she was with Jaxxson. For some reason, it was more pronounced than ever now.

Callan had caught Gabby's comment. "What do you have to tell us?"

Jaxxson put a proprietary arm around Gabby then announced, "Gabby and I have bonded. We are far more powerful now as a team."

Zilya gasped.

Kenja's eyebrows dropped low over her confused gaze. Kaz was neutral and Callan sliced a look at Rayen that said *we could have done that.*

Gabby's tentative gaze skittered around until it landed on Rayen. She smiled back but worried what that would mean for Gabby since there was no way for her and Jaxxson to end up together.

Kaz said, "Then let's get busy and try it with Gabby and Jaxxson."

Callan turned toward the ward, and everyone followed him, including Rayen. He shook his head at her. She backed up to watch, feeling useless for all the power she possessed.

The rest of them spread out six feet apart and raised their hands.

Jaxxson began the chant, then Gabby picked up his rhythm. Blue-green light radiated from the two of them and even Zilya's eyes widened with awe.

Callan jumped in as the chant repeated, followed by Kaz's bold voice and Zilya's murmuring.

Surprised, Rayen could see the spread of power and the spots that were getting stronger, especially where the streak of power originated with Jaxxson and Gabby.

But after five minutes, Kaz and Callan had sweat pouring down their backs, Zilya was trembling, and Gabby looked pale. Kenja and Jaxxson were gritting their teeth. Jaxxson took one look at Gabby and told Callan, "We have to stop."

Kenja shouted, "No. The ward is getting stronger."

Jaxxson turned to her. "We're pulling off in thirty seconds."

"We can't finish in thirty seconds," Kaz argued in a strained voice.

The heck with this. Rayen walked over and touched Callan's shoulders. He tensed and said, "What are you doing?"

She answered him by tapping on his mind. When he opened to her, she said, *We can do this with my power. I just need to find it without being upset and having my power run out of control.*

He surprised her by sweeping into her mind and telling her, *Follow me.*

She let go mentally of everything except focusing on him as he dove inside and found the red glow of her energy. As soon as she saw it, she drew the energy up and pushed it into Callan. His shoulders rolled with the surge of additional energy, and he took the power as fast as she could feed it.

Colors swirled and blurred, spinning into a vision as beautiful as it was chaotic. Rayen kept drawing from her core. It felt as if she had a bottomless supply of energy.

Then the flow slowed until she couldn't push it anymore.

What was wrong?

A noise pierced her mental sanctity. Voices shouting.

Oh, no. Had she destroyed the ward?

She opened her eyes and stared at the back of Callan's head. He said, "Are you going to release me?"

Her fingers were digging into his shoulders. She snatched them back. "Did I hurt you?"

Callan turned, rubbing his shoulder, but grinning. "No."

"You did it, Rayen," Gabby exclaimed and hugged her.

She looked up and the wall radiated energy so powerful it glowed. "I didn't blow it up."

Kaz laughed. "No, you would have blown up Callan first as the conduit."

Her skin chilled. She hadn't considered that.

Callan gave Kaz a censuring look. "I was never in danger."

Jaxxson said, "I'm being called to the healing hut." He thanked Rayen for her help and took Gabby's hand.

Zilya swiped at perspiration that ran along her neck. "You could have done that to begin with and saved the rest of us from wasting our time."

"Protecting your people is wasting time?" Kenja asked.

Speaking through a clenched jaw, Zilya said, "Don't twist my words, Kenja. I'm only saying that she's of no real use to this village. We should have had her power the ward on her own. She clearly has enough energy."

Callan's face turned darker with every word Zilya spewed. "You should be thanking her."

Etoi came storming up. "I will take Zilya's place for anything else today. She is too important to use in labor such as this."

Rayen cocked her head in question. Yes, Etoi was Zilya's shadow, but Etoi didn't have Zilya's power for things like the ward or she'd have been out here helping. Was Etoi trying to keep Zilya from using her power to shore up MystiK defenses?

Could Etoi be the traitor?

"Thank you," Zilya told Etoi. "I'm going to find a place to cool off and rest. We need pik-pik thread woven. You and I'll do that today."

Zilya basically dismissed herself from anything else and walked off.

Kenja murmured, "She is lucky she was not born Uberon."

Callan scrubbed a hand over his face. "I don't care as long as she stays out of my way. We've got to figure out Thylan's next move."

Neelah came from the direction of the prisoner hut. Callan and Kenja tensed, probably both thinking the first thought that came to Rayen.

Had she gone to see the prisoners? Was *she* the traitor? Tony had warned Rayen about her from their first visit to the Sphere. She was angry and bitter, not that he'd blamed her, since she was trapped here, but such a person could easily betray others to save her own skin. Rayen just recalled everything Tony had told her and needed to share it with Callan, but not out in the open.

Callan asked, "What is it, Neelah?"

"One of the prisoners is begging to be released from the binding."

Kenja said, "Why should we care?"

"He claims he will share something he knows if we will free him."

Callan and Kenja took off like arrows shot from a tightly strung bow. Rayen followed with Kaz right behind her. On the way, she tapped on Callan's mind. He was quick to ask, *What?*

I didn't want to say this out loud, because I don't want to falsely accuse anyone, but Tony told me after our first trip here that Neelah visited him when he was locked in the prison hut. She made the comment that she didn't care if he was TecKnati and, in fact, hoped he was because she was looking for a way out of here. She said she'd do anything to go home.

Thanks for telling me.

But that doesn't mean she's guilty, Callan.

I know. I won't accuse anyone without solid evidence.

When they reached the hut, Callan opened it and they all entered.

Before Kenja and Callan started in on this guy, Rayen had a question for the scout. "How is the traitor in this village communicating with Thylan?"

"Messages are left outside the village in the same spot every time. I can show you the spot, but I've never seen the traitor."

She nodded and stepped back.

Kenja looked down her nose at the prisoner who was still standing and warned him, "We do not have to negotiate with you."

"I know. Please don't do that biting, itching thing again. I'm offering this in good faith."

"TecKnati do not understand good faith," she tossed right back at him. "You have broken our treaty and killed our children."

The knot at his throat pumped up and down with a hard swallow. "That's SEOH, not all of us. I didn't sign on to do this. I've tried to hide the whole time here, because I don't agree with what SEOH is doing, but to go against him is to die. I know you don't believe this, but not all TecKnati are bad. We have families just like you and many of us want to live in peace."

Callan crossed his arms. "Your leader is trying to commit genocide against our race."

"I realize that, but no one back home knows it. There's a board of twelve members that he answers to on everything he does. My father works in communications, and I heard him tell my mother that he thought there was something odd about the Komaen Sphere project, but SEOH delivers Sphere reports on a regular basis to the board members who oversee all TecKnati developments."

"Are you trying to tell me that SEOH is keeping this secret from *all* of the TecKnati?"

The scout nodded.

Callan studied the scout. "Why are you willing to tell us this now?"

"I thought all the scouts would have been sent home by now because the BIRG Con is tonight. But Thylan hasn't even come to see what happened to *us*." The scout indicated himself and the guy on the ground who was sniffling and crying. "He said once he completes both parts of his plan we'll go home. But I think he's lying about that, too. I'll tell you anything you want to know, but please let me go. I've never hurt anyone." His attention was squarely on Callan when he said, "I wasn't allowed to get close to you when you were locked up or I'd have helped you escape. I didn't have enough rank to be inside the main building. I've been sleeping outside the entire time."

Rayen believed him, but she wasn't sure if Callan or Kenja did. Kaz had a wary expression on his face that made her think he battled internally for a fair decision.

Callan and Kenja exchanged a long look then Kenja nodded. Callan ordered the scout, "Tell us everything you know, and we'll release you once we can confirm what you share."

The hunched body on the floor begged, "Do it, Allen."

Allen, the one standing, looked as if his life had been spared. He didn't need the prodding. "Thylan was supposed to take possession of the computer she brought." He angled his head in Rayen's direction. "And send it to headquarters. SEOH intends to reverse engineer it first then destroy the computer before the BIRG Con. Thylan was only supposed to test the laser at twenty percent level. When it barely worked on the two boys you came to rescue, Thylan turned it up eighty percent on you."

Callan grunted but continued standing with his arms crossed.

"Thylan sent a report back about how much power it had required and that he didn't have the computer yet. SEOH sent more scouts and an order that no one could go home until Thylan captured Rayen and delivered the computer to SEOH. Thylan has always been weird, but he's acting scary strange."

Rayen could only wonder what Allen thought was weird compared to what she'd witnessed.

Callan shifted his stance, his hands clutching his arms tightly. "What's Thylan's plan?"

"He's having the laser field dismantled, then rewiring it into a machine he's going to use like a weapon to destroy the ward around this village."

Rayen looked to Callan. "Can he do that?"

Before Callan could answer, Allen interjected, "The laser field was designed in layers so that if one level of power didn't work, they could keep increasing to the next level at another layer. There are three levels. When he maxed out the power, it was only the one layer. Combining all of them would be ..." Allen hung his head, thinking. When he lifted his chin, horror blanketed his gaze. "I don't know, but my guess is apocalyptic power. He has no idea if it will break the ward, blow up this village or maybe even blow up the entire Sphere. He's nuts."

Now she understood Allen's motivation. He wanted to be anywhere except in this village when Thylan unleashed his weapon. Something he said niggled at the back of Rayen's mind. "Why do you think Thylan is lying to you about taking you home?"

"Because of him executing the first step in his plan today. Some of the TecKnati scouts arrived in the transenders with MystiKs, which means they must travel back in the same transender, or the molecules in their bodies will rearrange and explode upon arrival. Thylan's destroying all the transender sites before moonset except the one he arrived in."

CHAPTER 31

TONY CARRIED THE LAPTOP AND wished he could show it to leading technology creators back home. He grinned at the half-pint genius beside him who'd shown Tony things he couldn't use back home. Not for another nine years. He'd given V'ru his word and wouldn't break it.

But hot day-am! Tony couldn't wait to see this baby light up if Rayen could do her imitation of a power supply.

When he reached the common area, kids were running around eating some weird yellow and pink fruit that could be the offspring of a watermelon and a pineapple.

Two of the kids were levitating and tossing a circle of pink power the size of a tennis ball between them.

V'ru's face drooped with longing.

Tony assessed the situation, then paused, turning his head back and forth.

"What are you hunting for, Tony?" V'ru asked, looking around. He'd taken to mimicking any move Tony made.

"Rayen and Gabby. I need to talk to them about not sharing anything they see with this computer when we go home. Do you mind hanging out here for a little bit while I find them and talk?"

"You mean out here?" V'ru asked with a bubble of excitement in his voice.

"Sure. You don't mind do ya?"

"Think they'll let me stay?" V'ru was watching the kids his age running around and playing with their powers.

"Mind? Are you kidding? They'll be glad to have you. Go on and I'll be back soon."

"Okay," V'ru answered, not sounding too sure of himself, but he took a step toward the group.

Tony headed toward the healing hut. If anyone knew where Rayen was, it would be Gabby. He rounded one of the shelters where the kids slept then turned around and leaned forward to watch V'ru to make sure that no one made fun of him.

Or hurt him.

Tony had spent many days watching over his kid brother Vinny and sometimes stepped in to keep someone from bullying him. He'd teach Vinny how to defend himself once they were back together again. As soon as Tony got the MIT scholarship, doubled up on his classes, and blew through school to get his degree, he'd take any job that would pay enough for him to rescue Vinny from foster care.

The only problem with that plan was Nick setting Tony up for a theft at the Byzantine Institute. Tony hadn't stolen anything, but could he convince anyone he was innocent?

He'd worry about that when he made it home again.

V'ru had walked up to a group of five kids playing some weird game that resembled shooting marbles, but it was a holographic game played on a horizontal level with balls that looked more like tiny stars. When they hit each other, it resulted in a little pop of light and tiny fireworks.

The kids stopped playing as soon as they noticed V'ru.

One boy crossed his arms. Bad sign.

V'ru shoved his hand up in his hair, a nervous twitch.

A little girl stepped up and smiled at V'ru then said something. V'ru tentatively opened his hand, palm up.

The little girl handed him a glowing star that twirled and sparkled on his palm.

The boy with the crossed arms made a put-upon noise, then nodded at the girl and V'ru stepped into the circle.

Tony grinned. V'ru was careful not to rub elbows with the little girl. Not because V'ru considered her below him. The kid didn't have a malicious bone in his body. No, he was being a normal eleven-year-old boy encountering the female half of the species for the first time up close and personal.

V'ru was acting as if she had something contagious like ... cooties. Just thinking of that old term made Tony smile.

The kid was going to be okay.

Tony swung around to continue on to his mission and practically ran into Gabby. He put a hand up. "Whoa, Sweet Cakes. Last thing we need is for me to drop this work of art."

Gabby stared at the laptop, dismissed it, and raised worried eyes to Tony. "We have bigger problems than the prophecy."

"Then why did I stay up all night with V'ru trying to make this thing work?" Tony snapped.

"Don't yell at me. I'm not the one causing the problems."

True, but admitting she was right would do nothing to soothe his irritation. "Sure. Whatever."

Gabby stabbed a hand on one hip. "I'm starting to feel more sympathy for Hannah."

He wasn't sure if he should be angry on his or Hannah's behalf. "Tell me what has your panties in a wad, then I need help finding Rayen."

Bam. Say the right thing and Gabby forgot about being mad at him. She clasped her hands together. Praying or worrying?

Or both.

"Rayen is gone with Callan, Kenja, and Kaz."

He tucked the laptop under his arm and cracked his knuckles. "We have maybe four hours until the moon sets. Do they want to solve this prophecy or not?"

"That's not the problem!" she said, grabbing her head. "Listen to me."

He was going to throttle Gabby if she didn't start making sense. "Start sayin' somethin' intelligent and I will."

She glared at him and whispered, "The TecKnati are destroying all the transender sites."

"*What the—*"

"Keep your voice down so the children don't hear." She cut her eyes to the side then came back at him. "Jaxxson just got a telepathic message from Callan, telling us to keep everyone inside the ward. He said it's the safest place and there's nothing he, Kenja, Kaz, or Rayen can do to keep us any safer. They're trying to reach the sites first and stop the TecKnati."

Tony clamped a hand over his face, feeling nauseous. If they wrecked all the transender sites, none of these kids would make it home. V'ru would be here forever. Pulling his hand down, he said, "Someone needs to burn SEOH big time."

"That won't be one of us, but if we can figure out the prophecy SEOH will get his due."

That was putting a lot of faith in words written in ancient Greece, but Tony wisely avoided pointing that out. "Now you want the prophecy solved again, huh?"

"I always did. I just didn't want to talk about it until I told you about the transender sites." Compassion wrapped Gabby's next words. "If they destroy ours, I won't be able to go home, and you won't make it back to Vinny."

His gut clenched with panic at that thought until he processed it all the way through. “The TeKs don’t know about our site.”

“Are you sure?”

“No, I’m not, but work through the logic. They’ve never met us at our transender site for an arrival or a departure. If they knew, I’m thinkin’ they would have had scouts watching that site for us to arrive today and ambushed us to steal the laptop. We didn’t come in through their transenders, so I don’t think they know about ours.”

“Oh.” She stared off into the distance a moment then smiled with relief. “Okay, then let’s work on getting the prophecy sorted out and that computer operating so we have a way to send these MystiKs home.” That sounded like what Rayen had been getting at last night.

“Wait a minute, Sweet Cakes. Where’d you come up with the bit about using the computer to send them home?”

Talk about the classic deer in the headlights look, with the way Gabby’s face froze, the headlights belonged to a tractor-trailer bearing down on her. “Hey, Gab, chill. What’s the matter?”

She was back to wringing her hands. Something was up with their mouthy Gabby. “Don’t ask me how I know, Tony. I can’t tell you and even if I could, you wouldn’t believe me.”

He raised a hand to calm her. “You don’t have to tell me, but as far as not believing you? I’ve time traveled through a portal in a laptop five times, outrun a croggle, fought a killer plant, and watched you float around.”

“Right. Okay, I need to sit down with you and V’ru to work on the prophecy while they’re gone. Callan promised Jaxxson they would all be back before moonset, but he didn’t know how soon before moonset.”

“Let V’ru have another fifteen minutes for a break and meet us at his kamara.”

“Okay. Thanks for easing my mind about our transender.” She went rushing off.

Tony couldn’t share her elation. It just dawned on him that the traitor might know about their transender site. If that was the case, he hoped Rayen got to it first.

CHAPTER 32

2179 ACE, in ORD/City One

SEOH HAD HIS ASSISTANT BLOCK anyone from coming into his office. He tapped the controls on his desk and accessed the video feed from where he kept the three sentient beasts.

Even though he'd already planned to send them to the Sphere later, the truth was that he hated to give any of them up. He could send one early so long as no one in his world knew that he possessed the outlawed killing machines. Thylan had discovered SEOH's stable of sentient beasts, just like Thylan had found out about the laser grid program.

SEOH grinned at the obvious genetics. Thylan might just be the one son as devious and deadly as SEOH.

Thylan had sent a request for help.

The least SEOH could do was support the person who had no conscience when it came to executing a plan.

Tapping keys, SEOH entered the code that would deliver one of his sentient beasts to the transender waiting to take it to the Sphere. Thylan had sworn he could deliver that computer before moonset in the Sphere if he had the beast.

CHAPTER 33

RAYEN RAN THROUGH THE WARD opening behind Callan, then waited outside the perimeter until Kaz and Kenja passed through before clasping hands with Callan and sealing the opening.

Once that was done, she and Callan turned to face the other two. She asked, "How many transender sites are there?"

Kenja answered. "Four."

"But one transender site is closer to the TecKnati camp and a long distance away from this new village location," Kaz clarified. "I could take that one and you three could go to the others."

Callan didn't waste a second to consider that. "We stay in pairs so that we all have backup. You and Kenja start at the site closest to the TeK camp and the next one on the way when you head back. Rayen and I'll go to the other two. The one where she arrived is a fifth location. We're going there first."

"No, we're not." Rayen was standing firm on this. "The TecKnati don't know about our transender site, or we'd have seen them there at some point."

"They might," Callan argued, just as adamant to have his way. "We don't know for sure if they do or don't know."

She wanted these MystiK children to return home, but she had to take Tony and Gabby into consideration, too. "In relation to the other four sites, how far from the TecKnati camp is the one where my group landed?"

Kenja supplied the answer. "Farthest."

Callan wasn't happy with her reply. "That doesn't change anything."

Rayen put her foot down. "Yes, it does. We do this strategically, starting with the sites closest to the TeK camp, because Thylan is lazy. He'll do whatever is easiest first. Kaz and Kenja are going to the first two so you and I will start at the third one down from the TeK camp and work our way back."

Callan wasn't through debating it. "What if Thylan gets word from the traitor that we're on to him?"

Ah, victory. She reminded him, "You aren't turning the prisoners loose until we return and no one can get through that ward without me because I'm not MystiK."

Kenja grinned. "She has you there."

Callan finally gave in.

Kenja wouldn't let any of them depart until she wrapped them each in a spell that protected them from the hallucinogenic ground mist still cropping up in places. Rayen was the one most susceptible, so she thought Kaz and Callan went along with it just to keep her from feeling like the weak link.

Rayen snapped her fingers. "Wait! We'll take the tortalones."

Kaz sighed. "The mama left with her herd."

"What happened to you being the turtle whisperer?"

"I can't make a tortalone stay when she doesn't want to and evidently, she didn't want to, because she left. She was being so affectionate that I'm pretty sure it's mating season."

Just when they could use them, too. Shrugging, Rayen said, "Meet you back here."

Kaz and Kenja took off fast.

She and Callan ran to the first of their two locations and found a transender crushed, lying on its side, and still smoking. The big pink, fake flower that hid the switch for a holographic control panel had been smashed. Wires and metal parts were scattered around.

How many MystiKs would that deny the chance to go home?

With no time to waste, they made it to the next one and found it in much the same condition except what was left of the transender unit crackled and sparked with a sick sound. Tendrils of smoke curled from sections that had exploded and landed everywhere across the clearing. The flower for the holographic panel had been torched and melted into a puddle of gray and black.

Watching Callan hold back the agony he had to be feeling over this was killing her. She wanted to put her hands on SEOH and make him suffer pain equal to what he had inflicted on all MystiKs.

If the wraiths came for Callan and she couldn't save him ... she didn't know what she'd do, but she *would* find Thylan since he was the access to SEOH.

On the way to her transender location, she decided to talk about the prophecy more as a distraction than anything. "V'ru and Tony are making headway on the prophecy."

"It's good to keep them occupied." Callan's words fell flat as soon as they left his mouth.

"That sounds like you don't believe in the prophecy."

"Let's just say the days of my believing in everything MystiK have passed."

She didn't know if the prophecy would save them or not, but it was worth the effort to find out. "You have to believe in something, Callan."

"Why?" He cut his eyes at her for a moment before watching the uneven path through what had turned from purple-tinged woods to bright-red jungle spotted with orange, blue, and brown plants. "After tonight, we won't ever see each other again even in the afterlife."

This was about bonding?

How could she make him understand that she wasn't sure it would work with them? "Gabby and Jaxxson are both MystiK. What if the bonding doesn't work with me?"

"Then you'll be free to find someone else," he snapped back in an angry tone.

"Is that what you think? I'm not bonding with you because I want someone else?"

He didn't answer.

She started laughing.

He scowled at her and cursed to himself, ignoring her chuckles for a few steps. He finally asked, "What's so funny?"

"You." She let him pull her around a ground fog that looked just like one she'd seen strip the skin from a small animal while it was still alive.

As soon as they got beyond the deadly fog, Callan released her and nursed his foul mood.

She caught a breath and asked, "How can you think that I want anyone else, Callan? Let's be honest. I won't have a life without you. I'm trying as hard as I can to give you the chance at having someone and believe me that's not easy to accept."

"I understand." He ran along for another stretch then said, "Now that you mention it, I do have someone in mind that I'd consider for bonding."

Was he really going to tell her about another girl he was interested in? Rayen ignored him.

Lifting branches out of their way when the growth thickened, he continued sharing too much. "She's a warrior and strong."

Of course, she'd be from the Warrior House. Rayen could see that, but it didn't ease the ache in her chest.

He continued. "She's fast. *Very* fast, in fact. Great skills with a spear and incredible power." His voice dropped until it sounded as though he was thinking out loud, figuring it for himself. "Pretty, too. No, that's not fair."

She wasn't pretty? Good.

"She's gorgeous. I'll have my hands full just keeping the other warriors away from her, but she'll be worth the battle."

He was killing her mood. She had enough to worry about without hearing the details of the girl who would end up with him.

Was she as skilled a warrior as me? she wondered.

Sounded like it.

Was she prettier than me?

Callan must think so.

"Rayen?"

"What?" She snapped. That probably hadn't come out as pleasantly as it should have.

Another few steps and he said, "Rayen?"

"*What?*" This time she'd snarled, but it was unfair of him to do this to her.

He was stifling a laugh but smiling at her.

She sent him a death glare and he burst out laughing until he had to stop to catch his breath.

Served him right to choke on that thought.

Callan grabbed her, swinging her around, smiling in her face the whole time.

She put her hands around his throat. "Clearly the mist has gotten to you, and you've lost your mind. I may have to beat some sense into you." It was getting harder to maintain her anger in the face of his delight.

"I love that you're just as jealous as I am."

"The only difference is that I don't have someone to carry on about in front of you."

"Silly woman. I was describing you. I told you. You're all I want."

Her hands had forgotten about strangling him and cupped his head to her so she could kiss him. She loved the feel of his lips, the way he took over the kiss, powering into it with his usual Alpha approach. Everything had to be done his way and anything he cared for belonged to him.

The Warrior House, the MystiK village here, and her.

He would always have her even if she couldn't be with him.

Kaz had a point about what she was doing with Callan interfering with his future. She could hold back from bonding with him, but she couldn't resist him here.

She realized they were moving. He'd lifted her and she'd wrapped her legs around his waist content for him to kiss her as they walked.

At least he'd had enough sense to keep moving or they'd still be in the same spot. She pulled her lips from his. "Put me down so we can run."

"We don't have to. Your transender site is just ahead."

Twisting around to look, she noticed the jungle had begun to regenerate in areas from the destruction they'd found on the last trip. "Do you think the TecKnati are here?"

"I would have heard them by now, but they may be lying in wait."

He let her slide down, then they snuck toward the transender site where leaves and trees that had been burned the last time now leafed out in aqua blue, vibrant orange, and pink colors.

They found a spot to crouch behind wide palm fronds and watched the transender site for several minutes, then Callan stood up.

She popped up with him. "Is it clear?"

"Kaz just called and said they passed a party of five TecKnati heading toward the TeK camp. He and Kenja have their second site to check."

"I hope it's still intact."

"Doubtful if the TeKs are heading back to camp, but that gives me hope that this site is still secret."

But for how long? Rayen wondered. Unwilling to be defeated, she said, "Let's find the flower with the switch for the control panel."

CHAPTER 34

Byzantine Institute, Albuquerque, NM

PHEN HAD SEARCHED THREE ROOMS to find the perfect spot for the computer with the time portal once he had it in hand. He needed somewhere that no one would disturb him while he waited on Rayen and her group to return. The perfect location for containing all three of them as soon as they showed up.

Did Rayen's powers function here in the past?

He should have tested her somehow before she left again. It didn't matter. He'd bind her hands, her feet, anything that she could point at him. MystiKs pointed at something to throw their power, right?

How was he supposed to know?

Scouts were trained in isolated areas and taught to ask no questions. He wouldn't have known about what his father heard at work if Phen hadn't snuck around at home.

No one risked talking. SEOH scared everyone with his ability to get information. One wrong word and Phen would have landed in prison.

Wait. How would that be any worse than being sent back in time to historical hell?

"Phen."

He turned sharply at the sound of a familiar voice. "What are *you* doing here, Kurt?"

"Same thing as you. SEOH sent me here." Kurt had a year of age and about twenty pounds on Phen. His brown hair had been clipped into the new flatter style, rather than the crowned look most TecKnati scouts wore, and his eyes were too small for his wide face.

"When'd you get in?"

Kurt looked up, thinking. "Four, maybe five hours ago. I can't get used to this time change."

Had that been a joke?

Phen kept questioning him. "Why'd SEOH send you here? You screw up something?"

"No. I think it's because I was in the Sphere. I haven't heard of anyone going home from there." Kurt scratched his chin where it sprouted a few hairs. "SEOH used me to send a message to Brown about a schedule change."

If SEOH was so smart, why couldn't he figure out how to send a message back without needing a body to deliver it? Phen didn't really care. When he got home, and there was no question that he'd make Rayen take him to his world, he was finding somewhere to live far away from SEOH and his insanity.

Kurt had mentioned a schedule change. Phen asked, "What's going on back home? Why the change in schedule?"

"Thylan is in the Sphere now. He volunteered, no less, to test a new laser grid system that SEOH has kept secret."

That was news. SEOH's middle son was rumored to be a special level of degenerate. One you didn't want to get caught facing on a dead-end street after dark. Phen held his thoughts, letting the silence force Kurt to keep talking.

"Thylan used the grid to capture Callan of the Warrior House. Slick job doing that. Then he offered to trade Callan for the Genera-Y computer. That girl intruder brought a computer to Thylan, but Thylan doesn't believe it's the Genera-Y unit."

Phen suppressed a grin. Thylan had been denied the computer because the Genera-Y that SEOH wanted was here at the Byzantine Institute. Rayen and her two cohorts were using it to travel to the Sphere. "What's SEOH going to do with the computer when he gets it?"

"He just wants to destroy it."

"What about the prophecy crap?" Phen asked.

"SEOH seems to think that after the BIRG Con tonight, no that should be yesterday … uh, no that's wrong." Kurt scratched his head. "I have no idea how to figure the time difference."

Phen did. He'd been keeping track since he needed to get back before SEOH sent the K-Virus here. He cleared up Kurt's confusion. "The BIRG Con starts at sunset back home and that's in less than an hour here."

"Got it. Anyhow, SEOH believes once the ceremony starts the MystiKs will no longer be a problem. He's got something up his sleeve."

Just the way Kurt said that alerted Phen that Kurt had not shared everything. "What message did you bring back to Brown?"

Kurt hesitated, his gaze straying from Phen.

"Listen, Kurt. You and I are screwed in this deal. SEOH sent you back with no plan for you to go home. They know that neither of us is a threat here in the past." At least, not in SEOH's mind.

That convinced Kurt, who started talking so fast there was no doubt he'd wanted to share what he knew with someone. "SEOH's message was strange, but Brown seemed to understand. I told him the next TecKnati to come back will arrive tomorrow and that person will carry a final message. He'll be sent as soon as SEOH is done with the Sphere."

Phen felt the blood drain from his face. SEOH was injecting someone with the K-Virus and sending it to this world in twenty-four hours. That had to be what Brown was talking about this morning. "What about Rayen?"

"What do you mean?" Kurt cocked his head in question.

"The intruder girl. What happened after she gave Thylan the computer? Did she go back to the MystiK village with Callan?"

Kurt snorted. "Do you really think Thylan would let any female go? I heard she traded herself for that MystiK warrior. She's not ever leaving the TecKnati camp, not as long as Thylan is there."

Phen's palms were getting damp. "What about her powers?"

"Thylan buried a laser grid around the perimeter. It corrupts their power. She's caught."

Phen could hardly listen as his last hope of finding a way home and stopping the release of the K-Virus vanished. He had only a slim chance of survival and that depended upon timing.

How was he going to watch the TecKnati portal spot outside the school compound *and* guard the room for Rayen's return at the same time? Kurt would have to help, but without knowing why, because Kurt might be one of the mindless TecKnati who thought he was supposed to report everything to Brown and Maxwell.

Hard to tell which TecKnati were susceptible to the brainwashing.

Phen had always been careful to never let on that he was no robot. Keeping calm so Kurt wouldn't figure out anything was up, Phen told him, "We should keep an eye on that portal landing spot to see who else SEOH sends back. Why don't you do that and let me know as soon as he or she lands?"

"Can't get in. Brown sealed the location and has put it under guard. We'll see the next TecKnati soon enough. I'm going to find a place to crash. I'm starting to come down from the charge that crazy time travel gave me."

Phen nodded and shrugged. "See you later."

Not being able to prevent the person being sent back with the K-Virus from infecting this world changed everything.

As soon as Kurt walked away, Phen took the service elevator to the floor where he'd hidden in the storage room earlier while Brown and Maxwell had walked by talking. On the way there, Phen pulled his lizard out, stroking its scaly head. Once the elevator spit him out, he went to the storage room and closed the door softly. He flipped on the light and turned to where a ladder was still set up next to tall metal shelves.

A heavy-duty shelving construction that could hold a lot of weight at the top, where it stopped about two feet short of the ceiling. His gaze tracked to the two commercial-size gallon cans of tomato sauce.

Someone had thought they were clever.

Phen had been smarter.

He stroked his lizard one more time and let it hop to the floor where the lizard stretched and shifted, hair replacing scales until a large black dog stood there, flicking his tail back and forth.

Phen patted the dog's side. "Took me a while to figure out why you were so excited about that ladder. Nice job. You stay here."

Phen climbed quickly. When he stopped three rungs down from the top and pushed up, he was eye level with the computer he'd found earlier. The same three circles—silver, bronze, and gold—continued to swirl on the monitor. Someone here had called it a laptop.

Who'd want to have that heavy thing sitting in their lap? He missed holograms. He missed everything about his life.

Reaching over, he pulled the laptop to him and carried it down to place on the floor.

His sentient beast padded around happily. Its eyes glowed at times. Phen had wanted to keep him and now he could.

He curled his hands into fists that needed a target. SEOH's face came to mind with a crosshair in the center of his forehead. "If I can't go home, then no one else is either."

He lifted his foot and stomped the laptop with everything he had.

CHAPTER 35

"THAT FLOWER LOOKS FAKE." RAYEN pointed and ran to the pink bloom large enough to stick her hand down into. It was a perfect replica of the deadly one that had once ambushed Tony. To SEOH's credit, he'd chosen a great camouflage. Once the MystiKs knew the pink flower was connected to a deadly host plant, they wouldn't touch anything resembling that flower. If they didn't know, they'd go around testing all pink flowers for transender switches and die.

Some had.

Nausea threatened at the memory of tiny faces looking out from the tree where the host plant grew at the base.

Callan was right beside her when she reached inside the bloom and felt around until her fingers touched a knob. Tony had twisted it when he called up the panel for the transender, so she did the same thing.

A holographic panel appeared, the screen lit up and a feminine voice said, "*One hour, forty-seven minutes left to request transender return from Sphere.*"

That was how long they had until moonset, because transenders couldn't be called up once the moon disappeared.

It wasn't fair that the other sites had been destroyed, but her shoulders dropped in relief. At least she wouldn't let Tony and Gabby down. They were here because of her.

Callan murmured, "Thank goodness."

She turned to him, trying to think of anything that would comfort him over the loss of their transenders.

The feminine voice emitting from the panel said, "*Error. Error.*"

Rayen stared at the panel that flashed a red "Warning" over and over.

Wind whirled and spun in the open field.

The transender wavered into view, then blinked out and came back. She held her breath as the spinning continued then the transender turned solid, shook as if a giant hand used it as a toy, then burst into a ball of green and purple flames. Lightning bolts shot up toward the sky.

"*Error. Error. Transender terminating!*"

"*No!*" Rayen shoved her hand on the panel that glowed bright as a hot ember, then shattered into a thousand pieces that floated in the air for two heartbeats.

Then vanished.

Smoke billowed from the pink flower, and it sizzled the way water did when it struck a scorching rock. Within seconds, it was all over, and the entire flower structure had melted into a smoking pile that smelled of burned chemicals.

She stared at that pile then forced her gaze to the spot where the transender had disintegrated. "It's gone."

Callan's arms came around her, comforting her the only way possible right now.

Her words tumbled over each other in a mumbled mess. "I can't get Gabby and Tony home."

"I know. I'm so sorry. This was our fight, not yours, Tony's, or Gabby's. I should have found a way to stop you from coming back."

She turned on Callan whose eyes bled with guilt. "Everyone is *not* your responsibility. It's *not* your fault that the MystiKs are here, and it's *not* your fault that I'm here or that I brought Tony and Gabby back. We chose to return. *I* chose to be here right now."

Callan didn't answer, just stared past her to the debris field she couldn't look at again.

She reached for him and hugged her arms around him. "I wouldn't care about this if it was just me. I will never regret coming back for you. I just have to find a way to tell them."

He let out a pent-up breath, crushing her to him. "We'll do it together. Maybe Tony will be able to get the computer working and we can find another way to send you home."

Tony and Gabby's world was not her home.

More than that, she didn't have it in her to tell Callan that based on how Gabby explained it to her, if the computer Tony and V'ru worked on was the one required for the prophecy it couldn't be used to send even Tony and Gabby home.

It might send the MystiKs home, or it might not work at all.

She wasn't even sure that the computer would play an actual role in fulfilling the prophecy, which was supposed to put the world back into balance.

Whatever that meant.

CHAPTER 36

"CONCENTRATE, GABBY." TONY SHOULD HAVE calculations spilling out of his ears by now after nonstop work on this laptop.

"I am concentrating." She held the palm of her hand parallel to the keyboard and an inch above it.

Jaxxson stood to the side of where he'd set them up in his healing hut at a table with tree stumps for chairs. Jaxxson wanted to be able to monitor what happened with Gabby as she tried to power up the computer and to also be available for anyone in need of healing at the same time.

But right now, his hovering was getting on Tony's nerves. "Yo, buddy. You got some herbs to mix or something?"

"If I had any that would improve your temperament, I'd gladly start mixing," Jaxxson retorted.

"Very funny. Tell ya what. You spend all night trying to turn an inanimate object into something sentient instead of sleeping and we'll see how cheerful you are."

Gabby pulled her hand back and gave Tony her stink eye. "If you want my help, do not insult Jaxxson."

"I didn't insult him, Sweet Cakes."

"Don't call her that."

Tony started to pop off at Jaxxson about playing caveman when V'ru made a throat-clearing noise, grabbing everyone's attention. "Arguing at this point is unproductive."

How did a pipsqueak like him manage to sound so full of authority at times? "You're right, V'ru Man." Tony took a calming breath and told Jaxxson, "No insult meant."

Jaxxson gave a half smile. "None taken. Now what is it you expect Gabby to do with her power?"

"Heck if I know." Tony washed a hand over his face and rubbed eyes that felt as though grit lined the inside of his eyelids. "When Rayen puts her hand on a computer, things just happen."

Stepping behind Gabby, Jaxxson leaned down and reached around each side of her to put his hands on the sides of the laptop. "Try it now, Gabby."

She passed her hand over the keys again. Lines furrowed her brow with her deep concentration.

Tony kept the sarcastic comment that came to mind locked behind his teeth, but what *were* these two woo-woos doing now?

Light flickered on the screen.

Are you kidding me? Tony sat up and leaned closer to observe.

Sweat pebbled above Gabby's upper lip and muscles stood out on her neck from strain. Jaxxson's hands gripped the sides of the laptop, white-knuckle tight. The monitor tried to come on twice then the keys glowed for an instant before turning dark again.

Tony rubbed his hands. "Keep going."

Jaxxson pulled his hands back from the laptop. "That took all the power Gabby and I could generate combined as one force."

V'ru asked, "Combined as one?"

Jaxxson was slow to answer the kid. "Yes."

The shock hammering V'ru's face confused Tony. "What's the matter, V'ru Man?"

V'ru's gaze ping ponged between Jaxxson and Tony. The kid's little Adam's apple bobbed up and down.

Jaxxson must have taken pity on him and explained, "Gabby and I are bonded."

Tony had questions, but not for V'ru's ears. "How about you pull up the prophecy list, V'ru, and let's get moving on it?"

The change of subject turned the kid's discomfort into immediate relief. He jumped up. "Where do you want it?"

"Over on the far side." Tony waved him back. "Make it big like a chalkboard."

At the distant look on V'ru's face, Tony saved the kid from digging through millennia of archived information stored in that little head of his and said, "A chalkboard is just a big display. So, make the prophecy list in a font size large enough to see it from over here."

Nodding, V'ru walked several strides across the length of the hut.

While he did that, Tony whispered to Gabby, "Did you and Jaxxson, uh, do the horizontal tango?"

She wheeled on him with furious eyes. "No. Bonding is much more important than mere sex."

Tony tried to wrap his mind around *that* and just gave up. "How can that be?"

"We blended our powers and made an eternal commitment. For the rest of time, our souls will always find each other."

O-kay. Just a bunch of their weird mumbo-jumbo. He could go with that. She wasn't leaving here pregnant. "Got it."

"Is this large enough?" V'ru asked from across the room.

Tony gave him a nod of approval. "Looks good. You want to stand there and add or change things as we talk?"

V'ru gave a vigorous nod that threw clumps of black hair in his eyes. The kid needed a haircut. V'ru pointed a finger at the line that read *A bond of two will set us free.* Next to it, Gabby and Jaxxson's names appeared in a bracket.

That explained the bonding part of the equation.

Gabby must have wanted to stay off that subject. She asked, "What does 'three powers' mean? Why is it in a bracket by *Three must unite?"*

V'ru explained, "I added that. I think it means that it will take three specific powers combined to make all of this work."

"Why can't it mean that Rayen, Tony, and I united?"

Gabby threw V'ru a curve with that. The kid studied the display, trying to find an answer. He lived for information and answers.

Tony hadn't given that line much thought earlier, but if V'ru's explanation was correct, then Tony was concerned. Jaxxson and Gabby had only been able to draw a flicker from the laptop. If this prophecy was all about MystiKs, then Rayen's power was of no use.

V'ru wasn't often stumped, but he turned to Gabby and shrugged his narrow shoulders. "Maybe it *is* you, Tony, and Rayen," he allowed, thinking. He added, "but I think *When three become one* and *Three must unite* are tied together because they both reference an action that would require power. *When three become one, the End has begun. Three must unite, for the scales to right*. It almost sounds the same, especially if 'End' means the end of chaos and fighting."

Gabby's forehead was scrunched as she studied the list. "You think the line *An enemy departs as a friend* is Tony, right?"

"Yes. It's logical since the TecKnati are our enemy and Tony carries TecKnati markers in his blood." V'ru seemed to catch himself and hurry to add, "But Tony is our friend."

Tony smiled at the kid to ease V'ru's worry. "You bet, buddy."

Gabby continued with her hypothesizing. "If that's the case and Rayen seeking answers is part of this, plus my bonding with Jaxxson plays a role, then that would mean our presence is part of the equation, right?"

V'ru's eyebrows drew together, which meant he was processing and trying to calculate Gabby's answer before he shared it. But when V'ru replied, he only managed to say, "I suppose so."

Gabby sat back, arms crossed and looking smug. "Then just to play devil's advocate, here's another possibility. *When three become one* could mean when Tony, Rayen and I joined as one to travel here through the computer portal. If that's the case, our arrival here set the clock ticking on *The End has begun*."

That sounded ominous, but Psycho Babe did have a point.

After studying on it a moment, V'ru lifted a finger he waved over his shoulder without looking at the holographic display. The words "three powers" were replaced with "Rayen, Tony, and Gabby."

Just when Tony thought Gabby was on to something with deciphering the code, she admitted, "I don't get that scales comment."

Jaxxson mused, "*For the scales to right* would mean to balance something. Correct?"

V'ru said, "Yes," but he didn't rush in with any more ideas after Gabby had surprised him.

Gabby asked, "But what *specifically* is being balanced?"

The silence grew and expanded until Tony expected to hear crickets. He said, "Let's start at the beginning. Why did Damian write this thing?"

Eyes lighting with excitement, V'ru warmed to something he could lecture on. "Damianus wrote it before he met Antonis, the TecKnati sent back to ancient Greece."

Tony said, "Right. The guy who built an analog computer then sank the ship with it."

"Correct," V'ru said. "But Damianus knew a great deal about Antonis when he came to tell Antonis he was in trouble and had to leave. It's thought that Damianus had a vision of what was to come to pass. It was never stated in specific words, but from all that our historians have gathered, Damianus believed Antonis really wanted peace between the MystiKs and the TecKnati. That led to the conclusion that Antonis was the catalyst for writing the prophecy."

Gabby didn't look the least bit confused. Tony had heard the story behind this earlier or he'd have been lost. Why wasn't Gabby?

Jaxxson propped an elbow on his other arm folded across his chest. He supported his chin on bent fingers and glanced over at Gabby every so often. Maybe he was doing some Jedi mind trick with Gabby, keeping her up to speed.

Tony pushed his attention back to the prophecy list and took a stab. "Based on Damianus and Antonis, *For the scales to right* could mean to bring peace to your world, but it's also a reference to justice. Maybe it means to punish those who created the chaos, too, like SEOH."

"Good point," Jaxxson noted. "I agree with Callan's name next to *Day of birth as Red Moon rises*. I have always believed that Callan may have been the designated one to lead the Houses all along."

Gabby stared hard then said, "You have BIRG Con next to *Night of end when last Moon sets*. I'd call that our deadline."

V'ru quickly agreed. "Yes. I added the BIRG Con, because everything in the records I reviewed leads me to that conclusion."

Or was it just the wishful thinking of a child who missed his family and home?

Tony had the urge to go hug this kid. V'ru might talk as if he was a tenured professor at a top academy, but underneath all that incredible knowledge was a little boy who needed to believe in something.

He needed to believe he was going home.

Tony had wanted to rip into Rayen earlier today for giving V'ru false hopes—because nothing in that prophecy list said anything about the MystiKs going home—but maybe she was right.

Maybe a little bit of hope went a long way.

Tony angled his head left then right, making a show of studying the list. "That could be what Rayen was talking about this morning, V'ru. Maybe if we figure this out, you'll all go home tonight."

Gabby turned a concerned look at Tony. Was she taking issue with the whole going home tonight part? "What, Gab?"

"You're just throwing things out there."

"So? We're brainstorming here. Everything is allowed." He gave it a beat then said, "Unless you have firm data we haven't received."

"No. Keep brainstorming."

Jaxxson snapped his fingers and said, "*The gateway will open*. That might support the theory about the way home, too."

Tony grinned at Jaxxson's jumping onboard the Hope Train.

V'ru must have agreed, because he added Jaxxson's suggestion then asked, "Now, what does *A path will close* mean?"

Jaxxson's gaze slashed down at Gabby who looked up at him and blanched.

A path will close.

Crap. That had to be the transender sites.

Of course, that was assuming this prophecy was all about the MystiKs here in the Sphere. But if V'ru Man was anything, he was literal, and accurate. He and Jaxxson both thought this was about Callan's Birg Day and the BIRG Con. Even Zilya and a few others Tony had overheard talking about the prophecy referenced the BIRG Con.

Plus, if Tony looked at this objectively, everything *had* seemed to change for the MystiKs here when he, Gabby, and Rayen came together to travel as one through the portal. Did that constitute the beginning of the end?

Lot of possibilities.

Gabby and Jaxxson were still staring at each other. Were they doing that mind-to-mind talking thing again?

Tony was starting to feel like the lowest animal on the food chain around these MystiKs, and he could get into Mensa any day of the week. He just didn't need to sit around with a bunch of eggheads trying to prove who was the baddest when it came to crunching code and data.

He'd slam dunk them.

While Jaxxson and Gabby did their mental time out, Tony took in the list to see what they were missing.

The future is in the past [Prophecy]
One will seek and all will forfeit [Rayen]

When three become one [Rayen, Gabby and Tony]
The End has begun [end of chaos, return of peace]

The gateway will open [a way out of the Sphere]
A path will close

A friend enters as enemy [traitor]
An enemy departs as friend [Tony]

Day of birth as Red Moon rises [Callan]
Night of end when last Moon sets [deadline]

Three must unite [three powers]
For the scales to right [bring the world back into balance
and punish SEOH, maybe send the MystiKs home]

The last will lead when others cede [Callan]
All turn to the outcast

The past speaks to alter the present [Rayen's ghost]
A bond of two will set us free [Gabby and Jaxxson]

Tony mentally added destroyed transender sites as a possible *path will close* since that was the only known way home for these kids. That left *All turn to the outcast.*

Who was that?

Jaxxson announced, "We're done here."

When Tony jerked around at Jaxxson's stern words, it took less than a second to realize something had happened.

V'ru's eyebrows lifted. "We haven't figured it all out yet."

Tony chuckled and said, "Hey, I need a break. V'ru Man, would you mind running back to your kamara and grabbing my backpack for me?"

"No problem." The kid zipped out of the hut.

Tony gave him time to be out of earshot before turning on Gabby and Jaxxson. "Cut the woo woo crap and tell me why Gabby looks like she's ready to toss her cookies."

When Jaxxson frowned, Gabby said, "He means throw up." She still looked punched in the gut when she turned to Tony. "Jaxxson just heard from the security inside the ward that the TecKnati are setting up some machine outside, but no one can get through the ward to take the kids out if we have to evacuate. Rayen used her power to help reinforce the ward so now we need her to open it."

Tony didn't like the idea of taking these kids outside the protective cocoon of the ward. "What kind of machine?"

Jaxxson answered, "Before Kenja left, she told me the TecKnati prisoners we captured this morning warned about Thylan building a weapon from his laser grid. And the ward is weakening again."

"Thought Rayen and Callan shot it full of their juice."

"They did, which means it's being intentionally corrupted."

A blast rocked the camp, shaking it hard enough to toss Tony and Gabby off their stools.

Tony jumped up. "Jaxxson, you call V'ru and tell him to stay put then come with me. Gabby, you get the other kids locked down in the safest place you can find in the village."

Jaxxson followed Tony out the door. "What are *you* going to do?"

"You mean because I didn't come with an internal power pack?" Tony didn't wait for an answer. "I'm going to offer them a sentient computer in trade to stop bombing us."

"We don't have a working computer."

"The TecKnati don't know that."

Jaxxson was striding with Tony step for step. "What good will lying do?"

"You're thinking like someone who plays by the rules. I learned survival on the streets of Camden. When in a corner, bluff your way out or at least until backup shows up."

The ward took another hit, sending Tony stumbling and Jaxxson falling to the ground.

Tony jumped and offered Jaxxson a hand. "All we have to do is bluff until Rayen, Callan, Kaz, and Kenja get back. If they can't kick Thylan's butt, then we're out of moves."

CHAPTER 37

"HOW CLOSE ARE WE TO the village?" Rayen asked Callan, because she was completely turned around by the path they'd taken to check transender sites.

"Maybe another four or five minutes at this pace. Kaz and Kenja are a little more than thirty minutes behind us. We'll wait on them to keep from opening the ward more than once. I've got a bad feeling about it holding up."

They were running as fast as they could through the dense jungle. This part had fully recovered from SEOH's attack prior to her last trip. That man had to be stopped, but she had no idea how they could accomplish that now that all the transender sites were gone.

Kaz and Kenja had found the same destruction she and Callan had at the sites they'd checked.

A loud boom sounded in the distance and blue light flashed up in the air. Rayen said, "Was that—"

"The village. Let's go." Callan took the lead, using his kinetics to shove everything out of their way and clear a path.

She ran faster, leaping over everything in the way and trusting him that they wouldn't rush into a threat.

Another blast hit and she felt the shock waves from it.

Thylan was attacking a village filled with children for a stupid computer.

Heat swirled and built inside her, rushing through her body to flood her arms and legs. She fisted her hands to hold it in, so tightly that her fists glowed red.

But she might not need it. There hadn't been a third blast yet.

As soon as they reached an area where the undergrowth thinned out, Callan slowed and lifted his hand to indicate they needed to be cautious as they advanced. He whispered, "I just heard from Jaxxson. Tony is trying to negotiate with Thylan to trade for the computer."

"He can't do that!"

"Jaxxson said Tony is bluffing to buy us time to return, plus he can't get outside of the ward because you have to help open and close it. Tony's been yelling at them and Thylan finally sent one of his scouts to the ward with a message that he's giving Tony one minute to open the ward and hand over the computer. If not, Thylan is going to turn his machine up to full power."

They reached the edge of the tree line.

Thylan had built something that was twice as tall as her. It was on a cart dragged by a huge beast with scaly gray skin. Four spikes erupted from its head, and it stood at least twelve feet tall. The creature snarled and pawed the ground with three-toed hooves. When the thing swung toward her, its eyes were unnaturally yellow and black. A nasty stench burned her nostrils.

She knew that smell.

Callan murmured in a shocked voice, "There are no more sentient beasts."

Evidently, there were.

The beast was harnessed to a flat cart that Callan could lie on with his arms stretched out and not touch an outer edge. It was parked with the back end facing the village. Piles of metal components, gears, wires, and tubing covered most of the cart body.

Callan whispered, "Those three round barrels as thick as my thigh are set up like cannons.

"What's a cannon?" She knew the word but had no mental picture.

"It's an old device that was used to launch ammunition of some sort at a target. In this case, it looks like he's shooting lasers through them."

Thylan's voice called out, powered by some mechanical device so that it could be heard all the way across three hundred yards to the warded village. "Time's up. You dare to test my patience? That ward is coming down."

Then his voice changed back to normal when he lowered his amplifier and turned to his men. He called to his scouts, "Load up a full charge of all three levels and send it in there."

Someone argued, "It might blow up everything and I mean like the whole Sphere."

"Don't ever disagree with me."

A buzzing sound was followed by someone's scream of pain, then a scout stumbled back from those huddled around the cart and beast. He clutched his chest with both hands, screaming again, then fell to the ground and stopped moving. Blood ran from his mouth and nose.

Rayen looked at her hands and they still glowed. The power had permeated her body until she felt one with it.

Thylan yelled, "Get up there! Blue laser, silver laser, then the gold one.

Release the blasts in that exact order."

A scout close to her age climbed up on the machine with jerky movements. He pushed two levers and lights started glowing.

Rayen yelled, "*Stop!*"

Thylan's head stuck up from where he hid on the other side of the cart. He grinned. "Glad you're here. Watch what happens when you lie to me."

Callan lifted his hands and threw a kinetic blast at the machine. The blast hit it and bounced away. He looked at his hands as if they'd failed him.

Thylan hooted. "I enclosed this cart with laser protection. You lose." He pointed a thumb at the village. "And they die."

Power rumbled so loud in her body it was deafening. Nothing mattered beyond stopping Thylan.

A stream of blue shot from one of the cannons.

Callan took a step toward them, turning his kinetics on the cart again, but it was bouncing off every time and Thylan remained inside the protective area.

Blue washed across the ward.

She heard children screaming.

Lifting her fists and shaking them at Thylan, she roared, "*Tenadori!*"

The cart lifted ten feet off the ground and started spinning. Blue laser bursts were flying everywhere. TecKnati scouts near the cart were sucked into the vacuum as it picked up speed. Bodies and mechanical parts flew around and around, all of it ten feet off the ground like a huge disk of living bodies and machinery.

A whining noise started, then picked up in volume.

The sentient beast morphed, changing shape over and over from beast to bird to a dog and back to a bird as it was slung around the outer edges of the tornadic storm.

Everything sped up until it was impossible to tell machine parts from bodies.

She shook her fists again, wanting to close her ears against the screaming.

Then she realized she was screaming.

Callan called to her from a distance. She couldn't find him in the blur surrounding her.

He shouted in her mind, "*Rayen! Let me in!*"

She forgot about her spinning storm and answered him telepathically. *Where are you?*

That was all it took for him to slide inside her mind and instruct her in a calm voice. *Slow everything down and allow it all to stop, sweetheart.*

No, she argued. *It feels good to let out this energy. Thylan wants to kill the children and my friends. I won't let him.*

I won't either, Rayen, but your entire body is glowing red. Pull back the energy before it consumes you.

It won't hurt me. The burst of colors filling her eyes was beautiful. Couldn't Callan see them? How could he ask her to give this up? Her power was calling to her.

Rayen, you have to stop the spinning now!

Why?

It's heading for the village. Stop. The. Spinning!

She fought to see what he was talking about and blinked away the mash of colors blinding her. That's when she saw what she was doing as if from a distance.

Something was shaking her like a rag doll.

Callan yelled in her head again and again, but the sound was distorted until she finally heard, *Stop it before you kill everyone!*

Her mind cleared. She scrambled through the mental chaos and yanked all her power back inside.

The spinning bodies and machinery slowed, dropping to the ground until the cart bounced and landed upright. The sentient-beast-turned-bird wobbled around for a moment then took flight and disappeared.

Scouts lay scattered across the ground, moaning. They held their heads and rubbed their arms.

Callan put his arm around her shoulders, panting and hanging onto her for balance. His entire body was shaking.

What had she done? "I'm sorry."

"It's fine. No one was killed. But you had me scared there for a minute. I've never seen anything like that, and your body turned into a fiery red glow, so bright I was sure you would combust."

Callan was looking down at her, his eyes soft with relief, then his gaze slid past hers and turned murderous.

He shoved her away hard, stepping forward as he did.

She stumbled and rolled from the force of his shove. When she scrambled to her feet and turned, Thylan had jumped up behind his machine and pointed it at Callan, shouting, "Die you miserable MystiK!"

Blue light burst from the center cannon.

Callan threw up a field of power. The laser slammed it and battered Callan's invisible shield, chewing small holes through it.

The searing beam that poked through the holes hit Callan, beating him as if he was being pelleted with rocks. He jerked with every hit. Skin stripped off his arms and legs in areas two fingers wide.

It all happened in three seconds.

Blue rays that bypassed Callan shot toward Rayen in slow motion.

She started forward to meet the attack. Energy roared to the surface and saturated her hands. She raised two fists and jabbed them in Thylan's direction.

Holes blasted up from the ground on each side of him, rocking the machine and cart, but nothing touched Thylan. He was safe inside the protective shield around his machine.

Laser strikes popped her skin, singeing and cutting. If Callan hadn't been blocking the strongest part of the attack with his kinetics, they'd both be dead already.

He slid back a foot and dug in hard, pushing against the relentless blue blast, trying to hold his tattered kinetic field.

Noises warped in a hollow sound. A voice filled her head, telling her, *Rise up and protect, Ashkii Dighin.*

That was the voice of an ancestor she'd met in a dream. She'd called Rayen that as if it were her given name.

She had no time to talk to ancestors.

The old ghost wavered into view. His words came to her, too. *You must take possession of all your powers now, Ashkii Dighin. Your people need you.*

She didn't know what he was talking about. Her people had already died, but the minute the voices disappeared, everything came at her in real time again and twice as fast.

Instinct drove her and she went with it.

Holding her hands up, she willed a wall of energy to form, something she'd never done before. Moving forward to push that protective energy ahead of Callan, who was taking a beating, required more than willpower. Locking her muscles, she bent forward, shoving as hard as she could.

Pushing the Byzantine Institute building across the desert would be easier.

One foot, then another, and the wall moved.

When she reached Callan's side, his body shook with maintaining his kinetic force field. The second cannon spewed a silver laser beam that struck next, tearing new strips from Callan's shield, and attacking his body.

He fell to his knees. His face had been battered and seared. Skin ripped off his shoulder and chest.

She raged at Thylan and the TecKnati, calling up every bit of power she felt inside her. Energy unlike anything she'd ever experienced before exploded through her body.

She couldn't think about overloading and being consumed by the power. Not when Thylan was killing Callan. Her body felt twice its size and heavy as she moved forward, but her hands and arms looked the same as always.

Her arms shook, straining against the force. Her knees threatened to buckle.

Fight, Ashkii Dighin! her grandfather shouted inside her head.

I can't do this.

Yes, you can. You must save your people.

Why did her ancestors think she could save anyone?

The lasers pounded, pushing her back inch by inch.

The female ancestor returned, speaking in Rayen's mind, too. *End this now or say farewell to him.*

Him? As in Callan?

Noooo! Rayen screamed in her mind then forced her feet to dig in and her legs to move forward. One step, another step, then another, faster and faster. She bellowed at the top of her lungs, "*Tenadori!*"

Thylan stuck his head to the side of his machine. His face held the first sincere emotion she'd seen on it. Terror. He screamed, "Hit her with everything we've got!"

Gold energy boiled in a plume around the machine for a second then sucked into the weapon and shot out the last cannon with a vicious burst.

The thick laser beam struck her energy field, a blind serpent with gleaming gold fangs ready to kill.

Her power and the laser blast clashed.

Brilliant shades of glowing yellow-orange power splashed up and out, spreading across her wall of energy.

Then it slowed. Had she beaten the lasers?

The gold crawled, separating into sizzling rivers of boiling energy, snaking out further and further until it found the perimeter of her force field and curled around the backside toward her from every direction.

What now?

Molten gold struck her skin, burning as it dug in.

She shrieked in pain. Nausea climbed her throat from the smell of scorched skin, and the burns felt bone deep. Her power rushed to the surface and burst around her in a white-hot cloud, sucking her into the core and wrapping her in a protective case.

Callan had been right.

Her power had consumed her.

Thylan was going to win.

No! No! No! Thylan could not win. SEOH could not win. The MystiKs needed Callan.

She opened her eyes and stared through a wall of smoky white.

The lasers continued pulsing toward her. She was on her knees, arms lifted, but she knew if she just lay down it would all be over and the pain would go away. She was tired of being alone and of fighting. Why did it have to be so difficult?

Because the strong will never be given easy tasks, Ashkii Dighin. It is time to show who you are. It is time to protect your people.

How do I do that? she pleaded.

You will find the answers inside yourself. Do it now. You no longer need our protection.

She didn't have it in her to argue any more about how she couldn't save a doomed race of people, but in that moment, she thought of the ancestors she'd met in a dream and of riding horses with her father. She saw the faces of her parents and felt a stab of longing. Long black hair framed the soft brown skin of her mother's face. Tiny lines creased around her blue-green eyes when she smiled at Rayen and hugged her father who stood tall and proud.

Rayen's eyes swam with tears.

She wanted to be with them again. Even if going home meant she would die with her C'raydonian race, she wanted one more day with her mother and father.

She wanted a chance for Callan to have his life, too, and one more hour if that was all she'd have with him.

Determination pushed her to her feet. White light spun around her and flowed inside her body, pumping power so hard through her the pounding of blood in her ears muffled everything else.

Was that the protection her ancestor had been talking about?

Hadn't her power been red?

Raising her arms this time, she watched the gold bounce off the white glow around her arms and hands.

The lasers continued shooting, but nothing touched her. Maybe there was nothing left of her, and she was dead, but she could feel the strength and had no time to question it.

Thylan and his group of scouts finally realized she was back on her feet and walking toward them. They scrambled to do something, but their three cannons were unleashing maximum lasers and it was all bouncing away.

Everything became clear in her mind.

She held her arms straight out and dropped her head back, calling forth her power and directing it to attack.

All the white power surrounding her disappeared.

Glowing red energy burst from her chest and engulfed the world. The power slammed Thylan's machine, pulverizing it. Metal twisted and screeched, ripping parts off that flew across the field. In a heartbeat, her red wave washed over Thylan's army, knocking them to the ground.

Screaming mixed with metal banging against metal, the fallout smelling hot and full of chemicals.

She stood there, weaving until she realized everything had stopped.

The sudden silence terrified her more than the lasers had, then a noise scraped behind her.

She swung around and cried out at the abomination that had once been Callan. What skin was left on his body was covered in blood. Bone showed in places. He struggled to stand.

Running to him, she caught him around the waist and grunted under his weight. Where had all her power gone that she could barely hold him up?

His clothes were in tatters. One eye had closed completely on his swollen face, but the gaping holes in his body were leaking out his precious life. He probably had even more damage on the inside that she couldn't see.

Her hands trembled with fear when she carefully touched his chin, turning him to her. Her heart cried out at the savage damage. "Heal yourself, Callan."

"I ... I can't. Not yet."

"You can't wait. Please. You're bleeding to death."

He lifted a bloody hand and touched her face. "Love you. Always."

She panicked. "We'll bond. Do it now. Whatever it takes to use my power to heal you."

"No. You could die ... too."

His knees buckled and they both went down.

CHAPTER 38

RAYEN DROPPED DOWN IN FRONT of Callan and let his weight fall against her. She shouldn't turn her back on Thylan and his TecKnati scouts, but if she hadn't killed them yet and they attacked, then she would die with Callan in her arms.

"Callan, can you hear me?" she asked, her voice breaking.

His eyes had closed, and his breathing rasped worse by the second. She bumped his mind. *Callan, let me in.*

When he replied, his words came into her mind hoarse and lacking strength. *No. Too painful for you.*

I don't care.

When Callan didn't answer her, she bumped harder. *Let me in or I'll force my way in and that will hurt both of us.*

She feared hurting him more, but if that was what it took to keep him breathing, she would barge through his mental shields. He had entered her mind more than once to save her. He'd showed her how to use her power to heal. She could do it again.

But she didn't have his experience. She might do it wrong and kill him, but he wasn't going to survive this way.

His arms hung limp at each side of hers that were wrapped around his back, holding on to him with everything she had.

"Please, Callan," she begged in a raw voice, terrified he'd draw his last breath any second. "Don't make me hurt you more by forcing my way in."

One of his arms moved slowly, lifting to grasp her waist. No strength in those hands, but he finally entered her mind and said, *Prepare yourself.*

When he opened the passage fully between them, she rushed past his shields, ready to wrap her power around his.

But it was like diving into the inside of a fire monster. Hot claws and spiked teeth ripped at her. She sucked in a breath, fighting for air, and fighting to not scream.

He tried to push her out, but she was stronger than him right now.

Speaking softly in his mind, she clamped her jaw against the moan threatening to escape and reassured him. *I'm okay. Show me the worst injuries first and don't waste time arguing. I'm not leaving.*

Unless she passed out from the pain. She was only getting part of what he endured. She didn't see his power anywhere so he couldn't push her around his body to help.

Recalling what she'd learned following him when he'd healed her body, she sent her power first to his heart and gasped at what she found. His heart had been slashed repeatedly by the attack. How was he even alive?

See? Callan whispered telepathically. *You can't fix me.*

She was not giving up. *What if we bond, Callan? Gabby and Jaxxson are stronger now that they bonded.*

If we bond ... A pause followed his words. He was struggling to even speak telepathically. He finished, saying, *You will die if you're inside my mind when I draw my last breath.*

You're not dying.

I am, Rayen. I won't take you with me.

If she lost him now, she'd never find him again. But if they were bonded, their souls would hunt for each other.

That was what Callan had been trying to explain to her about bonding. It was all so clear now. Why had she refused?

Because it might not work with her being C'raydonian. It might leave his soul unable to bond with another.

But if it did work and they both died, their souls might find each other again in another life.

More than all that, she was willing to do whatever it took to keep him alive.

She made her decision and had to form the bond now before Callan died. Air sucked from her lungs at the idea of his lifeless body.

Do this for me, Callan, she begged, still speaking in his mind where it was easier for him. *Bond with me.*

No.

Please. I want our souls joined forever. I don't care if I die today or tomorrow or any other time if I know that our souls will always find each other. Don't leave me alone to never find you again. Do this for us. Do this for me. Tell me what I have to do to finish the bond.

He shuddered with another racking breath.

She pulled her hand around to barely touch his chest at the spot of his heart. *I love you, too, Callan. Please don't leave me alone.*

After a quiet moment and the terrifying possibility that she'd lost him, his fingers at her waist squeezed gently.

Or was that all of his strength?

He explained, *I started the bond when I pierced the veil in your mind so we could fight the Frazzle Vine. You must pierce my veil ... then we blend ... powers.*

His voice was fading. She was losing him.

The pain in his body continued to leach into hers, eating at her with jagged teeth. Callan wouldn't be able to tell her much more or show her anything. She had to get through the veil in his mind and blend with his power.

But how?

What had her ancestors told her?

Look inside yourself for the answers, Rayen.

Closing her eyes, her thoughts blurred with images. She forced her presence further inside Callan until she could see all of him at once and not just one or two spots. What she found was heartbreaking. She touched where a wound had gone to the bone and clenched her teeth against the pain it caused.

A hiss wheezed out of him.

How was he still here? The damage was everywhere and devastating. His heart fought for each ragged thump.

His pain overwhelmed her, flooding more misery into her mind. She steeled herself against it, ignoring everything so she could search for the veil. Where was it?

The next second stretched until it felt like an hour, and finally translucent colors shimmered into view. They moved softly as a butterfly wing in a gentle wind. That had to be the veil.

She swallowed and pushed on the protective wall.

For as sheer as it looked, the filmy membrane was resilient and denied her entrance.

No one was stopping her, least of all a veil. Backing up, she surged ahead and broke through.

Callan groaned and sagged.

No, no. Tell her she didn't kill him. She clutched him to her, waiting on a sign he was breathing.

His shallow breath brushed against her skin, barely noticeable.

Rushing now, she delved deeper inside him, hunting frantically for the core of his power that should be glowing bright as a beacon. Where was it?

She sensed Callan barely nudge her once more in another direction, then she couldn't feel him. His hand fell from her waist.

Stay with me, Callan. Please don't leave me, she begged with tears pouring down her face.

He couldn't be dead. She would not allow it.

She fought past the panic paralyzing her.

Had he tried to push her toward his power that last time? She dove in that direction, refusing to accept his death until she had the cold evidence of his power extinguished.

It was so dark and quiet inside him.

Her heart hurt at every empty turn she made.

Then she saw it. A glimmer of the force that had to be his power. There was barely enough pulsing to keep him breathing.

The tiny ball of bluish light brightened then dimmed. It glowed again then dimmed even more, shrinking.

He said they had to blend their powers.

She had no time to question her actions or to fear doing the wrong thing. Not trying was the only wrong choice.

Calling up her bright red power, she brought it slowly inside Callan, past his mental veil. Her power obeyed, moving carefully and in sync with her for once. She would forgive all the times her power had failed her if it performed now. When she drew it close to the core of Callan's energy source, she closed her mind to everything except their two powers.

Red swirled around and around in a gentle stream toward the ball of blue light that began to spin slowly.

Bright red spirals continued swirling.

She felt Callan's chest move with one shallow inhale. He whispered, "Rayen." It sounded like his last breath then he went perfectly still.

She wasn't doing something right or fast enough.

It was now or never.

She shoved more power into the stream. The red ribbons of energy wrapped around the blue glow faster and faster until blue light disappeared inside a fiery circle.

No, that couldn't be right. Her power would consume his.

Everything she did was wrong.

Heat flashed in an explosion of red flares.

Brilliant blue light burst through the red circles and detonated into silver-blue shards.

A surge of energy flooded her with an overwhelming sense of happiness, peace and contentment all rolled together. She knew with a soul-deep certainty that she'd never experienced anything like this before. She was floating and didn't care where she was, only that she was safe and loved.

Then everything went dark.

She couldn't see. Was she blinded? Or had Callan died?

"Callan! Callan!" she shouted out loud.

"I'm here, sweetheart," he whispered.

Arms she recognized were around her back. She opened her eyes. Two gorgeous brown eyes flecked with blue-green chips looked at her with undisguised love. His face was still cut and bruised, but the swelling had gone down, and cuts were closing.

She leaned back to look at his chest. Pink skin replaced the open wounds and blood had dried. She touched him to make sure this wasn't some dream. "You're alive, right?"

"Yes, because of you. Because of our bond."

Lifting her gaze back to his, she saw a flash of worry and hesitation. She shook her head at him. "Don't even wonder if I regret that. I should have agreed last night. Now all I can think about is hoping the bond will really help me find you again somewhere in time."

He reached a hand up to the back of her head and pulled her to him. He kissed her lightly but held tight. She would never get enough of him, ever. His mouth loved her and told her how much she meant to him.

Rayen gave that back two-fold.

His fingers slipped down to her shoulders, gently massaging the muscles that whimpered from what she'd put them through. With a tender squeeze, he pulled back and said, "We are connected forever and that is all that I could ever want."

"How do you know the bond took, Callan?"

"Look inside me again. You have only to think it and you'll be there, now that we're bonded."

She closed her eyes and slipped inside him with an ease that surprised her. What she observed shocked her. Both of their powers had turned into a dazzling purple glow.

She searched further to see his body rapidly repairing itself.

Withdrawing, she smiled at him. She would never get tired of this view. His eyes held a peace and happiness she hadn't seen before, and she would give anything to continue seeing for the rest of her life.

He used a finger to wipe a stream of tears off her face. She hadn't realized she was still crying. He kissed the path he left. Pulling his head up, he whispered, "Thank you."

"Did you really think I was going to let you get away from me that easily?" she teased, needing to breathe a moment now that he would live.

At least until dark. They still had to face the wraiths.

Was reaching eighteen this hard for everyone?

She bent her head back so she could see the moon's position in the sky. "We're getting close to moonset, Callan." Bringing her head forward again, she said, "I'm not giving up on getting you out of this Sphere alive."

Callan got to his feet and pulled her up.

His clothes were still shredded, but now revealed a slightly battered, yet still powerful body. One she had every intention of keeping out of the hands of those miserable wraiths tonight.

He glanced past her. "Are any of the TecKnati still alive?"

"I don't know." She didn't want to look at Thylan and his people—at what her power had done—but she had to at some point.

With Callan alive, she could face anything else.

The transender sites were gone. Even if Tony had the computer operating, they didn't know what the prophecy meant. No one could leave the Sphere at this point except the TeKs who'd come through Thylan's transender if they had survived her counterattack.

Callan took her hand and they walked across the fifty yards to where bodies were scattered over the open field. He frowned as his gaze scanned the fallout. "What happened to their hair?"

She'd been avoiding looking down until he said that.

All the TecKnati had white hair and eyebrows. Huh. She watched their chests move slowly. "They're breathing."

"More's the pity," Callan muttered.

She nudged him gently, but his body was back to rock hard again and not easily moved. "I don't like the TeKs either, but I didn't want to kill them. Well, maybe Thylan. But the others were raised to believe in their leaders like you were raised to believe in yours. From what you've told me, both TecKnati and MystiKs need new leadership. If we solve the prophecy, maybe that will be possible."

He squeezed her fingers. "There's Thylan. I want five minutes alone with him."

"No. We need him alive."

"Why?"

"Because I have a plan."

Callan wasn't acting too keen on allowing Thylan to live, so she laid out what she was thinking. "The TecKnati have the only transender location that can transport out of the Sphere. I'm betting that SEOH is capable of setting up all the original transenders again. We're going to hold Thylan hostage. If we don't solve the prophecy, then he's our backup plan."

Now, Callan grinned. "I love that devious mind of yours."

One little compliment from him and her insides turned into a gooey mess. "Can you use your kinetics to move Thylan into the village?"

"Not yet. I need maybe an hour to fully rebuild my body and power, but here come Kaz and Kenja."

She turned to catch the pair running toward them and glanced over at the red moon. There wasn't much space left between it and the horizon. "We might not have an hour."

CHAPTER 39

2179 ACE, in ORD/City One

"WHERE HAVE YOU BEEN?" SEOH barked at Rustaad who came striding into SEOH's office.

"Things are not going as simply as you'd thought."

"I never expect simple."

"No, but you expected the MystiKs to behave as they always do and that has not happened."

SEOH slapped his hand down and the holographic monitors on the side of his desk disappeared. "What's wrong?"

"We never found the last four G'ortians. I think three were smuggled into the city as part of the staff supporting those two Hy'bridts."

"We were led to believe G'ortians were the equivalent of all but deity level in the Houses. Why would they pretend to be staff?"

"My guess would be that those two young Hy'bridt's and the G'ortians got together and came up with a plan on their own that didn't include the leaders of the Houses."

SEOH paused, shocked that a bunch of teens had defied fifty years of MystiK customs and habits. "What are they doing?"

"I'm not sure, but the laser curtains are corrupting for no traceable reason. It has to be due to those MystiKs."

"What? Why would they do that and risk letting C'raydonians in?"

Rustaad's gaze narrowed at that comment, but SEOH was not going to open a discussion on C'raydonians right now. SEOH said, "Power up the laser grid now. Weaken the Hy'bridts."

"It's too soon," Rustaad argued.

"We're just under an hour from the opening ceremony for the BIRG Con. They'll all be too busy to notice anything, and the leaders obviously know nothing if the Hy'bridts and G'ortians are making a rogue attack on our laser curtains. In fact, we'll expose those brats to the House leaders as soon as we meet. The MystiK leaders may hate me, but they will not tolerate anyone daring to undermine their authority and put their lives at risk."

Rustaad rubbed his chin.

That action was the equivalent of someone else having a panic attack. "Is there something you want to tell me about the C'raydonians, SEOH?"

"No." Just as there was nothing SEOH intended to tell Rustaad about the sentient beasts he still possessed. "What are you waiting for?"

"You need to reconsider this laser grid entirely. If we power up and it doesn't perform as expected, the MystiKs will turn on us. All of us. I have real concerns about these G'ortians and Hy'bridts joining up."

"That bunch of weirdo kids has you running scared? Where's the Rustaad I hired?"

"I'm standing here trying to keep you from losing everything you've worked to build. I've seen what the MystiKs can do, but not this level of power from them. The combined strength of the G'ortians and Hy'bridts has to be the reason for our sporadic breakdown in the laser curtains. What bothers me is the uniform corruption, as if the MystiKs can actually target that much damage and be specific. Thylan's laser grid test proved we still have more to find out about this grid system. Powering it up for the first real test when the most powerful MystiKs are together in one city will be suicide if we fail."

"Then don't fail. Go activate the grids now or I'll send someone else."

CHAPTER 40

CALLAN WAITED FOR KAZ TO deliver Thylan to the center of the common area. He normally would never allow a TecKnati this close to the MystiK children, but there was little time left. Callan could not risk succumbing to the wraiths and leaving the Sphere without solving one last problem.

Thylan was regaining consciousness when Kaz dropped him on the hard ground. The TecKnati groaned and flopped over on his back.

MystiKs emerged from community structures, and some drifted in from the woods protected by the ward. All of them eyed the white-haired TecKnati who was sitting up and trying to pull his hands apart. Kenja had offered to bind him head to toe, but Callan only wanted his eyes covered, plus his wrists and ankles cuffed.

Neelah rushed in, pushing past several children, and shoving them behind her. She hesitated for a moment, staring at Thylan. Finally, she found her tongue. "You bring that scum inside here?" When no one answered her, she raised her gaze in Callan's direction. "Kill the TeK and toss his carcass outside the ward."

Rayen walked over to stand beside Callan and whispered, "She's always seemed shy, barely speaking the few times I've noticed her. Her showing up now would fit the traitor."

He nodded. "I thought the same thing."

"Any ideas yet?"

Callan said, "Yes, but I'll wait to see if I'm right."

Zilya and Etoi marched up to the central area and both paused, staring down at Thylan. Etoi twisted her face into a frown that wanted to be a threat and ended up just unattractive. "Why does he live? He tried to kill us." Etoi stepped up her anger when she pointed at Rayen, but her words were still for Callan. "She's made you soft. First you let her TecKnati friend stay in the village. Now you bring this pig to taint our air."

Zilya showed no reaction at all, which was unusual. Maybe she was trying to figure out which response would be of greatest advantage to her.

Callan asked Kenja, "Would you remove his blindfold?"

Kenja pointed a finger then made a flipping motion with it and the blindfold ripped off.

"Ow," Thylan complained. "That was stuck to my hair."

Zilya's eyebrows lifted, and she angled her head, which gave her a better position to see Thylan's face. She turned to Callan, her gaze snapping from him to Thylan and back. "This is perfect. Let's demand SEOH send us home or we'll kill his son."

Thylan twisted slowly around and stared at her.

She gave him a haughty snub. "Do not look at me, you worthless TecKnati."

Thylan chuckled. "That isn't going to play, Zilya."

"You do not know me," she argued a little too strongly.

Callan had heard enough. He addressed Zilya. "But you know who he is, and you were the only one who had the autonomy to make decisions that would hide your deceit."

"How dare you!" Zilya said, but not with the kind of certainty it should have had.

Callan continued, "And for a while I thought it was Etoi."

"What?" Etoi screeched.

"But then it dawned on me that she wasn't creative enough to do this on her own, plus I couldn't figure out her motivation for standing by as our children died."

Zilya's voice shook. "You will pay for accusing me of treason, Callan."

Thylan had scooted around to face Zilya, but he tossed his words over his shoulder at Callan. "You want to know her motivation?"

"Shut up, Thylan," Zilya ordered.

"Are you kidding? I'm sitting here tied up in the middle of a bunch of crazy MystiKs, stuck in a Sphere that there's only one way of leaving, and I'll never get to use it at this point. You were supposed to open the ward for my two scouts and make sure they got the computer."

"Shut. Up!" Zilya screeched, losing her superior composure.

Thylan's anger rose with his words. "I sent men inside right where you left a marker outside the ward. They never came out."

Callan offered, "We're turning those two loose as you speak. I made a deal with them."

Thylan grunted. "Figures. Zilya was doing this because she thinks she's going to end up as part of my father's inner circle with all the money and power she could ever want once the MystiKs are eliminated completely from our planet. She offered to be the MystiK consultant to the TecKnati to help them catch and prevent MystiK interference in our space program until that time, didn't you, fool?"

Etoi was staring at Zilya as if the woman she'd admired had changed into a croggle.

Zilya snarled at Etoi, "Don't look at me that way. You helped."

"I didn't know what you were up to. I thought you were going to get us out of here."

Children started shouting, "*Traitor. Traitor.*"

Callan's voice cut through the melee. "I've heard enough. Lock up Zilya and Etoi with this TeK.

"You can't do that," Zilya argued. She and Etoi backed away as one, but they froze, and their arms jerked down to their sides.

Screaming, Zilya tried to break loose, but Kenja appeared next to Zilya and continued moving her hands in a motion that spun a wrapping around Zilya and Etoi, pinning them back-to-back.

Etoi yelled at the Uberon leader, "You will die when I am free."

Kenja gave a tired shake of her head and gagged the traitors.

As Kenja transported all three prisoners in an impressive display of her kinetic strength, Rayen spoke to Callan in a low voice for his ears only. "How could she live with herself after the death of those kids and you-know-who?"

He understood that Rayen meant Mathias. Callan squeezed her fingers. "I don't know, and she will have to answer for her actions, maybe even to him some day."

Nodding, Rayen looked around. "Where are Tony, V'ru, Gabby, and Jaxxson? We have to find out if they've unraveled the prophecy."

Callan said, "That may not make any difference."

She swung around in front of him with her fierce warrior face. "We *will not* quit trying. Would you call to Jaxxson and find out—"

"I already called to him a few minutes ago. Here he comes now behind you."

Jaxxson and Gabby walked up with Tony and V'ru following. V'ru still wore Tony's hooded jacket that swallowed the kid, but Callan had to admit that Tony had reached V'ru on a level that no one else had, including Callan. V'ru had no brothers or sisters and Tony treated him as a brother.

Callan had never thought he'd feel a kindred spirit with a TecKnati, but Tony had surprised him.

"What are we doing, people?" Tony asked, reminding Callan why Tony still grated on his nerves at times.

Rayen asked, "Did you get the computer working?"

"Yes and no."

"This is not the time to joke around, Tony," Rayen snapped.

"Hey, do I look like I'm jokin'?" Tony handed the computer to Rayen. "That is beyond state of the art for the best we have to offer back home right now, even beyond our next ten years of technology."

V'ru lifted a worried gaze to Tony and prompted, "But?"

"But I'm not using that technology until six months before it will be discovered in our world." He patted V'ru on the shoulder. "My word is better than gold."

"I know." Still, V'ru now looked reassured.

Gabby piped up, "We have most of the prophecy figured out except the traitor and the outcast."

Callan filled them in on what happened, saying, "So Zilya's the traitor entering as a friend, but departing as an enemy. Who is the outcast?"

V'ru scratched his nose. "I think it's Rayen, because she's C'raydonian and in our world that would be an outcast." As soon as V'ru said that he looked over at Rayen, "But we don't think of you that way."

"It's okay, V'ru. I've felt like an outcast, and it has nothing to do with all of you. It's just because I don't understand why my family sent me through time, but I don't hold it against them either."

Tony searched the sky. "If this show has to happen by moonset, we have maybe fifteen minutes. Everyone needs to figure out their places and what we're doing."

"You're right," Rayen agreed. "We need somewhere to put the computer."

Jaxxson walked to the center of the common area, and everyone backed away. He pointed both hands toward the hut where Callan and Kaz had used a table to strategize ways to defend the village.

A small slab they'd used as a work spot floated to the center of the common area and paused waist-high in front of Jaxxson. He turned to Rayen. "Will this do?"

"I don't see any reason it shouldn't." She placed the computer in the center and the laptop covered most of the surface. "Okay, V'ru, what should we do now?"

V'ru said, "Me?"

"You're the one who knows the most about the prophecy, right?"

"Of course, he's the one," Tony said, giving V'ru a pat on the shoulder.

"Do your stuff, V'ru Man."

V'ru's shoulders squared, and Callan thought his chest puffed out some. Moving his hands up and out, V'ru produced a holographic display with "Damian Prophecy" at the top. The following lines read:

The future is in the past [Prophecy]
One will seek and all will forfeit [Rayen]

When three become one [Rayen, Gabby and Tony]
The End has begun [end of chaos, return of peace]

The gateway will open [a way out of the Sphere]
A path will close

A friend enters as enemy [Zilya]
An enemy departs as friend [Tony]

Day of birth as Red Moon rises [Callan]
Night of end when last Moon sets [deadline]

Three must unite [three powers]
For the scales to right [bring the world back into balance and punish SEOH, maybe send the MystiKs home]

The last will lead when others cede [Callan]
All turn to the outcast [Rayen]

The past speaks to alter the present [Rayen's ghost]
A bond of two will set us free [Gabby and Jaxxson]

Callan started to ask V'ru why he thought the prophecy meant the MystiKs would end up going home but changed his mind. Mathias had said to keep hope alive with these kids.

V'ru pointed out, "We haven't determined what *A path will close* means."

Gabby and Jaxxson exchanged a quiet look. Tony sent Rayen a little headshake that Callan read as saying to not mention the destroyed transender sites.

When Kaz quirked an eyebrow in Callan's direction, Callan said, "It means no more MystiKs will be sent here."

"Ah." V'ru pointed at the display and filled in that bracket. Sounding more confident of himself than he had in a while, V'ru started dictating instructions. "The prophecy requires power to activate the final stage."

"What is that final stage?" Jaxxson asked.

V'ru cut his eyes at Tony who nodded so V'ru said, "Tony and I think the prophecy will reach fulfillment when a time lock opens. Based on what we know about the history of Antonis, Lysandra, and Damianus, I believe the computer must be powered up to maximum capacity to activate that last step."

When he got head nods, V'ru said, "Based on the words *three must unite* and *a bond of two will set us free,* and the fact that it points to *one who will lead when all others cede*, I think Callan, Gabby and Jaxxson should power the computer."

Callan ignored the sick feeling that this wouldn't work and stepped up to the computer.

Gabby ran over to Rayen and hugged her. "I hope you manage to go home."

Rayen whispered something and Gabby said, "I'm at peace because of our bond."

That gained a smile from Rayen even though tears clung to her eyelashes.

Gabby hugged Tony who stiffened then shrugged and hugged her back. He said, "See you on the other side, Sweet Cheeks."

Hurrying, Gabby joined Jaxxson and Callan.

The last thing Callan wanted these children to witness was wraiths dragging him to his death. He paused and caught his breath at that thought.

He could do this.

Mathias had faced his final hour with honor.

Callan would do no less, but he could admit to himself that he had never expected eighteen to mean the end of his life and regretted losing the chance to experience that life.

Kaz's empathic gift meant he knew exactly what Callan was going through.

When Kaz took a step forward as if he wanted to help, Callan gave him a subtle hand signal to stay back. Nothing Kaz could do would change the fate Callan faced.

With effort, Callan calmed his breathing and prepared for the end. He'd shared the truth about Mathias with Kenja and Kaz. The two of them had been ordered to throw a shield spell over everyone except Callan and Rayen as soon as a wraith showed up.

She wouldn't want to be blinded during that moment any more than Callan would if the tables were turned.

But he had asked Kaz to do whatever it took to prevent Rayen from sacrificing herself.

Rayen said, "Hurry up you three."

Callan forgot about everyone except her. Would the bond hold and their souls eventually find each other?

He took one last look at her and swallowed the lump of regret clogging his throat. Why couldn't they have had more time together? He drank in his last vision of her.

This was worse than facing death.

He took a step toward her.

Rayen had been leaning forward, as if she was pulling against an invisible tether held only by her mind. When he moved, she ran into his arms, kissing him first.

He hugged her tightly. Why did he have to give her up? She was his reason for breathing and looking forward to the future. Closing his eyes against the onslaught of emotions, he pulled inside himself and opened his mind to her. *Rayen?*

She was there, filling him up and bursting with love, yet hurting at the same time. Purple energy misted around them in a soft haze. No one could intrude when they were together this way.

Her voice whispered, *I don't want you to go, but I don't want you in this Sphere any longer either.*

He would be strong for her. *When I do this and I'm gone, my soul will search for you. If I had the choice to lose only* my *life in trade for just one more minute with you, I would do it.* His throat moved with a hard swallow.

You said those words to me in a dream. I want to believe our bond is solid, but what if it didn't work with me? I might have doomed you to never having a life with anyone else, Callan.

I don't care. You're all I ever want. If this is all we get, then the memory of holding you will comfort me forever, because I will never replace you.

She shook with a sob. *I can't do this, but you have to go before the wraiths come.* Rayen pushed back from him, eyes red and tears glittering. She smiled past her sadness. "Go before it's too late."

He kissed her once more and walked back to the computer.

When he glanced over at V'ru, the kid had tears in his eyes. Callan forced a smile for him and said, "What do we do, V'ru?"

Scrubbing a hand over his face, V'ru said, "Each of you place a hand on the keyboard, starting with Gabby, then Jaxxson, then Callan."

Gabby and Jaxxson stacked their hands, then Callan put his on top. The computer whirled and the monitor brightened with one circle that was braided with gold, bronze … then silver.

CHAPTER 41

2179 ACE, in ORD/City One

RUSTAAD BURST INTO SEOH'S OFFICE, screaming, "We're under attack."

"What the—" SEOH had just walked around his desk to go to the BIRG Con. He'd planned to show up late enough to send the message that all others wait on him.

"The MystiKs are ripping apart our laser curtains. They're looking for the source of what's making some of their people sick."

"Then turn the furkken thing up to high!" SEOH shouted. "Why do I have to tell you that?"

Rustaad sounded like a vicious attack dog, snarling, "I did turn it up. The grid is failing. I think the Hy'bridts are interfering."

SEOH's assistant Leesa flashed into his office as a hologram. "The Hermes II Explorer has exploded, SEOH. ANASKO's research center foundation is being rocked by something with the seismic power of an earthquake." She disappeared.

Rustaad's tan skin lost its vitality, turning an unhealthy pallid shade. "That's no earthquake. It's the MystiKs. What are we going to do? The leaders are on the way here for you. Now!"

Those MystiKs wanted a war? He'd give them one.

SEOH pulled himself under control. He told Rustaad in a deadly calm voice, "How fast can you inject the K-Virus into our host body and send him back with a message to destroy all the MystiK eggs *now*?"

"I can have him launched through our time travel portal in three minutes, then it depends on how quickly Brown and Maxwell execute your orders."

That would run it to the minute for the official start of the BIRG Con. Brown knew that SEOH expected his orders executed immediately. SEOH smiled. He told Rustaad, "Do it."

Then SEOH rushed back to his desk and called up his monitor. Two holographic displays jumped into place.

Rustaad was on his communicator ordering the injection of the unaware TecKnati scout SEOH had chosen to be the incubator for the K-Virus. When Rustaad finished the call, he stepped over to stand at the side of SEOH's desk. "What are you doing?"

"Closing the last transender site in the Sphere."

"What? Your son is there."

"If he'd gotten the computer, he might have had a value to me."

"But why are you shutting down the transender?"

"Preventing a backlash of astronomical proportions." SEOH typed faster.

"We're facing war breaking out any second, SEOH. I'm betting the Hy'bridts have figured out we have those kids imprisoned somewhere. We need to be strategizing how to face the leaders and diffuse this."

SEOH ground out a scoffing sound. "Am I the only one who believes in the superiority of technology? The only one who realizes that we have more power than they do?"

Rustaad shouted, "If this goes to war, the destruction will be catastrophic. They will tear apart our cities."

"Only if they have all their soldiers and right now, we've got a major chunk of their MystiK power sitting in the Sphere. Remove that from the equation and we have the edge." SEOH continued tapping on the screen closest to him.

"What are you doing?"

SEOH waited for the last code to appear on screen then tapped in the other half that would begin the sequence. He did that and hit "Enter," then turned to Rustaad. "I'm ending project Komaen Sphere. In three minutes, the Sphere and all those furkken kids will be history."

CHAPTER 42

RAYEN WAS HOLDING HER BREATH, waiting on something to happen, but Gabby, Jaxxson and Callan still had their hands stacked on the computer. Nothing happened beyond the one multicolored circle appearing.

Children stood in a circle, almost shoulder to shoulder, around the common area, watching with a mix of wonder and fear.

Kenja had returned. "What's wrong?"

V'ru admitted, "I don't know."

The computer *had* responded. That should mean they were close to making it work. Right? She asked Tony, "What do you think?"

"Heck if I know, Xena. V'ru and I built a piece of technology that should launch spaceships, but it's not going to do squat unless it gets the power source it wants."

Did they have the wrong power mix? She asked V'ru, "Who else could be the three?"

He studied on her question then excitedly answered, "Maybe it's a Hy'bridt, a MystiK and C'raydonian?"

Callan's gaze fixed on a distant point.

She followed the direction to find the horizon had swallowed two-thirds of the red moon. At this point, it would disappear in another two minutes, maybe three. "Let's try it."

Jaxxson stepped away, opening a spot in front of the computer that Rayen filled.

Gabby asked, "What about the *bond of two* requirement?"

Oh, boy. What could she say?

Callan didn't hesitate. "Rayen and I are bonded."

Gasping sounds and murmurs raced around the common area. She glanced at Kaz who smiled and winked at her.

"Whatever, people," Tony said. "You know the drill. Put your hands together and let's see if that does it."

He was right. With time so short, they couldn't waste another minute.

Gabby put her hand down, then Callan covered hers, then Rayen's on top of his. The monitor blazed brightly. Her heart pounded out of control at that.

They'd done it.

Then the monitor screen's brightness dimmed, and the circle now switched from silver to bronze to gold, rotating through the colors.

Gabby whispered, "V'ru looks close to a panic attack."

Callan shot a quick look at V'ru then over at Tony, his face indicating that he weighed some decision. Then Callan told Tony, "V'ru is very important to all of us, but not just as a G'ortian or because of his extraordinary skills in the Records House. He is valued as a MystiK and someone I think of as a brother."

V'ru's face crumbled into a watery mess, but he stood there like a little soldier.

Speaking from his heart, Callan asked Tony, "Will you keep him safe until I can return to carry him home?"

Rayen's heart was breaking for Callan, because either they all went home, if V'ru was right, or the wraiths would succeed in tearing him from this world.

Tony announced, "I give you my word as Anthony Asklepios Scolerio that I will protect him like my own brother. Now, try that power thing again because the moon is almost gone."

V'ru's eyes rounded, and he became animated, bouncing on his toes. "What did you say, Tony? What's your name?"

Tony repeated it. "What's wrong, V'ru Man?"

"I didn't know. I didn't know that was your name."

"What's the problem with my name?"

"The original ancestor of SEOH was documented as having come to power in your time." V'ru lost all of his usual authoritarian sound and rattled on like a kid trying to get a story out faster than his mouth could work.

"That's where the name ANASKO came from," V'ru rattled on. "SEOH's ancestor was an international business mogul who changed the face of technology in the early third millennium. He was eventually known only as SEOH ANASKO, but he started out as CEO Anthony Asklepios Scolerio and he shortened that to form the acronym for his empire."

V'ru's gaze stayed glued on Tony when his voice dropped off into a whisper. "SEOH is your descendant."

All eyes turned to Tony.

As in *all eyes turn to the outcast.* Tony was the outcast.

Rayen's skin pebbled with fear at the realization that if the MystiKs killed Tony then SEOH would cease to exist.

Just as SEOH was trying to wipe out the MystiKs.

Callan stepped down away from the computer and crossed the short distance to Tony.

If he raised a hand to harm Tony, she would have to ... she couldn't consider that possibility.

She believed in who Callan was as a person.

Tony waited, calm in the face of being labeled as the origin of MystiK agony. "So, you think I'm the TecKnati devil incarnate now, huh?"

Callan shook his head. "No, you are not SEOH. You are our friend, but I ask one thing of you."

Answering with a hint of confusion, Tony asked, "What's that?"

"If you find a way home, and I hope you do, that you will show others how to bridge the differences between our people so that by the time my generation is born maybe we'll have a real chance at peace." Callan offered his hand.

Tony's voice came out thick and earnest. "You have my word on it."

They shook, then Callan returned to the computer.

Only a sliver of red moon remained. It would disappear in another minute.

Callan said to Rayen, "Let's try it again."

"*Wait!*" V'ru shouted.

They all turned to him.

V'ru said, "We need Tony instead of Gabby."

Gabby said, "Hey, I'm good with that, but Tony has no power."

Here came the voice of authority again from V'ru. "I told you once before that he does. Every human is born with powers, but it's recessive in TeKs because by our time they didn't believe in their powers so they stopped developing."

"Sorry," Gabby said. "You did tell me that."

But no one looked as though they believed V'ru. His eyes danced from person to person until V'ru rushed over to Callan.

Callan bent down to keep V'ru's words secret, but Rayen could hear them.

"I'm not supposed to admit this, because I'm the only G'ortian born to the Records House. That means I'm the only one who can read blood by touching it between my fingers. I figured out when I was four that our House is not the same as the other MystiK Houses, because we carry MystiK *and* ... TecKnati blood. I am a descendant of Antonis and Lysandra."

Poor kid sounded like he'd just admitted to killing a pupple.

Callan pulled V'ru to him and hugged him. "Thank you for telling me. No one will ever know." When Callan stood, he waved Tony forward as V'ru ran back over to stand with Kaz.

Tony faced Rayen with an I'll-try-but-don't-expect-woo-woo-from-me look.

She shouted, "Hurry up, Tony, we're out of time."

"Keep your shorts on."

That was the irritable Tony Rayen knew, cared for, and owed a debt to for all he'd done. "Thank you, Tony. I'm so glad I met you and Gabby. If we never see each other again, I'll miss you. I hope you live through this, find your brother, and get everything you want in life."

Tony's eyes were shiny. "It's been a trip with you and Psycho Babe, Xena. No regrets. Just take care of you."

"I will."

A rogue wind came out of nowhere, swirling.

The last slip of that blood red moon barely showed and would be gone in seconds. Her heart dropped to her stomach.

Tony stepped up on Rayen's left. Callan returned to her right.

Howling came from a distance.

Gabby yelled, "*Hurry up, Rayen! He said they're coming*!"

That would be Mathias talking to Gabby. What was it going to take to make this work?

Find the answers inside you, Rayen.

Had that been her thought or the voice of an ancestor? She didn't know, but when she lifted a hand toward the computer, her palm was yanked flat against the monitor.

She froze, waiting to be sucked in again.

Didn't happen.

Three circles appeared, identical to the silver, gold, and bronze ones on their time travel computer.

"Why didn't you do that the first time, Xena?"

A high screeching joined the howling that was approaching.

"Shut up, Tony, and do what I tell you."

"Whatever, just get on with it."

The wind batted her hair everywhere. She told Callan, "Put your hand on the keyboard."

He did it without hesitation and his eyes remained steady on her. He said, "I *will* find you."

Her heart was trying to climb out of her chest and cling to him. She nodded then told Tony, "Your hand on Callan's."

He did as she asked and muttered, "Can't believe I'm gonna die without getting laid."

She could see the black wraiths coming from far off toward Callan's back. They were flying fast as a laser beam toward their target.

This was it. She looked at Callan. "I *will* find you somehow."

Black wraiths flew in a mad dash for him.

As the first wraith extended black claws toward him, she slapped her left hand down on top of his.

Her world exploded, warping with twisted shapes and colors. She was pulled in three directions and whipped about like a tangled, broken kite. Where was everyone? What had she done?

The sound of air rushing past her blocked all other noise.

Faces of ancestors she'd met flew around her head, going in and out of focus. She could hear the wraiths screeching and calling for blood. Gabby and Tony flickered into view then stretched and disappeared. MystiK faces surrounded her, their gazes locked in shock then they were snatched away as if a giant hand had grabbed their feet and yanked.

Callan spun toward her. He reached out.

She lunged for him.

At the last second, he was pulled away, yelling her name the whole time.

She tumbled and flipped until she just gave up and let go of her struggle.

The swirling colors and shapes whipped into a spinning tunnel.

Then it all sucked into a vacuum, dragging her along with it.

CHAPTER 43

VOICES HUMMED NEARBY, DISTURBING RAYEN.

She stayed still, eyes closed, to discern where she was and who owned those voices.

Dry heat warmed her skin. That was familiar. It felt like a desert. She'd been in a desert before. Had awakened to a beast hunting her.

Her mind caught up to her body and memories came at her as fast as she could absorb them.

Albuquerque. Byzantine Institute. The Sphere.

Wraiths flying toward Callan.

Her heart came wide awake and pounded against her chest. She opened her eyes to soft light spilling in through a sheer window covering. The room wasn't large or small, but comfortable. Just big enough for the bed she was stretched out on, and a few other pieces of furniture. Two chests with drawers stood against the stone walls. The chests were carved from wood and trimmed with paintings of warriors on horses and a rocky setting.

She sat up and felt lightheaded, but it passed quickly.

The floor was covered in a woven geometric red and white rug. A rocking chair hewn from piñon pine waited in the corner. The blanket covering her had been woven with lightning designs she recognized. They were the same designs that had been on the clothes of ancestors she'd met in a dream.

The entire room came into focus as a sharp memory.

She knew this room and furniture.

A tear plopped on her face and her happiness struggled to push past the pain.

She was home, which meant she'd never see Callan again.

Climbing out of her bed, she padded over to find clothes and fished out a dress her mother had made for her. The tears wouldn't stop as her heart jumped from happy to miserable and back again, unable to make up its mind.

Once she had the pale blue dress and soft boots on, she walked out into the great room, the source of the low voices humming.

A man and woman stood up, staring at her as if she was a ghost. Next to them sat a boy who was V'ru's age. His name was Torg. Beside him stood a fifteen-year-old girl named Aleah. They both had blue-green eyes.

Rayen's brother and sister.

Her heart clenched at thinking of V'ru. Had he made it home, too?

Breathing hurt.

They all rushed her at once, hugging and crying. She allowed herself to enjoy being wrapped in the love of her family, being home again. She felt whole once more because little by little her memories were returning.

But she also had new ones from her time away. Now she knew what would happen to her family in the future.

How was she going to tell them what was to come? That they would all be exterminated like dangerous animals.

That conversation would have to wait for another day when her heart felt stronger. Right now, it was whimpering over all she'd gained and lost in one moment.

Her beautiful mother couldn't stop stroking her hair. "Let's let Rayen catch her breath."

Aleah and Torg hugged her, then left when her father echoed her mother's request.

Rayen panicked. "Don't let them go outside."

My father asked, "Why?"

"Sentient beasts."

"The beasts can't get past our barriers. They are safe as long as they stay inside the perimeter we protect."

Safe for now, but at some point, all that security would fall apart. She stood silently, wondering if she'd have to watch her brother and sister die at some point.

How had Callan survived losing a brother?

"Come sit with us, Rayen," her mother said, gently guiding her to a wide sofa covered with woven fabric. She gave Rayen a glass of water as the three of them sat down. "I was afraid you would never wake up."

"How long was I asleep?"

When her mother tried to talk, but couldn't speak past crying, her father said, "You just appeared, sleeping in your bed, ten days ago. Your mother found you, but you slept through everything we tried. Our elders performed a healing ceremony that should have brought you around. You didn't even stir."

Her father sat with his elbows propped on his knees, leaning forward. “I’m sorry about sending you to the shaman that night. We spent months trying to figure a better way, but when the elders came to us and said you, your brother, and sister would not survive unless we allowed you to fulfill your destiny, we ...” Her father looked away, blinking back tears before he turned to her again. “We didn’t want to lose any of you. I offered to take your place, but the elders said it would mean sure death for all of us. That you alone could fulfill your destiny.”

Her destiny, huh? If only they knew that she’d failed, because she never figured out what she was supposed to have done. She’d let her family and her people down.

Now she had guilt on top of heartbreak.

Someone had to shoulder the blame. She’d been the only one given an opportunity to save them, but she hadn’t come through so the end of their people would be her fault.

If she admitted that, would her father only feel worse for what he’d done? She might as well explain what she did know. “I understand that we have to follow our hearts and read signs in life along the way. As for destiny …”

Torg came running in. “Father, an army is outside our barriers.”

My father jumped up. “That can’t be. No one has ever found us here. How many?”

“The guards say it’s at least five hundred. The leader demands we send out Rayen.”

“*No!*” Rayen’s mother shouted. “I won’t lose her again.”

Her father hugged her mother.

Rayen stood. “Let me speak to them. If they aren’t attacking, they may only want to talk.”

“People of the cities cannot be trusted. We’ve hidden here for many years to avoid them. They kill C’raydonians on sight.”

Had the K-Virus been released in this world yet? “Are our people infected with a virus, Father?”

“Some were infected, but not for a long time now. We tried to treat them, but they went mad and died.”

“It’s contagious, right?”

“Yes, but those of us who heal protect ourselves and others from the deadly virus if we know someone is infected.”

That meant eventually someone would get inside these defenses and contaminate the entire race. “Let me talk to the leader waiting outside our gates.” Maybe this would be her chance to protect their people. If she could convince the TecKnati to allow them to quarantine in this location and prevent a major outbreak of the K-Virus among the C'raydonians, maybe they would leave her people be.

Maybe that was the reason her destiny was to go back in time.

This had to be the way to save her people. She could only hope that Callan was able to save his. She had to believe in her heart that if she was here, then he had made it home, too. That would have to be enough.

Her father walked over to get his spear. "I will not risk my children again. Not for the entire C'raydonian race or anyone else. We'll figure out how to save our people with you safely guarded."

"Allow me to walk with you. I think this may be part of my destiny. Trust me on this. Please."

My father lifted his spear and exchanged a look with her mother, who nodded even though she cried the whole time.

He held out a hand for Rayen and she joined him. Walking outside onto a fifteen-foot-wide ledge covered by an overhang of more rock, she looked around to find a circle of mountains enclosing a five-mile-diameter valley lush with plants, trees and a glistening lake.

Barns dotted the area. Horses grazed in a far section.

But they lived in a desert.

More memories bombarded her. Memories that had hidden the whole time she was gone now came rushing out to say hello. C'raydonians had found this canyon in the Sandia Mountains. Over time, they used magic to encourage the mountains to grow and completely enclose it, leaving only a narrow, ward-protected opening that allowed riders to pass.

From the outside, that warded section would appear like the rest of the mountain. From above, the valley looked like more mountain peaks.

How had the TecKnati found them?

She took in the hundreds of homes chiseled out of the face of the rock bowl. People moved around in the valley over a hundred feet below her. They tended to farms and animals. Some sat on ledges outside the entrance to their mountain-side homes, ledges furnished with hand-made furniture and plants in pots.

Looking down, she sucked in a fast breath. They were ten stories above the ground, and she saw no steps.

Before she could go into full-blown panic, her father took her hand, then he stepped off the ledge.

Following him had to be something she'd learned to do and trust, because it went against every instinct she had, but she also knew she would not fall.

They floated down.

Her pulse raced, but she trusted her father. They landed softly on the ground. He chuckled. "For a moment there, I thought you once again feared heights. Training with your powers cured that, but the look on your face when we stepped off had me worrying that your shamanic journey undid that work."

More memories—some from her training—filtered in. She had power inside her to control levitating to their home or dropping gently to the valley floor, too. But no one here knew she could destroy a croggle with it.

They walked toward the narrow passage in the mountains. Two men and a woman, all appearing to be around thirty, approached from that direction.

The woman addressed her father, referencing the strangers outside their compound. "The leader has not spoken other than to demand your daughter be brought to the gates."

Rayen's father digested that, then said, "No one knows of my children. No one should know of our location."

Her palms dampened.

Did they think she was infected? How would they know if they shouldn't even know about this valley?

What ancestor of SEOH had found them?

She and her father continued walking through two lines of guards, who filled in behind them.

Her father paused to open two wards on the way. She felt the power sizzle over her skin. They were as well protected as they could be from TecKnati, but not from the K-Virus if a C'raydonian brought it inside this area.

But how would that happen?

Was this unexpected meeting how the infection would end up inside the valley? She hesitated for a moment, and her father stopped beside her, his face full of questions. What a hideous irony if her destiny ended up destroying her family.

Always follow your heart.

She searched hers, and it told her to keep going, so she started forward again, playing possibilities over in her mind.

A traitor?

The MystiKs had suffered a traitor inside their village in the Sphere.

If her people had one here, that might explain how the K-Virus would eventually be brought in to infect the C'raydonians. As soon as this was over, she would tell her father that they had to find a way to flush out a potential traitor for any hope of surviving.

First, she had to be on guard to push her father back inside if this turned out to be a trap.

The twenty-foot-tall passage that they traversed was wide enough for two people on horseback to ride through side by side. With sun shining on both ends, they walked through a dark tunnel.

As they reached the exit into the desert, heat blanketed her. She covered her eyes and squinted against the glaring sun.

When her vision adjusted to the light, she was prepared to argue that they had a right to live here and to warn that the first sign of aggression would be met with a power unlike anything TecKnati could imagine.

She wasn't prepared for the deep voice that said, "Took long enough, but I found you."

CHAPTER 44

CALLAN SAT ATOP A CHESTNUT horse fifteen hands high. He rode bareback.

"You're alive," she whispered. Or was this even real?

He slid down in a lithe move and draped the reins over the neck of his horse.

When he turned to her, she tried to move forward.

Her father stopped her. "Do not go near them, Rayen. Have you forgotten? They are MystiKs. They hunt us. They're almost as bad as the TecKnati."

"I know this one, father."

"It is a trick. We have lost too many people to tricks."

"Not anymore," Callan called out, taking easy steps forward. "Things have changed. That is why I must speak with Rayen."

Callan continued moving toward her.

She sensed power rising behind her. "Callan, stop. They don't know everything yet and I'm not even sure how you are really here."

"I'm here and so are you because you were not born fifty years ago as you thought. You were born in my time." He smiled at her, not backing off one bit as he kept heading straight for her.

This was 2179. That thought struck her so hard she took a step back from the blow.

How were the C'raydonians still alive?

She turned to her father with questions on her tongue, but he was lifting his spear, preparing to attack.

Callan was unarmed, but MystiKs didn't need physical weapons.

She had to stop a potential battle, or war.

Calling up her power, she felt it roll through her in a gentle wave.

Careful not to break her father's arm, she burst past him, running to Callan.

Her father yelled, "No!"

Callan lunged forward, meeting her halfway. They collided in a mash of arms and lips. His kiss touched her all the way to her soul. It unwound the hurt and misery balled inside her, allowing her happiness to finally dance free. She didn't care if this was all a dream as long as she didn't wake up.

His powerful arms held her close, lifting her, and swinging her around as he turned. She felt him outside her mind and opened all the way to him. When he flowed inside, the world turned a beautiful shade of purple.

That was all the confirmation she needed.

She was laughing, then he joined her with a happy sound that came from deep inside, the kind that overflowed with joy. She'd never really heard that from him before. Not laughter with such abandon.

That was the sound she wanted to hear forever.

When he finally put her down and they pulled apart a few inches, they were surrounded by his riders on one side and an army of C'raydonians on the other side.

Hostility and heat threatened a meltdown.

She turned in Callan's arms to face her father, because Callan would not release her and she couldn't let him go either. "This is Callan of the Warrior House. I have promised myself to him."

"With your blessing we hope," Callan added, but whispered for my ears only, "You are mine regardless of what is decided here."

Her father stared at them without a word.

She whispered over her shoulder, "Father will come around."

But the C'raydonian warriors were making sounds that warned this was not going to end well.

Her father lifted his spear and stabbed it into the ground.

She hoped that was not a signal of war, but she honestly didn't know. She hadn't gotten *all* her memories back yet. How could this be 2179?

Father crossed his arms, staring at them. "Do you know of her destiny?"

"Yes." Callan stood tall and strong behind her. "I have seen her battle to save my people, to save her people, and to save people in other worlds. She is a gift to all of us, but now she is mine and her future is with me."

Rayen's smile should have been all the evidence needed to convince her father that she would not be deterred, but she could understand his being confused. She had hated it when she flailed around with no memories.

She squeezed Callan's arm. "Give me a minute."

He allowed her to step from his embrace, but his hand snagged hers and he stepped up beside her. "I'm not letting go of you again."

Her heart danced all around her chest at the determination in his voice.

Callan gave an order over his shoulder and his entire army dismounted, leaving their swords sheathed as the two of them walked to her father.

"You didn't have to bring an army to get to me, Callan," she whispered.

"I didn't bring it for that reason. I would have found you on my own no matter what. I brought an army to make a statement so that your father would know I will always protect you."

"You and I managed pretty well on our own."

"And I watched you too close to death more than once to go through it again. I also want the C'raydonians to know that I will defend them with every resource under my control."

Her throat thickened with emotion at that declaration.

When they'd reached her father, she stopped in front of him and said, "When our shaman sent me away, I went to another time and place. It's a long story and I'll share all the details, but Callan was there with me. If he hadn't been, I wouldn't be here now."

The look on her father's face was priceless. He took stock of Callan with one long perusal and after several tense seconds he extended his hand. "I will be forever grateful that she was returned to me."

"You're welcome."

Her father told her, "We must discuss this with your mother. She is just now speaking to me again. I didn't tell her before I took you to the shaman."

Rayen's poor father had taken on the decision to send her away on his own. By the grim look when he'd shared that, he'd suffered for it. One thing Rayen did recall was that her mother and father loved each other completely.

For that reason, she had no doubt her mother would understand about Callan once Rayen told her how she felt and that they'd bonded.

Father continued, "I see a lavender glow surrounding the two of you. I admit that I had hoped you would choose a C'raydonian to marry, but if this is who holds your heart—"

"He does," she answered quickly.

"Then I will honor your wishes if your mother agrees," father finished then turned to Callan. "This may create a conflict for you, though."

"There are none I can't overcome to have Rayen."

"That's good, because to have Rayen you must give up the Warrior House."

Rayen stepped out of the upstairs library in her parents' home onto a wide ledge decorated with furnishings created by her people, the C'raydonians.

The veranda overlooked their valley, but with the high railing and the memory of how she'd been trained to deal with heights, she wasn't panicked standing here. Torchlights and silk lanterns lit with magic-infused rocks glowed deep umber around the valley, shining a spray of light against the darkening sky.

Her father had explained that C'raydonians had always been reclusive, but prior to the virus outbreak they had begun to move away from this valley. Once the virus began spreading, many came back, running from the TecKnati and MystiKs.

C'raydonian healers quarantined those who were ill but in a different location to prevent the sickness from entering the area where her people now lived. Just as her father had said, those infected died.

The ones who did not catch the virus were allowed to return here and the C'raydonians sealed the valley, hiding it from both MystiKs and TecKnati for more than fifty years.

Until today.

Callan strolled out behind her and put his arms around her waist.

Dinner had been strange, especially when she recalled that she'd never been in a relationship with a boy before Callan. No wonder she'd been out of her depths when they met.

Her parents had drilled it into her that as the firstborn she was expected to take over as the leader of the C'raydonians at some point. Never had the firstborn been a girl in all the C'ray generations, which was another reason the elders were adamant that she had a destiny.

It boiled down to her being the C'ray princess.

Now she knew why the word princess had sounded familiar.

She smiled at finding out why no C'raydonian was allowed to grow peanuts. Every C'ray leader was born with that allergy. The elders had been perplexed when she was born a female, so they'd tested the peanut theory on her with a tiny bite. She'd become violently ill.

That confirmed she would be the next leader of the C'ray.

Her father had made the terms clear for his support of her and Callan's union. She had a responsibility to the C'raydonians.

But Callan had one to the Warrior House and the MystiKs.

Why do we have to always face difficult decisions?

Callan chuckled. "It's just part of becoming an adult."

"Did you hear that in my mind?"

"No. You mumbled the words. Stop worrying over your father's decree. I never wanted to lead the MystiKs. I plan to convince my House that Kaz will be a solid choice, because as much as Becka is high maintenance, she's also intelligent and fair. She'll be an asset for Kaz."

"Kaz and Becka? Really? Amazing. Okay, so what happened to Zilya, SEOH, Thylan, Etoi—"

"Hold it, sweetheart, and let me explain." He resettled his hold on her and said, "Let me think. First, every MystiK, and even the TeKs from our time, who was still alive in the Sphere when we activated the computer was returned home."

"Because of the computer?"

"Once we were back, the Hy'bridts came together to explain the elements of the prophecy. Evidently, we managed to bring the world back into balance when you, I, and Tony powered the computer, which turned it sentient."

"*Everyone* was sent back to their respective worlds?" she asked, thinking about Tony and Gabby.

"As far as I can tell, yes. The Sphere is gone, too. I heard that SEOH entered the code to destroy it, because the explosion was seen seconds after we appeared at home."

She'd missed that entire event while she slept for ten days. "What about Zilya and Etoi?"

"Zilya has been charged with treason against the MystiKs, which will have serious consequences. She will have to face each family who lost a child, then she'll spend the rest of her life in a MystiK prison. That is not somewhere you ever want to visit. We are expected to use our powers to benefit mankind, not destroy other humans."

She shuddered. That sounded like a fitting, but awful punishment. "And Etoi?"

"Unfortunately, she disappeared."

"You mean escaped?"

He shook his head. "No. She was from one of the last families to disappear due to the egg-harvesting program SEOH instigated at the schools in the past. Schools like the Byzantine Institute you told me about."

"Oh, that's awful." Rayen meant every word, then remembered, "That must be what they were going to do to Gabby until we found and released her."

"Then you saved her and all her descendants."

"And SEOH?"

"Thylan appeared at ANASKO headquarters among MystiK leaders surrounding SEOH and Rustaad, SEOH's right-hand man. SEOH was in the process of sending a TeK infected with the K-Virus back to the past to kill MystiK ancestors, but the MystiKs were able to prevent that. Thylan tried to roll on SEOH and Rustaad, but Thylan's testimony meant nothing. In the first few days that I was back, our world was filled with chaos and squabbling. Every House was still represented at the BIRG Con."

"So, you and the other MystiKs all appeared in the *same* location?"

"Yes."

"How did that happen? You were captured in different areas, right?"

"The only reason I can figure for us returning to one spot together is that either the united power of the Hy'bridts and G'ortians were pulling us to them, or the prophecy controlled it."

She thought back on what she'd learned of Hy'bridts and G'ortians while she was in the Sphere. "Aren't Hy'bridts reclusive? Basically, MystiKs who are not considered team players?"

"They were until two Hy'bridts, one nineteen and one twenty, crossed paths while searching for a lost MystiK. They talked and decided they would be more powerful as a team, something the older ones would never have considered. The Hy'bridts had a vision that clued them in that SEOH intended to attack MystiK power with technology of some sort during the BIRG Con. They convinced G'ortians to travel to the BIRG Con with them undercover."

"Is that why SEOH feared the Hy'bridts and G'ortians so much?" she asked, glad to hear Callan sound so relaxed.

"From everything I've learned over the past ten days it appears that SEOH was a fairly keen observer. Evidently, his spies reported that the reclusive Hy'bridts and younger G'ortians might be less resistant to change than their MystiK counterparts. Given a chance, they might communicate with one another and, by sharing information, come to conclusions SEOH didn't want reached until it was too late. And in this, he was correct."

She'd been so wrapped up in what was going on while they were on the Sphere that she hadn't considered what SEOH might be doing back in Callan's world.

Uhm, my world, she corrected herself.

She asked, "Did the Hy'bridts prevent the attack?"

"Yes, and over the past ten days they've met several times with the TecKnati ANASKO board members who admitted they feared what MystiKs would do so they agreed to sending the future leaders to the Komaen Sphere, but they all thought it was more like a summer camp based on what SEOH had shown them during progress reports."

"Summer camp my butt," she grumbled.

"And a very nice one." Callan leaned over and kissed her cheek. "Anyhow, the Hy'bridts and TecKnati joint council have come to several agreements. One is that they'll have a committee of ten TecKnati and ten MystiKs, including G'ortian leaders, to vet any decisions that affect this world or space travel. The list goes on and on, but basically for the first time since the K-Virus, the MystiKs and TecKnati are going to work together in a peaceful way."

"The world really is coming into balance," she murmured.

"I hope so. Only time will tell."

"You still didn't tell me what happened to SEOH, Thylan, and Rustaad."

"I did get off track. This joint committee heard enough evidence from the imprisoned MystiKs and Mathias, who spoke through a Hy'bridt, to convict SEOH of crimes against humanity, murder, theft of TecKnati funds, and maintaining a stable of sentient beasts, which have since been destroyed."

She had to interrupt. "What about the beast sent back in time? And what about Phen? He was at the school, too."

"V'ru was right about the time lock. Everyone the TecKnati sent back in time returned to our world when we activated the computer built by Tony and V'ru."

She studied on that. "Does that mean the laptop that Tony, Gabby, and I used to open the portal wasn't the only sentient computer?"

"Actually, the Hy'bridts said that neither computer was truly sentient. Not yours or the one Tony and V'ru built. The combined energy of you three—a MystiK ancestor, a TecKnati ancestor and a C'raydonian—is what opened the portal through the laptop to the Sphere."

She thought on the elements of the prophecy. "That's why it took the same combination to open the computer Tony and V'ru built."

"Technically, yes, but it was more than that," Callan explained. "As per the Hy'bridts, the prophecy was set in motion when the C'raydonian ancestor Damianus, the MystiK, Lysandra, and the TecKnati, Antonis joined their energies. The Damian Prophecy was fulfilled, and everyone sent back to their original places in time, by combining three *specific* energies, not just *any* C'raydonian, MystiK and TecKnati."

She closed her hands on Callan's, taking in every second of having him with her and continued sorting through everything out loud. "You were the one who leads when others cede. I was the one who will seek, and all will forfeit," she admitted, even though that part still bothered her. "Tony was the outcast who entered as an enemy and departed as a friend."

"Correct, but our bond was crucial to the outcome, too," Callan pointed out.

She'd almost prevented all of this by refusing to bond with him. She would have lost Callan forever, and her people would have been destroyed.

A lot of things might be different right now.

Angling her head, she mused, "Sounds like it was about the power of humans joining together for a common goal."

Callan's arms pulled her closer to him when he whispered, "The power of caring. And of love."

"Yes," she answered just as softly. But she still wanted something confirmed. "That means the sentient beast that attacked me in the past was definitely returned to our world, too, right?"

"Yes, but the Hy'bridts contained it the minute it showed up. Two men from that Byzantine Institute you told us about were convicted along with SEOH, Rustaad, and Thylan."

"Was one of them a Dr. Maxwell?"

"Yes, and the other one was called Brown."

She nodded, waiting on Callan to continue.

"SEOH, Rustaad, Thylan, Maxwell, and Brown were sentenced to spend the rest of their days on one of the planets discovered in ANASKO's space program."

"That doesn't sound like a tough punishment."

"Oh, but it is, sweetheart. All the dangerous plants and creatures in the Sphere came from *that* planet. The TecKnati board left the punishment to the MystiK leaders. SEOH and his group will be dropped off with the same rudimentary tools that we were given in the Sphere. They'll have to figure out how to survive croggles and killer plants on their own. And they'll have to find nonpoisonous food without the help of someone like V'ru."

"They won't last a day," she pointed out, but she couldn't feel any sympathy for men who had killed children and tried to wipe out a race of people. That was a fitting punishment. "How is V'ru?"

"He's good. Better than good. He slept for four days and scared everyone, but when he woke up, he said history had changed and he had needed the down time to reboot."

She was still in awe over V'ru's amazing mind.

Callan added, "Tony promised to leave V'ru a package buried like a time capsule. The first thing V'ru demanded was to go to the location Tony had told him. Everyone in the Records House quakes in their boots now with the new and improved V'ru."

That tickled her even though she missed Tony and Gabby just hearing this. "What did V'ru find?"

"The sealed container had a library of printed comics plus a letter that V'ru cried over, but they were happy tears. He shared some of it with me. Tony went to something called MIT, but it took him longer than he'd hoped to accomplish his goals because of the Byzantine Institute vanishing overnight. He did get his brother back, and brought him into Tony's company, which was where a woman named Hannah came to work. Tony married her. He had known her at the Byzantine Institute, but she hadn't recognized him when they met again."

"Hannah didn't remember anyone from the school?"

"No. Tony found Gabby once he had the money to do what he wanted. He said he and Gabby seemed to be the only ones in their time who could recall anything about the Byzantine Institute. It was as if the world had paused long enough for everything to swing back into balance. He and Gabby agreed to protect the secret."

"What about Gabby?" Rayen hurt thinking about how she and Jaxxson would not be together.

"Gabby created a world organization that focused on gifted children, regardless of the type of gift. She was a highly respected clairvoyant of her time and met a man that Tony said reminded him so much of Jaxxson that it was weird."

Rayen laughed as a breeze stirred and made a few strands of her hair dance across her cheeks. "Tony thought everything he didn't understand was weird." She breathed a deep sigh.

"What's wrong?"

"They're all gone."

"Yes and no." Callan rubbed a hand up and down her arm, his touch soothing her as much as his words. "Jaxxson is in our time and hasn't found his soul mate yet, but the Hy'bridt from the Healing House described a vision of Jaxxson in the future. He was with a young Hy'bridt who possessed a sharp wit, and the couple were surrounded by six kids. Oh, and Tony funded a special humanitarian program he called Woo-Woo, Inc. with Gabby on the board. SEOH was still SEOH when we returned, but there are positive signs that both Tony's and Gabby's efforts have influenced the world we now live in."

Callan squeezed her a little tighter and went on. "V'ru caused an uproar by declaring C'raydonians to be a race that deserved respect and recognition. He said SEOH's predecessors had believed C'raydonians were more powerful than even the MystiKs. The TeKs were fine with that so long as the C'raydonians remained in seclusion, but when the virus hit and some C'raydonians wanted to live in the cities, the SEOH in charge at that time refused entry. Then they feared C'raydonians retaliating at some point, which would force the TeKs to deal with two groups of people with unusual powers. That SEOH spread lies about the C'raydonians, which the current one continued to spread, gaining the support of paranoid MystiKs who helped TeKs determined to wipe out one race they saw as a threat."

She shuddered. "It's sad to think how many deaths were caused by those lies."

"Yes, but the MystiKs now see how their paranoia has been as much a part of the problem as the TecKnati leaders."

"Do you think these changes will last?"

Callan chuckled. "They will if V'ru has anything to say about it. He's turned into an eleven-year-old powerhouse. He's tossing out edicts and demanding that the houses live up to the changes he's seen. He told me off to the side that Tony convinced him that his opinion counts. That's another sign of Tony's influence."

"Yes, but I'm trying to picture skinny little V'ru when he's at home in his element. No doubt that formidable mind of his is turning the world upside down." It was hard to process all that had happened. She tried not to dwell on the children lost, but she couldn't stop thinking of one particular young man. "You said Mathias testified."

"Yes, a Hy'bridt called him to the committee meetings and transmitted his memory of the wraiths, plus she brought me in and drew from my memory of what happened to Mathias, then used her magic to show it to the committee. That was what convinced the TecKnati to defer to the MystiKs for SEOH's punishment."

"Is Mathias at peace?"

"Yes, he told our Hy'bridt that he had Gabby to thank and that he would watch over her descendants for the rest of time. The TecKnati are erecting a memorial to the dead MystiKs in every city, but they're casting a profile of Mathias on a new currency as an icon for reminding us of the selfless leadership we should all strive for."

"You don't need that reminder, Callan. You've always been selfless when it comes to others."

"Maybe at one time, but the minute I had a dream of where you were and knew how to find you in my own time, I would not allow anyone to deter me. I told the Warrior House and other MystiKs that anything else they needed would have to wait until I returned."

“What about uniting all your Houses?”

“Kaz and Becka will work with the Hy’bridts and the other G’ortians to that end.”

The sound of voices singing drifted up from far below.

Callan turned her to face him, and she dropped her head against his solid chest. She would have him forever, but she wanted to be with him right now. “I don’t want to wait, Callan.”

Her father cleared his throat on the ledge below them and everyone nearby heard it.

Callan’s warm breath teased against her cheek when he whispered, “Two years does seem like an eternity, but your father’s right about waiting until you turn twenty and that we should get to know each other without being under the stress of having our lives on the line. Plus, you have two years of training ahead of you to become the next leader of the C’raydonians. We don’t have to rush to start our life together.”

“What about you? You said all you ever wanted to do was lead your warriors.”

“Kenja told me she believes the Uberon Warriors and the Warrior House will be stronger together than apart, and that we need to present a united front as our leaders go into further negotiations and cooperation with the TeKs. She’ll take over the position of leading the Warrior House, which will be more powerful than ever in history. I have no problem moving here to live in the valley. I will train with your father’s warriors and learn their ways so that when the day comes for us to stand guard over your people, we will be a strong team.”

Callan looked down at her with the kind of love she knew only happened once in a lifetime. She didn’t think her heart could expand any more until he kissed her forehead and whispered, “Your people will be free to leave this valley whenever they choose, and our children will roam this entire country just as their forefathers once did.”

A tear ran down her cheek.

She’d turn eighteen in a month, and she’d celebrate it with Callan and her family. Eighteen no longer meant the possible end of his life, and here he was with her when she’d thought she’d *never* see him again. She could wait two years. It would be torture, but nowhere near as bad as the idea of watching him face the wraiths.

He would be here to share each precious day with her.

She whispered, “You’re right. There’s nothing we can’t overcome now that we have time.”

Standing there, she stared up at her destiny and saw her future in his eyes, as an unprecedented and unpredicted blood-red moon moved gently across the skies above them.

THANKS FOR READING THE RED Moon Trilogy. We hope you enjoyed it and will consider posting a review, which helps readers and authors. Reader enthusiasm has been special for us. We started this journey with a huge what-if question, and the ride has been a blast.

Watch for the spinoff series coming soon –
Red Moon Time Warriors

DEAR READER:

We could have made up a bunch of things – which we did *g* – but there's quite a bit of research and history that went into all three books. We used true elements for developing backgrounds for things like the C'raydonians. We built the C'raydonian history using the Navajos as our origin for their group. What part is true? There have been recent discoveries that indicate many of America's indigenous peoples may have originated in East Asia and crossed the Bering Sea on a land bridge 500 years ago, before it was lost into the sea. These same people spread to what was later known as Western Europe as well. The term shamanism was first used with Turks and Mongols and may have been a prevailing spiritual practice during the Paleolithic period. This gave us the basis for creating Damianus, our ancient Shaman with Siberian roots who was also a C'raydonian ancestor.

Thanks to Mary's husband Jim mentioning the early "analog computer" discovery made when divers happened on a wreck off the Antikythera Island in the 1990s, we had the seed of truth that bloomed into our "mythology" of computers. Just as we showed you in this story, there really is a device called the Antikythera computer which has scientists scratching their heads, so our explanation is as good as theirs right now.

As for the future, we can only imagine based on all the things we know in today's world. The one thing we do hope for is that the future will learn from the past.

***USA Today* Bestseller Micah Caida** is a blend of these two voices
New York Times Bestseller Dianna Love and
USA Today Bestseller Mary Buckham.

We love to hear from readers – micah@micahcaida.com
Website – http://www.MicahCaida.com
Facebook – Micah Caida

WHAT READERS ARE SAYING ABOUT

***Time Trap*, *Time Return*, and *Time Lock*:**

"*Time Trap* is amazingly original and unexpected...I loved every second of reading it!"

~~ Alexandra Fedor, 15, who has read *The Book Thief, The Hunger Games,* and *Anna Karenina.*

"Time Trap is a deliciously entrapping read you won't want to put down and leaves you thirsting for more when you finish."

~~Angela Catucci, young adult

"I really liked Time Trap and loved how Micah Caida created an entire world in the first pages. I liked reading from the different characters and hearing from each of them. I would definitely read more books of this series and really want to know what happens next. I've already recommended it to a friend."

~~Duncan Calem, 14, Georgetown, TX who reads the Inheritance Series, Dark Life and Percy Jackson

"*Time Trap* will be a delight to every reader! All the ingredients you would hope to expect: a strong-willed heroine, a dangerously sexy man, an intriguing setting, and lots of unexpected turns make *Time Trap* a real page turner."

~~ Lynn Fedor, adult/mom and has read *The Hangman's Daughter, The Curse: The Belador Series,* and *The BAD Agency Series*

"I loved reading this second book, *Time Return.* Everything developed fluidly from *Time Trap,* and the characters were true to themselves, and yet bold. *Time Return* certainly delivered what I was looking for-action, intrigue, and a lot of fun. Thank you, Micah Caida, for another book that I will be rereading a lot!"

~~Emily Gifford, 17, has also read *Divergent, The Codex of Alera*, and *The Lost World*

"What an incredible serial escalation! All in all, it's a masterful piece of work."

~~Angela Catucci, college student

"Time Return will grip you and keep you reading until the very end. The action is undoubtedly exciting, as well as the suspense. You won›t want to put it down!"

~~ Brooke McClure, teen

"*Time Return* is even better with the first one! The story heroes, Rayen, Tony, and Gabby, keep their promises and return to the future. But chaotic challenges ahead will test their loyalty and strength in the second book to the *Red Moon* trilogy. Absolute must read!"

~~Alexandra Fedor, 17, has also read the *Divergent* trilogy, *The Sea of Tranquility*, and *Thus Spoke Zarathustra*

"*Time Return* drew me in from the first page, it took hold of my attention and never let go until the last sentence."

~~Alex Bernier, teen, has also read also read all of *Rick Riordan's* books, the *Hunger Games*, the *Chronicles of Nick*, and the *Rangers Apprentice* series.

"As the thrilling conclusion to the *Red Moon* series, *Time Lock* does not disappoint and will leave you in awe...perfection on paper."

~~Angela Catucci, college student

"The issues addressed are timeless, and the characters are so realistic that I couldn't help but be drawn into their story. Thanks to Micah Caida for a great read for every age, this is a gem of a series."

~~ Emily Gifford, 17, read the Phantom of the Opera, A Princess of Mars, and the Dresden Files

"Time Lock, and the Red Moon Trilogy, is a fast-paced, exciting fantasy that is so well written that it meets my expectations as an adult reader too! Loved it!"

~~ Sharon Griffiths, adult

"Time Lock is an awesome read. The story grabbed my attention from the first chapter and wouldn't let go. The story is exciting and intense…"

~~ Hannah G, 12

"If I had found books like this (Time Trap) when I was a teen, I would have started reading much earlier, instead of waiting until my twenties!"

~~ Kay Barnes, adult

ACKNOWLEDGEMENTS

We really want to thank everyone who has helped with this entire trilogy. From the beginning, beta readers have been a huge support. We're going to list all of them in a moment, but there are some key people on our team who have been in the trenches with us throughout this project.

First, we thank our husbands for their incredible support that allowed us to spend many months immersed in this trilogy and gone when we needed to meet for brainstorming or editing sessions. Next, Cassondra Murray is our first reader before all others who has a sharp eye and Stacey Krug is our last who catches both obvious and subtle edits that make a big difference. She is a large reason for any continuity catches between books. Steve Doyle is one of our very early male readers who give us a new perspective on the story. Joyce Ann McLaughlin is the next one to read an early draft. She's been a major help with that and assisting us with the audio versions. Thank you to Sharon Griffiths read Time Lock early for us this time. Judy Carney is one of the last to read and edit through each book, catching those pesky typos. Kim Killion designs our amazing covers and Jennifer Jakes formats all the versions of this trilogy.

Additionally, Andrew LoVuolo is the genius behind our web graphics for MicahCaida.com and RedMoonTrilogy.com, plus he designed the Red Moon logo and created our T-shirt images.

Thank you to all the beta readers ranging in ages from 11 to 60, both male and female, for your valuable feedback, reviewing and helping us get these books in the hands of young readers:

Adam (Kentucky), Kym Amaral, Donna Antonio, Alex Bernier, Sally Blondiau, Brittany Bosse, Billie Jo Case, Nicole Case, Angela Catucci, Mary Cooper, Kathy Crouch, Alexandra Fedor, Lynn Fedor, Hannah Gunsallus, Sher Giambra, Emily Gifford, Sharon Griffiths, Dennis Jolley, Justin Jones, Tonya Kappes, Barbara Liebman, Ashley Love, Heather Machel, Leiha Mann, Brooke McClure, Heather Mitchell, Liz Mondragon, Marianne

Morea, Sophie Pajewski, Tara Pennington, Amelia Richards, Emily Skeel, Kelly L. Stone, Su Walker, Michelle Woods, Tammy Young and … thank you to all of you on our review team, who are incredibly generous when it comes to sharing our books.

ABOUT THE AUTHOR

USA Today* bestseller Micah Caida** is a melding of the two voices, two personalities and two minds of *USA Today bestseller* Mary Buckham and *New York Times* bestseller Dianna Love, a collaboration that often produces the strangest ideas. The authors enjoy exploring how different characters react and deal with unusual situations, because life is filled with the unexpected – both good and bad. While creating the Red Moon series, Micah hit upon a very unusual "what if" that exploded into an epic story filled with teenagers who face impossible odds but are the only ones who can save the world from itself. For more on Micah and the Red Moon Trilogy, plus future books, ***http://www.MicahCaida.com

www.ingramcontent.com/pod-product-compliance
Lightning Source LLC
Chambersburg PA
CBHW070828020826
48982CB00015B/807

9781940651019